Prime-Time Crime Time

Prime-Time Crime Time

By

Jay Dubya

Published by
Jay Dubya
Hammonton, NJ 08037
3835_7

Copyright © 2026 by Jay Dubya
All rights reserved. No part of this publication may be reproduced or
transmitted in any form or by any means, electronic or mechanical,
including photocopy, recording, or any information storage and
retrieval system, without permission in writing from the copyright
owner.

ISBN 978-161-863-45-04

For Michelle and Steve

Other Books by Jay Dubya

Adult Fiction

Black Leather and Blue Denim, A '50s Novel
The Great Teen Fruit War, A 1960' Novel
Ron Coyote, Man of La Mangia
Frat' Brats, A '60s Novel
Pieces of Eight
Pieces of Eight, Part II
Pieces of Eight, Part III
Pieces of Eight, Part IV
The Wholly Book of Genesis
The Wholly Book of Exodus
The Wholly Book of Doo-Doo-Rot-on-Me
Thirteen Sick Tasteless Classics
Thirteen Sick Tasteless Classics, Part II
Thirteen Sick Tasteless Classics, Part III
Thirteen Sick Tasteless Classics, Part IV
Thirteen Sick Tasteless Classics, Part V
So Ya' Wanna' Be A Teacher!
Mauled Maimed Mangled Mutilated Mythology
Fractured Frazzled Folk Fables & Fairy Farces
FFFF & FF, Part II
Nine New Novellas
Nine New Novellas, Part II
Nine New Novellas, Part III
Nine New Novellas, Part IV
One Baker's Dozen
Two Baker's Dozen
RAM: Random Articles and Manuscripts
Time Travel Tales
Modern Mythology
UFO: Utterly Fantastic Occurrences
Snake Eyes and Boxcars

Bee 17, Part IV, Short Stories
Bee 17, Part V, Short Storiea
Bee 17, Part VI, Short Stories

Young Adult Fantasy Novels and Stories

Pot of Gold
Enchanta
Space Bugs, Earth Invasion
The Eighteen Story Gingerbread House

Contents

The thirty-five novellas presented in *Prime-Time Crime Time* are works of pure fiction. The stories' themes deal with various types of crime and criminal motivation. Any character resemblance to anyone living on Planet Earth is positively coincidental. In addition, any fictional setting scenario is also coincidental.

"Story Behind the Headlines"

The relationship between big city police departments and the press is often both adversarial and contentious. It is with good reason and justification that many policemen possess a distinct animosity for the mass media. News commentators and on-the-scene reporters often interfere with crime-scene police activities and complicate arrests and indictments with *their* apparent ubiquitous presence. This narration verifies the disdain that many on-the-beat cops have for the ravenous media, particularly tenacious newspaper reporters. Relentless journalists have often been known to jeopardize investigations just so that they could develop a good "hook" to introduce their sensationalized front-page columns.

Detectives Mark Harmon and Dave Damon were sitting behind their cluttered desks in the third-floor office at the famously designed "Round House" police headquarters. Harmon was reading aloud an article from the *Philadelphia Inquirer's* "Metro Section" headlined "Cab Driver Killed on Job" while Damon was preoccupied staring out the grimy window and watching the traffic flowing between Pennsylvania and New Jersey on the very busy seven-lane *Ben Franklin Bridge.*

"The carnivorous newspaper writers ought to leave investigation work up to the police!" Mark Harmon criticized. "They're falsely reporting here on Metro Page One that cab driver Alfonso Giorno had been randomly killed on the job near his Kensington Apartment. The article maintains that an armed youthful-looking fellow deliberately murdered the cabby in cold blood by emptying six bullets from a .38 into the victim's head and chest."

"What was the motive?" Dave Damon asked as Harmon's have-seen-it-all companion apathetically observed the *Lindenwold High Speed Line* train crossing the *Ben Franklin* from downtown 'Philly heading eastbound toward Camden. "Was the cabby also robbed? If so, how much dough was stolen? Or did the young assailant have a personal grudge to settle with Alfonso Giorno?"

Mark Harmon deeply pondered his partner's question and briefly, his mind was in a mild quandary. "Violent crimes like this one tend to be more personal rather than simply being just committed at random by the perpetrator," Mark Harmon conjectured and pontificated from his twenty-four years of on-the-job experience. "As you know Dave, I had been assigned to *this* particular seemingly complicated murder case. The *Inquirer's* early morning edition had three separate related stories occurring on two distinct days, all of which today again appears on three separate pages describing the general facts, but the paper's devil-may-care amateur reporters didn't have the wherewithal to skillfully lace the three disparate accounts together. That's why the police should write the news stories *after* the trial instead of having the clueless press incompetents screw everything up, especially while certain precious evidence is being gathered and evaluated."

"Now that you've gotten my attention," Detective David Damon alertly answered, "how about filling me in on all the essential details. Actually, I have deep aspirations of becoming a journalist and also of evolving into an accomplished author after I retire from police work, that is, during my much-anticipated 'Golden Years'. Maybe then Mark I'll become rich and famous and finally earn the big bucks that I believe I now deserve. Kindly walk me through the specifics of your murder case."

Mark Harmon ignored his cynical colleague's typical prattle and momentarily focused on his already stated principal concern, the three distinct newspaper articles. The dedicated investigator casually thumbed through the bulky advertisement-laden early morning edition and his astute concentration soon noticed a small article appearing above a nondescript clothing store ad. Harmon then orally read, interpreted, and discussed the information provided in the suspect newspaper report.

"Dave, it explicitly states here on page thirty-eight that a young woman named Lisa Jacobs had her car stolen inside a high-rise parking garage near Eighth and Walnut. The article also indicates that Miss Jacobs is a nursing student at *Thomas Jefferson University Hospital* and that she also works part-time as a waitress at Portofino's Restaurant on Walnut near Broad."

"Ah, yes," Dave Damon recognized and acknowledged with a smile. "Portofino's has great Italian food. My wife and I eat there all the time. 1227 Walnut is the exact location, I believe. The place has really terrific cuisine and fabulous desserts. And I especially like the authentic white marble bar situated near the entrance. It gives the restaurant a rather special ambiance!"

"As usual, you're radically distracting me off subject," Detective Harmon mildly rebuked. "Thanks to the famous *Declaration of Independence* and the *U.S. Constitution* drafted just several blocks down the street, we have in this crazy country something known as Freedom of the Press, but as we were discussing earlier Dave," the argumentative-but-efficient detective affirmed, "cops ought to be writing the newspaper columns involving crime and not 'learning on the job' rank reporters that don't possess the proper education or the necessary investigative abilities or the basic strong ambition to get the front-page stories straight."

"Okay then, Mr. Sherlock Holmes," somewhat-amused Detective Damon countered while glancing at his friend's newspaper. "Review for me what happened to Miss Lisa Jacobs on illustrious page number thirty-eight. And please make your rendition short and sweet. I have a vital appointment to take my very fussy wife to a fancy restaurant and then clothes shopping at the *King of Prussia Mall* in just four short hours from now."

Mark Harmon cleared his throat and initiated divulging the "isolated" page thirty-eight story, explaining how Lisa Jacobs had been accosted and held at gunpoint by (according to the press release) an "in-need-of-a-fix" drug addict. After attempting to rob the frightened woman, the determined suspect next grabbed the lady's car keys from her pocketbook, hopped into the young female's pale green *Nissan Sentra*, started the engine and then sped-out of the high-rise parking facility. Miss Jacobs' fiancé, who was scheduled to meet her inside the parking garage, observed the familiar auto' speeding out of the building and then foolishly chased after it on foot.

"Of course, Mark, I presume that the *Inquirer* reporter failed to provide the name of Lisa Jacobs' fiancé," Dave Damon accurately interrupted his contemplative colleague. "I recall that I had read *that* same page thirty-eight article during a hasty desk breakfast and then clumsily spilled some freshly brewed coffee on my edition. The young woman's fiance' was described as a big, muscular fellow who was quite infuriated by the bold in-broad-daylight auto' theft," Dave Damon emphasized. "It's too bad the enraged guy didn't catch that vile thief, and then we would've had another easy murder to investigate and solve."

"Stop being so damned facetious!" Detective Mark Harmon admonished his all-too-jovial comrade. "As I was saying, it's no wonder that newspaper stories get so fragmented when unqualified reporters foolishly interview frivolous cops like you. And Dave, don't be surprised, but you happen to be closer to the pathetic truth than you might think!"

"Okay Mark, thanks for the backhanded compliment! I promise to be polite and courteous during the rest of your profound dissertation," Dave Damon cautiously pledged. "When your face turns as red as a beet like it is right now, I fully realize that it's time to drop the stupid drivel stuff and respectfully listen to your profound rhetoric. Tell me more about this rather remarkable case."

Harmon explained to his impatient partner that while Lisa Jacobs' muscular fiance' was preoccupied pursuing the stolen *Sentra* on foot, the disheveled victim gathered her composure, asked the startled garage cashier which way her *Sentra* had turned, exited the parking garage and anxiously flagged-down a taxi heading westbound on Walnut. A high-speed chase then ensued all the way from Eighth and Walnut across Broad all the way to Eighteenth Street, the location of ritzy *Rittenhouse Square*.

"They flew right by Portofino's Restaurant at 1227 Walnut without even stopping for pasta and some fine vino," Dave Damon sarcastically jested. "I'm mighty sorry Mark but I just couldn't resist the temptation of injecting *that* fantastic footnote into our mediocre bland conversation. Unfortunately for me, your drab story totally lacks suspense and drama!"

"You're just lucky you caught me in a good mood this dull afternoon!" Mark Harmon admitted with a degree of indignation. "The high-speed-chase eventually ended near *Rittenhouse Square* when the stolen *Sentra* smashed into a parked utility truck. The page-thirty-eight story ends with the madcap accident occurring, and the entire sequence of events is simply reported as an attempted robbery/pilfered car type item. As you can plainly determine Dave, so much for the *Inquirer's* inefficient staff for failing to stitch two seemingly unrelated things together! Do you follow my trend of thought here?"

"Well, what about the alluded-to third newspaper story?" Dave Damon demanded knowing. "Now that you've captured my curiosity about the *Sentra* theft and mentioned the resulting collision, exactly where does that third interesting alluded-to factor come into play? On *Inquirer* page seventy-two?"

"On page forty-seven," Mark Harmon corrected in an aggravated tone of voice. "The weak article linking the two seemingly isolated stories definitely appears on page forty-seven. Now if it were up to either you or me," the loquacious speaker authoritatively continued his blatant criticism, "then naturally…"

"Then naturally, the three Lisa Jacobs adventures would've been organized into one firm cohesive story instead of being disclosed in three seemingly unrelated incidents that have haphazardly been reported by journalistic imbeciles," Damon concluded and recklessly verbalized. "Certainly Mark, if allowed by fate to explore another profession we would've brought *justice* along with literary thoroughness to the art and science of newspaper journalism!"

"I don't know if you're being nastily candid or being obnoxiously deceitful!" Detective Harmon opined. "There's no doubt in my mind that you've been involved in the drudgery of police work at least five years beyond your tolerance level! I honestly believe it's time for you to take a much-deserved Sabbatical!"

"Was the nefarious assailant/carjacker finally apprehended?" Dave Damon apologetically asked. "I remember that I had glanced at a confidential report concerning the *Sentra* impact incident that had somehow accidentally crossed my desk while I was preoccupied munching on my morning doughnut."

"Yeah Dave; the parked city utility truck was parked and its driver was up in a cherry picker repairing a faulty traffic signal. The felon anxiously left the incapacitated damaged *Sentra* and then sprinted diagonally through *Rittenhouse Square,* but thanks to our well-trained department's quick response units, the repugnant thug was successfully collared two blocks away."

The now-captive listener concurred that two of the three stories were related and expressed interest in how the third "murder crime" story was connected with the two other newspaper reports. Inspector David Damon discreetly inquired about the third and most serious part of his friend's investigation, the bloody murder of cab driver Alphonso Giorno. The detective was now exceedingly intrigued and presently desired fathoming "the entire missing link".

"Well Dave," the senior detective proceeded with his stellar presentation, "I'll tell you my essential source of information at the conclusion of my story. I had learned from an anonymous waiter at Portofino's that Alfonso Giorno, the cooperative cab driver, had accepted Lisa's grateful invitation to take him out to dinner. The young-but-naive nursing student wanted to express her thanks for the cabby's help in having the police apprehend the man that had stolen her green car. Now you and I had casually discussed Portofino's Restaurant in our recent conversation and coincidentally, that's exactly where Lisa Jacobs and Alfonso Giorno had their arranged supper *that* evening," Harmon informed Damon. "After dinner the pair exited the premises and in an alley near the restaurant, Alfonso Giorno made romantic advances towards Lisa, who immediately refused his amorous overtures. According to a shocked eyewitness's account," Detective Harmon elaborated, "a terrible quarrel ensued and then Lisa fumbled in her pocketbook for her pepper spray but instead, the panic-stricken girl removed a steak knife that she always kept for protection purposes. During the wild scramble Alfonso Giorno had disarmed the knife from Lisa's grasp...."

"And Miss Jacobs was stabbed in the chest, abdomen and arm in the process," finished Dave Damon. "I recollect reading about the attack this morning on page fifty-eight of the *Inquirer,* but no names were given. But as *you* have related Mark, this third incident is really an extension of the second episode. I speculate that Lisa had later told her parents about Alfonso Giorno at the hospital right before she lapsed into unconsciousness. The hormone-driven cabby surely had a strange way of expressing his gratitude for a free dinner! Whatever happened to good old-fashioned American values and to the existence of common human courtesy?"

"Precisely, my Dear Watson!" agreed Detective Mark Harmon. "But the incapable local press never got the scattered pieces of the entire story systematically organized into a lucid-looking jigsaw puzzle. Now here's where Lisa's fiancé, a very jealous and possessive weightlifter again comes into the picture."

Detective Harmon next revealed to Damon that after Ronald Hutchinson had found out about Lisa Jacobs being assaulted and hospitalized at *Thomas Jefferson Hospital,* the jaded fellow went absolutely berserk. After talking with Lisa's father Mr. Jack Jacobs on *their* cell phones, and then conferring with me, the chief investigating detective, crazed Ron Hutchinson promptly researched Alfonso Giorno's address from a city telephone book. The incensed brute then drove his vehicle over to Giorno's apartment in the Kensington section and soon methodically proceeded to administer a brutal beating, and next, the livid young man emptied the contents of a .38 caliber into the aggressive flirt's head and chest. The coroner's men were summoned and soon arrived, pronouncing Giorno 'dead on the scene.' Quite a spectacular ending, huh Dave?"

"Well Mark," Detective Damon conjectured and stated to his astute associate in crime prevention and case solution, "where did you manage to arrest Hutchinson? To tell you the truth, I too would've probably gotten on the wrong side of crazy if a similar thing had happened to my wife or to my daughter. It's hard to be objective and rational when someone close to you is nearly killed!"

"That specific discovery was quite easy to find Dave," the veteran detective revealed. "Lisa had eventually regained consciousness over at *Jefferson Intensive Care Unit,* and she was able to recall and identify Ron Hutchinson's house number, and also, his street over in Bristol. I quickly contacted the Bristol Police, and we jointly raided the home and made the necessary apprehension. The rest of the matter is all criminal history! But the inept newspaper reporters don't have the intelligence to assemble three separate incidents into one in-progress series of events," the all-too-convincing speaker reminded his audience of one. "The high-rise garage robbery, the stolen *Sentra,* the high-speed chase down congested Walnut Street, the *Sentra's* collision with the parked utility company truck, the desperate on-foot pursuit through *Rittenhouse Square,* the violent altercation in the alley near Portofino's and the consequential murder of Alfonso Giorno up in the Kensington section were all relevant extensions of the single random criminal activity that had cruelly victimized Lisa Jacobs in the high-rise parking garage.

"Well then, who was the anonymous culprit that had heisted the girl's *Sentra* from the Walnut Street parking garage?" Dave Damon wanted to know.

"The original suspect that had stolen the *Sentra* is one Matthew Wilson, but ironically, his name is not cited anywhere in either the *Inquirer* or in the *Philadelphia Daily News.* Wilson had been released on bail for the auto' theft but has a record of being a common thief/drug addict with a chronic history of felonies."

"If those damned hare-brained reporters had as much on-the-ball as *we* do," Dave Damon egotistically boasted, "then the public would be much better informed and wouldn't have to watch TV *Action* or *Eyewitness News* for false details. Talk about lazy-minded journalists bein' bizarrely irresponsible! The city press and the local TV media inaccurately reported that Alphonso Giorno had been murdered as a cabby on the job *near* his Kensington Apartment when the man actually had been killed *at* his Kensington Apartment while off the job, and then the newspaper made the whole narrative sound like all three incidents had occurred on the exact same day. Say Mark, there's one aspect of this whole scenario that's now rather troubling me!"

"What's that Dave?" Detective Harmon nonchalantly answered. "What minor aspect has evaded *our* collective memory? As you well-know, I pride myself on being precise and thorough!"

"How did the distraught boyfriend Ron Hutchinson ever find out about this super-affectionate and horny cab driver Casanova, the now-deceased Mr. Alfonso Giorno, that is, if Lisa Jacobs had been unconscious in the *Jefferson Hospital* Emergency Ward? Was the angry fiance psychic, or what?"

"Well Dave, confidentially between you and me," Detective Harmon disclosed with a broad grin, "Lisa's dad, Mr. Jack Jacobs had divulged to me *that* particular information during an investigative interview, but her cooperative father has not yet learned of Ron Hutchinson's involvement regarding the cab driver's swift murder up in Kensington! I had inadvertently spilled the beans and told young

Hutchinson about Giorno's name and address two days ago during one of my impromptu interrogations. I had no idea that the former college football linebacker would take the law into his own hands and hostilely practice cold-blooded murder on the cab driver! Didn't he learn anything as a university student?"

"It was indeed a crime of passion, jealousy and revenge! Now Mark, I promise not to tell anyone of your unprofessional indiscretion in sharing confidential police information with the alleged murderer Ronald Hutchinson!" Dave Damon sincerely confided. "I'm certain that the Commissioner has bigger and more challenging obstacles and problems to deal with than suffering through a painful internal administrative-leave investigation that puts respectable *you* on the magic escape carpet! And thank goodness that the press is too encumbered and too lazy to sort and figure-out all of the pertinent facts relating to Miss Lisa Jacobs. Just think of all the expensive bureaucratic red tape you had effectively eliminated. Mark, I gotta' confess with admiration and envy that you're a true credit to the crime-solving business, and I'll never reveal your little secret to anyone, especially my garrulous wife!"

"And the lame media buffs actually think that all three newspaper stories that they themselves had written are entirely unrelated," Mark Harmon logically assessed and declared. "No wonder why the world seems so confusing to the average citizen that watches the daily news on TV or who innocently reads isolated fragments of minutia in the morning tabloids! I maintain Dave that the all-too-trustworthy residents of Philadelphia are doomed to experience news' mediocrity as long as the gullible public persists in getting its basic information from the lackluster mass media!"

"Ha, ha, ha," Detective Dave Damon laughed. "You oughta' be glad that the local news reporters are basically incapable blockheads because if they were really sharp and on-the-ball in regard to the Lisa Jacobs, Ron Hutchinson, Alphonso Giorno three story merry-go-round," Mark Harmon's partner continued while giggling, "then you my friend would be on administrative leave for unethical police conduct, and your retirement pension would be in grave jeopardy if you were found guilty of conduct unbecoming of a police officer!"

"Business Before Pleasure"

The late-model gray Chevy Suburban pulled out of the I-95 Chesapeake House parking area and rapidly re-entered congested southbound traffic heading toward metropolitan Baltimore. FBI Inspector Joe Giralo was behind the wheel, and his very serious passengers were agents Art Orsi and Dan Blachford seated in the rear and Agent Sal Velardi riding shotgun alongside the driver. Four bags of golf clubs and eight pieces of luggage had been conspicuously stored inside the large vehicle's rear compartment.

"Well Chief, you had promised that after having breakfast at the Chesapeake Rest Stop, you would divulge the true essence of this combination business and pleasure excursion," Agent Velardi diplomatically prefaced his inquiry. "And if our very capable director Chief Riley at our DC headquarters is the mastermind of this new mystery adventure, I'll maintain that, as usual, it's business before pleasure, or more specifically, business disguised as pleasure! Would my speculative assessment of the situation be correct?"

"Very perceptive observation Salvatore!" Inspector Giralo casually commended Agent Velardi as the other two loyal investigative associates Orsi and Blachford gave their undivided attention to the front-seat conversation. "Gentlemen, after getting to the Baltimore Beltway, we'll then be heading west on Route 40 in the direction of Frederick. Then using my trusty GPS navigation, I plan on eventually getting onto scenic Skyline Drive at Front Royal, Virginia. We'll feast our eyes on the picturesque Shenandoah Valley, stop at a few highway overlooks, and just around Luray, we'll next travel west through the majestic Blue Ridge Mountains until we reach Interstate 81. And incidentally," the grim-faced Inspector further revealed, "our top-secret destination happens to be the famous Greenbriar Lodge Plaza Hotel appropriately located near gorgeous White Sulphur Springs, West Virginia. As you all know very well," the driver continued his lengthy narrative, "that very exclusive place has a renowned championship golf course, but according to very explicit instructions from Riley's Office, only two of us at a time will be playing daily at the nearby Hickory Golf Green Course, commonly known to knowledgeable duffers as 'The Links'. It's a historic nine-hole Par 37, and it was the first functional golf course in America to ever sponsor championship competition!"

"Why can't we play a few challenging rounds over at the Greenbriar Lodge Plaza property?" Dan Blachford inquired from the back seat. "Have we been forbidden to do so from omnipotent Riley's instructions?"

"Yes Dan, apparently two of us are to strategically stay inside our well-appointed suite while the other two of us will be preoccupied a mile or so away exploring the fairways and greens at The Links," Inspector Giralo indicated. "Evidently, Riley fears that it would be entirely too dangerous on the Greenbriar Lodge Plaza grounds for all four of his highly trained government personnel. I believe the four of us will be watching our share of soap operas, woman talk shows and cable TV movies. And we've also been instructed to use room service as often as possible!"

"Exactly how far away is the Greenbriar Lodge Plaza from your home in Hammonton?" Agent Arthur Orsi asked the all-too-focused driver. "And what's so secret about this special activity we've been assigned? I need certainty and clarity in my mind and quite frankly," the twenty-year FBI veteran honestly admitted, "I just can't stand excessive suspense in my life! I'll leave *that* particular feature to Hollywood film studios!"

"Well Art, according to Map Quest on the Internet," Joe Giralo politely answered, "the classic vacation resort is approximately four hundred and eighty miles from my Jersey residence, about a nine-hour drive. But since we'll be cautiously taking a scenic roundabout route, then the trip will require about...."

"About ten total hours," Sal Velardi courteously interrupted his immediate superior. "But Joe, what's so uniquely perilous about this new exploit? I mean truthfully, golf seems to be a rather innocent and peaceful preoccupation."

Inspector Giralo cleared his throat and then very carefully uttered his lucid explanation. "Guys, I'll level with you about most that I've recently learned from Chief Riley's Washington Office. There's been some rather serious Internet chatter that's been slickly cloaked in encrypted messages. Much to Riley's satisfaction, our skillful Cryptology Department has capably intercepted and deciphered what constitutes significant domestic threats. And the name 'Operation Greenbriar' has now surfaced among certain terror group communications along with their disclosing of the designated summer dates August 7th to August 14th. In all his great wisdom," Joe Giralo summarized, "Riley has sternly warned me to have two of us alternately out playing the greens at 1 Montague Drive, Oakhurst Links while the remaining two of us are patiently doing surveillance and stationed inside our handsome West Virginia Wing hotel suite. And if and when something abnormal or drastic happens," Giralo hypothesized and genuinely stressed, "the agents doing due-diligent reconnaissance inside the suite are to cell phone the other two of us trekking out at The Links, and then the lucky players will promptly contact *this* very noteworthy confidential phone number. Such action will send a dependable response team into instant reaction!"

Inspector Giralo then reached into his shirt pocket and distributed three copies of the clandestine phone number to his subordinates and quickly requested that his trio of dedicated colleagues memorize the prescribed eleven digits and then rip-up the numerical information before arriving at their exclusive hotel paradise. The driver next articulated that the government operation might be either a massive false alarm or it could actually represent the initiation of a mammoth counter-espionage/terror plot operation, which extensively involved major coordinated police/military deployment.

From meandering I-81 the light gray Chevy Suburban soon progressed southward, and later the vehicle's four occupants were motoring on I-64 in the direction of U.S. 60. The determined agents' verbal exchanges again centered around their' highly-anticipated dramatic interaction with the incomparable landmark Greenbriar Lodge Plaza Hotel.

"Confidentially Men, we're masquerading as the Board of Directors of the Jersey Universal Construction Corporation," Joe Giralo informed his all-too-inquisitive riders, "so I want the three of you acting extremely professional while convincingly impersonating top Wall Street executives in quest of excellent gourmet dinners, the ultimate in golfing experience, and finally, some much-deserved rest and relaxation. Is that clear?"

"Tell us more about our mystery destination," Agent Orsi insisted. "It's got quite an excellent reputation if it's the same place I'm thinking about."

"I've found-out via Google that the luxurious hotel has 751 swanky guest rooms and suites, has nine terrific restaurants, sports a splendid tournament-caliber golf course, has three distinct coffee shops, possesses a marvelous health club, contains a quality casino and also boasts of a heated indoor pool worthy of European royalty. But allow me to emphasize," Inspector Giralo austerely expressed and then paused, "outside of us taking turns dining later in the week at the fancy ritzy restaurants in sets of two, we are to at all times during daylight hours be assigned as a pair of agents confined inside the West Virginia Wing suite and the corresponding duo positioned out at The Links on Montague Drive. Is that perfectly clear?"

"And I presume that Riley's efficient office secretaries had made our arrangements for our suite reservations, all on the government dime," Sal Velardi deducted and related. "Too bad I can't get a full body massage after we arrive on the job. My decrepit, deteriorating back is aching like you can't imagine! My vertebrae feel like I've been lying in a coffin for a full century!"

"Wasn't the hotel a surreptitious U.S. Government compound during the late '50s and early '60s Cold War era?" Art Orsi verbalized, deliberately ignoring Agent Velardi's futile attempt at sit-down comedy. "I remember reading something fascinating about that fairly interesting fact a couple of months ago."

"You have rather enviable reading comprehension skills," the normally no-nonsense driver humorously remarked, a trifle out of character. "When the West Virginia Wing had been shrewdly added in the 1950s, a spectacular underground 'Bunker' was also furtively constructed directly underneath the surface architecture, thus effectively concealing the Bunker's true purpose. There is enough space in the hidden labyrinth to accommodate at least a thousand people for months on end. Powerful subterranean generators could easily operate the sophisticated ventilation system along with the necessary sanitation waste facilities."

"Now I recall the magazine article I had read! The enormous Bunker was built to be a safe haven for the White House executive branch, for the Congress and for the Supreme Court to all hold meetings underground if Washington DC were to be destroyed by a foreign enemy, namely the Soviet Union, during a hostile nuclear attack," Agent Orsi eloquently contributed to the discussion. "I mean, the Senate and the House of Representatives' members would alone amount to around five hundred people to feed, to sleep and to provide adequate shelter. And if my erratic memory serves me correctly, during the 1950s, many households had their own fallout shelters, the apprehensive homeowners fearing radiation fallout from widespread atomic warfare!"

"Yes Art, and in addition, four large meeting rooms were designed and fabricated to accommodate the three separate branches of the federal government," Inspector Giralo conveyed to his still-alert three passengers. "But as I've already told you three amateur geniuses, the popular tourist-attraction Bunker will be off-limits to us. We're going to be strictly confined to The Links and to our West Virginia Wing suite until some obvious anomaly occurs," Giralo keenly reiterated. "And please don't forget! Seven hundred to a thousand other business executives will be holding various conferences and occasionally reveling at the hotel while we're conscientiously performing our stealthy FBI sleuth and gumshoe work!"

"Those seven-hundred to a thousand other hotel guests aren't FBI agents, too!" Agent Velardi joked.

"Say, there's the Greenbriar Lodge Plaza just ahead," Dan Blachford declared with relative enthusiasm as he excitedly pointed his right index finger. "Just look at those magnificent white columns and the fantastic garden flowers and shrub landscaping treatments near the main entrance. This place is quite impressive indeed. No wonder why it's classified and advertised as a 5 Star resort. Say Boss, please refresh my faulty memory. What was the name of the company we're supposed to be representing?"

"The Jersey Universal Construction Corporation," Inspector Giralo angrily commented, shaking his head in absolute disgust. "And may I remind you Dan, along with your two distinguished comrades, you Blachford are supposed to be the company Treasurer, Art, you're the Secretary, Sal, you're the business's President, and of course Gentlemen, I'm the revered Corporate CEO should anyone at the hotel ask our identities. It's very important that we all know our various company roles while we specialize in objectively keeping our eyes and ears open and our hyperactive mouths very scrupulously sealed!"

* * * * * * * * * * * *

After registering at the hotel's main lobby desk, the four federal men, accompanied by two friendly bellhops, took an elevator to their West Virginia Wing third-floor suite, which consisted of a spacious parlor area, two beautifully decorated bedrooms, plush green drapes and matching mint-colored carpets, and last but not least, a rather sensational window view of the ageless Allegheny Mountains. Under ordinary circumstances, the tasteful suite would have been a sensual pleasure to behold.

The accommodating Greenbriar Lodge Plaza bellhops were each rewarded with ten-dollar "expense account" tips, and next the cooperative and grateful resort employees exited the comfortable living quarters and soon, the weary travelers began unpacking their suitcases and methodically placing their clothing items into bureau drawers inside the two separate bedrooms. Agent Velardi was awarded "the privilege" (by his boss's authoritative decree) to share the first bedroom with Inspector Giralo. After those perfunctory tasks had been accomplished, the four government men ordered steak and potato dinners via room service. All was peaceful and tranquil with the outside world.

"We're basically stuck in a week-long Twilight Zone alternating between this fabulous suite and The Links Golf Course, which to the average person would be similar to being sandwiched somewhere between Heaven and Nirvana," skeptical Dan Blachford orally evaluated. "None of us will ever be able to stroll around the East and West Terrace sectors or for that matter, even venture-out to the Presidents' Cottage Museum. It states in this informative brochure that twenty-six U.S. Presidents have stayed here at one time or another, the most notable latest one being Dwight David Eisenhower. And even though all four of us live within driving distance of Atlantic City, we can't even try some entertainment gambling in the hotel's casino. I should've joined the IRS or the NSA like my mother wanted me to do."

"When you're on assignment," a somewhat-peeved Inspector Giralo explained the obvious, "you're on company duty twenty-four hours. That's the Bureau's principal rule that I must enforce and it's the standard 24/7 policy that *you* must obey. And unfortunately," the Boss continued, "for you Dan, the casino is seldom jam-packed because it's only available to regular guests staying at the hotel. No outside FBI visitors are allowed!"

"And it describes in *this* pamphlet I'm holding how this resort was originally built near a sulfur water spring that had been believed by locals to relieve agonizing pain associated with severe arthritis and rheumatism," Agent Orsi chimed-in. "Actually, the place was known as White Sulphur Springs for the first hundred and twenty-five years of its existence. But in 1858, a hotel was erected on the property, and during the Civil War the resort had been occupied by both Confederate and Union forces. But soon after the War Between the States, the popular hotel reopened for business. But in 1910, the property was then acquired by the...."

"By the Chesapeake and Ohio Railroad," added and embellished Agent Sal Velardi, who had been reading from the same pamphlet as Agent Art Orsi. "The structure was given the name Greenbriar Lodge Hotel and the original appellation has survived from 1913 right up to the present. And as you might be aware, the Chesapeake and Ohio is now CSX Corporation. In fact, there were several CSX executives down in the lobby when we were applying our alias John Hancocks to the traditional Registration Guest Book."

"Wow! An appellation in the Appalachians!" Arthur Orsi enthusiastically jested. "What wild irony!"

"Say Inspector," Dan Blachford butted-in. "Besides the fact that the noble Duke of Windsor, the wealthy Kennedy Clan and illustrious movie stars like Bing Crosby have vacationed here, what new pertinent details can you tell us about the Bunker from your elaborate Internet research. Just the thought of its basic purpose is both creepy and intriguing. I mean, the 1950s must've been very scary times all throughout America."

Joe Giralo gulped-down the remaining ounces of his delicious hot coffee and then typically grunted to intentionally gain everyone's attention. "In case of a nuclear holocaust, the Bunker was created under the West Virginia Wing as a clever emergency shelter to house the United States government officials. I had read that the Bunker contained radio and TV studios that could have broadcast explicit instructions and programs across the country to citizens that might have been still able to receive radio wave transmissions. Also," Inspector Giralo proceeded with his exposition, "patriotic flags and random familiar Washington backdrops were in the background, all designed to inspire a feeling of national pride and unity should a nuclear attack be initiated by the then Evil Empire, Soviet Russia. And incredibly Fellas', there were eighteen underground dormitories in the Bunker that could phenomenally sleep sixty people each. Give me a calculator, and I'll do the essential math."

"Precisely one thousand and eighty people," arithmetic wizard Art Orsi piped-up. "It was a pretty colossal engineering achievement. That's almost as many folks as the number of students now attending Hammonton High School."

"And each of the underground dormitories had accessible shower areas along with myriad toilets and an accompanying small lounge sector," Joe Giralo continued his general dissertation to his captive audience. "And there was even a hospital clinic situated inside the premises, the area having twelve beds manned by a staff of competent military physicians and reliable nurses. The entire enterprise was quite an amazing undertaking for the relatively primitive medical and scientific technologies that prevailed over a half-century ago. And here's one more relevant item that I failed to mention. The gigantic blueprint had the government code name Project Greek Island."

"Pretty extraordinary!" Agent Sal Velardi blustered. "But let's be totally candid here. The ugly downside of this strange mission is that none of us will be able to tour the Bunker. I feel like I'm being deprived of witnessing the vestiges of a huge part of 1950s Cold War

History. Let's face it. The Cuban Missile Crisis during the Kennedy Administration could've swiftly led to total worldwide human devastation."

"And the world is no safer today with plenty of terrorists, jihadists, along with drug and gun smuggling cartels running rampant all over the globe, including South, Central and most importantly, North America," the Boss reminded his all-too-garrulous underlings. "Our numerous duties and heavy responsibilities are being seriously challenged every single day!"

"And what about the exceptional championship golf course that we're prevented from playing," Dan Blachford mildly protested. "I believe this place is on the official PGA tour. I'm willing to bet a week's salary on it!"

"Yes Dan, you can keep your hard-earned money. The big tournament is held in early July right here on the ground's well-manicured Old White Course, which the hotel depicts as being somewhere between impeccable and immaculate," Inspector Giralo solemnly verified. "I guess that even a super resort such as this one has to once in a while engage in some nice, self-serving propaganda from time-to-time."

Before retiring to their separate bedrooms for the night, the four restive government men watched the local West Virginia evening news in the suite's handsome parlor, and during the ever-boring television commercials, the G-men conversed in an impromptu manner about the country's porous southern borders, about the perils of illegal immigration "coyote criminal activities," about militant hate groups abounding in the United States of America, about the ineffectiveness of Congress and finally, about the general decline of morality throughout the nation.

In the end, Inspector Joseph Giralo reviewed the vital ground rules for the agents' stay at the glorious Five Star Greenbriar Lodge Plaza Hotel, and the proud boss accentuated for all mission participants to always be on the same page. "I'm requesting that each man now states his individual role, duty and responsibility during the proposed enactment of "Operation Greenbriar Lodge Plaza Hotel. Our response to any developing dilemma must be fast, decisive and efficacious!"

* * * * * * * * * * * *

The agents' first four days at the acclaimed Greenbriar Lodge Plaza Hotel were fortuitously without incident or consequence. The relentless FBI men alternated in sets of two, a pair occupying the attractive third floor West Virginia Wing suite while the other duo engaged in morning and afternoon rounds of golf on the 9 Hole Links. Evenings were spent watching television, engaging in pleasant dialogue, playing poker and blackjack, and when feeling less energetic or being downright ambitious, reading several contemporary action/adventure novels that Agent Sal Velardi had brought along to neutralize the risk of ensuing boredom.

The three lower rank agents were observably thrilled when Inspector Joe Giralo imperatively announced early Thursday morning that *that* evening Art Orsi, Sal Velardi and Dan Blachford would be permitted to enjoy swallowing-down sumptuous suppers in the grand facility's main dining hall.

Friday morning, Agents Orsi and Blachford were scheduled to remain in the comfortable third floor suite while Joe Giralo and Sal Velardi rode in the gray Suburban over to Montague Drive to engage in their now-familiar repetitious golf course routine. Everything in the Universe seemed relatively copacetic until Inspector Giralo insisted on taking a Mulligan after topping his ball off the tee on his first wooden club swing.

"Don't feel bad Inspector!" Agent Velardi mockingly encouraged. "There's two acceptable ways to play golf. There's the fairway and then there's the unethical way!"

"You're more on the ridiculous side of hilarious than are either Art Orsi or Dan Blachford," the irritated Boss quickly chided and replied. "Learn to implement some common sense, which evidently today is not-too-common! At least your fellow agents, Salvatore, know how to exercise discretion in what they think and then say. Sometimes it's best and most advisable Sal to simply keep your ultra-critical thoughts exclusively to yourself!"

"Sorry Boss! We're all human!" Agent Velardi apologetically maintained. "Sometimes my valiant confederate Agent Orsi will miss the ball off the tee and almost violently corkscrew himself into the surrounding turf. And when not making a huge divot, sometimes Agent Blachford will smack the ball into the nearby woods or he'll inadvertently endanger unaware golfers putting for birdies on nearby greens. And once Dandy Dan crushed a ball so hard that it smashed directly through the large pane window at the Buena Vista Country Club back in South Jersey!"

"Well, Salvatore, I shot a seven on the first hole and those double pond water hazards tended to intimidate me," the befuddled Inspector begrudgingly retorted. "That lousy misfortune completely wrecked any chance of me ever arriving at a Par 4!"

"I'm not trying to pander to you, but quite frankly, you're much better at performing complex detective work than you are at imitating either Sam Snead or Tiger Woods!" Agent Velardi praised and then chuckled. "And furthermore Boss, we both shot lackluster eights on the 322-yard Par 5. But don't feel too depressed!" Velardi recommended. "At the clubhouse on Tuesday morning, I overheard several amused guys say that one Mississippi fella' several years back incredibly shot a 28 on #2. Based on *that* pretty remarkable statistic," Agent Velardi conjectured and rather persuasively expressed, "I'll wholeheartedly confess Boss that we're both having an outstanding day out here on The Links!"

"And the third tee we're now approaching is quite difficult even though it's only 102 yards to the pin," Inspector Giralo assessed and concluded. "That pond over to the right of the green is an awesome detriment and the sand traps are a bit deceiving. Maybe it's time for us to take-up the leisure-time sport of tennis, or even more propitious and beneficial yet, when we return to Jersey we ought to just become burned-out couch potatoes, sleepily watching the Masters at Augusta on our big screen den televisions!"

"That 52 I had shot Tuesday on this Par 37 nine-hole course was truly rather abominable, and confidentially Boss, I've always considered myself a sixteen handicap on typical Par 72s back home," Sal Velardi defensively elucidated. "That usual performance would be comparable to an eight handicap on this abbreviated course, and using *that* certain infallible metric," the agent continued his weird justification, "a round of 45 should be my average on *this* course. And carrying these heavy golf bags around in the hot summer sun is sort of an encumbrance all by itself. As you know, I'd much prefer zooming around the course in an electric cart, even with *you* in control sitting behind the wheel, Inspector. In all due respect Boss, you awkwardly drive a golf cart around as if you're carelessly piloting a bulky ponderous Chevy Suburban on a snake-like rural country road! Say Boss, why do they call some golf courses 'Links'?" Velardi inquired of his well-educated superior.

"Because Salvatore," Giralo said without any hesitation, "in the beginning days of the sport, most golf courses were built along bays and seas. The holes were positioned back-to-back just like the links in a chain, thus the origin, or should I say 'etymology' of the English nomenclature 'Links'!"

Just then Inspector Giralo's cell phone rang, and quickly forgetting his trivial quarrel with Agent Velardi, an expression of seriousness immediately was exhibited upon the Boss's facial features. On the line was Dan Blachford, and the distressed agent sounded as if he and Art Orsi were encountering imminent duress.

"Inspector!" Dan Blachford loudly gasped. "There was just an urgent call from the lobby desk, and the frightened employee stated that all guests in the hotel are to evacuate their rooms and report with dispatch to the downstairs Cold War Bunker. We've also been informed by management that some sort of bomb threat or some kind of security breach has necessitated this spontaneous action. Sorry Boss, but I must soon have to terminate this conversation!"

"There's a definite aberration in progress!" Joe Giralo determined and asserted. "If it's demanded of you Dan, both you and Art are to surrender your cell phones to any intruding radical perpetrators. They mustn't suspect that you're on duty FBI men! Whatever you do, don't resist or offer any struggle while attempting to defend yourselves. What's *that* terrible background noise I hear? Is there someone pounding on the door with their fists?"

"Yes, and they're demanding that we open the portal right this second!" Agent Blachford whispered into his cell phone. "And Art and I are looking out the window and there is a caravan of Avis, Hertz and Budget box trucks parked out front. And there are squads of what looks like armed Mexican bandits and Arab jihadists toting an array of rocket propelled grenades and AK-47s. The maniacs are hopping out of the backs of those box trucks, and Boss, they're presently storming into the building's main and side entrances like a herd of savages! The entire place is under siege. We're right in the middle of a ruthless terrorist attack! Boss, I've never been so scared in all my life! Everything sounds like pandemonium out there in the corridor! I think Art's hyperventilating in an advanced panic mode!"

"Dan, you and Art are to cooperate with the villains, er, I mean hostile insurgents!" the FBI Boss constructively suggested. "Open the damned door before the fanatics break it down, barge-in, and then wickedly do you two men physical harm! Do you read me Blachford! Give yourselves up without any violence!"

Boisterous shouting, obnoxious chaos, remote gunshots and overwhelming confusion dominated the other end of the line as yells of "Allah Akbar" blasted-out from Inspector Giralo's trusty cell phone. And then quite predictably, the electronic transmission went dead as the fierce motivated invaders took full control of the third-floor suite and next roughly confiscated the agents' apparently nondescript communication devices.

Inspector Giralo did not waste any time hesitating about initiating his next move. He instinctively pressed the memorized numbers of the secret alarm code into his cell phone, and then exercising full concentration, "the Boss" adroitly pushed the object's "Send" button. "Counter-operation Greenbriar Lodge Plaza Hotel" had successfully been launched.

"Now Sal!" unfazed Joe Giralo urgently commanded his momentarily paralyzed companion, "it's time for us to return to the besieged hotel and personally witness the upcoming battle unfold. Let's just hope that all of the Greenbriar's terrified visitors and guests have been safely escorted into the establishment's protective underground Bunker. I hope and pray that Dan and Art's lives are not at-this-moment in jeopardy!"

* * * * * * * * * * * *

Time was indeed of the essence. The austere-minded Inspector and his affable golfing partner speedily cut across a fairway and next quickly hastened to the Oakhurst Links half-empty asphalt parking lot. Upon reaching the dusty Chevy Suburban, the on-a-mission men anxiously deposited their heavy golf bags into the rear storage space. Surprisingly, Inspector Joe Giralo's cell phone again rang, and the muffled voice of flustered Agent Dan Blachford was discernible on the other end.

"Boss, I'm down here in a remote corner of the underground Bunker with at least a thousand other hotel guests. I'm crammed between an IBM executive, a Bank of America director and two panic-stricken guys from Alcoa!"

"Tell me Dan, is everyone now safe and sound inside the Bunker?" the FBI chieftain desired knowing.

"Yes, I do think we've all now been barricaded, inside," Dan Blachford nervously answered. "And the stinking terrorists have pilfered my cell phone along with my expensive Rolex watch that my wife had given me for our twentieth wedding anniversary. Boss, I'm now calling you from my miniature cell phone that I had hidden and stored in the hollow heel of my right shoe," the rattled agent rambled on. "The rambunctious marauders never once suspected for one iota that either Art Orsi or I are undercover G-men. And Boss, the vicious, reprehensible riffraff also heisted Art's wallet and cash as well as mine too!" totally frustrated Dan Blachford communicated and complained. "It's pretty darned scary being a helpless victim, that's for sure! But it's a good thing we didn't take our pistols and holsters along on this trip or else Art and I would probably be floating inside some huge black crucible's boiling hot water just about now!"

"Never mind the monotonous minutia!" Inspector Giralo adamantly rankled. "Hang-up immediately Dan! I gotta' call Army Colonel Bob Bauers right this second! He happens to be the head coordinator of this intensely complicated operation!" Click.

The very efficient FBI Investigator had Robert Bauers on his cell phone's speed dial, and upon making the prompt connection, Joe Giralo calmly advised the Colonel of the vital information that *he* had recently gleaned from hostage Agent Dan Blachford. "That's right Colonel. Everyone of importance is now locked inside the Bunker. That includes all the hotel guests, too! You can send your combat teams into the battle arena. Good luck accomplishing your imminent engagement, Sir!" Click.

On the short drive from The Oakhurst Links back to the embattled Greenbriar Lodge Plaza Hotel, Inspector Giralo thoroughly explained to Agent Velardi the major confrontation that was about to transpire both around and inside the popular resort, the comprehensive explanation occurring just as a swarm of Apache attack helicopters zoomed by, maneuvering a mere hundred feet or so above the commonplace Chevy Suburban.

According to the Inspector's very detailed litany, a diverse thousand-man conglomeration consisting of lethal military commandos, Delta Force, Navy Seals, expert Army snipers, along with experienced state and local SWAT squads, had been assembled to counteract the in-progress brazen terrorist attack upon a highly treasured iconic American landmark. Back-up helicopter units coming from as far away as Roanoke, Virginia had already been dispatched to the intensifying and very fluid scene of battle.

"The random accumulative chatter that's been received and interpreted from the most militant Jihadist websites has presented the stark scenario that the Arab and Iranian terrorists, who had reportedly crossed the Rio Grande from the El Paso and Brownsville, Texas areas into the United States, have maliciously planned to raid the Greenbriar Lodge Plaza Hotel, gain full control of the enormous facility, and then make an international political statement by dramatically dying in an Alamo-type shootout with our various law enforcement agencies," Inspector Giralo shared.

"And Boss, what about their criminal Mexican accomplices?" Sal Velardi curiously asked. "How do those evil felons fit into the rather egregious scheme of things?"

"The demented Arab and Iranian jihadists plan to become crusading martyrs, deliberately sacrificing their lives to Allah inside the hotel, but in the process, they had owed the formidable Mexican drug and gun smugglers a rather colossal debt for assisting them entering into the country and then soon getting the vile crusaders furtively transported from Texas up here to West Virginia," the Inspector verbally conveyed to his loyal cohort. "And Sal, the money, the jewelry and the other valuables that had been purloined from the thousand sequestered hotel guests sealed down inside the emergency Bunker would be used to pay off the Mexican criminals, who would gratefully stash their newly acquired plunder inside several of the rented box trucks and then speed away to local safe houses with their very valuable stolen loot."

"Wow!" exclaimed an astounded and excited Agent Velardi as another intimidating wave of descending Apache helicopters zipped-by above. "And Dan's prized Rolex watch represented a minor part of the thieves' tremendous payoff! If he loses it during this thrilling mission, I'll never hear the end of it! And tell me Boss," the thoroughly impressed agent switched his thinking, "where are these thousand or so American commandos coming from?"

"Many of the Apache helicopter units had been stationed at the Greenbriar County Airport. Another strategic staging area, where the Delta Force and Navy Seals are originating from, is the town of Lewisburg, situated about fifteen minutes in a chopper flight from here. And the quick response SWAT teams were being camped at another town named Caldwell, located directly between Lewisburg and White Sulphur Springs."

"Do you mean to tell me that you knew all of this secret information and never shared it with Dan, with Art or with me?" objected Agent Velardi. "What kind of Boss are you?"

"I figured that the less info' you mischievous fellas' knew, the better off you three lower-level sleuths would be, that is, having much less data to think and worry about!" Inspector Giralo confided as his gray Suburban suddenly arrived at the renowned hotel's entrance. "Now Sal, I've been specifically instructed by Colonel Bauers to stay in the car until this full-scale battle terminates. His Delta Force unit will conduct the full operation!"

"Holy cow pastures, Boss! There's a whole slew of dead bloody bodies strewn all throughout the front flower and shrub treatment areas!" shocked Agent Velardi panted and vociferated. "Mostly Mexican coyotes I presume, with several Arab and Iranian holy war warriors scattered around in between the other corpses! And notice that a half-dozen choppers have already landed on the hotel's roofs, and look around Boss," Velardi resumed his graphic description, "at least a dozen more have converged and landed all around the esteemed edifice! And just look at all of the empty military jeeps and troop transport trucks surrounding the blocked Avis, Hertz and Budget box getaway vehicles!"

A blazing battle royal ensued on all floors of the revered hotel as the Greenbriar Lodge Plaza was indeed horribly transformed into a modern-day Alamo. Forty-five minutes of close combat elapsed with perpetual gunfire rounds being gradually diminished, both in scope and sequence. Finally, all sounds of a variety of weapons being shot had ceased, and then a face that Inspector Joe Giralo immediately recognized appeared on the scene.

Colonel Robert Bauers exited his command-and-control jeep, slowly approached the now-grimy parked Chevy Suburban, and the Delta Force leader merrily shook hands with an old acquaintance, venerable Inspector Joe Giralo, who was still sitting stationary behind the steering wheel. All the while, rambunctious Agent Sal Velardi looked-on in sheer admiration.

"Congratulations Joe! I'll have to recommend to Matt Riley that *you* ought to be promoted at the Bureau. Your strategic involvement in this remarkable grand hotel siege will definitely be much appreciated and honored by the President!"

Inspector Giralo abruptly turned to Agent Velardi and matter-of-factly said, "Now your' good pal Dan will be able to retrieve his coveted Rolex from one of those rented box trucks! And it's a good thing that we were able to plant several of our elite personnel into the Mexican and terrorist organizations and suggest to them that the hotel guests be held as hostages in the Bunker. Pardon my oversight Colonel Bauers. I'd like to introduce you to Agent Salvatore Velardi, one of my most trusted men, who incidentally had been highly instrumental in contributing to the overall success of this very intricate quasi-military operation!"

"From the outset Colonel, I never once imagined the great magnitude of this immense operation!" Agent Velardi marveled and expressed. "I'm quite awed by it all! Your military strategy was outstanding!"

"And just think," Colonel Bauers declared and then momentarily hesitated to contemplate recent reality, "I nominally estimate that perhaps, conservatively speaking, two-to-three million dollars of extensive damage has been inflicted upon this noble queen venue of American resorts. This exquisite hotel was the perfect opportunity for *us* to get five hundred or so zealous enemies congregated into a small area to be systematically killed en-masse. Regrettably, there're plenty of doors that have been smashed, numerous walls riddled with bullet holes, ornate chandeliers demolished, and there's also scads of carpets smeared and stained with blood and flesh tissue. And that's not counting the multiple grenade explosions *we* had used to save American lives! But now, this historic structure will serve as a fine inspiration of national patriotism for all future visitors to amply value and appreciate! This magnificent grand hotel has been traditionally regarded as a tourist Mecca for well over a hundred years," Colonel Bauers emotionally emphasized, his fervent words meandering out of his normally stoic disposition lane, "and right now it sort of really looks like a morbid Middle East Mecca, especially with all of these lifeless dishonorable Arab and Iranian corpses lying around!"

"It looks like August of 2011 will be a calendar month for posterity to remember," Agent Velardi blurted-out. "Thank goodness the evil terrorist plot has been eliminated."

"Indeed!" Inspector Giralo concurred. "Salvatore, you've just spoken the bloody truth!" the Chief accurately concluded as his keen eyes surveyed the extensive human carnage strewn about the popular resort's violated grounds.

"Friendship"

Jeffrey Marsh was quite depressed after reviewing the contents of his *Oakcrest High School 1967 Yearbook.* Marsh's senior year had been a glorious one, all-state New Jersey quarterback in football, president of his senior class, and the handsome young man had also been head-cheerleader Samantha Ross's distinguished escort to the Oakcrest junior-senior prom. 'My life's been in a dreadful downward tailspin ever since 1967,' Jeff lamented as he disgustedly slammed his high school yearbook closed and then tossed it into an open desk drawer.

The proud former athlete pondered the nagging source of his melancholy. 'I flunked out of *Rutgers* second semester of my junior year, never was offered the pro football contract I had always wanted, have been divorced from Samantha for the past seven years, and now *she* has custody of Ricky and Caroline. And to top it off,' Marsh concluded, 'I need nine-hundred-thousand-bucks to buy out my incompetent unreliable partner in *our* foundering real estate business. Life's been a real miserable bummer for me since high school, a thorough and total disaster that's for damned sure!'

The doorbell ringing interrupted Jeffrey's very disconsolate daydreaming. He rose from his den's most comfortable red leather desk chair and briskly stepped to his modestly furnished Galloway Township townhouse's front door. Frank Donoghue was standing there with a handful of letters, bills and assorted junk mail.

"Hello Jeff," the jovial-but-efficient mailman began, "I have a registered letter for you to sign for."

"I hope it's not another nasty demand or legal threat from my wife's carnivorous attorney," Jeff abruptly answered. "I already pay more than my share of alimony and child support because of that money-hungry vulture."

"I don't think so," Postman Donoghue casually replied. "The registered letter looks more formal than official. I share your conviction about the legal system and I too have little affection for leeching lawyers and their bloodsucking profession."

"Thanks for endorsing my sentiments, Frank," Jeffrey Marsh returned as he anxiously signed for the unexpected item. "I'm glad someone else understands my animosity for sue-happy people and their viperous legal representatives. I'm now motivated to see exactly what this important correspondence is."

The resident re-entered his dwelling, waved farewell to his genial visitor and then gently closed the green wooden front door. Jeffrey's restive mind was suddenly filled with abundant curiosity. 'I wonder what sort of letter this is,' Marsh suspiciously considered. 'It's certainly much more interesting than any junk mail or telephone, cable or electric bill, that's for sure!'

The real estate broker quickly tore open the envelope and studied the eight-square-inch card's language, handsomely scrolled in calligraphy, which he immediately recognized as a special invitation from a long forgotten past acquaintance. Marsh's head shook from side-to-side in disbelief as the fascinated recipient examined and then comprehended the interesting letter's content.

  Jeffrey,

You are cordially invited to a party among old friends to be given at my palatial estate situated between Bethany Beach and Fenwick Island, Delaware on Monday, September 8, 2003.

I request that you drive to the Tuckahoe Inn at Beesley's Point where you can park your automobile. I have arranged for my widely acclaimed yacht *Friendship* to be docked at the pier adjacent to the restaurant. Be prepared to board my personal cruising ship at eight a.m. sharp. The captain of my pleasure craft will transport you from the Great Egg Harbor River and down the *Atlantic* from Ocean City, New Jersey to my elegant mansion on the Delaware Coast.

Jeff, I have a big surprise awaiting you. Wear casual attire for your once-in-a-lifetime cruise but please bring along a tuxedo for the formal, black-tie gala to be held at my mansion afterward.

I trust that you will be able to attend my exclusive affair. If you cannot, please write and another visit to my vast estate can be scheduled.

Your Oakcrest High School classmate,

Milo Cabot
1 Network Road
Bethany Beach, Delaware 19930

Jeffrey observed the date on his kitchen wall calendar, Tuesday, July 15th. Then he hastily perused his personal agenda book to determine if the Atlantic Coast cruise aboard the *Friendship* interfered with any important business appointments. 'No conflicts,' Marsh acknowledged. 'I'll leave Monday through Wednesday open to accommodate good old Milo. I haven't seen the skinny wimp since high school graduation. Who would have ever thought that the biggest and squarest egghead at Oakcrest would become a prominent American billionaire? Milo really hit it big in the computer networking industry and he's been on the cover of several national business magazines,' the real estate broker recalled. 'Maybe I can convince Cabot to lend me a paltry million bucks to buy out my lazy partner's half of our struggling real estate company. Milo might just be the Godsend I've been praying for to rescue me from a humiliating bankruptcy.'

Marsh opened the freezer compartment door and plunked four ice cubes into a glass. Then after shutting the refrigerator's bottom door, he advanced to the liquor cabinet and generously poured a *Jack Daniels* double. The dreamer sipped the powerful whiskey and contemplated how he would approach Milo Cabot in private and describe *his* unfortunate financial dilemma to the successful and now-famous entrepreneur. 'Milo always had a kind heart in high school back in 1967,' Jeffrey recollected, 'but unfortunately, he avoided all class reunions since 1985 when he systematically began accumulating his incredible fortune. He'll certainly help me out of my present difficulty once I convey the simple details. Milo always looked up to me as a role model and as a staunch ally,' the real estate man remembered with a broad grin. "A million bucks is chicken-feed to a rich guy like Milo Cabot!'

Jeffrey very deliberately crossed-off each day on his kitchen calendar from July 15th to September 7th. Following a restless night's sleep, finally the morning of his seven-week-long anticipation arrived. Marsh checked the red-number read-out on his alarm clock and sprang out of bed before the object would begin playing an FM station's music at six a.m. 'Only an hour to shave, get dressed and have some coffee and toast for breakfast. I'm glad I already have my tux carefully stashed away in my car's trunk,' the ecstatic fellow remembered.

After packing a suitcase in which he kept a change of casual clothes, underwear and his beige-zippered toiletry case, Jeffrey Marsh donned his black Bermudas and put on his colorful Hawaiian shirt. 'I almost feel like a hormone-driven teenager again,' he wishfully thought as he admired his well-groomed appearance in the bathroom's *vanity* mirror. 'I'm glad I inserted a fresh razor blade into my shaver. Who knows? I might be reunited with a long-lost high school sweetheart at Milo's posh get-together.'

Jeffrey Marsh toted his suitcase to the front porch, locked the townhouse's front door and paced out to his aqua green 2002 *Honda Accord*. He clicked his key chain's remote control and the trunk sprang open. After inserting his piece of luggage, Marsh was ready for his pleasant drive to the historic Tuckahoe Inn. "I'll take *Route 322* to scenic *Route 9*, the highway Bruce Springsteen always sings about. Of course, Asbury Park and the *Stone Pony* are about sixty miles north of Mays Landing,' the blithe man chuckled. 'The *Garden State Parkway* will be more crowded than usual so I'll just relax and take the old Beesley's Point Bridge across the bay to Tuckahoe. I can't wait to board and inspect Milo's yacht. Knowing *his* new reputation, it must be a real dandy!'

The early morning September 8th *Route 9* excursion was indeed pleasurable and soon the aqua green *Accord* was crossing the Beesley Point Bridge, which spanned the Great Egg Harbor Bay. 'It's called Egg Harbor Bay because birds often nest here to lay their eggs. And over there are the twin stacks of the South Jersey Power Plant,' Jeff noticed as his four-door vehicle approached the tollbooth situated in the center of the antiquated span. 'Wow, the toll's now a hefty sixty cents! I remember when it used to be a mere thin dime.'

The dual spans of the *Garden State Parkway Bridge* were to the driver's left and Marsh recognized the familiar bumper-to-bumper congestion of tourists motoring south from Philadelphia, New York and Atlantic City down to popular vacation resorts Ocean City, Sea Isle City, Avalon, Stone Harbor, Wildwood and Cape May.

After fumbling in his coin tray for the precise change, the traveler then handed the three silver-plated objects to the amiable collector. As soon as the *Honda* continued its transit across the quaint but in-need-of-repair bridge, Jeffrey's keen eyes spotted a glistening object reflecting morning sunlight from the vicinity of the Tuckahoe Inn. 'That must be Milo's sleek vessel!' Marsh jealously marveled. 'Its appearance is regal, somewhere between being spectacular and magnificent. Oh my God! The ship has three levels.'

The impressed man next drove his modest *Accord* into the almost-vacant Tuckahoe Inn asphalt lot and inconspicuously parked in the rear. After removing his suitcase and his rented black tuxedo from his common means of transportation's trunk, Jeffrey sauntered in the direction of the splendid custom-designed yacht. Upon reaching the gangplank, Marsh was surprised and thrilled to see two former high school acquaintances engaged in general conversation with the *Friendship's* captain.

"Hello Jeff!" greeted Kathy Landis, a friend of Samantha's that had always idolized the Oakcrest Falcons' first-string quarterback. "Fancy meeting you here!"

"Hi Jeff," a rather weak voice added. "Do you remember me from chemistry class?"

"Why if it isn't Richard Daniels," Marsh exclaimed. "I haven't seen you since the last class reunion at the Venice Plaza over in Berlin. You wrote the term paper on Archimedes that enabled me to get out of Oakcrest. And oh yes," Marsh recalled. "Hello Kathy! You were a terrific leader for the school debating team!"

"Jeff, I'd like to introduce you to Captain James," Richard Daniels formally insisted. "He's going to navigate this beauty down to Milo's place, or should I say 'palace' in Delaware."

"Quite a luxury ship, Captain James!" Marsh instantly evaluated. "I'll bet with the radar and triple-decks of opulence, this baby probably easily goes for between two and three million clams, even in the throes of a recession."

"Well, Mr. Marsh, that's really a humble low-ball figure you have alluded to," the tall Captain replied with a forced smile. "Mr. Cabot does everything first class, and with all of the *Friendship's* special amenities and fine ambiance, money is really no object to my employer, if you know what I mean!"

"How long will our ocean voyage take?" Kathy Landis asked. "I once got horribly seasick in a rocky rowboat at Lenape Lake Park in Mays Landing."

"About four and a half hours," the navigation specialist returned. "We'll be stopping off at Rehoboth Beach to pick up Mrs. Cabot. She's doing some casual shopping down in Delaware at the clothing mall outlets and should have an extensive new wardrobe to take back to Bethany Beach with her."

"Then Milo is married?" Jeffrey inquired. "I could never picture him in high school having a sound relationship with any female."

"Yes sir Mr. Marsh," Captain James confirmed. "Mr. Cabot married a former *Miss Maryland* finalist seven years ago. The two get along rather harmoniously. Now if you please," the slightly nervous pilot indicated to Marsh, "if you don't mind, I'll take your suitcase and tuxedo aboard and temporarily store them in a closet."

"Here they are," Jeffrey offered. "I believe I can trust them to your care," the new passenger jokingly added.

When Captain James departed up the gangplank and then stepped into the fabulous white yacht's interior, the remaining threesome struck up an impromptu cheerful chat.

"Tell me Jeff, are you still involved in real estate?" Kathy Landis innocently asked.

"Yes, and are you still working in banking?" her former heartthrob requested knowing.

"I got a recent promotion to branch CD Officer," Kathy indicated, "but I didn't tie the marriage knot for too long. Now that I'm getting older, I do regret not having any children or a faithful husband around the house. I guess I'm really loyally married to my job, and *my kids* now are those cherished Certificates of Deposit I sell to appreciative Mays Landing bank customers."

"And how about you?" Marsh asked the usually laconic Richard Daniels. "What are ya' doin' for a blessed living, and are you married?"

"I'm single and still playing the field," Richard informed. "I'm a political science teacher at *Camden Community College*. I had taught high school Social Studies for four years, but I got tired and frustrated of all the stupid discipline problems and educational bureaucracy. The college scene is much more satisfying to me than public school education ever was."

Just after Captain James accompanied by a teenage boy again appeared on the main deck and then shuffled-down the sturdy gangplank, the high school acquaintances observed a tanned, svelte female carrying two new suitcases to where the *Friendship* had been moored. Jeffrey almost swallowed his tongue and tonsils when he recognized that the attractive, dark-tan woman was none other than his former spouse.

"Samantha, what on Earth are you doing here?" wide-eyed Marsh stammered. "I mean, you look so ravishing!"

"Feast your deceitful eyes," the well-built lady replied with an air of contrived sophistication. "You had your chance with me, but fumbled the football, Mr. Quarterback," the exotic-looking woman cackled as she drew reactive forced smiles from Kathy Landis and from Richard Daniels. "Why Richie! So nice to see you again!" the former Miss Samantha Ross stated. "And Kathy, this is indeed a marvelous coincidence!" the all-too-wily female continued. "I still believe that you and Richie would make a terrific couple! And as for my former husband, I think that we'll both try and be old friends simply tolerating each other and we'll fake being genuinely sociable on this particularly pleasant ocean adventure."

Jeffrey Marsh figured that he would change the subject to avoid further embarrassment or conflict from his sharp-tongued ex'. "Who is your young mate there, Captain?" he asked while showing his general inquisitive nature.

"This is Jacob everyone," Captain James revealed. "Jacob is Mr. Cabot's only stepson. His wife Sierra's young lad by a previous marriage."

"Hello, and welcome aboard the *Friendship*," Jacob snottily and insincerely announced. "Miss Ross, I believe, I'll take your luggage inside."

"Why thank you Jacob," Samantha answered as courteously as she could. "That was very sweet of you. You seem to be a respectful and mannerly young man. That's a quality lacking in most youth now-a-days," she exaggerated.

"Thank you, Mam," Jacob mechanically replied. "I sometimes enjoy being first mate on this ship and being its only permanent porter. A little common labor once in a while never hurt anyone as my stepfather always says."

"Okay, you landlubbers; let's get this ark sailing," the yacht's Captain suggested as he waved everyone aboard and then signaled for four workers stationed at the dock to loosen the heavy ropes that moored the *Friendship* to the newly constructed Tuckahoe Inn pier that jutted out into Egg Harbor Bay. "I'll gently raise the gangplank by pressing a little red button as soon as everyone is safely aboard for departure."

"Oh Richard," Samantha uttered as she ascended the gangplank and attempted to ignore her handsome former husband. "I almost got lost driving here. I keep getting Tuckahoe geographically confused with Tuckerton."

"Actually Samantha," Richard Daniels qualified, "Tuckahoe is a village located right next to Beesley's Point and Tuckerton is a town situated ten miles or so on the mainland above Atlantic City."

"That's what I always admired about you Richie," Samantha Ross falsely complimented. "You know so much trivia that you put the rest of us to shame. Now tell me Captain, how long has Milo owned this fantastic ship."

Captain James explained to his guests that *his* employer had owned the *Friendship* for over a year. "Since as you know Mr. Cabot is partially paralyzed in his left arm, my employer seldom pilots the ship and has assigned me to perform that task. I was also Mr. Cabot's chauffeur for six years before I obtained my captain's license to navigate the *Friendship*."

"How long have you worked for Milo?" Kathy Landis inquired.

"For thirteen years," Captain James seriously replied. "Thirteen dedicated years of service as gardener, butler, chef, chauffeur and finally, as captain."

"Who's maneuvering the ship from the pier?" Jeffrey instinctively inquired. "Is there another pilot aboard?"

"Jacob," the captain related. "He's almost as skilled as I am and insists that he must practice the important chore to impress his stepfather." Then the gray-haired man with handsome features continued his standard monologue about the well-appointed ship. "The *Friendship* was custom-manufactured for Mr. Cabot. The Burger Boat Company of Manitowac, Michigan built this nifty ninety-five-foot-long gem. It has an enclosed bridge and as you know it possesses three breathtaking observation levels."

"Isn't *thirteen* years regarded as an unlucky number?" interrupted Jeffrey while referring to the tenure of Captain James' employment with wealthy Milo Cabot. "Some of us may be a tad superstitious, you know!"

"Thirteen is a number just like any other number," Captain James diplomatically and objectively countered. "But I must add that Mr. Cabot believed that Midwest boat builders produce a better ocean-worthy product than east coast companies do. That accounts for *his* preference."

"Tell us more interesting details," Samantha implored while again feigning sincerity. "I always like learning new things about the secret habits of the rich and famous."

"And so, this ship was launched in Michigan and I then piloted it from the Great Lakes through the St. Lawrence Seaway and next down the East Coast to its principal mooring just below Bethany Beach, Delaware. It was quite an exceptional adventure and also an honor for me to perform. Now if you all will excuse me," Captain James finished his answer, "I'll climb up to the bridge deck and assist Jacob with his challenging responsibility. I'd hate to have the Coast Guard board this flawless vessel and present me with a nasty citation. Please make yourself comfortable in the air-conditioned lounge. I'll soon dispatch Jacob to service your individual drinking and eating needs."

As the four guests leaned against the vessel's railing and scanned the bay's shore, along with the landmark Tuckahoe Inn, each was thinking of his or her own selfish design for agreeing to be entertained by the renowned and eccentric computer networking mogul, Milo Cabot.

'I know Milo will lend me the cool million to salvage my real estate business,' Jeffrey Marsh considered. 'He'll be more-than-happy to aid an old friend.'

'Maybe I'll flirt with Milo and turn him on. He always liked me back in high school,' Samantha imagined, not knowing that Sierra Cabot was just as treacherous and just as vivacious as she was. 'That would make my former husband jealous and perhaps I could have a secret affair and land a very rich husband in the process.'

'I want to quit teaching at the college and then start-up my own computer networking company,' Richard Daniels fantasized. 'Milo will surely give me the seed money I need to fulfill my ambition, and with a little luck, my corporation might grow into the next Cisco Systems or into the next Cabot Enterprises.'

'I need to quit my boring bank job,' Kathy Landis regretfully rehashed in her mind. 'I'll ask Milo for a management position in his wonderfully prosperous company. I'll be a steadfast employee. I feel a personal debt to Milo Cabot for what I had accidentally done to him in high school. I need to heal scars from the past and in the meantime guarantee my future security.'

Everyone's reverie was interrupted by Captain James's distinct voice over the ship's intercom speakers. "The *Friendship* is too huge for us to take the *Inter-Coastal Waterway*. This is an ocean-worthy vessel so we'll proceed south on the Atlantic rather than travel slowly down the bays that separate the barrier islands from the mainland," the licensed operator informatively divulged.

The four captivated guests stood and leaned against the main deck's railing as the *Friendship* gingerly left the marina next to the Tuckahoe Inn and soon Captain James adroitly steered the craft as it majestically glided under the twin spans of the *Garden State Parkway*. Even the huge cylindrical stacks of the South Jersey Power Plant suddenly appeared harmonious with the peaceful nautical and pine barren environments it shared.

"Every time I see that electric plant my mind thinks of some advanced form of Arab-inspired terrorism," Jeffrey related. "I know that violence is an obscure possibility, but the threat always seems to haunt my psyche."

"Ever since *9-11*," Richard Daniels said as he stared at the power company's twin towers, "everyone including me is a little paranoid. The safest and most innocent place could suddenly materialize into a mass disaster area. The possibility of sabotage is now present almost anywhere and everywhere in America!"

"I can't wait to see Milo after so many years," Samantha Ross stated off subject. "I wonder if he's still shy and introverted," the woman added as she glanced across at her ex-husband and contemplated *his* strong tan muscular forearms. "I think Milo Cabot was actually cute in his own peculiar way *our* junior year."

"You never know which direction fate will take you," Kathy Landis contributed. "Whoever suspected in their wildest imagination that Milo Cabot would become one of the wealthiest and one of most influential men on the whole planet. Every citizen from Main Street to Wall Street knows and reveres *his* name."

Soon the *Friendship* had gracefully left the tranquility of Great Egg Harbor Bay and smoothly entered the dark blue Atlantic. The Ocean City Boardwalk along with its many food concessions and amusements soon came into view. The four passengers scrutinized and relished the familiar stretch of white sandy beach along with the wide wooden commercial platform's popular pizza, popcorn, salt water taffy and souvenir shop businesses.

Captain James's baritone voice was again heard from overhead speakers. "We'll be cruising down the Jersey Coast at about twenty-two knots. Enjoy the spectacular scenery. The *Friendship* is fully capable of crossing *the pond* to Europe if it had to. It is a most dependable ship and I take great pride in being its captain."

"Look over there to our left," Kathy impulsively requested. "There's the old Flanders Hotel. It's been recently renovated and converted into plush condominiums."

"And there's Ninth Street to our right where the Chatterbox Restaurant is located three blocks down from the boardwalk," Jeffrey Marsh reminisced and reminded his listeners. "Samantha, remember when *we* used to eat at that place during our college year summers while working down there on the boardwalk earning money to pay for our tuition and textbooks?"

"Yes, and what about the Music Pier and Convention Center?" Richard Daniels mentioned and pointed to a familiar structure jutting out into the Atlantic. "The building looks almost exactly as it did back in good old 1967."

'Samantha sure has remained beautiful and alluring after thirty-six years of wear and tear,' Jeff Marsh assessed. 'Maybe I should have given our marriage a second chance like *she* had wanted.' Then the woeful real estate agent contemplated a troubling question his mind had been rehashing. "Say Samantha, who's taking care of Ricky and Caroline?"

"My sister Nancy," the beautiful blonde woman bluntly answered. "She has excellent rapport with both *our* children." And then Samantha had a rather covetous thought. 'I wish I was in bed with Jeff right now. His biceps and shoulders are looking better and better by the minute.'

"Let's go inside and have a drink," Kathy recommended. "We can review old times and classmates without this wind messing-up our hair."

The four guest passengers entered the ship's spacious air-conditioned lounge area and sat in comfortable green leather chairs around a circular solid oak table. Jacob entered dressed as a formal restaurant waiter. "Would you folks care for anything to drink?"

"Yes, I'll have a double of *Jack Daniels* on the rocks," insisted Jeffrey as he inadvertently licked his lips.

"I'll have a tall Tom Collins," Samantha ordered. 'I wish that Jeff wasn't such an avid alcoholic. That's the major reason why I divorced him,' she recalled.

Kathy Landis asked for a Pina Colada and Richard Daniels requested a Rusty Nail. Then the four reunited classmates engaged in nostalgic conversation. And after a second round of potent beverages, everyone had loosened-up their inhibitions enough to at last be honest about their communications.

"I always thought that Milo Cabot was a trifle peculiar," Samantha honestly admitted. "He was a *nerd* a full two decades before the terminology ever became part of the American pop culture scene. Milo was definitely somewhere between an egghead and a common fink back then!"

"Milo and I competed for the honor of being the best academic student in the graduating class," Richard recollected and mentioned. "He was much smarter than I was but I somehow managed to be his staunch rival throughout high school. Boy, now I wish he and I had been closer friends than we actually were. Milo was always a little aloof and distant," Daniels bluntly stated. "I believe he had additional eccentricities, but I suppose I'll never be privy to what those specific quirks might be."

"Richie, I absolutely concur with your on-target impressions," Kathy agreed. "Milo was a bit timid when it came to dating girls. But now I regret not having an affair with him. I mean I did marry Steve Hart and we stayed together for two years," she related, "but then we didn't hit it off and my life ever since has been one plagued with lonely drudgery and dreadful aggravation."

"You know what you should do, Samantha," Jeffrey Marsh playfully proposed to avoid hearing any more of Kathy Landis's grievances with life. "You could give us one of those old Oakcrest High fight cheers for old time's sake. You were one helluva' head cheerleader."

"I'll be ready, willing and able after another round of drinks," the gorgeous woman promised her flattering admirer. "It'll be easy once I warm up to the occasion."

Captain James skillfully guided the *Friendship* along the enchanting Jersey Coast. The ship seemed to be gliding along as if the eternal sea was a continuous sheet of wave-less navy-blue salt water. The four passengers exchanged fond memories as they sat in the lounge around the impeccable circular oak table. Meanwhile the vigilant skipper kept the vessel on a parallel path about a mile off the irregular Jersey coastline.

"Why do you think Milo invited the four of us to his mansion?" Kathy Landis boldly asked her fellow passengers.

"Actually, I believe he's looking for some sort of closure to an ugly chapter in his life," Jeffrey theorized and replied. "He's now looking for our acceptance. In his heart Milo craves to gain the lost prestige that he had missed during his formative years. Only the four of us, being the most popular kids in his high school class could satisfy his dire emotional need."

"What gives you that strange impression?" Samantha challenged while demonstrating her typical domineering attitude. "How can *you* even pretend forming such a strong opinion about someone we all hardly ever knew?"

"I do suspect there's a giant void in Milo's life," Jeff Marsh summarized. "He simply desires filling that vacuum with us giving him his lost recognition. I mean we were the four envied class officers and poor Milo was basically a non-entity," the former quarterback and class president hypothesized and shared.

"I believe Jeff's correct in his theory," Kathy Landis concurred. "I was vice-president, Richie was class treasurer and Samantha, you were the senior class secretary."

"Holy cow!" Richard Daniels exclaimed. "How time flies! I had forgotten that we were the four class officers forty-three years ago when Oakcrest High was brand new!"

"And now that Milo has gained international notoriety," Jeffrey Marsh continued, "he has to reinforce that new-found domination by validating himself to us. It's his way of making a proclamation that he's made it big in the real world. It's Milo's way of obtaining tribute and honor from those that had overshadowed him in high school. Milo was what you might call a late-bloomer!"

"I now agree with my ex after listening to *his* persuasive argument," Samantha reluctantly confessed. "I think Jeff's right on the money," she begrudgingly acceded. But then the conniving woman surreptitiously kept her secret thoughts to herself. 'Jeff is intelligent and physically alluring, but Milo's got the heavy-duty bank account. I'll try to use my feminine charms and entice *him* to buy me a new *Mercedes*. If I remember correctly,' the cunning woman speculated, 'Milo had a mild crush on me in high school. I don't care if he's now married to *Miss Universe*, or whatever she is. I'm gonna' get that expensive white convertible if it's the last blessed thing I ever do!'

The *Friendship* soon passed the coastal town of Strathmere and now several high rises from Sea Isle City could be seen to the southwest from the immaculate ship's spotless pane windows. The resort town was mostly residential and not nearly as commercially oriented as Atlantic City or Ocean City. Nevertheless, Sea Isle's exclusive ocean frontage sold at a premium price as did most limited, but in demand, land did along the heralded and enticing New Jersey Coast.

Five minutes later Jacob again awkwardly entered the ship's lounge and appeared with a tray having a coffee pot, four cups with saucers and a delicious-looking already-sliced cheesecake. After the encumbered junior waiter distributed plates, forks, knives and teaspoons and then poured four cups of the freshly brewed java, the guests indulged in consuming the delectable dessert by devouring two cheesecake slices each.

"This boat is almost as well-equipped as an ocean liner," Jeffrey Marsh mentioned to Jacob. "I'll bet it'll be yours some day when your stepfather buys a *Cunard*-ocean liner all for himself, and sails-off to the Mediterranean."

"Oh Jeff, just look at those expensive mansions in Avalon and Stone Harbor!" Samantha jealously shouted as she pointed out the ship's windows. "They go from anywhere between three and five million each. An acre of beachfront property sells for a cool million at bargain basement prices," the gorgeous woman elaborated. "Some rich people buy an old ocean front house for two million, have it demolished and then they effortlessly construct a five-million- dollar palace in its place."

"Big deal!" a somewhat perturbed Jacob snottily declared. "My stepfather's mansion cost fifteen million to build and now he's tired of the dump and plans to have a bigger and better beach residence erected. He's already discussed the details with his architect."

'I'm definitely going for an Ocean City condo' in addition to the white *Mercedes* convertible,' Samantha Ross decided. 'I now know I should have flirted with Milo back at Oakcrest. I was too into myself and into my vain popularity to seriously realize *his* great potential!'

The ship's ever-trusty propellers churned the outstanding seaworthy vessel past Wildwood, and the four travelers led by Jeffrey Marsh sang a dissonant version of Bobby Rydell's classic pop hit "Wildwood Days", which celebrated the glorious joys of spring and summer high school escapades at the amusement-laden boardwalk featuring sensational carnival-ride piers having mammoth waterslides. Richard Daniels thought about his college fraternity taking over the flashy town and *its* honky-tonk venues, Kathy remembered her friend's wild bachelorette party at a downtown Wildwood 50s'-style art deco motel, and Samantha and Jeffrey mused about their first experience at lovemaking underneath the expansive boardwalk while hundreds of unwary vacationers promenaded on wooden planks eight feet above *their* passionate embraces. Soon Jacob appeared with another round of potent drinks and after setting the tray on the sturdy oak table, Milo's egotistical stepson dutifully began cleaning-up the dessert plates.

"My stepfather demands that I learn life as he did from the bottom up," Jacob mildly complained to his audience in a melancholy tone of voice. "Someday, I'll be sitting in the chairman-of-the-board driver's seat and giving similar commands to my eldest son just to keep Pop's stupid slave tradition alive."

"We'll be cruising by Cape May in about half an hour," Richard observed and stated. "I just love all of the colorful Bed and Breakfast places. It's the most Victorian resort town on the entire East Coast."

"It's certainly an expensive tourist trap," Samantha opined. "But the town has lots of character, charm and history too to balance things out! A visit there is like taking a swell journey into the past. Sometimes the tour guides dress-up in turn-of-the-century costumes and you get the feeling that you're actually living in the 1890s."

"Anything in Cape May is a dump compared to my stepfather's castle," Jacob arrogantly interrupted, "and that's the plain simple truth without any bragging. One-day Pop will buy the dumb town and change it into something modern. He's the only person that I know of that could pull that maneuver off without a hitch!"

The picturesque Cape May Victorian edifices soon faded from view, the exquisite and historic lighthouse on New Jersey's southern peninsula was speedily passed, and without hesitation the *Friendship* was soon beyond the Cape May tip of New Jersey and crossing the mouth of the Delaware Bay.

"Look, there's the old concrete ship that sunk just off the inlet," Richard said while using his right index finger. "It was an experiment that was a dismal failure to conserve steel for army use during *World War II.*"

"And there's the Cape May-Lewes Ferry on its way to the Delaware shore," Kathy perceptively noted. "From a distance it looks like it's going to rendezvous with the ferry coming in the opposite direction from Lewes."

"I've been on several deep-sea fishing expeditions out of Cape May," Jeffrey Marsh informed his listeners, "and the Baltimore Canyon is about ten miles or so from here out in the Atlantic. It's a haven for serious anglers!"

'And *you* always came home from charter-boat fishing drunker than an Irish sailor,' Samantha concluded and kept to herself. 'That's when *your* erratic behavior was a total embarrassment to always have to explain to Caroline and to Ricky.'

"We'll be docking in about an hour and fifteen minutes at Rehoboth Beach to pick-up Mrs. Cabot," Captain James sternly announced over the intercom speakers. "All passengers can relax on chaise-longues out on the sundeck if you'd like. There's a whirlpool spa running for your convenience."

The *Friendship* cut across the seventeen-mile-long mouth of Delaware Bay as if it were a knife severing through a sea of soft butter. Jeffrey, Samantha, Richard and Kathy frolicked about on the wooden sundeck like school children exploring their first playground experience. All of their immediate world appeared innocent, carefree and full of gratifying luxuries as the foursome dangled and splashed their feet in the spa's swirling water.

When the streamlined yacht docked at the northern end of Rehoboth Beach, the four guests ceased their playful romping and dried off using towels that had been generously supplied by their wealthy absent host. It was now time to put on their shoes and sandals and formally meet the very stunning Mrs. Sierra Cabot.

A tall, tanned, radiant woman was standing on the side pier holding six bags of newly acquired apparel. "Over here Jacob!" she yelled to her apathetic spoiled son. "Come and help me with these horribly heavy packages!"

The gangplank was lowered and Captain James reached out to assist the temporarily overwhelmed lady onto the yacht. "Welcome aboard Mrs. Cabot!" 'the Admiral' courteously greeted. "May I introduce you to Jeffrey Marsh!"

Sierra Cabot took a glimpse at the man's handsome face, pearly-white teeth and powerful body and a sudden broad smile beamed just above her chin. The now-dazzling-looking auburn-hair woman suddenly abandoned her usual sarcastic demeanor. "And this is Samantha Ross, a fellow high school classmate of your husband," Captain James stated to Mrs. Cabot.

The two glamorous women fiercely stared at each other, both instantly recognizing a rival's charm and grace when those distinct qualities suddenly confronted each of them. The pair lovely ladies feigned brief smiles as their suspicious eyes made direct contact.

"And here are Richard Daniels and Kathy Landis," 'the Admiral' formally introduced the guests to Sierra Cabot. "They also had graduated Oakcrest High School with Mr. Cabot in 1967, back in New Jersey."

"Glad to make your acquaintance!" Sierra nonchalantly declared with a false degree of etiquette. "Now if you'll all excuse me, I'll retire to my stateroom. I'm completely exhausted from that ghastly shopping spree. And that bus ride to the dock with all those nasty tourists was rather atrocious and quite pedestrian to say the least. I should've gotten my husband's chauffeur to wait and drive me back to Bethany Beach, but Milo insisted that Paul had to drive *him* to Salisbury to close an important legal transaction. At any rate," Sierra Cabot protested in an exaggerated sophisticated manner, "here I am. Jacob, please be so accommodating as to carry my new belongings to the master cabin."

"Okay everyone, you may return to either the recreation den or to the sundeck spa area!" Captain James bellowed to his four original passengers. "Mrs. Cabot is fatigued from her lengthy shopping ordeal and requires her rest. We should be shoving off in about five minutes and are scheduled to arrive at South Bethany Beach in about one hour. Please enjoy the beautiful Delmarva peninsula viewed from the ocean."

The four travelers retreated to the sundeck where they discussed their various appraisals of Sierra Cabot. Opinions were flying around like bullets at the infamous O.K. Corral.

"Sierra is certainly a beautiful woman," Richard began his very honest analysis, "and she could probably win the Mrs. Delaware Beauty Pageant right now if she was a contestant. Next to Samantha, she's the most stunning creature I've ever seen."

"Thanks for the nice very polite compliment," Samantha Ross answered. "But it is quite obvious Milo's wife has a haughty disposition that won't quit. I can see where Jacob gets his ugly self-centered conceit. If my son Ricky ever acted like Jacob does, I would smack him across the face so hard that his teeth would rattle. That snooty kid needs his jaw fractured at least once!"

"Perhaps you're being a little too judgmental of Sierra and of Jacob," Kathy Landis cautioned her opinionated acquaintance. "Samantha, you don't know enough about either of them to even begin writing the preface to their biographies."

"True," Samantha defensively replied, "but I'm a devout believer in first impressions being accurate, and I think that Milo's snobby wife and *his* bratty stepson are ambitious parasites bent on exploiting Milo's extraordinary wealth."

"Samantha, I can't believe that you feel so damned threatened and insecure because of the presence of another formidable heavenly female in our midst," Jeffrey criticized. "The two of you stared at each other like a pair of felines about to claw each others' eyes out. And neither of you was openly acting out your hostility either! The animosity between the two of you was quite palpable and easily felt. It's a good thing Sierra retired to her cabin or else a vicious cat-fight between you and her was bound to occur."

"You should have been a child psychologist," Samantha sarcastically remarked and ridiculed. "You don't have the capacity to ever satisfactorily psychoanalyze adults," the sharp-tongued woman finished in one of her predictable, classic put-downs.

"Enough personality assassination! Let's change the topic to something more relaxing," Richard intelligently suggested. "I don't appreciate conflict in real life. I prefer vicariously encountering and experiencing it in the movies."

* * * * * * * * * * * *

Milo Cabot stood still as a statue peering-out from a window in his fabulous mansion's north tower. A faint white object was barely visible glistening like a white diamond floating on the calm-but-shimmering sea. The computer-networking tycoon's eyes were transfixed on the inimitable *Friendship* as it strategically approached its South Bethany Beach destination. Hatred gradually swelled in the wealthy man's normally cold heart.

'All I loathe and despise on this Earth is now sailing on my yacht,' Milo imagined. 'I hate you Sierra for cheating on me with that avaricious scoundrel Martin Jamison, alias Captain James, my disloyal yacht meister! Your little love affair has not gone unnoticed,' Milo angrily recalled. 'Yes Sierra, you've attempted stealing my vast fortune right after you succeeded in stealing my vulnerable heart, but your scheming, evil, black soul is destined to soon meet its demise.'

Milo Cabot paused for a moment to avoid acting too hastily and prematurely. He very methodically wiped some cold sweat from his forehead despite the good air-conditioning system inside his private, lofty "Tower of Meditation." 'And to you Master Jacob, my greedy and craven stepson, you want a fortune without working for it as I had diligently done. You are a dangerous nefarious punk ingrate dreaming of ways to eliminate me and making your mother and you my exclusive heirs. Yes Jacob, you and your greedy mother are identified as principal heirs in my recently written will, but I shall survive the both of you and then gleefully modify my last testament!' Cabot mentally predicted. 'Your vile spiteful conspiracy against me will be a total failure!'

Milo Cabot's diabolical heart was pounding loudly inside his frail chest cavity. The thin-but-tenacious man breathed heavily while garnering the required audacity and the resolute inspiration to perform his premeditated heinous misdeed. 'You three vile vipers have seriously wronged me. Captain James and Sierra, you shall pay for your infidelity and for your reckless scheming and you too Jacob shall be swiftly punished for your lusty covetous ambitions!' paranoid Milo Cabot thought in an almost maniacal trance.

And as the fabulous *Friendship* came within a mile of Milo's resplendent ocean estate, more wicked thoughts surfaced from the networking tycoon's turbulent soul up to the man's now-livid consciousness. 'And you four high school classmates had grossly violated my good intentions in the past,' the madman recollected. "You Samantha Ross had crushed my ego when you refused to go to the junior-senior prom with me. I have carried this lingering grudge for forty-three agonizing years, and now is my chance at obtaining retribution!" the highly irritated insane lunatic internalized and then mechanically whispered to the tower's window. "And you, Jeffrey Marsh, class president and fearless football quarterback, you used to taunt and pick on me in the halls and push me around for the amusement of your muscular jock friends. I have never forgotten your mean-spirited cruelty or the extreme humiliation that your insensitivity had caused me to suffer," Milo uttered in a lucid tone of voice. "Your perpetual browbeating and your incessant belittlement have not escaped my memory! Soon revenge will be mine! All mine; you despicable bully!"

And after a sobbing interval of self-pity, Milo proceeded with his demented muttering. "And oh yes, Richard Daniels, cunning Oakcrest fellow graduate. You had stolen Mr. Jenkins's final physics exam' and at the end of the school year beat me out by a tiny infallible fraction on grade-point-average. You cheated and became class valedictorian while I had to settle for salutatorian. I have never forgiven you for depriving me of my justly deserved academic distinction. I had to live with the disgrace of being second best after dedicating my whole high school life to being the top honors' student in our class," Milo muttered to the window and also to the timeless sea in a state of self-imposed hypnosis.

Milo Cabot's bloodshot eyes were now bulging out of their sockets. His right fist was clenched and the man's long fingernails were penetrating his white-sweaty-palm. The vengeful gaunt genius had one more individual to indict in his self-proclaimed dictatorial prosecution. "And finally, Kathy Landis; I wholly loved you when we were in eighth-grade, but you always gave me your cold shoulder. I hated being ignored and I had to live eighth grade and high school as a rejected subordinate and as a social isolate. And then the week after the high school prom, you and I were involved in that terrible automobile accident!" Milo Cabot cried. "I have been paralyzed in my left arm ever since that fateful collision. I know *you* claim it was an accident, but to me I have had to live these past four plus decades with physical injury added to painful emotional insult! You should have never recklessly sped through that stop sign Katherine Priscilla Landis. And yet, I've managed to overcome all those immense obstacles, and through much sacrifice, and plenty of trial and error, I've ascended to the great societal height I've achieved with steadfast determination, along with with focused perseverance!" Milo angrily panted and pouted.

The billionaire then very slowly and meticulously opened the center drawer of his fancy handcrafted semi-circular dark cherry-wood desk. His thumb slowtly touched a red button that had been cleverly concealed inside. Just as the *Friendship* came within a half-mile's range of *his* superb ocean-side mansion, the jaded aristocrat firmly pressed the remote-control button. A powerful bomb detonated aboard the gliding yacht, and then a distant flash followed by a booming explosion was discernible upon the sun-kissed, shimmering Atlantic.

The *Meditation Tower's* door swung open and the chief butler appeared in the portal, the servant having a pallid alarmed expression upon his countenance. "Excuse me Mr. Cabot, but did you just hear a loud booming noise!" the startled butler gasped.

"Yes, Simms. I believe there are scattered thunderstorms in the vicinity and lightning must be approaching South Bethany. Be sure to have all windows shut in case of an unexpected cloudburst."

"Certainly, Mr. Cabot. I'll see that your instructions are carried out immediately!" Simms vowed as he deftly closed the secluded tower's sole means of entrance and exit.

'It's a good thing I shrewdly had the *Friendship* insured for only a third of its actual value,' Milo contemplated in a more rational and calculating state of mind. 'Oh well, I really need a new yacht anyway.' Cabot paused for a moment to collect his next thoughts. 'And besides, I have effectively and simultaneously eradicated all of my enemies from the present, and all of my harassers from the past. I'll testify to the authorities that I believe that misguided Arab terrorists were conducting an economic jihad against an eminent American capitalist, and that *their* fundamentalist beliefs have been responsible for the shocking sea explosion,' Milo Cabot schemed. 'Naturally, the unscrupulous Arab terrorists had miscalculated that I would be entertaining some innocent guests on my luxury yacht with *my* illustrious presence on board. I can't wait to give my already-rehearsed deposition. I'm certain that the police will accept my practical theory as being both plausible and valid. Hello future! Goodbye *Friendship!'*

"Rock, Paper, Scissors"

Every area epicure of fine food from Cherry Hill to Vineland knows about Vianna's Restaurant on White Horse Road in Voorhees, New Jersey. The establishment's six-page menu offers the most palatable Italian, American and seafood selections at very reasonable prices and the clientele consists mostly of professionals including eminent doctors and lawyers. Since Vianna DiAngelo speaks fluent Italian, her restaurant is widely reputed to be a haven for local Mafia members. Usually everyone entering the beveled glass door (including an occasional suspected hit man) dresses formally in business suits and exhibits refined aristocratic manners.

Several minor fracases have sporadically surfaced at Vianna's, which tended to sully the place's otherwise stellar culinary reputation. Earlier in May of 2003 the main chef quit when Vianna refused to fire two obnoxiously snooty waiters that continually taunted the kitchen headman. On another busy night in July, one of the waitresses became so frustrated by the fussy chef's demanding disposition that she first imitated *his* heavy Italian accent and then threw a handful of forks and knives into the air during a fit of rage, accidentally gouging a chunk of skin out of an unsuspecting customer's bald scalp. Before the waitress could officially announce her quitting to Vianna, the man's wife got into an altercation with the already indignant waitress and two-reputed Mafia figures in pinstriped suits then had to skillfully separate the combatants, providing the remainder of the patrons with "the night's entertainment." Other than those trivial incidents, "Vianna's" is generally regarded as a "tranquil, civilized business serving very excellent cuisine."

The restaurant does not accept "Entertainment Book Discount Coupons" on Tuesday nights, because on that special evening, tables at opposite corners of the main dining room are reserved for three incompatible contingents: doctors, lawyers and Mafia. On Tuesday evening August 12th, 2003, a gathering of four prominent surgeons was preoccupied discussing "shop gossip" at *their* reserved table.

"I have a fairly funny story to tell you," Dr. James Burke of Cherry Hill's Kennedy Memorial Hospital related to his three distinguished colleagues seated at the physician's weekly round table. "This story happens to be a real gem!"

"What is it?" pleaded Dr. Phillip Campbell of Vineland's Newcombe Hospital. "I could use a healthy chuckle to cancel out my mild indigestion! And I haven't even been served tonight's delicious supper yet!"

"Yes, give us the scoop!" implored Dr. Thomas Wagner, veteran head surgeon at Hammonton's Kessler's Hospital. "I hope your story is funny. I could use a good laugh."

"Don't bark it too loudly!" insisted Dr. Robert Layton of Our Lady of Lourdes in Camden. "This place is a cultured and refined restaurant, and not a disorganized chaotic operating room!" the surgeon jovially bantered.

"Okay gentlemen, here it goes," Dr. Burke suavely continued his story. "In *our* x-ray department at Kennedy we have a new doctor, a callow radiologist named Harold Dexter. He's getting married to a very lovely lady next Saturday." Dr. Burke paused to determine if he still had everyone's undivided attention. He was well-aware that his introductory remarks had generated a great deal of interest amongst his three critical and sometimes hypocritical friends.

"So, what's so extraordinary about *that* rather commonplace event!" objected Dr. Campbell. "So far your tale is the typical dog bites man back-page newspaper story. What about giving us some man bites dog fodder?"

"Really Jim," interrupted Dr. Wagner. "In Hammonton, we have a young radiologist over at Kessler who's also tying the knot next month. Radiologists get married all the time, just the same as internists, neurologists and nose and throat specialists do. So far your story is rather nondescript."

"I see you were all intensively listening to my eloquent preface," Dr. Burke giggled and then laughed before sipping from a potent whiskey sour. "Now if you'll all just be a trifle more indulgent, I'll proceed with my little anecdote."

"Don't bore us to *death*," Dr. Layton sarcastically advised. "Your captive audience is too young and ill-equipped to enter the hereafter right this moment!"

Dr. James Burke waited for the levity to subside before advancing to phase two of his narrative. "Anyway," the speaker resumed in a whisper, "this vernal radiologist Harold Dexter had to get married because he knocked-up his bride-to-be!"

"What was she, a prostitute?" cackled a half-inebriated Dr. Campbell. "One must really be careful how he distributes his sperms in this day and age, now doesn't he?"

"You'll never believe this crazy yarn in a million years," Dr. James Burke replied with a rather stern face. "The woman that Dr. Harold Dexter made pregnant before marriage happened to be a gynecologist at my hospital. Isn't that one of the funniest ironies you ever heard? A gynecologist gets knocked-up and the real victim is the overzealous radiologist! If anyone should know any better about averting pregnancy, it's gotta' be the impregnated female doctor! Ha, ha, ha!"

"It sounds like a definite case of entrapment to me!" Dr. Wagner opined. "I'm laughing so hard at that ludicrous story that I think I'll have to use the facilities soon! That delightful tale really takes the cake, icing and all!"

The table of stoic lawyers in the opposite corner of Vianna's had noticed the doctors' levity and were curious about what exactly had caused it. The four attorneys shrugged their shoulders in response to the surgeons' "undignified public behavior." Several of the men in three-piece suits found the doctors' boisterous deportment abominable.

"I wonder what's so damned funny with those emergency-room sawbones," Richard Harper, Esquire cynically commented. "You'd think those scalpel-wielding professionals were grade-school children cavorting out on the playground during recess!"

"They're more like scalpel butchers than scalpel professionals!" Attorney Seth Ruberton chimed-in. "No wonder why so many of them are sued by innocent patients suffering operation complications. They're acting like a cabal of raucous alcoholics having a bad humor convention!"

"I concur with Seth's accurate assessment," the famous trial lawyer William Davis promptly agreed. "Irresponsible surgeons are to blame for thousands of lucrative malpractice cases all across America. They bring them on themselves by being negligent, incompetent or inebriated. Thank God for tort cases to keep the fools in check!"

"Seth and Bill are right on target," stated Attorney Dennis Martin. "Those medical lunatics are becoming more and more boisterous every Tuesday night. You'd think that David Letterman, Johnny Carson and Jay Leno were sitting at *their* table. They ought to be optometrists, because I believe that they're making a real spectacle out of themselves!"

The assembled surgeons were much fonder of their exotic desserts and their imported coffee than they were of their professional counterparts seated in the opposite corner of the popular dining room. The doctors were soon aware of *their* loud conversation when the rest of the room's diners suddenly became silent. So becoming more self-conscious, the physicians then engaged in more docile and hushed exchanges that centered upon how most politicians in state government and in the *United States Congress* were "greedy lawyers" that made legislation mostly to benefit the success of themselves and of their "ignoble profession".

"I'm not too enamored with any pathetic lawyer," Dr. Burke maintained. "They're all devious scoundrels and quick talkers looking for technicalities to affect the outcome of a case in their favor. As you gentlemen know," the eminent physician added, "lawyers and costly lawsuits are to blame for the colossal medical malpractice insurance *we* annually have to pay. And the more language and the more pages that exist in a Congressional bill, the more lawsuits that can be generated by the vile scoundrels!"

"I know a surgeon on Long Island that converted himself' into a corporation and then he shrewdly made his wife and his children the principal stockholders," Dr. Campbell informed his very astute listeners.

"Why did he ever do such a terribly foolish thing?" Dr. Wagner challenged. "I would never consider having my wife and children having economic dominion over *my* destiny. It's preposterous even to consider such an absurd idea."

"It's not quite as ridiculous as you might have believed upon first impression," Dr. Campbell politely responded. "The Long Island surgeon refuses to pay malpractice insurance, period. If any patient's lawyer ever sues him, he owns absolutely nothing. His wife and children control all *his* assets, and then give him a modest salary of thirty-five thousand from the dividends in their shares of *him* being the corporation."

"I see definite merit in what Campbell is suggesting," Dr. Robert Layton seriously declared. "I pay over three hundred thousand dollars a year for malpractice insurance. That's money out of *my* pocket and taken away from my expendable income all because some greedy parasitic lawyers promote the practice of generating patient grievances against doctors. I don't know of any doctor who deliberately injures a patient," Layton emphatically insisted. "And yet *we* all must pay steep sums before taxes for the wrongful actions of a few derelict physicians and for the lust for easy money by the nation's leeching settlement-grubbing lawyers."

"Layton for Governor! Layton for President!" Dr. Wagner jested and then saluted with his wine glass. "Just look at those cavalier attorneys sitting over there all smug and complacent with their corrupt lot in life. They're hungry fleas out looking for dogs to feast off of!" the disgruntled doctor cited. "Shakespeare was no dummy when the bard supposedly proclaimed that the first thing a new government should do is eliminate all the country's lawyers. And Old Honorable William used a less polite term to dispose of the rabble than the benign word *eliminate*."

But Dr. Robert Layton was a brain surgeon that also often outspokenly despised paying for exorbitant malpractice insurance. Presently Layton needed to ask pertinent questions to obtain relevant answers. "Now Phil," the skeptical doctor said to Campbell, "can that Long Island specialist avoid being directly sued by making himself' into a corporation and having the company's profits divided among the lucky shareholders in his family?" the medical guru rhetorically asked. "I don't know if I could ever trust my wife and kids to handle *my* earnings! They would squander every cent that I had and would make me into *their* personal slave until age ninety or death, whichever came first! I think I'd rather take my chances with malpractice insurance!"

"That's exactly the point!" Dr. Campbell strongly indicated. "The Long Island fellow hasn't to my knowledge been sued yet to determine whether or not his insurance-evasion strategy would work. Maybe he just buys the minimal insurance allowed in his state just like a driver gets the highest deductible on his car insurance policy to lower the rates. And also," the loquacious doctor stressed, "I understand that the corporation pays him the meager $35,000.00 up front and then quietly gives him the quarter-million savings he has reaped from not paying for the maximum malpractice insurance, which represents a quarter of the corporation's earnings."

"Phil may have introduced a pretty significant argument tonight," Thomas Wagner injected into the forum. "You have to be more devious than either the lawyers or the Mafia to make a sizable disposable income nowadays. The whole idea behind malpractice insurance that the bloodsucking lawyers use as their trump card is that each individual is responsible for his or her actions," Wagner pointed out. "If the doctor's wife and kids own all stock in the man's corporation, they are probably exempt from being liable for the Long Island surgeon's prospective negligence lawsuits."

"I predict things are about to change for the better," James Burke prognosticated to his highly concerned colleagues. "The time for procrastination has passed and soon surgeons will be retaliating. I know of a growing conspiracy and I'm going to reveal some of it to *you three* geniuses in a few minutes," Dr. Burke confidentially shared with his closest loyal friends.

The gray-haired well-respected heart surgeon then whispered a general introduction of his incredible conspiracy scheme to his associates, all of whom were shocked-but-supportive of the general theme. "Next Tuesday night I'll review for you gentlemen the exact nature of the reprisal against malpractice lawyers. But first before I become more specific," Dr. James Burke articulated with sparkling eyes accentuating his forceful language, "I need the three of you to take a pledge of loyalty to *our* fraternal brotherhood of surgeons. Is this agreeable to everyone at this table?"

The three other medical doctors conferred briefly among themselves, and then unanimously assented to Burke's extraordinary proposition. Then while the other medical men were finishing-up their scrumptious Banana Foster desserts, Dr. Burke conveyed in a low voice to his fellow healers more details of his secret knowledge involving operating room procedures being conducted at certain Philadelphia and New York hospitals. The essence of Burke's amazing revelation would be sufficient enough to make Hippocrates's skeleton turn over in its grave.

* * * * * * * * * *

The following Tuesday night at Vianna's, the connoisseurs seated at the corner Mafia table seemed quite cheerful along with the doctor delegation, but the three lawyers present appeared rather visibly disturbed. Attorney William Davis, a chronic smoker had undergone a scheduled cancer surgery at a major Philadelphia hospital, but he unexpectedly died shortly after the intricate lung operation had been performed. Davis's funeral had been arranged for Thursday and the three listless attorneys sat somberly at *their* table and were not nearly as animated or as convivial as they usually were. The lawyers used that Tuesday night's dinner at Vianna's to sadly reminisce about and grieve their dearly departed friend.

After Dr. James Burke nonchalantly ordered his standard surf and turf entrée, the instigator whispered several preliminary sentences designed to inform his fellow surgeons the relevant details concerning William Davis's untimely death. Burke then respectfully read the elderly attorney's impressive obituary, which had been published in that morning's edition of the *Philadelphia Inquirer.*

"What happened during the lung operation?" Dr. Thomas Wagner insisted on knowing while feigning a degree of sympathy for the deceased. "Was there a problem with the anesthesia? Did Davis suffer a heart attack or stroke during the operation?"

"Remember now, last week you good men swore your allegiance to a medical fellowship fraternity," Dr. Burke reminded his dearest comrades. "Well, my most trusted colleagues, cooperative teams of surgeons at Philadelphia and New York major hospitals are systematically putting an end to *their* profession's ugly malpractice woes. Attorney Davis's passing represents the mere beginning of the overall solution."

"Could you please be more specific?" Dr. Thomas Wagner requested while almost choking on his fresh garden salad smothered with French dressing. "It sounds like you're evasively speaking in zany riddles."

"Yes, please elaborate on this arcane conspiracy/fraternity business," Dr. Phillip Campbell also demanded. "I hope its subject matter is above and beyond tabloid publication!"

Dr. James Burke divulged over dinner in the then crowded main dining room the particulars of his disclosure. His audience of three sat spellbound listening to *his* astounding-but-solemn rhetoric. Six eyes at the table focused on every syllable uttered from the acrimonious-and-vengeful heart surgeon's mouth.

"Operating room doctors in Philly' and New York hospitals have begun eliminating malpractice trial lawyers when *they* come in for either routine procedures or for delicate organ operations," James Burke objectively conveyed without a trace of guilt or emotion evident in his tone of voice. "Now *they're* calling on other doctors in *our* profession to join them in abolishing malpractice lawsuits by virtually eliminating greedy trial lawyers. Our fraternal duty is to reciprocate with *our* esteemed colleagues. It's basically come-down to the survival of our noble profession versus the avaricious nature of *theirs!"*

"Exactly how does this *termination* process work?" asked an intrigued Robert Layton. "To tell you the truth, it sounds a little too Arnold Schwarzenegger-like to me."

"Yes, and how did Davis expire? What were the specific circumstances?" Dr. Phil Campbell asked. "He's been a real thorn in many doctors' rear ends for over three decades now. His name had to be high-up on the hit list. Davis wasn't too revered by the medical profession in the Greater Philadelphia area!"

"Well Gentlemen," Dr. Burke methodically proceeded as if *he* was mentally preparing to adroitly perform a triple bypass, "Rule Number One is that a surgeon never murders a lawyer that *he* has had conflict with in the court room. Other doctors in other hospitals do it for him. Each team in every operating suite affected works together to make sure that the patient dies in recovery by screwing up *his* or *her* vital organs and his or her immune system. It's all connected with the administration of a secret non-traceable chemical injection that is virtually foolproof and undetectable."

"How does this retribution involve *us* suburban surgeons?" a now-very concerned Dr. Thomas Wagner asked while wiping some sweat-beads from his wet brow. "Some doctors might prefer paying out-of-this-world malpractice insurance rather than be active accomplices to obvious criminal acts. Felony acts if I might add! How about first-degree murder?"

"The doctors only dispose of lawyers that have given other surgeons severe financial difficulty," Burke dispassionately reiterated. "Now they want us suburban sawbones to get into the battle arena and join the crusade. Eventually the clandestine revenge scheme will be widespread and implemented all over the country."

"Won't all of the random attorney hospital deaths trigger a wave of police investigations and courtroom litigations?" Dr. Robert Layton incisively argued. "This revenge conspiracy indeed sounds like a very precarious business to me."

"Maybe," James Burke calmly answered. "But that's the only way to get rid of the plague of malpractice attorneys and the scourge of malpractice lawsuits. Eventually the lawyers will become so afraid of dying that they'll cease bilking honest money from dedicated doctors and then prey on some other vulnerable professions like pharmacists, accountants or even other lawyers. It's essentially Darwinian ethics gentlemen. Only the strongest species survive, only now it's professions and not species! The parasitic lawyers will soon find weaker targets to exploit once *they* totally fear the secret medical retribution factor."

"What else do you know that we aren't yet aware of?" Dr. Phillip Campbell anxiously inquired. "I mean Jim, surely you can tell us more important facts about this bizarre scenario than you already have. You've successfully stimulated my curiosity."

"Yes Phil, I have two pertinent things I can reveal right now," Dr. James Burke announced in a quiet-but-strong bass voice. "Number one is that Attorney Dennis Martin is going into a North Philly' hospital for a routine arterial stent insertion. I don't think you'll see him comfortably sitting over there at his customary table next Tuesday evening!"

"What's the second relevant thing you want to tell us?" asked a fascinated-but-apprehensive Dr. Thomas Wagner.

"We'll be finishing dinner tonight way before Martin, Harper and Ruberton get done theirs," James Burke observed and related. "Then we'll saunter over to their table and express our condolences to the three predator barristers for William Davis's unexpected death before *we* casually depart from the premises."

"Anything else?" Dr. Campbell asked Dr. Burke. "Jim, you have the charismatic characteristics of a dictator. You could have given Hitler serious competition."

"Yes, and be sure to wave at the grim-faced Mafia guys on our way out of Vianna's," Burke aptly suggested. "You never know when we might need the cooperation of notorious South Jersey thugs like Tony Valentino, Frankie "the Assassin" Scardino, Carmen Campanella and Nicky Tassone."

The next seven days elapsed rather slowly for Drs. Phillip Campbell, Thomas Wagner and Robert Layton, with each of the restive surgeons awaiting news of Attorney Dennis Martin's demise. All local daily newspaper obituary pages from the *Camden Courier-Post* to the *Press of Atlantic City* were thoroughly scrutinized. The trio had been assiduously scanning all regional papers like possessed men endeavoring to obtain physical tangible verification of James Burke's rather disturbing prediction. On the following Monday morning the prominent lawyer's lengthy obituary appeared in the *Trenton Times*. The three researching physicians quickly notified one another of the shocking article's publication.

On Tuesday evening Dr. James Burke elucidated on the Dennis Martin sudden death situation. "You plainly see my dear friends, Dennis Martin is officially dead by all newspaper accounts and as you can presently observe, the viperous malpractice villain is not now seated at the corner lawyers' table. In fact, the damned table is completely empty tonight."

"I now believe that your conspiracy group's tactics are already showing significant positive results," Dr. Campbell complimented his wily mentor. "The attorneys are either overcome with grief at losing another key associate or the remaining two malpractice case prosecutors are home fearing for their very lives. My friends, it's no fun being a duck floating inside an active shooting gallery!"

"Don't worry!" Dr. Burke confidently boasted. "Their day will come sometime in the future. We doctors must stick together and thwart those lecherous bandits that legally rob us blind with mammoth unjustified malpractice settlements, all granted by naïve sympathetic juries. It is ironic that we doctors must exterminate an undesirable element of the public to keep society-at-large healthy.

Harper and Ruberton fully know that *they* are white-collar crooks, just like their legal profession cronies, the nation's judges and justices. The corrupt vermin have the privilege of robbing us blind without ever using handguns."

"The Mafia men sitting over in the other corner of Vianna's don't seem too disconsolate about Dennis Martin dying, or about the attorneys not sitting at *their* familiar table," Dr. Thomas Wagner objectively noticed and contributed. "I've seen more melancholy displayed at New Year's Eve parties!"

"Now, my dear friends," Dr. James Burke said in a firm-but-low manner, "I understand that Richard Harper is scheduled to go to a downtown Philly' hospital for analysis of an irregular heart rhythm. His examiner was an old college friend of mine, and we're both graduates of the *University of Pennsylvania*. The diagnosing physician will definitely recommend a quadruple bypass. I've been recently contacted at my home and I was happy to hear from my old med-school dorm' roommate," Burke qualified and smiled. "He wants *me* to assist in performing Harper's unneeded "precautionary bypass operation. Of course, for *us* to escape suspicion, the patient, or shall I say *victim,* will die in the recovery ward several days later from a mysterious delayed lethal injection administered just before *we* begin our routine procedure."

"Are you sure you want to get involved in murder?" a worried Dr. Robert Layton challenged his mentally-possessed colleague. "I've known you for a long time, Jim, and think you've gone absolutely overboard on this one."

"I assure you," James Burke answered with resolute blazing eyes. "I'm quite adamant about this direct threat to *our* profession. If it weren't for having to pay malpractice insurance, all of us would be happily retired in San Diego or Fort Lauderdale, and the biggest problem we would be having would be where to navigate our million-dollar fishing yachts. Murder is what you do to another human being," Burke argumentatively defined. "Killing is what you do to an animal. And let me make it perfectly clear that these despicable covetous trial lawyers are nothing more than extremely dangerous carnivorous scavenging human animals disguised in three-piece-suits!"

"And by disposing of malpractice case lawyers," Dr. Robert Layton cleverly theorized and stated, "we would all be *specialists* in the strictest sense of the word. Congratulations, Dr. Burke on enlightening us about *our* great civic duty as practicing American surgeons doing business in a most complicated free-enterprise economy!" The brain surgeon raised his glass of Merlot and he, Campbell and Wagner all showed praise for the presence and the audacity of the venerable Dr. James Burke. Everyone seated at the reserved doctors' table clicked their wine glasses in unison and then gulped down the vintage liquid.

No sooner had the three other doctor diners celebrated their endorsement of Dr. James Burke's sagacity that the glass front door to Vianna's Restaurant violently swung open and in stepped five sinister-looking characters wearing well-tailored pinstriped suits with matching color-coordinated shirts and ties. The five formidable-looking newcomers immediately caught the attention of all the elite unsuspecting diners sitting inside the establishment. A sudden and distinct five-second hush resulted from *their* unexpected appearance inside the main dining room.

Then, much to the alarm of most all in attendance the five nefarious henchmen pulled out revolvers and began firing their pistols at the four stunned still-seated surgeons. Everyone else in the room hopped off their comfortable green leather chairs and sought shelter from the ricocheting bullets as the customers frantically ducked under dinner tables and wildly overturned others for protection. After thirty seconds of savage carnage, the shooting stopped and the five vigilante intruders left the place of business and next speedily fled the scene in a waiting get-away white Lincoln.

Tony "the Bonebreaker" Valentino was the first person to arrive to render assistance to the dying Dr. James Burke. "Is there a doctor in the house?" the hefty Mafia don ironically yelled at the top of his lungs. "Someone; call an ambulance right away! The other three guys are dead, but this one is still breathing a little! Call an ambulance I said!"

* * * * * * * * * * * *

Five Mafia diners inconveniently met the following Tuesday night at Sugar Hill Restaurant and Bed and Breakfast in Mays Landing, the plush establishment being on the northern bank of the Great Egg Harbor River. Tony Valentino sat at a round table and presided over the impromptu thug conclave. His demeanor was as harsh and as gruff as usual.

"Look you punks," Tony "The Bonebreaker" imperatively began. "We had to switch to Sugar Hill until Vianna's can get back into business. There's lots of glass shards, and also broken furniture all over that place. And a big police investigation is in progress, too."

"Tell me Boss," Carmen "the Eliminator" Campanella piped-up in his squeaky staccato voice. "Why did Rocco's gang wipe-out that table of nice doctors. Who's gonna' operate on *me* now if my ticker goes out of whack?"

"Relax, Carmen baby," Tony Valentino recommended. "Rocco's gang from South Philly' was assigned to the job. Our gang and his gang have been getting extortion money from the area lawyers for around ten years now. Since they pay us and line our pockets with all the extra greenbacks we need, the Mafia owes the attorney fraternity a little favor when *they* ask for it!"

But something additional was perplexing Frankie "Fingers" Scardino's delicate cerebrum. "But Tony, why did the rub-out happen at Vianna's? I happen to like that place very much! No more lobster-tail there for me for a while!" he verbalized.

"Because numbskull," the Bonebreaker rankled as he brushed some random dandruff flakes from the right shoulder of his black pinstriped suit. "The cops ain't gonna' blame *my* boys for killin' the MDs. How can the Mafia be at fault when the Mafia was in the restaurant dinin' and actin' civilized and tryin' to save lives? Ya' get where I'm comin' from, you dumb Sicilian grease ball!"

Tony's three subordinates all slouched down in their chairs and lowered their chins to show their subordination to their boss's nasty temper. But then Nicky "The Fish" Tassone gathered up the courage to ask a salient question.

"But Boss," the Fish cautiously interrupted the general silence at the table, "who spilled the beans on the MDs? How did Rocco's gang get the go-ahead to make Vianna's place look like Mussolini's headquarters after the U.S. Army demolished it in the big war my Pappa used to talk about?"

"Stop actin' like a stupid scooch-a-mensa!" Tony Valentino loudly balked in the exclusive private dining room overlooking the river. "Can't ya' figure the gig out Nicky? Richard Harper was a big shot lawyer goin' in the hospital for a heart examination and stress test. He's got a buddy named Jason Dixon that's got both a degree in medicine and a degree in law. This Dixon jerk became a practicin' lawyer instead of a practicin' doctor. So then, Dixon decides,"….

"I get the gist now!" Frankie "Fingers" Scardino enthusiastically exclaimed. "Dixon found out about the doctor conspiracy to knock-off the lawyers and told Harper. Harper got wise to the pattern after his two pals Davis and Martin bit the dust. So naturally Dixon ratted to Harper about Burke and his fellas' havin' *their* contract out on the lawyers, and then,"….

"And then the climax to the stupid drama happened at Vianna's," Tony non-eloquently finished. "Rocco's gang really did a number on the docs', didn't they boys? The lawyers were legally extortin' big money from the doctors with their handsome malpractice lawsuit commissions, and the Mafia was illegally extortin' *insurance money* from the lawyers. The lawyers appealed to the syndicate, so we had no alternative other than to get rid of Burke and his high-falutin' chums to keep our revenue-flow goin'."

"How much dough did the rub-out cost the court jockeys?" Nicky Tassone asked. "I like it when lawyers get ripped-off! And the more doctors there are, the more *we* get to make from the lawyers!"

"Two million bucks!" Tony Valentino proudly announced to his avid and impressed listeners. "And it was worth every penny to 'em to terminate the crummy docs' once and for all!"

American kids often play a silly simple hand game called Rock, Paper, Scissors. A closed fist represents a rock, a flat hand signifies paper and two moving fingers thrown-down indicates scissors. Paper covers rock and it wins when the opponent has a closed fist. Scissors cuts paper so it prevails when the other player shows a flat hand. In the case of the traditional Tuesday night patrons of Vianna's Restaurant, the greedy lawyers were the rocks, the covetous doctors were the paper and the avaricious final-word Mafia was the inevitable lethal scissors.

"The Bounty Hunter"

"Very secretive and a scary lone wolf!" Those were the profound words describing Trevor Crawford printed in bold type just below his 1985 Hammonton High School senior yearbook black and white photo'. And family members who knew Trevor best could also throw into the mix the adjectives cunning, calculating, deceptive, scheming, shrewd, sly, wily, vindictive and efficient. Those relevant characteristics comprised Trevor Crawford's "stealthy personality" and the introverted young man privately reveled in being so irreverently perceived.

Trevor Crawford's fertile-but-sinister imagination had always fantasized devising and committing "the perfect crime." His often-contemplated opportunity suddenly materialized in early December of '87 when his family was feuding over hunting-land territory with a neighboring clan, the Wilsons. A shallow creek served as a border between the opposing families' homesteads for a half a mile, but then the remainder quarter mile separating the wooded Crawford and Wilson properties was not demarcated by any physical boundary. Deer season was about to commence in several days when a heated dispute between Trevor Crawford and Carlton Wilson (the loner's counterpart in the other hostile family) erupted inside the arbitrary median zone.

"That deer huntin' tree stand you've constructed is on my Pappy's property," huge Carlton Wilson accused Trevor after encountering his bitter enemy standing atop *his* newly constructed tree platform in the pine' barrens woods. "Now I want ya' to take it apart or there's gonna' be big trouble around here between you and me."

"I wonder if you're half as tough as your big mouth claims ya' are!" Trevor audaciously answered back. "I'm not intimidated by you! And I'm not your damned servant or slave either, Carlton! If ya' wanna' make somethin' of it why don't ya' show-up here on Sunday at three p.m. and we'll have a nice little bloody fistfight. And don't tell your ugly brothers or retarded Pappy anything about our little personal arrangement, ya' hear. Then we'll see exactly what kind of hero, or coward, or wimpy weakling ya' really are, tough guy!"

"Okay Charlie Atlas, just you and me and no other humans around," Carlton agreed. "Sunday will give ya' a couple more days to live and to worry. I always wanted to kick your butt and break your face open in high school and now's my chance. Get ready to be administered the beatin' that your daddy should've given ya' when you was in kindergarten!" Carlton egotistically predicted. "And it won't be any secret any longer after you're admitted to the hospital emergency ward with multiple fractures."

"Listen punk!" Trevor concurred from his small platform roost up in the tall pine tree. "Next Sunday at 3 in the afternoon right here at this exact spot. And the ground rules are no weapons; meaning no guns, knives, or chains. We'll just have a good old fashion fistfight, skin against skin, knuckles against jaws. What do ya' say?"

"That's perfectly fine with me, you obnoxious simpleton!" Carlton Wilson arrogantly and sarcastically retorted. "Get ready to be hospitalized. I don't know why I never beat ya' to a pulp in high school! You were lucky to stay out of my way!"

"Oh yeah!" Trevor vehemently yelled down from his perch. "Forget the hospital! Get ready for the funeral parlor Carlton. You're gonna' pay the price of being the bully you've always been. Prepare to be savagely pummeled!"

Trevor was keenly aware that mammoth Carlton Wilson had been a high school "All-State" wrestling champion, weighed a burly two hundred and fifty pounds and could easily vanquish Crawford in a one-on-one brawl. And after again seriously considering those extraordinary circumstances at noon on Sunday afternoon, the clever plotter drove his black *Ford 150* pickup truck to an Oak Road kennel on the other side of Hammonton where Crawford boarded his two attack-dog Doberman pinchers each hunting season.

The vicious dog fancier knew that Bret Hennings would be out inside the nearby *Wharton State Forest* getting *his* tree stand ready for deer hunting scheduled to begin the following morning and that the kennel owner would be returning to his Oak Road side-business at around 5 p m.

'This gives me an ideal two-hour window of opportunity to pick the locks on Prince and Duke's cages, to take the animals by back roads across town and then enact my nefarious scheme. After my hungry puppies bite and chew Carlton Wilson to shreds, I'll clean the pedigrees up, take them back to Bret Henning's kennel, and lock them safely in their cages,' Trevor imagined. 'If and when the cops interrogate Bret, he'll claim that the cages were locked and that the dogs never left the premises. Next, I'll hightail it over to the Pic-A-Lilli Inn over on *Route 206*, order a dozen delicious hot wings and several frosted mugs of beer and then casually watch some sports on the big screen TV. The cops won't discover Carlton's mutilated body until several days later, and if I'm ever interrogated,' the devious, young man plotted, 'I'll simply say I spent Sunday afternoon at the

Pic-A-Lilli and was just sittin' there with my huntin' acquaintances who will have no alternative other than to verify my sober story. What a fantastic alibi!'

At 2:45 that same Sunday afternoon, Carlton Wilson with clenched fists cockily and confidently approached the controversial deer-hunting stand in the disputed territory ready to engage in and emerge victorious from his slated altercation. As the livid giant haughtily jaunted over a hill in the direction of the aforementioned site of contention the trekker was horrified to witness his unscrupulous adversary yell out the command "Kill!" and spontaneously unleash his ferocious Dobermans.

The savage animals chased the screaming Carlton Wilson over the knoll and brutally and fiercely mauled and ravaged the helpless terrified screaming victim. Two minutes later, silence reigned supreme in that remote section of the South Jersey coniferous forest. Trevor Crawford's principal enemy had been permanently and mercilessly eliminated.

'No fingerprints, no evidence, no gunshot wound and no trace of any human clues whatsoever,' the vengeful young man concluded and snickered. 'Now to clean-up my faithful pets and wipe the blood from Prince and Duke's dependable fangs. Then, I'll transport my loyal hounds back to Bret Henning's Oak Road place, lock my doggies back in their respective pens and then merrily motor over to the Pic-A-Lilli. I'll dispose of the bloody rags I used to clean up my Dobermans' mouths on a familiar Wharton Forest Trail that parallels the old railroad tracks just off of Union Road,' Trevor Crawford speculated. 'Then it's directly off to Buffalo wings and draught beer land. Tomorrow I'll go huntin' with my daddy and three brothers and that slick deception at the Pic-A-Lilli oughta' seal-up my alibi. Goodbye you lousy degenerate!' Trevor contemplated as he hatefully stared down at the dead bloody body lying ten-foot away. 'This fate is exactly what ya' deserve, ya' dead fat worm!'

The town police did interrogate Trevor four days later about the "mysterious death of Carlton Wilson", but Crawford was a veteran psychopath who lied easier than he had ever told the truth. The state police next continued their thorough investigation at the Pic-A-Lilli Inn, at Bret Hennings dog kennel, and in the pine woods, and they eventually again returned to the popular "*Route 206* piney tavern" and questioned local patrons that had been at the establishment when Trevor had made his appearance at the sports bar on the ill-fated Sunday afternoon. But the authorities could never glean sufficient evidence to indict Trevor. Forest rangers had verified to the State

Police that imported wild coyotes were now straying in many of the local woods scavenging for food, and later the official documented report indicated that perhaps those itinerant hungry animals (clandestinely introduced into the local pine barrens' environment by anonymous area inhabitants and exotic pet collectors) had probably been responsible for what seemed to be Carlton Wilson's diabolical demise.

* * * * * * * * * * * *

Trevor Crawford never divulged his particular implication in Carlton Wilson's 'remote control animal murder' to his parents and brothers, all of whom instinctively believed *his* innocence, blaming the "strange death" on imported wild coyotes. The evader of justice entered *Stockton State College* in the fall of 1988 and ironically graduated with a degree in "Criminal Justice" in June of '93. After working four years in a South Jersey police department, Trevor logically reckoned he could make a much more lucrative income by becoming an ambitious entrepreneur and evolving into an independent national bounty hunter.

The adventurous bounty hunter's exploits took him all over the contiguous forty-eight states, where Crawford gained a stellar reputation for finding and apprehending thirty desperate renegades and fugitives running away from the long arms of law and order. Secretive Trevor perceptively realized that he enjoyed certain distinct advantages over his more public and more heralded bounty hunter competitors.

'I'm not married and have no children to support or worry or care about,' Trevor Crawford proudly rationalized. 'And I have no partners or accomplices that can expose my personal secrets. No one's ever going to convict me for Carlton Wilson's sudden departure from this evil Earth. But I still have to strive to be the best bounty hunter in the USA because I gloat in the fact that my rivals are intensely jealous and are equally as greedy as I am. I'll have to keep my' vigilance and be especially aware of their investigative activities and special projects.'

In early February of 2004 Trevor left his new home on Birch Drive and drove from Hammonton to the Lindenwold High Speed Train Terminal situated fifteen miles west of Hammonton. The freelance fugitive hunter had a routine doctor's appointment at Philadelphia's *Thomas Jefferson Hospital,* just two blocks away from the subway's heavily trafficked Tenth Street Station.

Upon driving west on *Route 30* past the Berlin Farmer's Market, a car coming eastbound crossed the double yellow line and smashed into Trevor's new black Ford pickup. The Berlin Police report determined that the driver heading east toward Hammonton had suffered a heart attack and had veered out of his passing lane. Trevor was taken unconscious from the accident scene and quickly hospitalized, and when he finally came out of his coma the man's mind felt quite different as if his senses had become keener. Crawford clearly imagined that his now-vivid daydreams involving other renowned bounty hunters were undeniably true, and the wary patient then astutely interpreted from his new-found visions that six of his illustrious-but-envious antagonists were mutually conspiring against him.

'I had learned basic survival skills after I had enlisted in the South Jersey Para-Militia,' Trevor rehashed in his mind while lying in his Stratford *Kennedy Hospital* bed. 'And I'll persevere and stalk the six creeps down one by one. I gotta' trust my newly acquired sixth sense and go after the half dozen sinister thugs before they find and eradicate me. And I think I know exactly what kind of battle plan to employ against them,' the injured man thought with a smile. 'I'll take a page out of my Doberman enterprise involving Carlton Wilson back in early December of 1987. Now that I believe I'm clairvoyant, I predict that my six adversaries are doomed to suffer some imaginative, well-orchestrated disasters, personally instigated by little old me,' the crazed hospital patient thought and snickered. 'Of course, I'll have to secretly coordinate geography and environment to sagely formulate six additional perfect crimes that will definitely defy police solution.'

The first suspected enemy to be targeted was Darren Branson, who resided near rock and roll icon Buddy Holly's old stomping grounds, Lubbock, Texas. On April 1, 2004 Trevor was a passenger on a *Continental Airlines* jet flying from *Philadelphia International* to Houston, and then an hour later the dangerous lone wolf boarded a *Southwest Air* plane to Lubbock. At his destination city Crawford rented a black *Ford Explorer SUV* at the *Lubbock Airport*, located a cheap motel on the outskirts of the west Texas city and then mentally pursued the next phase in stealthily committing his carefully contrived felony.

'I've studied and figured-out the terrain around Lubbock from various encyclopedias and from topography books, and know approximately where to find and catch two brown-recluse spiders. The dangerous species inject potentially lethal poisonous bites into their victims and the creatures are identifiable by dark violin-shaped marks located near the head,' Trevor reminded himself. 'And I'll have to catch several of the spiders in the wild and make sure their size is around a half-inch long each so that they'll have enough venom to render Darren Branson unconscious and dead within a half hour after being bitten. And if I can't locate and capture any deadly brown-recluse spiders,' Crawford wickedly surmised and chuckled, 'then I'm sure a pair of nasty bad-spirited desert rattlesnakes will do just fine!'

After two days of assiduous exploring and searching under rocks and inside sagebrush, Trevor was ecstatic to come across several of the remarkable tiny crawling creatures, which he instantly and deftly trapped inside an upside-down aluminum container. 'These special spiders are magnificent and quite distinguishable from other species by virtue of their six eyes. Most spiders have eight,' Trevor acknowledged from recollection of his pre-project research, 'and the dark violin-shaped marks near the head confirm that these specimens indeed are brown-recluses!'

Knowing Darren Branson's particular habits and schedule, just before dawn on the morning of April 3 Trevor drove west from Lubbock on Highway 114 to nearby Levelland, easily discovered his target's home inside a newly constructed housing development, used a master key to open the driver's side door of Branson's light blue *Cadillac De Ville* and then gently deposited the two hungry poisonous spiders inside.

The cunning felon then re-entered his rented vehicle and parked a block away to surreptitiously wait and alertly observe his "mark" open the door, and then sit-down behind the wheel of the *De Ville*. At eight-fifteen a.m. Darren Branson was seen standing at his front door and kissing his wife goodbye. In another minute the notorious targeted bounty hunter was entering his *Cadillac* parked in the concrete driveway. The death candidate never suspected that some devious enterprise had been cunningly initiated and at that precise moment the lethal activity was indeed in full progress.

The following morning, area newspapers reported that Darren Branson of Levelland, Texas had inexplicably died behind the wheel of his automobile on his way to *Lubbock Airport*. A full-scale autopsy had been authorized by the county coroner's office to determine the exact cause of death. A police investigation was pending awaiting full disclosure of the autopsy's revelations to be available to the press in three weeks' time.

'They'll have to conclude that the whole matter was an atrocious freak accident,' Trevor deducted and chuckled while putting the morning newspaper down on his motel room's 'island table.' 'The only logical question in their minds will be how did two venomous spiders manage to get inside Darren Branson's locked car. That mystery ought to confound the cops and completely stymie their probe,' the paranoid fanatic fantasized. 'And it all seems rather plausible because the brown-recluse spider is indigenous to this particular geographic region of northwestern Texas. I think I'll stay in the arachnid family to conduct my next devilish crime. Thank you, Carlton Wilson. If it weren't for you, I never would've figured-out how to put into motion the flawless foolproof crime I had just enacted using small spiders! But I gotta' act with dispatch before my avowed enemies realize that I've been the brains behind Darren Branson's premature death.'

Unfazed and undaunted by his ignominious fiendishness, the self-appointed executioner proceeded with resuming his nefarious perversion. 'No doubt the other five conspirators my mind has identified will be attending Darren's funeral,' the defensive-minded bounty hunter decided. 'I'll soon exterminate another of the dirty rotten-skunks before any of the remaining conspirators see a distinct coincidence between Carlton Wilson and Darren Branson's dual deaths. It's a good thing I had been involved in that February automobile accident or else I'd never have realized my psychic powers and would have never known who my true enemies are. And with each new foe that I eliminate, my value as a prized bounty hunter will go up!'

The second selectee to be terminated was Frank Carlino, a former Mafia associate turned bounty hunter living in Boulder, Colorado. 'I'll take a *Southwest Air* jet from Lubbock to Denver, rent a car and then motor to Boulder,' Trevor expediently connived. 'Then I'll begin the first segment of my well-conceived *sting* operation! Ha, ha, ha!' the demented vindictive fellow contemplated. 'I remember apprehending a convicted drug smuggler up in Ft. Collins three years ago, so I'm more than slightly familiar with the turf around that section of Colorado. Carlino should be back in Boulder from his Texas buddy's funeral by Sunday, so I have plenty of time to prepare his murder.'

After arriving in Denver and renting a gray *Ford Taurus* from *Hertz* at the bustling airport, the man-on-a-vile-mission drove up *Interstate 25* and quickly obtained lodging at the *Budget Inn Motel,* 3975 Colorado Boulevard. 'I'll rest-up until dusk. Scorpions are most active at twilight because they're nocturnal predators out looking for prey soon after the sun goes down. After using the brown-recluse spiders, I gotta' utilize some variety in the small deadly creatures' family. Ha, ha, ha!' the treacherous eliminator mused and indulgently laughed in the comfort of his modest suite.

At dusk, the deranged bounty hunter drove his *Taurus* into a wilderness area off a side road that paralleled *I-25* and tenaciously searched the terrain for his sought after "animal villains." Trevor Crawford's clandestine activity was rewarded two hours later with the discovery of a nest of the dangerous critters (found with the aid of a flashlight) located under a rotted fallen timber. 'I have to be careful and methodically grab and corral four of these ugly varmints. I'll have to grasp them under the thorax to avoid their stinging tails and pincers. I've fortunately come across this scorpion nest just before the hungry hunters have gone out scouting for insects. I figure that if four of the things get to sting Frank Carlino,' the crazed maniac conjectured, 'then that should be adequate poison to send my unwary adversary to the peaceful eternal hereafter. And the best part of this terrific plan is that Frank's a confirmed bachelor and there'll be nobody home sleeping at four a m except him.'

After exhibiting noteworthy dexterity and remarkable patience, Trevor captured four semi-active scorpions from the discovered nest. He gingerly placed each of the five-inch-long crawlers into a lidded plastic box while wearing thick protective gloves. The scheming killer then drove back to his motel and waited for the appropriate time to begin practicing his insanity. Finally, Sunday night arrived and the starving scorpions were very ready to satisfy their appetites, living the past several days on a minimal diet of ants, roaches and flies supplied by their captor. Then at three-thirty a.m., the crafty bounty hunter drove with his plastic container and its four famished occupants to Frank Carlino's secluded residence, located three miles north of Boulder.

'Under much more pleasant circumstances, I've been here twice before to Frank's pad and know the general area pretty well,' the focused man recollected. 'And Carlino hates with a passion pets and animals so I don't have to worry about disturbing any fierce canines inside his place. All I have to do is use my house skeleton key to gain entrance through the laundry room door,' Trevor reckoned, 'sneak and slink down the ranch home's hallway and gently place these four cooperative accomplices on his bed covers. The rest of the minor tragedy I'll leave up to *their* natural animalistic instincts.'

Three-hundred-pound Frank Carlino was snoring loudly inside his king-size bed when the night intruder entered his dimly-lit bedroom. With sly concentration, Trevor slowly lifted the lid and tilted the box, adroitly depositing the four deadly night hunters onto the unraveled bedspread. And then, demonstrating rather enviable perseverance, the inconspicuous interloper did a quiet one-eighty and retraced his steps back down the shadowy hallway to the main part of the attractive one-story rustic home. After gently exiting and then locking the laundry room door with his trusty skeleton key, Crawford methodically removed his surgical gloves and cautiously skulked a hundred yards down the asphalt lane to his parked *Taurus*.

'I'll throw a decoy factor into the equation,' the lunatic hypothesized as he slowly turned the ignition key. 'I'll cleverly hang around Boulder and faithfully read the daily newspapers. If my plan has been a success, I'll then attend Frank's viewing just to throw my other bounty hunter conspirator colleagues off my trail. That'll make the other four numbskulls think that I'm not suspected as the culprit, and possibly make the remaining four plotters vulnerable to my next creative scheme.'

Frank Carlino did die from "unknown sources presently under analysis" that on-the-case medical examiners believed to be "poisonous in nature." Because of a required autopsy that had been ordered, Trevor Crawford had to wait a full week to be able to show his presence at his rival's viewing. Although the funeral guest never chatted with any of his four remaining "hit-list targets," Crawford gave each an innocent polite salute after passing by the victim's casket and then nonchalantly leaving the crowded mortuary before he could be followed.

'I'll cool it for three months or so, and then I'll effectively take care of victim number three,' Trevor matter-of-factly considered on the smooth flight from Denver back to Philly'. 'By then the four others will have solidified their separate plans to erase me. But I'm not ready or anxious to become extinct right now, though. I'll keep Prince and Duke on guard inside my home, just to make sure there's no skullduggery occurring against me in the meantime,' Trevor assured himself. 'I'll have to think of some other animals I can pilfer from their natural habitats and then sensationally utilize against my final four antagonists. Then I'll ratchet-up my savvy battle strategy and if I have to fight an Alamo-type siege at 23 Birch Drive, I'll do just that! It's a good thing I had that para-militia training!'

Several months elapsed without any significant homicide operations being undertaken. Then on June 15th, 2005 Trevor

Crawford boarded a *United Airlines* flight from Philadelphia with its destination *McCarran International Airport* in Las Vegas. 'I'm staying at the magnificent *Venetian* on the Vegas strip and I'll be able to combine gambling pleasure with my daring bounty hunter murder escapade. Julius Murphy lives in nearby Henderson, so in a couple of days I'll rent an *SUV* with four-wheel-drive and take a side excursion out into the hot arid Nevada desert,' Trevor reviewed in his mind. 'I'm certain there's a friendly cold-blooded reptile lying under a rock somewhere out in the vast arid wilderness, conserving its energy to escape the torrid afternoon sun, and I'm absolutely sure that the diamondback would amply appreciate biting into some warm human flesh.'

After two lonely days of experiencing the glittery casino city and gambling activities at *New York, New York* and the *Mirage,* Trevor drove his rented *SUV* fifteen miles to the *Painted Desert,* an awe-inspiring hued environmental treasure open to the public. 'From my militia survival training I know where to find rattlesnakes in that type of rugged terrain,' Crawford evaluated en route. 'And I'll just put my designated assassin inside this laundry sack and tie a little hemp around the top. That ought to keep my temporary pet docile until I require its indispensable services.'

It took two whole hours of meticulous exploration until the accomplished bounty hunter/killer discovered a specimen worthy of capture, found shading itself upon the scorching sand behind a small red-hued boulder. Despite the detection of the diamondback's rattle warning, Trevor was cognizant of the imminent danger and kept his distance, as the pit viper coiled itself down, ready to lash-out at its intruding tormentor.

The intrepid trespasser dropped his white linen sack, waved his left hand to gain the snake's keen attention, and when the seven-foot-long rattler was totally distracted, Crawford swooped his right hand around and adroitly gripped the reptile behind the neck. The captor held his trophy high into the air and inspected and admired his 'in-custody quarry'.

At 2 a.m., the deft bounty hunter departed the *Venetian* parking garage, having his coveted snake snugly contained in the laundry bag, which he kept neatly stashed in the *SUV's* back storage compartment. 'I left all four windows open a tiny crack so that my sharp-fanged hostage didn't suffocate while I was having dinner and was later engrossed in playing blackjack. But as they say in the entertainment business, 'It's show time'!'

Rival Julius Murphy's Henderson, Nevada address was easily accessed and Trevor employed his sophisticated prowler skills to gain entry to the secluded residence. 'Although he's getting old Murphy's just as ruthless as I am,' Crawford reflected as he tiptoed down the dark hallway to the master bedroom. 'But Julius is allergic to fur, and he hates animals, particularly ferocious dogs; so that's why he doesn't have any barking canines meandering around the premises. It's too bad I can't stay around and interview old Murph's ghost about what his spirit thinks of my starving and soon-to-be aggressive rattler!'

The venomous reptile was then gently and expertly released from the open cloth sack and coyly left next to the sleeping man's pillow. Then, the very scrupulous encroacher slowly pivoted around and sneaked back down the dim hallway to the side entrance door. 'My trusty skeleton key keeps any alarm from being tripped,' Trevor momentarily and fondly considered. 'In another two minutes I'm off the property and driving back to glitzy Las Vegas. I'll simply toss this white linen sack into the first open garbage bin I see, remove my plastic gloves and the rest of the hit should be personal history. I'll just stick around the *Venetian*, take a gondola ride or two, hit the craps tables, and then consult the papers the next few days to ascertain that my very in-genius murder-by-proxy drama had actually occurred.'

On a bland Monday morning in mid-summer, the intrepid bounty hunter was inspired to organize another grisly human liquidation. His intended victim lived a hundred thirty miles northwest of Hammonton in historic Tarrytown, New York. After Trevor exited the *Garden State Parkway* and crossed the New Jersey State Line onto the *New York Freeway* he was soon heading east on *I-87* and *287* toward the landmark *Tappan Zee Bridge* spanning the majestic *Hudson River*. The relentless plotter reviewed in his mind the pertinent facts relating to the next victim designated to have dangerous animals efficiently execute "the mark."

'Today, I'll scope-out Ron Leadley's Tarrytown mansion on the *Hudson*,' Trevor reminded himself. 'He's my only major bounty hunter nemesis who's married with kids. If I remember correctly, each summer Ron's wife and family go to the Hamptons over on Long Island for a two-week mid-July vacation while Leadley stays home on the *Hudson* during the weekdays and joins his clan on weekends. I'll just visit the vicinity and determine if the wife and kids are around,' Trevor anticipated. 'If they've already left for the Hamptons, then I'll return on Thursday and put my competitor out of business before that filthy rat Leadley manages to team-up with Tom

Meritt and Harry Taylor; and the vile threesome then predictably comes after me.'

Much to the visitor's elation, there was no sign of Ron Leadley's family anywhere around the multimillionaire's handsome estate so the formidable eliminator traveled south on *Route 9* and checked out *Sunnyside*, the museum/mansion home of famous American post-colonial author Washington Irving. The beautiful well-designed structure offered a fantastic view of the stately *Hudson* with the New Jersey Palisades lording over the scenic river on the opposite shore. 'Washington Irving coined the phrase 'the Almighty Dollar!' Trevor thought while pretending to listen to his tour guide's fairly interesting-but-monotonous presentation. 'The outrageous Headless Horseman of Sleepy Hollow isn't the only specter that's gonna' be actively haunting this area around Tarrytown after I get through with one Ronald Patrick Leadley.'

Back in Hammonton early Thursday morning, July 14th Trevor ate breakfast at the Red Barn on *Route 206*, checked his chainsaw in his back storage box, smiled at his aluminum ladder and then nonchalantly drove out to a secluded section of the *Wharton State Forest* just beyond Tuckahoe Turf Farm on Hammonton's Oak Road. 'This fantastic caper will definitely work!' the paranoid constant schemer ruminated. 'If I remember correctly, Leadley has a huge oak tree planted in his back yard and one of the branches extends out and overlaps his swimming pool. And it's quite possible that a summer beehive could un-noticeably form in a few days on that branch and then accidentally snap free and plummet into the swimming pool right after good old Ron does an awkward cannonball off of his diving board. Ha, ha, ha! They have nasty beehives up in Tarrytown too; just like we got down here in South Jersey! Ha, ha, ha!'

Using a ladder stationed below a deciduous tree at the fringe of the *Wharton State Forest*, Trevor climbed the rungs wearing a beekeeper's outfit and mask, which he had recently acquired from a Delaware honey farmer. The clamberer placed a temperature-controlled metal box on the top rung, that was located directly below a suspended beehive. 'It's still early morning and the bees aren't active yet,' the insidious rogue contemptibly thought. 'Now I'll simply open the lid, descend the ladder, grab my chainsaw and next get the beehive to plummet into the metal container. Then before the bees get active and excited,' Trevor thoroughly evaluated his plan, 'I'll close the lid and trap the bees along with their hive inside. I'll then lower the temperature inside the controlled environment and keep the flying insects immobile until I need their assistance in good old Tarrytown.'

After accomplishing that first important phase of his mission, the madman descended the aluminum ladder, removed his bee safety mask and accompanying protective gloves, placed his equipment in the back of his truck, returned home to 23 Birch Drive and placed his ladder and chainsaw on a bench inside his utility shed. Then the homed-in man motored up *Route 206* past the Pic-A-Lilli Inn watering hole north to Bordentown, got onto the *New Jersey Turnpike* at Exit 7 and drove north again to Exit 11 where the recently repaired late model Ford truck transferred onto the *Garden State Parkway*.

'*The* pristine *Wharton Forest* was named after the Philadelphia millionaire who started the famous *Wharton School of Economics* over in Philly,' Trevor recalled for his own selfish amusement. 'Getting rid of Ron Leadley will definitely improve my own economics as a bounty hunter.'

Trevor distinctly remembered as he drove northwest on the *Parkway* that Ron Leadley had never liked or trusted him. Although there was heavy summer traffic heading south and east for the popular New Jersey and New York beaches, Trevor was soon again crossing the architecturally unique *Tappan Zee Bridge* and entering Tarrytown two hours and thirty minutes after departing Hammonton. Then Crawford halted outside a downtown restaurant and carefully adjusted the temperature inside the metal container from 45 to 75 degrees Fahrenheit in order to gradually shake the honeybees out of their lethargic inactive state.

'It's just before noon, and that pugnacious Ron Leadley likes to take a swim before he has lunch,' Trevor remembered and schemed. 'There's no doubt about it. Instead of feeling a stomach cramp, the ruthless thug is going to get the ultimate surprise of his life, or should I change that depiction to, the ultimate surprise of his death! Ha, ha, ha!'

Trevor parked his new black truck in Ron Leadley's driveway, grabbed his beekeeper's mask and gloves, mentally surveyed' the immediate surroundings for any trace of being observed and then exited the driver's side. After removing the metal containment receptacle from the cab's passenger side, the exterminator briskly stepped to the left side of the well-manicured lawn, followed a cement sidewalk around an exotic 'flower and shrub treatment,' stealthily opened a wrought iron gate, and sneakily proceeded to the quiet back yard.

The intruder quickly donned his beekeeper's mask, completely disguising and hiding his grim face. After putting on his trusty gloves, Trevor lifted the box and slowly lowered the metal container to the ground, gradually opened the lid, very deliberately raised the beehive from the box's interior and then defiantly approached his next victim, who was preoccupied swimming across the pool in Trevor's direction. Ron Leadley spontaneously became aware of the stranger's presence, stopped his daily exercise routine and incredulously stared at the impostor beekeeper with *his* mouth agape.

"What's goin' on?" Leadley squawked to camouflage his mounting fright of his incognito visitor. "Get your ugly butt the hell off my property you *Halloween* freak!" the shocked infamous bounty hunter imperatively demanded of the anonymous-but-determined beekeeper-garbed invader.

Without uttering a syllable, Trevor mechanically flung the huge beehive directly at the astonished and flabbergasted Ron Leadley, who immediately shrieked after the impact and then submerged and swam underwater. Surfacing for oxygen, the petrified victim was instantaneously enveloped by swarming angry bees. The tenacious insects were incessantly stinging away at Leadley's exposed face and instinctively sacrificing and drowning themselves in the water in hostile pursuit of the unfortunate fellow's flesh.

Three minutes later, Ron Leadley lay breathless floating upon his swimming pool's crystal-clear water. Trevor gazed-up at the oak tree's limb projecting out over the pool, evilly smiled at the results of his malevolent exploit, removed his sweat-drenched mask and gloves, picked-up his utilitarian metal box and then sauntered back to his truck mentally reciting 'Four down and just two more to go, and then after I rub out the ever-dangerous Tom Meritt and Harry "the Snoop" Taylor, I'll easily become by default the most acclaimed bounty hunter in America!'

Tom Meritt lived on the outskirts of urban Miami, Florida in a Hialeah housing development, just off *Route 41*. Trevor flew on a *Delta Air* jet from Philly' to Miami, registered at a well-maintained '60s vintage Coral Gables motel and mentally coordinated his tactics. 'I'll as usual do a surveillance of Meritt's place before I get into action. I'll visit an alligator farm just west of here shown on this airport tourist map, situated near the *Everglades*. Tomorrow night around midnight, I'll return to the gator haven and steal a seven-foot-long reptile and tape its mouth. Then, I'll wait until Monday at noon, cut the duct tape I had wrapped around the swamp resident's jaws and casually dump the sharp-toothed reptile into Tom's swimming pool.

It's a good thing I've been working-out with weights and am in excellent physical condition.'

Trevor paused for a moment to organize his random thoughts. 'After this job, I'll havta' get a little more mentally dynamic because this will be the second swimming pool-related murder I will have pulled-off. And it's a good thing that one summer during my youth I once trained and got experience as an alligator wrestler on a gator' farm up near St. Augustine back in the late '80s. That was before I decided to find a more profitable profession and eventually become the foremost premier bounty hunter in the whole country,' the conniving murderer reminisced. 'Now it's time to put my practical education to good use!'

Using his incomparable stamina along with his specialized grappling skills, Trevor Crawford purloined a sizable alligator from the Glades Gator' Swamp Preserve southeast of Fort Meyers and next transported the ornery beast under a heavy tarpaulin in the back of his rented *Pathfinder SUV* to Hialeah and then specifically motored to Tom Meritt's impeccable single-story residence. 'I gotta' be careful and watch my speed. I don't want to be confronted by any duty-minded patrolman in quest of promotion and wanting to make the rank of sergeant in a hurry! If my memory serves me accurately,' the villain continued thinking, 'my intended victim usually takes a midnight swim before hitting the bottle, and then his bed's mattress. Tom Meritt; you pathetic fool! Get ready to experience the surprise of your miserable life!'

The very efficient killer cautiously drove his rented dark blue vehicle near Tom Meritt's small mansion, dimmed his lights, and shut-off the engine after surreptitiously entering the middle-age fellow's paver-stone-driveway. Then Trevor furtively removed the tarp' that concealed the nasty-tempered beast. And after successfully dragging and lifting the taped-mouth gator' from the all-purpose vehicle's interior and carrying the writhing animal through the side gate, much to Crawford's satisfaction and relief, Thomas Matthew Meritt was seen in the distance floating inside his backyard swimming pool.

But instantly, fear and shock shot throughout every fiber of Trevor Crawford's entire nervous system. Tom Meritt's bloody and horribly chewed-up body was observed floating face-down in the pool's deep end, and two very aggressive carnivorous alligators similar to the one that Trevor was holding were maneuvering-around and pecking away at the victim's corpse.

'Oh my God!' the trespasser gulped and mentally realized. 'Someone's devised the exact same method of killing Meritt as I have! My educated guess is that this is the work of Harry the Snoop Taylor, the only other mark remaining on my hit list. Taylor probably concluded that either Meritt has been scheming to terminate *his* existence or that *we* were covertly collaborating against him so the killer figured that he'd delete Tom and then dedicate himself to expunging me. I gotta' think fast because now I know I'm the only name left scribbled in on Taylor's short list. And Tom Meritt certainly didn't expire because of hypothermia here in Miami, that's for damned sure!'

Wearing his usual heavy plastic gloves, Trevor transported the heavy reptile twenty-feet to his right and carefully deposited the heavy gator near the pool's edge. Then he deftly unraveled the duct tape that had held the gator's trap-like jaws shut, let go of the creature's mouth and gently nudged the beast into the pool's deep end to join its new companions in a carnal feast.

'Now, it'll look like whoever planned Tom's little misadventure used *three* famished gators' to conduct their evil treachery,' the un-repenting and un-relenting stalker decided. 'But Harry must know that I can be just as unscrupulous as he is! Now to use explicit Darwinian terms, it's all narrowed-down to primitive survival of the fittest between him and me! I eagerly accept the challenge!' Trevor reflected as he saw the three carnivorous gators biting at the victim's mortal remains.

Then, Trevor put everything into perspective as the trespassing bounty hunter watched the sordid spectacle occurring inside the swimming pool's red-hued water. 'But I must honestly confess that the bizarre alligator coincidence had really blown my mind and had shaken my confidence for a few minutes! I'm running out of original ideas, and am under extreme pressure to act quickly!' Crawford acknowledged. 'I don't have time to be inventive! I might have to duplicate what I had done with my Dobermans to long-gone Carlton Wilson. Taylor lives up in Wilkes-Barre and as soon as I rest-up from this Miami surprise I've encountered, I'll have to pay him a Pennsylvania showdown visit accompanied by my dear colleagues Prince and Duke.'

All during Trevor Crawford's return jet flight on *Delta Air* from Miami to Philadelphia, the self-proclaimed psychic kept thinking, 'I've got to get to Wilkes-Barre and dispense with Harry the Snoop before he shows-up in Hammonton to obliterate and annihilate me. This afternoon I'll reclaim Prince and Duke from the Oak Road

Kennel. I'll need them for protection if not for an early-warning-system should *that* wickedly insane Harry Taylor eventually find his way to 23 Birch Drive.'

After arriving back to his native, somnolent New Jersey community, and being reunited with his obedient attack canines, that July evening Trevor drove his recently purchased late-model *Ford* pickup north on *206* past *Atsion Lake* to the Pic-A-Lilli Inn Bar and Restaurant to devour some delicious hot wings and beer. The standard crowd of hunters and pineys that frequented the establishment were all there, but the bounty hunter had certain paramount issues dominating his somewhat-puzzled mind, and was reluctant to socialize with the boisterous and occasionally rowdy bar and restaurant regulars.

When Trevor returned south to Hammonton and 23 Birch Drive, the restless fellow alertly observed that everything in his neighborhood seemed normal and tranquil. The bounty hunter had the electronic garage door on his four-year-old house rise and soon drove his black truck inside. Very deliberately, he then used the automatic remote control to lower the paneled partition to the garage's cement floor. 'I'll go upstairs and get my revolver out of my wall safe just for security purposes and for mental peace-of-mind. I hope I don't have to use it to defend myself in my own house,' the homeowner seriously considered and worried.

Upon entering his den from the tiled laundry room, Trevor was momentarily stunned to notice that his two prized possessions Prince and Duke were lying prone on the bloodstained tan carpet. 'Poisoned and then shot with a rifle, probably having a silencer!' Trevor nervously assessed. 'I gotta' get out of here before I'm destined for the same kind of gruesome treatment!'

Just as the bewildered man tried recomposing his standard sensibilities, excessive barking was heard, and before Trevor Crawford could pivot and close the door to separate himself' from the animals, two voracious implacable Dobermans that were almost identical to Duke and Prince rounded the corner of the kitchen leading into the den and viciously attacked the astonished victim, first knocking Crawford to the floor and then mauling and tearing the flesh right off of his vulnerable hands, face and legs. Soon, the terrorized killer lay prone bleeding to death on the tiled laundry room floor, a victim of his own sinister-style stalking method.

'That completes my purpose in visiting the off-the-beaten-path *Blueberry Capital of the World!'* Harry "the Snoop" Taylor snidely thought. 'When we were on more favorable terms, Trevor had often invited me to visit his small-time town. Now I'm glad I finally took him up on his courteous invitation!'

The victor triumphantly stared-down without remorse at his most recent conquest, who had ceased breathing just before the imported Dobermans had quit growling. 'Now I'll just leave Count and King locked inside the house so that the imbecile local cops will think that Trevor was accidentally killed by his own ferocious Dobermans. But first, I gotta' make two trips and sneakily carry Crawford's dead pedigrees in separate laundry bags across the street and deposit them into the back of my *Chevy Suburban*, lock the side door with my trusty skeleton key, and then have a pleasant three-hour-drive back to good old mountain country up in Wilkes-Barre. The evidence will dry-up a full day before this poor excuse for a bounty hunter's body is ever discovered!'

"A Small World"

Eugene Derek Douglas was a puny, hundred and twenty-pound Hammonton High School weakling who had suffered from the embarrassment of having muscle-bound bullies (in front of their girlfriends) deliberately and ostentatiously kick sand in the wimp's face on Atlantic City, Wildwood, Cape May and Ocean City, New Jersey beaches. The cowardly-but-vindictive 1980 HHS graduate possessed a latent Napoleon Complex, and Eugene held huge personal grudges against twelve people from his academic past who he believed had excessively offended and grieved him. And the revenge-oriented individual never forgot certain demeaning "malignant insults" that had left "unforgivable emotional scars" on his delicate-but-unstable fragile psyche.

Eugene Derek Douglas had proudly graduated from Philadelphia's prestigious *Drexel University* with honors in 1985, and two years later earned, a Masters Degree in computer graphics from the *University of Pennsylvania*. After working for and being fired from an internally competitive computer firm, three years later the ambitious entrepreneur moved West and founded a fledgling Irvine, California software design company, which six years later in 1996 proliferated into a multimillion-dollar manufacturing concern', E. Douglas Computer Software Animation and Graphics Corporation. During the firm's 1998 *IPO,* Eugene had sold two million of his growth company's shares at forty-three dollars each and overnight became an instant multimillionaire with sufficient monetary resources to get even with those people Douglas believed had harmed him in the past.

'Now I still have six million shares left valued at a cool three hundred mil',' the wily risk-taker thought. 'And with my annual salary as *CEO* fixed at three million per year, and with my exercisable seven million stock options I paid two dollars apiece for currently valued at three-hundred and one million, I suppose my illustrious photo' is ready to be featured on the covers of *Business Week* and *Time* magazines,' Eugene mused while sitting behind his solid oak desk in his well-appointed Irvine office. 'Not bad for me being called a 'loser geek' and a 'hapless nerd' throughout my high school days when I was the varsity basketball team's equipment manager and the football squad's water boy. I suppose all of my high school and college enemies are wonderfully jealous of my daring recent spectacular business accomplishments! And I haven't forgotten about any of those malicious tormentors throughout my years of struggle and ridicule.'

The high-tech multimillionaire had purchased prime oceanfront real estate and had built for his own pleasure and ego a fabulous mansion on the Pacific Palisades just south of Los Angeles. Then on the East Coast the corporate executive purchased an eight-million-dollar summer palace in Stone Harbor, New Jersey, and finally to thoroughly aggravate and make his old Hammonton High School nemeses envious, Eugene oversaw and had constructed a magnificent eighteen-million-dollar residence on Fourteenth Street in Hammonton, which naturally became the "talk and gossip of the quaint rural New Jersey town". All the right dominoes were falling for Eugene Derek Douglas.

'Computers have been my salvation from a life fraught with despair' and mediocrity,' the software expert concluded as he looked out onto rural Fourteenth Street from his incomparable hundred-room "Taj Mahal". 'Now that I'm fabulously wealthy and don't have to answer to any blustery employer, I can devote my free time to experimenting and researching to gain revenge against all those who had abused me in the past,' the insecure introvert thought. 'Now is the time for me to contrive an appropriate scheme to implement against those mean-spirited people that had the audacity to proclaim themselves' my enemies. What I have in mind might seem a little far-fetched to the traditional world,' Eugene cunningly rationalized, 'but in modern technological history so were the miracles of the electric light bulb, the computer chip and the invention of television. And to think that I actually owe all my success to bored and addicted teenagers vicariously enjoying graphic violence while manipulating joysticks and playing interactive combat video games.'

Three additional years of intense experimentation had elapsed with trial and error being the dominant result sandwiched in between occasional causes for optimism. But Eugene was tenacious and resolute and persisted in his mania until his progress towards his clandestine goal eventually was showing a degree more promise than failure. It was towards the last stage of his exhaustive research that the jaded and emotionally disturbed "New-Age aristocrat" mentally reviewed those tormentors that had irritated and distressed him during the computer software prodigy's lackluster teenage and early adult life.

'I have about two-dozen key enemies that have embittered me over the years, but I'll narrow my targeted list down to twelve for now,' the crazed acrimonious tycoon thought. 'First, there's the three-wicked women. Desiree Conklin had accepted my invitation to the senior prom but then she dumped me at the last minute for the star basketball player. And then there was beautiful-but-elusive Lorraine Rice. The sorority queen rejected me after two weeks of going steady at *Drexel* and had also stood me up on our third big date,' Eugene lividly recollected. 'And I was out of college and was low man on the company totem pole at my first computer job in Philadelphia when that conniving witch Natalie Cirillo squealed on my using company time doing my personal work and promptly got me fired. I haven't forgotten the devastating impact you three sirens have had on my younger life! But through hard work I was resilient enough to persevere and gradually escalate my existence above all the reprehensible grief I've endured!'

And then Eugene considered his major male adversaries whom he also regarded as permanent lifelong enemies. 'I had lent Joshua Banks the hard-earned sum of $5,000.00 back in 1991 and he never re-paid me; in fact, the brawler beat me up when I demanded my money after the terms of our verbal agreement had expired. And I should never forget that sicko Nick Luciano, son of a small Hammonton Mafia junkyard operator who took me deer hunting and shot me in the leg saying to the local police that the incident was all an accident. And let's not exclude Richard Ryan, churchgoing and *Bible*-thumping St. Anthony of Padua parishioner and staunch Republican conservative who beat me out for town council when I was an aspiring Democratic candidate,' the livid and deranged Douglas recalled. 'I'll never forget that malicious dirty tactic smear campaign which that holier-than-thou Richard Ryan had utilized to defeat me.'

Other names were jotted-down on Eugene Derek Douglas's "short hit list". 'I was Aunt Jenny's favorite nephew, and she had promised to leave me fifty-thousand dollars in her will back when I really needed the money, and my slick cousin Stuart Townsend ruined my inheritance by convincing *his* aunt that he was more deserving of the windfall and would put the bonanza to better use, which basically translated into gambling it away in Atlantic City,' Eugene remembered and brooded. 'And how could I not include on my get-even list that disgusting bookworm, Ian Bates. That lousy egghead narrowly beat me out for high school Valedictorian after I had conscientiously devoted my whole four years from grades nine to twelve dedicated to achieving that special academic honor. And yes,' recalled Eugene, 'I must also remember one Arthur Cantor, my first stockbroker who unscrupulously manipulated my account and lost money playing the stock market just when a nasty recession set in. His enterprise cost me thirty thousand just when I needed to finance seed money to get my upstart computer software company launched and so I had to take out a high-interest loan. I hereby promise as God is my Witness that Stuart Townsend, Ian Bates and Arthur Cantor will receive their just compensations for crossing me.'

And then finally, Eugene sorted-out the final three resented names to appear on his "itemized hit list". 'Robert DuBois built my first house, made numerous mistakes and wound-up charging me forty thousand cold-cash bucks over and above the initial construction cost. I had to take out a second mortgage to pay the crook or else he threatened to hospitalize me with multiple injuries,' Eugene reflected. 'And then there's that repugnant, pugnacious bully Eric West who always slammed me against high school lockers in front of girls and incessantly berated and mocked me in the cafeteria. And finally, I have to add the name Allen Porter', a banker who dared calling me his "friend" after he denied my second mortgage to pay that slippery snake Robert DuBois. I guarantee that *your* time is coming soon Robert DuBois, Eric West and Allen Porter. My uncompromising heart demands that I have retribution for you three jerks matter-of-factly violating my dignity and denying me respect. Your abominable actions were humiliating to me, and I promise they'll be avenged!'

And then, Eugene contemplated exactly how he would lure his prospective victims into a clever trap just like a sly spider would attract flying insects into its imaginative-but-deceptive web. Eugene had always been fascinated with miniaturization, making objects smaller and lighter than they normally and naturally would be in everyday reality. His computer industry success and expertise allowed him adequate time and sufficient knowledge to combine his *3-D* software background with the theories he had learned studying advanced bio-chemical *DNA* formulas in college textbooks and professional research journal articles to fully organize the raw essence of his diabolical scheme.

'Thanks to Dollie the Sheep, politicians and church leaders are overly concerned about the prospect of human cloning,' Eugene evaluated with an evil smile on his face, 'when *they* really should be apprehensive about the advent of human miniaturization. And after I conveniently dispose of my twelve loathed past antagonists, I'll be able to triple my wealth by selling my new scientific secrets to the military. If it weren't for significant miniaturization technology developed in the 1960s and early '70s,' Eugene speculated and ascertained to justify his twisted motives, 'then the U.S. space program would've been stagnated and generally speaking, computers, circuit boards, microchips and software achievements would've never materialized.'

The egocentric and very inscrutable loner then mentally reviewed how his pertinent pioneering experimentation in the new uncharted field of "bio-chemical molecular miniaturization" had evolved from a wild reckless theory and amusing hobby into a relevant matter involving practical applied science. During Eugene's early laboratory endeavors, a dozen white rats had been "accidentally exploded" while *he* had been recording exploratory findings using four "shrink guns" to genetically rearrange and shrivel cellular structures in the sacrificed rodents. But despite those frustrating failures, the frail man possessing an indomitable will doggedly persisted in his mania.

Next, Eugene modified his revolutionary technique, and the new applied procedure utilized twelve "shrink guns", six of which recycled and fed *DNA* and red and white blood cells back into the animals being subjected to the bio-chemical laser penetrations. Seven rabbits had been disintegrated until Eugene systematically (by trial and error) delicately and intricately adjusted the amount of exposure in each "laser injection", and on the eighth "genesis", a normal healthy rabbit had been successfully diminished to two-inches in height and three and a half inches in length. 'I now know how to shrink highly specialized cells in all body systems and vital organs. I not only can miniaturize organs but also bones and even red and white blood cells and intestinal enzymes, too! My spectacular accomplishments will eventually be praised, taught and studied in high schools and universities all over the world for the remainder of history!'

More minute adjustments and alterations were done to the various factors in the complex *DNA* equations until a highly sophisticated paradigm had finally been achieved. Eugene then used his inexhaustible cash reserves to illegally acquire on the black market seven Rhesus monkeys, whose *DNA* molecules were most similar to that of humans out of any other mammal species on the face of the Earth. Five of the Rhesus monkeys had incidentally imploded in the madman's preliminary tests, but after making minor corrections to certain crucial algorithms that monitored the miniaturization process dynamics, the final two monkeys were astoundingly transformed into diminutive creatures, the seventh monkey representing valid verification of the method's integrity and reliability.

'Now that I've mastered the essential secrets of bio-chemical miniaturization,' Eugene Derek Douglas evilly plotted, 'it's almost time for me to execute the next innovative phase of my grandiose strategy. I've already had the 'miniaturization room' altered to accommodate my pre-selected twelve human guinea pigs and my sensational Hammonton model railroad landscape platform is also just about completed down in the basement. My human 'Lilliputian containment box' has been perfectly manufactured by an area metallurgist,' Eugene evaluated and reviewed, 'and now to cordially invite my twelve unsuspecting death candidates to a terrific party that they won't ignore and will undoubtedly accede to attend. And I always had thought that just the Mafia was in the 'can't refuse' business! Ha, ha, ha!'

The irrepressible grudge-keeper sat erect at his desktop computer and composed a cordial letter that would be individually addressed and printed and then sent to the twelve unfortunate designated recipients. One such letter read as follows:

276 Fourteenth Street
Hammonton, NJ 08037
September 1, 2005

Desiree Conklin
757 Grand Street
Hammonton, NJ 08037

Dear Desiree,

It's been years since I've seen you, and as you probably already know, luck has smiled in my direction and I've fortuitously become a multimillionaire. I would like to share my good fortune with twelve people that I have had happy memorable moments with in the past.

As you undoubtedly know, I'm a serious collector of fancy and rare classic automobiles, keeping three dozen of my valuable cars in my Pacific Palisades mansion and the other twelve in my Hammonton mansion, 276 Fourteenth Street. But recently, I regret that I've become bored with my New Jersey collection and plan to discard my twelve Hammonton classic autos', and then replace them with magnificent, expensive speed-oriented Ferraris, Porsches, Lamborghinis' and the like.

Here's what I intend to do at my lavish extravagant party to which I'm inviting you. I plan to have the keys to the twelve classic cars I wish to dispose of placed in twelve separate envelopes. A dozen face-down flash cards will correspond to each of the sealed envelopes. Each of my twelve invited guests will select a numbered flash card that will entitle each lucky individual to one of my twelve classic automobiles, all of which are currently valued at over three hundred thousand dollars each. The evening should prove to be one that provides you with some very exciting and rewarding amusement and me with the satisfaction of enjoying your valued company while *we* nostalgically review our past association.

Here are the twelve cars that I'll be awarding to lucky friends from my past.

1) 1932 Chrysler Custom Imperial Phaeton
2) 1931 Marmon V-16 Passenger Sedan
3) 1925 Vauxhall 30/98
4) 1931 Bugatti Royale, Berline Voyage
5) 1935 Mercedes-Benz 500K
6) 1926 Dusenberg Model A Phaeton
7) 1928 Rolls Royce Phantom 1 Limousine
8) 1931 Alfa Romeo
9) 1937 Jaguar SS 100 Roadster
10) 1938 Hispano-Suiza
11) 1936 Auburn Boattail; Speedster Model
12) 1929 Isotta-Fraschini Limousine

Please arrive at my 276 Fourteenth Street Hammonton residence at 7:30 p.m. on Friday evening October 7, 2005 to claim your wonderful prize in my suspense-filled lottery. Please come alone without an escort and also, kindly keep this information a secret or else your winning prize might indeed be jeopardized by default. You can appreciate how I would dislike the knowledge pertaining to this imaginative lottery to get out into the public domain before the fun event actually takes place.

I'm looking forward to seeing you on the evening of October 7th and pleasantly reminiscing a slue of sentimental memories from our mutual pasts. *RSVP*

Sincerely,

Eugene Derek Douglas
CEO, E. Douglas
Computer Animation and Graphics, Inc.

The twelve very carefully prepared letters were individually addressed, sealed in elaborate envelopes, and sent "Certified Mail" to Desiree Conklin, Natalie Cirillo, Lorraine Rice, Joshua Banks, Nick Luciano, Richard Ryan, Stuart Townsend, Ian Bates, Arthur Cantor, Robert DuBois, Eric West and Allen Porter. By Tuesday, September 13th Eugene Derek Douglas had received via post-delivery definite confirmations from all twelve invited guests stating that each lucky candidate would indeed be attending the multimillionaire's "generous giveaway party". It was now time for Eugene Derek Douglas to meticulously coordinate his secretive last-minute preparations.

On Thursday afternoon, October 6th the computer software expert had made final arrangements for the caterers to set-up tables and deliver the hot food and cold beverages to be served the following evening to his "distinguished guests" in the "entertainment lounge" that had been shrewdly and diabolically designed as the special "shrinking chamber".

That evening, Eugene stepped down to his elegantly furnished basement to admire his newly-constructed, treasured, scale-model miniature reproduction of downtown Hammonton featuring handsomely painted replicas of Bellevue Avenue banks, retail stores, office buildings and funeral parlors. And small renditions of actual homes scaled-down to every exact minuscule detail had been wonderfully handcrafted and duplicated and then bolted-down to the enormous-but-sturdy landscape platform.

Each miniature 16"x16"x16" home (having barred windows and doors) was cutely furnished, and each structure even came complete with running water and flush toilets to accommodate each of the twelve, intended, temporary "shrunken residents". A 1950s' black locomotive having twelve authentic-looking *Pullman* cars and an accompanying caboose rotated on the railroad tracks around the inimitable and impressive scale model of what Eugene described as "metropolitan downtown Hammonton".

'Tomorrow night my meticulous preparations and hard work will all be justified,' the pernicious schemer imagined with delight as he greedily rubbed his hands together. 'Those enemies that had egregiously wronged me in the past will finally pay for their malice.

My vengeful heart knows no mercy as far as the twelve-targeted dupes are concerned! And thanks to my fertile imagination, gloom will definitely precede doom!'

At six p.m. Friday evening, the event's caterers arrived, set-up the excellent food selections and beverages, and then (according to strict instructions), swiftly departed the Fourteenth Street premises by 7 o'clock. At 7:20, the guests started arriving and Eugene (dressed in a black tuxedo) acted like a proud host giving each of the bug-eyed arrivals a personal tour of the main parts of his splendid mansion. At a quarter to eight, the host cordially escorted all twelve of his exhilarated guests into his "exquisite museum-garage" to personally view, inspect and sit in the dozen vintage automobiles to be given away in the highly anticipated "limousine lottery". Everyone in attendance was thrilled and "tickled pink".

"Okay folks, you've all seen the terrific cars I'm going to be providing as gifts," Eugene yelled above the incessant chatter, "so let's all take a stroll to the food and libations room and eat, drink and share our fellowship before I initiate the grand lottery. Follow me, and I'll lead you to your sceumptious epicurean delights! And try not to eat too much caviar or drink too much *Jack Daniels*, imported scotch or fine Merlot!"

Everyone followed their amiable host to the "gourmet room", *not* realizing that they were about to become fatted cattle being prepared for execution. Champagne, bourbon, vodka, scotch, rum and rye were readily available along with other assorted soft beverages to concoct a variety of mixed drinks. Friendly conversations abounded throughout the diabolical 'shrink room without a psychiatrist', and no one dared mention any negative event from the past to the decadent multimillionaire doing the fantastic splurging.

"This is really a terrific excellent party, Eugene!" Desiree Conklin complimented without daring to allude to her treatment of Douglas before the Hammonton High School senior prom. "Your taste in food and lodging is both extraordinary and impeccable. There are no other adjectives that can adequately describe it! Thank you so much for inviting me!"

Natalie Cirillo never once mentioned her getting Eugene fired from his first employment in Philadelphia after he had graduated *Drexel University*. "I hear you have an outstanding summer home in Stone Harbor?" Natalie politely said to the seemingly benign automobile-lottery overseer. "I live just a stone's throw away in Avalon. Look me up when you're down the shore, and we could go out to dinner."

Lorraine Rice, Eugene's admired college sweetheart who had discourteously left him high and dry to have an intense romance with another man (that eventually ended in a very difficult divorce), also had plenteous accolades to bestow upon her gaunt-faced but dangerous host. "You've really made a name for yourself and are an important international figure," the former college beauty praised. "I always knew Eugene you possessed fantastic potential and a keen business mind. Congratulations for becoming Hammonton's most successful citizen!"

Joshua Banks, who had borrowed five thousand dollars from Eugene Derek Douglas and never repaid his debt, also had benevolent words for his "master of ceremonies." "Ya' know Eugene, we were pretty tight back at old Hammonton High. And many thanks for lending me your chemistry and biology homework from time to time. You were probably the one that was most responsible for me eventually graduating from that grueling institution of higher learning! I really *owe* a lot to you, and will forever be grateful!"

And the always-melancholy Nick Luciano never stated a single sentence about accidentally shooting Eugene in the leg inside the *Wharton State Forest* during deer hunting season. "Remember that time I took ya' to the rifle range to practice firing a shotgun," Nick glumly reminisced to the skinny computer mogul. "You gave it your best Eugene, and just look where your enviable determination got you: to the top of the heap; that's where you've climbed! I suppose that's what happens when you *aim* high!"

And garrulous Richard Ryan, a dye-in-the-wool Republican who had defeated Eugene for a town council seat during a bitter political campaign that featured many vitriolic exchanges, accusations and insinuations, was quite congratulatory when alluding to Eugene Douglas's present, highly-esteemed national reputation. "Well, my old friend. You've bravely shown everybody in this room the kind of guts we all wished we had!" Ryan generously opined to his unflattered host. "If anybody in this world deserves this fabulous palace, you my good buddy certainly are the one! Congratulations on your great success, and may you live in good health to be a hundred and ten!"

Stuart Townsend, who had deceitfully cheated Douglas out of a sizable inheritance from *their* Aunt Jenny, also had commendable things to say about his "favorite cousin." "Ya' know Eugene; we've been close pals ever since we were kids back in grammar school. Time's really been flyin' by, and I couldn't be happier for you about your phenomenal business enterprises. Remember dear cousin,"

Stuart stammered before imbibing a mouthful of potent *Jack Daniels* on the rocks, "I've always believed that charity begins at home, ha, ha, ha! I can't wait to see what kind of car I'm getting!"

And to each lauder chatting and mingling at the closed party, Eugene Derek Douglas tranquilly answered in a sedate voice, "Thank you very much for your kind words!"

As the host with the ulterior motive was ambling around the large square "reception and auto' lottery room," he took time to casually converse with each of his attendees. Ian Bates, who narrowly beat out Douglas for the coveted *HHS* Valedictorian award and attendant graduation speech told his former competitor, "You're now the most famous person to have ever graduated from Hammonton High! And Eugene, I mean this from the bottom of my heart when I tell ya', it couldn't have happened to a more deserving person!" Ian flattered and exaggerated. "May you live in good health until you reach a hundred and twenty!"

Arthur Cantor, the unethical stockbroker who had unilaterally gambled away a large chuck of Eugene's desperately needed cash-management account had some additional favorable words to share with his "gregarious philanthropist host." "Eugene, if you have any loose money available to invest in safe mutual funds and *Fortune 500 Company* preferred stock, then by all means, give me a buzz. I know you have many other investment opportunities out in California, but I can guarantee you a solid seven percent return on equity in what constitutes very fundamentally sound securities. Please think my proposition over and contact me!"

Robert DuBois, the slippery untrustworthy builder that had mercilessly bilked Eugene out of forty-thousand dollars when the young man needed the "lost money" to establish his corporate empire, was the next guest to aggrandize the "kindhearted benefactor". "I'd be thrilled to do any necessary remodeling work or scheduled renovations to your stupendous mansion," DuBois offered, showing a modicum of sincerity. "And I've always liked rustic Fourteenth Street. And this gorgeous palace Eugene is without a doubt the most opulent home in all of South Jersey."

Eric West, high school bully that had perpetually pestered, mocked, humiliated, and picked-on Eugene throughout his *HHS* student career, also had several pleasant comments to render. "If you need a loyal bodyguard to protect you from any nasty-minded rivals in the corporate world Eugene," West boastfully stated, "you be sure to look me up. Here's my personal monogrammed business card for you to keep in a safe place! And I'm very fussy about who I distribute these things to!"

And finally, there was Allen Porter, the hard-nosed banker that had denied Eugene a mortgage loan when the upstart really needed financial assistance and psychological confidence. Porter was the next thrilled guest to glorify the software game guru with orchestrated kudos. "Eugene, if you ever require underwriting of any major project, my bank will be available and right there' on the scene to lend our expert advice and financial support," Porter frivolously pledged. "No enterprise is too big or too small for us to subsidize, that is, when our liberal collateral terms are met by our many satisfied clients!"

And to each lavish compliment Eugene Derek Douglas graciously and calmly replied, "Thank you very much for your kind words!"

At eight forty-five, Eugene stood on a red leather chair to make a brief-but-important announcement. The room's nervous occupants hushed-up in a hurry as all ears strained to hear the wealthy software tycoon's important pronouncement.

"My dear friends, at nine o'clock we'll be conducting the much-anticipated lottery drawing right here in this very room!" the vengeful speaker prefaced. "Soon, I'll be returning here with the numbered envelopes and the corresponding marked flashcards to begin the lottery drawing by having each of you selecting random cards. Please enjoy yourselves while I go into another room to obtain the items needed to have our fun activity," Douglas politely suggested. "I'll return very shortly to initiate *our* drawing!"

When Eugene Derek Douglas had departed the meeting-room-chamber, everyone's interest spiked to a euphoric level, and low conversation gradually ascended into raucous clamor. And then, precisely when all of the "master-of-ceremonies" enthralled guests were immersed in the general enchantment of the moment, the host with the ulterior motive surreptitiously bolted and then barred the meeting room's door, stealthily confining all twelve of his chatting guests inside the "elaborate buffet chamber". But not one of the preoccupied and ecstatic, incarcerated invitees ever noticed the clever ruse that had just transpired.

Quickly, the mentally disturbed host entered his laboratory control room and activated his biochemical miniaturizing laser jets. The overhead recessed lights dimmed inside the square, enormous banquet room, and seconds later, an abundance of shouts and screams could be discerned three rooms away. 'The wonderful chamber is beautifully compressing, in addition to its vile occupants being simultaneously shrunk,' Eugene thought with a smirk on his countenance as the conniver carefully manipulated the dials on his instrument panel. 'Greedy, parasitic, wanna'-be-important, small-town hicks! I'll show you twelve imbeciles exactly how small I think you really are!'

Three minutes later, Eugene's miniaturization "demonstration" had been satisfactorily completed. The computer guru self-assuredly exited his "Experimental Control and Containment" facility, and the mad biochemical authority immediately observed that a large vacant area now occupied the space where the 'dissipated conference room' had previously been. Twelve high-pitched voices could be heard shrieking and cursing from within the vastly shrunken room, which now served as "a functional holding tank".

'I'll open the trapdoor hatch on the dwindled room's ceiling and use my trusty eyebrow tweezers to extricate my twelve little egomaniacs, one at a time; and then I'll carefully transfer them into my more human-compatible, metallic transport box,' Eugene mentally reviewed. 'After that, I'll carry the distressed two-inch-tall maniacs down to the basement and lock each one up inside a different miniature house bolted-down to the simulated Hammonton display train platform.'

Using a flashlight in his left hand and his eyebrow tweezers in his right, the fanatically insane, grudge-honoring multimillionaire one by one meticulously extracted his fully dressed enemies, each wearing his or her original clothes that incidentally, also had been deftly shrunken to suitably fit the wearers' new physical dimensions.

"What have you done to me?" shrieked a very incensed Desiree Conklin, sounding like a children's TV show puppet. "Turn me back to normal size! I demand that you do it immediately!"

But Eugene calmly and objectively ignored the myriad protests being rendered by his unfortunate victims and one by one transferred the vociferous balkers and hyperventilating squawkers from one container to the other "salvage box" having the wider lid. And after all dozen yellers had been accounted for and gingerly deposited into their new receptacle, Douglas cautiously closed the top and then carried the miniaturized "house of cacophony" down to his fully furnished basement.

The cache's lid was again opened, and the hollering and screaming confined neo-Lilliputians were cautiously and singly removed with the utilitarian eyebrow tweezers, and then inserted one at a time into various houses that comprised the miniature downtown Hammonton replication. Each tiny yelling prisoner was then locked inside a barred-window home, and the perpetual shrieking of shrill voices was akin to a convention of Oz Munchkins frenetically conducting a hectic Chinese fire drill inside an overcrowded Shanghai auditorium.

"Hello down there, my fellow Hammontonians! It's a small world isn't it, without even having to be in Disney World, you miniature, pathetic power trippers!" Eugene bellowed without any evident sympathy or discernible compassion distinguishable above the disconcerting din originating from various houses in the downtown Hammonton representation. "Why are you all so acerbic and unappreciative of your unique, petty predicament? Ha, ha, ha!" the demented man guffawed. "This experience will teach you idiots that you shouldn't have tinkered with my pride and attempted exploiting my vulnerabilities! Know what it feels like to suffer true mortification, you miserable, pathetic, trite riffraff! Scream your puny lungs right out of your tiny chests, for all I care! You know, I actually really like the sound of your cute high-pitched voices!"

Much to the frustration of the dozen distressed and shell-shocked temporary *"small town"* residents, Eugene Derek Douglas reached under the beautifully fabricated Hammonton landscape display, pressed a concealed button, and activated the black locomotive that had been stationary at the superbly handcrafted town depot. The 1950s-style train left its station platform and slowly chugged around the scale model community, tooting its shrill whistle as it passed the descended railroad gates situated at every key traffic intersection.

And then instant horror was incorporated into the general scenario when the dispassionate and calculating host lifted-up and then placed upon the landscape a stack of six dynamite sticks attached to a clicking time bomb set to go off precisely at midnight. "This explosion apparatus will blow all twelve of you screaming dolts to smithereens, and blast all dozen of you' egocentric creeps on a one-way excursion to Kingdom Come!" the crazed and demented lunatic laughed and cackled. "You must admit that this is really a dynamite idea! Ha, ha, ha!"

After cautiously placing the potent explosive sticks, along with the accompanying detonator, at the main intersection of Bellevue Avenue and Egg Harbor Road, the items then situated just adjacent to the scale-model platform's railroad gates, Eugene Derek Douglas bid his rambunctious two-inch-tall boisterous adversaries "Adieu!" and then nonchalantly ascended the tan carpeted steps up into the main section of his stellar Fourteenth Street palace.

'Now to relax and recline until 11:45 when I'll passively evacuate the house and make a routine trip to the local twenty-four-hour convenience store!' the psychopath callously considered. 'That's where I'll be when my under-insured ornate mansion accidentally explodes! What a coy and subtle alibi I'll have! And I hope there'll be several cops on night patrol at the local *WaWa* biting into doughnuts and drinking coffee when the dispatcher broadcasts the tragic news over the police radio! I could use a few reliable and reputable witnesses to support my alibi!' Then the chronic plotter considered some more self-serving notions. 'This mansion's thick walls are heavily plastered, and I can still hear those stupid squealing voices shrieking down in the basement. Oh well, time for a little libation to savor the moment!'

The self-satisfied avenger stepped to his mahogany liquor cabinet and plunked four ice cubes into a glass. Then, Eugene filled the glass with *Southern Comfort*, took a healthy sip, and next proceeded to sit down in his massive den's comfortable recliner chair. 'I'll set this loud alarm clock for 11:15 so that I'll be awake and can abandon my mansion just before the dynamite is triggered at midnight, and when my puny guests are quite effectively blown into oblivion. I'll just dim the lights, listen to the cable TV's uninterrupted 'Easy Listening' music channel, and if I doze-off, the alarm will awaken me. *Southern Comfort* never tasted so sweet and good! And my prized automobiles are far enough away from the explosion that they'll escape the catastrophe unscathed. This is better than living in Shangri-la, Mr. James Hilton! And I'll personally blame the ugly carnage on hateful, jealous town residents that want a capitalistic American entrepreneur like myself eliminated!'

Eugene noticed two ants enter a tiny wall crevice next to his stone fireplace. 'I would call an exterminator tomorrow if my whole house were still here,' the rich man mused before sipping more *Southern Comfort*. 'But the explosion at midnight ought to kill all of the insects roaming around, too!'

At ten thirty, the crazed, about-to-be-murderer slumped-down in his soft, white, leather recliner, shut his eyes, and went into a mild slumber. Eleven o'clock chimed in the hallway grandfather clock without ever interrupting Eugene Derek Douglas's sleep.

Ten minutes later, a voracious black widow spider crawled-out of an opening at a corner wall joint and then slowly climbed up the recliner, found an exposed piece of flesh on the multimillionaire's left leg, and instinctively injected its venom into a major artery. The snoring victim never stirred in the dimly lit room, and never reacted to the trusty alarm clock going-off. Soon, the half-intoxicated, unconscious, self-made multimillionaire had taken his last breath.

At precisely midnight, the dynamite sticks detonated down in the mansion's wall-to-wall carpeted basement. No trace of anyone that had been occupying space inside the Fourteenth Street mansion had ever been found. The Hammonton Police Department is still investigating the "terrible explosion" where all leads are now pointing to "home-grown terrorist activity".

"Missions Accomplished"

The lengthy five and a half-hour March 14th United Airlines flight from Philadelphia International Airport to San Diego's Charles Lindbergh Field was both smooth and enjoyable, except for a thirty-minute interval of minimal atmospheric turbulence over Nevada. Astute FBI Inspector Joe Giralo, accompanied by his loyal team of Agents Salvatore Velardi, Arthur Orsi and Dan Blachford, had been dispatched west to specifically investigate a very disturbing rash of violent explosions whereby eighteen unoccupied Catholic churches in three separate states had been destroyed or severely damaged by powerful dynamite detonations.

After retrieving their assorted luggage pieces from one of the airport's rotating baggage carousels, Chief Giralo took swift command of the operation and soon rented a comfortable *Ford Expedition* from Avis, and predictably, Sal Velardi was assigned the responsibility of driving the SUV and its fatigued passengers north up *Interstate 5* to where reservations for a pair of two-bedroom suites had been made at the La Jolla Marriott, situated on beautiful Village Drive not-too-far from the campus of *San Diego State University,* and also around two miles from coastal and scenic Torrey Pines Road.

"Say Chief," Sal Velardi announced from behind the steering wheel. "Many classic golf tournaments have been played just down the road from the Marriott at historic Torrey Pines. And here's a proletarian suggestion!" the chattering driver embellished his monologue. "There's a Denny's Restaurant in the vicinity further down on the way to *La Jolla,* which according to a colorful brochure I had casually read at the airport, means 'the jewel' when translated from Spanish into English."

"And what about the all-too-crowded Interstate Highways?" Agent Art Orsi eagerly chimed-in. "Everything in regard to motoring directions out here on the West Coast is that you have to take 'the 5' to travel up toward L.A., or you have to get onto 'the 15' to venture over toward San Bernardino or 'the 10' will get you heading in the direction of Palm Springs or Palm Desert. Back in Philly' and Jersey, equally congested interstate thoroughfares are just basically referred to as I-95 or I-80!"

"And they sure have some strange ecology habits out here in environmentally friendly California," Dan Blachford chipped-in, sitting erect in the back seat across from Agent Orsi and also directly behind stoic-faced Inspector Joe Giralo. "I was just speaking with a transplanted New Jersey gentleman at the luggage carousel, and he told me that the bridge spanning from San Diego over to Coronado Island doesn't require a toll if you have one or more passengers riding in your automobile. Car-pooling is definitely encouraged out here in the Golden State," Blachford continued his prattling. "A driver only has to pay the bridge toll if he or she is alone in the vehicle!"

"Boss," Agent Velardi respectfully addressed Inspector Giralo. "Will we be given some free time off during this caper to visit the famous Hotel Coronado? I've never had the pleasure of experiencing it since this is my first time in the area."

"Only if we're able to first solve this abominable series of horrendous church bombings," Chief Giralo bluntly answered. "After we check into the Marriott, I've made 6 pm reservations for four at the Chart House on the Prospect Street promenade down in gorgeous La Jolla. But Men, I've stayed at the luxurious Hotel Del on three occasions, twice on week-long vacations with my wife and two daughters, and then a third time on government business back in 1990. Now for the benefit of killing some time, what do you know Sal about *that* highly acclaimed tourist trap other than the popular notorious legend that several rooms at the Del are believed by some superstitious guests to be haunted with rather annoying, obnoxious ghosts!"

"Well, I know that the Hotel Del Coronado is a huge, white, wooden, Victorian structure featuring a fabulous red roof," Sal Velardi intelligently replied. "The place has several impressive spires, the largest one is located on top of the tremendous banquet and reception room. And I would be very remiss if I didn't mention that many Hollywood actors and actresses along with a plethora of multimillionaires have over the decades proudly vacationed there."

"Yes, the Del Coronado would be way-too-expensive for us to stay on this extended assignment. While organizing *my* final trip evaluation," the team leader assessed and then cleared his raspy throat, "it came down to a tough choice between the San Diego Sea Lodge nestled on the Pacific Coast or the very reputable La Jolla Marriott. As you're all well-aware, especially in this nasty tight economy, we have to be exceptionally frugal when it comes to spending the taxpayers' hard-earned dollars, and quite frankly, I didn't want to see you three fledgling sleuths constantly being distracted by curvaceous women out on the sandy beach, the alluring dolls all wearing skimpy bikinis. But back on subject, when the Del had opened its doors to the public in 1888," Chief Giralo authoritatively stated to his three-member captive audience, "it was the biggest resort hotel in the entire world. Despite its present noble age, the dignified seven-floor edifice is still one of the highest regarded hotels on all the continents. I remember especially relishing tremendous dining feasts at the resort's 1500 Ocean and Sheerwater restaurants. If we can break this top-secret church bombing case wide open, I promise to buy, with money out of my own wallet, yes Men, I'll generously treat the three of you' voracious chow-hounds to extravagant surf-and-turf dinners at one of the Del's very exclusive restaurants."

"I understand that much of the hotel's landscaping rivals that of a European palace's botanical garden," Agent Art Orsi contributed to the ongoing SUV conversation. "And I had read in a flight magazine on the airplane that Chinese laborers had been brought-in from San Francisco and subsequently relocated down here to semi-tropical Coronado Island in order to construct the original hotel main building."

"Yes, and the Del was the first hotel to ever have electricity," Chief Giralo articulated before squirming about to achieve a better riding position in his front passenger-side bucket seat. "Thomas Edison himself had arrived on the premises to inspect the final product and to conduct a comprehensive safety analysis. And Sal," Giralo then expounded. "You were right about powerful politicians and renowned celebrities frequenting the fantastic place: Presidents William McKinley, Woodrow Wilson, and also silent film stars Rudolph Valentino and Charlie Chaplin, just to name a few dignitaries! Even Richard Nixon, J.F.K., Jimmy Carter, Ronald Reagan and George W. Bush have stayed at the one-of-a-kind national treasure. Yes, and if I accurately recollect, L. Frank Baum, the distinguished author of the *Wizard of Oz,* well Guys, he had produced a good deal of his most creative literature at the totally inspirational Hotel del Coronado, and oh yes, finally Men," knowledgeable and long-winded Inspector Joe Giralo characteristically and incessantly declared. "At least a dozen classic movies have been filmed at the Del including *Some Like It Hot* starring Jack Lemmon, Marilyn Monroe and Tony Curtis."

"Well, Chief, I strongly recommend that we'd better get this bizarre church bombing investigation completed early in the week so that the four of us can spend a pleasant day ambling around at the San Diego Zoo in Balboa Park, after of course," Dan Blachford paused and then qualified, "we journey over to Coronado Island and tour the prestigious hotel's grand lobby and all-the-while appreciate the many terrific amenities the place has to offer! And let's not rule-out a sidebar visit to Sea World too!"

Agent Sal Velardi adroitly steered the rented black SUV off of "the 5's" typical traffic congestion and then navigated onto La Jolla Village Drive. After registering for two already-reserved fourth floor suites at the Marriott's main lobby desk, three ambitious, uniformed bellboys escorted the four New Jersey men to an empty elevator, which soon quickly ascended to the designated fourth floor. After tipping the cheerful accommodating hotel help, the quartet of federal employees spent the next three hours unpacking suitcases, hastily placing clothes into very clean bureau drawers, resting on comfortable emerald-green chairs and matching cloth sofas, and then later, washing-up in preparation for delicious steak and seafood combination dinners at the Chart House on La Jolla's picturesque waterfront. An hour before sunset, the four hungry FBI detectives were finally being seated at a fine table having a picturesque Pacific Ocean view by a very pretty tanned blonde hostess.

"Boss, while you and Sal were especially preoccupied relaxing on that Prospect Street bench just before we were summoned into the restaurant," Art Orsi smartly remarked to his immediate supervisor while the hungry group was busy consuming their various appetizers inside the Chart House's main dining room. "Dan and I strolled around the corner and we were lucky to observe a family of contented seals lazily basking upon enormous rocks out in the harbor. You don't see that type of extraordinary spectacle too often back in Atlantic City or Wildwood!"

"Did the docile creatures have long floppy ears?" Chief Giralo inquired and academically challenged before chewing and swallowing another morsel of luscious crab meat cocktail.

"Why no!" Arthur Orsi mildly exclaimed with a suddenly observable florid face. "There weren't any long floppy ears!"

"Well then, Arty," sagacious Inspector Joe Giralo verbally supplemented and elaborated. "Those particular animals that you and Dan had not-so-keenly witnessed dozing-off in the setting sun were actually lethargic sea lions and not phlegmatic ocean seals. Sea lions don't have long floppy ears like seals do!"

"Holy crustaceans!" Agent Orsi laughed as a skinny male waiter gently laid a sumptuous-looking combination plate of lobster and crab meat between the famished agent's silverware table settings. "If I'm ever fortunate enough to be promoted to the high rank of FBI Inspector, I only hope that I'll be half as erudite about certain esoteric matters as you are Chief!"

"Before my cluttered overtaxed mind forgets Sal," Joe Giralo confidently related to his favorite chauffeur, "tomorrow morning I want you to take 'the 5' down to San Diego. Here's the address of our local FBI bureau: 9797 Aero Drive," the mission coordinator disclosed as he handed Agent Velardi an official business card. "Enter the street and number coordinates you've just been given into the SUV's GPS system and then navigate your way to the appropriate location. And don't forget to take Art and Dan along with you on your vital information-gathering escapade!"

"Well Boss, exactly what's the nature of our secret assignment?" Sal Velardi anxiously asked. "As you might already know, I have a special penchant for finding-out pertinent background details in relation to cracking-open extremely complicated and frustrating crime wave riddles!"

"While you had inadvertently abandoned me on the Prospect Street sidewalk bench and were totally enamored with shopping for several cheap La Jolla souvenirs in three alluring novelty shops," Chief Giralo lightly admonished his sometimes-aberrant subordinate, "and while Art and Dan were around back mistaking despondent sea lions for depressed seals, I wisely utilized my government-issue cell phone and cleverly contacted old reliable Matt Riley back in Washington."

"And exactly what did that wily federal savant have to reveal that's remotely relevant to this incredible West Coast church bombing scenario?" Velardi asked.

"Here's the scoop, Guys!" Inspector Giralo lowly whispered towards the center of the round restaurant table. "Sal, you're to compile an adequate portfolio on the six malicious California church explosions. And Art, you're to glean sufficient info' on the half dozen parallel Arizona incidents. And finally, Dan," the Boss instructed, "your challenging task is to obtain all the essential data that you can muster pertaining to the six very distressing New Mexico church felonies!"

"Tell me Joe, er I mean Inspector," instantly embarrassed Sal Velardi awkwardly corrected his own deviant departure from common courtesy and standard FBI etiquette. "Have the horrible explosions occurred in all three states on the exact same dates?"

"Yes Sal, the same time at noon on the exact same dates, a full Monday apart, each set of three blasts happening at the exact same time," Chief Giralo indicated and confirmed. "That ongoing established pattern means that we only have until next Monday the

19th to satisfactorily figure-out the nuts and bolts to this most perplexing chain of disastrous church desecrations!"

"And tomorrow's already Thursday the 15th!" Agent Velardi contemplated and then gasped. "I'm no Alexander-the-Great by any stretch of the imagination, but this narrow five-day time-frame simply means that we have only a fraction of a week's precious days to unravel this very complex Gordian Knot!"

"That's right Sal!" Inspector Giralo promptly acknowledged. "And Men, if humanly possible, I want to keep the level of church destruction at a minimum. Several more sacrilegious bombings and I'll have to shamefully retire from the FBI as both an absolute disgrace and as a dishonorable failure! For my reputation's sake, please pray for a large miracle Fellas'!"

* * * * * * * * * * * *

At 9 a.m. sharp on Friday, March 16[th,] 2012, the four dedicated FBI men met as planned in the fourth floor Marriott suite currently shared by Inspector Joe Giralo and Agent Salvatore Velardi. Following their determined leader's explicit directions, the three investigators had brought along a wealth of recently obtained information neatly and carefully arranged inside their individual oak tag folders.

"Well Chief," Art Orsi began as the four men formally sat around a mahogany coffee table in the suite's tastefully decorated living room area. "What's your clever theory about who's wickedly committing these atrocious Catholic church bombings?"

"Actually Art, presently I don't know the identities of the individual culprits, but generally speaking," Inspector Giralo elucidated and then momentarily hesitated, "I suspect that we're dealing with a string of hate crimes here, yes indeed, hate crimes directed against the Catholic religion, all being deplorably enacted in three separate states. Now then Gentlemen, I'm inclined to believe that rather than us chasing-down crazed international terrorists, we're concerned with bringing to justice a batch of demented home-grown anarchists, probably zealous fanatics that greatly despise the church's dogmatic teachings, particularly in the areas of abortion, gay rights and also so-called women's *reproductive rights,* which obviously have nothing remotely to do with the normal process of female reproduction. Instead, the practice of reproduction rights conversely prevents reproduction from happening! The all-too-convenient politically correct phraseology is a modern-day euphemism for the use of contraception and for the employment of common birth control methods."

"So therefore, Boss, you hypothesize that radical pro-choice advocates, militant gay and lesbian marriage villains, along with crazed feminists are probably the central instigators of all of these contemptuous church attacks that appear to be deliberate, and not random or copy-cat criminal activities!" Dan Blachford deduced and verbally concluded.

"Exactly Dan," Chief Giralo tersely agreed. "There's nothing at all superficial about these extremely heinous church bombings! Usually though, humans are creatures of habit in their daily behavior patterns. But as a rule, crooks tend to give themselves away when the morally corrupt fools attempt becoming too sophisticated, and then the overconfident perpetrators think that they're uncommonly shrewd and soon audaciously deviate from their standard-but-effective M. O.'s, while interestingly enough, during *their* mania, attempting to send the state and federal authorities onto the wrong trail. That's the crucial tipping point when the cocky erroneous thugs are most vulnerable to being apprehended and then Gentlemen, ultimately being promptly indicted and convicted in like fashion."

"Your novel theory about the haughty nature of the criminal mindset is quite plausible," Agent Velardi commended his highly admired tutor and mentor. "Now Boss, with your permission, may I now begin my formal presentation about the mendacious California church explosions."

"Yes Salvatore, you may commence. But try being as succinct as possible," Giralo sternly insisted. "Conciseness and brevity should be this discussion's principal objectives!"

"Okay then," Agent Velardi almost neurotically replied as he slowly opened his oak tag folder containing his research that had been carefully obtained at 9797 Aero Drive. "As everyone's quite well-aware, six disgusting church bombings have occurred at seven-day intervals, each one on a consecutive Monday. This evolutionary pattern obviously suggests that the next human-caused California catastrophe will occur next Monday, March Nineteenth. No magical crystal ball is needed to prognosticate *that* bone-chilling prediction!"

"That mundane conclusion is both plausible and rational!" Chief Giralo assessed and expressed. "But please Sal, let's meticulously review the six abhorrent California church detonations in their precise chronological order."

"The first demolition regrettably happened right here in San Diego, the second one up in Carmel, the third destruction over in

Monterrey County, the fourth in San Gabriel, the fifth in San Luis Obispo County and finally," Velardi vociferated before inhaling an abundance of fresh oxygen to resume his important exposition, "the sixth germane tragedy occurred just last Monday at noon, March 12th up in San Francisco."

"Excellent information gathering," Chief Giralo complimented. "But Sal, you neglected to provide *us* the names of the old Spanish missions that are located nearest to the specific targeted Catholic churches that have been under siege!"

"Chief, I didn't consider *those* remote, minute facts that you had just alluded to as being material to this first stage of our investigation," Agent Velardi quite defensively answered. "And I sincerely apologize for the gross oversight!"

"Agents Art and Dan; do you two contemporary Dick Tracy impersonators have in your possession the names of the nearest missions to the destroyed churches over in Arizona and New Mexico respectively?" Chief Joe Giralo politely-but-directly reprimanded the suddenly surprised duo. "What about the original erection dates of the nearest missions to those affected parochial churches? Precisely, in what years had the nearest missions been established?"

"Why no Boss!" Orsi and Blachford simultaneously chorused, showing signs of instant humiliation.

"Well then, my illustrious trio of professional crime fighters, I want *those* particular vital construction facts available to me by 9 am, tomorrow," Joe Giralo imperatively commanded. "How can I ever make any valid interpretations about this insidious crime wave if I'm given totally mediocre and incomplete backgrounds to the eighteen unscrupulous nihilistic acts, all apparently performed by obsessed political ideologues!"

"Well Chief, what remarkable pearls of wisdom has *your* singular research obtained?" Agent Arthur Orsi intrepidly requested knowing. "Personally, I need to learn some enlightening guidance because right now, my mind is a little stifled by a lack of solid evidence in regard to the vexing Arizona crime spree that's gone way beyond acts of mere vandalism!"

Chief Joe Giralo patiently explained to his now-mortified men that originally, a series of twenty-one California coastal Spanish missions had been founded by Father Junipero Serra of the Franciscan Order. However, the Catholic missions that had been constructed in Arizona and in New Mexico had been established a century earlier by members of the rival Jesuit Order.

"The Jesuit missions outside California are much older than the Franciscan ones that were logically situated along the Pacific Coast," Giralo convincingly lectured with little body animation. "The Spanish were expressly motivated to explore the New World as a result of what history books describe as the Three G's: a quest for *gold*, the avaricious pursuit based on the fabled Indian tale of the lost city of El Dorado; secondly, there was the consuming desire of major, adventurous explorers and conquistadors like Balboa and Coronado to attain personal *glory*, and thirdly, there was the religious need for devout Spanish missionaries to spread the *gospel* and then successfully convert the various indigenous coastal Indian tribes to Christianity."

"Well, please educate me some more about local history. What labor force had built all of the various western missions?" Dan Blachford curiously inquired. "Each one, just like the venerable Alamo over in San Antonio, Texas is a unique architectural monument having its own distinct design and local personality."

"Great question Dan!" Inspector Giralo enthusiastically praised. "Local Indian populations had labored and toiled in the hot sun to obediently build the wonderful missions, that is," the Chief resumed his scholarly narrative, "that is *after* the tribes had been converted to Catholicism. But Men, when you show-up here with your newly compiled documentation tomorrow, Saturday morning, March 17th, better known as St. Patrick's Day, please have with you the exact dates that the missions in your assigned states had been built. But finally, Gentlemen, I want you to include, or should I say *exclude*, one vital thing in your reports."

"And exactly what's *that* salient item that we have to *exclude?*" Sal Velardi queried his mentor, the agent's confused mind presently addled with a lack of clarity.

"I desire for you three Fellas' on Saturday to *not* include any Franciscan or Jesuit mission that's presently in ruins," Chief Giralo decisively stipulated. "I only want the three of you to acquire the names of the original missions that are still standing and operating in California, in Arizona and in New Mexico. Can I be any more lucid about *that* very elementary specification?"

"Easier said than done," Sal Velardi reflexively complained. "But with Monday's March 19th deadline rapidly approaching, I assure you' Boss, your rather peculiar demands will be satisfied! Well then Guys, I suppose that it's back to the old drawing board! I'll drive *us* back over to the FBI Office on Aero Drive."

"Good then!" Chief Giralo rather blandly exclaimed. "I'll contact Matt Riley later today to synchronize a potential raid with Colonel Bob Bauers of Delta Force being in charge of logistical operations. All we have to do is winnow-down our present all-too-wide path of detective scrutiny and then incisively devise a probable time and place scenario so that Bauers and his competent commando units can swiftly collar or kill the Catholic-loathing anarchists who are recklessly participating in this all-too-sensational, horrible skein of reprehensible home-grown terror acts."

* * * * * * * * * * * *

On Tuesday morning, March 20th a much-relieved Inspector Joe Giralo entertained his three FBI associates with a delectable room service breakfast inside his deluxe fourth floor La Jolla Marriott suite. The three mentally out-of-sync agents were totally dumbfounded at exactly how their rather unorthodox boss had magically unraveled the very difficult hate crime California church bombing crime spree. The veteran FBI detective was immensely savoring every moment of his seemingly vague and obscure verbal rendition recounting recent events. Much to *his* great satisfaction, the abundant suspense existing within *his* all-too-curious agents' hyperactive minds was definitely escalating.

"Yes Men, my close friend Colonel Bob Bauers and his elite Delta Force storm-troopers easily made mincemeat and chopped liver out of the dozen clumsy domestic anarchists causing all of the troubling church havoc out here in sunny California. Confidentially," Inspector Giralo concisely disclosed, "three of the egregious home-grown terrorists had been seriously wounded during the brief military encounter."

"Then you were correct in your assumption that gay and lesbian political militants, abortion rights' radicals and a bevy of truculent woman's rights' fanatics were conspiring and collaborating to eliminate the chosen churches one by one because the crazed nihilists stridently opposed the Catholic religion's moral teachings about certain civil rights issues," Sal Velardi aptly summarized. "Evidently, *their* totally evil purpose represented a contemporary war of the First Ten Amendments versus the written-in-stone Ten Commandments of the Old Testament prophet Moses! Book of Exodus I do believe!"

"Very well put!" Joe Giralo congratulated his main crime-fighting apostle. "And Sal, when I was a kid, I had the distinct pleasure of attending St. Joseph Elementary School on North Third Street in metropolitan downtown Hammonton," Inspector Giralo esoterically mentioned, deliberately stressing every single syllable. "Yes indeed, Salvatore, that's how in my youth I knew from redundant classroom memorization that March 19th was always St. Joseph's Day, traditionally two days following St. Patrick's! Without exception, the school's ultra-strict nuns and austere priests had the ever-fearful student body attend mass on those two highly-revered March religious holidays!"

"What on Earth are you talking about!" a fully frustrated Arthur Orsi staunchly protested. "Boss, please stop being so darned evasive, elusive, vague and facetious!"

"Okay now, my totally confused investigative Gentlemen, let's academically review *our* formerly bewildering case one illuminating step at a time. But please remember, your stellar gumshoe research over at the San Diego FBI Office actually had been the magnificent springboard that got me thinking about how dangerous ruthless crooks have a certain propensity for outsmarting themselves when they foolishly attempt being tricky by accidentally wandering away from their ordinary habits and methods! And Guys, that's precisely how I had managed to dynamically exploit their vulnerability."

"But the other two anarchy squads patrolling over in Arizona and New Mexico did yesterday, Monday, March 19th, successfully dynamite two more churches!" alert Dan Blachford profoundly objected. "Please tell me why those two empty houses of worship had to be sacrificed!"

"Well Dan, Matt Riley was getting a lot of verbal static from powerful bishops and cardinals, and the Bureau was also receiving pressure from the persistent TV media about the widespread rash of church calamities being chronicled in local newspapers, but to simplify matters," Joe Giralo audaciously defended his erudite strategy, "in the end I was more certain where the next California attack would happen than I was about where the next surreptitious hate-crime church blowups intended for Arizona and New Mexico would occur."

"Well Chief, my exhausted mind's still in an absolute quandary about how you've miraculously cracked-open this rather oddball case!" Sal Velardi all-too-honestly maintained. "I'm going to again review for benefit of the assembled group sitting here my personal discoveries about the *disparate* California church explosions and then *you* can cast much-needed illumination upon the most recent St. Joseph Day Delta Force invasion!"

Velardi then once more orally conveyed to his three comrades that the first California church debacle had occurred in San Diego, the second in Carmel, the third in Monterey County, the fourth in San Gabriel, the fifth in San Luis Obispo County and the sixth calamity in San Francisco. "Now kindly tell us in plain, simple, unvarnished English lexicon Chief, how does all of this seemingly marble-cake data I've just divulged correlate nicely into a feasible FBI detective-oriented explanation?"

"As you know, Salvatore, I'm quite experienced at deciphering hidden meanings that are often furtively disguised inside certain given facts," Giralo affirmatively and arcanely revealed. "Now Sal, here's a nondescript map I've printed off the Internet showing the exact timeframe order that Franciscan Padre Junipero Serra had founded his original twenty-one California missions. Notice that the six places of worship that you had just identified, all situated in six separate counties, correspond perfectly with the first six original missions in exact chronological order. The San Diego mission was the first one built by Father Serra's Indians, its name being San Diego de Alcala as accurately recorded on this Internet map reproduction. The present Catholic Church, which is located nearest the first established mission, was the first one to be targeted. And the second church that had been destroyed up in Carmel was the closest one to Father Serra's second founded mission, San Carlos Borromeo de Carmelo!"

"How fantastically unbelievable! I now see the full magnitude of your brilliant methodology!" Agent Velardi marveled and exclaimed. "The Monterrey County Church that had been disrespectfully burned to a cinder was located near the third mission shown on *your* duplicated map, its name being San Antonio de Padua, located not-too-distant from the world-famous Hearst Mansion; and the fourth church that had been dynamited was in San Gabriel over in Los Angeles County, and it was conveniently positioned near the San Gabriel Archangel mission; and in a similar fashion, the fifth selected church that went-up in flames was close to the San Luis Obispo de Tolosa Mission up north in San Luis Obispo County; and finally Boss, the sixth church conflagration was not far from the San Francisco de Asis Delores, which had been the sixth mission erected in the northern city by the bay possessing the same San Francisco name."

"But what about the Jesuit missions along with the related diabolical church shenanigans' occurring in Arizona?" Art Orsi asked and then momentarily ceased speaking with his mouth temporarily agape. "How was *that* hellish skullduggery masterminded by yet-to-be-caught Anarchist Team B?"

"Well Art, I've already cited where criminals often foul themselves up by endeavoring to be too wily and then idiotically deviating from their regular routines," Chief Giralo prudently reviewed. "Well Guys, that's where creativity usually back-fires! If you think about the ugly crime-wave series involving each Arizona church incineration, the separate incidents follow a definite *reverse pattern* to that which had been demonstrated in the aforementioned California mission scheme. Instead of going from oldest to newest," Giralo persuasively emphasized, "the applied Arizona criminal strategy constituted a major backward approach going from a church situated near the newest Jesuit mission, then the second one slated for elimination being close to the second newest mission, and so on, and so on!"

"Well Chief, what about the New Mexico churches that were set ablaze from violent dynamite blasts?" Dan Blachford wondered and asked. "How about them?"

"The demolished churches located close to the chosen New Mexico Jesuit missions were deviously arranged and selected in an extremely deceptive, staggered pattern, actually a unique *alternating pattern,* Dan!" Joe Giralo very judiciously communicated. "The first burnt-to-a-crisp New Mexico church being situated near the oldest mission, the second modern-day church being constructed near the newest mission, the third targeted church being near the second oldest New Mexico mission, and in regard to the fourth designated Catholic house of worship, its specific geography was in close proximity to the second newest mission, and so on and so on!"

"This entire sordid sequence of parallel malicious events, all developing simultaneously in three separate states at precise seven-day intervals is without a doubt mind-boggling!" opined Agent Velardi. "I conjecture that intense, in-house, rough, no-nonsense interrogations of the captured California A-Team radicals will eventually lead to the apprehension of the equally wretched Arizona and New Mexico anarchists. But please tell me, Chief; how in God's holy name did you know about the seventh California scheduled attack being treacherously planned for the esteemed San Juan Capistrano Mission?"

"That's where my wonderful Catholic grammar school intuition, or should I pragmatically say 'my strict parochial school educational indoctrination' dramatically kicked-in!" the now-jubilant Inspector Giralo smiled and then consequentially chuckled. "I figured that the miserable vindictive anarchists were quite ready to branch-out of their normal practice for just one auspicious day, and subsequently, carelessly abandon their vile church destruction tactics in order to abruptly shock the public by eliminating the renowned landmark San Juan Capistrano Mission. They just couldn't resist the overwhelming temptation to make a dramatic public statement!"

"So, you had Matt Riley confer with Colonel Bob Bauers and have his ever-vigilant Delta Force units stationed all around the historic Capistrano Mission," Art Orsi surmised and concluded. "But how does the St. Joseph's Day March 19th jargon fit-in as a significant factor into your imaginative mental equation?"

"Here's the marvelous formula Arty! On St. Joseph's Day, March 19th of each year," Chief Giralo nonchalantly prefaced his superb discourse, "squadrons of swallows, yes, very tiny birds, habitually wing their way back to Southern California to roost for half a year at the San Juan Capistrano Mission. In fact, Art, there's an old song commemorating the annual phenomenon that's appropriately titled 'When the Swallows Come Back to Capistrano'! And quite amazingly," Inspector Giralo exhaled, fully enjoying every wonderful second, "on October 23rd of each year, which traditionally on the Catholic Calendar is designated as the 'Day of San Juan', the itinerant swallows obediently depart Capistrano, only to again faithfully return the following St. Joseph Day, March 19th!"

"And so Boss," Sal Velardi excitedly fathomed and generalized, "you had perceptively theorized that the California A Team anarchists would for one time only, imaginatively abandon their fanatical church implosions and stupidly concentrate on a much more colossal and tremendously more shocking violent act of discriminate terror, that is, heinously detonating the famous Capistrano Mission and killing-off most of the swallows in the process, just to make a brazen-but-potent ideological statement to the totally appalled world! I now see and comprehend Boss that incomparable San Juan Capistrano had been the seventh site founded by Father Junipero Serra that's prominently listed on *your* chronological order historical mission map!"

"And now *we* know why the local Major League baseball team is named the San Diego Padres!" Art Orsi declared.

"And why the team up in Anaheim is called the California Angels!" Dan Blachford laughed and related.

"What an outrageously preposterous, fundamentally deranged, maniacal conspiracy!" Art Orsi angrily determined. "And the entire outlandish fiasco was ignorantly based on a diabolical animosity for the Catholic Church's inflexible moral doctrines!"

"That's basically right, Arty," Joe Giralo gleefully verified. "The mendacious villains in all three states were radical, heterogeneous, home-grown anarchists who absolutely despised American History, Western Civilization and the U.S, Constitution in general, and the Catholic religion in particular!"

"And Chief, if it weren't for your notable wisdom," Dan Blachford opined to his eminent team captain, "the dastardly dissidents might've eventually advanced to eradicating epic cathedrals and basilicas! Maybe even initiating repulsively hideous crimes like blowing-up the Vatican!"

"Now I truly believe that you three inimitable geniuses have finally pieced-together the entire puzzle that's no longer an enormous perplexing mystery," Inspector Giralo stated with an artificial lugubrious expression upon his countenance. "So therefore, Gentlemen, contrary to my ordinarily parsimonious nature, I feel extremely obligated to honor my sacred pledge, and so consequently, as a direct result of my former irresponsible rhetoric," the enthralled FBI Chief very politely proceeded, "I feel quite compelled to treat the three of you rather fascinating amateur sleuths to a fabulous well-deserved five-course surf and turf supper inside the beautiful Hotel del Coronado's incomparable Sheerwater dining facility! In the final analysis, Gentlemen," self-satisfied Inspector Joe Giralo haughtily snickered, "dining ambiance just can't get any better than that!"

"Accidental Coincidence"

It was April Fools Day, and Hammonton, New Jersey CPA Troy Rogers was extremely stressed. The April 15th IRS tax deadline was looming only two weeks away, and the conscientious accountant's phone was constantly ringing with worried clients inquiring about their estimated or already tallied income tax burdens. 'I should run away to the South Pacific for the rest of my life, or else join the French Foreign Legion if the organization still exists!' the harried "numbers' cruncher" lamented and fantasized. 'It's a good thing I have a trusty secretary/assistant to help me through these especially rough times. Mrs. Cheryl Penza's a terrific aide, and I can't afford to lose her steadfast allegiance. In fact, in appreciation of her loyalty I've decided I'm going to offer her a two thousand dollar raise effective May 1st!'

The phone rang inside the anterior office, and Cheryl put the caller on hold and immediately relayed the message to the overwhelmed tax law authority, who was disgustedly staring at a stack of alphabetical order folders that had been accumulating over the past week upon his cluttered desk.

"Troy, it's Phil Caruso on Line 1," Cheryl announced in her normal pleasant tone of voice. "What should I tell him? He insists on talking to you."

"Tell that neurotic insurance salesman I just stepped out of the office to mail some important tax returns at the post office," the fatigued CPA instructed. "Tell Phil his tax return will be done within two days, and that I'll get on the horn to personally convey the dreaded bottom line to him. That feasible explanation ought to stave-off that annoying worry wart's incessant curiosity for at least forty-eight hours."

"Okay Boss," the cooperative office assistant concurred. "But I've also just got paranoid Hector Russo on Line 2. This time he's a little over the top, insisting that he's one of your biggest accounts and he's demanding that I get through to you or else he's going to take his coveted business elsewhere."

"Put the petulant maniac through, Cheryl!" the assets and debits expert directed. "I can't afford to lose that nutcase fanatic as a customer even though his nasty, mercurial temper is undeniably on the reprehensible side."

Cheryl Penza immediately honored her employer's command and transferred the call to *his* desk.

"Hello Hector! How's your seven-hundred-acre blueberry crop looking for this coming season?" Troy Rogers greeted his significant account subscriber. "I'll bet that pretty soon the honey bees will be buzzing around doing their vital field thing!"

"Don't try soft soaping me!" the vitriolic and volatile blueberry farm mogul yelled. "I've got a seven million dollar a year fruit operation going for me and if I need to scrape-up more than a quarter million bucks in a hurry to pay off that legal crook Uncle Sam, I have to know how much I owe the greedy thief pretty damned soon so that I can sell stocks in my UBS cash management account, which incidentally isn't performing too-well because of the terrible economic recession that's currently plaguing the country."

"Hector, I'm working diligently on your complex statistics, and I promise you I'll have the ballpark data in your possession by noon tomorrow," the numbers guru committed and vowed. "Now my preliminary evaluation is that you won't have to pay a penny over three hundred thousand! But truthfully," Troy Rogers qualified, "I'll be able to provide a more thorough and comprehensive analysis of your tax liability situation no later than four p.m. tomorrow, Greenwich, England time!"

"Stop being such a lousy, dumb, preposterous, sanctimonious Ignoramus!" prominent blueberry grower Hector Russo squawked and protested. "If I was standing next to you right now, I'd be inclined to beat the living daylights out of you after first making you swallow your front teeth! I used to be a middleweight boxer in the Navy before I inherited my father's fifty-acre farm and expanded it to over fourteen times its original size!" the obsessed blueberry empire agriculturalist egotistically bragged. "Now then Mr. Rogers, CPA, get my tax information to me by noon tomorrow, or else I'm gonna' find myself a more reliable and less difficult tax accountant to handle my personal money affairs! Ya' know Troy, it's wise guys like you that really get my dander up, and really make the world a rather lousy place to live in!" Click.

'I think that the inimitable Hector Russo should read the book *How to Win Friends and Influence People!*" Accountant Troy Rogers concluded as the numbers wizard gently placed his land-line phone back into its charging cradle. 'It's amazing how that belligerent Idiot could've ever become a successful influential businessman! Market conditions of supply and demand I suppose, especially when the great demand for fresh-picked New Jersey blueberries tremendously exceeds the available supply.'

Cheryl Penza again predictably buzzed her perturbed Boss. "Troy, it's Cynthia Harper on the line, and she wants to speak with you about her upcoming social event."

"All right," the fully beleaguered professional financial genius answered, shaking his head. "But from here on out, I'm not taking any additional calls today. Fact is Cheryl; I'm literally drowning in a sea of responsibility. Oh, hello Cynthia!"

"Troy, I just want to remind you that you've been invited to my masquerade party that's slated for this coming Saturday night, but I haven't yet received your RSVP," the vivacious, tanned blonde-hair hostess stated. "Are you attending my fabulous affair, or aren't you? I assure you; it'll be a real gala happening that you'll definitely regret missing!"

"Why Cindy, of course I'm going to be there! I wouldn't miss it for all the gold bullion in Fort Knox!" Troy communicated and exaggerated. "But honestly Cynthia, I've been deluged with a colossal workload this tax season, and I must've inadvertently forgotten to contact you. Please accept my genuine excuse! I sincerely apologize for the grievous oversight."

"Well Troy, I just want you to know that Rita Maimone is going to be a special guest at my party, and I've picked-up gossip around town that she has her eyes on you, and I've also heard through the local grapevine that you've taken more than a casual interest in her," Cynthia Harper confided and then giggled. "That luscious revelation alone oughta' be sufficient motivation for you to get your rear end in gear. Exactly what costume are you going to be wearing? As a personal policy, I really don't like having any costume duplications at a masquerade party; you can understand my position, don't you?"

"Wow Cindy! I'm more than thrilled that Rita will be there, fancy mask and all I presume," Troy "Buck" Rogers gleefully exclaimed. "And by the way, thanks for the confidential information! I'll treasure it and promise to keep my intel' source a secret!"

"Well Troy, here's a bit of indispensable news you can count on. She'll be wearing an exquisite Marie Antoinette outfit and won't be hard for you to identify!" Cynthia Harper voluntarily revealed. "But the big question is, what will *you* have as a suitable disguise so that I'll be able to recognize you when you enter?"

"I plan to arrive as a distinguished Egyptian pharaoh so that you'll easily be able to confirm my attendance," the CPA disclosed and joked. "Possibly Ramses II or King Tut!"

"Great! I don't have any pharaohs on my list!" the talkative party-giver enthusiastically divulged. "And Troy, don't forget to have your vizard on Saturday night!"

"What's a vizard?" the bewildered accountant asked.

"It's a type of mask, Silly! William Shakespeare himself often used *that* cool word 'vizard' in many of his comedy plays! See you at my place Saturday at eight!" Click.

Troy Rogers placed the phone into its cradle a little harder than usual. 'Oh, mercy me!' the CPA mentally anguished and languished, holding his aching head. 'It's Monday and I forgot to order a King Tut or Ramses II outfit for Cindy's big masquerade party. I know what I'll do! There's a historical costume rental store over in Mays Landing inside the Hamilton Mall, and it's only twenty miles away. Cheryl's not yet meltdown material, and definitely not too argumentative during the all-too-vexing tax season! And besides, my Girl Friday is very dependable and can keep her calm composure even during a major crisis!' Troy Rogers logically determined. 'I'll temporarily put her in charge of the office and let her diplomatically contend with all of the relentless mounting duress while I'm out of the vicinity; preoccupied on my weird in-quest-of-a-disguise shopping expedition!'

* * * * * * * * * * * *

Troy Rogers pulled his dark blue Lexus out of the Vine Street parking lot located next to Columbus Park, and then made a left turn onto Egg Harbor Road. Soon, he passed by Hammonton Lake Park and the Little League and Babe Ruth League baseball complexes. Several miles later on his all-too-familiar route was the blinking Red Traffic Light. After stopping at the four-way signal, a right was made onto County 559, better known to local motorists as Weymouth Road, and after the Lexus ascended the Atlantic City Expressway overpass, the two-lane highway meandered in a snake-like fashion left and right past the 1,300-acre Atlantic Blueberry Plantation, the largest cultivated blue fruit farm in the world. 'In five more minutes, I'll be heading east on Route 322, the Black Horse Pike and I'll be halfway to my destination,' Rogers reckoned.

The Alpha-minded CPA had his immediate itinerary already sketched-out in his belabored mind, for ever since his childhood days, Troy had always been a stickler for honoring minutia and enacting details. 'I'll now park my car in the Hamilton Mall lot, take the center mall escalator up to the food court for a couple of slices of pizza and a Coke, and then hasten over to the Acme Costume and Tuxedo Rental Store to obtain my gaudy pharaoh's garb for Cindy Harper's posh party.'

Fifteen minutes later, the very stressed-out man was sitting at a Food Court table staring at his rather mediocre lunch. 'Not exactly an Epicurean banquet but nevertheless these two tomato and cheese slices are adequate junk food substitutes,' Troy imagined as he began gobbling-down his fast-food meal. After downing his two savory pizza slices and his medium-sized cola, the pressed-for-time accountant took the convenient escalator downstairs to the mall's main corridor. A right-hand-side amble soon had Troy Rogers stepping into the desired retail rental place of business.

"Hello," a tall thin mustached clerk behind the counter amiably greeted the new arrival. "I'll bet you know exactly what you want without browsing around. May I help you?"

"Yes, I've been invited to a very special masquerade party extravaganza, and I'd like to go as an ancient Egyptian pharaoh, possibly either King Tut or Ramses II," Rogers concisely stipulated. "Ever since I was in middle school, I've been fascinated by ancient Egyptian culture, the Nile River, the Sphinx, the pyramids, and especially Cleopatra. You seem to have a vast inventory here on your racks. I believe that I've come to the right place!"

"Yes, you have Sir, but regrettably, our only pharaoh ensemble has already been rented and will not be returned until late Thursday morning," the suave store employee informed his disappointed visitor. "But Sir, I promise you that our dry cleaner can get the pharaoh getup spruced-up and shipped to your door via UPS no later than Friday afternoon; that is to say, if you luckily live in either Atlantic or Cape May County."

"Well now, I do live in Hammonton, Atlantic County," Troy stated, his overall demeanor suddenly reflecting mild relief. "But how can I be certain if the pharaoh outfit will fit me if I don't have the opportunity of trying it on for size."

"That's all quite easy to explain Sir," the pleasant store attendant insisted in a mellow tone of voice. "It states right hear in the company catalog that the pharaoh costume is specifically tailored to fit any man ranging between the heights of five foot eight inches and six foot two, and who weighs anywhere between one hundred seventy and two hundred and ten pounds," the affable salesman indicated. "Here is a glossy representation of the particular item on this page presented in vivid color. Notice Sir, that the handsome black mask accompanies the exotic-looking apparel and headdress. And if I may add Sir, it's at no additional charge. Now then, after viewing this color photo', what do you think about you impersonating Ramses II? Isn't the costume rather intriguing?"

"It's very outstanding, extremely top notch!" Rogers commended the persuasive salesperson. "That's my personal opinion. Exactly how much will it cost me to rent all of the Ramses II paraphernalia Friday through Sunday."

"A real bargain Sir. Only a hundred bucks plus ten dollars to cover the UPS express delivery," the clerk recited. "I say only a hundred smackers simply because the costume was not in stock when you had stepped through the store's main entrance to make your inquiry. I'm proud to say that *that's* our strict company discount policy. What's your pleasure Sir?"

"Okay, here's the hundred dollars up front," the convinced customer said, handing the clerk a crisp Ben Franklin note. "And here's an Alexander Hamilton to cover the express freight delivery charge. I believe you'll now need my residential address and phone numbers; both land-line and cell."

"Yes Sir, I'll gladly take down that pertinent information and give you a copy to keep as a receipt. Now I only have one further question. Is your girlfriend or wife going to attend the grandiose party as Cleopatra?"

"No," Troy laughed and grinned, shaking his head in mild amusement. "She's actually going to the big shindig as Marie Antoinette."

"Sounds like a definite conflict in historical eras to me," the congenial fellow behind the counter chuckled. "Oh well, Mr. Rogers, I guess it could've been even more problematic like Adolph Hitler and Dolly Madison, or diabolical Ivan the Terrible escorting dangerous Lucrezia Borgia, ha, ha, ha!"

At six p.m. Friday evening, a brown UPS truck pulled into the CPA's Walnut Street ranch home's asphalt driveway, and the harried carrier delivered a large package from the Acme Costume and Tuxedo Rental Store, Hamilton Mall, Mays Landing, NJ. Five minutes later, the excited recipient quickly unwrapped and opened the string-tied cardboard box, but was highly upset upon discovering and examining its mistaken contents.

'Oh no!' the disappointed resident thought. 'Those incompetent imbeciles sent me an ancient Greek warrior's regalia instead of the elaborate Ramses II getup.' The man's frustration was heightened upon him calling the Hamilton Mall store.

"Sir, we're sorry for the unusual mix-up!" an apologetic voice on the other end stated. "Wilhelm, the fellow who had rented you the pharaoh's costume is away on vacation in St. Thomas, Virgin Islands; so obviously, he's not available to speak with you about the matter. But from what I can determine," the sympathetic Acme employee related, "three costumes had been simultaneously sent to the wrong customers; your pharaoh outfit to someone else, the Greek warrior one that you've accidentally recently received, and a third one inadvertently addressed to an altogether separate party. I'll speak to the owner and arrange an appropriate refund for you because of the oddball shipping error."

"Never mind all the trivial explanations!" Troy angrily and vehemently protested. "I'll wear the erroneous Greek thing you've sent me, bronze sword, helmet, sandals and all to the masquerade party tomorrow night, but with truth as my witness, I'm never going to recommend or do any further business with your irresponsible company ever again!" Click.

Slowly regaining his emotional composure, the Walnut Street resident sat at his computer desk and typed in "Greek heroes" into the Google search box. After perusing the faces of battle uniformed Odysseus, Hercules, Agamemnon, Menelaus and Ajax, Troy Rogers eyes eventually focused upon the graphic color illustration of the magnificent champion Achilles.

'This is without a doubt the exact guy I'm going to impersonate!' Rogers concluded. 'It says here that Achilles was the mightiest of Greek warriors during the Trojan War, a ten-year conflict that happened around 1184 BC as chronicled by the supposedly blind poet Homer in his narrative epic poem the *Iliad*.'

Rogers reflected for a moment and then continued reading the language presented on his desktop computer screen. 'And this tragic hero figure Achilles, in spiteful revenge, had killed Hector, the King of Troy's son because Hector had previously killed Achilles' best friend Patroclus. But,' Rogers paused and gasped before resuming his fairly remarkable reading session, 'later in the adventure tale saga, King Priam's younger son Paris accurately shot an arrow and killed Achilles by hitting him in his most vulnerable area, the heel of his foot. Hence, that part of the human anatomy is now called the Achilles tendon. Oh my God!' Troy Rogers realized. 'The Trojan King Priam's son Hector in the *Iliad* bears the same name as Hector Russo, my unsavory nemesis in real life!' the superstitious CPA keenly evaluated. 'What a truly oddball set of coincidences with the names Troy, Hector and Achilles all seeming to spontaneously be intersecting.'

* * * * * * * * * * * *

Saturday evening eventually arrived, and after admiring his new-found appearance in the living room mirror, Achilles (alias Troy Rogers) climbed into his dark blue Lexus, meticulously exited his circular driveway onto Walnut Street, and then proceeded to turn left onto Third. The driver's mind was still troubled and distracted by the peculiar shipping error. The disgruntled motorist was heading his 'chariot' toward downtown Hammonton, and soon Troy had to slam on his brakes when a huge dump truck going south on Fairview Avenue rumbled through a yellow traffic signal. Instantly, Rogers' automobile was then unexpectedly and violently rear-ended by a shiny black Mercedes.

Immediately, two cursing masked men, one dressed as a Greek warrior and the second aggressive fellow as a Trojan Prince swiftly evacuated their respective vehicles. The enraged, vociferous pair soon confronted one another.

"See here you arrogant, clumsy Fool!" Troy wildly screamed at the Prince Paris impersonator. "You were not paying attention, recklessly speeding, and smashed into the back of my car. 'If you weren't going so damned fast, you rambunctious Fool, and also speeding as if you were driving an ambulance, and deliberately tailgating me like a cop on patrol, then this unnecessary collision would've never occurred!"

"Don't give me any stupid crap, or I'll decapitate you with your own sword!" the infuriated man regally dressed in the Trojan apparel bellowed as he pointed to Troy's bronze weapon. Then getting an impulsive evil inspiration, the incensed maniac removed an arrow from his quiver, inserted it into his bow, and aimed the primitive weapon at an astonished and suddenly intimidated Troy Rogers, who instantaneously turned and frantically fled onto a North Third Street home's front lawn.

The truly out-of-control and greatly irritated Prince Paris pretender shot his arrow, which accurately pierced the back of Troy Rogers right foot. The victim fell to the turf with a thud, agonizing, crying and then writhing about in excruciating pain as the arrow recipient futilely held his wounded. lower right appendage.

* * * * * * * * * * * *

Hammonton Chief-of-Police Henry Passarella sat behind his town hall office desk and was in the process of seriously reviewing and assessing the report of the outlandish Saturday evening traffic accident at the corner of Third Street and Fairview Avenue. The Chief was conversing with Sergeant Fred Ingemi, the equally confounded, on-duty investigating officer handling the case. The two guardians of the peace were putting together the complicated pieces of the strange sociological puzzle.

"Fred, you've written here in your incident report that Hector Russo, oddly dressed as Prince Paris of Troy, shot and wounded Troy Rogers in the right heel, using a primitive-looking bow and arrow, and you've also indicated that Mr. Rogers, at the time of the incident, was dressed as the Greek hero Achilles. And," Chief-of-Police Passarella proceeded with his oral analysis and interpretation, "a witness to the accident/crime, blueberry farmer Skeeter Bertino had been traveling as a passenger in Hector Russo's black Mercedes; and Officer Ingemi, your strange report states that the third party had been dressed as an Egyptian pharaoh named Ramses II! What kind of an insane anachronism is this incident Sergeant?" Chief Passarella bellowed. "The peculiar set of events will easily make national tabloid journalism news, along with unwanted cable chatter, once the ravenous Philly' newspapers and TV stations grab a-hold of this thoroughly demented story! Don't *you* get it? Our respectable town will become the laughing stock of the entire nation!"

"At least the two principal participants were driving cars and not riding in ancient war chariots!" Sergeant Ingemi humorously articulated, much to his superior's chagrin. "The arrow employed didn't exactly belong to Cupid, either! It seems Chief, that all three subjects were en route to a masquerade party down on Central Avenue given by that blonde knockout dame, Cindy Harper. I surmise that since all three men were wearing masks," Officer Ingemi hypothesized and nervously stated, "I believe that Troy Rogers and Hector Russo didn't recognize one another, even though they actually knew one another in real life!"

"And also Fred, the corresponding hospital report explicitly states that Mr. Rogers injury is only minor, and that the doctors in the Atlantic Care Emergency Room have determined that the arrow wound is only superficial," the Chief read and related. "Thank God for *that* minor miracle!"

"That's right, Hank!" Sergeant Ingemi confirmed in a more personal tone of voice. "Troy Rogers will not be hobbling around for long, and fortunately, the arrow victim won't be a cripple for life.

He'll be able to make a full recovery and be back on his feet without crutches in less than a week," the police officer disclosed to his boss. "I've also learned from interviewing Troy Rogers in his hospital room that he plans on suing that detestable bully Hector Russo for attempted manslaughter. And once the shrewd accountant wins the accident civil case in the local municipal court," Sergeant Ingemi predicted, "then Troy will be filing a felony criminal lawsuit at the county level, and if he wins that particular litigation," the policeman elucidated, "Rogers will be awarded a gigantic settlement by an empathetic jury. He'll possibly wind-up with perhaps half of Russo's prosperous blueberry farm empire. Being wounded by a non-poisonous arrow might actually be a blessing in disguise," Fred Ingemi divulged and punned.

"What incredible irony!" Chief Passarella exclaimed. "Hector Russo should've stopped his rage at *shooting-off* his big mouth! Now he's in real deep hot water for thinking that he was Prince Paris of Troy *shooting-off* an arrow at his avowed ancient Greek foe Achilles; alias Troy Rogers; coincidentally wounding him in *his* right heel. Now Fred," Chief Henry Passarella emphasized to his loyal and obedient subordinate, "I hope that you don't think that you're almighty Zeus and then angrily hurl a million-volt lightning bolt in my direction just two weeks before I can enjoy my long-awaited retirement from the Hammonton Police Force!"

"The Duck Pond"

Salvatore "Duke" Miduri, a diversified business mogul, owned three enormous junkyards in the Hammonton, New Jersey vicinity, and state authorities suspected that each of the trio of fairly profitable operations was a money-laundering front for illicit Philadelphia Mafia drug distribution, prostitution, loan sharking, and also gambling racketeering. Frustrated federal and state officials had often investigated notorious and controversial Salvatore Miduri, but the sly Sicilian culprit and his burly bodyguard lieutenants had never been convicted of engaging in criminal activity, even though "the Duke" was constantly under intense police scrutiny.

"The Duke" and his two brash bachelor cohorts lived in a fabulous mansion that had a long, winding, paved front entrance, and the rustic tree-lined lane leading to the estate was situated at the very end of Oak Road. Salvatore Miduri's seven-thousand square foot palace had been built next to a large three-acre duck pond that coincidentally bordered on New Jersey owned Wharton State Forest.

The State Pinelands Preservation Commission theorized that Salvatore Miduri had been polluting the oval-shaped duck pond, but since the reputed villain had owned the hundred-and-fifty-acre property years before the Commission had been appointed in the early 1980s, the regulatory body had no jurisdiction over the land because Miduri's extensive "boundary estate" had already been "grandfathered" into the Pinelands' statutes.

Much to the Duke's dissatisfaction, in 1997 the New Jersey State Police had obtained a search warrant to excavate the lawn on three sides of Salvatore's mansion, and to dig both to the left and right of Miduri's very massive maintenance building, where the "Palermo and Messina Construction Company" owner kept his heavy-duty equipment, including six dump trucks, four bulldozers, two front-end loaders and a still-functional, rusty steam shovel. The massive storage structure's rear wall was located only twenty feet from "the pristine duck pond", and over the years *that* particular "environmental hazard reality" had vastly irritated the concerned bureaucrats sitting on the State Pinelands Commission.

"The State Cops were searching for dead bodies, and the incompetent fools were relying on information supplied by a couple of stool pigeons just released out of the Trenton Prison," Salvatore orally reviewed for the ears of his personal henchmen Nick "Blitz" Bartuccio and Patsy "the Bonebreaker" Olivo. "The fuzz had conjectured that the corpses had been buried on my Oak Road property because my home was pretty rural, out here in the South Jersey sticks, and they thought it would be convenient for the Philly' mob to dump-off and bury certain uncooperative victims here as a safe haven."

"That's right, Boss!" hit man Nick Bartuccio promptly agreed. "You've not only been annoyed and pestered by the nosy Pinelands' jerks, but also by the feds, the state goon squads, and the lousy local cops, too. It's a good thing ya' hired those top-notch defense lawyers from Newark to represent you in court."

During the initial verbal exchange just shared by the other two underworld confederates, Patsy "the Bonebreaker" Olivo had been mentally engrossed in admiring an exquisite wall fresco rendition of the scenic duck pond. In the background, the cherished artwork featured thirteen colorful mallards passively swimming, while in the forefront, the mural portrayed six splendid ducks flying towards the pond on the left, and three pheasants marvelously hovering amongst the cedar trees to the right.

After glancing through the mammoth bay window and then gazing outside at the three-dimensional body of water, tough guy Olivo decided to join the casual conversation. "Ya' know Boss. I think the cops waited until 1997 to get their search warrant permittin' them to dig for bones because up until that time, you were friendly with some big Trenton and Atlantic City politicians, and also closely associated with some Philly' professional baseball and hockey players that would frequently go wild mallard hunting at the pond in the fall. But after your high-level political pals left office," Bonebreaker Olivo contributed and insisted, "that's when the crummy State Cops went to the county judge and..."

"And got their stinkin' permit to start shoveling turf, sand, and dirt away to try and discover some clues to indict the three of us and put our butts in the slammer," Nick "Blitz" Bartuccio boisterously finished Patsy "the Bonebreaker" Olivo's accurate background statement. "And when the State Cops failed to uncover any evidence, that's precisely when..."

"When I stepped-up and vigorously sued the State of New Jersey, and consequently, won a handsome ten-million-dollar defamation-of-character lawsuit," Salvatore "Duke" Miduri articulated and then indulgently laughed. "The damned State Cops were punished for not doin' their due diligence, and for naively listenin'-to unreliable witnesses. And next, the taxpayers got really riled-up because their precious, hard-earned revenue money had been neglectfully and stupidly squandered on an expensive wild goose chase, ha, ha, ha!"

"And Boss, you were smart enough to get those costly defense attorneys from Newark who make over ten times as much dough as the less-talented federal and state prosecutors do," Blitz Bartuccio haughtily chuckled. "There's a definite reason why the lawyers you had hired make ten times more than the prosecutors do. It's because they're more skilled at the art of evading the law than the district attorneys know about the science of enforcing it," the ruthless aide persuasively argued and then chuckled. "The highly paid defense lawyers that we had workin' for us knew every loophole, and technicality, to eventually win *our* case."

"But in the Boss's situation Blitz," Bonebreaker Patsy Olivo diplomatically challenged his counterpart's position, "there was no convicting evidence, and the jury regarded the inept State Police investigation team as bungling intruders violating our esteemed Mentor's First Amendment civil rights. Then, the State had to also pay for all of the bushes and landscaping that the embarrassed State Cops had damaged or ruined during their clumsy, frantic-but-futile ground rummaging."

"Boys, we've been together as close pals ever since we attended the Waterford School over in Winslow Township, and then barely graduated from Edgewood High," Salvatore Miduri nostalgically reminisced. "I mean Guys, I hate to sound too sentimental, but nearly everybody in Waterford is a Miduri, a Midilli, an Iannaco, a Bartuccio, a..."

"Calabria, a Mauriello, a Sarappa, an Illiucci, or a Sindoni," Blitz Bartuccio relevantly added. "Truly Boss, Waterford and Hammonton are like one big Cosa Nostra, with a lot of Sicilian inbreeding showing in each town!"

"Yeah Boss, most of our Waterford cousins are now either workin' construction for you, or seriously manning the three junkyards," Patsy Olivo matter-of-factly pointed-out. "If ya' study our family trees, us Waterford Italians are almost as inbred as Cleopatra's ancient Egyptian royal family was before Julius Caesar ever sailed his warship up the Nile! I think that *that's* the only fact I remember from my high school Ancient History seminar."

"Patsy, you remember more than I do from that boring class. But why do you two Imbeciles keep callin' me Boss!" cigar smoking Sal Miduri affectionately ridiculed and then characteristically cackled before casually flicking his ashes inside a convenient metal tray strategically located upon his expensive mahogany desk. "Who do ya' think I am, Bruce Springsteen! Ha, ha, ha!"

* * * * * * * * * * * *

In 1995, the local Hammonton Town Council had declared a building moratorium on all new house construction, done in order to abide by recently legislated strict New Jersey, forest and conservation laws. In the early 1980s, the Trenton lawmakers had established the creation of the omnipotent Pinelands Commission, which had the expressed authority to regulate population growth in and around the "environmentally sensitive" Wharton State Forest. Since Salvatore "Duke" Miduri had owned and already-occupied his hundred-and-fifty-acre duck pond property prior to the creation of the Pinelands Commission, the flamboyant Mafia figure was essentially exempt from the acting authority's powerful land and water management control.

According to careful definitions enforced by the established bureaucratic Commission, the "New Jersey Pinelands" extended from Absecon just west of Atlantic City to Atco, seven miles west of Hammonton; and from Vincentown seventeen miles north of the Hammonton/Waterford agricultural community district, all the way to Vineland, seventeen miles south.

The newly defined terminology "Pinelands" had Hammonton and its proud peach and blueberry farmers (along with third-generation large land owners) managing properties located directly in the middle of the "pine barrens core area", where building and population growth was both restricted and limited, and where new houses inside the town's jurisdiction (that weren't connected to water and sewer lines) were now required to have the expressed written approval of the "Almighty Pinelands Commission". However, as had been legally determined, Salvatore "Duke" Miduri's acreage, and his corresponding duck refuge, were not affected by the austere Pinelands Commission rules and mandates.

But Hammonton farmers, along with big acreage landowners like Miduri, were incidentally deeply affected by the Pinelands and its governing Commission. Since their land valuations were now exclusively restricted to farm use property value (that would ordinarily be worth a hundred thousand dollars an acre to an entrepreneurial real estate developer), the various "blocks" were now devalued to a meager five thousand dollars an acre, because presently, only other farmers or "wealthy environmentalists" would want to purchase the land for agricultural or for ecological preservation purposes. Real estate competition had virtually been eliminated for the sake of "green conservation".

Consequently, because of the enforcement of very stringent Pinelands regulations, Hammonton fruit and vegetable growers had trouble borrowing money from banks and from farm credit bureaus in order to conduct their businesses, since their credit lines were determined by using their now devalued land assessments as "basic collateral". It cost most area vegetable growers three hundred thousand dollars of "seed money" to get their operations started each spring, since big bucks had to be placed on the table as down payment to purchase the upcoming summer's fertilizers, sprays and special customized packages and cartons (with the farm's brand names printed on them). And in addition, payrolls had to be met before crops were ever picked, packed, and shipped, along with other myriad, miscellaneous, accumulative, spring farm expenses.

Duke Miduri had become disgusted and had gotten out of agriculture in 1998, defiantly stating publicly to the Hammonton Gazette that "Peach, apple, and blueberry growers would in the future be doomed by not being able to secure viable credit from banks and from other regional and national lending institutions."

Farmers doing business in Hammonton's "highly governed and restrictively regulated Pinelands Forest core area" were also limited in deciding exactly who could build houses on their property. Their children were allowed to build new homes on three-acre tracts, and if immediate family was not involved, desperate farmers had to otherwise have their land parceled into ten-acre zones if they wanted to sell those sub-divisions to non-family strangers (with a lot of money) desiring to erect rural dwellings on such sizable tracts.

Since the tremendously autocratic New Jersey State Pinelands Commission required "core area residents" to hook-up to Hammonton city water lines and to limited town sewer lines, new population growth was hampered by the State in the name of "natural environment preservation".

And when the old, outdated Hammonton sewer plant began operating at full capacity, a restrictive building moratorium was adopted and enforced, and the Town Council had to conform to the State's inflexible land-use mandates.

"Thanks to the liberals in Trenton, my land's now of little value or use," Sal Miduri had been quoted as complaining in the Hammonton News. "The State is driving honest area businessmen out of operation just to save the damned pristine water underneath the Pinelands, being reserved for the unworthy residents of Philly' and New York!"

The Hammonton area farmers, along with peeved real estate developers, boldly challenged the Pinelands Commission's authority in State courts, claiming that the new environmental laws were "Unconstitutional" and that the statutes violated the farmers' rights to own and sell land at face value. The disgusted real estate entrepreneurs maintained that their "civil rights" to build and make profits were also being abused. The costly litigations were aggressively pursued, but in the end, the various challenges to State Authority were to no avail. The Pinelands Commission prevailed and won every legal wrangle intensively argued before sympathetic judges, and the resultant court decisions maintained that the "State's general good" was being upheld by the intelligent, planned, regional conserving, and by ensuring the prudent preserving of South Jersey forests, lakes and wildlife.

But the wily Hammonton farmers suspected that the real reason for the "stranglehold" Pinelands legislation (and its accompanying land restrictions) was more than mere discrimination against fruit and vegetable growers.

Entrepreneur Joseph Wharton of Philadelphia, founder of the prestigious University of Pennsylvania Wharton School of Business, once owned extensive sections of South Jersey land, which today is known as the Wharton State Forest. Wharton was a venture capitalist at heart, whose ownership of the pineland forests (on either side of busy Route 206 surrounding Atsion Lake and vicinity), had by coincidence seven trillion gallons of excellent pristine water reserves laying directly under the virgin forestland, and the attendant Pinelands were fed by the close-to-the-surface Cohansey Aquifer.

Capitalist Joseph Wharton's grandiose scheme was to pump clean fresh water from the Wharton Forest Tract to the Philadelphia and New York metropolitan areas, and then economically profit from his diligent endeavor. But near the end of his life, the nineteenth century investor/entrepreneur changed his mind and heart, and benevolently donated the beautiful acreage to the State of New Jersey.

The shrewd Hammonton farmers had suspected all along that the Pinelands building restrictions were not so much about protecting the surface pine trees as the State of New Jersey had adamantly asserted, but that the real issue was undeniably about preserving the seven trillion gallons of pristine water lying beneath the forest trees as an emergency reserve water source for Philadelphia and New York during a future time of dire regional crisis.

* * * * * * * * * * * *

A Med-Evac helicopter along with a New Jersey State Police surveillance chopper were stationed at (and serviced inside) a maintenance hangar at the Hammonton Municipal Airport. Seated inside the small airport's coffee and snack shop were New Jersey State Police Colonel Ed Siscone and his helicopter pilot for the day, Lieutenant Greg Donio. The two diners were conversing at a square restaurant table, informally exchanging anecdotes, and mutually enjoying their respective bacon, eggs, potatoes and toast breakfasts. The pleasant dialogue was centered upon the pair's scheduled survey/observation flight over the nearby Wharton State Forest and the adjacent Atsion Lake area.

"I understand Greg," Colonel Ed Siscone mentioned between chews, "that there're over seven trillion gallons of fresh water lying directly under the Pinelands Forest. Could you ever imagine that? Over seven trillion, I said! Sounds almost as humungus as the upward spiraling national debt!"

"Yes, Colonel; and I believe the vast water supply is referred to as the Cohansey Aquifer," Lieutenant Donio keenly verified. "I've read where *that* water, along with its intended use, has been in heated dispute around South Jersey for over a century. But now, it finally looks like the environmentalists and the conservationists have gotten the upper hand over the covetous real estate developers, and the stubborn area farmers."

"And quite candidly, Greg," achievement-oriented Ed Siscone confided, "during our upcoming routine scouting patrol this morning, I'd like to fly over that unscrupulous thug Salvatore Miduri's plush mansion at the end of Oak Road. Do you know that vicinity well?"

"Yes indeed, Colonel!" the recently assigned helicopter pilot answered. "I've studied that section of Hammonton on various land and aerial maps. Wasn't Miduri the guy who…"

"Who took *us* to court and with the help of some slippery and unethical mob attorneys, the dastardly crook made the State Troopers look like a bunch of defective rank amateurs. If ever I get the opportunity," Colonel Siscone promised, "I'd like to get even with that no-good corrupt scumbag! Of course, Greg; my comments and opinions to you are strictly off the record!"

"Yes Colonel," Lieutenant Donio replied with a broad grin before sipping some hot coffee from his steaming cup. "I too would like to see justice served. That outrageous swindler Miduri and his two Sicilian henchmen deserve to be jailed for life, and I can honestly sympathize with your desire to incarcerate the whole pack of Hammonton affiliated Mafia types, none of whom are in any way a credit to humanity."

"Remind me to recommend you for a promotion right before I retire from the force in six months," Colonel Siscone facetiously suggested to his new trooper acquaintance. "What do ya' say, Greg!" the elder trooper then stated in a more imperative tone of voice. "Let's gulp the remainder of our delicious java down and get today's in-air action show initiated!"

The two state troopers ambled-out of the popular airport coffee shop, briskly paced to the helicopter pad, and then nonchalantly entered inside the expensive machine. After Lieutenant Donio confidently manned the chopper's pilot seat and checked the gauges on the control panel, the young pilot started the blades rotating, and the police whirlybird smoothly lifted off of its landing pad. As the craft glided over a desolate-but-dense, remote section of pine-barrens, Colonel Siscone and the amiable pilot rekindled their general repartee.

"It's a gorgeous day to be flying," the chopper operator cordially opined to his superior. "I know from perusing my assignment sheet that we're gonna' do some forest fire prevention observations with the rangers' division, and then perform some cursory air surveillance to see if any hunters are illegally prowling the woods with their shotguns. Which way should we be heading first?"

"Parallel Route 206 north up to Atsion Lake, and then swing over across Indian Mills and Shamong. That's where Route 541 skims Burlington County, and then travel southwest towards Atco. Next, we'll conduct a cursory inspection of Winslow and Waterford Townships over in Camden County, and after that episode is completed, we'll be returning back to Hammonton to terminate our itinerary. And easy on the throttle!" the Colonel commanded his enthusiastic subordinate. "I honestly get a trifle sea sick with even the slightest irregular motion, even when I'm on a deep-sea fishing boat, riding out a minor rain shower!"

Nothing extraordinary had been spotted within the perfunctory two-hour survey, so the trooper pilot began navigating his craft over that section of the Wharton Forest existing between Winslow and Waterford Townships. Suddenly, the alert State Police dispatcher at South Jersey Folsom headquarters voiced an urgent message to the Colonel and the Lieutenant.

"A seismograph up in New Brunswick has just recorded a 5.2 earthquake with its epicenter in western Atlantic County, and the scientists at Rutgers University indicated that the event had occurred only fifteen minutes ago," the on-the-ball dispatcher transmitting the verbal communiqué related. "This is a rather small vibration as earthquakes go, but whenever we rarely have a jolt here in New Jersey, it's usually in the range of 2.3 or 2.4. Nothing to worry about, but we figured we'd keep you two airborne guys updated about what's happening down here on Earth!"

"Thanks Seth," Greg Donio radioed back to central command at Folsom. "We'll be landing back at the Hammonton runway in about ten minutes. We appreciate hearing your informative update! Ten-Four Seth; over and out!"

"Well, if that doesn't beat all!" Colonel Siscone exclaimed as the helicopter zipped a thousand feet high over Flemington Pike; then it soon passed over Spring Road, Walker Road, followed by Pine Road. "An earthquake happening and shaking-up civilization right here in the good old Garden State. Say Lieutenant, what's that beehive of activity going on outside Sal Miduri's mansion! There's something weird occurring in the vicinity of the Duck Pond!"

"Oh my God!" Lieutenant Donio boomed as his pupils widened to their fullest. "The pond's completely empty, with only mud showing; and now I think I see objects sticking-out of the black, wet bottom. Colonel, grab those binoculars wedged between our seats and take a closer gander of what's actually down there."

"This is incredibly bizarre! Absolutely astounding!" the Colonel bellowed as the amazed passenger slowly focused the lenses to allow for a more accurate sighting of the radically altered Duck Pond just off of Oak Road. "There're bundles of cash sitting there in the black mud, and oh my God. And I can see human skeletal remains sticking-out from all over the drained pond. So *that's* where Miduri was keeping his skeletons, not in a back closet, or bured next to his mansion, but under his cherished Duck Pond!"

"Miduri and his two hit men have noticed us, and they're now scurrying to that black Lincoln parked next to the mansion," the vigilant pilot reported and pointed-out to his commander. "We'll follow them overhead until some of our colleagues in their highway cruisers can tail and arrest them."

"I'll bet ya' dollars to doughnuts Lieutenant that the brazen crooks are fleeing to Miduri's two-engine plane he keeps fueled at the airport," Colonel Siscone hypothesized and stated. "Hand me that microphone! I'll send out an emergency bulletin alerting our patrol cars to intercept the three thugs right there, if indeed the municipal airstrip is their intended departure destination."

* * * * * * * * * * * *

Driver Blitz Bartuccio, along with passengers Sal Miduri and Patsy Olivo, were apprehended and immediately handcuffed at the intersection of Union and Middle Road. Officers in four New Jersey State Police cars and in two Atlantic County Sheriff's Department patrol vehicles had participated in the chase that eventually ended less than a mile from the Hammonton Municipal Airport.

Much to the credit of the speed and efficiency of the pursuing lawmen, not a single bullet had been fired during the entire high-speed "containment operation". A week later, a gloating Colonel Ed Siscone met with Captain Ted Hoover and Sergeant Mark Bertram, the dedicated state troopers that had comprehensively conducted the extensive bone-search and cash excavations at Sal Miduri's ritzy Oak Road mansion.

"Colonel, back in the 1990s we had made what appeared to be an archeological dig at the suspect's place of interest," Captain Hoover firmly insisted. "The lawn on three sides of the manor house, along with the grounds on either side of the heavy equipment storage and maintenance building, had been roped-off into quadrants before we meticulously performed our investigation. But apparently, *our* efforts had been outsmarted by savvy cunning criminals."

"And furthermore, Colonel," Sergeant Mark Bertram chimed-in, "Ted and I had expert SCUBA divers from the Shore Division Barracks at Bass River scouring the length and breadth of the Duck Pond, delving for evidence. All aspects of our, please pardon the expression Colonel, of our *wild goose chase* came-up empty-handed. How could we have missed all of the cash hidden in the water, along with all of the skeletal remains that had surfaced? The whole complicated conundrum defies reason!"

"And how did the pond become drained down to its muddy floor, so that you and Lieutenant Donio could see the evidence in the mud from inside your whirlybird?" Captain Hoover asked. "Don't the laws of physics define the parameters of reality any more?"

"One meaningful question at a time please," Colonel Siscone suavely requested of his addled underlings. "You two very excellent men are not at fault in any way, shape or form; so kindly get off your guilt trips. Instead, Gentlemen, our very best minds were deceived by some very shrewd and deft criminal subterfuge. In fact," the unflappable Colonel Siscone calmly elaborated, "if it weren't for the minor 5.2 earthquake that South Jersey experienced just before noon on *that* extremely fortuitous morning, that nefarious thug Sal Miduri and his two sinister cohorts would not now be sitting in separate jail cells awaiting their individual arraignments in the Mays Landing County Courthouse today."

"What do you mean?" Sergeant Mark Bertram incredulously asked. "How could the minor earthquake have made the pond drain? It doesn't seem logical or plausible? Was that coincidence really a cause-effect phenomenon?"

"Ha. Ha, ha!" Colonel Siscone loudly laughed, relishing certain knowledge that his mind possessed to which his two inquiring fledglings were totally ignorant. "Here's the scoop, Men! Miduri had excavated a fifty-foot-deep tunnel originating from inside the side maintenance building that then rapidly descended down horizontally underneath the center of the Duck Pond. It appears that the contemptuous racketeer had taken a chapter out of either the Viet Cong, or out of the al Qaeda terrorists' playbook!"

"I can now visualize the basic scenario you're describing!" State Trooper Ted Hoover realized and exclaimed. "The tunnel was so deep that even if *we* had dug down six feet during our search, which we did, and even if the hollow had been directly underneath us, which it probably wasn't most of the time, then *our* digging team would've never discovered it, regardless of how conscientious and thorough our on-the-ground excavations had been."

"Well Ted, the original tunnel entrance hidden inside the maintenance building had been deliberately cemented over, so you never considered digging inside where the heavy construction equipment was being stored," Colonel Siscone revealed. "But unbeknownst to all of us, a second entrance has recently been discovered, fifty feet in back of the Duck Pond, where your search expedition never considered exploring or digging. Does that specific information illuminate the remainder of the mystery?"

"I now fathom what you're saying!" Captain Ted Hoover recognized, mechanically nodding his head up and down. "The concealed Wharton Forest back tunnel entrance was the only access used once the passageway had been dug-out and later covered-up from inside the metal-framed storage building. And so, we could never identify what was really happening from our frequent air reconnaissance flights because all of the initial tunnel activity had already obviously occurred from inside the enclosed heavy equipment storage structure!"

"Exactly!" the Colonel affirmed and concurred. "And when the larger-than-usual earthquake happened just before noon, the secret tunnel's wooden beam supports, similar to those in old abandoned gold mines out West, well, they shook and then consequently, an abundance of loose sand and dirt situated directly beneath the Duck Pond came pouring into the narrow cave-like passageway below. Soon, the assorted bundles of cash, along with the eerie-looking skeletal remains, became buoyant and surfaced; and then the convicting evidence instantly became visible from the air; all cash bundles and bare-bone anatomies, strangely lying in the black wet surface mud!”

“That’s really a very fantastic set of coincidences to *ponde*r! I suppose that the moral to this bizarre story is that it truly matters greatly to have all of your ducks in a row during a rare New Jersey earthquake!” Sergeant Mark Bertram imaginatively quipped. “It was not a wild goose chase; it was really a wild duck chase!”

“I don’t think you’re quite ready to replace either Jay Leno or David Letterman on late night television!” Colonel Siscone reflexively grinned, mildly admonishing Sergeant Mark Bertram. “But I do believe that one thing’s for sure, Men. I don’t think that Salvatore “Duke” Miduri and his nasty henchmen Nick “Blitz” Bartuccio and Patsy “the Bonebreaker” Olivo will ever again be prominent *movers and shakers* in the ever-proliferating New Jersey crime syndicate world!”

"May 27th, 2012"

The top brass at Washington FBI headquarters had assigned relentless Inspector Joe Giralo to the historic Balsams Resort in somnolent Dixville Notch, New Hampshire. The hotel would serve as the essential location where "the Boss" could supervise his strategic operations, which incidentally also involved his most trusted agents, Salvatore Velardi, Arthur Orsi and Dan Blachford.

Over the past week, the loyal FBI trio had been individually dispatched to distinct sections of the United States in order to gather very important undercover investigative information. On May 27th, 2012, the now-very-relaxed Chief Inspector amiably greeted his three arriving subordinates inside the famous New England resort's Tavern Restaurant.

"Glad you three accomplished sleuths could finally make it up here to the Balsams for a late lunch extravaganza," sometimes garrulous Joe Giralo merrily stated, showing a broad smile. "Originally, I had been slated to establish my incognito operational base at the Beacon Resort over in Lincoln, but our ever-vigilant boss Matt Riley at DC headquarters moved me an hour and a half north up here to the Balsams because this exclusive resort is temporarily closed to the public for the whole summer. The new owners are renovating the entire main and adjacent buildings."

"Thanks, Boss, for the swell three and a half-hour limo' ride from the Manchester Airport to way up here near the Canadian border," Agent Velardi rather cynically answered. "But actually, the ride was more comfortable than traveling up here to super-tranquil Dixville Notch on moose back! Too bad this fine Victorian resort is also closed for boating, fishing and golf!"

"Yes," Agent Art Orsi confirmed. "Sal flew into Manchester from Buffalo, Dan flew in from Vegas and I came in commercial early this morning from Rapid City, South Dakota via Cincinnati. After we ate a quick breakfast at the airport," Agent Orsi thoroughly reported, "your special black limousine picked us up, and now here we are, clandestinely meeting at your secret New Hampshire hideout somewhere north of the White Mountains."

"Doesn't this closed-for-repair hotel have some sort of political significance?" Agent Dan Blachford spontaneously asked. "I know I've often heard Dixville Notch mentioned on TV newscasts, but quite candidly Guys, I can't recollect the exact significance."

"Well Dan," Inspector Joe Giralo exhaled after gulping down several ounces of tasty regular coffee. "This famous hotel is where the first votes are cast just after midnight in each national Presidential Election. In fact, the voting room is situated upstairs just past the main dining room and can be found right behind where the attractive second floor corridor lounge ends. I believe that only a dozen or so local citizens actually participate in the much-publicized voting process," the all-too-knowledgeable speaker elaborated. "But as I've already stated, the unique political matter does generate widespread attention across the entire nation. And Guys, the new Balsams owners were quick to agree to us having our hastily arranged conference right here in the Tavern Restaurant, which has been kept open for the sole purpose of accommodating us and our culinary needs."

"Riley probably intimidated the new proprietors by threatening to have his pals over at the IRS scrutinize their past tax returns. But as usual Boss, and with all due respect," Agent Velardi carefully qualified his words, "Art, Dan and I are again totally confused about what this complicated case in all about. I mean Boss, we've successfully completed our separate surveillance responsibilities, and then we conscientiously reported our confidential observations exclusively to you via encrypted computer messages. But still, all three of us remain basically clueless about the big picture. We've all surmised that we're involved in identifying the central culprits of some surreptitious home-grown terror network," loyal Sal Velardi confided off-the-record. "But as to *us* being familiar with any particular relevant details, the hazy fog floating around inside our three noggins is as thick as Campbell's tomato soup!"

"Ha, ha, ha!" Inspector Giralo indulgently laughed. "Don't worry about the minutia my dear Salvatore. Colonel Bob Bauers of Delta Force should be arriving at the Balsams in about an hour to clarify all of your abundant mental vagueness. In the meantime, for me to attempt mitigating your general consternation," Joe Giralo amply chuckled, "I'll gladly disseminate to you vexed Gentlemen some rather pertinent background. I suppose that during the past week you three illustrious Einsteins have been assiduously functioning in the chrysalis stage of our present law enforcement probe."

"Please speak standard vernacular English, Boss," Agent Art Orsi sincerely requested. "What on Earth is the chrysalis stage? Have Madonna and Lady GaGa ever performed on it?"

"Don't be *fazed* by the chrysalis *phase*," Giralo joked. "In elementary biology, *that* development is the vital stage of the metamorphosis process. It's when a slow-moving caterpillar amazingly enters a chrysalis, or a small pouch inside a cocoon, and then in time, the creature miraculously transforms into a magnificent butterfly, which then instinctively breaks-out of its protective chrysalis shell and soon thereafter, marvelously flies away in quest of a new existence."

"Truthfully Boss; Art, Dan and I always feel like we're sort of individually incarcerated into three designated restricted areas, that is, we're kind of like mindless guinea pig hostages expected to hibernate inside FBI-designed cocoons too, just like those in-transition caterpillars you had just mentioned," an exasperated Sal Velardi evaluated and respectfully declared. "Now Boss, we're aware of some aspects of what's been occurring across the terror network spectrum, but frankly, we're cognizant of only a fraction of what you and *our* DC mastermind Matt Riley already know! Now please connect some of the remaining dots!"

"Okay, you three totally befuddled federal malcontents," a somewhat-amused Inspector Joe Giralo politely replied. "Why don't you review what you've witnessed over the course of the last week, and then I'll genuinely try educating you zany wanna' be Mike Hammer detectives on the true merits of your invaluable contributions to cracking this potentially catastrophic conspiracy crisis wide open. Let's start with you Arty."

Agent Arthur Orsi cleared his throat and then quickly reported that he had followed an itinerant Egyptian named Karim Chalthoum from the Rapid City, South Dakota Airport across regional prairie land to a remote makeshift campsite outside the town of Fairburn. Using powerful binoculars and reliable night vision spy goggles, the experienced FBI veteran had diligently recorded in his notes that a dozen box trucks had delivered certain camouflaged equipment and assorted large heavy boxes, and that the unidentified big and small items had been immediately transferred onto two large flatbed trucks. And next, the various packages were swiftly transported; soon, everything was deposited alongside the secluded and well-concealed wilderness retreat.

"You did well, Arty," Chief Giralo calmly commended. "Your intensive stake-out has led to the capture and arrest of four extremely dangerous Egyptian-born terrorists: jihadists Karim Chalthoum, Mustafa Sawalhi, Ahmad Wadi and Hassan Massri. I'm convinced that these four desperate enemy combatants had been receiving their instructions directly from internationally infamous Ayman Zawahiri, the overzealous Egyptian who has taken Osama bin Laden's place as the formidable inspirational leader of al Qaeda. Now Dan," Chief

Giralo next addressed nervous Agent Blachford. "Let's hear what indispensable evidence you've recently gleaned out there in Vegas. I understand that you were able to acquire valuable information without encountering any apparent aggravating snafus!"

Quite-puzzled Dan Blachford aptly described a similar scenario to the one that had been orally conveyed by still-mentally-disheveled Agent Arthur Orsi. The incessant crime-fighter had vigorously trailed a Pakistan-born American transplant possessing the I.D. of Monsin Bhatti from McCarran International Airport's United Airlines Terminal to the bustling hotel New York, New York. And then three days later, with the assistance of the Las Vegas Police Department's helicopter patrol unit, Blachford had followed the suspected malicious villain from the Vegas Strip to the vicinity of an isolated desert cabin that was surrounded by giant saguaro cactus, the ramshackle structure being five miles outside the corporate limits of Henderson. As in the previous episode graphically depicted by Agent Art Orsi, Blachford had alertly observed several different box trucks delivering undisclosed covered objects to the desolate terrorist base at nighttime, and the secret cargo had been cunningly loaded onto awaiting flatbed units, which then hauled the separate shipments away from the narrow asphalt access road and subsequently, re-located the goods nearer to the desert cabin.

"As you three fine Men readily know," Chief Joe Giralo assessed and prudently articulated, "there exists much animosity towards America in much of the Middle East, and in particular, Pakistan is a principal country expressly accountable for perpetuating fierce hostility towards the United States and its rather unassuming citizens. Indeed, al Qaeda and the Taliban skillfully harbor this ever-present rancor towards Uncle Sam, and Pakistan itself provides the unscrupulous insurgents with a safe haven to conduct lethal raids upon vulnerable American troops presently stationed in neighboring Afghanistan. But Dan, because of your noteworthy Nevada desert perseverance," the renowned FBI Inspector congratulated the still-somewhat-bewildered Agent Blachford, "our dedicated field men along with commandos dispatched from Colonel Bob Bauers' Delta Force team have promptly apprehended Pakistanis' Monsin Bhatti, Yasir Remani, Bilah Rizvi and Ayaz Shah."

It was now the completely-addled Agent Salvatore Velardi's turn to communicate his salient discoveries to the assembled "debriefing conference" members. The flustered crime-stopper orally shared that Saudi Arabian radical Abu Al Reshedi had impatiently obtained his luggage from the rotating American Airlines carousel inside the

Buffalo Airport and that the ever-alert defender of justice then had competently tailed Reshedi to an abandoned bungalow located in a shallow ravine on the outskirts of a rural town halfway between Buffalo and Rochester. Again, similar to suspicious parallel nocturnal events that had coincidentally transpired in South Dakota and in Nevada, a series of unmarked box trucks had stealthily delivered unrecognizable items in sealed boxes along with cloaked heavy machinery to the dilapidated half-collapsed shanty.

"Allow me to generously compliment you, Sir Salvatore, on accomplishing some exceptionally excellent detective work!"

Inspector Joe Giralo proudly praised. "Your intuitive talent for pursuing dastardly criminals is nothing short of superb! Because of your dedicated service," the esteemed Boss haughtily editorialized, "homegrown Saudi terrorists Abu Al Reshedi, Tariq Al Subaiee, Yousef Al Juhani and Saad Al Dosary have all been effectively collared and are now presumably imprisoned! And don't forget Sal," the internationally famous Chief provided his standard addendum. "Osama bin Laden was also a Saudi as were the vile perpetrators responsible for the colossal 9-11 Twin Towers' tragedy!"

"But Chief!" indignantly balked and squawked Sal Velardi. "Art, Dan and I are still very much like lazy caterpillars asleep inside our lousy cocoons. Please give us the big picture so that we can adequately erase the thick mystery that's associated with our most current FBI reconnaissance."

"Ha, ha, ha! This is all-too-rich for my hungry cerebrum to fully appreciate!" Joe Giralo enigmatically exclaimed. "Confidentially Sal, I too had been baffled by this unusual case until *your* targeted man, this Saudi desperado Abu Al Reshedi had led *you* Salvatore to a small town situated between Buffalo and Rochester. Then the complete labyrinth of disconnected, disparate facts suddenly became marvelously all-too-discernible to my sensitive mind's ever-acute comprehension!"

"Stop speaking all of this exotic esoteric gibberish Boss, and kindly tell me exactly what your nebulous nomenclature means before I go absolutely insane and become a fanatical terrorist myself!" Agent Velardi angrily rankled. "Needless to say, Chief, I positively despise your silly riddles, along with your absurd, redundant, verbal cryptograms!"

"Fundamentally, it's all a matter of simple history and grammar school geography!" Chief Giralo admirably divulged. "Now Sal, as you've already informed us in your coded e-mails, the town in New York State where you had followed this mendacious jerk Abu Al

Reshedi was called Medina, conveniently positioned almost midway between Buffalo and Rochester. Yes, my fine-feathered Friends, Medina happened to be the decisive key that had magically unlocked this whole Pandora's Box!"

"Medina?" Sal Velardi incredulously asked. "Is she a new obnoxious nauseating rock singer?"

"No Salvatore," Chief Giralo reflexively indicated with another grin evident upon his lips. "Medina is not only a town in upstate New York. It's also known as the sacred city of the prophet Mohammad over in western Saudi Arabia. Next to Mecca, Medina is the second holiest city in the Islam faith. In fact, according to my meticulous and fastidious research," the wily Inspector authoritatively and casually pontificated, "Islam's three oldest mosques had been constructed in Medina, which had been established by Mohammad in the year 622 on the Muslim Calendar. Indeed Gentlemen, much of the Quran had been composed in Medina, and just like Mecca, entrance into the Holy City is limited to Muslims only! And most certainly Fellas'," erudite Chief Giralo continued lecturing his long-winded narrative, "Mohammad had become more militant in his religious attitudes upon arriving in Medina from Mecca. And finally, Guys," Joe Giralo predictably expounded, "an American town with the appellation *Medina* would naturally appear to be fascinating, if not enticing to an ambitious Saudi terrorist because Medina had also been the Arabian city where the Prophet Mohammad had been buried!"

"Wow!" the now-enlightened Agent Salvatore Velardi finally realized and orally reacted. "How tremendously interesting! I honestly gotta' grant it to you Chief! It sure pays to be well-versed in basic world history and grammar school geography!"

* * * * * * * * * * * * *

The Balsams skeleton crew consisted of one chef, one waiter and one housemaid, all especially assigned to service the demands of Chief Joe Giralo and his three omnivorous agents. The abbreviated staff was most accommodating, thanks to the persuasive urging of FBI Boss Matt Riley and *his* influential colleagues, who had made several imperative government requests upon the prestigious hotel's new management. After mouth-watering pie and cake desserts had been devoured along with huge mugs brimming with delicious hot coffee, Inspector Giralo continued with his expert analysis of the FBI team's most recent crime adventure.

"Now Salvatore, given the essential clue of Medina," the Boss loquaciously prefaced his post-lunch remarks, "the nefarious Abu Al Reshedi and his three Saudi comrades were cruelly planning on firing a pair of Iranian Fateh missiles from Medina, New York; the first one directly into the gigantic water cascade commonly known as the great Canadian Horseshoe Falls, and the second one into the adjacent American Falls, together commonly called Niagara Falls, the pair obviously situated not-too-far from Buffalo, around seventeen or so miles away, according to MapQuest data on my laptop. Such a brazen horrific act, that is, deliberately destroying a major national landmark like Niagara Falls," Inspector Giralo stressed to his stunned colleagues, "would definitely send people all across America into a terror panic of monumental proportions!"

"Holy Houdini!" exclaimed Agent Arthur Orsi. "They'd be out to launch while everyone else would be out to lunch!"

"And most certainly, the heinous misdeed was evidently scheduled for execution tomorrow, Monday, May 28th, Memorial Day!" gasped parch-mouthed Salvatore Velardi. "The demonic Saudi jihadists absolutely desired to sabotage one of America's most revered holidays by committing a terribly despicable act of war! How deranged! How outrageously atrocious can a wickedly determined enemy get?"

"That's why good' must always discriminate against evil!" Joe Giralo attested and concluded. "As long as there is good, there will also be evil abounding in this unpredictable world!"

"The entire Niagara River area would've probably been drastically devastated by massive flooding!" semi-shocked Sal Velardi uttered in disbelief. "And just think, Boss. I had recently read in an edition of *National Geographic* that the Falls and the entire Hudson River Valley had been carved-out by Mother Nature when the enormous mile-high glacier had eventually retreated from what is now New York City back into the Arctic polar region; a mere ten thousand or so years ago!"

"And furthermore, Arty," Inspector Joe Giralo emphatically spoke to Agent Orsi while intentionally ignoring Sal Velardi's fairly irrelevant geological comment. "Your excursions out to Rapid City and to Fairburn, South Dakota were not-too-far from the white-stone visages of eminent George Washington, Abraham Lincoln, Thomas Jefferson and good old Theodore Roosevelt, all prominently displayed on the facade of Mt. Rushmore. It seems that our advanced intel' squad had intercepted enemy e-mails that had alluded to Mr. Karim Chalthoum and his three Egyptian accomplices firing another two imported Fateh missiles smack-dab into the treasured national landmark, diabolically blowing the top of Mt. Rushmore to smithereens. How bitterly ugly could *that* kind of rather stark, harsh reality get?"

"How totally abominable!" Agent Orsi bellowed and concurred. "Those Iranian Fateh missiles aren't just any ordinary, lackluster rockets, that's for sure. Those souped-up missiles have sophisticated GPS guidance systems that are much more accurate than those aboard any mediocre, randomly fired rockets."

"Yes, Arty," verified Inspector Giralo, "and our dependable, anonymous, collaborative sources theorize that the designated Niagara Falls' missiles and also the Mt. Rushmore Fateh missiles had been smuggled into the United States piece by piece from neighboring Canada, all via a porous Northern Border."

"But what about the surreptitious supplies delivered to the desert campsite outside Henderson, Nevada?" Dan Blachford inquisitively inquired. "Was that oddball, distant situation a prospective missile launch site, too?"

"Very perceptive insight, Dan!" the Chief bluntly replied. "Monsin Bhatti and his three Pakistani cohorts had configured modified versions of the deadly Fateh missiles that they planned on aiming at Lake Mead and at nearby Hoover Dam. Could you imagine the national chaos that would have prevailed if the four crazed lunatic terrorists had succeeded in simultaneously blowing-up Niagara Falls, Mt. Rushmore and Hoover Dam on Memorial Day, May 28th, 2012? Those three calamitous events would have been the second terrible day to 'live in infamy' as Franklin Roosevelt had so precisely described the violent unwarranted Japanese sneak-attack on Pearl Harbor on December 7th, 1941!"

"And quite incredibly Chief, we owe it all to *your* impeccable familiarity with Medina!" Sal Velardi respectfully marveled and admitted. "I fully understand that those Fateh missiles are extraordinarily accurate from within a range of one hundred miles. Say Fellas', what's that whirling sound I hear outside!"

"It's Colonel Bob Bauers arriving to brief us on exactly what had developed in Medina, New York, in Fairburn, South Dakota and in Henderson, Nevada!" Chief Joe Giralo ascertained. "That's the sound of chopper blades rotating!"

Five minutes later, the irrepressible Colonel Bob Bauers sauntered into the Balsams' Tavern Restaurant wearing his traditional polished combat boots, and the inimitable American patriot immediately saluted the four almost-hypnotized men seated at their round table.

Then without hesitation or delay, the highly decorated military soldier spoke to Chief Giralo and his three confederates in an impressively strong baritone voice.

"The New Hampshire Air National Guard had sent a helicopter from the Pease Air Base over in Portsmouth and the very capable pilot met me at the Manchester Airport," Colonel Bauers sternly revealed. "Then, we flew north, had a refueling in Berlin and before I knew it, we had arrived at this world-class Balsams Hotel up here in good old historic Dixville Notch. Since this place is currently undergoing mammoth renovations," Colonel Bauers noted, "it was quite convenient for us five to secretly rendezvous here!"

"What's happened to the three respective conspiracy groups in New York State, in South Dakota and in Nevada?" Sal Velardi intrepidly asked the austere Delta Force officer. "If the on-a-mission terrorists have been corralled, then most certainly, the President should declare this wonderful day May 27th to be designated as a fabulous national holiday!"

Then Agent Art Orsi had the audacity to ask the prominent Commander a very direct question. "In all honesty Colonel, it is rumored at FBI headquarters that whenever wanton home-grown or foreign terrorists are apprehended here in the United States, and if Iranian Fateh missiles are involved in enacting *their* hideous schemes, then Delta Force operatives will enthusiastically strap the terrorists to the aforementioned missiles and then deliberately propel the destructive objects off their mobile launch pads through the atmosphere, hurtling wildly into the hinterlands, thus fantastically terrorizing the victimized terrorists all the way to their appointed deaths. Now please tell me Colonel. Is this outrageous scuttlebutt I've recently heard true or false?"

Colonel Bauers paused for a pregnant moment and then after reorganizing his scruples, the well-disciplined veteran soldier cleverly initiated his rather shrewd verbal response. "Well Art, er, I meant to say Agent Orsi," the military guru quite adroitly corrected himself. "It's my sincere opinion that we owe these demented crusading enemies of the United States no ethical courtesy whatsoever, nor should the homegrown or foreign terrorists that are caught red-handed in the act deserve any legal due process either."

"But Colonel, please don't evade my question!" Agent Orsi diplomatically insisted. "Does Delta Force actually harness apprehended terrorists to *their* own Fateh missiles, or don't they? Wouldn't *that* vindictive act be a glaring violation of the United

States Constitution? Give it to us straight, in common. everyday English vernacular."

"Well now, as you four distinguished Gentlemen very well-know, the American media, comprised mostly of ultra-liberal newspaper and TV journalists, often masquerade as enemy combatants' sympathizers and as lily-white Muslim apologists! So, in answer to your very serious question Agent Orsi," Colonel Bauers eloquently expressed with a broad frown firmly exhibited upon his grim countenance, "Delta Force does indeed have its deep dark secrets pertaining to the special destiny of captured enemy combatants. Now, please consider this sage advice, you four dedicated FBI Savants. I wholeheartedly suggest that you forget all about the merits of enhanced interrogation methods employed by virtue of regular water-boarding procedure! And as far as tethering the arrested disgruntled ignoramuses to mediocre Fateh rockets goes," Colonel Bauers keenly vociferated without even blinking an eye, "all that I can confidentially convey to you all-too-curious federal government bureaucrats is that you'll never read about the ultimate fate of these twelve captured evil-minded conspirators in the daily newspapers or in the weekly magazines!"

"Return from Honolulu"

Ludwik Wisniewski and his wife Olga had originated from Krakow, Poland, and then daringly journeyed to the United States by ship, being processed through Ellis Island immigration in 1901. Proud of their Polish heritage, Ludwik and Olga joined other members of the relocated Wisniewski clan, soon residing outside Posen near Alpena, Michigan; the long grueling train ride from bustling New York City to Alpena being financed by Ludwik's brother Stanislaus.

"Stan" had already established himself in the "New World" and had successfully founded a logging business, leasing a thousand acres of prime forest ground from the federal government. The ambitious Wisniewski immigrants believed that the eastern Michigan lower peninsula's climate was similar to that of their native Poland, and that crucial opportunities for social and economic upward mobility would abound in their "new country".

Almost always during nightly family conversations, Ludwik and Stanislaus Wisniewski would remind their wives Olga and Agatha about their wealthy aristocratic cousin Teodor Radziwill of Warsaw, Poland, who was the chieftain of a rich family that had accumulated a colossal fortune in the proliferating steel manufacturing business. But greedy Teodor was too sanctimonious and quite parsimonious about amassing his awesome wealth, and the reclusive industrialist never bothered communicating with his struggling Michigan cousins Ludwik and Stanislaus, electing to live a secluded life with his wife Isabel and his pampered son Henryk.

In the summer of 1908, the logging camp owned and operated by Ludwik and Stanislaus Wisniewski had caught fire, and Stanislaus and wife Agatha had perished in the wild inferno. Broken hearted and financially ruined, defeated Ludwik and disconsolate Olga (along with their three children) migrated to live with relatives in Baltimore, Maryland, where several years later, the bad-luck elders had unfortunately died of pneumonia during the great influenza epidemic that had plagued major American cities just prior to the advent of World War I.

Ten years later, during the Roaring Twenties, the deceased couple's oldest son Josef married an Italian girl named Rita Monzo, whom he had met at an East Baltimore wedding reception, and soon thereafter, the newlyweds moved from Dundalk, Maryland to Hammonton, New Jersey, where Josef was employed as a conscientious construction laborer, eventually saving enough money to finally initiate his own business enterprise.

Josef Wisniewski's construction business was on the verge of bankruptcy during the very disappointing 1930s Great Depression, but the World War II years between 1941 and 1947 were rather fortuitous and profitable, and the post war 1950s created an economic boon for industrious, hard-working entrepreneurs. Josef's "second-life" construction company grew and prospered. But still, the exotic legend of the Teodor and Henryk Radziwill cousins' connection became a popular "Old World tale" often discussed over Josef Wisniewski's dinner table with wife Rita, son Michal and daughter Gretchen. Honoring respect for tradition and ancestral heritage, the family's Polish genealogical history always dominated the children's Sicilian background that had been provided on the mother's side.

"Yes Kids, your grandfather Ludwik was a great man who with his brother Stanislaus ran into overwhelming misfortune when their logging camp went up in flames, just outside Alpena, Michigan," Josef would review at least once a month for the benefit of Michal and Gretchen to hear and appreciate. "And then, that widespread 1917 influenza plague that ravaged Baltimore was absolutely devastating. So many people along with your grandfather Ludwik and your Grandmother Olga had perished during that abominable time period, and your grandparents even had to be buried in mass graves, since individual funerals were impossible to perform because of the great numbers that had died. Yes," Josef regularly emphasized, "you Kids don't know how difficult things were way back then! Human existence was a far cry from Paradise!"

Josef Wisniewski had died of a massive heart attack in 1980, and his wife Rita had passed-away from diabetes complications four years later in 1984. Now, it was up to Michal to orally carry on and transfer the Wisniewski family legends to his son Frederick, to his daughter Mary Ellen, and to his apathetic wife, Janet.

"What kind of work did our great-grandfather Ludwik and his brother Stanislaus do in Poland before they decided to immigrate to Michigan?" high school sophomore Frederick Wisniewski asked his father Michal. "Were they so poor that they had to travel across the Atlantic on a cattle boat to seek fresh new lives here in America?"

"Well, first of all Fred," Michal said as his fuzzy mind attempted to organize the family history story. "As I understand it, Ludwik and Stanislaus had worked very hard in the famous Wieliczka Salt Mines in Southern Poland, and were not once helped by their wealthy Captain of Industry cousin Teodor Radziwill of Warsaw. But just before Hitler and his wicked minions began taking over most of northern Europe in the late 1930s," Michal Wisniewski continued his recollection of significant past events, "Teodor and his son Henryk had advantageously sold their thriving Warsaw steel mill and haven't been heard of since. It's been nearly eighty years following their intelligent financial maneuver and then their subsequent escape to Geneva, and rumor has it that the fabulous Radziwill fortune has been accumulating interest in a Swiss bank account and that Henryk's only heir and bachelor son Leo is living high on the hog, and is gradually dwindling-down the fantastic estate's value. But as to exactly where the mysterious phantom Leo Radziwill might be living now," Michal summarized and concluded his narrative, "your guess, Fred, is as good as mine."

"Why do we have to have such a goofy last name like Wisniewski?" seventh-grader Mary Ellen asked her seventy-year-old father. "The other kids at my school think it sounds funny and too old-fashioned!"

"Actually Mary Ellen, Wisniewski is a very common surname in Poland, and I believe that it is the third most common last name after Nowak and Kowalski," Michal explained to his somewhat-concerned daughter. "And translated into English, 'Wisniewski' roughly means 'from the village of the cherry tree.' That's about all I can tell you about our illustrious family name."

"Oh Mike, I think that the old story about multi-millionaires Teodor Radziwill and his son Henryk, and Henryk's spoiled jet-setting oddball son Leo, is just a lot of hot air that's only really designed to generate some much-craved Polish family pride," spouse Janet opined and criticized, much to her husband's general disgust. "And what do you care about foreign cousins you've never seen or known Mike? You've inherited a good business from your father and have been extremely successful on your own without any help from any of those remote and eccentric Radziwills over in Europe."

"Yes Honey, I guess you're right on that issue!" Michal reluctantly agreed with his totally bored marital mate. "Yes, perhaps the Wisniewskis' of Hammonton, New Jersey are now better-off than my distant aristocratic cousin Leo Radziwill is. But you have to understand one vital thing, Janet. That is, family pride is very important to people of Polish descent, and I just have to recognize and value the sacrifices and travails that my ancestors had to endure, especially bravely venturing here to America and boldly seeking their separate fates in a strange new land. I just very much admire their pioneering spirit; that's all!"

"Well, sometimes I wish that I could be given equal time bragging about *my* just-as-relevant Irish heritage," the former Janet Sullivan argued with her left hand on her hip while obediently pouring her demanding husband a second cup of freshly-brewed hot coffee. "In the 1890s, there was a serious dreadful potato famine back in Ireland you know," Janet maintained from her standing position. "And my valiant ancestors had to overcome obstacles and dilemmas too, while trying to make a living subsisting in Boston and New York! I want you to appreciate that *your* Krakow folks weren't the only ones to pass through Ellis Island while desperately seeking advancement and improvement in their lives!"

"Okay Janet, I'll concede *that* excellent point to you," Michal diplomatically compromised. "I suppose that I shouldn't be jealous one iota of that anonymous mogul Leo Radziwell, and I must admit that the Irish Sullivans are just as equally as vital to our family's identity and development as are the Polish Wisniewskis of yesteryear. Now Dear Wife," the apologetic husband politely expressed. "Fred and Mary Ellen can swallow-down their hot dogs and relish, but as a token of *our* domestic peace, please pass the kielbasa and the sauerkraut, since I'm the only person in this American household that ever eats the delicious stuff!"

* * * * * * * * * * * * *.

Contracts from highway paving bids and from Atlantic County municipal building improvements had been signed, and Michal Wisniewski's M.W. Enterprises, Incorporated was able to purchase three additional dump trucks, bringing the company fleet up to twenty-five. But because of the high cost of heavy equipment, the chief executive had trouble saving cash, always having to reinvest his firm's profits into new machinery and heavy-duty apparatus.

Sitting behind his cluttered office desk on Tuesday morning, December 1st, 2009, Michal received a registered letter from Honolulu, Hawaii that the mailman insisted Wisniewski must sign in order to claim. 'I wonder what this must be!' the surprised and curious recipient pondered. 'Oh well, let's see what it is!'

Adalbert Kaminski, Attorney-at-Law
Waikiki Beach Hotel
Honolulu, Oahu Hawaii 96815

November 23rd, 2009

Dear Mr. Michal Wisniewski:

Greetings, Sir! It gives me great pleasure to inform you that I have been the principal legal council for Mr. Leonardo "Leo" Radziwill for the past thirty-five years, and I have the paramount responsibility of conducting all of Mr. Radziwill's business matters.

As you probably already know from your family's genealogy, Mr. Teodor Radziwill had owned and operated a large steel mill outside Warsaw, Poland, just prior to World War II's ravaging most of Northern Europe. Teodor and his son Henryk Radziwill had fortunately sold their flourishing steel plant a year before Adolph Hitler and his Nazi regime had destructively invaded Poland. In a necessary flight to safety, the Radziwills had moved to Geneva, Switzerland where Teodor had died in 1947, and as you might be aware, then Henryk had passed away in 1976.

The surprise letter received went on to explain that Michal's distant cousin Leonardo Radziwill had been suffering from cirrhosis of the liver for ten years prior to succumbing to the dreaded disease on October 6th of 2009. The flamboyant international playboy client Mr. Leonardo Radziwill had been a bachelor who had led a very extravagant lifestyle, owning fabulous mansions in Geneva, Tuscany, and Monaco. But having no children or immediate family members, in his hospital room Mr. Radziwill decided to conduct a simple lottery among his remaining distant cousins to determine whom his next-of-kin heir would actually be. The attorney's letter then congratulated Mr. Michal Wisniewski for *his* good fortune in being selected from thirteen cousins' names that had been placed into an ordinary shoebox. The Honolulu lawyer further stated in his missive that Michal was entitled to receive what was left of Mr. Leonardo Radziwill's dwindling-yet-impressive estate.

Mr. Leonardo Radziwill had inherited the equivalent of thirty million Euros (43 million U.S. dollars) from his frugal father

Henryk, and upon your fine benefactor's death, a sum of fifteen million Euros (approximately 19.6 million dollars) still remains in three separate Swiss bank and stock brokerage accounts.

Now Mr. Wisniewski, in order to facilitate the appropriate transfer of the willed money over to you, and since I will be conducting business for other clients over the course of the next month here in Honolulu, I strongly suggest that you meet me at noon on Wednesday, December 30th in your already booked Suite #428 at the Waikiki Beach Hotel.

As part of the will settlement (and as the will's assigned exclusive legal executor), I have already had my personal secretary send you four United Airlines plane tickets (upon separate cover) with departure being from Philadelphia International Airport to Honolulu with a refueling stopover in San Francisco: one for yourself, one for your wife, and a pair for your two children to vacation on Oahu for ten days during the Christmas holidays from Monday December 21st to Friday, January 1st, 2010, of course, with all expenses paid for by benevolent Mr. Leonardo Radizill's Last Will and Testament.

I am looking forward to meeting you and your family at noon on Wednesday, December 30th at your already booked suite at the Waikiki Beach Hotel.

Sincerely,

Adalbert Kaminski, Attorney-at-Law

Feeling a surge of pure ecstasy, Michal's heart surrendered to impulse, and Wisniewski anxiously picked-up the phone and called Janet at home to relate to his cynical wife the rather incredible postal news. Janet insisted that her emotionally charged husband read the extraordinary letter over the phone so that she could jot-down the more pertinent details on a clean sheet of paper. The construction chief's mind was without a doubt majestically floating on Cloud 9 as he faithfully recited the text word by word.

"I'll have Marge call Hawaii to confirm our paid reservations at the Waikiki Beach Hotel in Honolulu," the husband excitedly suggested. "The construction business is pretty inactive between Thanksgiving and March. My secretary has nothing else more important to do than to call Hawaii about this hotel reservation item.

The matter ought to occupy some of Marge's time on such a lazy December 1ˢᵗ morning."

"Better yet, Mike," distrustful wife Janet voluntarily answered. "I'll call Hawaii myself and verify the reservations for the prescribed dates that have been pre-scheduled for later-on this month. I just want to make sure that we're not being victimized by a fantastic mean hoax of some sort."

"Okay, Honey," Michal eagerly agreed while the consummate dreamer was secretly contemplating the magnitude of his great inheritance. "If it is some sort of quirky trick, it's a most expensive one at that for the unscrupulous person perpetrating it!"

A half-hour later, Janet contacted Michal and enthusiastically confirmed that everything appeared to be on the up and up, both at the Waikiki Beach Hotel main desk and with the United Airlines ticket counter. Both marriage partners were satisfied that the exceptional provisions depicted in Leonardo Radziwill's will (as described in Adalbert Kaminski's letter) were authentic, and that the dispensing of the multimillionaire's huge estate was indeed perfectly legitimate and on the level.

"And Mike, our four placements are in the first-class section of the plane, which automatically entitles us to more comfortable seats than the passengers riding in coach, along with more terrific food choices on our meals' menu."

"Janet, I've told you, well, at least countless times, that there was a definite close connection between the Radziwill and the Wisniewski families back in Poland during the late 1800s," Mike bragged and gloated. "And truthfully, I've never had anything negative to say about anyone in the Radziwill clan except the notion that Teodor, Henryk, and Leo were all a trifle on the odd side; although I must qualify *that* poignant statement right now because at this moment, despite *his* cad-like eccentric reputation, I fully appreciate Cousin Leo's abundant generosity."

The United Airlines flight from Philadelphia to San Francisco was quite smooth, and the exciting transcontinental trip was only surpassed by the wonderful Pacific flight from the "City-on-the-Bay" to Oahu. The accommodations at the luxurious Waikiki Beach Hotel were quite luxurious, and the view of the shoreline and the incomparable sight of Diamond Head from Suite #428 were as magnificent as magnificent gets. Even normally sarcastic Frederick and typically contrary Mary Ellen appeared to be mesmerized by the resplendence of the Pacific tropical paradise.

"I can't say enough superlatives to describe this exotic place," Janet marveled and offered upon assessing the panorama from the suite's balcony. "It's a dream come true, and perhaps the finest experience of my life!"

"And don't neglect to mention my unbelievable nineteen million six hundred-thousand-dollar miracle bonanza!" Michal laughed as he casually observed several honeymooners frolicking in the surf. "Who ever said that blood wasn't thicker than water? Make sure that tonight at dinner I offer a heartfelt toast to the memory of the great and noble Leonardo Radziwill! May his immortal soul dwell forever in Heaven!"

The next seven days passed by rapidly with junkets and jaunts to popular Honolulu tourist destinations such as Pearl Harbor and the revered Battleship Arizona Memorial, the Hanauma Bay Marine Preserve, the Diamond Head State Monument, and Volcanic Crater Park, the Iolani Palace, the Honolulu Zoo, and the nearby Waikiki Aquarium where colorful fish (indigenous to the island's bays and currents) were on exhibit. And besides those inimitable wonders, the flight over Oahu provided by Island Seaplane Services was both spectacular and sensational.

Finally, noon on Wednesday December 30th arrived on the end-of-year calendar, but much to Michal Wisniewski's instant frustration, Adalbert Kaminski, distinguished Attorney-at-Law, failed to show-up at Suite #428. By suppertime, Michal had realistically suspected that he had been the victim of an elaborate and outlandish canard, or a very complicated ruse.

"I'm telling you Janet, there's something more putrid and rancid in Honolulu than that normally heard *other something* being rotten in Denmark!" the totally distressed husband ranted. "I've never felt as used and as exploited as I do right now! But all of this scheming and planning being done for what reason? I simply don't get it!"

"Yes Mike; the picnic's officially over! I just called the airport and we have to fly coach all the way back to Philly'," Janet disclosed and reported. "No more filet mignon or lobster tails!"

"When we get back to Hammonton, I'm going to get to the bottom of this weird puzzle if I have to sell three dump trucks to pay for a thorough background investigation," the angry husband vowed with a look of consternation dominating his facial features. "I've never been so befuddled in my entire life, and I don't relish the empty bewildered feeling one bit either!"

* * * * * * * * * * * *

On Monday morning, February 1st 2010, experienced private investigator Frank Meyers paid a vital visit to Michal Wisniewski's comfortable Hammonton residence on upper middle-class Golf Drive. Frederick and Mary Ellen were attending their respective public schools, so the construction contractor and the veteran private eye were able to conduct a forthright and confidential conversation.

"Well Frank, nearly five weeks ago I had hired you, and you've been paid a nice five-thousand-dollar retainer," Michal nervously prefaced his remarks. "Tell me now, what has your research discovered, or should I say 'uncovered'?"

"I'll be perfectly candid with you right from the outset Mike," the bald-headed and rotund P. I. began his comprehensive narrative. "I had twenty-five years in a patrol car on the Atlantic City Police Force and Mr. Wisniewski, I've been a private investigator for thirteen more yearly campaigns. Quite honestly, Mr. Wisniewski," the extremely competent investigator qualified, "I've never before been involved in a case like this one; a multi-faceted riddle that required plenty of ingenuity and hard delving and probing to eventually solve. It's extremely unique and complex in many ways, and after a great degree of adversity," Frank Meyers swore solemnly, raising his right hand above his shoulder, "I've amazingly managed to piece it all together."

"Well then, Mr. Meyers, first of all," the flustered and deceived Hammonton businessmen verbalized, "what happened to my wife and where is my missing nine-hundred-thousand-dollars? How's that for a double whammy loss?"

After loudly clearing his larynx, Frank Meyers first explained that both the local and the state police departments had been advised of what peculiar circumstances had surfaced and materialized and that the 'All Points Bulletin' that had been sent-out to apprehend the two suspected felons had been canceled in order to protect and insulate the 'reputable victim'. Michal Wisniewski. from IRS scrutiny and prosecution.

"I'm a little confused," Michal honestly stated. "Could you be a little more specific?"

"Mike, the Devil is always in the details," the shrewd. reputable detective declared. "Now kindly tell me. Sir. Did you ever have a devious fellow named Vladimir Kozlowski work for you?" Meyers asked in a slow enunciation.

"Why yes! Kozlowski was a road tar foreman for my firm for about seven years until we had an explosive argument over a paving and slurry seal contract job that we were doing down in Stone

Harbor," Michal recollected and stated. "Vladimir was generally a good industrious worker, but he had a chronic problem with alcohol that induced his nasty temper to surface from time to time; especially when he wasn't completely rested or sober. Why are you asking me about this indignant fellow, Kozlowski?"

"Well Mike, after your wife Janet had found-out that you were having an affair with your vivacious secretary Marge Dixon, who incidentally has been married three times as you probably know," Frank Meyers added and vociferated, "your spouse began seeing your fired guy, this love-competitor nemesis Vladimir Kozlowski when you weren't around. And of course, their every rendezvous was stealthily done, arranged out of your wife Janet's overall spite and jealousy!"

"And so," Michal replied after taking a much-needed deep breath, "my wife wasn't molested or kidnapped like I had originally thought. She had run away with that two-bit loser Kozlowski. What an unfaithful Jezebel Janet turned out to be!"

"Precisely," the loyal private investigator concurred with his paying client's opinion, nodding his head in full agreement. "And your wife knew all about the nine-hundred-thousand-dollars that you had skimmed from the business over the course of the last decade. She fully knew that you had kept the accumulated dough stashed in your cellar inside the slat vent to your air conditioning duct. So, while you were away merrily vacationing with the family in Honolulu," Meyers continued his rather fascinating exposition, "Janet's lover/accomplice Vladimir Kozlowski, alias Swiss Barrister Adalbert Kaminski, Attorney-at-Law, decided to pull a clever scam on you as vindictive punishment for your infidelity to your wife and for your incidental firing of your amorous, on-the-prowl, former road foreman."

"This is all very bizarre and incredibly sophisticated!" Michal acknowledged, exhibiting a stern, grim expression on his now-florid face. "I fully understand that since the nine hundred thousand had never been reported to the IRS on my past tax returns, I would then have to pay hundreds of thousands of dollars in back taxes that I don't really have at hand. What a tight Gordian knot I had tied for myself!" the thoroughly duped man verbally realized. "When the skimmed money was finally noticed stolen from the cellar air conditioning duct, I couldn't report it to the local authorities because then eventually, an IRS investigation would have me losing my business. But tell me Frank," Michal Wisniewski questioned with an astonished look showing on his face. "What was this roundabout Hawaii adventure and inheritance marathon all about?"

"That's all quite simple; basic elementary school logic," Frank Meyers answered and indulgently chuckled, and then the hired researcher begged for forgiveness after admitting to his gross indiscretion that had been inadvertently directed toward his shocked and beleaguered client. "I figured that your cheating, scorned wife and this Kozlowski gigolo knew all about your historic infatuation with the Radziwill steel moguls from Warsaw. Consequently," the savvy detective concluded his extraordinary exposition, "after you had coincidentally fired Mr. Kozlowski, he couldn't be hanging-around your house and deliberately be breaking into your air conditioning duct by removing the latticed vent cover. And so, the audacious pair concocted this magnificently creative scheme where...."

"Where I temporarily forgot all about my nine-hundred-thousand dollars concealed in the cellar air conditioning duct and foolishly focused my concentration on the nineteen and a half million-dollar non-existent reward; the perilous illusion at the end of my fantasy rainbow," Michal gasped and uttered in complete animosity. "The two creative rogues capitalized on my desire to become twenty times as wealthy as I presently am, or was, and they next coyly sweetened the pot and enticed me with an all-expense-covered Hawaiian vacation for me and my family. That was the maraschino cherry on top of the all-too-tantalizing hot fudge sundae," Wisniewski regretfully determined. "And while I had been unsuspectingly touring the splendid sights of Oahu with my cheating wife, Vladimir Kozlowski, alias Lawyer Adalbert Kaminski, sneakily entered my house with a door key provided by my wife and then..."

"And then unimpeded, the deplorable scoundrel without any interruption, easily pilfered your stashed nine-hundred-thousand clams that had been concealed inside your cellar air conditioning vent!" Frank Meyers attested. "The entire Hawaii ruse was just a neat scam to skillfully scam you and get you away from Hammonton for a week or so, just in order for the common thief to casually purloin your hidden basement treasure."

"But the whole deceitful plot must've cost Kozlowski at least thirty thousand dollars when you consider the round-trip plane tickets for four, the lavish hotel accommodations and the cash allotted for the trip's food expense account!" the still-astounded Michal Wisniewski vigorously complained. "And the worst aspect of the entire fiasco is that I had been betrayed by my formerly trusted, two-timing wife!"

"Indeed!" P.I. Frank Meyers exclaimed. "In effect, this Vladimir Kozlowski character and your deceitful wife had ingeniously collaborated to achieve something mighty imaginative. They offered you an artificial twenty-million-dollar whale in exchange for a real nine hundred-and-sixty-thousand-dollar rare tuna, and you, in a gullible manner, swallowed their absurdly outrageous proposal, hook, line and sinker! And when you and your family arrived in Hawaii, that was Mr. Kozlowski's confirmation signal to fly back to New Jersey from Honolulu to enact his sly cellar duct heist, which naturally you will never report to the local authorities out of fear of punitive IRS retribution."

"I suppose that I deserve this uncouth outcome as atonement for me being so covetous," Michal generalized and confessed. "I guess I've been pummeled both in love and in money, because I had been a naïve, foolish, greedy dreamer believing that the high-flying aristocratic and super-sophisticated wealthy Radziwill family of Warsaw, Poland had cared one tiny scintilla about the lowly, impoverished Wisniewskis of Krakow."

"The Trespassers"

Judd Lenox and Ted Owens had been acquaintances ever since kindergarten. The duo had played on the DiDonato's Bowling *Little League Baseball* team, were the starting guards on the Hammonton High School basketball team, and the pair had double-dated twin sisters to the senior prom. The close chums even were classmates majoring in agriculture at *Cook College of Rutgers University.* Way before becoming successful New Jersey fruit farmers, Judd and Ted's close fraternity had been remarkable in one respect. Their friendship had to be done on the sly because their fathers had been fierce competitors in the local peach-growing industry. Each elder thought *he* grew the best peaches in the area.

After the feuding Lenox and Owens' patriarchs finally journeyed to their eternal rewards, Judd and Ted became as inseparable as salt and pepper. The pair masterminded and formed a lucrative "peach cooperative" that protected the unit price of each grower's accurately measured, size-graded "fancy fruit". Over the years, the comrades' personalities seemed to fuse into one kindred spirit. Their similarities in taste were appropriately demonstrated when Judd and Ted married the same twin sisters that they had escorted to the Hammonton High School senior prom.

Judd Lenox managed an impressive four hundred acres of well-maintained peach orchards. Ted Owens supervised a similar impressive operation, but the proud, ambitious man harvested a hundred acres of apples to complement his fourteen peach varieties planted on his remaining three hundred acres. Their well-maintained farms abutted between Oak and Walker Roads, partitioned by a mile-long dirt path that stretched between the White Horse Pike (*Route 30*) and Union Road.

Each morning, the conscientious brothers-in-laws alternated picking the other up at six a.m. Augie's Diner was the local early morning haven for the more prominent and garrulous Hammonton, New Jersey peach, apple and blueberry farmers. The area growers congregated at the popular Route 30 eatery to discuss crop prices, to exchange gossip, to study local newspapers, and to engage in good-natured banter.

"Mornin' Ted," Judd greeted his buddy from his new red Ford truck driver's window.

"You ain't happy 'til ya' wake up my roosters," Ted amiably answered before entering the familiar cab. "I ain't got no hen-house, and you're out bright and early lookin' for chicken hawks."

Judd drove his favorite vehicle down the White Horse Pike in the direction of Augie's breakfast place. Lenox was the more vociferous brothers-in-law. He was certain to dominate all their friendly conversations with his myriad opinions and verbal editorials.

"Ya' know Ted," Judd began his morning lecture. "We're gonna' have another great peach harvest. Those dim-witted vegetable growers will never learn how to master fundamental agricultural economics. They're dumber than a barn of jackasses wantin' to become plow horses!"

"And more stubborn than jackasses, too!" Ted alertly added. "They're blind to the truth; that's for sure!"

"They ain't never gonna' make money foolin' around with plants," Judd Lenox interrupted his pal. "The farmin' dollars grow on trees and bushes; not on plants. They ain't never gonna' learn *that* simple fact of life."

"You're right on the money," Ted wholeheartedly agreed. "The dough's definitely in fruit. Vegetables ain't where it's at!"

"Peaches, apples, nectarines, and blueberries," Lenox orated. "Those dandies' will always be the money crops. Tomatoes, peppers, corn, and cucumbers just barely pay the bills," the very opinionated grower related to his receptive brother-in-law.

"You know it," Ted Owens reflexively concurred. "Hammonton and Vineland vegetable farmers are too independent. They won't help each other. Fact is Judd; they ain't like the Amish over in Pennsylvania Dutch country! Local farmers will never help each other, even after experiencin' a brutal hurricane."

"It's a good thing we're close friends and brother-in-laws," Judd acknowledged. "We're there for each other through thick and thin, through trauma and drama, and also through life and death. That's more than I can say for the others around these parts. The idea of cooperative farmin' to them is like the word communism. It rings like something unpatriotic and un-American."

"If the Mexicans and Orientals have to stoop to pick it, the crop ain't worth a flyin' fiddler's fig in a forest fire!" Ted solemnly declared and alliterated.

"Maybe cash doesn't grow on trees or bushes," Judd hypothesized and opined, "but the money crops sure do. Fruit is king here in South Jersey. Remember when that numbskull Brent Collins planted those five hundred acres of zucchini over in Nesco."

"Lost his shirt," Ted tersely replied.

"And remember when Curt Miller over in Minotola sowed five hundred acres of soybeans," Judd stated.

"Lost his shirt," Owens answered and chanted.

"And don't forget Bob Miller over on *206* up in Indian Mills," Judd persisted. "That misadventure has to be a classic textbook mistake!"

"Old Bob planted stupidly a thousand acres of corn," recollected and related Ted, "and he. . ."

"Lost his shirt, pants, and underwear, too!" agreeable Judd Lenox indulgently laughed.

Lenox sucked in more air so that he could expand his valuable contribution to the conversation. "Ted, ya' don't have to be a rocket scientist professor from one of those *Ivy League* schools to figure it out," Judd pontificated. "The 'Queen of Fruit' takes us on exotic vacations all over the world. Last year we got eighteen dollars per thirty-eight-pound box of two-and-a-halves. And during the height of the season, two-and-a-quarter inch peaches brought..."

"Twelve dollars all summer," Ted corrected and inserted.

"What I'm getting at," Judd quite loudly insisted, "is that in comparison, tomatoes brought only four bucks per twenty-five-pound box. And a crate of corn brought..."

"Five puny dollars all summer long," Ted aptly remembered and explicitly verified.

"And the crate cost a dollar, so the revenue per unit was really only four dollars before broker commissions!" Judd yelled over to his rider. "Ya' don't have to be Einstein's brother to know what's happenin' in the overall produce market. It's not all that academic or all that scientific, either!"

The verbose driver stopped his red truck in the left-hand lane at the White Horse Pike and *Route 206* traffic light. A construction crew was preoccupied installing a new traffic signal at the busy intersection. An old shabby lavender van coughed its way to a stop in the lane next to the shiny new Ford pickup. The strange-looking vehicle's engine incessantly wheezed and sputtered. The paneled van's light purple background was supplemented with an assortment of daisies, pansies, daffodils, and petunias painted over the exterior lavender facade.

The van's driver-side window had been rolled-down, and the peculiar-looking man's facial features were very distinguishable to Judd and Ted. The operator had a long unkempt beard, wore huge oval earrings, had a dirty Arab turban covering his head, and "the hippie" also puffed incessantly on what the farmers at first believed to be a miniature cigarette.

Judd gawked at the bizarre spectacle that his eyes beheld. "Ted, what in tar-nation is wrong with this all-too-crazy world?" Lenox questioned. "If I didn't know any better, I'd think *that* itinerant hippie freak was funny."

"It sure looks funny to me," Ted replied and concurred. "Must be a circus that's come to town!"

"I gotta' confess, he does look like circus sideshow material to me," Judd elaborated to Owens. "We're livin' in a sick, perverted, Godless society. These hippies, gypsies, or whatever they are, don't have our proper Christian values. They lack basic decency," Lenox persuasively stereotyped.

Ted nodded his head in support of his brother-in-law's statement. "The lazy fool don't know that the *Vietnam War* ended almost forty years ago when we was in high school," Owens sympathized.

"Ted, I blame his father for not kickin' his butt when the pink was growin' up," Judd criticized. "Ya' know as well as I do that peach trees are hard to straighten-out after they've grown crooked after only two short years bein' in the ground. The same principle goes for people. All that guy wants to do is listen to rap music and smoke his share of pot."

"I hear ya' loud and clear," Ted typically agreed. "And I'll bet he don't hold no job or live normal. Prob'ly can't speak good English like Shakespeare or us, either!"

"I'll tell ya'," Judd insisted. "Hippies' are a damned cancer to American civilization. They're Satan's livin' curse. They're an abomination, a burden and a..."

"A disgrace to humanity," Ted finished. "A curse worse than the most terrible plague!"

"You and I gotta' support 'em though on welfare, and pay for their food stamps and Medicaid, so that they can get diseases like *AIDS* and waste our hard-earned tax dollars stayin' in hospitals after actin' immoral," Judd generalized.

Ted also was not enamored with the threat of subculture-types thriving in America. "I gotta' agree with ya' on that count," Owens admitted. "I don't like the way they cavort about on that *MTV* cable channel, singin' that sickenin' rap crap."

"Or what about the way they try and disrupt political conventions and Presidential parades," Judd indicated. "Or the way they riot and destroy other people's properties. We ougha' petition the federal government to send 'em all to Cuba or North Korea, or some other disgustin' communist place like that."

A New Jersey *DOT* highway construction crew was assisting the local power company workmen in installing the new traffic signal. Finally, the alert flagman signaled for traffic coming from the opposite direction to halt, and then the worker aggressively waved Judd forward. The red Ford pickup pulled-out in front of the noisy lavender van. Judd resumed his verbal dissatisfaction with contemptible, subculture types.

"Well Ted, I'd better not catch any hippie freeloaders stealin' fruit off of my farm," Judd warned, "or else, a few pellets from my double barrel shotgun will make the trespassers wiggle their carcasses outa' there in a hurry."

"Yeah, Judd. That sort of activity oughta' loosen-up their bowels a bit," Ted assured his brother-in-law. "Sometimes a gun represents the best solution!"

Lenox and Owens perceived themselves and each other as being vastly superior to itinerant "lowlife social deviates". The enterprising farmers had cash, credit, land, stability, the Protestant work ethic, and economic security. The peach farmers had influential relatives in high places that shared their mutual attitudes about societal troublemakers. If any conflict with undesirable "out-of-town scum" should arise, Judd and Ted had more-than-sufficient clout with local law enforcement authorities. Judd's cousin was legendary Atlantic County Sheriff Conrad Grant. Ted's notorious uncle was town Chief-of-Police Ben Turner.

The illustrious fruit growers proceeded westward toward Augie's Diner. Judd's truck's acceleration left the "pathetic love van" far behind to swallow-up the trail of carbon monoxide being emitted from his powerful Ford's dual exhaust pipes. Several minutes later, the humored peach farmers exited their vehicle, entered Augie's with the expressed intention of relating their brief encounter with the "hippie weirdo" to "the boys", and then the new arrivals would learn the latest town scuttlebutt and obituary news from the other assembled growers.

It was late September. All of the peaches were off the trees, and the ones that were not already packed and sold had been safely stored in standard wooden bins, which were stacked four high in Judd and Ted's "state-of-the-art" cold storage facilities.

"Ted, we ain't got nothin' to worry about," Judd remarked as the pair made their grand entrance. "All our remaining precious fruit will be sold by brokers and sent to chain stores from Boston to Richmond by October 1ˢᵗ."

"Ya' forgot something important, didn't ya'?" Owens answered in a mild challenge. "I still got a couple of Roman Beauty and Wine sap apple orchards to pick off in early October. Then, I'll finally be caught up to you."

"Maybe ya' can hire that-there hippie fella' to prune your trees this fall and then fix your tractors and your irrigation pumps, too," Judd joked.

"No thanks," Ted politely responded. "I'd rather get dirty and do those jobs right, all by myself. I need that hippie freak like I need a doctor's second opinion about nothin'!"

After sauntering into Augie's dining establishment, the hungry new arrivals eagerly plopped-down on counter-stools, ordered their standard bacon and eggs breakfast, and then discussed the art of farming with their fellow fruit growers. The assembled men talked about attending the upcoming annual fruit and vegetable growers' convention in February at *Resorts Hotel Casino* in Atlantic City. The farmers then reviewed the well-deserved work slowdown between October and March, a welcomed relief following the hectic growing and packing season. Now there was more time to socialize with cronies, to work at a casual pace, and to visit exotic vacation paradises all over the globe.

"Why go to Vegas or Atlantic City to gamble?" Judd rhetorically asked his captive Augie's Restaurant audience. "Farmin' is such a big gamble with the unpredictable weather that we're all sick and tired of gamblin' when the harvest season's finally over." All the other growers howled in appreciation of Judd Lenox's perceptive analogy. "Now just wait until I tell ya' guys about this here light purple van Ted and I just saw on the Pike. You'll all laugh your fat guts and buttocks off!"

At noon the following day, Judd made an urgent phone call to his brother-in-law, and the caller's voice was full of anger. "Ted, my blood pressure is gonna' make the mercury explode right out of my barometer tube!" Lenox lividly shouted.

"Now Judd, calm-down and start from the beginning!" Ted advised. "Let's not jump to conclusions until all the evidence comes to light!"

"Ya' know that punk hippie we saw drivin' the purple van with all them flowers painted on it yesterday?" Lenox recalled and loudly reminded his listener.

"The one up on the Pike and *206*?" Owens asked.

"That's the one," Judd confirmed. "Well, he and some freaky friends are camped-out right now near Butterton Woods, smack dab between our farms. I'll be arrivin' at your homestead in five minutes. We're gonna' scare the love beads right off their ugly necks. Be ready to go in five!"

Ted was a bit more rational than Judd Lenox was. The grower never liked confrontation and always tried avoiding conflict. Owens would rather call the local police and have Uncle Ben Turner's boys in blue take care of the matter.

"Okay Judd, but don't get your guts stuck in your intestines over crummy lowlife," Owens wisely suggested. "Because the lousy freaks ain't worth you sufferin' a heart attack or stroke."

"I'll take a couple aspirins before I stop by to pick you up," Judd sarcastically promised.

Lenox's red Ford truck suddenly stopped on the asphalt driveway behind Ted's back door in exactly five minutes. Owens hopped inside on the passenger side, and then Judd took-off down Walker Road until he reached Butterton Woods. Lenox turned the 4 X 4 into a peach orchard situated just before Ted's main irrigation pond. A cloud of dust followed the red pickup as it accelerated and barreled down the dirt and gravel road. "Now don't do anything desperate or foolish!" Ted cautioned the reckless driver.

"I'll do what I gotta'!" Judd exclaimed. "That's me and it's always been me!"

A minute later, Lenox reached his destination, the narrow dirt road that served as the official boundary between their prosperous orchards. Ted Owens was much more deliberate in exiting the cab than his rambunctious brother-in-law was. The more assertive farmer stepped briskly toward the band of trespassers as if they were a horde of invading barbarians.

The interlopers were aware of the owner's arrival, but the squatters acted apathetic to his presence. Two tall, muscular, bearded men glared at Judd menacingly. The hippies had skull and crossbones tattooed on their arms, wore earrings in both ears, and small diamonds had been pierced through their noses. The encroachers had been nonchalantly standing with their arms folded, watching three female companions systematically laying down and examining tarot cards while kneeling on the ground.

"Looky here folks, I'm tryin' my best to be as polite as possible," Judd addressed the hippie wearing the Arab headdress. "I own this here land and the sign over near the woods says 'No Trespassin'!"

The intruder with the turban, Mexican poncho and grimy denim jeans spit some phlegm onto the ground next to Judd's work shoes. "So?" the hippie defiantly asked.

"So, you say!" admonished and objected Judd. "No Trespassin' means 'Keep out!' I put my heart and soul into developin' this here land to make it productive, and I don't appreciate lazy dolts like you violatin' my property rights. Get off now, or else there's gonna' be big trouble!"

The leader of the hippie entourage sneered and then answered the irate land baron as Judd's less hostile brother-in-law stood alongside Lenox. "Look man. Cool it, ya' dig dude!" the huge leader replied. "We're just passin' through the territory, got it dude!" the fellow qualified. "Chill brother, before ya' cardiac out!"

Before Judd could muster the wherewithal to formulate a reply, the other burly fellow sporting long scruffy hair and wearing a tie-dyed t-shirt had something to say. "Hey dude, don't get so uptight over nothing," the second trespasser implored. "We're groovin' on the fresh air and sunshine, the blue sky, the white clouds, and the magical changin' of the leaves. Ya' got the picture, Fly Guy?"

Judd raised a clenched fist, but Ted restrained his more demonstrative neighbor from starting a melee, or doing something drastic that Lenox might regret later on. The hippie leader with the turban headgear laughed and again and then he spoke his mind.

"Your jive talkin' is a crock, man," the massive leader protested. "The earth belongs to everybody, ya' dig Big Daddy? No one really owns the land 'cept good old Mother Nature," the hippie honcho proclaimed. "Now Mr. Bluejeans, you're just a temporary steward of this here land. It really belongs to the people. John Lennon had it right, man! Power to the people."

Two of the other eavesdropping hippie campers heard the cliché and yelled out in unison, "Power to the people! Power to the people!" the group reiterated.

Lenox was fit to be tied. His face turned as red as a beet. "Is that so!" Judd yelled. "Well, I've got a deed on record over in Mays Landing that says I'm the legal owner, and that I pay ample taxes on this property, too!"

The two giant male hippies had been unaffected by Judd's belligerence, which they interpreted as mere bravado. Lenox stared contemptuously at the nomadic clan's leader and his monstrous sidekick, finally noticing that the burly intruders were as big and as brawny as he was. And besides their enormous size, the itinerants were just as adamant about staying on the property as Lenox was about evicting them from *his* sacred land.

Judd quickly paced back to his Ford pickup. Ted interpreted Lenox's actions to mean he should strike-up a brief conversation with the trespassers to temporarily distract them from his brother-in-law's furtive activity. Owens stepped over to the three young women who were now sitting upon the ground with their legs crossed like *Campfire Girls.* Two of the females were deciphering the symbolism of selected tarot cards, while the third was busy sewing a strange-looking furry garment.

"What's your name?" Ted innocently asked the suspected hippie leader, showing more civility than his totally incensed brother-in-law had exhibited.

"I'm Abdul, and this big dude here is my amigo, Jupiter. We're travelin' cross-country in my van with those three lovely ladies over there; Cassandra, Esmerelda and Delphi."

"Esmerelda is actin' strange, like I ain't even here," Ted observed and declared.

"Esmerelda is deaf and dumb," Abdul informed. "And all she does all day long is sew, sew, sew. Can't get her to do nothin' else constructive 'cept smoke an occasional joint, or play cards with us every once in a while."

"How about the other two young ladies?" Ted diplomatically asked to stall for more time to cover for Judd's absence. "Tell me somethin' about them."

"Cassandra is Esmerelda's twin sister, but ya' can't really tell by lookin'," Abdul confided to Ted.

"Cassandra's dumb and mute and can't speak a word either," Jupiter interrupted. "Her and Esmerelda's parents were both acid-heads, and I do believe the two girls' genetics got all screwed-up because of it."

"And then of course there's beautiful Delphi," Abdul indicated. "Yes indeed; Delphi is *my* special woman! Sometimes we sleep in the van. Sometimes we sleep under the stars. It's all groovy, ya' know, Dude. Communion with nature, that's where it's all at. Ya' dig the good news, Daddy? That's what turns me on! It's a natural high without drugs, Man!" Abdul loudly summarized before taking a deep drag from his reefer.

Ted then asked Delphi how the tarot cards worked. While Delphi explained the intricate basics of how to understand the occult world, Cassandra was laying-out a new pattern of the cards on the ground. Ted seemed intrigued with the phenomenon.

Judd hollered over to his easily distracted brother-in-law from the red Ford truck. "Ted, ya' got a minute? I gotta' tell ya' somethin' special."

"Hold on a second Judd!" Owens insisted. "Hold your cotton-pickin' horses! I wanna' find out somethin' interestin' that's goin' on over here!"

Judd took personal offense and interpreted Ted's fascination with the hippie women as being an act of disloyalty. Lenox hustled from his truck carrying his loaded double barrel shotgun. The impulsive brother-in-law grabbed Owens by the arm, attempting to tear him away from the paranormal conference in progress. "What's gotten into you?" Judd demanded. "These ragpickin' welfare collectors must have ya' under their confounded spell."

"Quiet-down for a second Judd," Ted grinned. "Pay attention and learn somethin'."

"Ted, those stupid cards layin' on the ground down there are as phony as a three-dollar bill in February. If ya' believe in that evil crap, you're doomed! You're gonna' burn in hell. They're against the *Bible!*"

Abdul snickered at the wrangling farmers. Jupiter noticed Judd's shotgun and brought it to Abdul's now-groggy attention. The hippie leader suddenly became tense and defensive as he angrily flicked his marijuana joint to the dirt.

"Ted, there ain't no truth in those cards. I don't like or trust 'em. Never have, never will!" Lenox futilely argued. "That's the devil's deck for sure!"

"Judd, I just want to see how they work. Just a trifle curious; that's it all in a nutshell!"

"Listen Ted," Lenox ordered in an imperative tone of voice. "They's the Devil's diabolical work, yes they are. These here hippies are the Devil's children, sinful demons they are. And old Lucifer and me ain't the best of friends."

"If you don't believe in the power of the cards," Delphi said in an enchanting tone of voice, "then you shouldn't be afraid of what they have to say!"

"Man, there's nothin' worse than a redneck with plenty of land and lots of money," Jupiter whispered to Abdul so that Judd couldn't hear. 'These two dudes are far out, brother!"

Cassandra had methodically placed three stacks of tarot cards faced down upon the ground. Delphi instructed Ted to randomly remove any two cards from the second pile. "And you," Delphi emphatically said to Judd, "you can take any one card you wish from the first pile."

Judd Lenox refused to participate in the activity because the hippies had initiated the direct commands. Being intrigued, Ted turned over the two cards he had been instructed to select. Owens studied the two medieval knights on horseback, both brandishing swords in their right hands. The more sedate brother-in-law chuckled at the ridiculous mail and armor worn by identical charging cavaliers, but Lenox was not quite as amused.

"See Judd, just like you said, there's nothin' to it," Ted declared. "Show these here trespassers you ain't afraid to have your fortune read. Just pretend you're attendin' the July carnival in the tent with a gypsy fortune teller."

Judd hesitated for a moment. The farmer reluctantly reached-down and roughly flipped-over the third card from the first stack. Horror momentarily beamed from the superstitious man's face. The skeleton figure of Death immediately haunted Lenox's perception. Then, the startled grower laughed out loud in mockery of the macabre figure represented on the card. "Ted, I ain't afraid of no cardboard Grim Reaper. I got old Nellie here to protect me," Lenox boasted as his left hand pointed to his loaded shotgun.

Ted instinctively turned toward Esmerelda and noticed that the girl was not paying any attention to the tarot reading. The deaf and dumb teen just sat there and continued industriously sewing the strange furry brown garment.

Delphi motioned for Cassandra to select a card from the third stack. Cassandra did as commanded and diligently studied the four chosen cards on the ground. The oracle then communicated with Delphi in an indecipherable sign language. Delphi soon conveyed Cassandra's interpretations to everyone else.

"You two greedy farmers will both die within six weeks," Delphi mechanically prophesied. "You'll both be murdered by the police. You sir," Delphi determined as she formidably pointed to Judd, "you will be violently murdered by your cousin, the County Sheriff I believe, and you sir," Delphi said as she swiftly pointed to Ted, "you will be savagely killed by your favorite uncle, who is the town Chief-of-Police."

Lenox and Owens stood stunned and dumbfounded, looking at each other in sheer astonishment. 'How did Delphi know they were related to the County Sheriff and to the local Chief-of-Police?' each farmer wondered and instinctively worried.

Judd felt a compulsion of breaking-out of his apprehension with a boisterous roar. Lenox evaluated the prospect of his future demise as "pure nonsense". Ted was not quite as jovial about the recent ominous predictions as his mercurial brother-in-law was.

"Wait 'till the boys sittin' over at Augie's hear this one!" Judd skeptically bellowed. "I've heard plenty of malarkey in my time, but this one really takes the cake, frosting and all!"

Abdul and Jupiter lit-up new "pot" reefers that had been rolled in cigarette paper and passed their marijuana "joints" around to Cassandra, Delphi, and Esmerelda. The five uninhibited trespassers inhaled deep drags, and then they again passed their joints around to share amongst themselves.

Judd resented the strange celebration as much as he despised the hippie's undesired presence on his property. His anger had snapped him back to his original purpose in confronting the five "aimless vagabonds". Judd pulled Ted aside and gave his partner several specific directions. Lenox then twice fired his double barrel shotgun into the air and quickly reloaded it with two more cartridges.

The hippies' mirth instantly transformed into silence when Lenox forcefully snapped the firearm shut and pointed the weapon directly at the intruders. Delphi grabbed Esmerelda's arm and rotated her in the direction of Judd and his shotgun. The five visitors' disoriented minds tried differentiating between fantasy and reality. Delphi's prophecy had instilled fear into Judd's mind, while Lenox's shotgun had created anxiety in the visitors' hearts.

"Listen-up freaks!" Judd demanded, not realizing that Esmerelda and Cassandra were unable to hear his commands. "I'll gladly use force if I have to show I mean business. I never wanna' see your rear ends in my neck of the woods again. If I catch you despicable weasels snoopin' around here, next time I won't think twice. I'll blast the fat right off your fannies! Is that clear?"

Lenox aimed his weapon at Abdul and Jupiter and instructed the pair to turn around under threat of death. Ted was directed to go to Judd's pickup and soon returned with five lengths of five-foot-long rope, which Lenox had ordinarily used for securing newly planted peach trees to poles. Owens tied the hippies' hands behind their backs, employing the same double knots the farmer had used to keep his young trees straight and attached to the poles.

Abdul was the first to protest Judd's vigilante style of justice. "You rednecks will pay for this! The tarot card prediction will definitely come true!" the group leader screamed. "In six weeks, you'll both be dead as predicted! I guarantee it!"

164

Ted did the same knot-tying procedure to the three young women's hands as Judd steadily pointed his trusty shotgun. Lenox next told the five campers to slide into the rear of the lavender van. Then Judd requested Ted to commandeer the "gaudy-lookin' hippie wagon" and meet him in thirty minutes at Pennypot, an old abandoned piney village that was located four miles southeast of Hammonton.

Thirty minutes later, Judd pulled into the woods where the hamlet of Pennypot used to be located. Lenox's traveling companions were his two ferocious Doberman pinschers sitting next to him besides the steering wheel in the red Ford cab. The anxious farmer pulled-up to the lavender van, removed his unfriendly canines, and vigorously walked them in the direction of the other previously arrived vehicle.

"Been here long, Ted?" Judd yelled above the vicious dogs' incessant barking.

"No!" Owens hollered back. "That damned purple tin pig can't go over thirty with my foot pressed through the floorboard! What a horrible contraption that piece of junk is!"

Judd was employing all his strength to tug his excited Dobermans over to an oak tree next to the hippie van. The incensed fellow then tied the dogs' six-foot-long leashes around the sturdy tree's girth as the ferocious animals bared their teeth, jumped about, and wickedly growled and snarled. All Lenox would have to yell was the word "Attack!" and the canines would then go completely haywire.

Judd then told his brother-in-law to remove the "vermin scoundrels" from the back of the dilapidated van. The livid peach farmer drew a line in the muddy ground eight feet or so from the Dobermans' fangs, and with his shotgun pointing at Abdul, Lenox advised *him* to stand on the drawn line or be immediately shot. The crazed farmer next carefully motioned with his gun aimed at the other captives, tacitly communicating that they should imitate their leader's example.

"Now listen good!" Judd shouted above the savage Dobermans' wild barking. "I'm gonna' give ya' five minutes to run for your lives into the woods in that direction. Then I'm gonna' release my dogs after ya.' They already got a whiff of the skunky rags you're all wearin'. You scumbag critters better run faster than greyhounds, or you might not live to see the sun rise tomorrow! My advice is to just pretend you're five desperate foxes, ha, ha, ha!"

Ted then cut Jupiter's bindings and the frightened hippie sprinted down the muddy road like a decathlon champion. The same procedure was done to the three women, and Abdul was the last to be liberated from his bondage. Lenox laughed mercilessly at the panic-stricken hippies disappearing from view in the opposite direction from which they had entered the woods as van captives.

Judd Lenox was entertained by the fury of his ill-tempered pedigrees. Foam had formed in the gaps between the Dobermans' jagged, carnivorous fangs. "Good boys!" Judd praised as he expertly calmed his attack dogs down.

"King and Prince will chew those five up when ya' let 'em go and do your dirty work!" Ted declared. "Judd, don't take the law into your own hands. It ain't right!"

"Those stupid donkeys should've read about their adventure with my frisky dogs in those phony cards they got," Judd strongly laughed. "Those cards are as fake as an Arkansas outhouse without a toilet seat hole in it!"

Ted Owens did not share Judd's excessive enthusiasm. The brother-in-law was worried about the fate of the five hippies. "Three minutes have already gone by. Are ya' gonna' release your mutts on their prospective victims?"

"Don't you worry," Judd guffawed. "I was only scarin' 'em. I just wanted to create the fear of hell into those freakin' hippies. Creeps like them got to fear somethin' once-in-a-while to experience a reality check. I ain't gonna' set my puppies loose, this time. Next time, I might, though."

Ted Owens broke-out in a smile when the relieved grower realized that Judd was not going to resort to utilizing savage animal violence against his imagined adversaries. "Their underwear will be dark brown by the time they stop runnin'," the peach and apple producer said, grinning from cheek to cheek like a happy chimpanzee.

"Do ya' think they even wear underwear?" Judd cackled with amusement. "Those hippies went to the dogs long before my puppies ever wanted to get to their hides."

"But what about the van?" Ted inquisitively asked. "Are ya' gonna' leave it parked out here in the woods? On second thought, it looks like it's now right in its natural environment."

"You just leave that matter up to old Judd," Lenox explained. "Drive that pathetic junker down to the rear corner of my old Loring peach orchard. Stay there 'til I arrive. I'll take care of that ugly contraption. Ted, my mind's workin' fast today. I've thought of just about everything."

Ted Owens drove the grotesque-looking lavender van to the designated corner of Judd's recently uprooted Loring variety peach trees. In the meantime, Owens drove his Dobermans to *their* chain-link pen, entered his house, downed three generous jiggers of *Southern Comfort*, walked to his large storage shed, hopped onto his bulldozer, and next the crazed fellow drove the huge machine out to the prescribed corner of his Loring peach orchard.

Judd Lenox had always replaced (on a rotating basis) his immaculately maintained orchards every fifteen years, and the old Loring orchard's five hundred trees had just been uprooted. Judd quickly used his bulldozer to push piles of downed Loring trees and branches against and above all four sides of the lavender hippie vehicle. In twenty minutes of brush manipulation, the vehicle had been neatly concealed inside the huge heap of dead fruit trees.

The next morning, Judd divulged his imaginative act of *vandalism* to "the regular boys" at Augie's Restaurant. The breakfast faithful laughed incessantly when the comrades heard about the antics of the fierce Dobermans and about the thoroughly camouflaged van. Instantly Judd Lenox had become a local hero and legend to the other farmers, ascending to become a contemporary crusader defending Christian morality and the *United States Constitution* against the dangerous revolutionary threat of the hippie subculture.

"Judd, I'm treatin' ya' to breakfast this mornin'," promised Dennis DeMarco, a jovial area peach and plum grower. "That tale ya' just told us beats all!"

"You successfully defended God, mother, baseball, and apple pie against modern day barbarians," added Larry Galletta, a prosperous area blueberry czar.

A full month passed without any evidence of reprisal or incident. Judd presumed that Abdul and his disciples had learned their lesson and had fled the Hammonton vicinity for more hospitable sanctuaries devoid of Doberman pinschers. Lenox's presumptuous tranquility was disturbed when he received an unexpected afternoon phone call on the last day of November.

"Hate to bother you with some bad news, Judd," Ted diplomatically apologized over the phone. "But there's another one of those queer hippie vans parked in the back of your Blake peach orchard on the Oak Road side of Butterton Woods. This one is painted pink with elephants, bananas and volcanoes drawn all over it. What a lousy work of art! It belongs next to the *Mona Lisa* we once saw over in that French museum!" Owens facetiously exclaimed.

"I'll bring my shotgun and investigate this shenanigan," Lenox replied. "Our farms are becoming magnets for society's scum!"

"Judd, why not get Conrad or Ben over there to do your damned dirty work? The Sheriff or the Police Chief are better trained and equipped than we are. They're the ones that oughta' handle this trespassin' situation," Ted recommended.

"Farmers in these parts are very independent minded, you know that Ted," Lenox indicated. "I'll only call for help as a last resort if the uncouth intruders don't cooperate."

"I'll pick ya' up in five minutes, then," Ted informed his more volatile brother-in-law. "And don't overreact. Let's allow the local police to deal with these hippie trespassers. Put your tax dollars to work, so to speak."

Judd Lenox was infuriated by the new information Owens had just communicated. He impatiently waited for Ted's aqua blue Chevy truck to pull into his driveway. Ted's 4 X 4 entered the well-landscaped property and halted outside Judd's back door. Lenox threw his double barrel shotgun behind the front seat and then hopped inside the cab.

"They look like different hippies this time," Owens related. "I don't think they're the same batch."

"Doesn't matter," Judd angrily returned. "We gotta' nip these flower children in the bud. This is becomin' an ugly habit. My farm ain't Woodstock, ya' know!"

"Go easy on 'em Judd," Ted cautioned. "And don't take 'em so seriously," Owens further advised his passenger as the calmer brother-in-law piloted his Chevy pickup out of the impeccably clean asphalt driveway onto the White Horse Pike.

"Look Ted, it ain't so bad when these hippies begin crappin' on my head," Judd objected. "But when the brown juice rolls down my face and I gotta' taste it, that's when I gotta' do somethin' in the realm of problem solvin'. If word gets around that I can't handle these parasite hippie trespassers, I'll be the laughin' stock and gossip of all Hammonton agriculture."

"I see what ya' mean," Ted readily agreed. Owens' aqua blue pickup soon sped-down Walker Road and finally reached Butterton Woods when the nervous dialogue continued.

"Next time this happens, I'll get Conrad or Ben over here and throw these derelicts into the slammer," Judd assured the driver. "Ted, there ain't no respect for private ownership no more. Our grandpas' and pappies worked damned hard with mules and horses right through the *Depression* and *World War II* to keep this here land plow worthy. I ain't about to share it with any good-for-nothin' riff-raff!" Lenox insisted.

The aqua blue truck veered left and soon cruised-down the long dirt road that conveniently partitioned the parallel estates. A continuous dust cloud swirled-up from the 4 X 4's rear tires. After Ted rounded the large irrigation pond that the two farmers shared, the pink van with the ostentatious artwork suddenly became visible three-hundred-feet ahead. Soon, the aqua blue vehicle slid to a halt. The two peach farmers leaped from the truck. Judd was so crazed that he forgot his shotgun behind the seat inside Ted's 4 X 4.

Two formidable-looking men arose from the warmth of their campfire. The first wore Apache Indian apparel with an enormous gold medallion dangling around his neck that complemented his brown buckskin outfit and matching moccasins. The second trespasser wore a black motorcycle jacket and accompanying engineer boots. Metal chains draped-down (against the character's hairy chest) from around his neck, and other chains hung out of the pockets of the fellow's filthy, faded blue jeans. The second intruder had greasy hair, thick bushy sideburns, and featured a gruesome scar on the left side of his face.

"Hey there man, what's happenin'!" the Indian-type greeted the newcomers to the peach orchard. "I'm Geronimo, and this here's my good buddy, Studs. We don't mean you dudes no harm, man. We're just out here in the sticks lookin' for harmony with nature. I mean dudes, love is where it's at!"

Judd tried remaining externally subdued although the livid owner very consciously believed that Geronimo and Studs had violated his sacred property rights. Lenox felt that the new delinquents should be punished just as Abdul, Jupiter, and their three female disciples had been dealt with back in October.

"I've had it up to my gills with inconsiderate trespassers," Judd exclaimed. "And now I'm givin' you two irresponsible bums ten minutes to gather your gear and hit the road!"

Ted attempted to diplomatically pacify his aggrieved brother-in-law. Owens did not want to witness verbal conflict erupt into wild lawlessness. He wanted to evade a serious altercation.

"My friend here is overreactin' a bit," Ted conceded. "He gets too frantic sometimes with his temper," Owens apologized. "I'll try and simmer him down."

"We ain't botherin' nobody," Studs maintained. "Just tryin' to keep a low profile and make it to tomorrow, ya' freaks know."

Judd marched back to Ted's pickup to retrieve his shotgun. As the man-on-a-mission got to the 4 X 4, the enraged farmer turned-around and shouted some insults at the two standing happy campers. "You vile scumbags are more disgustin' than a hog's infected hemorrhoids. Hop into your pink puddle jumper and hit the Pike before it's too late."

Judd confidently reached behind the blue truck's seat and grabbed his weapon. The infuriated farmer opened the stock and inserted the cartridges. Lenox snapped the shotgun shut and rapidly approached the two new trespassers, who appeared quite surprised by the landowner's overreaction to their unannounced presence.

"Don't shoot man! We like breathin'," Geronimo implored his new-found enemy. "Keep your cool, Big Daddy!"

"We'll do whatever you fat cats say," Studs promised with his hands raised over his head to indicate his eager willingness to surrender and comply.

"If I catch you skunks loiterin' and hangin' around these parts again, I'll shoot first and ask unnecessary questions later!" Judd threatened. 'Now it's time for you punks to adios!"

Just then two large men leaped-out of the nearby thicket and ambushed Judd from behind. The shotgun blasted into the air, knocking-off an overhead branch from a huge tulip tree. Geronimo and Studs joined the struggle, and soon Judd and Ted were overpowered and strenuously wrestled to the ground.

Horror shone from Judd's eyes when he observed that his two ambushers had been former adversaries Abdul and Jupiter. Geronimo easily wrested the shotgun from Judd's clutches. While the farmers were being strenuously pinned to the ground, Esmerelda, Cassandra, and Delphi emerged from the back doors of the pink van.

The surprised captives were hastily shackled with hemp rope, and Studs meticulously bound the hostages' feet with chains he had stored inside *his* paneled pink van. Judd futilely screamed a barrage of derogatory remarks, but his boisterous cursing was regarded as sheer amusement by his bizarre-looking-captors.

Abdul especially relished his sweet revenge. "Look here, you jive turkey!" the maniac indignantly shouted. "It's now *your* turn to listen to me! I want my wheels back, and I want 'em back now! No more freakin' double talk, man! You flakes make me sick to my stomach and make me wanna' vomit!"

"That's right!" Jupiter boldly interrupted. "We don't wanna' hear any more horse crap! Let's get down to brass tacks, shall we? Where's the purple van?"

"Look, we're very sorry!" Ted gasped in horror. "We'll get your van back in a jiffy! You have my pledge!"

"Where is it?" Abdul demanded. "I miss navigatin' around in my favorite machine."

"It's hidden," Judd dreadfully panted; "inside that-there huge brush pile way down the road there!"

"You must really think I got a pea-brain functionin' inside my skull," Abdul said while holding Judd in a rather devastating headlock to further indicate his utter dissatisfaction. "You now tellin' me my love wagon is inside that wood garbage branch pile over there. You must be trippin' out on *LSD* or meth'!"

"I think his brain's melted-down to the intelligence of a peach pit!" Geronimo quipped. "What a freakin' loser!"

The seven trespassers laughed relentlessly at their desperate prisoners' captivity. "If you're not lyin' and actually tellin' the truth, how ya' gonna' get my purple van outa' there?" laughed Abdul in a fit of hysterics. "Ya' gonna' use dynamite? Ha, ha, ha!"

"With my bulldozer," Judd answered before struggling for his next air inhalation. "It'll get your van back!"

"With his bulldozer!" Abdul yelled as all the hippies (except Esmerelda and Cassandra) roared deliriously. "With his bulldozer!" the hippie chieftain repeated and laughed.

Abdul puffed diligently on his freshly-lit marijuana joint. Then the chronic trespasser divulged some deleterious remarks to the disabled orchard barons. "You two annoyin' clowns are regular meat-heads, ya' know that!" the hippie chieftain venomously chided. "Tell 'em a thing or two to enlighten 'em, will ya' Jupiter!"

"You two pompous dingbats think you're so damned smart and important, but you're really stupid retards," Jupiter berated. "Ya' pay a lot of taxes, ya' pompously dress-up and go to church every Sunday, and ya' think you're somethin' special when ya' break-down and then guiltily give to charity," the inspired flower-child savant insulted and laughed.

Abdul continued the briefing by telling Judd and Ted that the hippies were also "shrewd businessmen", but that the captured farmers were too dumb to ever realize it. The self-appointed Arab then informed Lenox and Owens that the two encumbered individuals were the ones now trespassing on the hippies' sacred land, and that the seven intruders were really practicing successful farmers in their own right.

"What do you grow?" Ted meekly asked from his tied position sitting on the ground.

In unison, the four male hippies chortled themselves into hysterics. The wandering band thought that Ted's inquiry was absolutely hilarious. Abdul nearly suffocated trying to uncurl his tongue. But then, the awesome giant reached inside his pants pocket and produced a palm full of strange-looking green leaves.

"Hey man," Abdul giggled. "You hamsters are so funny ya' both belong on the *Animal Channel*. These here green leaves are from the cannabis bush. Marijuana man!"

"We've been growin' hundreds of these plants all over your two farms," Jupiter informatively added, "and you two simpleton patriots never paid any attention to 'em because they look just like your typical tall orchard weeds, and they aren't planted in neat rows like your stupid peach and apple trees."

"This here land is *our* farm now," Abdul unofficially declared his victorious confiscation by force. "And you two freaks thought all along that *our weeds* were just your regular weeds!" the fanatic cackled. "What a pair of dimwitted ninnies."

Judd and Ted struggled to liberate themselves from their bondage, but their restraints had been too securely tied. And the 'abominable hippies' represented the ruination of everything the two farmers respected and revered. To Judd and Ted, the intruders were barbaric iconoclasts that loathed traditional religion, that had abandoned the institution of marriage, that had practiced illegitimate sex, that had disregarded personal property rights, that didn't pay taxes and finally, that were illegal drug users and pushers. Now the clever hippies were drug growers shamelessly profiting on the private land of two decent, law-abiding citizens.

"You valueless dirtbags don't honor the *Ten Commandments*. You know nothing about the need for Christian principles!" Judd foolishly accused his tormentors.

"I want you to know Idiot King," Abdul explained, "that this past summer we've made over four hundred thousand tax-free dollars growin' pot on your two farms. We're capitalists without any major capital expenses. That's probably as much money as you two imbeciles made growin' your dumb pretty red and yellow peaches after foolishly paying taxes and business expenses."

"Yeah, we've created the perfect gig here," Geronimo verified. "We have no tractors, pumps, packinghouses, cold storages to maintain, or expensive machines to buy or keep. We have no electric or phone bills. If our *grass scheme* was ever discovered, we blow the town and move on. It's on *your* property and you gotta' answer for it if we got caught. We did our homework, man," Geronimo disclosed to his distressed hostages, now sitting on the cold hard ground with their encumbered hands tied behind their backs.

Studs filled-in several more missing pieces to the amazing jigsaw puzzle. "We keep a constant lookout for the fuzz. We know you screwed-up rednecks are related to the Sheriff and the local Chief-of-Police. The pigs would never come and arrest you two jerks for growin' marijuana and make a big scandal around these pinelands. We're thought of everything, dudes!" Studs chuckled and reminded his captives.

"And now," Abdul announced, "both of you lily-white *WASPS* thinkin' your detectives or somethin' like that, and ya' had to stupidly snoop around too much and ruin our cover. We have no choice now. We gotta' waste ya' because ya' both know too much about our operations!"

The band of hippies who were not deaf and mute broke-out in a chorus of wild revelry. Judd and Ted didn't know what to expect.

Owens tried one last entreaty. "Look folks, just let us go!" Owens begged. "We'll forget everything that's happened, and we'll all live in harmony. We'll bury the hatchet. My brother-in-law and I will pretend nothin' negative ever occurred!"

Abdul was not-too-impressed with Ted's feckless rhetoric. "It's too late for that, you self-righteous pigs. Your doom is sealed, and there's no turnin' back the clock. You guys go to church each Sunday. You oughta' be prepared to die pretty soon and finally get to meet your Divine Maker."

"Yeah Abdul," Geronimo followed suit, "they oughta' get to heaven real fast. St. Peter will let them use the escalator instead of the stairs. Then these two knuckleheads won't have to deal with us sinful creatures interferin' with their precious land any more."

The entire company of onlookers rejoiced after hearing Abdul and Geronimo's exceptional eloquence. Jupiter was not to be outdone by his slick associates. "And we'll keep your prized shotgun as a special memento," the hippie bragged and promised. "We're all dedicated vegetarians, and we hate people like you that eat meat. We especially hate hunters that go out and kill poor innocent animals. Your gun is proof that man is evil and that nature is good."

Judd argued in vain that he and Ted only hunted for sport and for pleasure, and that the local hunting season kept deer and rabbit populations in check, or else *their* crops would be overrun and destroyed by ravenous animals on the prowl. "The deer would overpopulate the forests, and many would die from starvation while competing for food," Judd futilely explained from his subordinate prone position upon the ground.

"And we don't waste what we shoot," Ted academically added. "Our gunning club gives the deer and rabbit meat to their families and friends, and some to charity organizations, too."

Again, Abdul was hardly impressed and persuaded by Judd and Ted's various explanations. His heart desired vengeance for his unforgettable Pennypot encounter with awesome King and Prince. The hippie leader also despised the captured land barons because he believed that the duo frowned on pleasure; conjectured that they exploited the poor with their harmful profit incentive; theorized that they polluted nature with chemicals and pesticides, and evaluated that the two farmers were mindless puppets obeying the nefarious, powerful political/military combine in Washington.

The hippies thought that Lenox and Owens represented the ultimate in American hypocrisy. The farmers were too narrow-minded and Puritanical to ever appreciate the value of beauty, peace, love, sex, sharing, and harmony with nature.

Abdul then gave Studs a tacit signal. The male monster readily picked-up a two-foot-long pipe, and as Geronimo and Jupiter pinned Judd and Ted's shoulders to the earth, Studs hit the two hostages on the back of their heads, immediately knocking each of the captives unconscious. Abdul then exhibited a large hypodermic needle, and the instigator maliciously administered massive heroin injections into Judd and Ted's left arms. "This ain't exactly penicillin," the psychopath snickered as he enacted his madness.

Esmerelda retreated into the pink van and opened the back panels. The deaf and dumb girl returned with two unusual furry costumes she had been assiduously sewing for the past seven weeks. The fortuneteller proudly displayed what Delphi's hand-signaling described as "authentic-looking forest bear uniforms" to her very amused colleagues. The imaginative disguises had been uniquely tailored to conform to Judd Lenox and Ted Owens's general physical measurements.

"This here fur material was purchased by me at a trading post up in Bushkill, Pennsylvania," Abdul reminded everyone. "Do ya' all remember that trip?"

"Yeah, *Pocono Mountain* bear country," Jupiter clarified. "Now's our opportunity to put the material to good use."

The hippies generously sprinkled several bags of cocaine into the costumes' bear heads. The unconscious farmers were untied and then roughly placed inside the brown-furred outfits, unaware that their disguises were the main part of a sick, lethal masquerade about to commence.

Judd and Ted were rudely rolled-over onto their stomachs, and Esmerelda used long leather laces threaded through huge sewing needles to mend the narrow gaps close together. Next, the bear heads were roughly put on the landowners, and then Esmerelda quickly sewed the new material to the fabric of the heavy furred costumes.

The twin bears were next deposited inside the rear of Geronimo's pink van. After the hippie band climbed inside the back, the vehicle's rear panels were closed tight and then locked. Abdul stepped to the driver's side, hopped inside, closed the door, and after starting the noisy engine, maneuvered the weird-looking contraption off the premises.

The decrepit-looking thing made a right turn onto Walker Road and proceeded north. It crossed Union Road and moved onto a dirt trail that divided a huge section of privately-owned woods. The road continued through tall hedgerows on both sides, and then passed through the property of Tuckahoe Turf and Sod Farm.

Soon Abdul reached his ultimate destination; the *Wharton State Forest*. The large tract of virgin pine lands had been protected from commercial development by strict New Jersey environmental laws. The pink van continued onward onto a sandy trail that penetrated ten miles into the dense woodlands, with the dusty road extending all the way to *Atsion Lake* on *Route 206*.

"Tomorrow's December 1st," Abdul reminded his entourage as the fanatic drove further into the protected wilderness. "December 1st is something special to the male residents around here."

"First day of Jersey deer huntin' season," Geronimo answered from the van's rear compartment. "This forest is gonna' be crawlin' with anxious trigger-happy hunters."

After advancing a bumpy four miles into the aforementioned *Wharton State Forest,* the pink van came to a stop at two sandy cross trails. The back panels were opened, and Judd Lenox and Ted Owens were rudely deposited onto the ground in the center of the intersecting trails, deep inside the coniferous forest.

"Bye, bye, you holier-than-thou idiots!" Abdul ridiculed. "Stupid fools! You've always been the great white hunters. Now you're the great white hunted! Ha, ha, ha!"

The itinerant van turned right and slowly followed the sandy trail three miles east to *Route 206*. Abdul's delighted male apostles loudly cheered the very obvious defeat of their most recent enemies.

An hour later, Judd awoke from his unconscious state. The disguised fellow turned-over on the forest ground and became frightened when he observed a dreadful-looking, huge, brown bear sleeping alongside of him. Lenox superficially inspected his own arms and legs to astonishingly discover that he had similar characteristics to the furry animal lying next to him. Then Judd realized that the other immobile bear must indeed be his furry brother-in-law, Ted Owens.

"Ted, wake up!" Lenox anxiously begged. "It's me Judd," the petrified man implored as perspiration beads from the hot black bear suit rolled down his face, chest, back, and legs.

The effects of the heroin injections and of the cocaine powder that had been sprinkled inside the bear heads now made both men very groggy and disoriented. The afflicted duo gradually regained a degree of sensibility within an hour, and vainly endeavored ripping the strong thick laces that kept them trapped inside their burdensome costumes. Their valiant and awkward efforts proved futile. The leather bonds could not be torn and were so thick that only a sharp hunting knife could ever sever the cords.

Judd and Ted were now subject to nature's will and whim. The overburdened pair now needed the cunning of wild forest bucks to escape the cross hairs of hunters' shotguns. The two unfortunate masqueraders trudged south along the dreadful trail in their very heavy, furry, cumbersome costumes.

Judd had a vague idea of their location, and was momentarily inspired by a moment of fleeting hope. The gunning club member had hunted the *Wharton Forest* many times and knew most of the paths and trails by heart. As the two ponderous forms advanced southward, Lenox saw the shine from the setting sun flickering through the dense pine tree canopy, and the forest trekker instinctively knew that *that* direction was 'west'. Judd's blurry mind had the ability to determine that the south trail which, they were trudging along on, would eventually lead Ted and him back to the expansive Tuckahoe Turf Farm.

Judd Lenox knew he had to remain calm and rational in order to conquer the insensitive, uncaring, cruel, environment that now surrounded him and his ill-starred companion. Ted Owens was not as strong-willed as his more dominant brother-in-law was. The pathetic victim began whimpering and sobbing inside his heavy, brown-furred, exterior; half his beleaguered mind hallucinating on heroin and cocaine, and the other half of his brain comprehending that his very life was certainly in grave jeopardy.

Early December heralded the advance of the winter solstice and the advent of *Christmas*. Nightfall would be descending before five p.m. The ursine amblers had to abandon their hopes of ever being

176

rescued before daybreak. The dismal pair hobbled and stumbled south down the desolate sandy trail toward imaginary civilization. The potent drugs that had been administered were still clouding their thought processes and slurring their speech. The men soon sank-down to the ground, embracing each other. The late fall air was cold and crisp. The unfortunate twosome clumsily huddled together to keep warm. Eventually, the discouraged brothers-in-laws fell asleep.

Judd woke-up first, sweating profusely. Ominous noises from the forest's interior had suddenly awakened him. The sound of a flitting owl swooping through the tall pines in quest of unsuspecting prey immediately gained his attention. The terror, the drugs, the total disorientation, and Lenox's overwhelming paranoia sent Judd's already greatly-disturbed mind into a tremendous quandary. His aching body had gone beyond mere exhaustion. The emotionally defeated dupe slumped over onto the forest floor and then out of sheer fatigue, fell back to sleep.

The following morning, *Wharton State Forest* was teeming with ambitious hunters in quest of big buck antlers. Sheriff Conrad Grant and local Chief-of-Police Ben Turner were prepared to spot their first "big rack" of the new hunting season. The on-a-mission lawmen were avid hunters who took the seven-day-long annual ritual very seriously, as did other members of their infamous Boot Hill Gunning Club. The first buck kills always brought along exclusive bragging rights at the very remote cabin clubhouse.

Honorable Sheriff Conrad Grant and Chief-of-Police Ben Turner slowly climbed-up the sturdy makeshift ladder to the deer observation platform that they had skillfully constructed on a large oak tree, a full mile inside the dense forest. The two excited men carried huge paunches that would become even more expansive after a week of feasting on delectable venison, pizza, Italian bread, *Jack Daniels* and homemade "dago wine""

"I just can't rightly understand it, Ben," Conrad Grant began while scratching his bald-head. "Judd and Ted weren't present for roll call at the Boot Hill cabin this mornin'. Ain't like them to miss somethin' so important."

"Maybe they ran-off to become hippies," the Chief-of-Police jokingly replied to his best friend, who also absolutely detested dreadlocks, longhairs, body piercing, and male earrings.

"I'm more than a little concerned about their absence," Conrad confidentially admitted. "They ain't ever missed the first day of deer season, yet. They're both always there to christen my homemade wine and sample your dandy strawberry brandy."

"You're right there," Ben Turner promptly attested. "Half the fun of huntin' is male bondin', and the other half is getting sick on the booze and the lousy food. Huntin's just an excuse for male bonding, and the fall season's a really good reason to successfully get away from the bossy wives and obnoxious kids. Maybe Judd and Ted are turnin' into advanced senior citizens and boycottin' us this year."

"Nonsense Ben," Conrad contradicted. "Ain't like 'em at all. Those boys have been comin' out with us for over thirty years, ever since they were young bucks. I wouldn't be surprised to see 'em show-up tardy any minute now."

The two keepers of the peace heard a distinct rustling originating from the near woods to their north. The avid marksmen perceptively peered-down into the thick forest from their lofty tree stand. The silent pair deftly raised their shotguns to their shoulders, ready to fire at the sighting of buck antlers. Ben Turner was the first to spot two oncoming forms.

"Jesus, Mary, and Joseph, will ya' look at that!" Chief-of-Police Turner marveled and lowly uttered. "This has gotta' be a mirage. Bears haven't been seen in these here woods for nearly a century!"

"Quiet Ben!" Sheriff Grant commanded. "Don't scare them off with your big mouth. It's gonna' be quite a story to tell if we can bag those two fantastic trophies," Conrad whispered.

Hammonton Police Chief Ben Turner was quite ecstatic. "I can positively see the head of that one on the right hangin' over my fireplace right now," the local cop softly whispered to the Atlantic County Sheriff. "No law says we can't kill bears in *Wharton Forest* because there haven't been any bears here since before 1900. Especially, black bears!"

The two expert shooters took aim at their respective targets, which were clumsily meandering, weaving, and stumbling onward directly towards them. The trigger-happy marksmen studied their quarry as the wobbly bears lumbered onward, desperately seeking the security and safety of human civilization. The doomed creatures were now within shooting range.

Dual discernible shotgun blasts echoed amid the majestic pine trees. Two furry figures simultaneously collapsed to the forest ground. Two jubilant lawmen danced upon their sturdy tree platform, elated at their great achievement, and thrilled by their remarkable once-in-a-lifetime good fortune.

"Too Much Monkey Business"

Inspector Joe Giralo cautiously drove his huge, gray Chevy Suburban north from Route 54 and then across Route 30 onto New Jersey State Highway 206. Seated in the front passenger seat was true-blue FBI Agent Salvatore Velardi, with dependable Agent Arthur Orsi seated directly behind the grim-faced driver, and conscientious-but-reticent Agent Dan Blachford occupying the rear seat behind Agent Velardi. The four government men had promptly departed the Hammonton, New Jersey Third Street Carnival Grounds, but as usual, only the very shrewd Inspector was acquainted in-depth with all of the vital circumstances associated with the team's mission-in-progress.

"I'll tell you, Boss, I don't like the way that certain local traditions are rapidly being dismantled, piece-by-piece," opinionated Agent Salvatore Velardi commented. "Take the annual 16th of July Mt. Carmel Festival, for instance. For over a century, the town church sponsoring the event had been known as St. Joseph, but now with parish consolidations being the vogue," the overzealous passenger riding shotgun elaborated, "the diocese has changed the church's name from St. Joseph to St. Mary of Mt. Carmel. I don't want to sound sacrilegious or anything," Velardi diplomatically qualified. "But it's as if venerable St. Joseph has had a gender surgery performed, and is now transformed into his New Testament Biblical wife, St. Mary. But let me emphasize that it had been the Camden Diocesan Bishop who had mandated the gender name change, and not me! Now Boss, as I said, I fully realize that the changing of names was sort of done out of being politically correct, or should I more accurately say, out of 'religiously correct' necessity!"

"But the local Catholic elementary and high school are still called St. Joseph," reminded don't-rock-the-boat Agent Arthur Orsi. "The controversial name-change to St. Mary of Mt. Carmel had been judiciously decided because the three Hammonton churches, St. Anthony of Padua, St. Martin de Porres. and St. Joseph have now been incorporated into one entity. Obviously, the Bishop didn't want to be perceived favoring the name St. Joseph Church over the other two town parishes."

"Well Guys, at least the identity of the Mt. Carmel Beer Garden that's situated at the rear of the carnival grounds hasn't been altered one iota," normally quiet Agent Dan Blachford merrily contributed to the general conversation. "Say, Boss; why did you use your cell phone and yank Sal, Art, and me out of the crowded beer garden so suddenly? I was just finishing-up gobbling-down a terribly delicious pepper and sausage sandwich!"

"Well frankly, my loyal Confederates," Chief Giralo keenly prefaced. "As you can plainly see on my state-of-the-art government issue GPS tracking device, we're in hot pursuit of a white van that's seven miles ahead of us; somewhere in the vicinity of Atsion Lake. Pretty soon our designated suspects will be passing by *that* notorious den of iniquity, the ever-popular Pic-A-Lilli Inn, the rather unique pinelands' Mecca for area motorcycle gangs and rowdy Wharton State Forest hunters and pineys. I must truly admit, Gentlemen," Joe Giralo pontificated, "this super-advanced 2007 dashboard GPS map is a major improvement over James Bond 60s' tracking technology. It's rather impressive, to say the least! Thank goodness the Bureau's top brass guys sitting behind *their* big desks down in Washington have dramatically increased our budget expenditures."

"Look Boss, I don't wish to be sounding too impertinent or too blatantly disrespectful," Agent Velardi boldly verbalized, "but most of the time you make Art, Dan, and me feel like we're three hapless, incompetent buffoons. We're quite familiar with specific fragments of the overall colossal puzzle we're involved in, but only you and Matt Riley down there at DC headquarters are knowledgeable of the entire big-portrait scenario. In my unsolicited judgment, it just isn't fair! Well, quite realistically Chief; *that* happens to be my exclusive personal conclusion!"

"On the contrary Salvatore," Inspector Giralo answered as the light gray Suburban sped by the landmark Red Barn Farm Market and Restaurant situated on the left. "I must confess; you three professional crime-fighters are a tad more sagacious than Moe, Larry and Curly ever were. I've never especially referred to you three potential geniuses as clumsy Stooges; now have I ever?"

"No Sir, but always being out of the loop does not enhance our faltering self-esteem," Agent Orsi intrepidly stated in support of Agent Velardi's brazen allegation. "And please don't give us your standard enigmatic reply; your predictable cavalier response reiterating the strange notion that 'the true accurate picture is commonly developed in the photographer's dark room'."

"Okay Fellas'," Joe Giralo gleefully chuckled. "I'll fill you in on several essential details, but as is my normal habit, I can't divulge anything that's based on mere speculation. Honestly, in a few days, Matt Riley and I will have all of the principal facts logically organized in neat fashion, and at *that* time, I hope to reveal the whole amazing situation to you three amateur sleuths over a delectable spaghetti and meatball supper at the Maplewood Inn; of course, at my generous expense and treat. But first Sal," Joe Giralo pragmatically stipulated, "please kindly review for us how you had successfully executed *your* very important assignment in regard to this complicated investigation."

After assiduously scribbling-down the aforementioned possible dinner engagement date of Monday night, July 16th, 2007 into his trusty notepad, Agent Velardi reviewed and reported that he had followed suspect Anthony Sullivan's black Lexus SUV from the 400 block Arch Street Holiday Inn in Old City Philadelphia across the Ben Franklin Bridge into Camden, and then all-the-way up the New Jersey Turnpike into downtown Manhattan.

"Just like you, Boss, I also had used the modernized James Bond-type homing device, placing the sensitive signal mechanism in a concealed area under the SUV's rear bumper. It's the same sort of sophisticated electronic transmitter that you're presently using to pursue at a distance *that* white paneled van up 206!"

"Excellent field work, Sal!" congratulated Inspector Giralo. "Notice that the van is now in the vicinity of the Red Lion Circle as we're whizzing past the bustling Pic-A-Lilli Inn. Now then," the renowned FBI Chief wanted to know. "Exactly where in New York City did this obviously unscrupulous, charlatan person-of-interest Anthony Sullivan unwittingly lead you?"

"To 10 West 47th Street, and that's where I soon linked-up with my pal Dan here, who had been nonchalantly staking-out the vicinity according to *your* precise instructions," Salvatore Velardi enthusiastically shared. "Dan had been stealthily following another possible perpetrator named. . ."

"Jamie Miduri," Agent Blachford articulated with relative certainty from the back seat. "Then this Miduri jerk and his probable accomplice Anthony Sullivan proceeded to journey north in Miduri's white van, which incidentally we're now following. It's a good thing that I had smartly attached a suitable GPS tracking apparatus to the under-frame of Jamie Miduri's rather mediocre-looking mode of transportation! I then tailed the vehicle from Manhattan all the way up to Yonkers."

"And who in Yonkers did Anthony Sullivan and Jamie Miduri visit?" Chief Giralo very seriously asked.

"A man named Michael Farren," Agent Orsi confidently declared from the Chevy Suburban's rear. "The three men had a half-hour conference inside Farren's Yonkers row-house, which I had been diligently observing for a full week! Then the three of *us* in three separate cars trailed the white van over to Flatbush Avenue in Brooklyn; that is, until elusive suspects Anthony Sullivan and Jamie Miduri anxiously entered the Farro Plush Toy Company's sole manufacturing facility!"

"What do *you* have to say about those incidental developments that Art had just mentioned, Chief?" Agent Velardi inquired of inimitable Inspector Giralo. "A prospective Irish crook with the appellation Sullivan hanging-out with a suspected Italian thug having the surname Miduri?"

Unperturbed and introspective Chief Joe Giralo intentionally ignored his inquisitive subordinate's interrogative and quickly pointed to his indispensable GPS. "Look Fellas'. The white van is now turning off 206 onto Woodlane, and heading due west toward Burlington City. And I conjecture that it'll be crossing the Burlington-Bristol Bridge in around twenty minutes or so, and soon venturing into Bucks County Pennsylvania, again foolishly making *their* fairly complex caper a federal crime occurring across state lines. It certainly warrants our FBI attention," Joe Giralo confirmed. "Now, which of you three budding Einsteins can tell me where the infamous white van had traveled to after leaving the Farro Plush Toy Company over in Brooklyn?"

Sal Velardi thoroughly explained to his immediate superior that two large boxes had been carefully loaded into the white van's interior and that the itinerant vehicle had then been driven from Flatbush Avenue across the Brooklyn Bridge, and next through the congested Lincoln Tunnel into New Jersey. The unassuming driver had navigated onto the New Jersey Turnpike, and after proceeding seventy miles south, veered-off onto the Exit 7 ramp at Bordentown. Then the van driver motored-down Route 206, ironically stopping at the Hammonton Carnival Grounds on the French Street side.

"All three of us had followed the white van down the Turnpike in our identical black autos; of course, at a safe distance, since we could conveniently monitor the mobile suspects with our various GPS tracking equipment," loquacious Sal Velardi indicated and embellished. "Naturally Boss; Dan's car was first, since he was able to easily hunt-down the villain's rather ugly means of transportation with *his* awesome upgraded GPS!"

Just as the gray Suburban was approaching the EZ-Pass toll of the two-lane Burlington-Bristol Bridge, Agent Velardi had the courage to ask his mentor a very relevant question. "Where do you suppose *their* final destination is?"

"24 Dahlia Lane in the Dogwood Hollow section of Levittown, Pennsylvania," the seemingly omniscient Chief firmly announced with a stern expression upon his countenance. "In Dogwood Hollow, all the streets begin with the letter D. According to my reliable GPS readout," Inspector Giralo added, "you have Dogwood Drive being the circumference of the whole housing section. Inside the oval, you have streets bearing the names Daffodil Lane, Dewberry Lane, Disk Lane, Daisy Lane, Darkleaf Lane, Deepgreen Lane, Deerfield Lane and oh yes, how could I ever forget? Finally, there's our destination; good old Dahlia Lane!"

"But Inspector Joe; how do you know this obscure information about 24 Dahlia Lane?" objected an astonished-but-frustrated Sal Velardi. "Are you inherently psychic or clairvoyant; a true crime-solving wizard, or what?"

Just then, Chief Joe Giralo totally befuddled his three nebulous-minded colleagues by turning-off the low-volume background news transmission being broadcast on Sirius XM Radio, and next inserting an old Chuck Berry stereo music disc into the appropriate dashboard slot, deliberately surprising his already-stunned men because prior to *that* exceptional moment, the nationally acclaimed Inspector had always preferred listening to classical renditions when driving.

"Here's a definite clue that should satisfactorily lead you three marvelous savants out of your very vexing mental labyrinths!" Chief Giralo critically vociferated in his typical, arcane-language manner, which was obviously designed to fully confuse his three exasperated disciples. "I strongly suggest that *you* listen closely to the catchy song's lyrics to be able to comprehensively decipher this wonderfully perplexing riddle."

The 1956 smash-hit "Too Much Monkey Business" was loudly played, and upon the tune's completion, the erudite driver instantly shut-off the radio speakers. "Now then, you fledgling Jack Webbs, what fine clue have you just learned from this remarkable, up-tempo rock and roll classic?"

"Well Boss," Agent Velardi spoke-up. "Chuck Berry sang 'Been to Yokohama, been fightin' in the war'. Does this mystery adventure we're now on have anything to do with Japan?"

"Not even close!" Chief Giralo replied with a prodigious grin evident upon his face. "What say you, Art?"

"Chuck Berry sang 'Army bunk, Army chow, Army clothes, Army car'!" Agent Orsi recollected and mentioned. "Is your friend Colonel Bob Bauers of Delta Force somehow involved in the execution of this extremely intricate operation?"

"Great guess, Arty. But you aren't even in left field with your hypothesis! In fact, you're entirely out of the stadium! Now please Dan; give us *your* educated evaluation of the all-too-apparent significance of the song 'Too Much Monkey Business'!"

"Is some local academic institution in imminent jeopardy?" Agent Blachford deducted and orally summarized. "The unique words 'Same thing every day, getting up, goin' to school' seem to imply and support *that* particular school building assumption of mine!"

"Wrong again!" Inspector Giralo exclaimed and indulgently laughed as his gray Suburban exited Route 413, zipped under the ancient, rusty Pennsylvania Railroad Bridge, and then swiftly turned right onto dual highway Route 13; heading north toward Levittown. "But if my fuzzy memory serves me correctly, I recall that cover versions of 'Too Much Monkey Business' had been later recorded by both the Beatles and the Hollies. Pardon me for switching gears, but by now, Guys," the more-than-clever Chief grimly stated, "the dilapidated white van is slowly cruising around Dogwood Hollow, its occupants meticulously casing the unfamiliar D Street environment in search of 24 Dahlia Lane."

"Boss, I don't want to appear impolite or obnoxious," Sal Velardi guiltily remarked. "But how the heck do you know that the white van is going to stop outside 24 Dahlia Lane? Are you Edgar Cayce reincarnated?"

"Because Salvatore, for the last forty-one miles the van had been following an innocent family riding in a dark blue Ford Explorer all the way from the Third Street Carnival Grounds in Hammonton, New Jersey to 24 Dahlia Lane, Levittown, Pennsylvania!" Joe Giralo adamantly narrated, adding new confusing information, much to his passengers' general bewilderment. "How plain and simple can I actually describe it to you? I mean Sal; I learned *those* valuable nuggets of info' from the targeted family that had been munching sweet junk food at the carnival's all-too-popular cotton candy stand. And furthermore, Gentlemen; the key element to *our* seemingly weird jigsaw puzzle can be found in the song's outstanding title, 'Too Much Monkey Business'."

The Chevy Suburban was gently steered to the right off of Route 13, and soon was crossing the busy north-south thoroughfare and heading west on Haines Road, in seconds, with the vehicle moving past the dried-up Delaware Canal and quickly motoring past the adjacent Windsor Pharmacy.

"That's the Junewood section on our left with its numerous J Streets, and there's Kenwood on the right with its corresponding

K's," Joe Giralo routinely uttered to his still semi-shocked car audience. And after readily passing the James Buchanan Elementary School on the right, Chief Giralo succinctly declared, "Farmbrook is next on *your* side Sal, and now we're coming near Dogwood Hollow with the entrance to Dogwood Drive on our immediate left. I recommend that you have your handguns available for swift action just in case there's an unexpected snag in the forthcoming SWAT-team raid!"

Agent Sal Velardi was about to aggressively challenge his Boss's mental sanity when the highly-focused driver adroitly halted his gray Chevy Suburban along the right-side Daffodil Lane curb, which coincidentally paralleled Dahlia Lane. Then the illustrious Chief Inspector advised his three addled passengers to remain silent while the foursome would view between houses an assigned elite Bucks County SWAT unit decisively moving-in to apprehend the unwary occupants of the now-parked Dahlia Lane white van.

"Ha, ha, ha! Mission accomplished!" gushed and roared Inspector Giralo, much to the consternation of his trio of companions. "As I've already promised, I'll provide all of the juicy data to you three mesmerized Dick Tracy wannabes' on Monday night at the Maplewood Inn; that is, after I confer with Matt Riley down in Washington and wrap-up my latest investigative report. By the way," now-jovial Joe Giralo elucidated. "By Monday evening, I'll be familiar with all of the salient bits and pieces that have yet to be recognized. Of course, Fellas', a splendid four-course Italian dinner will be *your* special treat; my way of commemorating another FBI job well-done! Just remember these dynamic words, Men! 'Too Much Monkey Business'! Ha, ha, ha!"

* * * * * * * * * * * *

On Monday night, July 16th the four refreshed FBI men met at the Route 30 Maplewood Inn's front bar, and were soon escorted by the accommodating owner Jimmy Italiano to a secluded back dining room where the government detectives could conduct their important private discussion pertaining to recent FBI events. After crab meat cocktail appetizers and spaghetti and meatball main course suppers had been ordered, Salvatore Velardi, Arthur Orsi, and Dan Blachford's deep desire to fully fathom all of the prominent details of the 'Too Much Monkey Business' escapade was finally addressed by their often-evasive superior.

"Okay now Guys; to satisfy your intense curiosity, first up, please review for me the names of the dastardly culprits you three had been relentlessly trailing. Matt Riley has given me the official government 'okay' to divulge the mechanics of this most secret case to you rather extraordinary, potential rocket scientists! I'll attempt to make it brief so that we can enjoy the fabulous 16th of July fireworks at 9 p.m. tonight with our families over at the town carnival grounds."

"The punk in the black Lexus SUV, was Anthony Sullivan!" Agent Velardi reflexively exclaimed.

"Jamie Miduri; the Manhattan-based idiot with the lackluster white van having grimy New York license plates!" Agent Blachford orally conveyed.

"Michael Farren; the sinister Yonkers row-house dude!" Agent Orsi incisively communicated. "And allow me to reiterate that the dull, white, decrepit, van in need of a Maaco paint job eventually led us to Flatbush Avenue over in Brooklyn; stopping at the Farro Plush Toy Manufacturing Company."

The courteous waitress delivered the scrumptious-looking crab meat cocktail appetizers to the men's table, and without asking his agents for their additional culinary preferences, Inspector Giralo promptly ordered four bottles of Coor's Light beer along with four large slices of carrot cake to be consumed for dessert. After the experienced amiable waitress departed the virtually empty back dining room and re-entered the establishment's kitchen, Chief Joe Giralo eloquently articulated his rather astounding revelations.

"Well Guys, thanks to our ever-vigilant Washington agents' nimble ability to infiltrate certain radical home-grown terrorist organizations here in the USA," the group leader suavely began his stark exposition, "we've determined that Anthony Sullivan's real name is Antwan Sulimoni; that Jamie Miduri was born Jamal Madari; and that Michael Farren happened to enter this chaotic world as one Malic Faraj. Those three diabolical crazies are all Saudi Arabians by ancestry. And as far as Farro Plush Toy Manufacturing Company is concerned," the Chief very forcefully enunciated, "the shell firm is owned by a not-so-stellar individual named Omar Farrahkan; a very dangerous Egyptian bombmaker now-residing in Brooklyn. I was sure that one of you three brilliant investigators would've finally seen the particular nomenclature relationship between the similar-sounding words 'Farro' and 'Pharaoh', and between the names Farrahkan and the Farro Plush Toy Manufacturing Company. And in the final interpretation Gentlemen," Joe Giralo continued his fascinating disclosure, "this home-grown jihadist, Omar Farrahkan, had his bomb-making laboratory in the basement situated below the stuffed animal toy company; a very convenient front to effectively launder pilfered money for the expressed acquisition of cell phone IED detonations; the powerful ingredients constituting plastic putty-like explosives such as C-4 and Semtex, and the like! This ruthless fellow Farrahkan was a highly-skilled artist at producing high-quality weapons of mass destruction."

"Holy heavenly Houdini!" bellowed an almost-delirious Sal Velardi. "And what integral roles did Antwan, Jamal and Malic play in this very preposterous enemy enterprise? I presume that the three Arab devils were co-conspirators directly dealing with this avowed treacherous terrorist, Omar Farrahkan!"

"Precisely, Sal!" Joe Giralo commended and verified. "Here's the entire big-picture explanation. Antwan Sulimoni traveled from 'Philly to Manhattan to obtain stolen diamonds from Jamal Madari, a dishonorable employee at the New York Diamond Exchange, located at 10 West 47th Street in midtown New York. Madari then visited a wealthy black-market fence named Malic Faraj at the crook's modest Yonkers row-house, one of six safe-house residences positioned all over the U.S. that are owned by the extremely corrupt middle-man stolen-goods' specialist. The pilfered diamonds would be traded for cash to buy additional explosives that the formidable Saudis and their demonic Egyptian counterpart Farrahkan were clandestinely seeking to obtain."

Just then, the very affable Maplewood Inn waitress brought to the table a loaf of soft Italian bread on a cutting board, along with a full bowl of fresh vegetable salad and a handsome-looking cut-glass set of oil and vinegar cruets. When the attractive brunette hastily left the rear "overflow room" to attend to the needs of regular patrons sitting in the main dining area, Inspector Giralo re-commenced his rather mindboggling monologue.

"As I had alluded to earlier, this mastermind criminal Omar Farrahkan, alias Mr. Oliver Farro, was illegally manufacturing C-4 and Semtex, two distinct varieties of plastic explosives. And our very expert Washington DC intel' team had recently learned that the demented Egyptian maniac and his equally warped Saudi comrades planned to blow-up the Empire State Building, since it's now quite difficult to heist a 737 airplane and pilot it into a New York skyscraper as had been done to the Twin Tower World Trade Buildings on that infamous morning, September 11th! Matt Riley and I had believed that the conspirators' Empire State Building attack would soon occur on a work day when the popular edifice would be fully occupied with office workers and tourists."

"And I'll bet that this lunatic Omar Farrahkan of Farro Plush Toy Company, that Jamal Madari, and that Malic Faraj all maintained recently rented offices on different floors of the Empire State Building!" marveled and expressed Agent Arthur Orsi. "How absolutely psychologically deranged those four totally wicked homegrown terrorists must be!"

"Exactly!" Joe Giralo affirmatively answered. "But fortunately, our astute-minded undercover team members soon discovered that the IRS had been investigating Farro Plush Toy Company for income tax evasion, so nefarious Omar Farrahkan had to temporarily hide his new-found purloined diamond cache in a remote safe place; and out of sheer necessity, the nutcase jihadist had his acquaintance Jamal Madari transport two enormous stuffed baby monkeys all the way from Brooklyn to the traveling carnival down in our hometown, Hammonton, NJ. What a phenomenal-but-fortuitous coincidence!"

The veteran waitress, accompanied by a young male restaurant employee, then carefully carried the four spaghetti and meatball entrees to the men's back-room table. The FBI agents gradually resumed their confidential dialogue after being again left alone.

"Well then, Chief," flustered Sal Velardi declared after finally regaining his mental equilibrium. "How did that oddball 24 Dahlia Lane, Levittown excursion and the subsequent criminal arrests fit neatly into your exceptional investigative equation?"

Inspector Giralo momentarily paused, inhaled a deep breath, cleared his throat, and then expounded that the ubiquitous white van had delivered two mammoth boxes of stuffed baby monkeys to the basketball shooting game, located on the French Street side of the town carnival grounds. The basketball-oriented game had been operated by another Saudi, a lower echelon fellow named Sammy Astaire, whose native name was Samir Asir. The low-ranking Asir had made a crucial mistake in recklessly hiring a mentally challenged American carnie bearing the name Frank Dawson. From documented, on-the-scene FBI interviews, Frank Dawson had been asked to manage the basketball shooting game while Samir Asir had been preoccupied at the Mt. Carmel Society's Beer Garden enjoying a fine platter of terrific Italian food.

"But Boss; what about the targeted family residing at 24 Dahlia Lane?" Dan Blachford insisted on learning. "How do they fit into the weird scheme of events?"

"Well Dan, a middle-class couple, Bob and Sarah Abbott of 24 Dahlia Lane, along with their two daughters Sierra, age sixteen and Lindsey, age ten, were in Hammonton visiting cousins Charles and Marie Sceia of Fernwood Drive," Chief Giralo academically disclosed. "I found-out just yesterday that Sierra Abbott is a remarkable star athlete, and more specifically, the young lady's an accomplished girls' basketball player at Levittown's Harry S. Truman High School. At least thirty colleges are offering the talented junior scholarships, since Sierra has a fifty-two percent three-point shooting average, along with an enviable ninety-three percent free throw shooting reputation!"

"Let me hypothesize the rest," Agent Sal Velardi volunteered his personal assessment. "Sierra had beaten the odds, and easily made three consecutive baskets, and so Frank Dawson was compelled to award her the immense baby monkey prize containing the recently transported stolen diamonds!"

"Almost a home run, but no cigar!" mildly reprimanded an animated Chief Giralo. "After Sierra had sunk three straight free throws, she requested the top prize; the first fantastic stuffed monkey that was on display. But then, her younger sister Lindsey yelled that she wanted one too, and at the urging of Bob and Sarah Abbott, mentally-challenged Frank Dawson broke-down and consented to their request to allow Sierra to shoot again. Incredibly, Sierra Abbott made three more free throws and at the doting parents' demand," Chief Giralo clarified, "Dawson entered the concession's rear stock area, turned the huge box upside-down, thus ignoring the warning instruction scribbled on the top ordering employees to not open the package. Next, this illiterate, itinerant carnie named Francis Dawson eagerly opened the box, and then inadvertently presented the second giant stuffed monkey to thoroughly delighted, ten-year-old Lindsey Abbott. But honestly, Sierra Abbott swishing six straight foul shots at a carnival game of chance is indeed positively surreal!"

"Positively unbelievable! What exactly happened next?" asked totally intrigued Art Orsi.

"That evening, the Abbotts drove back to Levittown not knowing that they were being pursued by desperate terrorists endeavoring to regain possession of their pouch of heisted diamonds that had been sewn inside the gargantuan second baby monkey. However, athletically talented Sierra Abbott needed to return to Pennsylvania because the future court hoops' star had just been hired as a summer basketball camp counselor. As a result of *that* development, that evening Bob and Sarah Abbott had to reluctantly travel back to 24

Dahlia Lane. In conclusion," the incomparable Inspector Giralo lectured, "you fine Men must fully understand and appreciate that in the final analysis, most human matters and most people events are basically determined by chance, by circumstance or by uncanny coincidence! And that's precisely how Jamal Madari and Samir Asir had been collared outside 24 Dahlia Lane. Now my stouthearted Companions," Inspector Joe Giralo snickered, "let's indulge and eat to our souls' content, so that we can later tonight enjoy the spectacular July 16th fireworks' extravaganza!"

Agent Salvatore Velardi instinctively raised his brown Coor's Light bottle, extended it toward the center of the table, and then humorously exclaimed in an exaggerated-but-exhilarated voice, "Too Much Monkey Business! Long live Chuck Berry!"

The other three ecstatic diners seated comfortably at the round Maplewood Inn table lifted their separate cold brown bottles in unison, and ambitiously joined the proposed toast, an admirable salute dedicated to the celebrated, sensational 1950s rock and roll recording artist, and his "Monkey Business" smash hit.

"Double Trouble"

Little honor exists between ignominious human beings, and this graphic story confirms *that* very valid social/ethical axiom. Charles Carlucci nervously fidgeted with his wristwatch during another boring Hammonton Lions Club meeting. The apathetic service club member hastily had eaten his delectable veal parmagiana meal, drank-down two glasses of merlot wine, paid a dollar fine to the Tail-Twister (for forgetting to wear his membership badge), and was remotely listening to the litany of fundraising reports. The club's pie and muffin concession stand at the July 2nd blueberry festival had netted three thousand dollars profit, the gold raffle dinner had earned twelve thousand dollars, and the '50s dance committee chairman was now giving his glib presentation on the upcoming event.

After the lengthy civic club meeting, Charles Carlucci deliberately stayed another half hour, conversing with the club's President and with the guest speaker for the evening, the distinguished Governor of New Jersey Lions Club District 16-C. 'By now Hank Cardone has murdered my wife!' Carlucci was thinking as the Governor was commenting on how inspiring and dynamic (and what a model organization) the Hammonton Club was when compared to less active and smaller charity clubs in District 16-C. 'Yes; by now Sandra is dead. All I have to do is pay that scoundrel Cardone $25,000.00, and then after the funeral, collect on my wife's hefty $500,000.00 insurance policy. And I have a great alibi being here at the Lions Club dinner until 9:30 p.m. It sure pays to have out-of-state Mafia connections!' the conniving husband concluded. 'My wife has betrayed me a final time!'

Charles and Sandra Carlucci had been sweethearts at Hammonton High School, and both had graduated in 1960. After Charles attended Rutgers University in New Brunswick, and Sandra eventually graduated from Glassboro State College, the couple tied the marital knot. Then, the ambitious husband became a local new car salesman at a Hammonton GM dealership, and the wife, an elementary school teacher in nearby Folsom. Everything went all right with a son Daniel being born in 1965, and then twenty years quickly passed; but after the Carlucci's only child left the nest for higher education at Boston University, Sandra and Charles' relationship drastically changed. Each accused the other of "cheating", and at least three prolonged arguments developed every week with one spouse accusing the other of infidelity. The couple's happiness bubble had completely burst, and hatred now dominated their rapidly eroding marriage partnership. Things were getting ugly in a hurry, with the relationship's accelerated deterioration.

'I'll hang around another ten minutes and pay the club treasurer my back dues that I owe,' Charles decided. 'I don't want to barge in on a brutal murder-in-progress. I'll wait until Hank Cardone finishes the job without any complications or interruptions. Then, I'll pay him the 25 Gs I have stashed in a suitcase in my car's trunk, wait a half hour for my hired gunman to get out of town, and next phone the Hammonton cops about my gruesome discovery. By the time the police cordon-off the house with their yellow crime scene tape, Hank will be driving across the Delaware Memorial Bridge into Wilmington,' the lazy problem-solving Lion fantasized. 'I'm sure glad I had contacted the Delaware Mafia and not the Philly' mob'. The cops will never be able to trace Cardone because he's told me his next contract obligation is out west in sunny Palm Springs.'

Upon steering his aqua Buick LeSabre into his Oak Road asphalt driveway, Charles Carlucci observed a late model black Cadillac parked beside his backyard garage. 'That's Cardone's vehicle,' Charles determined. Carlucci exited the Buick, removed the black suitcase from his trunk, and after slamming the auto's door shut, the new car salesman rushed across the back lawn and excitedly climbed up the concrete steps leading to the kitchen. Hank Cardone was waiting for his "employer" with his .38 caliber handgun gripped in his right palm.

"I guess you've done the job!" Charles awkwardly began the conversation. "Yes, I can see my wife lying there in the living room. You do mighty good work Hank. You're efficient and professional; no doubt about it."

"Two slugs in the head finished her off!" Cardone bragged. "It's a good thing ya' live far away from any neighbors. No one was around at precisely 9:15 when the rub-out took place; not even any random traffic passing by. Sorry I got some blood on your expensive Oriental rug, Charlie."

"That's perfectly okay Hank, but now you're goin' to have to get out of Hammonton fast so that I can report the crime to the cops. Soon, I'll be callin' the police dispatcher by dialin' 911. And Hank, please don't peel-out of the driveway and leave any skid marks. And I'm glad to see that you're still wearin' your plastic gloves! Ya' never know about evidence; fingerprints, DNA, and the like."

"Ya' got the cash?" Cardone anxiously asked. "I hope ya' didn't withdraw it all at one time from a stock brokerage or bank account!

The more-savvy higher-up State Police investigators will look into that type of thing right away."

"No Hank, I've been secretly savin' this money and keepin' it from my wife's scrutiny for three years now," Charles replied without showing any remorse for his spouse's horrible fate. "Here's all twenty-five-thousand clams in this black suitcase. Thanks for your very reliable services."

"Well now, Charles, thanks for the loot payment," Hank Cardone facetiously answered as he opened the suitcase and inspected and admired his remuneration. "Believe me Charlie, I've earned every penny of it. But before I leave your stellar company, I have something important involvin' arithmetic to say to you. One-half only equals one-third."

"What kind of illogical math' is that?" Charles questioned. "Your arithmetic doesn't make any sense at all! One-half can't possibly equal one-third!"

"I guess that's a weird fraction puzzle you'll never understand!" Hank Cardone chuckled with an evil frown suddenly appearing upon his countenance. "Now, it's time to officially join your wife in the afterlife. I'm not a cheap, everyday, run-of-the-mill thug, ya' know. You shouldn't be so frugal when dealin' with a professional murderer! You oughta' know better than that, Charles!"

"But, but! What's the meaning of all this?" Charles pleaded, almost crying as the widower frightfully and then hysterically stared down the barrel of the .38 caliber gun. "A deal's a deal! Why are you doin' this atrocious thing to me?"

"There ain't no guaranteed ethics when it comes down to basic crime and money!" Hank Cardone countered, his frown gradually converting into a smirk. "Now it's your time Charlie to meet the legendary Grim Reaper! Just remember in your final thought that one half equals only one third! But I assure you, ya' won't be able to figure the math' problem out before your butt hits the floor!"

The hired hit-man calmly aimed his weapon at his most recent acquaintance's forehead, and then without showing any pity or compassion, pulled the trigger twice. Charles Carlucci's body fell to the tan, square-tiled kitchen floor. Since no phone call to the local police would be forthcoming, the ruthless murderer had more than sufficient time to escape the premises, drive back to Delaware, and meet another client. Then, two days later, the very busy Hank Cardone planned to catch a jet from Baltimore out to sunny Southern California. The highly proficient criminal looked-down at his latest victim and smiled at his most recent conquest.

＊＊＊＊＊＊＊＊＊＊＊＊

Before the cold-hearted hit-man departed the grisly-murder-scene, Hank Cardone made certain that he had pilfered Sandra Carlucci's pearl necklace, diamond earrings, and other elegant jewelry from the woman's bedroom bureau. 'This way the local cops will think that robbery was the original motive, and they'll be foolishly searching for clues locally while on the wrong trail. The fuzz will think the Carluccis' accidentally discovered a robber in their house, and then had to face the consequences. That sort of confrontation happens all the time on Action News! Ha, ha, ha! This double homicide might someday be made into a Hollywood movie! I might even be called in as a consultant! Ha, ha, ha!'

The accomplished villain nonchalantly sneaked-out of the house with his cash bonanza, put the black suitcase into his Cadillac's trunk, and after slamming it shut, Hank Cardone climbed into his classy getaway vehicle. Then, the cold-blooded killer carefully removed his plastic gloves and stashed them under his seat. Fifteen minutes later, the ruthless murderer was motoring west on Route 40 heading towards the Delaware Memorial Bridge. But his destination was not Wilmington. It was Smyrna, Delaware.

'There used to be a really neat place down a mile or so south of here in Penns Grove called Riverview Amusement Park,' Cardone remembered as his black Cadillac reached the summit of the landmark bridge connecting New Jersey and Delaware. 'I was thirteen years old when I had won a subscription contest delivering newspapers for the Philadelphia Bulletin, and my reward was a free boat trip down the Delaware to Riverview Park. How times have changed! The Bulletin went bankrupt thirty some years ago, and Riverview Park is now defunct, also. And I'm no longer a paperboy, but I've advanced to doin' big-time criminal activity all over the USA from coast to coast!'

Then, the cunning murderer's mind exited its whimsical mood and seriously focused on the essential business at hand. 'When I finish crossing the bridge, I'll take Route 40 south to Route 13 just past the airport, and then head east in the direction of Smyrna. There's a McDonald's I'll stop at and catch a bite to eat,' the syndicate's dangerous player decided. 'After that, I'll have just enough time to meet good old Danny Boy at midnight in the parking lot behind his Smyrna video store.'

Dan Carlucci was impatiently waiting in his dark blue Honda Accord for Hank Cardone to arrive at the designated rendezvous point behind his "Route 13 Movie Rental Store". When the black Cadillac halted, the store's proprietor immediately exited his automobile with a satchel filled with hundred-dollar-bills, and next Dan Carlucci promptly entered Hank Cardone's vehicle.

"The Smyrna cops are on patrol tonight in this lazy hick town, but at midnight, they're usually at the diner getting coffee and doughnuts. So just to be safe Hank, let's make the transaction fast and sweet," greedy Dan Carlucci suggested. "Did ya' pull the job off? Are they both dead? Did they both die instantly?"

"Sure are, with two slugs into each of their heads," the heartless mercenary hit-man replied. "Your Mother was an easy target. She thought that I was your Pop returnin' home from his lousy Lions Club meeting. When she turned the corner from the hall into the living room, I blasted her twice at point-blank-range," the killer admitted without remorse or conscience. "I gotta' confess; it was a little messy and bloody. By the way, Danny Boy; here's your old key I had used to get in the back kitchen door. The baby still works like a charm, so I didn't have to use Plan B and break into the house. Either way; I'm glad that Oak Road is so desolate. I got a little tense when I heard myself breathin' before the back door lock clicked."

"Great!" Danny Carlucci jubilantly exclaimed. "My alibi is intact. Ironically, I had attended the Smyrna Rotary Club's boring meeting, and hung around the restaurant bar with several members until around 10 p.m. As you know Hank, the video rental business is on a nation-wide decline with cable television havin' 'On Demand' movies, so this cache of cash is really hard-earned money I'm offerin' you in this bag."

"I suppose tomorrow you'll get an urgent phone call from the minor league Hammonton cops about the Oak Road twin killings, and then you'll have to leave Delaware and arrange two funerals after the coroner's office staff performs routine autopsies," the hired assassin speculated and stated. "Be sure, Danny Boy to look shocked and melancholy when the cops get around to interviewin' you. Sorry that I'll be settin' up shop out west, and I won't be able to make the dual viewings at…."

"Marinella's Funeral Home on North Third Street!" Dan Carlucci matter-of-factly finished his hired gun's sentence. "That's the best mortuary in Hammonton. But I fully understand that you'll be out in California workin' on your next important assignment. Here's the dough we had agreed on; fifty thousand cash-on-delivery, and it's all in hundred and in fifty-dollar bills. It's half my life's savings I've kept stashed away from the IRS in my cellar. I'll tell ya' Hank. If I didn't skim profits off the top, then Uncle Sam would definitely own my soul, considering all my detrimental gamblin' habits!"

"Thanks a lot, Danny Boy!" Hank Cardone callously remarked. "It better all be stored in here, or else I'll come back from my shabby motel suite and hunt ya' down and shoot ya' in cold blood just like ya' see on TV. It's been a pleasure doin' business with ya'. I guess you'll have to wait a few months before receivin' your expected big compensation."

"Correct Hank!" Dan Carlucci concurred. "I figure my end will come to over a million bucks, includin' the house that has no mortgage, their bank accounts, stocks, bonds and their hefty insurance policies, plus the three building lots in Florida, and the one in the Poconos. I've thoroughly read their wills and each one would inherit the other's assets, but if both of them die accidentally or otherwise...."

"Then you bein' the only child are the chief beneficiary!" Cardone concluded and verified from past experience with other "clients". "Thanks for the fifty thousand, Danny Boy'! And just to think that your old man introduced you to me at a family picnic when you were still a young buck attendin' Hammonton High. Just like I told your old man, Danny Boy, right before I pulled the trigger, 'one third equals one half'!"

"What kind of strange math' riddle is that?" Dan Carlucci asked the wanton criminal. "How can one third equal one half? I'm no Einstein, but that equation's absolutely irrational!"

"I'll make the explanation good and brief," the unscrupulous hit-man indicated. "Your Pop had paid me $25,000.00 to eliminate your Mom; which I did. I had previously asked him for $50,000.00 to do the job, but your frugal Father was obstinate and refused to agree to the higher amount. Let me tell ya' Danny Boy; it doesn't pay to be a lousy cheapskate in this business, or you're askin' for trouble, but in your father's case, askin' for double trouble!"

"It still doesn't make any sense with the two fractions you've mentioned," Dan Carlucci deducted and related. "One-third can't be the same as one-half, no way!"

"Ha, ha, ha!" the remorseless thug indulgently laughed. "The way I figure it, usin' my very limited high school education, your Old Man gave me twenty-five thousand for eradicatin' your Mom; and then you upped the ante and have paid me an additional fifty thousand to shoot and kill your Old Man. The sum of the payoffs comes to seventy-five thousand smackers. Your Pop paid one-third of the seventy-five thousand clams, and you paid twice as much to have him rubbed-out."

"I get it!" Dan Carlucci exclaimed in amazement. "Pop's twenty-five thousand was one-third of your seventy-five thousand total fee, and my fifty thousand was twice what my dead old man was willin' to pay. So, in effect, Pop paid you half of what I did to have someone killed. But I don't think that your creative math' would work on any Algebra teacher's arithmetic test. Your final answer is just too bizarre and incorrect!"

The two connivers shook hands to consummate the settlement, and then Daniel Matthew Carlucci departed the expensive black Cadillac, and the prospective heir merrily re-entered his mediocre-looking dark blue Honda Accord. Daniel then realized that liars, thieves, plotters, and murderers could only be trusted as cash recipients if the client happens to be the highest bidder in a deleterious Mafia-style auction. 'If Pop had raised his offer to seventy-five grand,' Dan Carlucci hypothesized, 'then he and Mom would be makin' arrangements to attend my funeral. Ya' just gotta' be both careful and lucky when sealing deals with unscrupulous and treacherous Mafia hit-men!'

"Family Resentment"

Established in 1935, the Bronson Family Vegetable Farm, remotely situated on rustic rural Third Road in Hammonton, New Jersey, was a brand name famous for quality produce in food distribution centers along the East Coast from Baltimore to Boston. The business started-out during the Great Depression as a modest truck farm, hauling its freshly-picked and packed vegetables to Dock Street commission houses in Philadelphia, and to Hunts Point food centers in New York City's Bronx.

In 1960, old Joseph Bronson faced reality and handed-over the reins of the reputable operation to his two sons, Dennis and Ben, who specialized in raising asparagus, corn, green peppers, zucchini squash, cucumbers, eggplants, and tomatoes. Over the past several decades, the farm gradually expanded from the original hundred-fifty acres to a huge plantation of six hundred.

The industrious Bronson brothers missed-out on the post-World War II peach boom when the luscious fuzzy fruit was the top producer in the Hammonton area, where over eight thousand acres of the "Queen of Fruit" were annually grown and harvested. But then in the 1960s, blueberries began rivaling peaches as Hammonton's chief crop, and the eight-week short-season "blue fruit" eventually dominated the town's agriculture when the chain-store-popular California O. Henry variety knocked New Jersey peaches out of popularity, and virtually out of production.

But all through the evolutionary transformation from peaches to blueberries (in the local Hammonton farming economy), the Bronson brothers still stuck to what they knew best, growing and harvesting vegetables. even though the Town of Hammonton to this day prides and promotes itself as "The Blueberry Capital of the World". Two shopping centers on Route 30 attest to and verify the municipality's past and present agricultural glory; Peach Tree Plaza and Blueberry Crossing.

Like many working partnerships on various South Jersey farms, conflict between hard-headed owners often arise when one sibling desires to either be the dominant corporate authority in the daily operations, or wants to create and develop a reputation as a successful independent grower on his or her own. The harmony that prevailed between Dennis and Ben Bronson in the early 1960s gradually disintegrated into distrust, discord, and animosity by the year 2000. The formerly compatible owners decided to divide-up all their equipment, assets, irrigation lines, buildings, and families into two separate entities on either side of Third Road: Dennis Bronson agreed to own and farm three hundred acres on the north-side of the two-lane county highway, and Ben Bronson consented to owning and operating the three hundred acres that existed on the south-side of Third Road.

Over the ensuing five years, the two brothers became resentful and envious of one another, and their families didn't openly quarrel or feud but instead, virtually ignored each other, even at relatives' weddings, funerals, Baptisms, Communions, Confirmations, and also at graduation parties. Cousins living on opposite sides of Third Road never acknowledged each other's passing on tractors or in pickup trucks, and the two competing clans pretended that "the other entity" wasn't of the same blood, sweat, tears, and genetics.

In mid-January of 2005, Dennis Bronson really splurged and took his wife and family on an expensive two-month South Pacific vacation, including stops and stays in exotic paradises Honolulu, Tahiti, New Zealand, Bali, and Australia. The Dennis Bronson family returned from their sixty-day hiatus refreshed, renewed, and ready to engage in the redundant annual activities known as planting, cultivating, irrigating, fertilizing, growing, harvesting, packing, and selling their high-quality fancy vegetables. But unfortunately, memorable South Pacific leisure and pleasure soon turned into heartbreaking tragedy. On April 7, 2005, Dennis Bronson unexpectedly died of a massive heart attack after all desperate attempts at reviving him (by first his frantic delirious sons and then by Hammonton Rescue Squad paramedics) had failed.

On Monday evening, April 10th a viewing was held for sixt-seven-year-old Dennis Bronson at the spacious Marinella Funeral Home on North Third Street, and over five hundred local socialites including prominent Hammonton farmers, politicians, school board members and doctors and lawyers filed-past the casket and expressed their condolences to the grieving family. Everyone expected to attend was observed in the long line, but the family of Ben Bronson had been conspicuously absent. In fact, the south side Third Road Bronsons weren't even mentioned in Dennis Bronson's extensive obituary appearing in the Hammonton News, the Hammonton Gazette, and the Atlantic City Press.

And then on Tuesday morning, Ben Bronson, his wife and his sons and daughters did not have the decency or the courtesy to be present at Dennis Bronson's well-attended High Mass at St. Joseph

Church on Third Street, and his subsequent burial in a magnificent marble mausoleum in the First Road Greenmount Cemetery.

* * * * * * * * * * * *

Dennis Bronson was indeed the more gregarious of the two feuding brothers. While sixty-two-year-old Ben Bronson was introverted and introspective, the grower's older "sibling rival" Dennis was outgoing and more "public friendly". Dennis had belonged to service clubs like the Hammonton Lions and the Knights of Columbus, and Ben Bronson contemptuously resented his older brother's cordial nature, especially when the elder Bronson ran for Town Council on the Republican ticket and easily won a seat by campaigning vigorously, and decisively beating his Democratic rival in a landslide election.

Indeed, Dennis had been the more community-oriented and citizen-popular of the brothers. The likeable elder sibling enjoyed public speaking, club leadership responsibilities, and also working the grills and promoting good will at political banquets and at church barbecues. But the local politician further incurred his brother's jealousy when Dennis Bronson had used his political influence for what Ben and his envious family believed to be "excessive and decadent personal gain".

In 1995, the local Town Council had declared a building moratorium on all new house construction to abide by recently legislated, strict, "New Jersey Forest conservation laws". In the early 1980s, the Jersey lawmakers in Trenton had established the creation of the Pinelands Commission, which had the expressed authority to regulate population growth in and around the environmentally sensitive Wharton State Forest.

According to careful definitions enforced by the new bureaucratic Commission, the "New Jersey Pinelands" extended from Absecon just west of Atlantic City to Atco, seven miles west of Hammonton, and from Vincentown seventeen miles north of the agricultural community to Vineland, seventeen miles south. The "Pinelands" had Hammonton and its proud farmers located directly in the middle of the "core area", where building and population growth were both restricted and limited. New houses in the town's jurisdiction that weren't connected to water and sewer lines required approval of the "Almighty Pinelands Commission".

Hammonton farmers were deeply affected by the Pinelands and its governing Commission. Since their land value was now exclusively restricted to farm use property (that would ordinarily be worth a hundred thousand dollars an acre to an entrepreneurial real estate developer), the farm properties were now devalued to a meager five thousand dollars an acre because presently, only other farmers (and no ome else) would want to purchase the available land for agricultural purposes.

Consequently, because of stringent Pinelands Forest regulations, Hammonton fruit and vegetable growers had trouble borrowing money from banks and from farm credit bureaus to conduct their businesses, since their credit lines were determined by using their now devalued land assessments as "collateral". It cost most area vegetable growers like Dennis and Ben Bronson three hundred thousand dollars of "seed money" to get started each spring because big bucks had to be placed on the table to purchase the upcoming summer's fertilizers, sprays and special customized packages (with the farm's brand names printed on them). and payrolls before crops were picked, packed. and shipped, along with myriad other miscellaneous accumulative spring expenses.

Farmers doing business in the Hammonton "highly governed and restricted Pinelands Core Area" were also limited in deciding who could build houses on their property. Their children were allowed to build new homes on three-acre tracts, and desperate farmers had to otherwise have their land divided into ten-acre zones if they wanted to sell those sub-divisions to non-family strangers (with a lot of money) desiring to erect dwellings on such sizable tracts.

Since the very autocratic New Jersey State Pinelands Commission required "core area residents" to hook-up to Hammonton city water lines and to town sewer lines, new growth was hampered by the State in the name of "natural environment preservation". And when the old outdated Hammonton sewer plant began operating at full capacity, a restrictive building moratorium was adopted and enforced, and the Town Council (including staunch Republican Dennis Bronson) had no alternative other than to abide by the State's inflexible, land-use mandates.

The Hammonton area farmers, along with peeved real estate developers, boldly challenged the Pinelands Commission's authority in State courts, claiming that the new environmental laws were "Unconstitutional" and violated the farmers' rights to own and sell land at face value. The disgusted real estate moguls maintained that their "civil rights" to build and make profits were being abused. The costly litigations were aggressively pursued but, in the end, the challenges to State Authority were to no avail. The Pinelands

Commission prevailed and won every legal wrangle intensively argued before sympathetic state judges, and the court decisions maintained that the "State's general good" was being upheld by the intelligent, planned, regional conserving and by the prudent preserving of South Jersey forests, lakes and wildlife.

But the wily Hammonton farmers suspected that the real reason for the "stranglehold" Pinelands legislation (and its accompanying land restrictions) was more than mere discrimination against fruit and vegetable growers. Joseph Wharton of Philadelphia, founder of the prestigious University of Pennsylvania Wharton School of Business. once owned the South Jersey land today known as the Wharton State Forest. Wharton was a venture capitalist at heart whose ownership of the pineland forests (on either side of Route 206 surrounding Atsion Lake and vicinity) had by coincidence seven trillion gallons of excellent pristine water reserves directly under the virgin forestland, and the attendant Pinelands were fed by the close-to-the-surface Cohansey Aquifer. Venture Capitalist Joseph Wharton's grandiose scheme was to pump clean fresh water from the Wharton Forest Tract over to the Philadelphia and New York metropolitan areas and economically profit from his diligent endeavor, but near the end of his life, the nineteenth century investor changed his mind and heart, and benevolently donated the beautiful acreage to the State of New Jersey.

The shrewd Hammonton farmers had suspected all along that the Pinelands building restrictions were not so much about protecting the pine trees, as the State had asserted, but actually about preserving the seven trillion gallons of pristine water lying beneath the forest trees as a reserve emergency water supply for Philadelphia and New York City.

* * * * * * * * * * * * *

In the late 1990's, the colossal rift between the Bronson brothers became more intensified when the Town Council (of which Dennis Bronson was an influential member) passed a resolution to have a new city sewage plant constructed (with Pinelands Commission approval) at local taxpayers' expense. When the Town's petition was studied and finally endorsed by the State, plans for new Hammonton sewage and water lines were quickly drawn-up. With the acceptance of the new high-capacity sewer system, some lucky farmers in the correct "building zones" could then sell one-acre parcels to real estate developers at a hundred thousand dollars an acre, because those properties could now link-up with city water and sewer usage, and did not require sophisticated septic systems and water wells that were very strictly regulated by the supreme New Jersey Pinelands Commission.

Dennis Bronson was well-networked in the community, and through his strong contacts with the City Zoning Board and with his noteworthy "political clout" on Town Council, the elder brother had convinced other people in city government that (with the State approval of the new higher capacity sewage facility) it would be wise and judicious for the Town to have new water and sewer lines installed along the north side of Third Road that was more conveniently situated "closer to downtown." The town politicos supported Bronson's proposal, and in 2002, the new water and sewer lines were installed to Dennis's benefit.

Ben Bronson and his jealous family despised what had transpired in what they labeled "Dennis's selfish and arrogant actions". The older brother's three hundred acres on the north side of Third Road was then much more valuable than Ben's three hundred acres on the south side of the Atlantic County highway. By political savvy and by virtue of shrewd legal manipulation, Dennis's land was worth approximately 60 million dollars, while Ben's property (under the jurisdiction of strict Pinelands' regulation) was valued at only 1.5 million at five thousand dollars an acre (when exclusively sold to another farmer interested in acquiring additional land). Needless to say, Ben Bronson and his family felt that they had become victims of Dennis Bronson's greed and cunning political maneuvering.

In March of 2003 Ben Bronson requested through his lawyer that the original six-hundred-acres be "re-divided equitably", but then the older brother, acting through his attorney's advice, bluntly refused the "retroactive suggestion." Then six months later, Ben had requested through his accountant that his older brother purchase his undervalued land for five million dollars, but the older brother answered through a letter from his accountant that the price was "three million dollars too much".

Finally. Ben ate humble pie and requested through his lawyer that Dennis lend him five-hundred-thousand-dollars so that the younger sibling could avoid declaring bankruptcy, and thus, could continue the operation of his faltering vegetable farm, but the older brother declined to cooperate, citing that Ben's three-hundred acres were no longer considered part of the "family legacy". The mounting antipathy between the two Bronson families was reaching a crescendo. The Bronson brothers were no longer sibling adversaries; they were now bona fide bitter sibling enemies.

* * * * * * * * * * * *

Police Chief Anthony Presti summoned Detective Mark Cirillo into his office (located inside the police department in the basement of Town Hall on Central Avenue) for a private conference. The topic of discussion was the sudden, unexpected death of prominent Hammontonian Dennis Bronson.

"You know Mark," the Chief prefaced. "Dennis Bronson and I were really close friends. In fact, confidentially, I own ten acres of ground on Chew Road between several large sections of the Bronson brothers' farms. I had acquired the ground dirt-cheap after Denny clued me in about the probable lifting of the building moratorium and about the sewer and water lines goin' in on Third Road," the burly Chief elaborated. "I saw my pal's advice as an excellent opportunity to make a good quick capital gain on my recently acquired real estate property, that incidentally Mark, has been changed from farm zoning to residential. That's one advantage of bein' a public official in this town," the Chief expressed to his loyal subordinate before lighting-up his long, fat, expensive cigar. "You kinda' know what's goin' to happen before it actually does happen, and a savvy inside person like myself can capitalize on the special knowledge before it becomes public."

"Well Chief, why did you call me in?" the sharp-minded young detective asked his superior. "Are ya' thinkin' about getting a real estate license, or what?"

"Mark, I'm warnin' ya' to stop bein' so sarcastic and please kindly show your superior more respect. I'm a little suspicious about the circumstances surrounding Dennis Bronson's death," the Chief confided as he heavily puffed on his immense cigar. "I want to see if *you* can dig-up any vital information about possible foul play bein' involved. Your off-the-record investigation might be able to pin something tangible on that rotten skunk Ben, who didn't even have the common decency to pay his last respects to his brother. That's gratitude for ya'!"

The conscientious detective reflected deeply for a moment and then had several inspirations to share. "Well Chief," Detective Mark Cirillo commented, "a couple years ago I understand that Ben had asked Dennis to re-divide their original six hundred acres so that each brother would have the same valued land assessments, but your good buddy Dennis nixed the idea when it was certain that the new Third Road sewer and water lines were to be laid-down. Those combined factors would certainly give Ben a definite motive for wantin' to eliminate his brother."

"A motive does not constitute a crime," Chief Presti impressively articulated while remembering something salient from Law Enforcement 101. "And the exact cause of death was officially determined to be a heart attack. Now Mark, I believe that something sinister might've triggered the massive coronary, but I can't prove it; it's just a suspicion, a hunch without any substantial evidence. And the Atlantic County coroner's office's autopsy found no signs of poison or drugs present in Dennis's body. But I still have an inkling that there's more to his sudden death than meets the eye."

"Well then, Chief. It's rumored all over town in every barber shop and beauty salon that Dennis refused to buy his financially-strapped brother out for five million smackers, but your friend declined and rejected Ben's humble solicitation. And then, Dennis again denied Ben's request for a $500,000.00 loan according to coffee shop conversations. All of these facts could easily provide Ben with a good motive to eliminate Dennis, but like you said Chief, motives don't constitute crimes."

"Look Mark," the Chief expounded on his hypothesis. "We know that Dennis's property is valued at over sixty million with the re-zoning of Third Road, and with the heavy-duty north-side sewer and water lines bein' operational. We also know that Ben feels dejected and cheated because his three hundred acres is only worth 1.5 million if sold to another farmer, because of the lousy Pinelands' regulations. There's still another viable motive, but like we already know, motives...."

"Do not constitute crimes!" Detective Cirillo robotically answered. "So, what do you want me to do, Chief? Watch some old Peter Falk Columbo stories on cable TV and develop some brilliant idea?"

"Stop actin' so juvenile and bein' so damned cynical!" the Chief admonished his favorite detective on the force. "I want you to figure-out some new angle that somehow implicates Ben Bronson in his brother's untimely death. I hate the no-good scoundrel with a passion and would like to see the callow-minded punk put behind bars; maybe not for murder, but for some less egregious offense. It could even be common trespassin', or spittin' on the sidewalk, or loiterin' as far as I'm concerned. Now get on that secret detail and find me something relevant!"

Detective Mark Cirillo left Chief Anthony Presti's downstairs office with a resolute mind to excavate some heretofore unknown, significant facts within the community that were relative to Dennis Bronson's much-grieved departure from this Earth. The investigator did not employ the conventional direct approach; that is, using interviews and interrogations. Instead, the alert plainclothes cop kept his eyes and ears open and closely listened to community gossip. 'If skulduggery were involved in Dennis Bronson's death that had not been indicated in the coroner's bland report,' Mark Cirillo conjectured, 'then surely someone in Ben Bronson's family would eventually slip-up and make a boastful comment to a close friend or to a casual acquaintance at a bar or at a Confirmation party.'

Two weeks later, a very exuberant Detective Cirillo entered Chief Presti's downstairs office, all out of breath. The Chief cavalierly glanced-up from reading the front-page headlines of the Atlantic City Press in order to precisely discern what his principal informant had to divulge.

"Well Mark, what is it?" the Chief rhetorically asked. "Did your ridiculous girlfriend propose to you again, or what?"

"No Chief. It's something more essential and important than that!" Detective Cirillo replied without realizing exactly what his mentor had remarked. "There's something pretty pertinent in the wind concerning Dennis Bronson's death that wasn't chronicled in his obituary, and wasn't specifically identified and cited in the coroner's autopsy report."

"Well, Sherlock Holmes, gather your breath and collect your senses and please tell me!" the usually-skeptical Chief-of-Police characteristically chided. "Get to the point, even though I believe that points are for pinheads!"

"Well, I just contacted the EPA and the New Jersey Pinelands Commission on the phone and discovered that a week before Dennis Bronson's unexpected death, his three hundred acres of choice real estate had failed the State's harsh pollution standards for property development," the Detective revealed to his highly-focused boss. "It seems that the farm ground north of Third Road was saturated with DDT, a banned toxic chemical-pesticide that had been popular among local farmers in the 1950s. His entire farm is contaminated. The ground has been condemned!"

"Were soil tests performed in the past?" the Chief wanted to know.

"Yes, four years ago, while the building moratorium was in effect, Dennis Bronson's farm had passed the environmental tests with flying colors," Detective Cirillo stated. "It's my theory that while Dennis and his family were vacationing in Hawaii and Tahiti for two solid months, that Ben and his sons mutually conspired and poisoned the north side Third Road three hundred acres with an abundance of illegal DDT. But I believe we need additional evidence to substantiate my findings, and build a case against that dastardly hermit Ben and his ornery sons."

"Well Mark, DDT shouldn't be hard to trace because the chemical is both obsolete and forbidden to be used," Chief Presti related. "We might not be able to prove murder, but we might be capable of sending Ben Bronson to the county clinker for a couple years on charges of polluting the environment, for trespassing, for vandalism, and for crop devastation. Now I got a stellar idea that might help us in arrestin' and convictin' that slippery weasel, Ben Bronson. I truly now believe Mark that Dennis had suffered his lethal heart attack wonderin' how his ground had gotten poisoned with an obsolete chemical, and then theorizing who would have the unmitigated audacity to commit such a cruel deed."

"What is your instruction?" the young detective demanded. "Give me your corroborative evidence so that we can conduct a collaborative investigation," Detective Cirillo reflexively laughed as he thoroughly appreciated his slightly clever play-on-words.

"Well Mark, while you were yappin' away, I've just made a brilliant deduction," the egocentric Chief commended himself as was his bad habit. "As you know, I own a fairly large parcel of ground on Chew Road situated directly between sections of the Bronson brothers' farms. Now if Ben and his sons drove their tractors and sprayers across my land to get to Dennis's back acres while the older brother and his entire family were celebratin' their prospective sixty-million-dollar bonanza in the South Pacific," the Chief objectively pontificated, "then some of the poisonous chemical would've leaked-out of their sprayers' tanks and left an invisible toxic trail clear across my ten acres. That'll be all the corroborative evidence necessary to launch charges against that yellow-bellied rogue, Ben Bronson. I order you to get in touch with some soil testing experts right-away and have sand, dirt and gravel samples taken from the main roads runnin' through my property, and then have the evidence fully analyzed. Like they say Mark," Chief Presti elucidated, "there's more than one way to skin a cat; whatever the hell that means!"

"Yes Sir, even though Ben probably caused his brother's death, if we can't get the culprit for murder," the quick-learning detective insisted to his vindictive superior, "then we'll throw him in the Mays Landing County slammer for other less horrendous violations."

"The Pondarosa"

In 1990, Stanley Adler had sold his very successful garden mart, greenhouses, and fifty acres of Colts Neck, New Jersey land to a real estate consortium, and (with his wife Sylvia) moved a hundred and thirty miles south to rural Vineland. The couple had a son, Jason, who was struggling as an aspiring stage actor and who loathed his father's good fortune and his mother's domineering nature. Despite many attempts by Stanley and Sylvia to make amends with their stubborn, impractical, gay son, Jason eschewed his parents' truce-overtures and lived with his male-companion-boyfriend in sunny Glendale, California.

Stanley Adler loved to tinker around in greenhouses, and so the all-too-restive man used some of his excessive profits the business tycoon had received from the multi-million-dollar Colts Neck real estate deal to purchase a thousand acres of prime, virgin, land on Route 47, Delsea Drive near Wheat Road; just several miles west of downtown Vineland.

Stanley and Sylvia had good instincts in regard to intelligent land investments, and had thoroughly researched their Vineland area acquisition, since the rustic property was situated just outside the New Jersey Pinelands environmental restrictive area, which limited housing development and building construction in order to preserve the natural pine barrens environment, and to adequately protect the accompanying seven trillion gallons of pristine water lying beneath the bountiful coniferous trees.

"That's why we used our brains and chose land outside the Vineland city limits and not that similar property we were considering twenty miles north in Hammonton," Stanley orally reviewed with Sylvia. "That's why it always pays to do your homework and use your imagination where New Jersey real estate is concerned. As is often said: Location, location, location!"

"Bravo!" his supportive spouse commended over Saturday morning breakfast. "The Vineland, Bridgeton, and Millville areas are growing like gangbusters, but Hammonton is fiscally stagnant because of the severe Pinelands' restrictions. And we now already have three interested syndicates bidding on our valuable thousand acres. And you're right Stanley about your bright idea that it pays doing our homework, especially the math'."

"That's pretty humorous!" Stanley concurred with a smile. "Our five hundred-thousand-dollar investment has proliferated into a top bid of eighteen million for the planned construction of a mammoth hundred and fifty store shopping mall. Life can't get any better than that! Say Sylvia; do ya' have any appointments for this afternoon?"

"I'll be gone most of the day," the prudish wife informed. "This morning, I'll be at the hairdresser's getting beautified; and then I'm going over to my girlfriend Sarah's place to have lunch and play cards with our bridge club. And finally, later this afternoon, I'll be hitting the Wal-Mart and ShopRite scenes, so as you can see, I have a full plate on my hands. I'll probably be checking back home around 5 p.m.," the wife rambled-on, without ever taking a breath. "What happens to be on your agenda today?"

"I just have to mow the front lawn, since I got the back and sides done yesterday before it started to rain," Stanley related. "It's not that easy taking care of a one-acre property, but after we sell our valuable land to the highest bidder, we'll be on Easy Street, spending the winters in Florida, the springs in California, and the summers and falls right here in good old New Jersey. That is, after we buy a splendid four-million-dollar house near the ocean in either Stone Harbor or Avalon. Ya' know Sylvia, I don't really like Sea Isle City, Ocean City, or Cape May because they get too many tourists there. And Atlantic City is definitely out of the question."

"Okay Stanley, I'll see you later this afternoon," Sylvia promised as she gave her spouse the customary little peck on his right cheek. "Have fun mowing the front lawn."

Sylvia Adler merrily departed the new, handsome, South Jersey ranch home, and Stanley then lethargically ambled-out to the backyard utility shed to fire-up his ten-year-old sit-down lawnmower. Just before noon, a white Cadillac with a twenty-foot-long fishing boat attached to the rear pulled into the concrete driveway of the well-secluded Vineland Main Road home. Three casually dressed gentlemen exited the luxury automobile and approached Stanley, who was just finishing-up mowing his front lawn. The curious rider shut-off his sit-down's Briggs and Stratton engine to hear what his unexpected visitors had to say.

"Mr. Adler; do you recognize who we are?" the first tall, husky gentleman asked without waiting for an answer. "I'm Victor Conrad; but you can call me Vic. And this here is George Griffith, and the third fella' is Alex McMillan. We're the three...."

"The three gentlemen interested in buyin' my thousand acres to erect a fancy shopping mall on Delsea Drive just below Wheat Road," Stanley alertly responded after formally shaking the men's hands from his position sitting atop the old red mower. "I remember you three gentlemen from a meeting four months ago we had over at the Trump Plaza on the Atlantic City boardwalk. Welcome to my humble Vineland home."

"I have a Toro sit-down mower," Vic Conrad voluntarily explained, "and George here has a John Deere; and old Alex has a Kobota because he prefers those Japanese products to American ingenuity. How do you like that baby you're riding; I mean, for reliability and maintenance?"

"Well Mr. Conrad, it's always served me fine. Now let's cut to the chase and find-out what really brought you here besides our common interest in lawnmowers."

"Now, Mr. Adler," Vic Conrad uttered very deliberately, "the boys and I figured we'd come out here and up the ante for your thousand acres from fourteen million to fifteen. What do ya' think of our new offer?"

"To be honest with you, Mr. Conrad," Stanley replied while gathering his thoughts, "there are three consortiums including yours that's bidding on the property and wantin' to build an ultra-modern shopping center to compete with the newly renovated Cumberland Mall on the other side of town. And quite frankly," Stanley expressly qualified, "yesterday I received an offer of eighteen million plus several performance incentives, and the ownership of two of the proposed hundred and fifty stores if I go along with the sweetened deal. Sorry to say that *your* alternate bid isn't anywhere near the highest at this moment."

The three disappointed men debated with the property negotiator for five full minutes, and then Victor Conrad noticed that Stanley Adler had a small fishing boat resting on a trailer parked behind his backyard utility shed. The tall, muscular, astute businessman brought the remarkable coincidence to Adler's attention.

"Mr. Adler, I see you have a fishin' boat, too," the determined visitor commented. "Do ya' enjoy fishin' as much as ya' like mowin' your lawn?"

"More so," Stanley promptly returned. "I don't like to fish. I love to fish, particularly in large well-stocked fresh water lakes like they have over near Glassboro and around Hammonton."

"Well now, we really do share common hobbies!" the slick Vic Conrad noted and stated while his two companions grinned like contented Cheshire cats. "The boys here and I have a terrific log cabin over near Winslow, west of Hammonton that we affectionately call the Pondarosa."

"After the Ben Cartwright homestead outside Virginia City, Nevada that was made famous on the TV show Bonanza?" Stanley curiously asked his visitor.

"That's correct!" Vic Conrad confirmed as George Griffith and Alex McMillan nodded their heads and smiled. "But that ranch was spelled 'P-o-n-d-e-r-o-s-a' and ours is spelled 'P-o-n-d-a-r-o-s-a.' Anyway Mr. Adler, your idea of association was generally right! Now our secluded Pondarosa getaway is situated near Turtle Lake in an area that the local Winslow Village residents call Inskips. The lake's very isolated, as I've already said, and it's stocked with fantastic pike and huge catfish. And since we have exclusive access to the Pondarosa Lodge, we also have the privilege of fishin' at Inskips all the time."

"Well, what are you suggesting?" Stanley bluntly asked. "Are you in the process of invitin' me to accompany you on an exploratory fishin' expedition?"

"Now that you've mentioned it'," Vic Conrad affirmed with his two pugnacious-looking escorts very obviously nodding their heads in approval, "as sure as God made little green apples, you're definitely invited to accompany us."

"Well then, Mr. Conrad, I'll go along with you on two conditions. That I can bring my boat along, and that you and I ride in my car that I'll hitch my boat trailer to," Stanley stipulated. "And when we're on the lake, you and I will fish from my boat, and your two buddies can fish out of yours. Maybe if you fellas' sweeten your cash offer a little bit, and sprinkle it with a few enticing incentives, let's say a total package to the tune of a nice round twenty million, then I'll be inclined to ink my signature to an official contract; first thing Monday morning."

"Okay, Mr. Adler. Your terms seem satisfactory and quite amenable, too," Victor Conrad attested as the deal negotiator appointed himself official spokesman for his more laconic, muscular partners. "Now get that old rusty red lawnmower into your utility shed and we'll help ya' connect your boat trailer to your vehicle. Is that your brown Lincoln parked over there?"

"Yes, it is!" the dedicated fresh-water fisherman verified. "I can't wait to start castin' my line into that lake ya' mentioned!"

"And after we do some serious fishin', we'll have a few cold beers out of the 'fridge over at the Pondarosa," Victor persuasively added. "And you'll just love Turtle Lake. It has a very convenient concrete ramp where we can easily launch our boats. Mr. Adler, you've really made my day by sayin' ya' relish fishin'!"

The old. red, rusty lawnmower was quickly returned to the backyard utility shed, the boat and trailer were connected to the rear mount of the brown Lincoln, and Stanley Adler (with Victor Conrad as his front seat passenger) followed the white Cadillac driven by George Griffith and the accompanying trailer onto busy Delsea Drive, their final destination being Inskips near Winslow Village, five miles southwest of Hammonton.

The conversation between Stanley Adler and Victor Conrad during the pleasant twenty-mile-long excursion encompassed a variety of subjects ranging from fishing to baseball, and from bowling to stock market investing, but not once did the two businessmen discuss the sale of the thousand acres of ideally located Vineland land for the specific purpose of shopping center development. At last, the two vehicles and their attached boat trailers pulled off of Winslow Village's Hall Street onto a desolate, bumpy, side dirt road that led to isolated Inskips.

In another fifteen minutes, the two boats had been successfully launched down the concrete ramp, and Mr. Conrad proposed that he and Stanley engage in a friendly two-hour fishing contest with the occupants of the second boat, George Griffith and Alex McMillan. "The winners get to drink as many beers as they want, but the losers are limited to imbibing just two bottles each!" Victor Conrad mandated and laughed in a jovial tone of voice. "And then Stanley; the disgruntled losers will have to watch the *victors,* including me Victor, ha, ha, ha; and you, ha, ha, ha, drink as many brews as our thirsts desire."

"This lake is quite immense, and also so clean!" Stanley admiringly observed and vocalized. "How come I've never seen it on any South Jersey map?"

"It's our little secret rendezvous that we keep hidden from the rest of the world!" Victor Conrad explained and chuckled. "And when you join our select fraternity, Stanley, you'll have complete access to the lake and to the Pondarosa Lodge whenever your greedy heart desires doin' some serious fishin'."

George Griffith and Alex McMillan were having better luck at the contest's outset, reeling-in several foot-long pikes. But then Stanley felt a fierce tug on his line, and instantly, a gleeful expression instantaneously appeared upon his visage. Soon, the veteran angler was wildly and enthusiastically reeling-in an enormous pike that certainly dwarfed the two beauties that had been caught on the competing boat.

The very thrilled fisherman lifted his line out of the water, proudly exposing a really healthy eighteen-inch-long fresh water fish. The jubilant fellow hoisted the wriggling prized catch up to waist-high level and was about to triumphantly show his trophy to Victor Conrad and also to the two men seated in the adjacent boat. Suddenly, Victor leaned forward and violently pushed his fishing companion into a six-foot-deep section of Turtle Lake.

"What did you do that for?" Stanley complained to Victor Conrad as the surprised speaker bobbed up and down in the six-foot-deep-water. "That was not funny! Get me out of here, right this instant! Now I'm not gonna' sell you my thousand acres, just for spite!"

"We don't really think you have much of a choice in the matter!" Mr. Conrad arrogantly exclaimed. "Pretty soon you'll be feelin' a few hard tugs at your pants and legs."

"What do ya' mean?" Stanley Adler yelled back in a frightened tone of voice just as several tugs confirmed Victor Conrad's rather stark prediction.

"Why do ya' think they call this here remote body of water Turtle Lake?" Victor Conrad joyfully hollered back like a possessed madman as his two brawny colleagues in the other boat let out a boisterous roar. "Besides a few random pike and catfish swimming about, this here scenic lake is stocked with an abundance of hungry snapper turtles that could bite flesh off of a man as if they were a school of piranhas, yes sir. Nice knowin' ya' Mr. Adler!" the heartless tormentor yelled to the duped victim as a pool of blood surfaced and surrounded the petrified hysterical man hopping around in the shallow lake.

"George Griffith skillfully maneuvered the second boat to be parallel to Stanley Adler's "Love to Fish", and then Victor Conrad gingerly clambered into the other craft "Catch of the Day," climbing aboard just in front of the Mercury outboard motor. The three men laughed indulgently at the completion of their nefarious scheme, while poor Stanley Adler's head descended and instantly submerged beneath the crimson-colored water's surface.

"Don't forget to re-install the 'Danger: No Swimming: Snapper Turtles' sign next to the boat ramp," Mafia chieftain Victor Conradi reminded his associates-in-crime, Georgio Griffani and Alexandre Milano. It goes to the right of the concrete boat ramp."

"Boss, I gotta' confess that the Pondarosa story was a terrific setup," Georgio 'the Snake" Griffani commended with a wide grin. "We ain't got no damned log cabin out here in the Pinelands' wilderness, but it's not such a bad idea after all. That imaginary log cabin next to Turtle Lake was just thrown into the mix to enhance and embellish our foolproof murder setup," Georgio noted with very evident admiration for the ruse's success. "But on second thought, Boss, it ain't such a bad notion to make fiction into reality!"

"If Mr. Adler wasn't so damned greedy, he'd still be alive and nearly sixteen million bucks richer," Alexandre "the Brute" Milano (alias Alex McMillan) effectively reminded his villainous "syndicate comrades". "The papers are gonna' erroneously report that Mr. Adler went alone on a fishin' trip, clumsily fell-off his boat, and was viciously attacked and eaten by snapper turtles that he never suspected were prowlin' around in the water. What a shame!"

"And that snoopin' around Vineland that you two guys did the past month has paid-off handsome dividends," Mafia kingpin Victor "the Moose" Conradi praised his henchmen. "You guys figured-out through workin' the grapevine that Stanley's wife was gonna' be away from the house doin' her weekly beautification appointment that she had made at the hairdressers; and later playin' bridge with her card club, and then goin' to Wal-Mart and the Vineland ShopRite, so the stupid dame never got the privilege of meetin' us in person. Only her deceased, money-hungry husband ever got the wonderful opportunity to greet us face to face."

"And Adler's gay kid Jason that we contacted out in California has agreed to sell us the thousand acres for a paltry ten million. He's gonna' inherit the land in good old Stanley's Last Will and Testament," Georgio Griffani reminded his avaricious confederates. "It's a good thing that the kid hated his old man, and that we were smart enough to capitalize on the tense situation. And Adler and his gullible wife never imagined in a million years that Stanley would accidentally die before the sale of their thousand-acres was ever consummated," Georgio verbally reviewed. "The greedy, idiotic fool didn't even trust havin' his wife's name on the deed, or even listed in his Will as the surviving heir. What a pathetic dolt that egotistical bozo was! Only his raunchy kid's name is listed! I've reviewed the whole document in the Cumberland County Surrogate's Office!"

"That only proves that a dead guy ain't worth a plug nickel in the eyes of the law," Alexandre "the Brute" Milano philosophized. "Even if the dumb punk was a multimillionaire before he kicked the bucket! And thanks to our good team work, we knew that Stanley loved fishing, and that he had an old tub of a boat sittin' in his backyard on that rusty trailer. Those facts were bits of information that we could easily exploit. And the imbecile even promptly drove his own car and attached boat to the death scene!"

"Hey, fellas'!" Victor "the Moose" Conradi bellowed with a lusty laugh. "Guess what kind of red riding lawnmower Mr. Stanley Adler was sittin' on this morning?"

"A Snapper!" Griffani and Milano simultaneously boomed in amazed, amused voices. "He was ridin' on a damned Snapper!" the thoroughly entertained hit-men simultaneously declared and then boisterously laughed.

"Swarming Killer Bees"

Of all the baffling crime scenarios that have both challenged and intrigued FBI Inspector Joe Giralo, none has ever been more mysterious and bewildering than the difficult case of the "Swarming Killer Bees", which all amazingly transpired in April of 2012. Accompanied by his squad of loyal agents consisting of FBI men Salvatore Velardi, Arthur Orsi and Dan Blachford, Giralo and his trio of dedicated government investigators have once again relentlessly sought-out specific answers to what had constituted a very sinister, perplexing, but fascinating crime puzzle.

Fatigued Inspector Joe Giralo was on a week-long spring vacation temporarily away from his grueling investigative responsibilities, and the revered sleuth was presently engaged in performing some perfunctory family grocery shopping chores for his wife Gina, who was on an academic field trip with her older daughter's middle school class to the Franklin Institute over in Philadelphia. While casually ambling with a squeaky-wheeled cart inside the Hammonton, New Jersey Wal*Mart well-stocked dairy aisle, the now-domesticated husband abruptly stopped to choose between a half gallon of vanilla fudge or a similar-sized container of butter pecan ice cream. The famed inspector's cell phone rang, and Giralo immediately read and recognized the caller I.D. to be that of his trusty assistant, mercurial-tempered and typically garrulous Agent Salvatore Velardi.

"Hi Sal! What's up?" the call's recipient asked. "I told you not to get in touch with me about FBI business matters during my brief hiatus, unless the message was somewhere between crucial and urgent! Where are you right this minute, Sal?"

"I'm soon leaving Bagliani's Italian Market here on Twelfth Street after I pick-up a watermelon and some fresh lunch meat for my wife," Velardi quickly complained, feigning a degree of bland aggravation. "She claims the melon's too heavy for her to lift and transport from the store and then deposit inside her car, while also trying to stay alive inside the chaotic Bagliani's parking lot. Then, after I successfully deliver the perfect ripe watermelon to my laundry room sink counter," the thoroughly flustered agent continued his exaggerated explanation, "I'm immediately off to Cherry Hill to meet-up with Orsi and Blachford to continue our gumshoe work in the complex, ongoing Warren, Gibase, and Anastasia interstate drug smuggling operation."

"Well Sal, I already know all about the intricate probe that's delving into the burgeoning local drug trafficking crime spree," Inspector Giralo rankled. "Please don't say that you're callin' me about how to exactly select a ripe watermelon! But just for the general record, I always look for a yellow spot on the bottom, an accompanying black withered stem, and most of all; a hollow sound when the dark green item's being gently thumped!"

"Well Boss," Agent Velardi respectfully replied, "even though *this* most recent oddball story I'm about to share doesn't cross state lines, it's all quite uniquely interesting to say the least. Here's the scoop! An adult female named Jennifer Carlson of Medford, New Jersey, has just early this morning been egregiously attacked and killed by a dangerous swarm of fanatical bees while innocently walking alone in the Laurel Hill Cemetery over in Burlington Township. This type of blatant, nature-gone-wild, animal instinct aggression is rather inordinate indeed; wouldn't you tend to agree?"

"Indeed, yes Sal; it most certainly is," Giralo conjectured and then concurred. "An indiscriminate random attack you say? What species of bees? Has *that* essential fact been determined yet?"

"Yes Boss. The stingers that have been removed from the victim's body by the Burlington County Coroner indicate that the invading creatures happened to be formidable African Killer Bees. But according to the most up-to-date available info'," Agent Velardi complemented his personal analysis, "*that* particular kind of lethal bee hasn't yet gotten north of Oklahoma; let alone an insect invasion being able to geographically travel up here to Jersey, and consequently cause extreme havoc, pandemonium, and panic among the local population!"

"From your graphic description Sal, it could be a rogue colony specifically and deliberately harvested by a demented South Jersey beekeeper; perhaps the crazed enthusiast having the necessary skill to develop a demonic hive, and then unleashing the ravaging insects for revenge on some unassuming mortal target," Inspector Giralo evaluated and surmised. "This regrettable event that you've just mentioned could evolve into a fairly big case, if the attack becomes a distinct pattern also showing-up in other places like Delaware, New York, or Pennsylvania. As of now though, Sal, it sounds like a singular weird-but-sensational incident, and nothing more; pretty similar to the analogous classic journalism cliché 'man-bites-dog' example that's prevalent and often cited by editors in the newspaper publishing industry!"

"Okay Chief, I'll do some preliminary background research on this poor, deceased Burlington Township woman, Jennifer Carlson, to determine if she had had in her past any lunatic enemies that would stoop to such nefarious illicit activity, that is, Boss," Velardi scrupulously qualified to his immediate federal government superior, "my professional services being performed with your expressed permission to begin initiating an unofficial inquiry."

"As usual, you have my total approval to proceed," Chief Giralo agreeably consented. "Say, Sal; my weary mind's now in a quandary! Please tell me. What flavor of ice cream do you prefer? I'm at Wal*Mart attempting to select between either vanilla fudge or butter pecan!"

"Definitely vanilla fudge, without a single doubt," Agent Velardi automatically declared. "Confidentially Boss, I prefer the Turkey Hill brand. Now kindly inform me. Where will your exciting travels take you after your nondescript Wal*Mart excursion? Are you off to Siberia, or perhaps Death Valley?"

"After I deliver the ice cream to the kitchen freezer compartment, and the other grocery items to the refrigerator and the pantry," Joe Giralo revealed, "I'll be off to Oak Grove Cemetery where the family mausoleum is finally finishing-up construction. I mean Sal; I don't plan on dying soon, but truthfully, I want *that* major project fully completed so that my heirs will have a place to eventually bury my human remains. The impressive granite edifice can contain six embalmed bodies, and it's only costing me a hundred and fifty thousand bucks to build!"

"Oak Grove's a nice cemetery for a pair of morbid romantics like us to eternally rest in peace," Velardi reluctantly commented. "It's got plenty of tall, shady oak and elm trees, and the ancient graveyard has both history and character. In fact, Boss, I prefer Oak Grove to Hammonton's Greenmount Cemetery over on First Road. Oak Grove dates back to the Civil War era; even before the town was incorporated, I do believe. I suppose I'll soon have to acknowledge the inevitable, also!"

"Try to stay on the green side of the dirt for as long as possible," Joe Giralo jested. "It's usually a lot warmer there!"

"I think I'll purchase six or eight grave plots over there on the Old Forks Road side, while there's still a good selection from which to choose. Maybe someday, I'll be able to afford *your* kind of expensive macabre investment; that is, if I'm ever promoted to the rank of Inspector; that isk of course, after you retire from service Boss," Velardi anxiously emphasized. "Then, I'll be able to legally save enough dough to arrange for my own dignified-and-impressive family stone mausoleum."

"I'll recommend *you* for a decent promotion, when I gracefully retire in twenty-three years," Joe Giralo promised with a very evident, sarcastic chuckle, terminating his humor-oriented remark. "Get back to me after you meet-up with Orsi and Blachford over in Cherry Hill. Quite frankly Sal, thanks to your alert reporting, I've certainly become more than a trifle curious about the fate of this unfortunate lady Jennifer Carlson."

After returning home with his assorted food packages, and then methodically inserting the acquired products into the correct kitchen cabinets and refrigerator compartments, Inspector Giralo carefully prepared a cup of instant coffee, removed two white powdered doughnuts from a cupboard box, and then promptly sat-down at the Canadian oak oval table to indulge in his late morning brunch. 'My age is catching-up with me. I really need this time off,' the serious-minded crime-fighter considered. 'But I also realize that I truly love my meritorious FBI career. I wonder if Salvatore has successfully excavated any additional clues pertaining to the untimely strange death of Jennifer Carlson!'

Just then the land-line phone rang, and Agent Art Orsi's voice was discernible on the other end of the call. "Guess what Boss?" the FBI agent rhetorically asked. "Dan Blachford and I are over here at the recently remodeled Cherry Hill Mall. We're gonna' meet Sal at Maggiano's Little Italy Restaurant for a spaghetti and meatball lunch at around 1 p.m., and we'll be discussing the complicated Warren, Gibase and Anastasia drug smuggling syndicate," Orsi swiftly elaborated, predictably and characteristically pausing to catch his breath. "Anyway Boss, Dan and I know all about the Jennifer Carlson killer bee tragedy over in Burlington Township, but there's been an associated bizarre case that's just been reported on the area police bulletin wires; the new extraordinary situation occurring just forty miles southeast of Cherry Hill, over in Vineland."

"Another inexplicable killer bee attack?" a fully now-intrigued Inspector Giralo hypothesized and assertively asked. "Give me the precise details, Art!"

"Sorry to interrupt your well-deserved time-off Boss! But this incredible news I'm currently divulging isn't any frivolous routine stuff, either!" Agent Orsi assessed and remarked. "An elderly fellow named Jerome Esposito has just been assaulted and violently killed by a vicious swarm of angry bees over in Sacred Heart Catholic Cemetery in Vineland. Hundreds of bites have been detected all over his lifeless body. Apparently, Mr. Esposito had been doing some spring exercise strolling, and before he knew it, the victimized fellow was covered head-to-toe with belligerent killer bees, which obviously, as you're well-aware, Boss, are not indigenous to either Vineland or South Jersey!"

"Yes, and if the deadly killer bees populate all regions of South Jersey," Chief Giralo logically theorized and contributed, "then they'll soon eliminate all native honey bees while they're instinctively in pursuit of territorial conquest! Arty, I want you, Dan and Sal to see if there're any significant connection between Jennifer Carlson and this new victim, Jerome Esposito. Get back to me with any pertinent discovery, or better yet, contact me with any other vital information that you might obtain. One wild bee attack, in itself, is important! Two brutal invasions in the same day! That's absolutely something more than simply being dramatically coincidental!"

"Okay Boss, I'm no Arabian genie escaped from a bottle," Agent Orsi imaginatively responded from his cell phone, "but I'll see what kind of magical research I can organize."

"Alright Arty," Joe Giralo objectively comprehended. "I'll go onto Google and learn some more significant info' about radical bee behavior. Entomology is one science where my basic knowledge is rather limited!"

"You're concerned about studying the origin of words?" Agent Orsi incredulously questioned.

"No Arty! I said 'Entomology' and not 'Etymology'. Entomology happens to represent the study of insects!"

* * * * * * * * * * * *

The following morning, Inspector Joe Giralo was savoring a hardy breakfast while anonymously seated at the counter of the Silver Coin Diner, situated on Hammonton's Route 30, the White Horse Pike. The man's consumption of delectable bacon and eggs was rudely interrupted by a cell phone call from Agent Dan Blachford, who had been secretly stationed on crime-watch surveillance in Cherry Hill with his trustworthy colleagues, Arthur Orsi and Salvatore Velardi.

"Boss, we've got some more pretty bad killer bee news to report!" an overworked Agent Blachford prefaced with woeful rhetoric. "Two additional African bee attacks have occurred early this morning in separate parts of South Jersey. The first gruesome bombardment happened inside the normally tranquil Haddonfield Baptist Cemetery. The victim has been identified as a female named Lisa Serappa."

"Well, Dan;" Joe Giralo calmly stated in declarative terms. "At least these rambunctious killer bees don't discriminate. Yesterday, that fellow Jerome Esposito had been savagely brutalized inside a Vineland Catholic Cemetery, Sacred Heart I believe; and today this newly-discovered woman Lisa Serappa has met her demise in a Haddonfield Baptist graveyard. Tell me, Dan," the sagacious crime crusader resumed his inquisitive narrative. "Describe the second ferocious swarming assault Dan! These very voracious, volatile flying insects don't seem to ever gender differentiate between men and women, regardless of whether the terrorized person that's being targeted is a devout Catholic or a Godfearing Protestant!"

"The fourth horrendous mutilation has just come across the closed-circuit FBI network wire," Blachford almost-hysterically answered. "The latest New Jersey casualty is, or should I say 'was' an independent-minded, backwoods' piney; actually, a neurotic, paranoid loner named Joseph Frederico, who incidentally was horribly attacked by a frenetic swarm while attempting to illegally shoot a squirrel inside Holy Cross Cemetery over in Mays Landing. There was one eyewitness to the ghastly debacle, a completely shocked guy who had observed the grisly onslaught from afar; a now-petrified cemetery caretaker, Stephen Prince!"

"This entire phenomenon is as incongruous as a bill in Congress!" Chief Giralo marveled and commented. "Thanks Dan, for providing the very thorough and efficient update!"

"Boss!" Agent Blachford then very optimistically exclaimed, his excited voice competing with the dissonant din prevailing inside the hectic and crowded Silver Coin Diner. "This very evening, local police, and a competent Camden County SWAT team, along with *your* three FBI men will be raiding the homes of Henry Warren, Jack Gibase, and Antonio Anastasia. We now have sufficient evidence to convict those three drug-smuggling thugs in a federal courtroom, and we're now in the process of obtaining a judge's search warrant. Guess where the notorious scoundrels live?" the on-a-mission agent wildly asked. "The trio are neighbors over here in Cherry Hill, frolicking around on Chapel Avenue! Pretty righteous, ethical, moral, and religious fellows, wouldn't you agree! Of all the ironic absurdity! Warren, Gibase and Anastasia all nonchalantly residing side-by-side on Chapel Avenue, not far from Church Street!"

"Dan, getting back to this rather confusing killer bee swarming mystery," Chief Joe Giralo objectively insisted. "If any more scurrilous attacks occur, especially outside New Jersey, let me know immediately! I'll instantly contact Matt Riley down in Washington and get his direct permission to launch a comprehensive investigation into this enormously perplexing killer bee problem. In the meantime," Giralo bluntly summarized, "I plan on learning as much data as I possibly can about the peculiar mannerisms of these dreadful, lethal, hostile insects!"

"And Boss," Dan Blachford emotionally indicated. "Orsi and Velardi are presently preoccupied doing fundamental research on any unique relationships existing between the four deceased human prey: Jennifer Carlson of Burlington Township, Jerome Esposito of Vineland, Lisa Serappa over in swanky, upscale Haddonfield, and bad-luck Joseph Frederico; found dead over in the Atlantic County Seat, Mays Landing."

"My formerly latent curiosity has now been strongly stimulated," usually stoic Joe Giralo confessed. "I'm just as inspired and motivated as you are Dan to professionally get to the bottom of this totally confounding enigma! If you derive any key connections between the four-dead people and the prolific killer bees," the FBI supervisor imperatively instructed, "get on the horn and fill me in about the relevant details! Take care Dan; and use your trained discretion when dealing with those armed and dangerous Mafia punks! And be awfully careful when dealing with the whole ruthless Cherry Hill mob syndicate!" Click.

* * * * * * * * * * * *

That Thursday afternoon in April, Inspector Joe Giralo was quite active surfing the Internet and aggressively studying the various characteristics of bees in general, and of African killer bees in particular. From his intensive academic inquiry, the conscientious FBI official now fully fathomed that ordinary bee swarming constituted a distinctly natural method of facilitating the insects' regular reproduction cycle, which is predictably demonstrated among honey bees and killer bees alike. A traveling bee caravan is usually in quest of a new colony home. A new royal queen leaves the previous hive, and then is escorted and accompanied to a secondary location by industrious worker bees. A swarm might involve up to ten thousand bees that are exceedingly loyal to the in-transition new queen, and the old queen is left behind with perhaps just 40% of the original beehive population. And also, the mass migration to a new physical environment usually occurs in the spring during the months of April through early June.

'This entire frustrating examination is quite odd! Definitely an anomaly, but certainly not an exercise in futility,' the esteemed FBI Inspector concluded. 'Bee swarms usually *are,* under everyday circumstances, not regarded as dangerous, that is, unless the entire colony feels threatened, trespassed upon, or suddenly invaded. There're only a few soldier bees in the new transitory brood on hand to defend the single-minded on-the-move bee swarm,' Joe Giralo meticulously considered. 'I've also learned that individual bees have little chance of survival on their own. They must be a contributing part of a productive colony in order to feel safe and integrated; all the while sharing mutual food gathering responsibilities for the new queen and her young. And in my superficial cursory analysis, I've also discovered that loyal scouts wander out to explore new-found nectar sources besides also endeavoring to find a desirable safe place for the moving swarm to permanently re-locate!

After reading more information, Joe Giralo thought: But contrary to what I had previously surmised,' Giralo aptly conjectured, 'swarming bees are not wild and dangerous during the initial stages of new colony development! However, if the queen perishes, the remainder of the colony is then placed in automatic jeopardy; the now-vulnerable swarm would be losing its central purpose for social existence! Everything makes sense except these random attacks on South Jersey humans.'

Just then the den phone rang, and the now bee-enamored FBI Chief Joseph Giralo hastily picked-up the telecommunication device from its vertical cradle. "Hi; Arty! Congratulations on your successful Cherry Hill Mafia raid last night! Those three wicked crooks Warren, Gibase and Anastasia deserve twenty-year incarcerations apiece. Now tell me, have Sal, Dan and you unearthed anything significant with the inexplicable bee killing pattern? As I've often reiterated to you and your dependable cohorts, first intensively search for clues. And if you don't find anything tangible, Arty, then stubbornly *search* again! That's precisely why *this* intricate, rather illustrious methodology that I'm at the moment carefully reviewing for you is just what happens to be ingeniously called *re-search!*

"Here's some salient news flash information that's recently been made available to us from headquarters!" Agent Orsi hesitated and then proudly communicated. "New Jersey has company! Two freshly-fierce bee attacks have just transpired around noon in other nearby East Coast states!"

"Okay Art, you've successfully gotten my cerebrum activated!" Giralo sternly answered. "But needless to say, this extremely nebulous bee-stalking scenario greatly defies scientific plausibility! Bees usually only swarm and fly around in a several-mile radius from their original colony; their primary focus being to create a new base of operation. These disturbing killing incidents are at least ten-to-fifty miles apart, so therefore," the experienced FBI Chief dubiously speculated and profoundly articulated, "the uniquely separate attacking killer bee hordes must come from a variety of swarming colonies throughout the Delaware Valley. And besides *that* very obvious common fact, Art, I've just read from reliable sources that swarming bees are ordinarily docile, and basically harmless if left undisturbed!"

"Wow Boss!" Agent Orsi loudly replied with great admiration. "I'm becoming as skeptical as that ancient cynic, Diogenes. All of these fantastic angry bee incidents are indubitably contrary to normal bee conduct. Anyway, I'll get back on subject, Chief. Around noon today, over in Smyrna, Delaware's Glenwood Cemetery, a fella' by the name of Franklin Metz, pardon the forthcoming pun-like expression Boss, but while the designated victim Mr. Metz was merrily ambling about the grounds and then planting pansies in his family's grave plot section," Orsi expounded and then inhaled sufficient oxygen to continue his lengthy report, "the deadly killer insects made a straight *bee-line* and soon swiftly eliminated poor oblivious Franklin Metz from the face of the Earth! The pugnacious militant killer bees mystically acted in a spectacular frenzy, almost as if the ravaging, vengeful swarm possessed a single evil mind!"

"Just like subterranean ants, bees need to cooperate and protect a central queen in order for the collaborative colony to thrive! And please enlighten me Art. What about the parallel abominable incursion to the one that had occurred in Delaware?" Giralo inquisitively queried. "Exactly where did *that* other devastating onslaught happen? And how come all of these atrocious attacks have coincidentally taken place in different town cemeteries?"

"Well Boss, the sixth seemingly demonic surprise bee barrage happened over in West Chester, Pennsylvania inside the normally serene St. Agnes Cemetery. A prominent local small-time politician named Harold Porter was unexpectedly and perversely besieged, beleaguered and soon efficiently terminated by an incensed bee swarm; all happening while the unfortunate guy was simply standing there meditating at a deceased relative's stone monument!"

"Alright, Art. I've heard enough supporting evidence about this outrageous in-progress, cemetery-pattern bee dilemma! I'll dial-up Matt Riley down in DC and get the go-ahead to conduct a full-scale investigation into this extraordinary interstate bee-killing skein."

"Fine with me!" Agent Orsi respectfully concurred. "Sal's been piecing together some exceptional fragments related to this rather fantastic African bee case, and by noon tomorrow, we promise to fully disclose the entire tremendously unbelievable crime landscape to you! This weird killer bee investigation is sort of like putting together an immensely insane jigsaw puzzle!"

"Maybe if we could somehow intercept one of these migrating swarms, then a licensed beekeeper could be employed who could effectively isolate the queen, and then adroitly capture the entire insect gang. Then, our sage experts over at the lab' could examine the individual specimens within a controlled experimental environment to determine the exact causes that are influencing *their* consistent, aberrant, destructive deportment. Keep up the good work Art! I want to praise your high spirit, enacted all for the good of the order!" Chief Giralo complimented and encouraged. "But more importantly Arty; please keep the faith!"

"This killer bee thing goes way beyond religion, Boss!" Agent Orsi opined. "I now do honestly believe that we have to hire the services of a well-trained professional exorcist!" Click.

* * * * * * * * * * * *

Saturday morning, Gina Giralo was traveling in her late-model SUV twelve miles east out of Hammonton on *Route 30* heading to Schuster's Shoes in Berlin, her immediate mission being to purchase summer boardwalk and beach footwear for the family's two daughters. Joe Giralo prudently utilized the coveted, rare, free time to engage-in additional research on the subject of mass bee societal habits within a hive or active swarm.

'Bees don't have motives to kill people like humans do,' the Inspector reasonable contemplated. 'The species merely acts out of genetically programmed instinct; that is, unless they're somehow trained to attack and kill unsuspecting humans by some heinous-minded mortal. And what's so marvelously remarkable about honey bee behavior is that the busy creatures actually accidentally pick-up pollen on their legs while exploring for sources of nectar; thus, unintentionally pollinating area fruit and vegetable crops as the busy insects are simultaneously preoccupied gathering food, while maneuvering from flower-to-flower, their existential purpose being to produce sufficient honey to keep the colony or hive members productive, and also to keep the constantly hungry queen fertile! Besides being potentially dangerous when provoked, these buzzing, regular honey bees are quite vital to the world of agriculture!'

Just then, the Chief's cell phone rang, and the stammering voice of Agent Velardi was instantly recognizable to *his* distinguished FBI superior. Joe Giralo listened intently to his excited employee's new-found revelations. "Boss, yesterday, Art, Dan, and I burned the midnight oil over at the Philly' Office, and this morning we've finally gotten all our ducks in a row," Velardi quite nervously asserted and affirmed. "What I have to disclose to you right now is absolutely astounding!"

"Okay Sal, compose yourself and start again at square one," Joe Giralo patiently advised. "I sincerely suggest that you take five deep breaths and then relate to me your new evidence!"

"Boss, all substantial clues linking the six dead killer bee victims point directly to a certain New Jersey beekeeper named Oliver Norton, who had lived in the village of Elwood, to the east of Hammonton, over in Mullica Township," Velardi orally conveyed via the cell phone transmission. "But imagine this! This suspicious character Oliver Norton in the past had supplied area blueberry, peach and vegetable farmers with honeybees each spring, so that the growers could cross-pollinate their annual crops. But the most staggering aspect about this lone-wolf man identified as Oliver Norton is that this beekeeper person-of-interest had died a year ago, and that his tombstone and attendant grave are in Oak Grove Cemetery. Norton's final resting place is situated about twenty gravestones off the Old Forks Road entrance, just across from Hammonton High School!"

"I believe I've noticed *that* impressive-sized-but-plain Norton gravestone more than once," Chief Giralo recollected and verbally acknowledged. "Yes, I know exactly where it is, because I've just had the family mausoleum constructed on the opposite side of the cemetery's thick oak tree canopy. Everything on the project has been finished except the name 'Giralo' being inscribed onto the granite space just below the structure's pinnacle."

"Yes Boss," Agent Velardi reflexively and courteously replied. "According to the latest online cemetery map, the large Norton gravestone is around ten plots west of the very unique Jason St. John marker. But Boss, wait until I divulge how all six morbid deaths are connected in regard to this formerly cantankerous, deceased Elwood beekeeper named Oliver Norton!"

"I think I have to sit-down in a sturdy chair before you continue your dramatic exposition," Inspector Giralo firmly stated. "My ancient mind can only handle one uncanny, alien iota at a time!"

"Okay Chief. I have my notes all prepared on paper in exact chronological order," Sal Velardi vociferated. "Jennifer Carlson, the first victim attacked by killer bees inside the Laurel Hill Cemetery over in Burlington Township, was once married to Oliver Norton, but the estranged pair became divorced in 1985. And the second deceased individual, Jerome Esposito, who had met his fate in Vineland's Sacred Heart Cemetery, was once a business partner of this now-dead beekeeper Oliver Norton. According to Atlantic County records, the two men mutually owned a hundred acres of land just off the Egg Harbor Interchange on the Atlantic City Expressway. The overall deal went sour when apparently, Esposito fraudulently cheated Norton out of a percentage of the sale's profit. Hence, a feasible motive accounting for Jerome Esposito's brutal death has been established, and it's all verified through valid government deed documentation."

"But if Oliver Norton is currently residing in spirit form in the undefined afterlife," Joe Giralo deducted and verbally shared, "how could he ever train killer bees in April of 2012 AD to enact revenge on his purported Earthly Enemies? Several hidden factors to this mendaciously arcane equation must be missing!"

"And the third killer bee victim, Lisa Serappa, who came face-to-face with her ultimate destiny in Haddonfield's Baptist Cemetery, well Chief; the scorned woman once had sued Oliver Norton, and she actually won a case of sexual harassment against the deceased beekeeper way back in 1992," a perspiring Agent Velardi divulged. "Source records from the court proceedings show that Lisa Serappa refused to date this obnoxious philanderer, Oliver Norton, when the beekeeper had awkwardly proposed the not-so-romantic idea while visiting the woman's father's Camden County blueberry farm over in Blue Anchor. And in relation to the fourth corpse, Joseph Frederico, who had been mauled by antagonized flying bees over at the Holy Cross Cemetery in Mays Landing," Agent Velardi rather ambitiously disseminated. "Well Chief, this Frederico guy had in April of 1997 deliberately shot Oliver Norton in the left leg after the despicable beekeeper had trespassed onto the territorial piney's land, the remote property being not-too-far from the backwoodsman's dilapidated cabin, situated on the south bank of the Mullica River."

"All of these interesting factual events make perfect, rational, investigative sense under ordinary circumstances," the befuddled FBI inspector reluctantly admitted. "But the resolute key detail confirming that this suspected perpetrator Oliver Norton has been dead for a year adds a dimension of hazy confusion to my already cynical, clouded mind. Say Sal; what about the dual out-of-state Delaware and Pennsylvania cadavers! Obviously, scientific clinical autopsies have to be performed by coroner examiners!"

"Well Chief, Franklin Metz, who had been viciously enveloped by killer bees over in the Glenwood Cemetery in Smyrna, Delaware," Agent Velardi eagerly expressed and then paused, "that dead man was once Oliver Norton's brother-in-law. According to a Camden County police report, Metz had severely beaten-up Oliver Norton in 1997 at a bar over in Winslow Township, the loud dispute and subsequent violent altercation resulting over certain stock investments that had terribly gone south!

"What about the Pennsylvania victim?" Giralo asked.

"And as far as Harold Porter being mauled by barbaric-like bees over in West Chester's St. Agnes Cemetery is concerned," addled Sal Velardi cautiously mentioned to his boss, "Porter had moved from Hammonton west to Pennsylvania in September of 2007. It seems that before living in Hammonton, this itinerant fellow Harold Porter had resided in Elwood. Yes indeed, Harold Porter was an incompatible neighbor of volatile Oliver Norton. Well Chief, this guy Porter had legitimately defeated Norton for a political seat on the Mullica Township Council. After Oliver Norton became bellicose and exhibited a plethora of nasty threats to Mr. Porter over the span of four consecutive years, Mr. Harold Porter became totally intimidated with the constant physical encounters and soon abruptly abandoned Elwood for the tranquil, passive atmosphere of West Chester, Pennsylvania."

"Listen Sal, I must wholeheartedly commend you, Art, and Dan for doing an excellent job in compiling a sophisticated history of Oliver Norton's biographical background," Chief Giralo politely lauded. "But this ugly epidemic of killer bee felonies positively transcends history, geography, science and just about any other standard academic discipline, too. Indeed, regular conventional wisdom seems to have been made ludicrously irrelevant by virtue of the accumulative evidence that has been so impeccably gleaned by you, Art, and Dan."

"What's our next step Boss?" Sal Velardi curiously inquired. "Should the four of us venture over to Ancora State Hospital and undergo a comprehensive battery of psychiatric evaluations?"

"Don't be so blatantly ridiculous, or so foolishly facetious when describing serious criminal cases," Inspector Giralo mildly reprimanded and demanded. "I intend to drive over to Oak Grove Cemetery, take a perceptive gander at the large Oliver Norton headstone, and then I'll check-out my newly fabricated granite mausoleum on the cemetery's north side. I need the mental luxury of Oak Grove's special solitude to be able to genuinely assess the myriad, strange facets of this radically labyrinth-like case!"

"Good luck and God speed!" Agent Sal Velardi candidly declared, carefully arranging his nomenclature so as not to offend his austere, no-nonsense superior. "I hope and trust that there's a soon-to-be-found magic silver bullet that'll shed much-needed illumination upon this totally aggravating killer bee mystery."

Chief Giralo slowly exited his two-story colonial home's laundry room, entered his musty garage, and cautiously climbed-inside his late-model gray Chevy Suburban. The car's remote control reliably raised the garage door, and the G-man behind the wheel gingerly backed his automobile out onto his asphalt driveway, and then electronically lowered the dark blue exit portal.

Soon, the rejuvenated FBI detective was turning left off of Orchard Street, and next taking Tilton west to a familiar right onto Fairview Avenue. A left turn onto Fourth Street was soon negotiated, and after passing the Warren E. Sooy Elementary School, the huge Suburban was next steered right onto Walnut Street, which a mile later ended precisely at Old Forks Road. Across from Hammonton High School, the intensely focused Inspector turned left into stately and majestic Oak Grove Cemetery. After passing the noticeably distinctive Jason St. John monument, ten graves down the lane from the deceased sea captain's faded, dull-blue monument was a very outstanding-but-plain gray headston; the huge ominous object bearing the prominent appellation "Norton".

Upon halting his vehicle, Chief Giralo was astonished to perceive a colossal migratory bee colony resting directly upon Oliver Norton's massive granite gravestone; the listless swarm enveloping the total gray area surrounding the very visible engraved surname. The almost paralyzed veteran FBI guru stared in wonder at the bewildering silent spectacle, indeed a rather disconcerting visualization that his awestruck eyes had been witnessing.

'This whole grotesque phenomenon is absolutely surreal!' pallid faced Inspector Giralo imagined and then gasped. 'I'm going to swiftly evacuate this frightening section of Oak Grove and speed over to the safe haven area of my newly constructed mausoleum. Everything's done *there* with the mere exception of the inscription of the family name to be etched just below the apex!'

Just after the now-paranoid FBI Chief removed his right foot from the brake pedal and began applying soft pressure to the accelerator, the killer bee swarm slowly rose from the massive Norton tombstone, and as if governed by a single mental impulse, the entire colony, concealing its protected, regal queen, flew north in precise unison, buzzing directly through the dense oak tree canopy, and then virtually systematically, migrating in the direction of the newly-erected Giralo mausoleum.

Upon arriving at *his* now-eerie destination, the Chief Inspector was both flabbergasted and dumfounded to observe the colossal killer bee colony occupying the two vertical parallel pillars existing alongside the stone structure's recently installed glass door entrance. And much to Joe Giralo's overwhelming alarm and dismay, an assortment of specialized killer bees formed and accurately spelled-out the surname "G-I-R-A-L-O" upon the formerly blank block of granite, positioned just below the tomb's A-frame gray slate roof.

'That does it!' ordinarily non-superstitious Inspector Joe Giralo quickly determined. 'I must honor this repugnant, paranormal omen that's somehow mercilessly haunting me from the sordid depths of Hell! I hereby surrender to my diabolical, satanic, deceased adversary, the undeniably demonic Mr. Oliver Norton! I have neither the desire, nor the wherewithal, or the courageous will to do battle with *this* devilish, supernatural, black spirit! Discretion dictates that I should not tamper with what I can't readily comprehend!' Inspector Giralo fearfully realized.

Finally, Inspector Giralo gained control of his rational senses. 'It's best to avoid confrontation with Satan's appointed evil representative. Mortals are no match fighting the supernatural! I must cease and desist from any futile mission that guarantees a losing crusade against the invisible world's superior-yet-unknown diabolical forces. I seek an immediate truce with this implacable Devil's Disciple, a vile demon whose black soul formerly existed in human flesh as the vengeful area beekeeper, Oliver Norton!'

"What Goes Around Comes Around"

Harold Campbell had led a rather normal life for thirty-two years. In the late 1970s, the boy's elementary school teachers described "Harry" as a "compatible and amiable student". In the mid-1980s, Harold had earned academic honor on the prestigious Principal's List at southern New Jersey's Buena Regional High School, played two undistinguished years of varsity football, and as a senior, the likeable teen scholar was ceremonially inducted into the *National Honor Society*.

After graduating from Buena Regional High, Harold attended *Glassboro State College*. His freshman year Campbell dated Carol Simpson, and the two became amorously involved as college juniors. Following four years of intensive preparation, Harold Campbell finally graduated and proudly became an English instructor at his wife's former Alma Mater, Vineland High. Carol found employment in the same New Jersey school district as Harold had, serving as a kindergarten teacher. The idealistic lovebirds were soon engaged, and after a second year of serious courtship, Harold and Carol became husband and wife.

Carol's doting father was a reputable South Jersey physician. Jason Simpson had spoiled his daughter with the luxuries that accompany financial success. Harold's meager teaching salary could barely furnish the necessities of life: food, clothing and shelter. But the couple's combined wages enabled them to live at modest middle-class standards.

Love and idealism nourished the initial four years of Harold and Carol's marriage. The young husband coached a *Little League* baseball team to an area championship, and Harry also became benevolently active in the local *Kiwanis Club*. Carol was elected treasurer of her Women's Bowling League, and in addition, the wife became secretary of the local ladies' civic organization. The couple's relationship seemed blessed by heaven, and a worthy model for other newlyweds to actively imitate.

After four years of struggling with moody and demanding kindergartners, Mrs. Carol Campbell grew tired of teaching small bratty children and dealing with problem parents along with overbearing school administrators. Harold's spouse yearned for the freedom and the status that affluence had afforded her before she had married Harold. Campbell's "spoiled" wife soon quit her stressful teaching job and commanded her husband to "make more money".

Carol's life up to her wedding day had been a happy one. The teenager had taken extravagance for granted and had taken money and the things that money could buy as expected "givens". Dr. Jason Simpson hated Harold Campbell, saying to close friends at the wedding reception that his daughter's husband had only enough ambition to become a "paltry schoolteacher". After four years of monotonous wedlock, Carol Campbell had to struggle to balance the meager family budget against house payments, groceries, utility bills, car remittances, income tax, and automobile insurance.

"I can no longer go to the mall and shop the swanky stores," Carol confided over the telephone to Susan Jackson, a former teaching colleague. "Married life has been a big disappointment as far as I'm concerned. I now regret it!"

"Well Carol; why don't you just eat a little crow and go back to work?" Susan suggested.

"I'd rather commit hara-kiri than put myself through the nasty torture of again teaching kindergarten," Carol admitted. "Those little rascals can amount to modern day excruciation."

"Well then, how about pursuing other employment outside of teaching?" Carol Campbell's concerned friend suggested. "Certainly, you could find something to earn some extra cash."

"They're all lousy minimum wage positions," Carol complained. "That's all that's available in the Want Ads. Who really desires to be stuffing pills into bottles on an assembly line next to some snot-nosed know-it-all high school dropout?"

Carol's uncle, a prominent dentist in the community, offered his niece some "sympathetic financial assistance". But Harry Campbell was stubborn and forbade his wife to accept any "charity", or "family welfare", from well-to-do relatives.

'Daddy always warned me,' Carol thought, 'that a girl should never marry someone under her rung on the monetary ladder. Now I know exactly what he meant.'

Unfortunately for Carol's dwindling bank account, love had prevailed over her father's wisdom. But after six years of frustration and economic tread-milling, the wife finally admitted the validity of her father's sage advice. Quarreling over money had effectively eroded the foundations of marital trust and respect. The honeymoon was gone. The husband-wife arrangement seemed doomed to failure.

"Harold, how could you be content with your teaching job and the meager salary that you earn?" Carol plainly criticized. "We're actually living like paupers."

"I like teaching kids," Harold defended his choice of profession. "It gives me a psychological satisfaction that's hard to explain."

"Harold, Jerry Gares and Bill Burns used to be teachers too, but they've shown motivation and moved-on out of the classroom and improved themselves," the wife pointed out. "Jerry has a Masters Degree and is guidance director at your school, and Bill's a principal working on his *PhD* with hopes of being a district superintendent. And you; you're still a damned high school English teacher!"

"I'm sorry if that offends you Carol, but if I remember correctly," the husband argued, "you married me for what I was and not for what I had."

"Don't remind me of the biggest mistake of my life!" the irate wife screamed as she slammed the bedroom door and then dashed into the hall bathroom. "I'm the best thing that ever happened to you!"

Carol hated to admit it, but she was bored with her limited economic lifestyle. Other more prosperous couples were taking two-week vacations to Bermuda and the Bahamas, while she and Harold went to the mall movies and strolled in the city park. Carol was aggravated that her spouse was completely content with his lackluster income, and the mediocre lifestyle that it supported. Harold cared little about social status, prestige, *Wall Street,* or Barbados. Friction between the two had become a daily reality. Carol Simpson Campbell was becoming increasingly annoyed at the "lowly shelf of life" Harold's occupation could provide. 'My mother never had to work,' she sadly thought. 'Daddy always provided more than we ever needed.'

The marriage would have faltered sooner had it not been for a very extraordinary stroke of luck. From early youth, "Harry" had always been a dreamer. The English instructor loved to gamble at carnival games and at church raffles. Even in high school, Harold Campbell believed that wealth would come his way, not by hard work, but by him taking dangerous risks. After being pestered continuously by his nagging wife, Harold Campbell boldly withdrew the couple's ten-thousand-dollar bank savings and invested the hard-earned money in gold stocks.

Fortune broadly smiled in Harold Campbell's direction. A wild escalation in spot market crude oil prices sent the value of gold spiraling-up from two-hundred-fifty-dollars an ounce to four hundred seventy-five. The English teacher's speculative gold stocks quadrupled in value within six short months as the price of the precious metal skyrocketed.

"Honey, you wanted money; now we've got some to be extravagant with!" Harold joyfully yelled.

"How much of your windfall is mine?" Carol defiantly asked.

"I'll give you half; twenty-thousand dollars!" the happy husband proclaimed. "I hope that your little bonanza will stop you from complaining for a while."

Carol wasted little time squandering her share of the fantastic profits. She immediately purchased a fox coat, a ruby ring with matching pendant, a lavish Mediterranean-styled dining room ensemble, and a down payment on a new *Buick LeSabre*; thus exhausting her share of the money windfall.

Harry had delusions that he possessed superior writing talent to be a successful novelist. Campbell knew the high school grammar books inside-out'; he studied the stories and novels of Edgar Allan Poe, Jack London, Mark Twain and Arthur Conan Doyle, and the high school pedagogue possessed a very prolific and enviable vocabulary. The English teacher believed that he could make it big in the literary world in a similar way that he had hit the jackpot with his gold stock speculation. Another bold venture would result in good fortune smiling upon him once again. While the dice were hot, Harry wanted to stay "on a roll".

The following summer, the quixotic teacher worked assiduously on his first masterpiece eighteen hours a day, seven days a week from June to *Labor Day*. While his "dumb academic colleagues" were taking graduate courses to advance to higher echelons in the educational world, Harry was authoring the first book of a trilogy of "period novels" he was certain would-become best sellers. When completed, the novels would trace the erotic escapades of a wealthy Southern plantation family from the *Civil War* era through *WWI,* and then into the *Great Depression.*

Throughout the fall months, Harry was so enthralled with his mammoth enterprise that the aspiring novelist figured more money could be made if he published the three books himself rather than have a New York "big house" keep most of the profits. Campbell intrepidly gambled *his* twenty thousand-dollars into his ambitious "subsidy publishing" venture, but no reputable newspapers or journals would review his "vanity printing enterprise". The great project resulted in a disastrous economic failure.

"Daddy always said you were a foolish dreamer," Carol indicted and declared, "and now you have to go and prove him right! You naïve fool! You could've used that money you saved for a house down payment!"

Harold Campbell was extremely depressed because he had grossly miscalculated the press and the public's apathetic acceptance of his work. He felt "rejected"; a total failure. Husband and wife altercations soon led to sleeping in separate bedrooms. Things were becoming bleaker with each passing day.

"Can't I somehow make it up to you?" Harold pleaded to his thoroughly aggravated spouse. "I'm lucky. I got lucky once. I'll get lucky again."

"*I'm* beyond the shadow of a doubt the luckiest thing that's ever happened to you!" Carol mocked and belittled, "And *you're* the most-unlucky thing that's ever happened to me!"

"Carol, you've changed so much since college," the dejected author observed and shared. "Maybe we can go get help. You know, professional counseling."

"The basic problem is *I* have changed since college and you haven't," Carol criticized. "I've grown-up. Your mind is still meandering around in a high school mode. *We've* gone way beyond counseling!" the wife shouted as she slammed shut the modest apartment's hall bathroom door.

Three days later, Harold Campbell's heart was again devastated. Carol had left a "Dear Harold note" on the kitchen table, wishing him "Good luck". The wife explained in the memo' that she had run-off to New York with a well-to-do fruit and vegetable tycoon whose produce business netted, after taxes, a whopping seven hundred thousand a year.

Harold Campbell felt wicked sorrow and self-pity swell-up inside his chest. The jilted fellow decided to take a drive and spill his soul at the Riviera Lounge over on Wheat Road. Campbell talked openly to the affable bartender, who quickly realized that his new-found customer was doing some major-league drinking to neutralize a serious love problem.

"Where did your wife meet this guy from New York?" the bartender empathetically asked.

"I know that a few of the women in her civics club have husbands that are brokers over in the Vineland Produce Auction," Harold divulged. "I'm pretty sure *that* was the basic connection."

"And you think these brokers do business with that big shot up in New York your wife flew the coop with?" the mixologist theorized and inquired.

"Yeah; Hunts Point is probably where his commission house is," Campbell sniffed and replied. "I asked around town, and that seems to be the consensus."

"How's this guy make all that dough?" the talkative bartender asked as he generously poured the depressed English teacher his third scotch on the rocks.

"He sells everything from peaches to onions to all the major chain stores on the East Coast," Harold glumly answered. "He really makes me feel inadequate."

Harold Campbell became a regular patron at the Riviera Lounge. Within a month Harry and bartender Bill "Lefty" Walker became good pals. Walker got Harold to join the Never There Gunning Club, buy expensive season's tickets to *Philadelphia 76ers* pro basketball games, and during the warmer months, the two frequented the Monmouth Race Track up in Central Jersey. During the winter months, the new friends often visited *Bally's Casino* on the famous Atlantic City Boardwalk.

The men had much in common. Both were separated from wives; both liked to gamble, and both were wild dreamers. Their joint fantasy was to gain instant, enormous unearned, tax-free income.

"Lefty, I detest punchin' the proverbial time-clock," Harry admitted as he forcefully rolled the dice at a craps table inside *Bally's*. "I've had it with teaching English to wise guy kids!"

"I know exactly what ya' mean, Harry," Bill "Lefty" Walker agreed. "We're gonna' be in debt up to our eyeballs the rest of our lives if we don't figure-out how to find the proverbial cash cow and stay away from alluring money pits."

"I'm getting pretty tired of reading and teaching Hemingway, Steinbeck, Shakespeare, and Chaucer," Harold confessed. "Lefty, ya' got any ideas on how I can escape my misery?"

The men liked fantasizing the American dream, but each loathed working for it. The dual losers were both lazy, and certainly as contented as non-cash cows. The principles of sweat and sacrifice were alien to their basic psyches.

"I know a couple of guys who come into the Riviera to chill-out once in a while," Lefty confided. "They've tried recruitin' me on several occasions. Try this on for size."

Lefty Walker had made casual contact with fringe surrogates of the local Sicilian criminal element. Several tough-but-dapper henchmen often stopped by the Riviera to obtain "info" on local men that owed area bookies racing and football pool debts. Lefty always cooperated with the interrogating "bone-breakers," and the dreadful thugs liked *his* genial disposition. One goon, Tony "Mugsy" Tomasello, invited Lefty to get started in the business by doing some small "shakedowns" for area mobster Joey "the Brute" Campanella.

In the beginning, Harry was very adamant about not wanting any part in illicit gang activities. But Lefty was a persistent debater and had an edge in the rhetorical exchanges.

"Ya' know Harry, ya' make a respectable fifty thousand a year teachin' school," Walker prefaced, "but after Uncle Sam gets done with ya' with income tax, Social Security, Medicare, state taxes, sales taxes, property taxes; the whole nine yards; you're comin' home with maybe a meager twenty G's."

"You're right with the arithmetic," Harry concurred, "and I can only live one notch above lazy welfare recipients and grungy minimum wagers. The government owns half *our* rear ends the minute we're born, even before we get our personalized Social Security numbers. Everything ya' do that's legit', Washington, Trenton. and Vineland are your fifty percent partners on salary, capital gains, everything. Lefty, there's a lot to say about the benefits of the underground economy."

"Look Harry, I know you love teachin' kids and tryin' to make them academic scholars, but let's face it, you're on a merry-go-round to nowhere," Lefty argued. "I can get you out of that thankless profession and make ya' an instant tax-free soldier of fortune in the crime syndicate. What do ya' say about them apples?"

Two months later, Lefty Walker had finally persuaded Harold Campbell to cross the line from being a pauper in legitimate society to being a participant in profitable, illegal, underworld activity. Lefty soon abandoned the doldrums of mixology, and Harry traded his lectern in for a set of brass knuckles.

"Lefty, did you know that our English word 'left' derives its origin from the Latin word *sinestre*?" Harold asked at an Atlantic City *Harrah's Casino* craps table.

"Why no!" Bill Walker exclaimed. "So!"

"So," Harold went on, "our English word sinister comes from the Latin *sinestre*. In olden times, *left-handed* people were thought to have a predisposition for bad luck, because right-handed people were the majority that did things the standard or correct way. I hope the same is not true for you, because now Good Buddy, you're my new business partner."

"How do ya' know all this stupid unimportant academic stuff?" Lefty asked. "Is your brain a dry sponge, or what?"

"That word *sinister* was on my seniors' 'Etymology List' at Vineland High," Harold further explained.

"I thought you was an English teacher," Lefty heartily laughed. "Science teachers study insects."

"You really crack me up," Campbell cackled. "You're thinking of entomology; not etymology."

The former teacher and the ex-bartender each splurged and purchased a week's supply of pinstriped suits at a ritzy Vineland Landis Avenue haberdashery. Joey "the Brute" Campanella hooked the pair up with the notorious South Philly' Frankie Calabrese gang. Initially, the new "partners" were assigned routine "low risk" liaisons duties. The duo worked in tandem, alternating as "front man" and accompanying "back-up, which was the Philadelphia Mafia's standard version of "good cop" and "bad cop".

The novices picked-up extortion money, gambling debts, thirty-percent loan-shark interest, and the neophytes were introduced to some minor drug trafficking "operations" that were very profitable for all parties involved. In a mere year, the two "privates" moved-up to "corporals", chauffeuring Cosa Nostra lieutenants to Italian-American banquets, to political fund raisers, and to pizza-front operations between the cities of Baltimore, Philly', and Brooklyn.

"Harry, how do ya' like your new line of work?" Lefty asked his comrade-in-crime as the two motored east down the *Atlantic City Expressway* to pay cash for a new black Lincoln sedan for "the Brute" in "A.C."

"It sure beats correcting a hundred and ten eight-paragraph compositions a week, and teaching six pressure-packed classes a day," Harold Campbell, answered, shaking his head. "I taught for almost ten years, broke-up at least a hundred fights, mostly in the school cafeteria. Haven't seen one punch thrown since I've been affiliated with the mob. I do believe Lefty, that the real violence in America is in our schools!"

"So far, it ain't nearly half as rough working for the syndicate as we had thought it would be," Lefty amiably agreed. "Now I'm makin' over a hundred thou' and change; clear, tax-free. Already paid-off my credit cards. All I show Uncle Sam is twenty-grand token income I get from a phony change of occupation to chauffeurin' clients around for the Ritz Spaghetti Company."

"Yeah Lefty," Harry concurred. "Now I report I make twenty thou' legit for teaching English to recently arrived legal aliens from Italy. Of course, those legal aliens are smuggling in dope on their private Lear jets."

"Can't beat the hours we put in, either," Walker said as he sped past the second Pleasantville exit on the busy *Expressway*. "Easy Street smells a lot better than Manure Lane, that's for sure, Harry. The only way Joe-Blow beats the system in the nine-to-five world is

240

when he goes into business, makes two-hundred-thousand a year, gives a hundred thou' to *Sam*, and then uses the balance to live as good as we do now with triple the stress we got."

"Right on Pal," the former educator dittoed while using hippie phraseology from the late '60s. "And I finally found a job I like with short hours and good benefits. Lefty, stop at the next coin-operated washing machine place so that I can *launder* some of our dirty money," Harold joked and laughed.

Johnny "the Turk" Salvo took a liking to the crime organization's two new, aspiring upstarts. The notorious alley hustler employed their "services" to assist in several high-level felonies. "The Turk" specialized in targeting tax-evaders, especially ones that owned small "cash businesses". His men would break into the evaders' houses and then steal "skimmed cash", stashed "off the top" that would never be reported to the *Internal Revenue Service*. When the unwary homeowners were out to dinner, or away on business, "the boys" would break-in and "get the stashed loot". The larcenies were never reported to the police because the money had been "non-reportable" to the *IRS,* and the Feds naturally would want to know how the money was made, and why the victims' dough was not in the bank making a meager five-percent interest, which also would be government taxed.

Lefty and Harold became quite skillful at performing stealth larceny. The duo made strong connections with associates in Chicago, Detroit and L.A. Mafia circles. Soon, both distinguished gentlemen were driving their own Jaguars, owned condos overlooking the Ocean City, N.J. Boardwalk, and Harold and Lefty proudly wore expensive diamond rings on their pinky fingers and exhibited large, gold medallions dangling from their necks. The pair carried false identifications provided by the mob that worked perfectly at airports and at car rental agencies. The two budding hoodlums were establishing "reputations" in the underworld's participation in the ever-thriving "black market economy".

But the ambitious "partners" were now tired of being mere accomplices and low-profile subordinates. The eager gents were driven by greed more than by need. It was time to move up to the next more precarious rung on the crime ladder.

"I wanna' live in Hawaii December to March, and then come back to Jersey for the remainder of the year," Lefty told Harold on a side trip to Ocean City, Maryland. That's my goal; my finest dream!"

"Now that I got a nice car and a decent expense account," Harold commented, "all of a sudden all kinds of gorgeous women are showin' an interest in my masculinity. I used to naively think ladies liked ya' for what ya' were. Now Lefty, I know they like ya' for what ya' have."

"We need bigger and better jobs in the mob," Lefty indicated, "and I wanna' be a big fish in the big pond, and not a tiny guppy drowning in a miniature fishbowl."

"I don't know about that," Harold apprehensively replied before downing his scotch on the rocks at the boardwalk's Dutch Bar. "You're talkin' about a small fresh water pond, but there's plenty of hungry sharks out there in the big salt water ocean," Campbell retorted as he pointed across the Ocean City, Maryland boardwalk at the *Atlantic*. "The higher ya' go in the Mafia, the more dangerous the competition; the more intense the power struggles, and the greater the overall aggravation. That's when ya' have the killings and the gangster wars. Be happy Lefty, right where you are. I mean good Buddy, just look what ambition did to Julius Caesar."

"Frankie the Fish is gonna' meet us here in ten minutes," Bill Walker informed Harold. "The Capo said on the phone he has a nifty proposition for us."

"Be very careful Lefty," the suspicious former high school educator warned. "We're both of British descent, and the guys at the top of this organization are ruthless Sidgees. That's the long and the short of it as I see our reality."

Frankie the Fish showed-up at the boardwalk Dutch Bar about ten minutes late. Lefty and Frankie vigorously endeavored convincing Harold to get involved with performing simple armed robberies for the ruthless mob.

"I don't like it," Campbell stubbornly protested, "because you carry a heater, and if ya' get caught, it represents big time trouble and major jail time."

"You carry a heater already," the Fish pointed-out, "but in the new equation, the jobs you're gonna' do are more specialized and intricate than what you're doin' now for less dough. Ya' wanna' be a small sack of potatoes the rest of your life?" the Fish forcefully asked. "Ya' wanna' always be a lightweight?"

"Well, no," Harold replied with a degree of embarrassment.

"Well then, do as I say or we'll breaka' both your legs and then work on your skinny toothpick arms, too," the Fish laughed.

Harold Campbell didn't know whether Frankie the Fish was being facetious, or if the disreputable thug was being serious, but the former English instructor did understand that *he* was seriously being recruited, and the former teacher did know a few uncooperative "mob sergeants" that had been bruised-up and battered because they had refused to be compliant with their brutal Capos' wishes.

"Okay Frankie, as long as I have support in high places," Harold reluctantly answered. "Lefty and I can work together as a team and get things done without fireworks or unwanted media publicity."

"Looka'," Frankie declared to his sponsored recruits, "ya' gotta' carry the more advanced heaters 'cause ya' gotta' protect yourself in an emergency. The cops carry guns for protection, right? Now you guys gotta' tote one to all your jobs, too! The marks you're gonna' target will be set-up by *our* terrific scout guys. We'll send ya' somewhere to lie low durin' the customary coolin'-off period; that is, after the job is pulled and the smoke clears away."

"Look Harry, the syndicate does all the vital research," Lefty added. "All *we* have to do is execute the master blueprint."

"Okay Fellas', I have to concede. You persuasive guys win," Harold worriedly consented. "But you fellas' make it sound all-too-easy. I don't wanna' be ducking any low-flying bullets."

"I knew you'd eventually go for it, Harry," Frankie commended before chugging-down his fourth shot of *Jack Daniels*. "If ya' know the habits and the whereabouts of your mark, and if the mob tells ya' exactly where the loot's hidden in the guy's house, then in terms of cash, each half hour's work is worth a year of teachin'."

"Why do I need to carry a gun then if the jobs are goin' to be so simple? "Harold asked. "Honestly; I absolutely detest violence!"

"In case the owner comes home unexpectedly," Frankie clarified. "He ain't gonna' be too happy seein' his quarter mill of stashed cash bein' pilfered. But don't worry too much, Harry. That scenario never happens. The gun's only there for an emergency situation that seldom, if ever happens."

"Yeah," Lefty automatically verified. "The guy we're targetin' is prob'ly out hustlin' his wife's best girlfriend. The mark's too busy thinkin' about what *he's* doin' at *her* house while the mark's wife's out shoppin' at *Sachs* or at *Tiffany's*, while you're inside his place for thirty minutes doin' your thing. Doin' *our thing;* Cosa Nostra, get it, Harry? Ha, ha, ha."

"The creeps we rob never report the theft to the cops," Frankie elaborated while still laughing at Lefty's keen witticism. "They're too scared of bein' investigated, and then getting the *IRS* in on the case. As far as we're concerned, their skimmed money they're hiding from the government is just bein' professionally transferred from the mark's pockets directly into our cash accounts. After the quick heist takes place, the mark thinks about his choices, writes it off as a little bad luck experience, and then merrily goes back to skimmin' the froth off the top of his business enterprise, and keepin' it safe for himself."

Harold considered his essential role in the overall scheme of things. The former educator desperately desired to become filthy rich. Eventually, Carol would find-out about her estranged husband's new-found wealth, and soon the avaricious woman would desire Campbell back if the dreamer miraculously became more powerful in the material world than her Hunts Point Produce Commission House sugar daddy. Harold and Lefty talked about their new thrilling monetary possibilities while sailing north on the *Cape May-Lewes Ferry* midway between Delaware and Jersey.

"Well Lefty," Harold summarized, "just like you, I'm also tired of being a rank amateur. As long as no one gets hurt or killed, I'll play hard ball."

"This ferry's rockin' back and forth is makin' me seasick," Lefty observed and related. "I believe it's more dangerous than stealin' stashed cash from an assigned mark."

"Lefty; I don't want to spend the culminating years of my life in ignoble incarceration," the former English authority orated and laughed. "Such a lengthy, grotesque punishment would be exceedingly reprehensible!"

"Harry, stop usin' those fifty-dollar words!" Lefty exclaimed as the distracted ferry passenger threw some scraps from his roast beef sandwich to sea gulls hovering above the ship's deck, the birds scavenging for food. "You ain't in the classroom anymore! Stop pretendin' to be Shakespeare or Homer, or one of those other ancient writers!" the evolved bartender admonished.

"I only occasionally use that kind of nomenclature to improve *your* lexicon," Harold kidded. "That's my rudimentary modus operandi!"

"Listen-up Mr. Webster," Lefty testily commanded, "I only took the Commercial Course in high school. The nuns thought I wasn't good enough for the rigors of College Prep'. And I think Hemingway himself would have to look-up in a dictionary whatever ridiculous jargon ya' just said to me."

The following Saturday, the pair drove up to Boston to attend an underworld workshop on the theme "sophisticated armed robbery when no one's around". Twenty aspiring recently persuaded candidates were now enthusiastic students seated in uncomfortable school desks at "the professional heisting seminar," which was skillfully conducted by Tony "Bananas" Falcone in a warehouse.

Harold and Lefty speedily learned a variety of new techniques to add to their ever-expanding crime repertoire. The twosome mastered how to wear deceptive disguises; they learned fundamental judo and karate maneuvers, and the rookie fledglings diligently studied "situational psychology" should the home intruders be confronted by their "surprised mark" during a heist in progress.

"If ya' guys learn to talk in plain English," Tony "Bananas" explained to his new crop of greenhorn students, "then your mark will understand exactly where you're comin' from. But the less words the better."

Lefty winked at Harold and whispered a corrupted quote the former teacher had once communicated to him, "This won't *culverate* in your *car's cerration.*"

"Lefty, ya' mean to say 'this won't *culminate* in your *incarceration*'!" Harold giggled. "Your use of advanced terminology and nomenclature is quite abominable, indeed."

"Hey over there in the back; what's you jive turkeys laughin' about?" Tony Falcone demanded.

"Harry's a former high school English teacher," Lefty told the others. "And my pal knows the value of usin' small words and short sentences to get the right message across."

"A former English teacher joinin' the mob!" Bananas roared. "That's funnier than a purple pizza pie with polka dot anchovies! A former English teacher learnin' how to talk right to his mark! Ha, ha, ha. Hey Harry, how much does your former superintendent of schools make down there in Jersey?" Falcone curiously asked.

"About a hundred fifty G's a year," Campbell quickly returned.

"Well then, if ya' play your poker cards right," Bananas arrogantly promised, "you'll be easily makin' over two hundred G's *clear*. No taxes, no deductions, period. Your former *super* is only gonna' come home with about seventy-five G's, after taxes. His gross ain't that bad, but his net absolutely stinks."

The eighteen other novice students attending the informative seminar spontaneously broke-out in a raucous round of applause in support of Falcone's persuasive logic. "Bananas" next thought he'd better get back to the theme of his crash course in racketeering.

"Less is always best," Falcone instructed his oddball attentive class. "Especially when it comes to words, less is definitely best. Use your heater and hand gestures to get your message across."

In six months, Lefty and Harold's reputations were rapidly gaining mobster big-time attention from Maine to California. Job orders were coming in from all over the North American continent.

The comrades in crime successfully pulled-off a hundred-fifty-thousand-dollar rare coin and jewelry theft from a prominent Chicago banker's home. Then, the dynamic duo was sent down to Dallas and hit a similar "jackpot" in stashed cash from an internationally famous defense attorney who didn't accept checks from half his clients. Later that same week, an independent Miami drug dealer was suddenly missing a "quarter of a mill'," and a Denver new car dealer was "set-up" and hit for a similar "take".

The illustrious villains fifth big assignment was the mansion of a business tycoon that resided in exclusive West Chester County, New York. The now-confident bandits cased the vast Tudor estate for a week while manning various mobbed-owned vehicles. The studious pair had received background information that the mogul and his mistress were scheduled to attend a charity benefit dinner that Saturday night. Lefty and Harold impatiently waited in their television repair van until a white limo' pulled-up. Five minutes later, the expensive vehicle whisked the unsuspecting couple away in the direction of Manhattan.

A black Lincoln Continental and a gray Mercedes had been parked in the majestic Tudor home's brick-paved driveway. The neighborhood was quiet except for some noisy teenagers playing basketball in a nearby resident's yard. Harold and Lefty both donned ski masks, and next meticulously put on their thin rubber gloves. The partners-in-crime brought along pistols and some rope should the trespassing confiscators be forced to tie-up any unexpected servants or visitors that might be inside the house.

Lefty even carried two sets of handcuffs should the restraining devices be needed. The highly-focused robbers cut across the estate's well-manicured lawn, which was bordered by neatly cut evergreen shrubs and rhododendron bushes. The bold thieves dashed through the late twilight shadows, their sprint heading directly to the mansion's laundry room door. Before using his trusty master key, Harold tried the lock. "It's open," Campbell noted to his partner with a degree of amazement evident in his voice's whisper.

"Why not?" Lefty softly replied. "No crimes have been committed in this area of town for years. Maybe decades!"

The stealthy encroachers were inside the suburban estate in a matter of seconds. They furtively advanced with guns drawn through the spacious den. The trespassers leaped-up two steps to a magnificent kitchen that featured Canadian-oak paneled cabinets and matching wood-façade, major appliances. Harold and Lefty had no time to stop and admire the beautiful orange and green patterned

Italian tile that they soon scurried across. "They don't turn the lights out in this neck of the woods," Lefty observed and remarked.

"Electric bills don't matter one iota to them," Harold returned. "I suppose that the handsome dividends from their utility stocks matter just a little bit more than utility fees."

The pair darted-down a wide hallway to an immense spiral staircase. An elaborate crystal chandelier hung over the luxurious manor's front foyer entrance. Harold and Lefty ascended the steps, and flung open the master bedroom door. No one was in the room, so Harold searched the bureau drawers and immediately found three diamond rings, eight pair of expensive earrings, three gold pendants, two pearl necklaces, and a stunning woman's watch studded with dazzling rubies and sparkling diamonds.

Lefty adroitly located the homeowner's safe, which was unimaginatively hidden behind a painting on a side bedroom wall, and using the secret combination obtained by sophisticated Mafia intelligence, the Mafia thief opened the door in a jiffy. The already bundled hundred-dollar bills were quickly stuffed inside a laundry bag, and the two audacious pilferers quietly retraced their path down the spiral staircase to the expensive kitchen, and then retreated back to the mudroom.

"That was too easy," Lefty admitted, breathing a sigh of relief. "A real honest-to-goodness snap."

"Let's have ourselves a swell bonus tonight," Harold intrepidly suggested. "The lights are out next door. Let's hit that place, too. There's no car parked in the driveway."

"What about in the garage?" Bill Walker curiously asked his adventuresome companion.

"It really doesn't matter. We've both been very well-trained," Harold reminded his wary accomplice. "If people are home, Bananas Falcone told us how to handle 'em. Remember Lefty; we're each accomplished professional crooks, now."

The brazen burglars slouched-down and slinked and skulked their way across the freshly cut lawn to the neighbor's opulent residence, almost an exact facsimile to the beautiful palace the two had just robbed. This time the laundry room door had been locked, but Lefty's dependable master key did the trick.

The robbers donned their trusty ski masks, entered the fabulous house, made it through the kitchen to the spiral staircase, and then confidently vaulted-up the white-rugged steps. Harold flung open the master bedroom door and regrettably caught the horrified owner trying to insert a cufflink into his starched shirt.

"Nice tuxedo you have there," Harold Campbell yelled through his gruesome-looking ski mask as the brazen intruder noticed the formal white jacket upon a green and white brocaded chair, while menacingly pointing his heater directly at the horrified resident.

"Make one false move," Lefty loudly threatened from behind his ski mask, "and your brains will be oozin' out of your skull."

"Don't shoot!" the rich man pleaded. "I'll do anything you say! Just don't shoot! I value my life over property!"

"Just listen very carefully," Walker austerely demanded. "We only want your money; not your cherished life! Play ball with us and you'll live to see tomorrow."

The on-a-mission robbers then forced the alarmed victim onto the bedroom's very plush Oriental rug. Lefty held his pistol next to the fat man's temple to further intimidate the already-exasperated multimillionaire. Beads of sweat were forming on the petrified suburban aristocrat's balding head.

"We know ya' got money stashed," Harold declaratively stated. "Tell us where your safe is, and give the right combination; or you'll soon be baskin' in Hades with Napoleon, Hitler and Caesar. You'll be history! Dead! Get it? Now take your time, speak slow, and get it right on the first attempt," Lefty ordered the corpulent victim. "If ya' screw-up, I might have to blow your temple right off your noggin because I got little patience and have a very itchy trigger finger."

The distraught, obese, bald man was now trapped in Harold's mighty headlock, and the encumbered victim's air supply was being cut-off. The tense gentleman was snorting in panic, sounding like a wounded wild boar. Under extreme duress, the duped homeowner managed to gain enough composure to provide the essential information that had been requested. Harold released his choker hold, but Lefty Walker still threateningly pointed his gun at the petrified man's right temple.

"The safe's located in the wall behind the full-length mink coat; in the walk-in closet!" the frightened victim gasped, sounding like someone having a major panic attack. "The combination is twenty-seven left, thirteen right, after a full circle, and six left," he panted.

"Ya' sure about that!" Harold emphasized as he again grabbed the jittery fat man's neck and applied more pressure.

"I'm sure!" the exhausted mansion dweller exhaled. "Please don't kill me! I'll cooperate fully!" the very scared occupant cried.

An alarmed female voice then yelled-out from behind the master bedroom's bathroom door. "Charles, is everything all right? Who are you talking to? Or is it only the television I hear with the volume turned-up?"

Harold's ears instantly pricked-up, and his eyes widened when the Mafia hit-man acutely heard the enunciation of those rather ordinary words. The apprehensive woman continued speaking from behind the closed bathroom door.

"Charles, who in the world were you talking to?"

Lefty impressively reached into the right-hand pocket of his jacket and found the roll of duct tape he was searching for. The Mafia trainee quickly ripped-off a length, and then stretched the wide piece of duct tape straight across the portly husband's mouth. Walker then gave his partner several instructions.

"I've got the cuffs. Let go of the guy's arm and throat, and I'll shackle him to the bed's brass headboard. You go take care of the dame yelling in the bathroom," Walker instructed Campbell. "I'll hit the safe and grab the loot!"

While Lefty skillfully applied the manacles to his terrified hostage, Harold kicked-open the master bathroom door. Campbell grabbed the hysterical woman, grappled with her for a second, spun the blonde lady around to face his frightening ski mask camouflage, and after her shower towel fell to the tiled floor, the totally delirious naked woman let out an ear-shattering scream.

Harold Campbell became a man possessed. The now-incensed thief threw the appalled female to the tiled floor, removed a blackjack from his back pocket, and then knocked the frantic screamer unconscious with two swift strikes. The almost-berserk intruder reached into his other back pocket and removed *his* roll of adhesive tape, which Harold mentally measured and then ripped, smoothing the outer surface against the beautiful, limp woman's mouth and lips.

The desperate thief quickly left the master bathroom and stepped to the phone, which was on the table next to the bed. Campbell wildly yanked the jack wire from the wall, and then pulled the other end from the back of the telephone. Harold quickly scurried to the dresser, flipped open a mint-green, cameo-lidded jewelry box, and euphorically removed three precious rings, six sets of stunning earrings, and four lavishly decorated jeweled pendants.

After stuffing the newly discovered gems inside his pants' pockets, Harry Campbell stepped rapidly to the elegant master bathroom, lifted the unconscious woman up over his shoulder like Quasimodo handling La Esmerelda, and with dynamic dispatch, made his sinister way to the spiral stairway overlooking the mansion's palatial pink marble foyer.

Harold violently threw the woman onto the thick, plush, tan carpet as if he were dropping a heavy sack of Texas onions. The almost-possessed thief dragged the listless woman feet first and face-down to the wooden banister, pushed her heels and ankles through the separations, hoisted her up, and then tossed the nude female backwards over the handrail. The lady's body was anchored to the banister by her feet and knees, which were positioned on opposite sides of the banister's spokes. The beautiful, naked form resembled a circus trapeze performer dangling upside-down.

To further tether his victim to the banister, Harold Campbell shrewdly tied the telephone wire he had taken from the master bedroom around the woman's legs, and then wrapped the cord around the closest banister spokes.

Harold momentarily came-out of his in-progress trance when his perceptive ears discerned footsteps shuffling in the distance, approaching the upstairs hallway in his direction. Lefty had stuffed an additional two hundred thousand dollars into the burgeoning laundry bag, and the accomplished accomplice now-needed a pillowcase in which to fit the rest of the booty. Bill Walker stopped in a hurry when the larcenist shockingly observed the result of his partner's recent mania.

"Are you super nuts, Harry?" Lefty vehemently screamed. "You some kind of sadist psycho' I didn't know about? I think, Tarzan, that you've fallen-off your flimsy vine once too often!"

"I'll explain later," Harold managed to pant through the mouth hole in his hideous-in-appearance ski mask.

"That broad's beautiful, but she looks like she's dead hangin' there like that!" Lefty stuttered as was his habit when excessively nervous. "Let's get the hell outa' here before we spend fifty years apiece in the nearest slammer!"

The Mafia men exited the resplendent mansion with extreme cautious. The thieves ducked-down and scurried across the manor's picturesque lawn, and next quickly hopped into the stolen television service van that had been part of their marvelous deception. Lefty started the engine and slowly steered the vehicle away from the curb. The escape vehicle was piloted very deliberately down the wide street, which was lined on both sides with similar castles to the ones the robbers had just competently burglarized.

Lefty pulled-off his cumbersome ski mask, and then Harold did likewise. "Okay Einstein, now that we're away from there, what in God's name has gotten into you?" Walker indicted and exclaimed. "Why did ya' go totally bonkers back there on that gorgeous broad?"

250

"Lefty, what was the occupation of the first house's owner the mob assigned to us tonight?" Harold asked as Walker steered the service van around a wide turn.

"The guy was a big shot at one of the large insurance companies in Manhattan. Why?" Lefty wanted to know.

"Well Lefty, the fat bald-headed jerk in the second house was a big produce magnet in nearby New York City," Harold related with relative certainty.

"How do ya' know that?" Walker wondered and asked. "The mob ain't done no research on that guy. That hit was purely *our* own job we randomly do on the side."

"It's a good thing we didn't go back into the house, or I'd be a murderer now," Harold related. "Yes Lefty; I'd be a certain cold-blooded killer!"

"What are ya' talkin' about, Harry? Speak some common sense, will ya'! I ain't never heard ya' talk like this before!" Bill Walker answered with great alarm evident in his tone of voice.

"Lefty, you'll never believe this in a million years," Harold went on as the now-neurotic passenger struggled for the right amount of oxygen to continue speaking. Campbell was puffing out loud. His bloodshot, bulging blue eyes were wholly glazed.

"Look Har', stop talkin' in lousy, stupid riddles. Speak simple plain English!" Lefty demanded. "Tony Falcone was right. The more words a person knows, the harder it is for the turkey to say something that oughta' be easy."

"How many people live in the United States?" Harold rhetorically asked. "There're about two hundred and ninety to three hundred and thirty million inhabitants. The rich fat bald-headed dude I had encountered was the ugly creep my wife ran away with! What are the strange odds of that kind of crazy coincidence ever happening?"

"Ya' don't mean?" Lefty stammered and asked as Walker rounded a sharp corner driving the mob's stolen television repair van. "The vivacious, stark-naked, blonde dame was your former wife?"

"Exactly," Harold confirmed. "And when I kicked the bathroom door open, I saw Carol standing there like a voluptuous magazine centerfold. All *she* saw was a horrible ski mask that almost sent her into instant trauma. I just felt so much rage and jealousy that I went totally ballistic. I freaked-out! Went postal is not a strong enough phrase to describe my frantic reaction!"

"How does it feel Har to get some sweet revenge?" Lefty asked as the driver stopped for a red traffic signal.

"Sweet and fulfilling," Harold savored and emphasized. "Real sweet. In English class we call that 'poetic justice'."

Campbell deftly slid his right hand into his pants' pocket and removed several stolen rings obtained from Carol's mint-green cameo jewelry chest. His hand's search eventually found several hard objects, and soon Harold's eyes closely scrutinized the smallest diamond in the haul; a one-carat ring.

"Check this out, will ya' Lefty," Harold implored while gesturing with his free left hand. "Here's the four-thousand-dollar engagement ring I had given Carol. It took me two whole years of teaching to save enough money to finally buy it. She never sent it back after she ran away with that fat, ugly, bald-headed wholesale fruit and produce gorilla. Now it's in the custody of its rightful owner."

"It had to be in the stars, Harold; it simply just had to be authored in the stars," an amazed Lefty Walker marveled and repeated.

"Poetic justice," the former English teacher cleverly reiterated.

* * * * * * * * * * * *

The two obedient thieves turned-over all the pilfered cash and jewels from the first West Chester, New York heist, and half the treasure from the second productive robbery, telling "the Brute" that the second raid had been a lucky bonus from a spur-of-the-moment second job inspiration. The Brute gave Harold and Lefty each a ten-thousand-dollar "incentive bonus" after saying, "Loyalty deserves *renumeration*," which Harold was at first inclined to correct, but fortunately, *his* better judgment prevailed against his impetuosity. Campbell kept his cherished diamond engagement ring, which meant more than ten Fort Knox gold bullion bars to the former "teacher" turned "professional".

The Brute got several "fences" to skillfully redistribute the stolen jewelry, and when the profits from the first raid were finally distributed, Harold and Lefty received dividends of twenty-five thousand each for the "scheduled first job".

"You two punk turkeys better lie low for a while," the six-foot-eight-inch Brute aptly suggested. "Where ya' headin' to cool-off before your next big plunder?"

"To tropical Aruba," Harold perkily replied. "I hear it's an ideal island paradise to just relax and crash."

"If ya' see a ruby in Aruba, steal the damned sucker!" the Brute lustily laughed. Lefty and Harold felt obligated to share the mobster's zany merriment.

"Where ya' guys stayin'?"

"At a fancy resort called the Divi-Divi," Harold suavely replied.

"Is that some kind of wacky tropical bird?" the Brute inquired. "Divi-Divi sounds like a pretty stupid place to me!"

"No Capa Brute," Campbell declared and smiled, "it's a type of tree that has branches growing in the opposite direction of the wind. There're lots of divi-divi trees in Aruba."

"Sounds quiet, better than Atlantic City or Wildwood," the Brute observed and described.

"We would go to A.C., only as a *last resort*," Lefty laughed, as the self-appointed jester fondly recalled a former conversation with Harold. "The Casino Control Commission keeps a close watch on suspicious guys like us," Walker humorously explained.

Harold Campbell and Bill "Lefty" Walker were soon relaxing on the Dutch Antilles Island of Aruba, just off the Venezuelan Coast. The satisfied vacationers royally basked on the Divi-Divi's pure white beach, drank the gamut of Caribbean rum drinks, ate a number of sumptuous outdoor luau-type feasts, and also found abundant time to flirt and mingle with all available females.

"How'd ya' know about that slanted tree you told the Brute about?" Lefty asked his partner-in-crime as the tanned sunbather rotated to his stomach upon his white-latticed beach recliner.

"I read all about it in the *Encyclopedia Britannica*," Harold orally and courteously conveyed. "I still enjoy perusing through books despite my new, daring career."

"You schoolteachers," Lefty remarked with a sizable grin expressed upon his face. "You're all into academics and meaningless unconnected stuff. Ya' know what the sports announcers say if a football game is already decided, don't you? They say '*it's all academic*', meaning that the rest of the minor contest is of little public importance."

"You're right there," Harold indicated. "But that's a part of me that's hard to shake. I've always liked learning trivial details and minute historical facts."

"Tell me, Mr. Answer Book," Lefty continued his critical evaluation. "How's it feel making four times as much after taxes as the Vineland Public School Superintendent?"

"It feels absolutely great, because I'm also making four times as much as the New Jersey Commissioner of Education after the jerk pays his taxes," Campbell figured and bragged. "Why do we have to waste our time discussing people existing under our social strata?"

Nighttime found the nonchalant pair gambling at the Aruba *Holiday Inn* where they tried their luck at roulette and craps. Lefty Walker was down two thousand "bazookas", but later that evening, Harold got a hot streak going with the dice and came out of his entertainment activity a very excellent six grand ahead. Campbell exhibited the same recklessness at the gaming tables that he had demonstrated playing the stock market, and also when he had lost the big money investment in his vanity-publishing catastrophe. But true to his frivolous nature, Harry generously gave Lefty "a consolation" two thousand bucks as compensation "to break even".

The next morning, the vacationing pair again relaxed in beach chairs above the Divi-Divi's hot white sands. Neither vacationer had a care in the world. Harold amused himself by watching a lizard flee the hot sun and instinctively scurry into a small cluster of thorny beach shrubs. "Ya' know Lefty, this armed robbery business could be rather treacherous stuff," Harold maintained. "If the mark has a gun in the house, things could get mighty hairy really quick."

"Harry, we ain't wildly robbin' gas stations or Wal-Marts in broad daylight," Lefty pointed-out while deftly changing the focus of discussion. "Our marks are clearly defined. And it ain't armed robbery. We try not to confront our marks with raised guns. They're usually out of the house when we arrive for work. That deal with your former wife has got to be the exception."

"It's a good thing we're both well-trained and know exactly what we're doing," Campbell assessed and stated. "If we ever get caught, we'll spend the rest of our lives in prison hammerin' out cheap license plates for the New Jersey Division of Motor Vehicles."

Lefty Walker was not quite as pessimistic as his encyclopedic confederate was. "You forget Harry," Lefty reminded his closest friend. "We're now skilled pros. The street punks that rob candy stores and shoot the owners for ten bucks are rank amateurs. But I gotta' admit, ya' really scared the daylights outa' me when you viciously hung your former old lady over the banister railing. What a frightful caper! I thought for a moment that she was visitin' St. Peter at the fabled Pearly Gates when I first saw the dame suspended upside-down above the downstairs foyer."

Harold Campbell, who usually practiced suavity and civility, was ready with an appropriate reply to offset William Walker's aggressive questioning. "You know that murder and barbarism are not my style," the sentimental and sensitive partner insisted. "I just hung Carol up there over the railing for dramatic effects. But I had to restrain myself from savagely lancing her jugular. I guess I just wanted to leave her suspended there, in a sense, like she had left me suspended back in Vineland," Harry weakly justified. "I never once suspected she'd leave me for money and power. I wonder what her rich, snobbish doctor daddy thinks of her wimpy fruit and vegetable sugar daddy?"

Contrary to his generally garrulous nature, Lefty was at a loss for words and could only shrug his shoulders as an immediate response. Hypothesizing and speculating were not Walker's strong suites.

Harold paused for a few seconds to gauge Lefty's facial expression. "But Carol would never suspect me being the diabolical villain behind the hideous ski mask," Campbell continued his assessment of recent events. "I never abused her until that night up in her West Chester mansion. She still thinks I'm a meek, hapless donkey livin' the rest of his mediocre life tryin' to educate high school kids," Harold spilled-out, his words precisely originating from his abused heart.

When the two travelers returned to Jersey's Ocean City, a courier "bone-breaker" hand-delivered them an important message from Tony "the Knife" Tassone. The Chicago mobster wanted to bag "the Williamson Diamond," a widely coveted, three-hundred-carat gemstone. "Our guys could break it down and hustle it on the black market for a fantastic fortune," the unsigned note read. "This could mean early retirement for you two guys. I'll give ya' well-rested punks the details when ya' fly out to the Windy City for a briefing."

"This could be the big one we've been waiting for," Harold anticipated and said with a wide grin.

"This *is* definitely the big one," Lefty solemnly clarified. "I predict the gig might actually materialize into a real bonanza! Yes; the big enchilada we've both been dreaming about!"

The two aspiring millionaires booked a flight from New York's *Kennedy International Airport* to Chicago's *O'Hare*. After renting a black Ford from Avis, soon Harold and Lefty met-up with Tony "the Knife" Tassone, who resided in an expansive twenty-five-room palace in suburban Oak Grove. "Boys, I giva' you my blessin' to steala' that sparklin' rock. We gotta' three diamond cutters that can chop it down to size. You getta' the Williamson; I giva' you hundred-fifty thousand each, cash on the barrel-head."

Harold and Lefty quickly learned more specifics about the renowned diamond. Tassone revealed that the giant stone was on loan to Illinois from a Johannesburg, South African museum. The colossal gem had been transported under heavy security to be exhibited at large banks and stock exchanges all across the U.S. The diamond was to be brought into the Chicago area by an armored truck. The mob had learned that a large cache of money was also being transferred in the same ordinary armored truck, its destination being a popular bank in suburban Oak Lawn. Then the heavily guarded transport vehicle carrying the incomparable Williamson Diamond would be secretly driven into Chicago.

"We got any confederate henchmen working on this important job?" Harold cockily asked.

"Confederates?" the Knife laughed, defusing Harry's fragile ego. "This ain't the *Civil War* you're doin' at the Oak Lawn bank, ha, ha, ha. Do ya' mean helpers when ya' say confederates?"

"I'm sorry," Harold apologized to his predictably unpredictable host. "That's what I really meant to say."

Tony the Knife explained that the driver of the armored car "is one of *our* guys". The transport and delivery had not yet been publicized in Illinois newspapers or on local television. When the diamond would be safely stored inside the Chicago bank, the ever-vigilant press would then be permitted to announce the exact place and the time schedule of the magnificent stone's exhibition.

Security in the armored truck would consist of the mob-affiliated driver, a company-hired side guard, and a third guard, also a mob associate, seated in the rear compartment, supposedly guarding the coveted Williamson.

The Williamson Diamond heist was without a doubt Harold and Lefty's most daring and most diffucult assignment. The obsessed twosome intensely studied the security truck's itinerary, knowing every side street, intersection, and manhole cover along the route. Their secret intent was that the priceless gem would never be delivered from Oak Lawn to the Chicago banking institution the following Saturday morning.

On the designated date, the steel-plated red truck conveying the Williamson rumbled into the rear parking lot of the Oak Lawn bank. The avaricious New Jersey hoods anxiously waited inside a mob-stolen automobile parked near the bank. Harry and Lefty were dressed in security guard uniforms similar to those worn by their two accomplices seated inside the armored truck. The disguised bandits exited their vehicle and casually strolled-over to the newly arrived transport truck, which was in the process of backing-up to the bank's rear entrance. The driver nonchalantly hopped-out, leaving the motor running and the door opened as had been planned.

Lefty immediately shot a tear gas canister into the truck's open cab. The company-hired guard, who had ridden shotgun, leaped-out the driver's side, coughing erratically. Harold dragged the gasping guard to the driver's side window and immediately handcuffed the sneezing man to the steering wheel. The Mafia accomplice that had been driving the armored vehicle was also briskly handcuffed to the steering wheel, making it appear as if the Tassone "plant" was an overwhelmed innocent holdup victim.

The rear door sprung open as tear gas smoke wafted outside the back compartment's panels. The third guard was pulled-out and handcuffed by Harold, while Lefty grabbed the driver's gun from *his* waist holster. Having the necessary "inside information", Campbell stepped through the dense tear gas cloud inside the truck's interior, located the small safe containing the Williamson, and quickly tossed the sturdy metal object outside to Lefty, who securely tucked it under his arm. Harold next snatched three sacks of cash and hustled out of the rear compartment, showing excellent dexterity by adroitly jumping-down to the asphalt parking lot.

The all-too-confident thieves rushed to their getaway car, just as a clanging bank alarm sounded. Lefty started the blue Chevy's engine and took-off as sirens from distant police cruisers were racing toward the developing crime scene from the opposite direction. The former teacher opened the small safe with the already-acquired combination numbers that "the Knife" had conveniently provided, removed a red velvet pouch, stuck his hand inside, and then meticulously examined with admiration the celebrated mineral hunk.

"Just look at this incredible piece of compressed coal!" Harold marveled and exclaimed. "The Knife and us are entirely too smart for the cops, aren't we Lefty?" Harold haughtily asked.

"Wait until 'the Knife' takes a long gander at that terrific glittering rock," Lefty gasped and answered. "This has to be the most spectacular heist this side of the famous old Brinks job."

The ecstatic felons felt compelled to contemplate their rising fame and prestige inside the national crime syndicate. "Lefty, I'm a little worried," Harry confessed. "The grab went off all-too-easily, as if it were rehearsed, ya' know what I mean?"

"That's why we're accomplished pros," Lefty argued as the self-satisfied felon carefully stayed within the speed limit. "We make hard jobs look easy. Amateurs make easy jobs look hard. The biggest thing we gotta' worry about is returnin' the black rented car to Avis tomorrow over near the airport."

* * * * * * * * * * * *

The following morning the *Chicago Tribune's* front page featured two seemingly unrelated stories. The first article headlined *South African Diamond Rescued from Grand Theft*, read as follows:

"The famed Williamson Diamond is still in the hands of bank officials, thanks to the intuition of a senior bank executive, who wishes to remain anonymous. Yesterday, a bold armed robbery attempt was made on the rare gem. The scene was the Oak Lawn Savings and Deposits Bank.

The famous diamond was being transported en route to the Chicago National Bank where it was to be on public display until next Friday. Two highly dangerous bandits ambushed the diamond's armored truck at the back entrance to the suburban Oak Lawn bank. But unknowingly, the incompetent robbers had escaped the scene with an imitation facsimile of the much-heralded precious stone. The crooks also made-off with three bags of cash, but the one-dollar bills were all dyed and serial-numbered, and all major banks across the country are looking-out for any petty thieves trying to pass them off as legal tender.

The actual authentic Williamson Diamond is now safely in the custody of Samuel Conklin, President of the Chicago National Bank. When asked about the extraordinary incident, Mr. Conklin stated, "I always disliked the idea of armored cars transporting cargo more valuable than either gold or cash. I had a strange premonition that something unorthodox was going to be attempted. From early childhood, I had always shown certain psychic abilities."

The newspaper article further described how Samuel Conklin couldn't convince the Chicago bank's board of directors to change the armored car's itinerary simply "on a hunch". Consequently, Samuel Conklin had safely transported the Williamson Diamond from a Milwaukee bank to the aforementioned Chicago National Bank in his own private limousine. "I must confess," Conklin told the *Tribune.* "The artificial twin appears to be almost impossible to distinguish from its genuine counterpart. But expert gemologists could easily tell the difference in a Chicago second. My deepest condolences are extended to the blunderers who had attempted stealing the authentic Williamson, but instead, wound-up with a cheap counterfeit. No doubt their ulterior purpose was to plunder and disintegrate the Williamson into countless smaller diamonds."

The article closed by revealing that the Chicago Police were conducting an extensive investigation into the incident. Security had been light because the designated armored truck had only been carrying the bogus Williamson along with bags of marked, small denomination, U.S. bills. Detectives could only rely on vague descriptions of the unscrupulous bandits that had been provided by armored truck security guards, whose accounts are sketchy because of their slow recovery from exposure to a massive dose of tear gas. The *Tribune* finally reported that additional details of the "sensational story" would be chronicled in the following day's edition.

The second *Tribune* front-page headline read: *Gangland Killings Still Mar Chicago's Image.* "

Although the Al Capone Prohibition Era is still an ugly blemish to Chicago's public image, the city is still haunted by occasional gangland-style murders. Last night, city police discovered the dismembered bodies of two unidentified men. Their remains had been stuffed into plastic bags and put into the trunk of a late model Cadillac. The authorities are baffled by a lack of clues. Chief investigator Jack Pagano said, "The mob apparently had little respect for the victims. Whenever corpses are sliced-up like these two were, the killers are showing their contempt for their bloody dupes."

Police Lieutenant William Francis Burns then added, "From the looks of things, the dual executions fit the mold of a couple of past classic gangland killings. It's without a doubt the messiest job I've witnessed committed in my twenty-nine years on the force."

This afternoon, Coroner Robert "Duke" Southard will perform autopsies on the unidentified remains at the city morgue. Multiple bullet wounds were discovered in the victims' decapitated heads, and also in their disjointed chests. The police special investigations' unit has been assigned the task of unraveling the motive and interrogating suspects believed to be responsible for the gruesome murders. Police Commissioner Allen Mason said, "These heinous acts of atrocity must cease. We want our public streets safe from mobster rule. Crime only begets more mindless crime."

The horrible homicides hit the news wires shortly before press time. An exclusive follow-up will be published in tomorrow's *Tribune*."

As Harold Campbell had found-out and learned in his lackluster publishing venture, in marriage, and finally in crime, life in America is often a very risky dice roll.

"A Video Horoscope"

Middle age had taken its toll on William Edwards. The man's receding hairline, the silver streaks in his thinning brown hair, and a round bald spot located on top of his head were undeniable proof of Bill's aging. Two false teeth bridges and a forty-six-inch paunch verified that Bill Edwards was an obsessive and compulsive junk food eater. The auto' mechanic also loved drinking a six-pack of beer while watching television sports events, especially baseball and football games. In stark reality, in terms of physical appearance, William Edwards was forty-five going on sixty-two.

"Bill; you're a prime candidate for diabetes and heart disease," his very concerned wife criticized a week after her husband's forty-fifth birthday. "Watch your high blood sugar readings!"

"Thelma, if ya' think I'll ever use that gift certificate you gave me to exercise over at the health club," Bill Edwards countered from his comfortable couch, "then you're totally wrong. I might die on the treadmill or on the stair climber. I'd rather take my chances Monday through Friday on the treadmill of everyday life."

"I'm only looking out for your welfare," Thelma Edwards thoughtfully replied. "Soon your general health will be in jeopardy."

"You don't want to kill me, do ya'?" Bill joked. "Overexertion is liable to give me the coronary ya' just mentioned," Bill laughed. "I'm no young buck anymore. But medical doctors and hospitals will kill a person sooner than any convenience store junk food will!"

Over the years, the automobile mechanic had earned a good reputation working out of the garage next to the couple's modest bungalow on Old Forks Road in Hammonton, New Jersey. Bill was regarded as an expert on repairing camshafts, valves, ignitions, transmissions and carburetors on older model cars. Working on dirty engines contributed to the auto' doctor's gross, untidy appearance. Grease was always embedded underneath Edwards' long fingernails. Oil stains decorated his undershirts, many of which looked like abstract art designs. Thelma often accused her grimy husband of being "allergic to soap, detergent and water".

Thelma Edwards' cleanliness habits were the complete opposite of her unkempt husband's proclivities for filthiness. Bill's wife prided herself on keeping an attractive body and a pretty face. The wife spent at least an hour each day combing her lengthy brunette tresses in front of her bathroom vanity's mirror. The well-preserved woman would constantly search for the slightest wrinkle on her silky-smooth, light complexion. Going to the gym three times a week also helped Thelma maintain her youthful, slender appearance.

Bill and Thelma Edwards were verification of the popular maxim, "Opposites attract". The pretty lady was neat, self-conscious, fastidious, and refined. The only thing *refined* about Bill was the motor oil smeared on his hands and clothes.

The wife spent the daylight hours 9 to 5, Monday through Friday, as a receptionist-secretary for Dr. Paul Lacy, a dedicated downtown Hammonton family physician. The townspeople held the doctor in high esteem, as if he were a contemporary Hippocrates. Paul Lacy was the most patronized medical man in the small town, without any rival coming in a close second.

Thelma Edwards tried to be a financially independent woman. Her husband managed the house mortgage, car payments, utility bills, health care remittances, automobile and house insurance policies, along with the usual home maintenance expenses. The pretty wife bought the groceries, and after the weekly food supplies were purchased, the remainder of her salary was *her* business. Mrs. Edwards often visited ritzy boutiques in area malls, and was one of the best-dressed ladies in the entire rural community.

Although Bill Edwards was often crass and sullen when at home, the mechanic was affable and well-liked by his cronies at the local Italian/Irish Club. When not watching sports' events and drinking his standard six pack of beer, the engine and muffler guru was widely regarded as the best poker player in the somnolent community. Edwards really relished his Tuesday and Thursday "bachelor nights out" with his buddies at the local Route 30 club, which happened to be notorious for its male bonding and its "lewd and risque girlie stage strippers".

"Are you going out again?" Thelma complained one Thursday night. "You have a home, Bill, you know. Try living in it once in a while on nights that begin with the letter T."

"I guess I just like bein' with the fellas' a couple of evenings a week," William answered in a low monotone. "That gives ya' more time to admire yourself in the mirror or hit the shops at the *Hamilton Mall*, so *you* oughta' be happy, too."

Bill Edwards seldom took his wife out to dinner, to the movies, to the theater, or on vacation. When he wasn't playing cards, darts, and shuffleboard at the club with "the guys", the man was out in the garage working on backlogged "puddle jumper repair jobs". Edwards preferred sausage and roast beef sandwiches to filet mignon and lobster tails. Bill would rather guzzle down a six-pack of *Coor's Light* at home or "at the club" than sip Chablis with his wife at a fancy restaurant.

"Bill, can't we adopt a child?" Thelma repeated a question she had been asking for a quarter of a century. "I always wanted to have a son or a daughter."

"Listen; if we can't have kids naturally," Bill bluntly answered, "ya' don't know what kind of genetics you're getting involved with when ya' take somebody else's kid for adoption. I know three guys at the club who have adopted what turned-out to become juvenile delinquents, and not even one of the three adopted imports have ever developed respect and courtesy. Ya' just can't trust strangers' *chromosomes*. Say Thel, how'd you like that fifty-cent word my mind just came up with!"

"It's too bad the fertility drugs I took didn't work," Thelma complained and regretted. "Now, I'm too old to have children biologically. I know you think I'm too sentimental, but I often feel like my maternal role has not been fulfilled. It's sort of like a relentless guilt gnawing away at my soul."

"Are *the Phillies* playin' on TV tonight?" the self-centered husband asked his attractive wife. "I think they're playing an American League team tonight."

Thelma didn't respond. She promptly stepped into the bathroom, slammed the door, looked at her beautiful, aging face in the mirror, and began to cry out of self-pity.

The normally phlegmatic husband shocked his wife by opening the squeaky bathroom door. "Honey, we're both too set in our ways," Bill admitted. "Thel, we're too old to be parents. Why don't we just pretend that I'm your son and that you're my daughter 'til death do us part."

Mrs. Edwards found little merit or humor in her mate's attempt to ease things over. "That's very selfish of you," the wife sobbed and indicted. "I always thought people got married to want and have children, one way or another."

"Thel, that used to be true when people could afford 'em," Bill tried to explain. "The family guys at the club complain all the time about the cost of college, clothes, proms, cars, and weddings. Not that I never wanted to be a father," Bill profusely lied while inadvertently employing a double negative as was his bad habit, "but I've gotten too used to not bein' one."

Such imagination and rational argumentation were rare for William Edwards. The auto' mechanic was seldom suave or creative. Bill was not a polished college graduate like Nelson Howell, the family attorney, or Paul Lacy, the family doctor, or Tom Machise, the family accountant. The devil-may-care husband didn't enjoy the company of the town's sophisticated elite at annual *Christmas* or at *New Year's Eve* parties when the upwardly mobile citizens talked about literature, high technology, and local history. Bill Edwards could care less about Thelma's activity on the Hammonton Cultural and Historical Society, where his community-minded spouse served as the new club secretary.

"Bill, you again forgot our wedding anniversary yesterday," Thelma reminded her often-negligent housemate. "You never seem to remember important dates like birthdays, Mothers Day, anniversaries, or *Valentine's Day*."

"Thel, the *Phils* have the bases loaded in the bottom of the fifth and are only down two runs," Bill yelled-out to intentionally change the subject. "Tell me all about it later after the post-game show."

The TV baseball game lasted fourteen innings, and Bill did not take his shower until after midnight. Thelma was sleeping by the time her groggy-headed spouse finally got to bed. When no anniversary gift arrived by post or was affectionately presented the next day, the wife protested her husband's negligence by journeying to the Mays Landing *Hamilton Mall* and treating herself to an expensive black "designer dress".

"Bill, I want you to take me out in my new black dress to celebrate our upcoming twenty-fourth wedding anniversary," Thelma requested. "We can go to the Gourmet Room at the Venice Plaza over in Berlin. They have the greatest crab cakes and desserts I've ever tasted."

"Sorry Thel, but Bucky Sooy is havin' major trouble with his car," Bill haughtily declared. "He needs a complete tune-up, transmission work, and tailpipe and muffler replacements right away. Maybe next week, we'll go out to supper. And that new black dress looks like a morbid funeral gown. I'm too young to be planted in the cemetery," the husband crudely jested, "so there's no need for ya' to be wearin' widow's weeds."

"You need a muffler installed in your mouth!" the irate woman shouted as she slammed the bedroom door shut and rushed to the bathroom vanity's mirror. Her husband's insensitivity to her feminine needs along with his perpetual litany of lame excuses were beginning to make Thelma Edwards regret she had ever met the "arrogant grease monkey".

Thelma felt as if she had become a helpless victim always being constantly exploited by an excess of male chauvinism. "He never tells me I'm pretty," the wife sobbed to her mirror's image. "He's still living in the nineteenth century when a wife was the husband's personal property. Love is blind when you're a naïve teenager and don't know any better, at least, that's the way it was with me being attracted to Bill."

The all-too-patient wife had remarkably endured twenty-four years of hollow pledges and broken promises. In the beginning, Bill would give meaningful tokens to Thelma like a dozen roses on her birthday, and a box of *Godiva* chocolates on *Valentine's Day*. But as the years marched on to the new millennium, Bill spent more time working until midnight on cars and drinking beer at the club, or characteristically sitting in front of the television as a "devout couch potato". In her final analysis, Thelma ultimately believed that her derelict husband had become blatantly oblivious to her very ignored emotional needs.

Since Bill had been remiss, not buying his deserving wife any anniversary present for the past twelve years, Thelma wanted to remind him that she still was aware of the importance of May 24 in *their* lives. The next evening, the still-attractive woman approached her husband in the expensive black silk dress she had purchased at the ritzy mall shop. The inspired wife was carrying two special gift-wrapped packages for her mate's personal scrutiny. Her listless, marital companion was fairly busy thinking about an engine overhaul while watching another *Phillies* baseball game and drinking a bottle of cold brew. A wedding anniversary was the farthest thing from his mind.

"Happy wedding anniversary Dear!" Thelma hollered while standing above her husband sitting slouched-down on the family room's couch. "Here darling; I bought you a few little presents you may find interesting. I hope you like the gifts if and when you ever get around to seeing what's inside the wrappers."

Bill reluctantly placed his fifth bottle of *Coor's Light* on the gray granite-slate table positioned next to the den's sofa. The husband accepted the presents and thanked his wife in a mildly embarrassed tone of voice. "I promise Thel; I'll take ya' to Vegas just like I said I would," Bill stammered. "We'll stay at the *Mirage*, or maybe even at the *Venetian* I always see advertised on TV."

"That's okay, Honey," Thelma replied with a trace of sarcasm in her voice. "Whenever you can get around to it or can fit the Nevada casino trip into your busy schedule."

"Bucky's car now also needs new pistons," Bill added, "and Bob Zeltman's pickup needs new plugs and a radiator transplant. I'll see if

I have time tomorrow to get you a *Whitman Sampler* over at the Mainline Gift Shop."

"Now, I understand you're very busy," the distressed wife answered. "Those car repairs do pay the basic bills."

While Bill Edwards carelessly ripped the wrapping off the first gift, his wife furtively placed a plastic pharmacy medicine vial on the end table near *his* couch. Inside the package Bill found a beige tie to match his three-year-old brown sport jacket. The second present had a more dramatic effect upon the auto mechanic. It was a videocassette ready to be played on the den *VCR*. Bill read the title aloud. "A Video Horoscope. July 18, 1955. William Samuel Edwards. Sign: Cancer. Born 10:42 a.m., Jefferson Hospital, Philadelphia, Pennsylvania." A momentary mental pause was followed by a reaction. "Why Thelma, this is very clever!" Bill exclaimed, showing rare emotion. "That's the exact time and place of my birth. Where did you buy this unusual item?"

"At a neat novelty store I had discovered on the way back from the mall," Thelma replied. "They customized it to match your birth date. I thought it was a cute idea, different from the run-of-the-mill everyday gift. Since you watch a lot of TV," the wife explained, "I thought a video horoscope would be a pleasant surprise for you. You're always watching mediocre B movies on cable and are enamored with those horribly monotonous baseball games. I thought *this* particular gift would be a nice change of pace for you."

William had never placed much credence in astrology. His need to be practical while fixing motors placed "cute stuff" like horoscopes and zodiac signs in the same fanciful category with palmistry, tarot cards, and crystal balls.

"Now Thelma, how could planets and stars millions of miles away have anything to do with life here on Earth?" Bill cynically asked. "I've always believed that fortune-tellin' and the like were ridiculous pursuits and not worth any special consideration at all."

"Honey, it's only a novelty gift item," the wife answered. "Don't tale the gift so seriously! How many beers have you had so far tonight?" the wife asked as her eyes counted the five empty brown bottles set upon the table.

"I mean, people born on the same day as me have different jobs and different interests," Bill typically argued before imbibing another mouthful of beer. "Horoscopes are about as accurate as a blind man throwin' darts at a thimble thirty feet away. And Thel, please don't criticize my two favorite recreational pastimes, beer and baseball."

"Bill, don't be so argumentative and stubborn about what you like and what you dislike," his spouse suggested. "I thought it would be a little fun giving you a birthday horoscope on our anniversary; a change of pace, that's all."

"It's really dumb and juvenile," Bill slurred. "Really dumb! A lot of bull, ya' know what I mean, Thel. Sometimes, I think you're tryin' to insult my intelligence with this simpleton pseudo-intellectual crap," the disturbed husband protested before belching like a drunken Viking attending a medieval banquet. "Say, the *Phils'* are havin' a rally and getting back into the game."

Thelma wisely refused to escalate the debate with her intoxicated husband. She knew from experience that Bill could become defensive and even bellicose if irritated after consuming a six-pack of his delicious brew. "Bill, whatever happened to your famous sense of humor you used to have back in high school?" Edwards' wife asked. "You're too uptight. I have to now go and do some light grocery shopping. We're out of bread and milk and a few other things. I'll get you two more cold beers out of the 'fridge so you can relax and watch the game on the couch," the wife offered. "I know how you hate surprises and interruptions!"

The perturbed wife removed her pocketbook from the hall closet shelf, put on a light-colored rabbit-furred jacket, stepped to the refrigerator, removed two brown bottles of beer, and then brought the new refreshments to her ungrateful husband.

"*Phillies* winning tonight?" she mechanically asked the repair guru. "Do they even know how to win?"

"No way," Bill verbally responded with disappointment. "They're gonna' lose again to those stupid lousy *Mets*. They're behind five to one, and it's still early in the contest. Philadelphia fans ain't gonna' see another pennant year until the middle of next century. We'll both be long dead by the time the fightin' *Phils'* get around to winnin' their next *World Series*."

"Well then, here's two more beers so that your throat doesn't become parched," the pretty wife said. "Enjoy the game, but if you get bored, you could always view your novel video horoscope. You might find it quite interesting. I'll leave the item safe and sound next to the television."

Several minutes later, Thelma walked through the kitchen and into the small bungalow's laundry room, which had a side door leading to the garage. The disgruntled lady entered her car, wondering if Bill's curiosity had been stimulated about watching the horoscope cassette. The wife started the engine, pressed the automatic garage door opener, backed-out into the driveway, and then pushed the electronic remote to close the overhead door.

Bill suffered through three more innings of *the Mets* clobbering the *Phillies*, drinking the two additional beers that Thelma had given him. When the score became more lopsided and reached eight to two, the drunken viewer became thoroughly disgusted with the recent baseball developments being telecast from *Shea Stadium*. Edwards rose from the sofa, staggered into the kitchen, opened the refrigerator, and plunked three ice cubes into a glass.

Then the half-inebriated man pathetically trudged over to the liquor cabinet and removed a nearly full decanter of *Amaretto*. The disgusted baseball fan generously poured the rich liquid into the glass, and then carried the almost-full bottle over to the faded black leather sofa. After plopping down on the old faded and wrinkled couch, the disenchanted fellow swirled the ice cubes and *Amaretto* around inside the glass with his left index finger.

William sipped and then drank-down a mouthful of the smooth liquor. When the *Mets* scored three additional runs in the top of the sixth inning, the devout *Phillies* fan became angry, got up, sauntered to the *VCR*, and forcefully inserted the video horoscope that Thelma had gotten him into the slot. The plastered fellow dizzily wobbled his way back to the comfortable sofa, poured a second glass of *Amaretto*, manipulated the TV remote control, and figured that the video horoscope would be a welcomed departure from the already decided *Phillies'* game. The disenchanted viewer reckoned it was time to enjoy the folly of his own personalized video horoscope.

The disgruntled baseball fan matter-of-factly flicked the remote control to *VCR* mode, sat back on his black leather sofa, and sipped some more of the sweet-tasting liquor. A veiled oracle suddenly appeared upon the picture tube, and the strange-looking gypsy was gazing into the depths of a crystal ball. A dense mist enveloped the weird-in-appearance woman, who mystically waved her hands over the glass sphere, seemingly eliciting mysterious truths from inside the round object. The fortuneteller's facial features were vague and indistinguishable because of the thick fog that surrounded her.

The fascinated video viewer chuckled with delight as Mr. Edwards gulped-down another mouthful of the delicious-flavored *Amaretto*. Bill's distorted mind imagined that fortune-telling was a silly travesty left over from a superstitious past, as archaic as Neanderthal men and prehistoric cave drawings. Then, eerie organ music blared-out from the television speakers. Bill Edwards laughed indulgently at what his brain perceived to be 'hilarious entertainment'. The mechanic poured himself a third full glass of *Amaretto*, which certainly would heighten his beer-induced, delusional state.

A male baritone voice then addressed the groggy-minded viewer. The voice's distinct delivery along with its pitch and rhythm sounded somewhat familiar to the stunned and virtually paralyzed listener, but Bill's present fuzzy state of mind prevented him from associating the vocal cords' tonality with any one person.

"Hello Bill," the remotely-familiar voice very discernibly greeted. "Congratulations on you having your twenty-fourth-wedding-anniversary. Consider yourself fortunate to be able to now witness nostalgic highlights from *your* life. Just sit back, Bill. Relax, ease your mind, and enjoy reliving some of your most happy and memorable childhood experiences."

The narrator's haunting introduction then next described an old postcard photograph of downtown Philadelphia's Thomas Jefferson Hospital with the accompanying caption, "July 18, 1955. The Life of William Samuel Edwards."

A black and white picture portraying Bill as a young boy sitting on the fender of a '58 Chevy flashed onto the screen. "That's when I first became interested in cars," Bill mumbled to himself while sporting a contrived smile. "That picture's a classic. I wonder where and how they got it?"

A second photo' soon replaced the first upon the television screen. It showed young William pushing a miniature wheelbarrow across his grandfather's front lawn. The phantom narrator reminisced about Bill's joyful childhood. A succession of black and white still pictures followed at ten second intervals. The clear images from the 1950s were appropriately arranged in chronological order.

The astonished viewer was captured in stills eating an ice cream cone while being held in his mother's arms. Then there were snapshots of Edwards sitting and standing with parents, aunts, uncles, and various cousins. Several of the older relatives were now deceased, and *that* negative thought made the video spectator experience rarely felt sentimentality. The emotion known as sadness made the already-groggy man pour an additional glass of *Amaretto* while keeping his faltering eyes riveted on the TV monitor.

The drunken observer's negative thoughts quickly converted to happy remembrances as the video subject matter changed from still photo' presentations to an old home movies' format. Bill was shown playing *Little League* baseball, *Pee-Wee League* football, and wading with his parents in the *Atlantic* on a Wildwood summer vacation.

Sentimentality both dwelled and swelled inside Bill Edwards' aching heart.

The next amazing part of the fascinating video depicted Edwards as a freshman offensive guard on the Hammonton High School football squad. The lineman was standing with the team quarterback; tall, muscular Paul Lacy. And the very interesting video then reviewed a handsome Bill Edwards escorting a very beautiful Thelma Celia to the high school senior prom. Another sequence had the two dreamy-eyed teenagers dancing below a banner that appropriately spelled-out the prom's romantic theme, *Rainbows and Dreams Forever*.

Feeling very nervous, Bill Edwards anxiously chugged-down the balance of his potent *Amaretto,* and the chronic alcoholic instinctively poured another glass half-full. The enamored observer then redirected his attention to watching the re-creation of his past life as Edwards' right hand very deliberately tipped the decanter downward, and the thirsty man emptied the remainder of the sweet liquor into his formerly half-full glass.

High school graduation exercises popped onto the TV screen. Bill and Thelma were shown proudly displaying their diplomas in what the viewer's bleary eyes recognized as 'color motion film'. The next color scenes reviewed the couple's gala wedding reception at Hammonton's Lillian on the Lake restaurant, and then, the weird visual presentation exhibited their subsequent honeymoon occurring at Miami Beach's exclusive *Fountainbleau Hotel*.

Bill felt inclined to sip his liquor more indulgently. His vulnerable mind had been captivated by the well-coordinated re-creation of *his* almost-forgotten past. Edwards was then portrayed on motion picture film as a young ambitious mechanic working on a racing car's powerful engine. The burly video horoscope witness suddenly became misty-eyed from witnessing past nostalgia. The observer's heart yearned for a return to his carefree and innocent teenage years when life was simple, and certainly less burdensome.

'These forgotten films were taken by my mom, by my dad, and by Thelma. I haven't seen many of 'em in over ten years,' Bill's disheveled mind recollected. "Thelma did a great job piecin' it together," Bill groggily mumbled to himself. "She ought to change careers and become a Hollywood film editor!"

After twenty minutes featuring more sentimental memories, there was a full ten-second pause in the video. Edwards realized that he had virtually drained his final glass of *Amaretto.* 'This oddball film's better than the lousy *Phillies* game,' Bill whimsically thought. "It's a real gem and a half," the couch potato appreciated and laughed as he clumsily nursed-down the last ounce of delicious liquor.

"Now Bill," the anonymous narrator continued. "Your illustrious past has been seen and fully enjoyed. It is now time for us to take a look *at your* present life. You will observe how other people appreciate your marvelous companionship. You are well-liked by many people, Bill Edwards."

The mechanic was presented in the biographical video winning the pie-eating contest at the annual July 1st Hammonton Blueberry Festival. Next a heavy-set, balding Bill Edwards was captured on film leaving Dan's Stationary Store in downtown Hammonton. Edwards was next seen holding his bowling ball against his chest after his team, the Marks Brothers, had won the Adult League championship at DiDonato's Lanes. And then confused Bill viewed himself on tape entering Alice's Restaurant, a local eatery notorious for soggy French fries and greasy hamburgers.

The new scenes very much disturbed Bill Edwards' usually non-fragile psyche. The drunken mechanic's nebulous mind could not remember the events ever being filmed, and the unfaithful marriage cheater wondered how the home cinema footage had ever been obtained. "Somebody's invaded my privacy, and I don't relish it one bit," Bill muttered to the distant television screen. "Someone's usin' a secret camera and spyin' on me," Edwards guiltily grieved and complained. "And whose voice is that I hear? I know it, but can't place it. It sure ain't Allen Funt's."

The next revealing scene captured the grease monkey and his bowling cronies feasting and partying at the raucous Silver Fox Inn, a popular area Route 30 tavern. Doubt and alcohol were making Edwards extremely paranoid. His loudly thumping heart was swelling with anxiety. Sweat beads began rolling-down from his forehead down to his chin. Random thoughts eddied around inside his addled head. The now-melancholy engine and transmission repairman was becoming worried, neurotic, and suspicious. A wicked migraine throbbed behind and between his ears.

The next video representations were not-at-all charitable to the viewer's conscience. The bizarre astrology film depicted and exposed Bill's secret faults and sins. Several scenes caught the gambler wagering large sums at Monmouth Racetrack's "Trifecta" and "Daily Double" betting windows. Edwards' horse race mental anguish was followed by a scene showing the compulsive gambler and Italian/Irish Club friends seated at Atlantic City blackjack tables. "Bill, you gambled away over a thousand dollars a month at the racetrack and at the casinos," the narrator's smooth voice reminded. "You've maxed-out your credit cards, mortgaged your house, and will never escape debt's terrible spider's web. You're a loser Bill Edwards; a classic example of a real true bona fide loser."

The gambling embarrassment was succeeded by an even more indicting series of events. The film frames showed Bill involved in an extra-marital affair with Dottie Wilson, a short, middle-aged tavern waitress that worked nights at the Silver Fox where Bill and his bowling chums often banqueted. Bill's eyes now perceived exactly how clumsy and unromantic he had been during his amorous extra-curricular bed adventures, always sacrificing emotional gratification for pure biological pleasure. Edwards' soul was instantly laden with guilt and mortification. Several tears streamed out from bloodshot eyes, and then trickled-down his pallid cheeks.

And next the fantastic video exposed Bill under the sheets with Sylvia Clarke, an overweight cashier employed at Dan's Stationery Store, the Bellevue Avenue business where Bill faithfully purchased fifty, or more, one-dollar *Pick-Six Lottery* tickets twice a week. The awkward pair caught on film was playfully wrestling around on the mattress like two hormone-driven bears during mating season.

The graphic sex scenes had made Bill wonder how a camera had ever captured his out-of-home antics on tape. The video spectator was inclined to rise and smash his fist through the now-annoying picture tube, but the intoxicants the man had imbibed were so potent that the mesmerized victim had now almost become unconscious; his flabby buttocks virtually trapped in the deep pocket of his sofa's soft cushion. The man's body could not execute his anemic mind's feeble commands. But Bill Edwards' stimulated curiosity actually wished to see more of the intriguing, mentally agonizing video.

The next taped episode really challenged Bill's sanity. Thelma was standing in a dark room stark naked. A man, whose face had been partially obscured by dim lighting, was standing behind her curvaceous hips, gently massaging her breasts. Edwards felt his pride severely hurt because the betrayed husband was incapable of such sensuous affection as Thelma's unknown bed partner had been prolifically demonstrating. The wife's hips slowly swayed back and forth like a grandfather clock's hypnotizing pendulum, showing her passionate desire to escalate her mortal soul higher into ecstasy. Bill was absolutely stunned, despite his intoxicated fantasy condition. The in-shock fellow's altered mind imaginatively believed that his alluring blonde wife had suddenly transformed into a gorgeous pornographic movie star.

Thelma and her suitor sank-upon the plush room's bed, lost in a flurry of extended kisses and embraces. Several tantalizing moments of lusty foreplay followed. The steamy scene would have been an erotic movie to anyone other than Bill Edwards, who presently was gravely smitten by great jealousy.

The face of Thelma's muscular bed partner remained obscured from recognition. The suitor's silhouetted physique was familiar, but dark shadows hid the man's defining features. Bill's troubled mind was so much in turmoil that he could not associate a name with the sleek male body. The intimate caressing continued, much to Bill Edwards' ever-mounting chagrin.

'I've seen that guy in a locker room somewhere,' Bill imagined as rage surged throughout his mind and spirit. Edwards felt quite jilted and betrayed. The mechanic's trademark over the years had been that he was chauvinistic and selfish in his immorality, believing that extramarital affairs were a male privilege that the sinful husband assumed *his* wife never even thought about. Abundant frustration was converting into kinetic fury. Bill's heart was wildly palpitating. A severe chest pain made him grimace. An intense burst of agony pulsated between his lungs.

The crisp, clear narrator's baritone again resounded from the TV's speakers. The knot in Bill's chest was accompanied by excruciating emotional pain as the distressed sufferer struggled to inhale more oxygen. His dizzy mind still grappled with the riddle of the muscular man's identity. 'Yes, the narrator is the man making passionate love to Thelma. But who is he?' Bill wondered, as he now tightly held his chest with both hands.

"Well, William, now that we have carefully analyzed your past and your adventurous present," the narrator objectively stated, "we shall take a look at *your* future. After all Bill, this is *your* horoscope. The final scene brings to you the tranquility that your immortal soul yearns. May peace be with you, William Henry Edwards!"

The mellow, resonant narrator's voice echoed throughout the density of Bill's unstable mind. Despite his intense physical chest pain, William Henry Edwards' heart still sought revenge on his wife and her unidentified lover. No doubt Thelma had been a deceitful conspirator in producing the loathsome video. 'Her involvement is unforgivable,' the drunken, jealous husband considered. "Thelma must be punished for her infidelity; for her immoral betrayal," Bill swore to the empty *Amaretto* bottle positioned atop the gray granite-slate table.

Another aching spasm raced through the viewer's chest and seemed to maliciously pierce Bill's emotionally damaged heart. The physical pain momentarily eclipsed the terrible, guilty, spiritual bitterness the man dually felt, both in his conscience and in his soul.

The television monitor now displayed a still frame of a doctor's pharmacy prescription. As the camera angle zoomed-in, the plastic container read "Heart Tablets". In his present mental and physical condition, Bill was vulnerable to the subtlest suggestion of relief. His brain recalled a certain parallel situation, and his head turned to the left. His fatigued eyes noticed a similar plastic container that had been left by Thelma at the back of the granite-slate end table, positioned next to the faded black leather sofa. Edwards lunged for the available vial, fumbled with the protective lid, finally managing to twist it off. His frenetic tactile, hand search discovered only two pill capsules existing inside.

Bill Edwards had little time to honor better judgment. His brain was still confused from the excessive alcohol he had imbibed, and his limp body was now deeply in need of comfort from overwhelming distress. The drunken man's survival instincts were exclusively governed by fear. The knot in his chest was tightening. The sufferer frantically removed the two pills from the container and awkwardly popped the capsules into his mouth. The intoxicated victim slumped deeply into the black leather couch, his dazed eyes attempting to again refocus on the distant television screen.

"Bill," the video horoscope's obscure narrator stated in a low monotone voice, "I am very happy to report that *you* have *no future*. Bill Edwards, I repeat, you have no future! Bill, you have no future! May your erratic, mortal soul from your mediocre past now rest in eternal peace!"

Fifteen minutes later, Thelma returned to the wood-frame bungalow with Dr. Paul Lacy. The pair rushed-over to the den's sofa and found a motionless corpse with a horrible expression of rage seemingly welded upon its face. Dr. Lacy felt Bill's pulse for any evidence of vital signs. Then, the revered town physician made his authoritative pronouncement. "He's dead. Thelma. Bill's dead." Grief and shock were totally absent from their reactions.

"Paul, you've figured everything out, right to the letter," Thelma said rather matter-of-factly. "*Our* creative plan was a fine success."

"The stupid fool committed suicide being affected by the power of suggestion," the medical doctor objectively agreed. "There are no more obstacles standing in our way. Happiness is now ours!"

The couple embraced standing over Bill Edward's lifeless body, still slumped-down on the wrinkled, black leather sofa. Dr. Lacy and Thelma Edwards were savoring their wonderful moment of triumph.

"Paul, you figured-out everything to the letter. A sly fox has a lot to learn from you," Thelma praised her champion rescuer. "I couldn't live with his atrocious arrogance; his addiction to *Phillies* games; his habitual gambling debts; his excessive drinking; his gross infidelity, and his ugly marital apathy any longer."

"The smartest thing I ever did was have you hire that out-of-town freelance video photographer to document Bill's extra-curricular activities on film," the eminent MD admitted and summarized. "The rest of the inventive plot was quite easy to enact."

"And your amateur hobby of editing videotapes came in handy," Thelma added to the conversation. "You did a terrific job putting together the still photos', the old eight-millimeter home movies, along with the freelance video photographer's work. No one in town will ever suspect foul play. You're just too reputable and respected."

"Yes Thel, and the nice insurance policy will pay us five times Bill's annual income. The two-hundred-thousand-dollars will add-up to plenty of great vacations we're going to enjoy together. We'll start with a round-the-world cruise a year from now to celebrate Bill's regrettable passing. After your week of mourning, I want you to look at a *Cunard* brochure I have at home."

Paul Lacy walked-over to the *VCR* and methodically rewound the unique video horoscope cassette. The scheming doctor then pushed the "Play" and the "Record" buttons to effectively erase all evidence of convicting documentation from the tape.

"This is almost an infallible crime, if it is a crime at all," Dr. Lacy calmly articulated. "Your unfaithful husband actually killed himself by swallowing-down too much alcohol and then gulping cyanide capsules that he wrongfully thought were heart pills. That lapse of rational judgment could be construed as suicide."

"I didn't have the courage to murder him myself," Thelma acknowledged and revealed. "And I didn't want to take the risk of going to jail. Poor Bill; he's not even cold yet," Thelma Edwards acknowledged and said as she touched her dead husband's brow. "Thank God for the power of suggestion."

"Thelma, if you'll remember, I was high school quarterback and Bill was an offensive lineman who blocked for me on passing downs," Paul Lacy recollected and stated. "It looks like I'm still calling the plays for dearly departed Bill, even his last one; his video personalized *horrorscope!* the doctor cunningly laughed.

"Paul, what if there's an autopsy?" the future Mrs. Thelma Lacy wondered and asked. "Surely, the cyanide traces would be detected. Won't there be questions?"

"Don't you worry one iota Honey," Paul Lacy confidently replied. "I'm a prestigious doctor in this community, and Bill was one of my loyal patients. He had a history of heart disease and was a definite candidate for diabetes along with hardening of the arteries. Those debilitating conditions culminated in a massive cardiac arrest. I'll gladly sign the death certificate citing those details, and I guarantee you Thel that no one in the county government will ever come forth and publicly challenge my professional integrity."

Mrs. Edwards smiled at her longtime lover. The woman's mind had the cunning of Eve, and her heart the deceit of Pandora. Now Thelma had the full adoration of a divorced man, a suave, reputable professional who knew exactly how to treat her like a lady.

"I've thought of everything," Dr. Lacy remarked. "The wake will be over at my cousin's mortuary. Tom Murphy operates the most decent funeral parlor in town. His reputation as an ethical undertaker is equal to mine as a doctor. I've already briefed Tom about *our* intimate relationship, and incidentally, he owes me several big favors. Tom will be more-than-glad to help us out."

"His wife Sylvia worked as a cashier at Dan's Stationary for two years against Tom's will," Thelma recalled and declared.

"That's right," Dr. Paul Lacy confirmed. "Tom was furious when I showed him the video of Sylvia and Bill in bed together. He'll be more- than-happy to receive the body. Now let's get that blank Death Certificate out of my doctor's bag that's laying on the back seat of my car."

"I won't have to buy a black dress for Bill's funeral," Thelma commented to her devoted accomplice. "I had the foresight to recently purchase my funeral garb at the *Hamilton Mall*."

"City Councilmen"

The thriving New Jersey coast has a number of excellent boardwalks famous for amusement arcades, piers, rides, hotels, motels, gift shops, pizza parlors, and various games of chance. With the legalization of gambling, Atlantic City's revived boardwalk now features multi-million-dollar casino venues, which have significantly revitalized the city's economy. Other popular boardwalks exist along the Jersey shore in Seaside Heights, Asbury Park, Ocean City, Cape May and Wildwood, with all of those terrific beach towns being annually commercially promoted as "traditional family resorts".

The popular Wildwood Boardwalk is best known for its marvelous amusement piers and for its numerous games of chance and myriad summer gift shops. A typical boardwalk block facing the white sandy beach would feature a hot dog/hamburger stand, a pizza place, several several video game amusement arcades, a candy shop selling homemade chocolates and salt water taffy, a glassblower's shop, a gift shop, and several games of chance featuring stuffed animals for prizes. "Old Money" landlords charge exorbitant rents of up to two thousand five hundred dollars per frontage foot, with the average store occupying twenty-two feet along the wooden promenade. Many of the hard-working store renters diligently labor from Memorial Day to Labor Day just to pay their enormous expenses and in reality, the diligent merchants earn their annual profits when laboriously staying open before May 31st and after September 1st.

Thomas and Warren Wallace have owned and operated the Atlantis Coastal Hotel, which had burned down twice since 1900, when the landmark structure had first opened its doors for business. Brick-façade storefronts had been built in 1965 with ambitious tenets signing long-term leases to launch their prospective enterprises. In the year 2002, "agreed upon rents" were paid sixty percent by check (reportable to the IRS) to the greedy Wallace brothers and the remaining forty percent "hush money" was involuntarily contributed by means of "cash under the table".

Clint Vaughn was a wily Wildwood entrepreneur that owned a novelty shop along with a shuffleboard bowling game since 1994, the two stores being on the Wallace Brothers' lucrative boardwalk block. But Clint Vaughn had high aspirations of becoming "a serious boardwalk operator". and eventually, the determined and industrious young merchant acquired other establishments on other well-trafficked city boardwalk blocks, which represented a rather bold practice that jealous and greedy landlords Thomas and Warren Wallace did not entirely savor.

In the winter of 2002, Clint purchased from an elderly gentleman the Surf Bar located two blocks north of the Atlantis Coastal Hotel, and then two years later, the conscientious out-of-town shop-owner acquired a busy and profitable lemonade and pretzel concession situated next door to his notorious "Surf Bar drinking hole". And then, a nifty haunted house was added to Vaughn's holdings in the fall of 2004, and a water gun game at the boardwalk's south end was obtained in 2005. To say the least, Clint Vaughn's burgeoning Wildwood boardwalk rental portfolio certainly was becoming quite impressive. The all-too-wary envious Wallace Brothers thought that Clint Vaughn (and his ever-growing retail empire) was getting "too big for his britches".

"Something's got to be done with that sneaky rattlesnake upstart Clint Vaughn," Warren Wallace said to his older brother in late July of 2005 in the Atlantis Coastal's Victorian-style lobby. "That guy came here in 1994 and didn't have two nickels to rub together, and now the ambitious huckster is takin' over half the damned boardwalk," the younger Wallace brother complained to his elder sibling. "I say let's boot him the heck out of his novelty shop and out of his shuffle bowling game arcade, and we'll get two new tenets into those properties. And Tom," Warren Wallace continued with his tyrannical diatribe. "I think we oughta' consider changing the current rental formula into one havin' *us* ownin' a percentage of any new businesses comin' into our block. That new monetary equation oughta' generate more hidden off-the-books revenue for our corporation than the present basic store rental system does."

"Clint Vaughn's a good proprietor who always gets his rent in on time," Thomas Wallace corrected and challenged his younger and more callow-minded brother's proposal regarding the clever boardwalk maverick, Clint Vaughn. "He always pays his under-the-table debts on schedule, but you're right Warren. He's getting too big for his own sake, and his bar is a general nuisance with all the drunken derelicts it attracts. It caters to too many town mendicants and to underage drinkers havin' false IDs, too! Mr. Vaughn's walkin' a thin tightrope, and the guy's bound to tumble from grace by stumblin' over his own clumsy feet. Let's just bide our time with good old Clint and see what happens," Thomas Wallace prudently suggested. "I hear he's now negotiatin' to get the Telescope Picture business up on Boardwalk and Pine. Clint's definitely walkin' on quicksand Warren, and pretty soon the avaricious fellow's about to sink-down over his head."

"Old Money" that had been *will*fully transferred from generation to generation (like the big bucks belonging to the Wallace brothers) was at odds with the "New Money" being made and invested by upstart wheeler-dealers like Clint Vaughn. The Wallace brothers deeply resented their risk-taking tenet, because the shrewd operator was acting independently in the free enterprise marketplace without *their* expressed permission, input or consent. The all-too-perceptive power-oriented brothers wanted Clint Vaughn to be answerable to their dictatorial fiat, and obediently subordinate himself to their personal whims and inflexible fancies. Escalating conflict between the two egomaniac landlords and their adventurous boardwalk shopkeeper/tenet seemed quite inevitable.

Meanwhile, "the wily rogue" Clint Vaughn had become dissatisfied with the Wildwood Police "relentlessly harassin' and arrestin' my Surf Bar patrons" right outside *his* centrally-located drinking establishment, with the numerous cop arrests happening usually after midnight. The daring boardwalk bar owner soon rallied some political support among his loyal local customers (along with obtaining verbal commitments and endorsements from certain well-networked town contacts that positively resented the wealthy Wallace brothers). In a bold radio interview, courageous newcomer Mr. Clint Robert Vaughn announced his desire to seek a seat for city council, the chair presently occupied by the rich and well-connected old codger, the very formidable Thomas Bartholomew Wallace. The novice politician felt motivated to publicly broadcast his unique political campaign on the Jersey Shore TV and radio airwaves; the adamant upstart radically expressing to Wildwood's liquor-loving supporters *his* expressed intention of controlling and/or influencing the local police department.

But a major obstacle stood in Clint's political path: his Atlantis Coastal Hotel landlord Thomas Theodore Wallace was already a prominent member of the city council, and his seat was scheduled to be contested on the upcoming November ballot. Clint Vaughn's risky maneuver would certainly cause imminent friction between the aggressive tenet and his grudge-holding, senior landlord.

Clint had become the Wildwood citizens' favorite candidate, and Vaughn boldly predicted that he would win the "up for grabs" council seat, much to his envious opponent's total chagrin. Thomas Wallace's animosity for his industrious property tenet now rivaled the extreme rancor of *his* more argumentative and demonstrative, younger brother.

Just before August 10th of 2005, Clint Vaughn received his termination of leases (eviction notices) for his novelty shop and for his shuffle-bowling arcade. But the "hungry newcomer" continued to aggravate his former landlords by announcing in the local papers that he was relocating the two businesses four blocks south with Henry Thompson, a fourth generation Wildwood tycoon who absolutely despised the snobbish Wallace Brothers. And when it became public knowledge that Henry Thompson and Clint Vaughn had agreed in principle to form a partnership to construct "fifty top-shelf bay-side condominiums," the beleaguered Wallace Brothers' blood pressure levels climbed to very high danger readings.

"Warren, Clint's goin' big time with our rival Henry Thompson," Thomas Wallace informed his more outspoken younger brother. "Ya' know Warren, pretty soon those two chummy clowns are goin' to take over Wildwood if we allow them the opportunity. We gotta' do something about it, and something drastic mighty soon, too!"

"Don't worry Tom," Warren cavalierly answered. "I got some Mafia friends over in South Philly' that'll help us out. They're just itchin' for a little out-of-the-city job money. It pays to have the right alliances both in warfare and in local money battles. Those two connivin' boardwalk rip-off artists will get their just punishments; but right now Tom, I happen to loathe that slippery weasel Clint Vaughn a lot worse than I despise our long-time enemy Mr. Henry Thompson, whose despicable father and insane grandfather our pappy and granddad had hated with a passion. Now Thomas," Warren Wallace cautiously indicated, "let me give you the pertinent details of the exact plan I have in mind."

* * * * * * * * * * * *

In late August of 2005, Thomas and Warren Wallace put their combined strategy (to "once and for all reprimand Clint Vaughn") into swift action. Like other boardwalk merchants, Clint skimmed cash from his businesses and kept his "off-the-top" cache of hundred-dollar bills stashed in a large safe in his apartment that was conveniently situated above his popular Surf Bar. The unscrupulous Wallace brothers had a South Philadelphia Mafia hit squad conduct a secret operation by breaking into the small upstairs residence from a rear window, cracking-open Vaughn's unsophisticated safe, and then easily heisting a hefty hundred-twenty thousand dollars from the enclosure. The "found loot" was then split fifty-fifty between the appreciative mob members and the always-scheming Wallace brothers, who had been awarded the handsome "finders' fee".

Thomas and Warren Wallace were ecstatic upon reviewing their half of the recently confiscated booty. The ecstatic pair merrily sat and chatted about their fantastic good fortune in their tiffany-lamp-lit Atlantis Coastal Hotel office.

"Yes Sir, Warren. This is the easiest sixty thousand we've ever made," Thomas proudly bragged. "Clint's probably havin' severe conniptions and naggin' hemorrhoid flare-ups as I speak. And Councilman Vaughn will never go to the police because his money that had been expertly pilfered would not have been reported to the IRS because…"

"Because the hidden loot wasn't designated for reporting to the IRS in the first place!" Warren Wallace confirmed with a healthy laugh. "That's the fabulous benefit of ownin' cash businesses, Tom. The downside is that it's hard to keep a secret from your enemies, and when Clint least expected it, whammo! The targeted hustler gets robbed but can't call the authorities into the fray because he's been skimmin' cash from Uncle Sam for over a decade now. Tom, ya' can count this most recent, wonderful treasure as beautiful found money! Vaughn's already blown his main gasket, I betcha'!"

"Clint's loss is our gain; our capital gain, ha, ha, ha!" Thomas Wallace verified and chortled. "Now if that rotten skunk Vaughn had played his cards right by not runnin' against me for city council, then he'd be a hundred and twenty thousand dollars richer now, and would still have his two stores conductin' legitimate trade on our boardwalk block! Renters oughta' know their place in Wildwood society and stay humble and subordinate!"

"Say Tom," Warren mentioned after some lengthy rumination, "I got this here idea in my head, and I wanna' know what you think of it! Here's some logistics I have in mind."

"Sure thing, Warren!" the older Wallace sibling acknowledged. "If your concoction is half as decent as this Mafia grand larceny cash theft job has been, then my sensitive ears will prick-up and listen to your monologue. I always enjoy kickin' an enemy when he's down! Makes me feel mighty glad it's not me bein' stomped on!"

A week later in early September, the unethical Wallace brothers made a surprise afternoon visit to the Surf Bar, specifically to fake commiserating with Clint Vaughn and to offer their condolences at his "rumored financial loss". Contrary to his better judgment, Clint invited the two unexpected guests into his establishment's rear office to provide an appropriate setting for the impromptu conference.

"What are you two guys here for?" the surprised bar owner began. "Can I get ya' a couple of beers from the tap? How about some whiskey on the rocks?"

"No thanks!" Thomas Wallace promptly and politely answered. "There's scuttlebutt along the boardwalk that you've recently been robbed. Estimates range anywhere from a hundred fifty-thousand to a half million."

"People tend to exaggerate after hearin' some random juicy gossip like that," Clint Vaughn readily admitted. "By the end of the day, it'll probably reach a staggerin' million dollars! But I don't know how the theft news ever leaked-out, since I haven't told anyone except my mother; that is, after I swore her to secrecy."

"Well Clint," Warren Wallace articulated with a grim face. "If your mother ever goes to a beauty shop or to a charity function, the gossip is bound to slip-out. Women can't control their need to prattle all day long, especially when in the dignified company of other talkative females. It's their form of oral tabloid journalism."

"You might be fairly accurate this time," Clint verbally returned. "Now why are you gentlemen really gracin' me with your presence? Do ya' want me to relinquish my council seat? If that's your goal, forget it. I can't be bribed."

"No, not exactly," Thomas Wallace snickered in an effort to conceal his ongoing contempt for his principal adversary. "We just want you to know that we sympathize with your plight because we had a terrible robbery occur to us, too."

"What happened?" Clint asked, showing a degree of sincerity. "Who do ya' think pulled the caper? How much was stolen? Where did the theft take place?"

"Four days ago, our hotel office safe was broken into, and three hundred thousand had been removed," Thomas dramatically lied to his despised adversary. "We couldn't go to the cops, or else big problems might result after the newspapers and the Feds got ahold of the sensitive personal information. Can't trust anybody nowadays, Clint. But as soon as Warren and I heard from the boardwalk grapevine that you had experienced something similar in terms of a major burglary, we figured we'd pay you a little visit and let you know that we're sufferin' a gigantic monetary loss, too."

"Thanks for stoppin' by," Vaughn said. "Is there anything else you'd like to discuss?"

"My brother and I were thinkin' things over," Thomas Wallace emphasized. "Particularly recent negative events. I think that you and us oughta' be friends again in light of our similar unfortunate circumstances. Next Monday is Labor Day, and things slow-down on the boardwalk to almost a standstill until the following weekend. What do ya' say Clint that you come out on our yacht for a private fishin' party?" the older Wallace brother rhetorically asked. "We'll reminisce old times, drink a few beers, catch a few white marlins, and then get your opinion on a possible business deal we're gonna' cut you in on. How about accompanyin' us on our scheduled fishin' expedition next Tuesday morning? I guarantee you'll be excited at the nifty offer we got in mind."

"What time next Tuesday?" Clint wondered and asked with avaricious-looking, sparkling brown eyes. "But first, I gotta' check my calendar appointment schedule."

"Nine a.m. at Thomas's house on the other side of the bay," Warren indicated. "And whatever ya' do, don't disclose anything to anyone, including your aging mother. If we find-out that you've spilled the beans about any aspect of our dynamic proposition," Warren Wallace threatened, "then the deal's off, and we're all back to negative square one again. Are our cordial and genuine terms of consultation acceptable to you?"

"Sure thing!" Clint replied, ineffectively holding back his mounting interest and enthusiasm. "I'll meet you at your dock at quarter to nine on Tuesday. I gotta' confess that I'm really speculatin' about what you fellas' have cookin' on the drawin' board. Maybe we can find some middle ground and agree on something substantial, and finally call a permanent truce to our past disputes. Cooperation is always better than hostility; that's my family credo, even though I gotta' confess that my slick father was a notorious Hammonton loan shark!"

Clint Vaughn shook hands with both clever brothers to seal the general terms of their "prospective financial arrangement". "I've always wanted to take a ride on your terrific cabin cruiser," the Surf Bar owner confided to his prominent visitors. "I hear that baby is worth over a half million. Where are we goin'? I'm not the best fisherman when it comes to deep sea big game."

"That's perfectly all right," Warren Wallace diplomatically stated with a false grin forming upon his wrinkled countenance. "We're goin' out to the Baltimore Canyon just southeast of Cape May. And don't worry about a thing, Clint. The Atlantic in early September is as calm as Lake Placid. Our very terrific mission will be accomplished, and everything's gonna' be peaceful and friendly."

* * * * * * * * * * * *

At 8:45 a.m. on the Tuesday after Labor Day, Clint Vaughn showed-up at Tom Wallace's dock for his ocean fishing excursion out to the renowned Baltimore Canyon. The conniving Wallace Brothers greeted their guest and extended to Vaughn full courtesy and hospitality. Soon, the three sailors boarded the impressive "Point of No Return", and after the mooring ropes had been unraveled from the dock posts, the awesome fishing yacht gently left the pier and slowly headed south toward the Cape May inlet, directly where the Delaware Bay meets the majestic Atlantic.

"Never had the pleasure of riding in something so fabulous!" Clint praised Warren Wallace as the sleek craft opened-up its dual inboards to three-quarters-throttle just east of Cape May, as the luxurious cruising ship was heading straight south towards its Cape Henlopen, Delaware destination. "When are you' fellas' gonna' tell me your big investment plan? Not that I don't relish white marlin fishin', but frankly, sooner or later, I know that my mounting curiosity is definitely gonna' be getting the better of me."

"Here's a cold beer!" Thomas Wallace offered his inquisitive passenger, the beverage presented to the brothers' curious passenger in an ice-chilled brown bottle. "After each of us reels in a white marlin, then we'll stop our deep-sea activity, and my brother and I will sit down and confidentially disclose our benign intentions. And my brother and I are absolutely sure you won't be disappointed."

"Show some patience and self-discipline!" the equally devious Point of No Return co-navigator chided his anxious passenger. "The summer boardwalk season's just about over, and it's now time to relax and reflect on the great business trade we all enjoyed. There's plenty of time to settle-down and converse about our grand opportunity," Warren Wallace advised his impulsive, invited guest. "But let's collect those three white marlins as taxidermy trophies, and I assure you Mr. Vaughn that by high noon, you'll fully learn about our special project," the younger Wallace brother insisted. "The purpose of this little sea-cruise trip is to solidify our trust so that we can be three respecting partners in an ironclad joint development venture that'll make you glad you've accompanied us today on this splendid white marlin exploit. We'll cross Delaware Bay, and when we're finally parallel to Rehoboth Beach," the yacht copilot elaborated, "then we'll swing east to the Baltimore Canyon."

"All right," Clint amiably acceded. "But you guys oughta' write mystery novels, because you really know how to keep an already intrigued passenger in suspense."

A mere forty-five minutes later, the ultra-magnificent pleasure yacht/fishing boat finally arrived at its twenty-five-mile offshore objective. The handsome craft was now stopped with its engines off so that the three "mariners" aboard could conduct their friendly fishing contest. By eleven-thirty, Clint had admirably reeled-in a forty-five-pound white marlin, which eliminated him from continued participation in the competition because Warren was able to bring in and gaff a forty-nine-pound fish, and Thomas Wallace later skillfully landed an enviable fifty-three pounder that was laid writhing and wriggling on the Point of No Return's planked wooden deck.

"Looks like you lost our little contest!" Warren snidely related to the now-fatigued Clint Vaughn. "But I gotta' tell ya' Mr. Vaughn; you're gonna' badly lose in an even bigger way. But this second time with your precious life!"

"What are ya' talkin' about?" Vaughn vehemently objected. "I think you've had one beer too many, or maybe the hot sun has melted your brain cells."

Just then three awesome Mafia hit-men rapidly climbed the steps from the cabin cruiser's galley, and the fearsome mobsters menacingly confronted Clint with their shiny raised revolvers. Warren and Thomas Wallace laughed exceedingly as the surrounded boardwalk mogul finally realized the true gravity of his predicament.

"What's this ugly-lookin' scam all about?" Vaughn adamantly protested. "This is a lousy setup! I've been duped!"

"Exactly," Warren Wallace replied with a huge smirk apparent on his rosy sunburned face. "My brother and I have been thinkin' about disposin' of you ever since you foolishly decided to challenge Thomas and run and obtain your coveted city council seat. Now distinguished Sir, it's time for you to leave this evil, wretched, diabolical, dog-eat-dog world and visit the afterlife, so that you'll never be around to annoy and aggravate us again."

"That's what the hell you think!" Clint audaciously answered. "Tony, Lucky, Frankie; let these two obnoxious turkeys have it!" Clint commanded the three hired Sicilians. "These two aristocrat punks have been a thorn in my side for all-too-long now!"

The three dedicated Mafia hit-men turned their bodies and their revolvers, and the thugs pointed their weapons at the two suddenly flabbergasted Wallace Brothers. Before either Thomas or Warren could ever utter a plea (or even a defiant shout), three triggers were pulled six times each, and the two dastardly boardwalk tycoons fell like heavy sacks of potatoes onto the Point of No Return's now-bloodied deck.

"Thanks for agreein' to get involved in the neat double-cross!" Clint commended his three hired henchmen. "It was well worth three hundred thousand bucks to quickly exterminate both those pathetic miserable creeps."

"It pays not to be too frugal when dealin' with professional hit men!" Mafia confederate Tony "Bulldog" Brigandi concluded and expressed. "You were lucky enough, Mr. Vaughn, to be the highest bidder to do an assassination; actually, to do two assassinations!"

"First, we'll tie these two deceased creeps up and chain them to portable anchors," accomplice Joe "Lucky" Battaglia chimed-in. "Then we'll toss the scumbag evidence overboard."

"Hey guys," Sicilian associate Jimmy 'Gorilla" Noto pointed-out. "There comes our boat that's right on schedule for our planned rendezvous at sea. Say, we can tie each guy to a white marlin that could serve as chum for other big fish to nibble on! After that, we'll tow the Point of No Return five miles from here and dynamite it. That ought to confuse anybody investigatin' the two missing persons lost at sea theory. I never did like that pair of pompous, dirtbag WASPS now lying dead at our feet!"

"Okay men," Clint Vaughn finished with a broad smile. "Let's do those things before anybody accidentally spots us floating around out here. And as a generous reward to express my sincere gratitude, you three Philly' guys can keep the sixty thousand portion ya' had stolen from me, and then later gave back to me. And thanks for getting out the word to the Wallace Brothers and givin' those dead knuckleheads the dual boardwalk theft idea, too! I almost laughed my rear end off after the arrogant clowns came and visited me at my Surf Bar. And gentlemen, as a special added bonus, I'm goin' to give your boss Frankie "the Fish" Errera the remaining third white marlin as a special bonus to be mounted in his office for his stellar loyalty, and for his superb cooperation!"

"Dual Events"

My wife and I had never been to Bermuda. Joanne and I had always previously vacationed at various resorts on popular islands in the *Caribbean*. We had enjoyed week-long hiatuses on exotic isles like Barbados, Puerto Rico, Aruba, and St. Thomas. We once took a *Cunard* cruise from San Juan to Venezuela, which featured scenic stops in Grenada, St. Lucia, St. Marten, St. John, and St. Croix.

"Ginger" and I have always been warm-weather people. We prefer sunbathing and snorkeling to winter lodges, snowmobiles, and skiing. Our travel agent had recommended Bermuda anytime from May to October in order to experience the best possible weather. My wife and I looked-over some descriptive literature about the famous *Atlantic* paradise several weeks before boarding Flight #98 out of *Philadelphia International Airport*.

The takeoff from Philly' was very smooth and easy. When the "Unfasten Your Seatbelts" light flashed-on, Joanne and I became engaged in a casual conversation. It felt good getting away from the mayhem and the myriad demanding routines of American mass society as the sleek jet gently lifting into the wild blue yonder.

"It says in this excellent brochure that Bermuda is a British territory and only a mere two-hour flight from Philly'," my wife read out loud. "It takes us longer to drive from our South Jersey home to New York than to fly from the *Quaker City* to Bermuda."

"We'll probably spend more time going through customs in the *Bermuda International Airport* than we will traveling on the plane," I cynically answered. "Let me take a gander at the map on the back of that pamphlet when you're through with it. I need to know exactly where everything is located in our new semi-tropical environment."

I immediately observed that Bermuda was not an island, but actually a chain of about three hundred islands. I learned from my reading that nine of the coral masses are populated, and they are connected by a series of well-designed drawbridges and causeways.

"Claire said at the travel agency that the island's capital Hamilton is a tourist's paradise," I recalled and shared. "It's remarkable that a cluster of tiny specks could be populated, and yet so isolated in the *Atlantic* six hundred miles off the coast of North Carolina."

"I don't think the Wright Brothers would've made it from Kitty Hawk to Hamilton," my clever spouse, a veteran middle school Geography, English and History teacher laughed. "If I remember correctly their initial flight was just over a hundred feet."

"I read that the *Princess Hotel* has perhaps the finest accommodations on the main island," I added, "and just by coincidence that *that's* our exotic destination. Actually, I can't wait until we land and get situated."

"It's pink, my favorite color," Joanne observed and related with a smile and a wink. "Just like my bikini and my nightgown."

The entire *Boeing 727* flight out of Philly' was as smooth as satin. My wife was perusing some more pertinent literature about Bermuda's myriad sites of interest, while I was examining a small booklet that described in detail our choice of lodging. At that moment the entire Universe seemed tranquil and harmonious.

"Joanne, I gotta' admit; the *Princess Hotel* is really gorgeous, in this advertising photo'," I said before taking another sip of my *Seagram's Seven* on the rocks. "It's situated on a scenic harbor, has both a salt-water and a fresh-water swimming pool, and the facility has four splendid gourmet dining facilities. It even has fishing charters and glass bottom tour boats docked right on the harbor."

"And we also have beach privileges at the *Southampton Princess* on the other side of the harbor," my wife contributed and informed. "They have a ferry shuttle that transports guests between the sister hotels. I'm definitely going to check-out the *Southampton* facility the first chance I get."

"Honey, that sounds really great," I amiably agreed, "and I just know that this hiatus is going to be a memorable vacation; I just know it. I'm glad we chose this gorgeous hotel and this fabulous island. This is goin' to be an unforgettable pleasure adventure."

"Look here at this article describing our hotel," Joanne pointed-out. "It states that Mark Twain used to stay at the *Hamilton Princess*. It says it was the author's favorite place on the island. If it's good enough for Samuel Langhorne Clemens," the social studies/language arts teacher told me; "then the place oughta' be good enough for us."

It all seemed like a wonderful fantasy. There we were, escaping hectic work responsibilities and flying thirty-five thousand feet above the gleaming *Atlantic,* leaving the doldrums of jobs and home chores back in New Jersey. And Bermuda guaranteed us floral splendor and radiant sunshine. I looked at my watch to confirm reality. It was Monday, July 8. We were on a jet heading towards semi-tropical leisure and elegance. I was at peace with the Universe.

I again glanced at my wristwatch, which I had received as a college graduation present and noticed that the trade name was *Hamilton.* Then I realized a small coincidence; Hamilton, Bermuda and Hamilton wristwatch. My name is Hamilton Alexander, and remarkably, my face did bear a strong resemblance to Alexander Hamilton's singular portrait engraved on the ten-dollar bill, but I refused to acknowledge *that* similarity when someone would insist that I looked like someone else.

I chuckled at the cute parallelism that my mind had coordinated. 'Life is full of such unique associations,' I mused and thought. It came to mind that my birthday was July 27, or 7/27, and we were flying southeast on a *Boeing 727*. I conveyed those subtle vignettes to Joanne, who indulgently laughed and snickered at my "absurd superstitious imagination".

I glimpsed across the jet's aisle in the midst of our merriment. My eyes scrupulously observed a dark-complexioned gentleman seemingly staring at Joanne and me. I suspiciously thought I had caught him peering at us several times before during the flight, ever since we had left Philly'. At first, I mentally wrote the matter off as 'someone who disliked others that were a little loud and having a good time.' Instinctively though, I almost automatically loathed the stranger without ever verbally communicating with him.

At that moment, bad vibrations pulsated-down to the marrow in my bones. I turned and sipped the last ounce from my delicious rye whiskey on the rocks. My sixth sense perceived a bad chemistry existing between *him* and me. I whispered my secret feeling to my wife. Joanne casually dismissed my intuition as "an acute case of badly jangled nerves" and as "possessing a too-distrusting nature."

"Maybe you're right about my imagination and my twisted nerves," I answered as politely as I could. "I'm gonna' hit the lavatory and wash my face. That *Seagram's Seven* was supposed to tranquilize me, and not activate my defense mechanisms along with my kidneys. Maybe I'll be a better evaluator of character when I return," I softly expressed to my wife. "But my sixth sense is seldom wrong when it comes to evaluating another man's sinister motives and his malicious intent."

I freshened-up in the small bathroom cubicle, and then returned to my seat five minutes later. I was deeply disturbed seeing the suspicious-looking stranger now sitting across the aisle engaged in polite conversation with my all-too-garrulous, lovely wife. The new acquaintances were jovially exchanging anecdotes about freak accidents each had experienced on past vacations. Joanne introduced me to our fellow passenger, but I must confess that I felt very uncomfortable and self-conscious in Nolan Phillips' presence.

'Nolan Phillips; where had I heard that name before?' I pondered as I briefly peered into the man's cold gray eyes. The name had a definite familiar ring. 'Something to do with history or literature,' I guessed. 'It has to be another bizarre coincidence like Hamilton and 727,' I surmised. 'Nolan Phillips seems to register some academic association. but I can't exactly identity what it is.'

My natural audacity was tempted to ask Nolan and Joanne what person in history or literature shared Phillips' vaguely familiar name, but I did not want to impress the stranger as being academically deficient in common cultural knowledge. As a rule, I generally try avoiding public embarrassment or awkward situations at all costs.

'My mind must be really fatigued,' I determined in my defense. 'I need this *Princess Hotel* escape from the pressures of everyday reality,' I concluded. 'Joanne's right. I'm probably overacting to something that doesn't even warrant a second thought.'

Our new acquaintance tried his best to be affable. I was certain that the appellation Nolan Phillips, which my distrustful mind had been considering, was not a contemporary name but instead, was somehow connected with the past; the remote past. As I intensely studied the man's very distinct facial features, I believed his name might have been that of a former high school classmate, or perhaps someone from twenty years ago from a picture in an old *Rutgers* college seminar. His name was like one of those trivial facts my high school teachers made me memorize, only to be forgotten a week after the final exam' had been administered. It was there in my memory, yet it wasn't.

As Joanne and Nolan Phillips amused each other with broken elbow and sprained ankle stories, I promised myself that I would research the gentleman's name when I could find quiet sanctuary and sufficient time to fully analyze the situation in a Hamilton public library. There I could fully investigate the matter, if indeed it were a matter at all.

"Hamilton, Nolan would like to buy us drinks," Joanne informed me. I acceded to the stranger's friendly request, simply to be cordial, but I did not relish one iota my wife socializing with Phillips. I was puzzled that she hadn't sensed the danger in him that my perceptive instincts had felt. Maybe it was my strict neo-Puritan childhood resurfacing. Joanne had always called me "a prude". 'Could it all be jealousy in disguise?' I wondered. 'I don't even know this man,' I further contemplated. 'Why should every cell in my being instinctively hate him? He doesn't look like a criminal, after all!'

Moments after a pleasant blonde stewardess served us our particular drinks, much to my displeasure, Nolan Phillips disclosed that he would also be staying at the *Hamilton Princess Hotel*. The impertinent fellow then related to me that I looked exactly like someone he had known in the past, but he couldn't pin it down exactly who that anonymous person was. His odd observation rattled my consciousness. I felt that Phillips possessed the sixth sense, too.

"Nolan, everybody says that same thing to me," I deceivingly answered, "and I do have a pretty standard-looking face. Just today. the *American Airlines* receptionist back in Philly' mentioned the exact same notion. But Nolan, unfortunately, nobody seems to be able to tell me who my anonymous facsimile is," I responded as courteously as I could feign.

I conjectured what Nolan Phillips might have looked like wearing a white colonial wig or a tilted confederate hat. He too looked vaguely familiar, but my rampant imagination couldn't pinpoint his identity, if at that very moment, my life immediately depended on it.

"Well then, who do you think I look like?" I candidly challenged. "The President, the British Prime Minister, the Pope, Bill Gates?"

"I don't know," Nolan replied with an element of regret in his voice. "I can't seem to associate it right this minute. I've seen a portrait of you somewhere, perhaps in the *Guggenheim*, the *Metropolitan Museum of Art*, possibly the *Louvre*, or maybe in the *Smithsonian*. But the mystery gentleman I have in mind has a long nose. A trifle curved-up at the end, just like yours!"

Joanne was amused with Nolan Phillips' insulting comparative description, but I was deeply mortified. 'Is he trying to harass and ridicule me in front of my wife? Does he have malicious intentions?' I reflected and fumed. 'If we had lived in olden days, I would probably be motivated to challenge him to a duel with swords or pistols,' I thought.

Much to my chagrin, Joanne had not detected any malevolence in Nolan Phillips' disposition, or in his uncouth, graphic language. She considered his vile comment about my different-looking nose as being "cute and on-target".

'Maybe it's your strict upbringing that makes you skeptical of anyone that appears too convivial upon first contact,' I rationalized. 'It must be my *WASP*ish childhood, my jangled nerves, and my fertile imagination,' I speculated. 'Learn to just get along!'

The *727* gracefully landed at *Bermuda International Airport,* and the passengers eagerly disembarked. Inside the terminal, courteous Customs Officials dressed in khaki Bermuda shorts thoroughly inspected the anxious tourists' luggage. The three long arrival lines moved forward at a fairly rapid pace.

My wife was talking-up a storm with two lady passengers she had
met before boarding the *727* in Philly', and Joanne was vividly
relating her excitement about being there, a visitor "in paradise". My
nervous mind ignored her prattling and focused on getting our
traveling credentials together for impending inspection. And to add to
my quandary, my brain was preoccupied with fears, doubts, and
suspicions concerning Nolan Phillips, and those turbulent thoughts
were all rotating simultaneously in my mind like strange patterns
inside a mental kaleidoscope turning in many directions.

Contrary to my ordinarily calm disposition, I angrily admonished
Joanne about her apparent friendliness with Nolan Phillips. My wife
indicated that she was tired of being embarrassed by my unwarranted
"public hostility toward perfectly *friendly strangers*".

"Now that's an oxymoron if I ever heard one," I criticized, "and I
think your false observation about me is downright *pretty ugly*."

"Sometimes, you don't realize how cruel and offensive you can
be," my wife flippantly snapped back. "And you must learn to control
your nasty temper or seek psychiatric help. Did you hear me
Hamilton? Calm down! We're here on vacation to relax!"

"You're possibly right," I guiltily acknowledged. "I'm sorry for
overreacting like that. I'll be better tomorrow once I get acclimated to
this new environment. You know Joanne, I always have trouble
adjusting to new places. I promise to treat you like a lady for the rest
of our glorious stay here."

My spouse applied a big hug around my neck right in the center of
the waiting line. Several other travelers smiled in recognition of her
affectionate gesture. I looked behind me and noticed Nolan Phillips
snidely gazing in our direction; his evil eyes hidden behind thick dark
sunglasses. I immediately felt antagonism toward his deliberate visual
intrusion into our brief romantic interlude.

I felt compelled to go over and shatter his big protruding mandible
into a dozen or more fragments. Fortunately, I resisted that very
strong impulse, and reason prevailed over reckless inclination. An
attack of that nature would confirm to my wife that I was indeed
paranoid, and that I indeed lacked maturity and self-esteem.

Finally, much to my relief, *Ginger* and I proceeded through
Customs without incident or difficulty. A representative from the
Hamilton Princess Hotel was holding a sign over his head to attract
the resort's prospective guests to gather around him. Soon, the
employee assembled an entourage of thirteen people. 'Thirteen is an
unlucky number,' I automatically thought. 'If it weren't for the
presence of Nolan Phillips, who was traveling alone, the number of

292

people being transported would be a more acceptable dozen,' I reckoned. Then the accommodating hotel driver very efficiently loaded everyone's luggage inside the rear compartment of the large pink van, and the excited tourists all found comfortable seats after clambering inside.

The trip from the airport on St. George's Island to downtown Hamilton on Bermuda Island was about six scenic miles. The vehicle passed merry tourists riding on mopeds, which was the basic means of transportation for the more courageous and independent-minded island visitors.

The driver courteously pointed-out various places of interest on our splendid route. The hotel van traveled over a picturesque bridge, and then it motored through the village of Flatts. Stately boats gently rocked back and forth in a majestic canal of crystal-clear, aqua-green water. The friendly driver stopped and told us to scan the canal for varicolored tropical fish flitting about in the shallows, and we all claimed to have seen at least five apiece, even though I never saw even one during the "mass hallucination".

Fifteen minutes later, the large pink van pulled into the main entrance to the elegant *Hamilton Princess Hotel*. The edifice was truly worthy of its dignified royal name. The impressive structure was a pastel pink castle enveloped in and abounding with lush green semi-tropical landscaping. The extremely beautiful palace regally lorded over placid *Hamilton Harbor*.

I sauntered up to the mahogany registration counter, showed my reservation voucher to the desk attendant, and then presented my *MasterCard*. I received prompt, polite service from an attractive brunette hotel clerk who possessed a distinctive British accent.

"Here are some terrific pamphlets on sites of interest you might want to visit, or itineraries you might desire taking during your stay," the pretty young lady communicated. "Be sure not to miss the colorful military band parade on Front Street on Wednesday night at eight. It's a must. Be sure to take your camera."

"I understand you have a ferry that goes over to the *Southampton Princess*," I inquired. "That's quite a convenience for your guests."

"Yes, and they leave every two hours," the registration clerk shared. "And don't forget the glass bottom boats that take you out to some really wonderful coral reefs," the young lady reminded me. "People often tell me they come back here just to see the beauty of it all over again."

I thanked the well-mannered, obliging young woman for her assistance, and then turned toward Joanne and was troubled to see

Nolan Phillips standing several yards behind us in a parallel long registration line. I tried ignoring his presence, but then my wife gave the ubiquitous annoyance a half-hearted wave. My concentration was interrupted by the voice of the charming brunette female clerk. "By the way, Sir. I must tell you that you do have a very familiar face," she strangely stated. "Have you ever been told about that resemblance before?"

I felt like screaming-out, 'Just look on a U.S. ten-dollar-bill, remove the guy's wig by placing your thumb over *his* head, and see if you could figure-out the great mystery; you ridiculous fool!' But I miraculously controlled myself along with reigning-in my notorious volatile temper.

The young lady's question really pestered me because its timing coincided with the disquieting appearance of Nolan Phillips at the registration counter. I knew that the young female's inquiry was purely innocent but nevertheless, at that particular time, its utterance really irritated me.

"I only wish I knew who my anonymous twin is," I answered the clerk's innocuous commentary. "You can't imagine how many people ask me that same question. I think I'm getting some sort of phobia over it," I added. "But somehow, I've managed to live with the vexing riddle."

A cheerful bellhop brought our four luggage pieces down the magnificent mahogany-paneled lobby that featured an exquisite pink marble floor. Expensive vases, paintings, wall tapestries, and statues ornamented the stately corridor on both sides. Our room guide next conducted Joanne and me through several smaller hallways, and then into the oldest section of the well-constructed palace. We were swiftly led across a verdant garden that featured hibiscus bushes and tall royal palm trees, which could have rivaled any that might have flourished in Eden. We finally arrived at our well-appointed suite, situated in the newest section of the inimitable hotel.

Our luxurious accommodations overlooked the salt-water pool in the forefront, and also the tranquil waters of aqua-blue *Hamilton Harbor* in the serene background.

"This is no doubt the same view that Mark Twain enjoyed here at the *Princess*," I theorized and reported to Joanne while feigning rare enthusiasm. "The guy had good taste and good eyesight, too."

"We gotta' commend my favorite literary genius on his terrific selection of accommodations," my wife replied. "I'll have my Advanced English class read a selection of chapters from *Tom Sawyer* after I'm assigned my new teaching schedule in September."

Being in a blithe spirit, I gave a five-dollar tip to the appreciative bellboy. Joanne and I unpacked our suitcases, and she put away her cosmetics in the bathroom vanity while I stored-away our toiletries inside two matching bureaus. After getting the remainder of our things situated, we donned our bathing suits and scampered-out to the salt-water pool as if we were a couple of carefree school kids.

A friendly employee advised me that beach towels could be obtained near the fresh water pool on the opposite side of the hotel's central promenade. Upon returning from my errand with the towels, I became angered when I noticed Nolan Phillips, in a tight-fitting French bathing suit, casually talking with my wife. Sensing that I was distraught with his presence, the bothersome fellow dismissed himself from *our* company before certain confrontation would ensue.

"I'm going to try a rum-swizzle at the hotel's Flamingo Bar," Phillips announced just before departing our company. "Care to join me for a few libations?"

"Maybe tomorrow, Nolan," I rankled, "because we're just getting used to the place. And besides, Joanne and I are still a little exhausted from the flight and from the long waiting lines in the airport and in the hotel."

When Nolan Phillips left our presence, I jealously interrogated my wife. "What did he talk to you about?" I demanded to Joanne. "And what was so amusing between you two? The gigolo must think our relationship is weak and vulnerable."

"Just wait a minute," my wife warned. "You're overreacting a bit, don't you' think?"

"Before this week's up, that obnoxious creep's gonna' swallow his teeth!" I threatened. "All twelve of them," I sarcastically added.

"Please stop being so nasty Hamilton," Joanne insisted. "Nolan seems like a very lonely man. He's just trying to be friendly. I can't understand for the life of me why *you* despise him so. You must have had an unhappy childhood and very few close friends!"

I had difficulty concealing the extreme animosity my total being felt for Nolan Phillips. "Maybe you're right, but I have my doubts about him having any honorable motives," I lectured Joanne like a modern-day Diogenes. "I just don't like how he boldly approaches you when I'm in the airplane's lavatory, or when I'm off for forty seconds to pick-up a pair of beach towels. I really trust you, Honey," I confided. "But I don't trust Phillips as far as I can throw him. I guess I'm basically a very possessive husband."

That Monday evening, Joanne and I had supper on the American Dinner Plan in the regal *Three Crowns Restaurant*. My emotions had finally adjusted back to an even keel from the afternoon's brief encounter with rather-aggravating Nolan Phillips. Originating from a small nearby lounge, my wife and I heard a band playing a nostalgic medley of Frank Sinatra hit tunes.

After sumptuous dinners of shrimp and crab-meat delicacies, Ginger and I stepped to the romantic musical lounge where we were enjoying tropical rum-based cocktails. We intimately danced and romanced to the familiar powerful lyrics of "My Way".

"Ginger, I didn't mean to explode like I did at the pool today," I confessed and apologized. "I'm a little edgy being in a foreign place with so many strangers surrounding me."

"You always do things *your way* regardless of the circumstances," my spouse declared while alluding to the Sinatra song to which we were dancing. "Give Nolan a chance to prove himself," Joanne objectively suggested. "He seems lonelier than you are, as hard as that is to believe. At least you have me to lean on."

The six-piece band took an intermission break. My wife and I made peace and strolled like two newly-weds hand-in-hand back to our secluded table. I glanced across the almost empty room and saw Nolan Phillips sitting all by his lonesome. Joanne followed a whim and suggested that I invite him over for a drink. I stubbornly refused.

Much to my utter astonishment, my wife signaled for the reprehensible acquaintance to join our company. I was deeply distressed by Joanne's gesture of sympathy. Nolan Phillips casually strolled over to our cozy table. We ordered a round of tropical drinks, and randomly talked about college fraternities, pro' football, and the Venus and Mars natures of men and women. After we consumed a few more rounds of cocktails, Phillips didn't seem like such a bad fellow after all.

"Where did you go to college?" I inquired. "You have a North Jersey accent. I'll bet you attended either *Seton Hall,* or perhaps *Fairleigh Dickinson.*"

"*New York University,*" Phillips corrected. "I'm a prosecutor assigned to the Manhattan *DA's* office. What fraternity did you belong to?"

"Lambda Phi Sigma at *Glassboro State College,*" I said. "And then I transferred to *Rutgers University* in New Brunswick and became a Kappa Phi, studied architecture, and am now a builder. I also loyally serve as a Hammonton town councilman back in Jersey."

I volunteered to amble over to the bar and get a third round of tropical rum cocktails, since our waiter was nowhere in sight. The beleaguered bartender had trouble hearing my order because the band had returned from its break and started playing again, and I had to loudly scream my requests above the catchy melody of "New York, New York".

As I turned my shoulders around, my soul became infected with grief and inflamed with hate. I detected Nolan Phillips jitterbugging with Joanne. My next reaction was thinking that I did not want to cause a wild scene. 'Could this creep be so insanely stupid that he can't read my absolute contempt of him?' I angrily wondered. 'When the time and place are right, I'll gladly read him the riot act for sure,' I promised my ego.

When the two nimble dancers returned to *our* table, I told Joanne that I was experiencing a very vicious headache. I insisted that *we* should return to our luxury suite so that I could relax. Nolan noticed my sudden discomfort, and sensing my enmity toward him, the deceitful jerk diplomatically asked to be excused from our presence for the evening. As the idiot nonchalantly walked away, I glared menacingly at his back like a mongoose scrutinizing a cobra.

On the return to our suite, Joanne and I stopped to converse at Adams Lounge, a large colonial hall of great grandeur inside the hotel. Our conversation, which centered upon deplorable Nolan Phillips, became a little too raucous for our fellow pedestrians to overhear in *our* sophisticated, public environment. The argument continued as we stepped briskly down the corridor to the privacy of our hotel quarters. Inside, I had to control myself from angrily slapping Joanne across her face. I recalled wishing that we had gone to the Bahamas instead.

"I never want to see you dancing with that lousy creep again, do you hear?" I wildly demanded. "He's up to no good! Can't you sense that in him?"

"You're a very vain, shallow, and jealous man!" my wife shouted back. "You're an ingrate!"

"Maybe so, but I'm really going to hurt that wise-guy if he doesn't figure-out which women he can't become aggressive with! He needs a good pulverizing!"

Tuesday morning, Joanne and I rented mopeds to further explore the city of Hamilton and its vicinity. It was great fun sightseeing the island and leisurely stopping at various unscheduled destinations. The general warmth in our fragile relationship seemed to be somewhat rekindled.

At noon, we took a lunch break at a side-street fast food stand, several miles outside Hamilton. A blue-and-white-striped canopy covered a rear garden area where customers could eat in American picnic style, insulated from distracting highway noise. Joanne and I had hamburgers, French fries, *Cokes,* and some frank conversation.

After consuming the well-prepared "American cuisine", we decided to ride our motorbikes over to Flatts Village to again enjoy the fantastic view that the place provided. But then Joanne's moped refused to start. I was never mechanically inclined, and my futile attempts at correcting the annoying malfunction proved it. Then, a very suspicious and repugnant thing happened.

Nolan Phillips climbed out of a nearby rented car and offered to transport Joanne's incapacitated bike in his trunk back to the *Princess Hotel* Rental Agency. I reluctantly agreed to *his* cavalier show of friendship. I didn't trust his basic intentions or his phony sincerity. I wondered how he had managed to show-up right in the height of the motorbike crisis. Nolan Phillips was the last person in the world I wanted to owe a favor.

My mind hypothesized that Phillips had surreptitiously tampered with Joanne's motorbike, rendering it immobile, so that the devious fellow could arrive on the scene and role-play "Mr. Messiah". I did not relish the notion that the obnoxious man had been keeping *our* private movements on the islands under his close surveillance.

I drove Joanne to the *Hamilton Princess Hotel* with her riding on the back of my moped, with her arms wrapped around my waist. I told her en route to Hamilton that it had been more than coincidental that Phillips showed-up at the exact same time as when the moped suddenly became inoperable. My wife saw matters differently.

"The guy's doing us a really big favor by taking my rented moped back to the hotel, and now you're being totally vindictive and ungrateful for him helping us out," my wife chided. "You wouldn't be happy if you had a hundred-dollar-bill and were the only kid inside a candy store."

Nolan Phillips had dropped Joanne's moped off at the Princess Rental Agency, minutes before Ginger and I got back to the Hamilton resort. I observed the 'Bad Samaritan' standing next to the outdoor business counter, casually smoking a cigarette and glancing nervously every now and then at his *Rolex* wristwatch.

At the counter, the rentals' manager gave my wife and me a twenty-dollar rebate for our "unfortunate moped inconvenience". The amiable employee then said that I looked exactly like someone else. I became a little peeved at his observation, and told the startled fellow to mind his "own moped business".

"Sir, I didn't mean to offend or quarrel with you," the gentleman qualified in a British accent. "And believe me when I say I don't want to pry into your personal life."

"You've been on Bermuda for too long and are suffering from a warm-climate version of cabin fever," I retorted to the congenial moped agent living six hundred miles away from the nearest continent. "You probably also think that my wife looks like Miss America; perhaps Miss Universe!"

"Now that you've mentioned it, Sir" the British gentleman-turned comedian responded. The moped manager then excessively laughed while Joanne gave me a Medusa-like stare that should have turned me into stone.

I slowly walked over to Nolan Phillips and reluctantly thanked him for his unexpected assistance. The jackass very deliberately winked at Joanne and me and then articulated, "It was the least I could do, Hamilton." I wondered what "the most" Phillips could do really might be.

That night, my wife and I again dined at the *Three Crowns*. I had filet mignon and Joanne raved throughout the meal about her "fantastic" shrimp, clams, and mussel combo' meal. I was happy to see and realize that Nolan Phillips was not around to torment my faltering sanity. "Thank God *he's* nowhere in sight to further instigate me," I mentioned to my traveling mate.

"You're just envious because Nolan is acting like Superman, or behaving like the Lone Ranger," my lady companion very effectively needled. "He always comes to the rescue right when we need him. He's a Johnny with spots everywhere to be standing on."

"I need him like I need three broken ribs and two massive, malignant brain tumors," I sneered like a true chauvinist pig. "That guy's trouble with a capital T!"

Wednesday morning, Ginger and I sampled a delicious continental breakfast inside our well-appointed suite. We donned our swim suits and took the early morning ferry across Hamilton Harbor to the magnificent *Southampton Princess*. We improved our rapport by frolicking in the surf, snorkeling, and later sleeping for an hour on the pink-sanded beach.

At noon, my pretty Italian wife and I enjoyed a sumptuous seafood buffet at the resort's Whaler Inn, and then we rode the ferry back to the more conservative *Hamilton Princess Hotel*. Joanne and I took turns showering, and next, decided to have room service deliver our ordered dinners.

Just before dusk, Ginger and I dressed in typical tourist attire and strolled six blocks to downtown Hamilton for the Wednesday night military parade that the girl at the hotel's reception counter had strongly recommended for us to experience. The colorful event celebrated the *British Empire's* former glory days during the late-colonial-Victorian era. I sensed Nolan Phillips' presence in the crowd of spectators, but thankfully, I did not see him anywhere in the assembled throng throughout the hour-long elaborate military march spectacle.

"Will you please learn to relax and become a pleasant, cooperative tourist," my wife reprimanded me towards the end of the parade pomp and pageantry. "You're obsessed over nothing! Why do you keep turning around? You're going to need a chiropractor before this trip is done. You should only rubberneck back in the states where reality is more informal."

"He's here in our midst. I know he's here scrutinizing our every move," I sullenly replied. "I know he's secretly spying on us, that uncouth uncivil intruder."

"I think you're developing agoraphobia, claustrophobia, and Nolan Phillips' phobia all at the same time," Ginger smartly and spontaneously answered my obvious paranoia. "You need to lie down on a psychiatrist's couch and tell the mind doctor everything you know about your mother!"

On Thursday morning, I ambled-down to the lobby's Registration Desk and purchased two glass bottom boat tickets for a late morning coral reef expedition. When the genteel male clerk handed me the tickets, I instinctively checked the immediate vicinity to ascertain that Nolan Phillips was not stealthily observing my personal activity occurring at the main desk.

Later that morning, Joanne and I boarded the ominous-sounding *Perils of Fate* and were inadvertently standing near the stern of the glass bottom boat. I gritted my teeth when my keen eyes perceived Nolan Phillips sauntering down the long, narrow dock ramp heading in the direction of the sightseeing boat. The sinister rogue was the last passenger to board the *Perils of Fate*, which soon eased from its mooring and cruised into *Hamilton Harbor*, hardly leaving a wake.

The genial captain was quite knowledgeable and pointed-out various places of interest to his captivated, all-tourist audience. Joanne gave Nolan Phillips a tentative wave. I gave the distrustful passenger the absolute cold-shoulder treatment. I immediately sensed that potential conflict was imminent, but tried appearing generally civil and benign.

The *Perils of Fate* passed through an open drawbridge that connected two parts of Somerset Island, which was the last major link in the eastern Bermuda chain. The likeable captain navigated his vessel to a rendezvous point about a quarter of a mile out to sea, where *we* joined-up with four other glass-bottom boats originating from other Bermuda hotels and marinas; the vessels forming what my erratic mind synthesized as a "sightseeing armada".

The ship's pilot explained over the intercom speakers that the five boats would motor out to the nearby coral reef and view the spectacle one ship at a time in a "caravan on water", gradually enacted so that the exquisite sea animals below would not be disturbed in their natural habitat.

While the jovial captain was busy addressing his alert and enchanted passengers over the intercom, I overheard Ginger chatting with the same talkative ladies that had been on our flight from Philly'. The gossipers were exchanging ideas about different merchandise and clothing bargains available for purchase on Front Street. In the meantime, I was involved in deeply thinking about how to resolve certain negotiations of my own.

I decided to define some basic terms with my assumed adversary. I figured it was time to let Nolan Phillips know my exact sentiments about his constant, aggressive intrusions. I approached the agitator's standing position near a railing on the other side of the glass bottom boat. The scoundrel leech was looking-down at the colorful coral reef, seemingly admiring its natural beauty.

"I'll level with you Phillips," I sternly-but diplomatically began. "I would like to be on friendly terms with you for the remainder of my vacation here. I'm basically a very jealous man," I strongly maintained, "and I would appreciate it if you would stay away from my wife. That means keeping your eyes and hands off of her, is that perfectly clear?"

"Look here Hamilton; I'm not trying to make time with your wife, if that's what you're implying!" Phillips defensively stated with a florid face. "Your spouse reminds me of an attractive girl I used to date in Manhattan. Joanne brings back pleasant memories of Cindy."

"That's a very unimaginative and completely lackluster excuse," I curtly answered. "But I'm officially warning you, Nolan; lay off, or else there's going to be big trouble in paradise. Stop stalking my wife like you're some kind of urban predator!"

The captain's voice came over the intercom's speakers, and the navigator instructed all passengers to report to the "below deck". He then maneuvered the *Perils of Fate* to a favorable position directly above a marvelous array of tropical fish, thick vegetation, and coral resplendence. Soon, everyone aboard was stationed below and partaking of the real-life visual fantasy; that is, everyone except Nolan Phillips and me. My intent was for us to continue our disagreement in private.

"Look Phillips; it's not my fault Joanne looks like an old flame of yours," I firmly emphasized. "Just remember pal; she's still *my* wife, regardless of how your warped mind associates her with your past! One thing's for sure. I'm not going to allow *your* amorous past to interfere with *my* present!"

"Ya' know, Hamilton. Your mind contrives situations that don't really exist. You're always trying to reinvent reality, and then define it in your own neurotic terms," Phillips assertively accused. "And I seriously do believe, if I may add, that you need professional psychological help!"

"Tell me the truth," I adamantly insisted. "Did you follow us to the luncheonette outside Hamilton the other day and tamper with Joanne's moped while we were eating? Did you stoop to committing that kind of vile sabotage?"

"You've really gone off the deep end!" Phillips hollered while losing his temper. "You're crazy! Neurotic! Psychotic! You need the services of a competent shrink, quick!"

I roughly grabbed Nolan's arm to indicate my seriousness. He attempted escaping my tight grasp. We violently wrestled against the railing above the boat's stern. Phillips frantically swung his clenched right fist twice at my jaw. I blocked his first and second punches, but his third blow caught me solidly in the chest. We fiercely grappled some more as the captain, monotonously speaking below, continued his loud lecture into his microphone; his voice being amplified over the boat's loud speakers.

I managed to get my right hand free from my tormentor's grasp, and savagely smashed Phillips with an uppercut to his chin. It was a lucky, clean shot that I had delivered, and my attack stunned him in his tracks. The lummox staggered backwards from my blow's force. We had degenerated into two desperate Darwinian animals, primitively struggling for survival of th fittest. Danger was not a concern. The laws of civilization had been abandoned. We were strenuously battling for dominance in a two-man jungle.

I wrapped my hands around Phillips' throat, and squeezed firmly with all my might. My heart and wrists wanted to strangle the detestable jerk in the worst possible way, in order for me to achieve my ultimate victory. We were both wildly gasping for air, panting like two lung cancer patients. Adrenaline liberally rushed through my arteries and veins, giving me extra strength. I twisted all my weight to the left and maniacally shoved Nolan Phillips over the boat's stern railing. My ears heard a loud splash. Thirty seconds went by on my *Hamilton* wristwatch. Nolan Phillips did not surface.

My obstinate ego defensively justified to my conscience that my extreme violence had been performed in self-defense. I considered leaping into the *Atlantic,* but I instantly thought that the salvaging of *his* life wasn't sufficient motivation to convert me into a Good Samaritan exercising self-sacrifice. '*He* wouldn't do the same for me if our roles were reversed,' I selfishly speculated. 'I will live to enjoy the rest of my life at Nolan Phillips' expense,' I decided.

My pupils again intensely scanned the azure-emerald water below, searching for some evidence of the despicable brute, but there was no sign of his body. 'He's drowned and good riddance,' I surmised. 'He's probably hit his head against the coral rock, and went unconscious and drowned,' my stubborn mind concluded.

My lungs inhaled and exhaled ten deep breaths to help me regain my composure and my normal sanity. I tucked my light blue cotton shirt inside my blue denim jeans and then pretending that everything was business-as-normal, I furtively descended the black metal steps to listen to the captain's drab narration. Everyone standing in a circle below deck was preoccupied, all passengers visually appreciating the fantastic coral reef. No one ever noticed my stealthy arrival.

Joanne was still intermittently gossiping with her lady tourist friends and did not observe my quiet appearance below deck. My conscience was now saturated with guilt, but my heart felt little sorrow for Nolan Phillips' well-deserved demise. My mind truly believed that I had vanquished a terrible foe. Phillips had been bent on wooing my wife, and then destroying me in the process. I observed that the other more docile tourists were content staring-down at the fabulous reef through the boat's crystal-clear glass bottom, so I pretended to do likewise in order to cunningly conceal the atrocious felony I had recently committed.

"If you'll all direct your attention to the direction of the bow," the captain suggested, "you'll see some really splendid tropical fish. Those two yellow ones are known as long-nosed butterflies. Those multicolored ones are queen angelfish. Look at those lobsters crawling near the center of the reef next to that impressive white brain coral."

The other tourists' eyes keenly focused on the colorful underwater enchantment. I still was breathing heavily and perspiring from my traumatic ordeal, that incidentally, had exhausted most of my energy. My mind was spinning in a quandary as the euphoric captain continued his boring monologue.

"Have you ever seen such beauty anywhere before?" the boat's official lecturer rhetorically asked. "There's a spotted goat fish over to your right, and that mean-looking critter over there on the left is called a Nassau grouper."

The captain's glib presentation was rudely interrupted by an elderly woman's horrendous shriek. The startled lady pointed her forefinger to the right side of the glass bottom's underwater, coral reef view. Everyone reflexively turned to witness the source of her terror. Soon, there were numerous cries of shock and loud exclamations of disbelief.

Nolan Phillips' rigid body was seen floating beneath the boat, face down, and the corpse was slowly drifting toward the ridge of coral rock. The dead man's forehead then roughly banged into the coral reef, and everyone aboard the vessel cringed except me. The impact turned the corpse sideways, facing the boat's bottom. Nolan's eyeballs were bulging out of their sockets. Screams of horror echoed throughout the cluster of shock-stricken passengers. The captain pleaded with the crowd to "quiet down; please don't panic"! But much to his dismay, the mass hysteria continued.

Everyone else observing the gruesome phenomenon gasped as Phillips' remains continued drifting with the current underneath the *Perils of Fate*, with the cadaver eventually wedging between the boat's hull and the immovable coral formation. Blood seeped out of the corpse's forehead, and traces floated upwards from his mouth. The red water plume then filtered-outward in the direction of the boat's glass bottomed pane. The stressed-out captain ineffectively commanded for his now-delirious passengers to climb-up to the main deck to escape viewing the ongoing, morbid spectacle.

The Harbor Police were notified of the recent tragedy. The local government sent an expert *SCUBA* team down, and the divers soon located and successfully removed Nolan Phillips' body from the azure sea, and the victim was immediately transported to the Hamilton Hospital Morgue.

That afternoon, I was visited in my hotel suite by a team of very intelligent detectives conducting a "routine investigation". The chief inspector believed Nolan's death "an apparent suicide" rather than an official homicide. "Nolan Phillips had confided to me that he had been despondent, lonely, and depressed," I divulged to the investigators. "He was in a total state of anxiety; sort of bipolar, if you know what I mean," I clarified and continued my elaboration. "I believe the man was psychotic, or perhaps even paranoid. When the visiting loner was finally left alone, I suspect that Nolan willfully surrendered to his death wish, and decided to abandon this cruel world once and for all."

Joanne related to the authorities that Nolan Phillips was "a lonely sort of man in search of friendship". Our corroborative statements were accepted as appropriate depositions to be presented during the coroner's inquest. The team of investigating officers thanked us for our "cooperative, helpful observations and comments".

"His body does have a broken jaw," the chief inspector noted. "We know *that* fact even before any autopsy has been performed. Do you know anything about how that injury might have happened?"

"I saw his chin hit up against the coral reef as his head drifted below the glass bottom boat," I calmly testified under duress. The policemen conscientiously jotted-down my testimony on their report pads. I wisely hid the sore knuckles of my right hand behind my back while I was providing the examiners with the false information.

"Unless there's some radical change in venue," the chief inspector said, "you won't be detained on Bermuda for further questioning. I think you've both satisfied all our immediate concerns."

Friday was our last scheduled day on the heavenly main isle. Joanne wanted to purchase some souvenirs for our two nephews and niece. We agreed to separate, and then meet again an hour later in front of the *Atlantic,* a huge tourist ship out of New York docked along Front Street.

I casually strolled the pavement, sauntering past a strip of shop window displays colorfully designed to lure American and European tourists inside. I glanced into a novelty photography store that took old time black and white pictures of vacationers dressed in "authentic historical period costumes". I stepped inside the cheerfully decorated establishment out of sheer curiosity. I must honestly confess that some mysterious psychic force seemed to attract my attention, and then magnetically draw me into the store.

My eyes perceptively surveyed the wide variety of outfits on exhibit from different periods in history, and I observed that the apparel was hanging on long display racks. I decided to try on a colonial costume along with an accompanying white wig. My fancy thought that Joanne would be delighted with a photo' of me attired in eighteenth-century garb. 'She desperately needs me to show her something amusing so that she'll think I still possess a sense of humor,' I reckoned. My hands eagerly put on my chosen ensemble. A sprite British sales clerk assisted me with maneuvering into my complementing silk, long-tailed coat. My blue eyes examined and appreciated my stellar appearance in a full-length mirror.

"Sir, if I may say so, you look just like that chap on the American ten-dollar-bill," the salesman alertly observed and stated. "Hamilton, I believe the man's name was. Never made it to President, did he?"

"No," I replied. "He was assassinated in a duel before he could ever attain that high office."

The genial salesman was elated when I ordered ten reproductions of the original photo' he had taken of me dressed in the colonial haberdashery. I paid the affable gent in fifty and twenty-dollar denominations. I did not want to give him a ten-dollar bill and have him meticulously compare the note's portrait to my profile, and I certainly didn't wish to give him my *MasterCard* with my name "Hamilton Alexander" on it standing-out in bold relief.

At that odd moment, I was grateful that I didn't have to explain those particular details to the cheerful clerk, who was delightedly preoccupied making arrangements to send the ten duplicate photos' to my New Jersey residence. I then asked for and received directions from the blithe salesman to the Hamilton Library. I shrewdly told the clerk that I was a visiting college professor who needed to study an "important academic matter".

At the library, I located *Encyclopedia Britannica* H. My eyes avidly read the biographical account of Alexander Hamilton. My mind's keen interest was impressed that Alexander Hamilton had been the first U.S. Secretary of the Treasury and that both he and Benjamin Franklin were the only two "non-presidents" honored by having their portraits engraved on American paper currency. The informative article further stated that Hamilton had been killed in a pistol duel with Aaron Burr in Weehawken, New Jersey, on July 11, 1804. 'July 11!' I thought in amazement. 'That was yesterday, the same day that Nolan Phillips had met his demise.'

I rushed to grab *Encyclopedia Britannica* N. I thumbed-through the pages and found the exact information for Philip Nolan, which was the coincidental name reversal of my deceased former enemy. Next to the listing was the instruction "See Edward Everett Hale". I directed my attention back to Encyclopedia H and anxiously leafed through the pages with great anticipation. My comprehensive research yielded some satisfactorily staggering results.

Edward Everett Hale (1822-1909) was a distinguished clergyman, editor, humanitarian and noteworthy author. He is most remembered for his popular novella *Man without a Country*. The creative tale, the encyclopedia explained, was about a young officer named Philip Nolan, who had exclaimed during a court martial hearing, "I never want to hear of the United States again." As punishment for his lack of patriotism, Nolan was then assigned to and placed on a warship, and his commanding officers were instructed that no one would be permitted to provide "the prisoner" with any relevant news about the United States until *his* death. Philip Nolan was the notorious *Man without a Country*.

The informative article further indicated that Nolan had been court-martialed by the Army because the defiant young soldier had been suspected of being a disciple of Aaron Burr, a former maverick United States Vice President serving under Thomas Jefferson. The encyclopedia description detailed that according to Edward Everett Hale's story, Aaron Burr desired to carve-out a new independent territory for aristocrats and Federalists in the American frontier. The article finished by clarifying that Philip Nolan was actually a fictitious character, but that the story *Man without a Country* had been written in the style of a factual account, and the famous tale was especially designed to muster Northern patriotism during the *Civil War*.

'Philip Nolan, a fictional character,' I pensively thought. My inquisitiveness had reached its ultimate peak. I found *Britannica Encyclopedia* B and frantically flipped through its pages until I located "Aaron Burr". I felt a trifle dizzy and giddy when I examined his portrait. The dimensions of the library room seemed to expand and contract several times during my intense scrutiny. Aaron Burr's documented portrait looked identical to the Nolan Phillips that I had briefly known on my Bermuda vacation.

Burr had murdered Alexander Hamilton in a gun duel on July 11, 1804. I looked very much like Hamilton. Nolan Phillips looked almost identical to Aaron Burr. I had been responsible for Nolan Phillips' death on July 11. The incredible 'dual events' were really 'duel events.'

'I've gotten revenge for a spectacular pistol duel that had occurred back in 1804,' I thought and considered while sitting inside the stone-silent library. But quite confidentially, I felt no particular guilt or remorse for performing my evil deed aboard the ironically named *Perils of Fate*. After all, according to the infallible *Encyclopedia Britannica's* text, Philip Nolan was a fictitious character. In my mind, Nolan Phillips had to be a reincarnation of that same fictitious character. I've objectively concluded that I did not murder Nolan Phillips. Let me be completely rational about this entire matter. It is absolutely impossible to kill a recycled, imaginary, fictional character from American literature. I must be genuinely specific in organizing and presenting my astute analysis. 'In logical truth, only a delusional crazy person would ever think otherwise,' I intelligently evaluated and concluded.

"Loyalty to Duty"

Carl Taylor has been dead for nine months. The county coroner had issued a death certificate verifying Carl Taylor's one-way passage into the hereafter. A lengthy memorial service had featured a series of wonderful eulogies delivered by mourning family members and friends.

The deceased had enjoyed being dead the first six months following his memorial service. The man has twice visited the quiet cemetery where his marble tombstone rests beneath tall, shady oak and elm trees. Taylor was truly happy not occupying the grave beneath the impressive stone monument. Carl was glad that *his last will and testament* had left provisions for such a magnificent granite tribute to himself.

Carl had been a very successful computer systems-networker for a large Philadelphia banking institution. Taylor and his family lived on the other side of the *Delaware* in Cherry Hill, a fast-paced New Jersey suburb where every yuppie driveway featured a new Lincoln or Jaguar accompanied by a nifty *Sports Utility Vehicle*. Cherry Hill was a haven for well-to-do, ambitious executives whose chief concern was upward mobility on the greed-oriented American corporate escalator.

Carl had been married to the former Helen Weston (once a contestant in the Miss New Jersey Pageant) for twelve years. The couple had an eleven-year-old son Joey, and Stacy was their nine-year-old daughter.

The lovebird newlyweds were very compatible the first several years of marriage. The enthralled pair went out to dinner twice a week; the couple socialized with friends who shared their vivid perception of the "American dream", and the merry bliss-seekers afforded each other ample love and emotional encouragement.

"Helen, after I finally get my Master's Degree in Business Administration from *Temple U.*," Carl explained one summer night before the affectionate duo ventured-out to an *Outback Steakhouse* for dinner, "then you can quit your guidance post at the high school."

Similar conversations were exchanged in later years after the Taylors had their two bratty children. But with each passing twelve months, the verbal communications between the sexes became more and more confrontational.

"I like my job helping kids with their problems and making key life decisions," Helen answered. "And I certainly don't like the idea of being a full-time housewife. I think I'd rather enter the Mrs. New Jersey Contest instead."

"What about being a full-time mother?" Carl interrupted in a fairly demanding tone of voice. "You shouldn't worry about those kids at the high school more than you care for your own flesh and blood. Our son and daughter's needs should always come first. Joey and Stacy have our superior genes."

"Are you trying to send me on some kind of a wild guilt trip?" the slightly-peeved female educator replied. "If you are Carl, it's definitely not working!"

"You're a good wife Helen, and all of that kind of mushy stuff," the dominant male parent carefully stated. "But there comes a time when the man of the house has to make enough money so that his spouse can be a full-time mother."

"Carl, I like how you help by doing the dishes three times a week. You even vacuum the rugs and wash the clothes every other day," Helen complimented. "As long as you can do those things for me, I'll still be able to have a career in education, and also be a devoted wife, and a basic responsible mother, too."

"Soon Helen," Carl paused, searching for the right words, "I'll be making enough money to hire a maid so that *we* can have more free time for ourselves. The brass ring isn't far out of my reach any more. You'll soon see!"

As Carl made his gradual ascent into the higher echelons of the computer-banking world, the couple's fragile interdependency diminished. When more wealth was accumulating in their joint high-tech-oriented stock brokerage account, the high-tech computer-networking whiz became more selfish and less cooperative with Helen and her chosen profession. Both truculent adults possessed very stubborn personalities. Their nuptial vows were much safer during their newlywed years when the almost-destitute Taylors had few material comforts. Escalating conflict between the alpha husband and his obstinate wife was both predictable and inevitable.

"Helen, I'm disenchanted with my redundant job," Carl complained while helping his wife prepare a Thursday meatloaf dinner in their home's spacious, custom-designed kitchen. "I see the same unhappy faces and the same monotonous problems day in and day out. It's a cruel existence to suffer five days a week just so that we can live in this big suburban mansion and drive around in expensive cars. Sometimes, I think I'm livin' a hollow life. There has to be more to happiness than what I'm experiencin'."

Helen had little consolation to offer. The formerly affable wife had become contrary and non-supportive of Carl's chameleon-ever-changing character. "You've become too materialistic," Mrs. Taylor complained, "and now you're looking for a shortcut; an express elevator to the top! I'm keeping my guidance job just in case you prematurely burn yourself out like a defective light bulb."

"Please stop badgering me with your adolescent guidance psychology bull!" Carl snapped. "You aren't talkin' to a confused acne-faced senior tryin' to gain admission into a two-year community college!"

Carl and Helen's marital ship was navigating through a series of dangerous dire straits. The couple no longer sought entertainment at fancy nightclubs, or attended *Walnut Street Theater* performances in Philadelphia. Over the past several years, Helen had become more wrapped-up in her challenging school responsibility when she was surprisingly promoted to "Guidance Director" with a staff of seven subordinates under her leadership. In the meantime, Carl had been preoccupied saving money for a Margate or Ventnor beach house down payment, so that the addicted gambler could be nearer to Atlantic City's hot casino action.

"Carl, you never take me to the *Society Hill Playhouse,* or to the *Walnut Street Theater* anymore," Helen commented one Friday night. "Your selfish attitude makes me wish I could travel back to high school and decide on some different life choices about boyfriends and courtship."

"I hate Philly' more and more each passing day," Helen's burned-out husband declared. "And worst of all, I have to work downtown Monday through Friday, and go to night school uptown three nights a week." The husband paused to harness his next fleeting thought. "I can't stand crossing the *Ben Franklin Bridge* any more, even with the *E-Z Pass* convenience. And I can't help with the dishes tonight because I have to finish a major networking job at a new branch office way out in Springfield. My company's goin' to pay each member of my team double time to finish the bank's newest state-of-the-art *ATM* installation."

Joey and Stacy were much closer to Helen than they were to Carl, partly because their father was often absent from the home front earning sufficient money to sustain their high-on-the-hog lifestyle. Although the children had everything that they might want or need in terms of *things,* the self-centered son and daughter were almost unappreciative of their dad's financial contributions to *their* welfare.

Carl frequently complained to Helen about *their* "argumentative and totally ungrateful kids."

"Helen, don't ignore my comments as if they're old discarded junk collectin' cobwebs in the attic," the husband warned a month following the couple's last fierce argument. "I've been workin' my fingertips down to the bone to get ahead in this cruel dog-eat-dog world. If Uncle Sam didn't take almost half my salary to develop missile defenses and to keep the welfare and food stamp systems alive for the millions and millions of deadbeat citizens, then we'd have more free time to tour the world and smell the roses."

"You love things more than you love your own family," Helen bluntly retorted. "You're without a doubt an egotistical, male chauvinist pig of the first degree!"

"If it weren't for me and my work ethic," Carl nastily returned, "you and the kids would be livin' in a cardboard box house and wearin' genuine burlap clothes!"

Ever since the house mortgage had been paid-off, Carl and Helen quarreled ten times as often as they actually had made love. Trust had disintegrated into suspicion, and mutual admiration had subtly transformed into disrespect.

Joey and Stacy were perilously caught in the turbulent, emotional riptide that flourished in the *dire straits,* and Carl instantly became sullen every time he sensed that *his* children favored their mother's point of view over his. Taylor felt betrayed by the loss of his son and daughter's allegiance, and by their "disloyal" alliance with his "small-time-career" guidance department wife.

The troubled man needed an escape mechanism to compensate for his general loss of pride. The networking guru came under the influence of a major vice the husband believed he could afford. Once a week, Carl frequented Atlantic City casinos and wagered tall stacks of chips at roulette, blackjack, and craps tables.

When a high school girls' gym teacher confidentially informed Helen of her husband's secret and excessive gambling addiction, the angered wife threatened "separation followed by imminent divorce". These new family problems caused more pressure on the Taylors' already strained relationship.

"You're tryin' to henpeck me!" the indignant husband curtly accused his main antagonist. "So, what! I hit the casinos once a week! Big deal! I can afford it! It's not like Lady Luck is another woman I'm havin' an affair with! I'm not blowin' away my only income Social Security check! So, stop acting so freakin' jealous!"

"If it weren't for the children," Helen answered in a peeved voice, "I'd definitely seek a separation tomorrow! Unfortunately, you value the Queen of Diamonds over the Queen of Hearts!'"

Carl considered his wife's proclaimed independence as "an attempt at creating female dominance". The man of the house viewed her increasing defiance with increasing repugnance. Taylor despised what he frequently called "Dame Van Winkle petticoat tyranny". "Stop bein' such a vicious shrew!" Taylor madly accused. "I'm the best thing that ever happened to your existence, and you ought to remember that! Before you met and dated me, your future was mediocre at best!"

"Don't flatter yourself! You're living a big ugly lie every single day!" the wife yelled as she slammed the down-stairs powder room door behind her.

Ten minutes later, Helen exited the down-stair's small bathroom and found her husband sitting on the family room's soft, cordovan leather sofa. "Carl, I know from reliable sources that you're gambling heavily down at the boardwalk," Helen alleged, "so from now on, I want *you* to give *me* the same amount of money you're losing at the tables. I'll put the amount aside for the children's education. You were a much better human being when you had nothing, and when I had to slave as a less-than-minimum-wage deli waitress to put you through college. Now, I can't tolerate you and your obnoxious greed any longer. Honestly, I think I even despise and loathe you!"

"Helen, you resent me because I'm successful in the corporate world while you're mired-down working in the going-nowhere-fast public sector," the husband vehemently replied. "I know we had a better rapport when we had to drink out of plastic cups and didn't have two quarters to rub together. The casino is simply a safety valve for me to relax and to let off a little steam, that's all!"

Carl Taylor paused to gauge the impact of his remarks. His wife started trembling and sobbing. "Helen, I have to get away from the pressure caused by *your* continuous contempt," the boorish husband justified. "Maybe subconsciously I'm actively gambling to simply lose everything we have so that we can go back to the happy days before money and property changed us for the worse," Taylor finished, trying to show a bit more feigned consideration to cover his excessive arrogance.

Helen easily saw through her husband's façade, and persisted in her already outlined demands. "I want four hundred dollars a week for the kids' savings accounts," the wife firmly stipulated. "And I want a new red fox coat for myself. I also insist on having a new

Jaguar. Is that clear Carl! I want those *things* only because I can't stand to see you throwing your hard-earned money away to Donald Trump and his greedy casino friends," the wife emphatically chastised. "Maybe those additional expenses will force *you* to stay home and finally learn to become a decent father."

The husband was in his usual haughty, sarcastic mood. "That's a deal!" Taylor immediately and astonishingly agreed. "I've been winnin' big down the shore, not losin' big, Helen. Winning! Did you hear me? W-I-N-N-I-N-G-B-I-G! Do you understand! Not losing B-I-G, but winning B-I-G! So, according to *your* most recent equal payment demand, if I lose my bets at the tables," Carl angrily argued, "you get *nothing* until my luck drastically changes for the better, and I begin winning money again over in good old *A.C.*"

"You have a granite heart that has no desire of elevating itself to become wooden," Helen aggressively insinuated. "And if I may add, the important word 'humble' isn't found anywhere in your tiny self-centered vocabulary!"

"Stop tryin' to mock and berate me!" Carl yelled back. "My ego needs praise; not criticism! Wives like you have made lesser men commit suicide."

"Your cocky attitude makes me want to vomit!" Helen returned. "You were a more sensitive person when I first met you in *McDonald's* where you were wiping crumbs off of messy customers' tables!" The adamant wife's tirade was just as scornful and unrelenting as her husband's ill temper had been. "Now you've turned into a lousy *crumb* yourself!"

"If you can't say anything good about me," Carl Taylor screamed back, "then keep your pathetic trap shut! Sometimes you think you're the County Prosecutor out for fresh blood while preaching nonsense on your own personal warpath!"

"I'm not going to dignify this conversation by answering your pigheaded ridicule!" the wife hollered as she hastily abandoned the family room and re-entered the powder room, again slamming and rattling the door behind her. 'I would have slapped him across the face if it weren't for the children hearing our argument and then getting upset,' Helen thought and sobbed to the mirror above the sink. "Lord, give me strength!"

Antagonism, derision and discord between the feuding pair soon became a daily ritual. Salvos of abusive remarks were exchanged every night after supper, usually when the children were at friends' houses or were occupied in their respective rooms listening to loud pop' music and playing violent fantasy video games.

Carl eventually surrendered the master bedroom to Helen. The oppressed spouse began sleeping in the spare "guest room" with Candy, the family's prized golden retriever. The irritated guidance department employee suggested *their* need of consulting a skilled marriage counselor, but Carl refused to put any faith in the opinions of "some loser" who earned less than a third of his hefty take-home salary. Livid Helen Taylor had angrily wished her husband dead on more than one occasion.

One Saturday morning in May of 2000. Carl received a surprise telephone call from his Aunt Harriet, who lived thirty miles east of Cherry Hill in Egg Harbor City. The eccentric widow was a wealthy matron, and perhaps the richest citizen in the small Jersey pinelands' town. Harriet's enterprising husband had amassed a sizable fortune in the oil distribution business, and since Harriet Wilson had no children, Carl was her favorite nephew and favored heir apparent. The computer whiz would never refuse any reasonable request from her snobbish, aristocratic lips.

"Carl Darling; how's everything?" Aunt Harriet pleasantly asked over the telephone. "It's been so long since I've heard your wonderful voice, either over the phone or in person."

"Just fine Auntie. Things couldn't be better!" Taylor politely lied. "The children and I were plannin' to visit you soon!"

"Why that would be simply marvelous!" Aunt Harriet exclaimed. "And how are the children doing?" the caller asked without ever mentioning Helen's accursed name.

"They're both as chipper and as ornery as ever," the spoiled nephew fibbed and attested. "Joey's the star of his *Little League* baseball team, and Stacy made the honor roll with flying colors again. I'm very proud of their achievements," Taylor bragged without ever referring to Helen in the all-too-phony conversation.

"Why that's absolutely fantastic!" Harriet Wilson marveled and exclaimed. Finally, Taylor's aunt got down to the purpose of her unexpected call. "Carl, I'd like to ask a special favor of you. My bridge club is coming over to my place for a special session next Saturday, May 20th."

"Aunt Harriet, I haven't played bridge since you had taught me how when I was in elementary school," Carl interrupted. "I wouldn't know where to begin, and truthfully, my unskilled playing might actually embarrass you!"

"No, Dear Nephew; I don't want *you* to play bridge," Aunt Harriet clarified. "Now, for amusement purposes only, I've engaged the services of a fortuneteller to read for my friends at the bridge get-together. The wonderful woman is reputed to have amazing psychic talents. But the gifted lady will come only if I can get six clients. My closest friend Irene Gares can't make the session because of her grandson's wedding. Could you possibly drive down to Egg Harbor next Saturday so that I can satisfy the wonderful reader's six-customer quota? It certainly portends to be a most unique psychic experience. I'll remember your favor, always."

Carl considered his favorite aunt's peculiar request and then offered his affirmative reply. "Well, Aunt Harriet; *my wife's* takin' the kids to New York on a shoppin' trip next Saturday. And they'll be stayin' overnight with her parents up in Paramus. You're only twenty minutes away from Atlantic City, so after I'm through with your astrologer, or whatever she is, I'll high-tail it to the casinos to try my luck. I really need a little R and R."

Aunt Harriet was elated with her nephew's positive response. "I knew you wouldn't let me down," the elderly woman thankfully replied. "You're the most dependable relative I have."

"Now Aunt Harriet, I want you to know that I don't place that much credence in soothsayers, but for *you* I would show-up as an Arab on a camel if you had insisted on it. Count me in. What time should I be there?"

"That's absolutely sensational!" Aunt Harriet excitedly remarked. "And I'm sure the girls will be delighted to make your acquaintance. You've met Fran Burns. She'll also be there along with her friend, the new woman in town, Denise Fascetta from Arizona. Seven p.m. will be fine. Ta-ta Carl, and don't forget to say 'hello' to Joey and Stacy for me."

Carl smiled as he placed the telephone down into its cradle. 'Aunt Harriet has always been fascinated by the bizarre,' Taylor thought. 'I have to go make a showing, even if the whole scenario seems too ludicrous. Her place is only fifteen miles down *Route 30* from *Harrah's* and the *Trump Marina*,' Taylor concluded with a smile appearing upon his countenance.

The computer wizard's stereotype of a fortuneteller was a mental image of a cheap, gypsy charlatan with a large crystal ball and a stacked deck of tarot cards lying on a flimsy card table. But the novel suggestion of going to a seer for a private reading did stir-up an element of mild curiosity in Taylor's very skeptical and materialistically-oriented mind.

Saturday, May 20th arrived on the calendar, and Carl Taylor drove his brown Lincoln Town Car to Egg Harbor City to be in the company of Aunt Harriet's 'old hen gossiping bridge ensemble'. The

316

loyal nephew tried his best to act cordial amidst the assemblage of pretentious, snobbish, wrinkled, old, gray-hair ladies. Harriet Wilson made a big fuss over her "favorite nephew", and Carl relished the "celebrity status" that his glib aunt lavishly conferred on him to her dear lady invitees.

Aunt Harriet announced to her guests Carl's expressed intention of proceeding onward to Atlantic City immediately after *his* reading, and the cooperative old ladies graciously consented to allowing him to be the first of Harriet Wilson's guests to confer with Marian Brenner, the visiting oracle.

"How much is the reading fee?" the nephew inquired. "I've never been to one before."

"A crisp *Ulysses S. Grant* will suffice and cover everything," Aunt Harriet enthusiastically and theatrically replied, as her sophisticated bridge associates giggled at their host's imaginative choice of descriptive terminology.

Taylor descended the thirteen steps to the finished wood-paneled basement, which had tables, chairs, and an oval bar, the spacious room being arranged and configured in the pattern of a small 1940s-style nightclub.

The computer networking genius had always been cynical of the occult. Carl walked across the black and white checkered tile floor and boldly introduced himself to the lady seer, plucked-down a crisp fifty-dollar bill to satisfy the requisite reading fee, and then the impetuous client awaited formal instructions from the very attractive woman seated opposite him.

"Carl, my name is Marian Brenner. Now here is a regular *Bible*," the woman in the black chiffon dress announced as she handed Taylor a thick black-leather book. "When I direct you," the serious-looking reader instructed, "choose a page and then a verse from that page at random. As you read and think about your passage from the *Holy Scripture,* I'll closely study the aura radiating-out from your body, particularly from your head. Make sure your selection is from the *New Testament,* which is located toward the back of the *Bible.* "

"Is that all?" Carl haughtily asked. "It sounds entirely too simple and not very arcane at all!"

"I will then read aloud the same passage that you have randomly selected," Marian Brenner solemnly and soberly stated. "And then I shall incorporate the *Bible*'s sacred words with my perceptions of the energy field surrounding your flesh. That is what I really will be reading Carl; your aura. I then shall be able to interpret God's divine words in relation to *your* life force."

Taylor reflexively smiled and nodded, indicating that he perfectly understood the simple but rather unusual directions.

"Now Carl," Marian Brenner softly directed, "choose a page from the *Holy Gospel.* I remind you; take my instructions seriously; please limit your choice to the *New Testament.*"

The meeting was not exactly the preposterous fiasco Carl Taylor had anticipated. Marian Brenner spoke very deliberately and appeared extremely sincere about her sacred endeavor. The middle-age woman's prudent implementation of the *Holy Bible* added an element of solemnity to the eerie atmosphere that her presence in the dark-lit basement presented.

The invited oracle was indeed a very polished, intelligent woman. Her strong resilient voice added a dimension of validity to the incidental parley with the seated non-believer. Only the reader's bleached blonde hair, her large circular earrings, her golden bracelets, and her penetrating brown eyes conformed to Carl's stereotype of what a common fortuneteller should look like. Despite being a tarot card apostate, Carl Taylor opened the *Bible* to the *New Testament,* and the intrigued visitor then randomly selected a passage from the *Gospel of Luke.*

The prognosticator's revelations soon amazed the listener and quickly and effectively captured his undivided attention. Marian Brenner revealed that Carl was a very prosperous "computer professional" who had come from "very humble beginnings".

'Aunt Harriet probably told her that specific information,' Taylor skeptically ascertained. 'This peculiar woman couldn't have pulled *that* relevant knowledge out of thin air, and I don't put too much credence in this crazy aura radiance business, either!'

"You have a son and a daughter Carl; you like gambling, and you're not presently having a harmonious relationship with your marital partner," the reader calmly and accurately revealed.

Marian Brenner paused to see what kind of impact her valid statements were having upon her subject. Taylor again suspected that Aunt Harriet had given the psychic adequate background to describe everything she had so far disclosed and so, the basement guest acted unfazed and unperturbed.

"I also sense powerful ominous vibrations that indicate you are about to be betrayed by a woman. And I also detect that you will have exceptional good luck tonight if you stay away from *Harrah's Casino* and visit the *Trump Marina* instead. And whatever you do Carl, and I honestly mean this with all my heart, please remember to not travel long distances on Friday, October 13th."

318

The impatient gambler thanked Marian Brenner for her sage forecasts, gave the woman a generous twenty-dollar tip, and next uttered a very hasty "good bye".

After quickly ascending the basement steps, Carl Taylor bid adieu to Aunt Harriet and her ostentatious lady friends, departed the rich widow's mansion, climbed into his light brown Lincoln Town Car, and then motored down Philadelphia Avenue onto the *White Horse Pike*. The magical neon glitter of Atlantic City was only fifteen miles east on *Route 30*. Very carefully, Carl's active mind reconstructed and reviewed the fortuneteller's particular predictions.

Certainly, a preliminary chat between the psychic reader and Aunt Harriet could have accidentally communicated the facts about gambling, the children, Carl's career, his ongoing problems with Helen, and the possibility of his wife being deceitful. The business of having a terrific night at the *Trump Marina* remained to be seen. And as far as journeying out of New Jersey on Friday October 13th, *that* prospect represented nothing more than a crucible of absurd superstition as far as Carl Taylor was concerned.

But the seer's unexpected usage of the *Holy Bible* had added a degree of credibility to what Taylor's mind aptly classified as 'the strange event'. The *New Testament* method somewhat surprised the avowed skeptic, who was more than a little awe-struck. Seeking escape from harsh reality, and anticipating a huge jackpot at the casino, a rejuvenated Carl Taylor drove his brown Lincoln through Pomona and then Absecon on busy *Highway 30*.

Twenty minute later, feeling quite superstitious, Carl pulled into the valet parking area of the *Trump Marina Casino,* and soon the new arrival entrusted his car keys to a cheerful and efficient parking attendant. The new arrival then wondered whether his predicted good fortune would magically manifest itself. The avid gambler anxiously meandered his way through the crowded glittering adult fantasy world, all the while desiring to immediately test Marian Brenner's uncanny prophecy.

The Cherry Hill visitor sat down next to a roulette wheel having a hundred-dollar minimum. Much to the man's utter astonishment, the casino addict had won big eighteen out of the first twenty spins. The astounded dealers and their floor "pit manager" were all-together becoming extremely nervous and jittery. Noticing the sweat beads accumulating on the employees' foreheads, and feeling embarrassed with his extraordinary winning streak, the successful high-roller greedily gathered his chips into a disorganized pile. Before departing the *Trump Marina* gaming table, the lucky, on-a-roll customer graciously accepted a generous "comp" from the all-too-suspicious pit boss, who after the winner had left the table, prognosticated to his stunned subordinates that "the house" would get even with Mr. Carl Taylor on "the lucky stiff's" next impromptu visit.

'I'm glad I didn't go to Harrah's Casino tonight and came here instead,' the Atlantic City patron assessed. Then the casino attendee confidently strolled over to the more crowded dice tables. The on a hot-streak player started-out with purchasing five thousand dollars in casino chips, amd soon meticulously arranged them into five parallel and identical neat stacks.

The avid gambler was equally as invincible at craps as he earlier had been at roulette. Every half hour, the lucky chance-taker would ramble over to the "Redemption Window" and cash his chip winnings into a thousand dollars at a time in order to avoid having the patriotic duty of filling-out the required federal income tax withholding forms to report his enormous winnings.

Two triumphant hours later, the winner purchased a black attache case at a Trump Marina Gift Shop. Taylor shuttled back and forth to a nearby Men's Room at least a dozen times over a seven-hour period, and the leather container was just large enough to cram four-hundred-and-twenty-five thousand dollars worth of *Ben Franklins* inside its closed hinges. The "unearned income bonanza" was a happy secret that Carl vowed to conceal from his "detestable interrogating wife's" knowledge.

On the drive back to Cherry Hill, Carl marveled at the accuracy of Marian Brenner's incredible gambling forecast. And now more relevance had been added to the oracle's warnings about a treacherous woman betraying the lucky winner and about the sinister aspects of Carl traveling afar on Friday, July 13th. 'Maybe my wife is going to find and attempt to steal *my* money on that day,' the suddenly superstitious driver imagined. When Taylor finally arrived home, the apprehensive fellow stealthily locked the cache of hundred-dollar-bills in a large wooden storage cabinet located inside his garage, for the distrustful casino winner didn't want Helen "to discover and confiscate" half of his extraordinary winnings.

'The freedom-seeking homeowner paused inside his 'sanctuary garage', and his troubled mind momentarily measured his current economic predicament. 'The tidy sum is sufficient for me to start an exciting new life somewhere else in the good old USA', the gambler covetously considered. 'I'll finally have complete refuge from my wife's perpetual harangues.'

The fanciful dreamer believed that ultimately his suffering conscience would be guilt-free, because in the final analysis, Carl Taylor would leave Joey and Stacy a considerable fortune in *his* will. 'Helen could keep the hundred-twenty-thousand-dollar balance in the Merrill Lynch Cash Management Account,' the Atlantic City winner imagined, 'and she could also enjoy spending the seventy-nine-thousand-dollars in bank *CDs,* along with the Cherry Hill house deed,' the lucky gambler calculated in his all-too-shrewd mind.

Each successive day, Carl then envisioned his grand escape from his mediocre past life. Mr. Paul Warren, Taylor's immediate supervisor at the bank, sent out a memo' to Carl's department, the administrative note writer summoning the ambitious network coordinator to *his* office. Taylor was keenly delighted to discover that his name had been selected by the company's top executives to represent the corporation at a national computer convention scheduled to convene Sunday night, October 15th in Seattle.

"C.T., the bank's travel agency department has already made your transportation and hotel arrangements," Mr. Warren jovially informed. "Flight 721 to Chicago will depart *Philadelphia International* at 7 a.m., October 13th. A transfer at *O'Hare* has been arranged, and the connection will be made onto Flight 94, bound for Seattle," the astute supervisor explained.

The computer-networking genius left Mr. Paul Warren's plush green-carpeted office with mixed emotions. 'The date is October 13th, which is the twenty-four-hour danger period that had been specifically outlined by Marian Brenner,' Carl speculated. 'Forget about the negative prophecy! I could leave Cherry Hill behind and start a new life,' Taylor optimistically imagined.

The somewhat-worried networking wizard feigned a smile while walking past several bank acquaintances, just as the energized corporate employee entered the company's impressive marble-column main lobby. 'I simply have to be careful about Friday the 13th,' Carl scrupulously remembered while his overactive brain further contemplated his delightfully unexpected 'good news from Mr. Warren'.

On the eastbound drive home across the busy *Ben Franklin Bridge* from Pennsylvania to New Jersey, the computer systems installer conjectured that he could cancel *his* flight from Philadelphia to O'Hare at the last moment on October 13th. Then, the prospective fugitive from marriage theorized that he could wait a day at the airport motor lodge, carefully guarding and concealing his attache case brimming with cash, and then the 'husband on the lam' could easily fly to a distant region of the vast country where devious Taylor could assume another identity and start a new exciting life.

Upon arriving home in Cherry Hill, Carl kept a low profile, generally ignoring his combative wife and keeping to himself. Spring soon became summer, and summer majestically transformed into autumn. The ominous date Friday, October 13th finally arrived on the monthly calendar.

The anxious man rose early at five a.m., had a quick breakfast of toast and coffee, and very casually gave Helen a very perfunctory and mechanical final good-bye kiss on her left cheek before departing via the front door.

The jubilant conniver hopped into his brown Lincoln, took familiar *Inter-State 295* south to the Freeway, which then led directly to the always hectic *Walt Whitman Bridge* into South Philadelphia. Soon, Taylor was heading south on *I-95,* zipping past the *Phillies and Eagles* stadiums, and next traveling over the Interstate's long bridge, whizzing past the legendary *Philadelphia Navy Yard* while motoring toward the Quaker City's main airport.

Carl locked his luxury sedan in a high-rise airport parking facility, and then carried his full attache case into Terminal C. The divorce court escapee eagerly trekked Concourse C to reach the designated airline's customer service counter.

'I'll try selling my ticket to someone impatiently waiting in line,' Jack thought. "Miss, I have to get to Chicago by noon," a bald-headed man pleaded with the airline employee. "It's a business emergency! My future depends on it."

"I'm very sorry, sir. Flight 721 to Chicago is booked solid without any cancellations. The same businessmen take it every week. You can try 'Stand-By', but I doubt if there will be any seats available. There never are on this very popular flight."

Carl Taylor stepped forward to seize the opportunity to unload his already purchased 'coach ticket' to the desperate and denied traveling businessman. The Cherry Hill traveler held and offered a viable solution to the perplexed gentleman's 'urgent problem' right there in *his* left hand.

"Excuse me, Sir," Taylor said. "But I just happen to have a round-trip ticket reservation for Chicago with a transfer to Seattle that you might be interested in. My business meeting in the *Windy City* has been postponed until later this week. I'll sell it to you at face value."

The formerly disconsolate man answered, "That's great! I'll pay you three hundred dollars cash right this minute. You don't know how much I appreciate this!"

"I'm Carl Taylor, and it's a pleasure doing business with you," the seller related. "Here's your ticket. It's authentic! Don't worry about the bonus flight to Seattle. You can sell it to someone waiting in line and frustrated at *O'Hare*."

"I'm Bob Simpson," the thankful man identified himself, "and I'm a confused lawyer trying to get from Buffalo to Chicago, via Philadelphia. I've a very important presentation to make at a big corporate executive meeting, and you've really helped me out in my time of need. Are ya' sure you're not an angel?" Mr. Robert Simpson appreciatively joked.

The men shook hands in the standard American tradition to validate their quickly accomplished verbal transaction. Cash was exchanged for the ticket reservation voucher, and soon the happy traders went their separate ways.

Before departing the airport terminal to register at a nearby motor lodge, Carl decided to follow a silly hunch and purchase five-hundred-thousand-dollars worth of flight travel insurance, spitefully naming 'Helen' his beneficiary. After negotiating the terms with an easy-to-use computerized machine dispenser, and also using his *Merrill Lynch Visa* debit card for the "last time", the blithe-spirited, liberated "free man" nonchalantly ambled back down lengthy Concourse C toward the main section of the expansive airport.

The idea of total emancipation from life's drudgeries and family responsibility filled and dominated Carl's heart with new-found excitement. Although it was only seven in the morning, the jubilant fellow figured he would enter an airport bar and celebrate his newly discovered freedom

The computer-network-engineer climbed onto a red-leather stool, ordered bourbon on the rocks "to wake me up", and exchanged common pleasantries with the congenial bartender. During Taylor's second hard whiskey on ice, an attractive brunette entered the "24-7 Tavern" and sat-down on the stool just to the right of the nervous computer-network-installer. After several minutes of silence, a polite adult conservation blossomed between the lonely, transient patrons.

"Hi, I'm Bob Simpson," Carl fibbed while his stressed mind managed to remember the lawyer's name who had purchased *his* ticket to Chicago. "Can I buy you a drink, or maybe breakfast?"

"Why not! I think I could use a stiff cocktail right now. My name's Sarah Cassario," the woman answered with a smile. "In happier days I was Sarah McCarthy. That was my maiden-name before I made the horrendous mistake of getting married to a chauvinistic Italian; actually, and more specifically, to a pig-headed Sicilian," the beautiful blue-eyed lady lamented.

Carl could relate to Sarah Cassario's marital difficulties. The woman was very attractive and possessed a well-endowed, curvaceous, hourglass body. Her new admirer decided that he would commiserate with his female acquaintance as long as she wanted to converse with him.

"Marital un-bliss, I know all about it," Taylor began his sympathetic reply. "My marriage has been on the skids lately, too. Bartender give the lady a...."

"A Sloe Gin Fizz, please," Sarah alertly responded. "That's about the only bar mixture I can drink this early in the morning."

The two new acquaintances bartered personal anecdotes, and soon their initial conversation became more intriguing and intimate. Small-talk eventually mushroomed into more meaningful dialogue. Their discussions encompassed families, nationalities, politics, their religions, hobbies, sports, children, employments, high school experiences, and then the central subject switched to community service clubs. Immediately, the coincidental airport travelers quickly became immensely fond of one another.

Before either had realized it, three hours had advanced on the tavern wall clock. Sarah had consumed six Sloe Gin Fizzes, and Carl was nursing his seventh potent *Old Grand Dad* on the rocks.

The new acquaintances were temporarily able to escape their cultural shells, and the morning affect of the all-too-available alcohol made the chatty pair easily shed their initial inhibitions, with the seated pair divulging secrets as if the new friends were long lost comrades attending a high school reunion. Their personality compatibility was rather remarkable. After the first hour and a half, giddiness was evidently prevailing over adult maturity.

Sarah was becoming worried that *their* overt conduct was turning a bit too loud and that their verbal exchanges were becoming too discernible to the other 24-7 patrons, so she and Carl silently and discreetly transferred to an inconspicuous booth for the purpose of achieving more social privacy.

"Sarah, you say your husband was cruel to you. How was he?" the half-intoxicated bourbon drinker asked the pretty doll as C,T. began sipping his second cup of strong -flavored coffee.

"Bob, I've never shared this truth with anyone else before, but somehow I trust you," Sarah intimated. "My husband is a chronic alcoholic. He drinks more rye than a diabetic does water. And Tony becomes extremely violent when under the influence."

"Did your spouse ever physically abuse you?" Carl inquired, recklessly slurring the first and third words.

"It reached a point where there was more Mr. Hyde in him than Dr. Jekyll," Sarah divulged. "Tony would batter me for no reason to feed his arrogant ego." Sarah took a long drag on her cigarette and made direct eye contact with her new admirer. "I decided I couldn't take it any more, Bob," the dazzling woman confided. "Tony was an absolute martinet who often practiced his brutality on my face and head. That's really why I'm here right now. I've come to Philly' to run away from Pittsburgh, and somehow start a new life!"

"What about your children you had mentioned?" Carl asked. "You're leaving them behind?"

Sarah then forcefully crushed her cigarette into an amber glass ashtray. "Thank God they're almost old enough to provide for themselves," the knockout doll related. "Carol is a college freshman at *Duquesne,* and Jimmy is a high school senior. As you can see, Bob, I got married very young."

"Did your children know you were plannin' on leavin' your husband?" Sarah's attentive listener asked. "I mean, *that* was a really big decision you've made."

"I discussed it with Carol, and my daughter had told Jimmy about my intentions just yesterday," Sarah disclosed with tears forming in her eyes. "They both readily approved and understood my motive. I promised I'd write to Carol at her dorm' as soon as I got settled-down to a new beginning."

"I've a confession to make," the Pittsburgh woman's avid listener guiltily uttered. "Sarah, my name is not Bob Simpson. It's Carl Taylor. My boss at work calls me C.T."

The computer-networker then revealed the whole gamut of events leading-up to their Philly' Airport meeting, the revelations including the Atlantic City bonanza, Carl's extended rift with Helen, and finally, his recent ticket sale to traveling attorney Bob Simpson.

"Sarah, this might sound rash, but how about running away with me?" Carl Taylor impetuously proposed. "I assure you; I'll treat you with kindness and affection. We're sort of like two peas in a pod. We need to lean on each other for strength during this time of mutual crisis in our lives."

"Well, I don't know," the gorgeous woman stammered. "I have to think…"

"Sarah, we can be fugitives from society and see how things work-out between us," Carl interrupted, "and if the experiment fails, we can forget the whole defective deal, and then go our separate ways. Agreed?"

Sarah was astounded by the acutely bizarre, surprise proposition. She looked Carl squarely in the eyes. "That has to be the craziest suggestion I've ever heard," the vivacious blonde beauty claimed. "Leaving here for lush greener pastures sounds mighty inviting, I must confess. I want to really forget all about Tony's nasty temper, about the continual physical battering, about Pittsburgh, and all I only want to concentrate on is a brighter future that's free of cruel, jealous male domination."

At that particular moment, an important news bulletin flashed-upon the now-busy tavern's overhead television screen. The bartender adjusted the volume so that everyone seated in the airport restaurant could hear the "special emergency announcement". A familiar Philadelphia news commentator appeared upon the monitor with a very grim expression showing on his face.

"Ladies and Gentlemen; I'm sorry to report that a terrible airplane disaster has occurred just five minutes ago outside a Cleveland, Ohio suburb. Flight 721 from Philadelphia to Chicago has crashed. The plane had been delayed at *Philadelphia International Airport* for two-and-a-half hours for mechanical adjustments. Initial reports from the crash scene have found no evidence of survivors. Debris is scattered over a five-mile radius, which suggests a possible internal explosion; perhaps a terrorist bomb, but of course, this is only conjecture at the moment."

Carl Taylor and Sarah Cassario looked blankly at one another, with their dual mouths fully agape. The stark announcement made the new friends promptly sober-up in a hurry. The Philly' TV news commentator continued with his shocking announcement.

"Sources say that *FAA* investigators are on their way to the scene of the catastrophe. Film crews have been dispatched to the site. We will have additional details to relate to you when more information becomes available. We repeat. Flight 721 en route to Chicago, which had been delayed in Philadelphia, has crashed outside a Cleveland suburb. We now return to our regularly scheduled programming."

"Oh my God!" Carl exclaimed. "Sarah; that was *my* scheduled flight! Poor Bob Simpson! May Heaven bless *his* mortal soul! He was sacrificed for *my* sake! He died so that I could live!"

"Carl, your New Jersey psychic; the one you were telling me about, was amazingly right!" Sarah indicated in an astonished tone of voice. "It's simply too incredible and incomprehensible to fathom and believe!"

"I'm still having trouble processing it all!" Taylor gasped before gulping-down the remainder of his hot coffee. Carl looked at Sarah's pallid face and then glanced-down at his gorgeous companion's trembling fingers.

"Sarah, if it weren't for Robert Simpson and Marian Brenner," Taylor hypothesized and related, "I would certainly be dead now; and *we* definitely would've never met! Call it either fate, or serendipity, or whatever ya' want!"

"Carl, this sad news this morning to me is a sign that I should accept your very interesting companionship offer," Sarah acceded, fully accepting Taylor's rather astounding proposition. "I'll be your traveling soul-mate."

Sarah Cassario leaned forward in the booth and affectionately kissed Carl on his cheek. Taylor was still stunned by the startling news bulletin, and now the itinerant husband and father totally savored the Pittsburgh woman's 'surprise commitment'.

"Sarah, I don't want to travel far today," the now-superstitious Bible-believing man fearfully stated. "It's still Friday, October 13th. I already told you what Marian Brenner predicted about this day."

"I think you'd better heed your psychic's sage advice," the beautiful escaping woman agreed. "Her fantastic predictions have been too accurate to be ignored."

Carl summoned a waitress over so that he could pay the escalated tab. The couple stood and left the crowded airport tavern, which was now doing a swift early lunch business. The addled couple together stepped outside the air conditioned 24-7 Tavern's glass doors, their bold departure symbolically representing their new lives of mutual freedom, and then, the lovebirds strolled the length of Concourse C hand in hand, ambling all the way to the airport's central parking area. Taylor flagged-down a taxi, deliberately leaving his Lincoln Town Car in the high-rise garage for his pretentious, grieving wife to claim later. The driver of the yellow vehicle transported Sarah and her still shell-shocked escort to the Airport Motor Lodge, where the two attempted checking-in as Mr. and Mrs. Robert Simpson.

"Do you have a credit card?" the concerned desk attendant asked. "It's required that you present one."

"Sorry about that," the hotel's next prospective male guest answered. "I left it home. I'll have to pay cash."

"What about another form of identification to collaborate your identity? A photo' ID perhaps?" the all-too-demanding clerk asked. "I need to have some record of who you are."

"Look," Taylor imperatively said. "If my money's not good here, my bride and I could go somewhere else. I'm a bit nervous and stressed-out because we're both in a little hurry to get to *our* room, if ya' know what I mean."

"Yes sir, yes sir," the slightly-embarrassed and now-blushing main desk clerk answered as the nervous fellow gave Carl an understanding wink while beautiful Sarah was still seated in a lobby chair looking the other way.

The couple entered an elevator, and C. T. pushed the appropriate button. Soon he and Sarah were getting settled in their temporary accommodations. Inside the third-floor room, Taylor quietly closed the entrance door, and then he and Sarah passionately embraced.

"It's a good thing you had your suitcase from Pittsburgh," Carl said with a broad grin. "It would've been difficult for a husband and wife to check in carrying only a black attache case, regardless of their inordinate circumstances."

After a romantic overnight stay, the following morning the lovestruck couple outlined their future plans at the airport lodge's breakfast/snack bar. "Sarah, if no one was there to buy my ticket," Carl observed and verbalized, "I would be dead as Napoleon right now. In fact, I *am* now dead as Napoleon according to the official airline and police records and tomorrow's newspaper reporting."

"It's a good thing Bob Simpson had never gone to see Marian Brenner," Sarah replied, shaking her perfect face and head side-to-side in absolute disbelief. "I'm glad *you* had fate in your corner. It can be a strong ally, you know."

"Do ya' believe in fate?" Sarah's escort wondered and inquired.

"I do Carl, and I want you to know I do feel remorse for Bob Simpson and the other unfortunate passengers on that doomed plane. How do you think Helen is taking *your* presumed sudden death? I think she's been notified by now."

Carl Taylor inhaled a very deep breath and then shook his head to demonstrate his great uncertainty. "I don't really know," the still-stunned man shared. "Knowing her, she must feel guilty about how I had left our relationship on bad terms. That's probably her only real regret. Our marriage had been strained to its limit over the past several years, and that's putting it mildly."

"You left her quite a remarkable inheritance, didn't you?" Sarah asked. "She ought to be happy about *that* unexpected windfall."

"Well, quite truthfully, she gets the house free and clear, and that's worth over half a million," Carl recollected and indicated. "And the two hundred thousand bucks sitting in our joint banking and brokerage accounts, plus the half-million-dollar flight insurance policy that she doesn't even know about yet, well Sarah; those significant financial circumstances ought to make poor old Helen Taylor mourn my sudden passing from this cruel world even more."

"You've left her a very sad-but-lucky widow," Sarah logically added. "I should be so lucky with Tony. He's going to be a chronic loser for the rest of his life."

"Sarah, if I had met you last week, I would've made you my second beneficiary. You'd have wound-up with at least a quarter of a million if I were on that plane that went down outside Cleveland."

"Wouldn't Helen have contested *that* suspicious inheritance?" the former beauty queen asked. "Your vindictive wife sounds like a real witchy spitfire when it comes-down to the money inheritance issue!"

"No, because I would've changed *my will* to state that if *she* did contest *your* share, my wife would risk losing everything that she was originally entitled to," Taylor candidly replied. "That provision. or should I say *stipulation,* would've definitely been put into concise legal language."

"Did you have any other insurance policies?" the pretty female inquired. "I know that I don't have one myself!"

"Yes, Doll. as a matter of fact, I do," Carl affirmatively noted. "My pension life insurance will pay Helen five times my annual salary of over a hundred-fifty-thousand a year, and I also owned a three-hundred-thousand-dollar term life policy containing a double indemnity accidental death clause."

"Helen's now a bona fide, true-blue millionaire," Sarah confirmed. "That monetary fact ought to make her wearing a black funeral dress a little easier to bear at *your* upcoming memorial service."

"You know Sarah," the runaway husband suddenly realized and emphasized. "It really offends my pride knowing that I'm worth more dead than I am alive. I'm sure Helen will put on a good act wearin' her widow weeds and mournin' my sudden departure from earthly existence. I actually feel more sorrow for Joey and Stacy than I do right now for Helen."

"How much dough did you really win at the Atlantic City casino?" Sarah curiously asked. "You said to me last night that you were extremely lucky!"

"Almost a half million total," Carl bragged. "And you might say that this attache case between my knees is a portable bank. You should've seen the expression on the pit boss's face when I was on my incredible roll," the newly-rejuvenated dead man laughed. "The petulant idiot was on the brink of sufferin' either a major coronary or a mental meltdown. But the *half mil* contained in this black case is actually peanuts compared to what I've left Helen."

Carl then revealed that he planned to assume forever the identity of Robert Simpson as tribute to the deceased Flight 721 passenger. "I figure Sarah that I'm now livin' on borrowed time," the abused lady's new companion philosophically opined. "Who would ever imagine such a weird set of singular factors? Ironically, Babe; I hate lawyers and their ignoble profession, and ironically again, one of *their* reprehensible kind inadvertently sacrificed *his* life for me in the jet plane disaster."

Carl Taylor was classified by bureaucratic county, state, and federal authorities as being officially and legally dead. The new Robert Simpson was totally happy with every minute of *his* miraculous resurrection from death. *He* occasionally missed his wife's criticism and his children's apathy. But the man's soul had been genuinely liberated from guilt, and his mind had fortunately escaped the throes of unhappiness. Sarah's supportive love now filled the remaining void in Carl's rehabilitating heart.

Sarah used her Visa Card and rented a suitable automobile at the airport's *Hertz* booth, and the invigorated pair alternated driving responsibilities all the way from Philadelphia down to their ultimate destination, Venice, Florida.

"Sarah, I've always loved the *Gulf of Mexico*," the former beauty pageant contestant's new lover admitted as their white Nissan Altima crossed the border on *Inter-State 95* from Georgia into the *Sunshine State*. "It's where I always wanted to settle-down after retirement. I guess it's *now* early retirement for me, whether I like it or not!" the totally thrilled driver merrily remarked.

The couple purchased a modest three-bedroom home situated a block from the bay, played golf on weekends, joined a vacation travel club, bought a small motorboat, and soon mastered the finer skills associated with water-skiing.

Carl made several underworld acquaintances in the Venice, Florida area, and had a legitimate-looking *Temple University* Masters Degree diploma expertly counterfeited in the name of Robert Peter Simpson. The extremely shrewd-but-talented computer networking specialist then performed professional computer maintenance and networking installations "for cash", performing vital services for grateful retail stores and various wholesale vendors in the Venice area. The networking guru even found time to thrice fly north, rent an AVIS airport car, and three times pay his respects at his own previously purchased empty grave site inside a well-maintained Cherry Hill, New Jersey cemetery.

The two blissful "honeymooners" maintained an ideal relationship for six wonderful months. On the morning of April 16th, 2001, Sarah announced some very unsatisfactory and distasteful news to her suddenly appalled male companion.

"Carl, I want you to meet Chief Investigator Robert Rebek of the *Internal Revenue Service's* Tampa Bay office. I'm really Sarah McCarthy, Agent Sarah McCarthy, formerly of Pittsburgh, but now affiliated with the Philadelphia *IRS* division. I still professionally use my former maiden name when doing behind-the-scenes' government work. I had just finished making a settlement in the early morning of Friday, October 13th with a slippery airport gift shop owner that had been skimming cash," the female IRS agent factually revealed. "I figured I would go into the 24-7 bar and celebrate the two-hundred-thousand-dollar settlement with a much-deserved morning cocktail. I was about to get-up and leave the premises, but then you told me about your terrific casino junket and how you traded-in your chips a thousand dollars at a time over a twenty-four-hour period to avoid reporting federal taxes."

"When Flight 721 went-down, Sarah was specifically interested in exactly how much money you had stashed in the attache case," Investigator Rebek communicated. "She called her supervisor at his home with her cell phone that she kept in her handbag, all of this happening while you were preoccupied taking your shower in your airport motor lodge suite," the Tampa based federal official stated. "When the tax deadline passed just yesterday, April 15th, and *you* Carl Taylor failed to *report your* 'extraordinary monetary gains earnings'," Investigator Rebek continued his bad news narrative, "Sarah notified me to meet you here. We've been analyzing *your* records and activities with a fine-tooth comb for over six months now. Carl, I believe *you* owe Uncle Sam a nice tidy settlement."

Carl Taylor was dumbfounded upon learning that he had been the targeted victim of a surreptitious government IRS sting operation. Tears filled his bloodshot eyes. He felt betrayed by Sarah Cassario, a.k.a. Agent Sarah McCarthy.

"That's not all," Chief Inspector Rebek added. "We thoroughly investigated your stock dealings and discovered sizable unreported capital gains. You had specialized in buying and selling high tech' over-the-counter stocks that didn't pay dividends. You thought that those gains would go unnoticed because there were no dividends to report," Investigator Rebek articulated. "You, Carl Taylor, alias

Robert Simpson, then shrewdly reinvested those nice unreported gains in legitimate New York Stock Exchange blue chip companies. However, you never disclosed your blue-chip dividends to the *IRS* from 1995 to 1999. Now needless to say Carl, anyone could easily become rich if they never paid federal income taxes!"

IRS Agent Sarah McCarthy studied the dismayed and bewildered look on Carl Taylor's melancholy face. "Of course, Carl," the lovely IRS Agent explained, "your tax problems do not take into consideration your fraudulent identity as Robert Peter Simpson; your brazen falsification of *Temple University* official documents; your defrauding of insurance companies, and your pension embezzlement by deliberately faking your sudden death. These other important matters will be adequately addressed by other government law enforcement agencies."

"Getting back to your illicit income tax evasion," Chief Agent Rebek injected, "you were already in a high tax bracket before you hit it big at *Trump Marina*. The casino has all your gambling activity documented on videotape. The *IRS* estimates that you owe the government approximately two-hundred and fifty thousand dollars, not including ever-accumulating interest and penalties on your principal debt."

Carl's heart sank with sorrow, and the embittered man felt and knew the true meaning of the word 'despondency'. "Sarah, how could you do this horrible thing to me?" the puzzled dupe stammered. "I love you! We could've lived happily together here in Venice. Marian Brenner was right on target when she amazingly predicted that a woman would deceive me. Why couldn't I have been more intelligent? It's too bad she didn't tell me *who* that devious woman would be!"

"Carl, I want you to know that I truly do love you," Sarah sympathetically sniffed with ample tears welling-up inside her blue eyes. "These past eight months have convinced me that you're basically a good, decent man. I want to divorce Tony and marry you; that is, after you promise to get a legal divorce settlement from Helen and also promise to go straight after paying-off your massive government tax debt. First, you must liquidate all of your assets to expunge all of your currently-owed taxes off the Bureau's records. I estimate that after your tax liability is satisfied, you'll then have about ten-thousand left to start your new life."

"But you betrayed my confidence!" Carl insisted. "I trusted you!"

"Carl, when I became an *IRS* agent," Sarah authentically sobbed, "I took a solemn oath of loyalty to uphold *the public trust*. I could not allow my love for you to overshadow *that* sacred pledge. I still possess my ethical integrity, Carl. I want you to know that!"

"Mr. Taylor, Sarah is a very dedicated agent. She felt she could not betray her oath by doing anything dishonorable," Investigator Rebek informed. "That's it in a nutshell!"

"Carl, I could never in good faith live a double standard type of life," Agent Sarah McCarthy moaned and cried. "Believe me; my conscience gave me no viable alternative. I still love you with all my heart," the upset woman honestly whimpered and wept. "You might think me an idealistic fool, but in the end, I had to be loyal to my duty."

"Boardwalk Mania"

At 9 a.m. sharp on Monday July 16th, 2012, veteran FBI Inspector Joe Giralo summoned his team of steadfast agents consisting of Salvatore Velardi, Arthur Orsi and Dan Blachford into his third-floor office inside the Federal Building at 600 Arch Street, Philadelphia, Pennsylvania. Immediately, the three standing agents curiously detected an element of urgency evident in their mercurial-tempered boss's raspy voice. But according to standard conversation protocol, small-talk had to precede the more important crime business discussion to follow.

"Today's the 16th of July back home in Hammonton," Chief Giralo solemnly prefaced his intended, more serious, comments. "The annual carnival has arrived in *our* New Jersey town, and the folks are celebrating the Feast of Our Lady of Mt. Carmel. But much to my total dismay Fellas', each year the religious procession is getting smaller and smaller!"

"I always stop at the Assumption Food Stand and buy a pepper and sausage sandwich and a cold *Coke* to wash it down," Sal Velardi reminded everyone about his legendary, enormous appetite. "For some obscure reason, those pepper and sausage sandwiches always taste better at the carnival than they do when prepared at home. I think it's quite like buttered popcorn that always tastes better at a movie theater than the microwave variety does when being eaten at home while watching a pay-for-view cable TV movie! And then before leaving the carnival refreshment area," Agent Velardi continued his bland commentary, "I habitually consume two slices of pizza, a plate of French fries, and some sticky cotton candy for dessert!"

"I prefer swallowing-down the delicious pepper and eggs sandwiches that are served at the jam-packed Mt. Carmel Society Beer Garden that's conveniently situated at the rear of the carnival grounds," Art Orsi felt inspired to opine. "And I really savor lots of fried onions to sample as a delectable side dish!"

"Well, now that we're all stranded on the same general subject, usually I tramp around the carnival grounds with my wife, making two quick rotations of all the rides and attractions," Dan Blachford contributed to the ongoing trite dialogue. "But over the years, I've learned not to wear sandals because of the carnival grounds' rough gravel surface. But Guys, just like the Chief, I'm also afraid that small-town festivals and carnivals are rapidly becoming a lost tradition. I mean, giant amusement parks like Six Flags Great Adventure up in Jackson, Dorney Park over in Allentown, and Hershey Park out in Pennsylvania Dutch Country are now the popular attractions that are slowly-but-surely easily eliminating small town traveling carnivals."

"And I know plenty of friends in Hammonton who take their wives and kids on summer vacations to Busch Gardens down in Williamsburg and to Kings Dominion in northern Virginia," Sal Velardi orally volunteered. "Big business seems to be dominating every phase of our daily lives, and it's a downright shame that lots of good Americana is being lost in the ugly process. Regrettably, old honored customs are gradually becoming irrelevant and obsolete, thanks mostly to modern technology."

"But new traditions are constantly being created to replace the ones that are diminishing into oblivion," feisty Art Orsi challenged. "For instance, Hammonton has recently started a successful blueberry festival in late June that's almost now as big as the mid-July Mt. Carmel Feast. In fact, last year's one-day blueberry shindig drew twenty-five thousand eager visitors!"

"It's too bad that the blueberry harvest season lasts just eight short weeks," Dan Blachford honestly stated. "That's the one local South Jersey crop that I wish lasted all year long. And as we all fully know, Hammonton's monicker is that it's the Blueberry Capital of the World with over eight thousand cultivated acres being farmed to give the town undisputed bragging rights to *that* coveted title."

"Boss, is this why you've really called us into your office?" respectfully interrogated all-too-practical Agent Sal Velardi. "Do you want us to solely think about town carnivals, colossal theme amusement parks, religious processions, and the Hammonton Blueberry Festival? I don't believe so! From years of personal past experience, *we* know you much better than that!"

"No Fellas'!" Inspector Giralo candidly admitted as the Boss opened a Manila folder and then meticulously removed its printed paper contents. "Please get-out your notepads and your ball-point pens to jot-down some fairly pertinent information that I'm now prepared to communicate."

The men immediately obeyed their fearless leader's particular instruction and were now ready to scribble-down vital new-found facts and details. Seeing that his conscientious investigators were alert and listening attentively, Inspector Joe Giralo referred to his hand-held confidential government documents and began speaking in a monotonous drone, his deep voice reading from the printed sheets while occasionally peering-up at his three very competent agents' grim-looking faces.

"Look Guys; it now seems that illustrious Matt Riley down at Washington headquarters is understandably concerned about a series of boardwalk merchant disappearances up and down the East Coast, the onerous events occurring over the span of the last thirty-five years," the internationally famous, esteemed FBI sleuth commenced his official narrative. "Now Men, the latest missing businessman has been definitely identified as Manny Hammerstein, who had owned several very profitable boardwalk gift shops down in Ocean City, Maryland. But unfortunately, Guys, Hammerstein's body was never found, even though he's been gone from his profitable store for two whole weeks now."

"Well, logically, Boss," Sal Velardi courteously interrupted. "If this guy Hammerstein's corpse was never discovered, how does Matt Riley know who the heck the victim was if there's no sign of any dead body? How do we know that Manny Hammerstein just didn't run away from a nagging wife?"

"Good rational question!" Joe Giralo reluctantly commended while still sitting in his very comfortable black leather swivel chair that was positioned directly behind his expensive Canadian oak desk. "First of all, Salvatore; the Ocean City Police were completely baffled when Hammerstein's devoted seventy-year-old wife Rebecca frantically declared him missing-in-action. Second of all, Manny Hammerstein's fishing boat was located five miles out in the *Atlantic* with no one aboard. And third and most significantly, traces of Hammerstein's blood had been isolated and gleaned from the abandoned boat's starboard railing. When compared with corresponding evidence obtained from Mr. Hammerstein's medical records," Chief Giralo sanctimoniously summarized, "the correlated DNA boat samples matched perfectly with the victim's past hospital blood tests!"

"Then can *we* plausibly deduce that the dead man had been killed on board by fairly careless amateur criminals?" surmised and verbally concluded Agent Orsi. "Their non-thorough methods seem to be both awkward and clumsy!"

"Not exactly as elementary as you might think Arty!" Chief Giralo objectively answered. "Apparently, mild-mannered senior citizen Manny Hammerstein's blood stains discovered on his boat's railing were a result of an accidental cut the avid fisherman had received several hours before him being rubbed-out; ironically, while the targeted merchant/angler was deep sea fishing."

"Well Chief, what do *you* suppose actually happened?" Dan Blachford cautiously inquired. "This minor mystery is quickly transforming into to a rather major conundrum!"

"Now quite obviously, someone strongly desired to have Manny Hammerstein's Ocean City, Maryland lucrative boardwalk existence permanently eradicated!" Joe Giralo reasonably determined and orally conveyed to his three-man committee. "I suspect that his well-equipped boat probably had responded to a distress horn signal falsely given by another nearby approaching craft. Then, without warning, I theorize that a gang of villainous thugs speedily boarded Mr. Hammerstein's fishing vessel, and the vile punks probably knocked him out with a blackjack, or with some other heavy blunt object. Next, I conjecture that poor Manny was swiftly taken aboard the felons' escape boat, which probably then headed north to the infamous Baltimore Canyon, twenty-miles or so off the Rehoboth Beach, Delaware coast. That infamous deep ocean trench is a common dropping-off point for recently killed murder victims."

"I see!" Sal Velardi suavely exclaimed, nodding his head in absolute concurrence. "No doubt Hammerstein was ruthlessly chained to a huge cement slab, and then wickedly thrown overboard, left to sink to the bottom, becoming instant fish fodder! I only hope that the poor man had already been dead before being mercilessly hurled-down to Davy Jones's locker!"

Then, erudite Inspector Giralo graphically described three other associated cases of vanishing boardwalk merchants: Isaac Eichberg of Coney Island, New York in 1981; Obadiah Dorfman of Virginia Beach, Virginia in 1992, and Tobin Kessler of Myrtle Beach, South Carolina in 2003. "At first impression, Gentlemen, I had erroneously theorized that these other suspected felonies were hate crimes in-progress because all four missing victims were shrewd Jewish boardwalk businessmen."

"Well, according to *their* first and last names, aren't they all of Hebrew descent?" Sal Velardi asked with an element of certainty exhibited in his tone of voice. "And incidentally. Boss, Coney Island, Virginia Beach, and Myrtle Beach are all out of *our* territorial jurisdiction! So why are these other three guys Eichberg, Dorfman and Kessler deserving of *our* scrutiny?"

"Very keen observation indeed, Salvatore!" Chief Giralo promptly congratulated and praised his astute principal disciple. "I imagine that our Manhattan office will professionally examine the Isaac Eichberg Coney Island matter; our Richmond office will intensively study the Obadiah Dorfman Virginia Beach scenario, and

I believe that our on-the-ball FBI Charleston office will thoroughly analyze the 2003 disappearance of Mr. Tobin Kessler down in sunny Myrtle Beach, South Carolina!"

"Then, we only have to be involved with helping the Ocean City, Maryland Police unravel the very troubling Manny Hammerstein suspected murder riddle," Art Orsi prematurely decided and declared. "That special task shouldn't be too difficult for the four of us to systematically evaluate and eventually solve!"

Always vigilant Chief Giralo then again read from his detailed papers, and chronologically disclosed to his investigative team that other similar strange boardwalk merchant disappearances had occurred over the course of the last three and a half decades, and that the designated victims were not all Jewish by nationality or religion. Inspector Giralo reviewed that in 1994 Zachary Greenspan had vanished from Asbury Park, New Jersey; in 1987, Nabil Al-Karachi and Khalid Al-Razi were reported as missing from the Rehoboth Beach, Delaware boardwalk scene; in 1997, Gabriel Eckstein seemed to have evaporated into thin air from the Wildwood, New Jersey boardwalk oceanfront; in 2008, Phineas Tannenbaum was last seen inside his amusement arcade on the Ocean City, New Jersey board promenade; and finally, in 2010, Taziq Anwar and Hussein Zuabi no longer were visible proprietors selling souvenirs and colorful summer apparel inventory inside their Seaside Heights, New Jersey boardwalk tee shirt, merchandise, and beachwear emporium.

"This diabolical crime wave now sounds like some weird American extension of the ongoing Israeli-Palestinian West Bank conflict," Dan Blachford ascertained and somewhat-sagaciously remarked. "Could this very fascinating development be some sort of Arab-Jew conflict; a terrible Mid-East war of attrition going on; yes, happening right here on American soil? Er, I really meant to say *on American beaches!*"

"That special responsibility is for you three eminent men to genuinely hypothesize and then ultimately prove!" Joe Giralo imperatively communicated to his trio of ambitious government crimefighters. "But it's not simply Arabs versus Jews. In 1983, a Seaside Heights game operator named Robert Ryan had suddenly disappeared from sight; in 2001, a hamburger stand entrepreneur named Jack Thomas rang his Ocean City, Maryland cash register for the final time, and also, Men, in 2006, a Wildwood/Cape May popcorn and French fry vendor named Mickey Santora deposited his last daily receipts inside the local beach bank."

"Well then, tell me what's *our* specific official assignments?" indispensable Art Orsi impatiently demanded learning. "I can't stand attempting to cope with too much excessive drama and suspense! Frankly, I prefer peace, harmony, and tranquility!"

"Copy-down these relevant details I'm about to relate on your separate notepads!" Inspector Giralo directed his loyal subordinates. "My very capable secretary Sue Johnson has already made your individual two-week room reservations. Now Sal; your vital job is to snoop around the Asbury Park and Seaside Heights boardwalks, and if I may add, your more-than-adequate two-week-long late July accommodations will be at the Aztec Ocean Resort, 901 Boardwalk, Seaside Heights."

Inspector Giralo then drank several ounces of warm coffee from his frequently used desk mug and next proceeded to deliver his additional declarations. "Art, you're to do your typical gumshoe patrols, but this time ambling around on the Ocean City, New Jersey, Wildwood, and Cape May boardwalks. I've verified that Mrs. Johnson has gotten you into the Days Inn Motor Lodge, which is not-too-far from the Wildwood Convention Hall where *we* often attend fall oldies rock and roll shows!"

"I know exactly where the place is!" Agent Orsi automatically acknowledged and bellowed. "The Days Inn is at the end of Rio Grande Avenue right near the beach," the excited fellow elaborated. "Yes, Rio Grande is really Route 47 going into Wildwood! It's not too far from the Crusader Motor Lodge where I had taken my family for a week's hiatus just last September."

"And Dan," Inspector Giralo continued his duty roster while deliberately ignoring Agent Orsi's almost-delirious histrionics. "I want you to take the Cape-May-Lewes Ferry from Jersey over to Delaware. The pleasant hour and fifteen-minute bay crossing cuts around sixty miles of driving time from the lengthy trip that I'm presently proposing to you; a decent ramble down to Ocean City, Maryland to exclusively work with the town's police detectives on the perplexing Manny Hammerstein case. You have a two-week reservation at the ultra-deluxe Holiday Inn on 64th Street," the highly revered Inspector expounded. "As you're well-aware, Dan; I've spent several rather enjoyable family jaunts down to that terrific resort town. I think you'll find the inn's Reflections Restaurant, much to your overall satisfaction; that is, after gorging your hungry stomach with Thrasher's French Fries, Lombardi's Pizza, Alaska Stand hotdogs, Dollie's Popcorn, and finally, Bull on the Beach beef sandwiches; all of those wonderful eating establishments situated up on the crowded boardwalk."

"Any more pertinent and relevant instructions?" a rather impatient Agent Velardi anxiously asked his immediate superior.

"And last but not least, Men," Joe Giralo characteristically smiled and commanded, "stay away from the angry vacationers who had been effectively bumped-from their original room reservations. Just like we often do with airplane flights," the Chief explained, "prospective airline passengers can become extremely hostile when unexpectedly moved from first class seats into coach. Well, the same phenomenon can happen at an exclusive lodge when unappreciative guests become very belligerent after learning that their two-bedroom suite has been changed into a small single bedroom efficiency without an exotic ocean view!"

"Any other important central items you have to relay to us?" a now-peeved Agent Velardi repeated to his all-too-garrulous administrative supervisor. "I know from past practice you're not telling us all that you've accumulated in your preliminary research about these tremendously strange and arcane boardwalk merchant disappearances. Quite truthfully, Boss. Sometimes you treat us like we're brainless baby cave mushrooms. You keep us in the dark, and then predictably feed us a lot of trivial fecal matter!"

"Well, Salvatore, while you're industriously gathering information on foot patrol over on the Seaside Heights and Asbury Park boardwalks," the wily Philadelphia FBI Inspector reiterated, "don't go meandering over to Manhattan and take the Brooklyn-bound subway out to Coney Island as you had often done with teenage friends in your self-proclaimed glorious youth. I'm pretty cognizant of the fact that you had been enamored with the boardwalk Parachute Ride along with the famous Cyclone wooden roller coaster; both amusement venues still being very much in existence! And I also recall you having a mammoth propensity for consuming those tasty Nathan's hotdogs."

"And what about Dan and me?" Arthur Orsi instinctively asked, realizing that he too would soon be loquaciously admonished.

"Arty, I don't want you hanging-out at Shriver's Candy Store on the Ocean City, New Jersey boardwalk, and when gleaning your background information down in Wildwood, keep your distance from the Mariner's Landing water-slide park, and also maintain separation from the rather alluring roller coaster thrill rides operating on the various Morey Piers."

"And what about me?" Dan Blachford asked, feeling a trifle left out of the loop. "Am I chopped liver, always being treated last?"

"And finally, Dan, I want you to stay focused on your essential two-week-long summer mission, and keep *your* distance from the scary Zipper Ride and the notorious Haunted House excursion at Trimper's Amusements on the south end of the Ocean City, Maryland boardwalk; which are, if my memory serves me correctly, both situated near the inlet jetty," omniscient Inspector Joe Giralo uttered with feigned sincerity. "Now Men, in the final analysis, I want the three of you Mike Hammers to be again standing in my office on Wednesday, August 1st at 9 a.m. sharp, to comprehensively review everything germane that needs to be explored in regard to this bewildering boardwalk crime spree that's oddly occurred over the years in all of these different states. And also, Dan; don't forget to check-out all possible leads at Rehoboth Beach, too!"

* * * * * * * * * * * *

At 9 a.m. on August 1st dedicated Agents Sal Velardi, Art Orsi and Dan Blachford again stood in FBI Chief Joe Giralo's Arch Street office to enthusiastically deliver their most recent well-documented investigative reports. Their very accomplished mentor was in good spirits as he cordially greeted his team of concerned subordinates.

"As you know Men, detective work is based on the sound principles of the scientific method, an approach that's employed daily by laboratory researchers around the world," Inspector Giralo academically prefaced his standard lecture. "And the great literary master Edgar Allan Poe had imaginatively transferred the idea of the scientific method into the present crime-solving procedure when the genius had creatively authored the first detective stories involving Inspector Auguste Dupin, who had dynamically cracked-open the very difficult cases of 'The Murders in the Rue Morgue' and 'The Purloined Letter'; two classic tales that are among my favorites in American literature. Now Salvatore, do you recall the five basic steps associated with the scientific method as being noteworthy and applicable to everyday FBI detective work."

"Well yes, Chief;" Agent Velardi confidently replied and then momentarily paused, gathering his recollection. "First, there's the act of making a valid observation, which then is followed by the practice of fundamental objective experimentation."

"That analysis is precisely correct!" interrupted the always-alert Boss, casually sitting behind his enormous Canadian oak desk. "Over the course of the past two weeks, you three terrific gumshoes have been dispatched to different boardwalk communities to make observations and to gather pertinent details. That assiduous endeavor certainly covers the first two stages of the modern scientific method as it pertains to standard police work, as accurately outlined and prescribed almost two centuries ago by the inimitable literary giant, Edgar Allan Poe!"

"And if I fully remember, the third essential step is making a clever hypothesis; the fourth facet of the scientific method is to verify or prove the relevant hypothesis in the form of finding significant clues, perhaps a dead body, maybe fingerprints, or perhaps even obtaining a decent confession from a key suspect," Agent Velardi proudly articulated. "And the fifth and final phase of the scientific method of reasoning as it applies to police investigation is making reliable, consistent conclusions that are supported by appropriate facts and not by mere assumptions or faulty first impressions. Do I now get a free value meal at Burger King?"

"Excellent presentation, Salvatore!" Joe Giralo complimented his loyal underling. "As you three all-too-diligent workaholics can plainly determine, and with me being *your* immediate supervisor, my involvement with the scientific method is represented in stages three through five. while your direct connection in the process is evident in steps one and two!"

"Chief," Art Orsi piped-up, "in all due respect, the fabled Greek Sphinx standing on a mountain cliff outside the city of Thebes, well Boss, that female monster's crazy riddles that she offered to Oedipus actually made more straight sense than your obscure FBI rhetoric does. How come Sal, Dan and I typically know all the facts in a new case, but have no definite clues about the genuine motives of the criminals committing the deplorable crimes? It just seems that the hypothesis advantage that you and your DC comrade Matt Riley enjoy over *us* is way too awesome for *me* to ever fathom! In every case study scenario, Sal, Dan, and I get to see less than half of the total puzzle! On the other hand, you and your comrade Matt Riley get to view the entire cross-section!"

Inspector Giralo grinned from ear-to-ear like a pleased shark possessing a satisfied appetite, and then specifically asked his three agents to describe what they had respectively learned while prowling around the popular Seaside Heights, Wildwood, and Ocean City, Maryland boardwalks. Sal Velardi responsively disclosed that likeable merchants Elijah Friedman, Jonas Goldberg, and Mohamed Ba' Albaki had *also* been missing from the Seaside Heights

Boardwalk since the genesis year 1978, and that Hezikiah Rosen, Malik Wasti, and American Fred Kaminski had also vanished over the same thirty-four-year span from the ancient Asbury Park boards.

"Well, *that* diverse last name pattern undeniably demonstrates that the problem's not exclusively Arabs versus Jews," Joe Giralo persuasively stated. "And remember Guys, everyone with the exception of Manny Hammerstein had been reported as a missing person with no indication whatsoever of any murder ever being committed. Now Arty, what's actually happened down there in Wildwood, in Cape May, and in Ocean City, New Jersey since 1978; the auspicious year when this entire grotesque kidnapping evolution began developing?"

Agent Orsi declared that boardwalk store-owners having the names Thaddeus Herzog, Solomon Levin, Saul Kaufmann, Jamal bin Haji, Kareem Al Shahrani, Alex Murphy and Joseph Miller had, over the duration of the last thirty-four years, been listed as vanishing from the business world in those three separate-but-popular South Jersey beach municipalities.

"And what wildly inexplicable, clandestine boardwalk activities have simultaneously evolved down in Delaware and Maryland?" Giralo next asked Dan Blachford.

"Well Boss, businessmen Simon Epstein, Ruben Weinberg, Jacob Garfunkel, Rashaad Ta' Anari, Philip Turner, and Thomas Spencer had disappeared in Ocean City, Maryland since 1978; and also, Yasser Raboud, Akeem Assad, Efraim Schwartz, Ebenezer Lieberman, Aaron Cohen, John Palmer, and Henry Kelly had all mysteriously vanished from Rehoboth Beach in the last quarter century! Exactly what's going on here Chief? What's your esoteric hypothesis? I mean, we've thoroughly interviewed dozens of fearful and apprehensive acquaintances of the suspected kidnapping victims in three separate states, and no one had a remote clue as to what has become of the aforementioned missing merchants!"

"Okay then, you rank amateur Einsteins," Joe Giralo mildly chided and addressed his now-confused apostles. "Missing-in-action boardwalk proprietors have been individually reported to local authorities in Coney Island, in Virginia Beach, in Myrtle Beach, in Asbury Park, in Seaside Heights, in Ocean City, New Jersey, in Wildwood, in Cape May, in Rehoboth Beach, Delaware, and finally, in Ocean City Maryland?"

"Boss, we've already established those very elementary, redundant facts!" frustrated Sal Velardi vigorously reminded his highly regarded superior. "Honestly now; you haven't shared with us anything that we didn't already know!"

"Okay then, my fine colleague, Agent Salvatore," Inspector Giralo amiably-but-sarcastically agreed. "Think very hard, now using your entire cerebral capacity. Which New Jersey beach resort *hasn't* reported any missing boardwalk proprietors? I'll give you a powerful hint! It was once known as the Queen of Resorts that featured magnificent, elegant, boardwalk hotels!"

"Why Atlantic City!" Dan Blachford realized and exuberantly exclaimed. "Yes! Atlantic City! Casino gambling was introduced for the purpose of rejuvenating the aging resort back to its Pre-Depression glory days!"

"Exactly!" the virtually all-knowing Philadelphia FBI Boss confirmed. "And as a noteworthy parallel relationship, that is, coincidentally speaking, casino gambling had become a reality in Atlantic City on May 26th, 1978; the historic event being a direct result of a New Jersey public referendum conducted on the voting ballot in 1976. Yes Guys, it all came to fruition on *that* marvelous late spring day in 1978. That's precisely the year when Resorts International ushered in the new legal gambling era and opened its posh doors to enthralled table and slot machine bettors. And then in 1983, the three-floor Playboy Casino opened for business. and after *that* hasty enterprise ran into overwhelming financial difficulties, the Playboy project was quickly taken over by a new corporate entity and renamed the 'Atlantis', which soon lost its operating license and consequently went belly-up," Inspector Giralo verbally reviewed.

"Is that so?" Agent Orsi challenged. "You're simply describing meaningless past history to us. I mean Boss: Oz really gave nothing to the Tin Man, that he didn't already have!"

"Please allow me to continue," Inspector Giralo suavely declared. "A while later, investment mogul Donald Trump converted the former casino building into a hotel property named 'Trump Regency', but without a viable casino to support it, the doomed Trump Regency hotel enterprise declared bankruptcy in 1985. The Playboy Atlantis-Regency structure was located near the old Boardwalk Convention Hall where the popular Miss America pageants had been originally held. In fact, the old Playboy boardwalk grounds are now owned by a condominium speculator/developer."

"I've attended several big stage concerts at the Boardwalk Convention Hall, the most recent ones being given by Fleetwood Mac and Elton John," Sal Velardi instinctively remarked. "I think Stevie Nicks is the greatest!"

"Anyway Men," Chief Giralo proceeded with his long-winded exposition, paying little attention to Agent Velardi's singular rock music preferences. "Other A.C. casinos have gone totally defunct besides the ill-fated Playboy and the also humbled Atlantis. Another venture had been established in 1980; the Sands, formerly the Brighton. That misadventure eventually went the way of the dinosaur, but remarkably, the operation lasted until 1998. The place was recently purchased by the Pinnacle Corporation, but the new Pinnacle Casino Hotel never materialized. So, as you conscientious Men can feasibly determine, success in the highly competitive casino industry is not necessarily guaranteed!"

"But formidable Donald Trump did eventually get good traction in the new Atlantic City casino market," Art Orsi contributed to the mini-conference. "The Donald boldly opened the Trump Plaza and later unveiled the gaudy Taj Mahal up on the north end of the boardwalk, and let's not forget about the Trump Marina constructed near historic Gardner's Basin, over near Brigantine."

"And don't neglect mentioning the classy Borgata over in the Marina District, and let's not fail to include the swanky Revel up on the boardwalk; and let's also throw into the mix the four related sister hotel casinos: Harrahs, the Showboat, Caesar's World, and of course, Bally's. And as a footnote Boss," knowledgeable Agent Orsi expanded his loquacious discourse, "the Trump Marina has now morphed into the new, elegant Golden Nugget."

"And let's not neglect to mention the Tropicana and the Atlantic City Hilton, formerly known as the 'Grand'," Agent Dan Blachford vociferated. "But Chief, what-on-earth does Atlantic City casino gambling have to do with the disappearance of all these apparently vulnerable boardwalk merchants in other East Coast beach resort towns? It just doesn't add up!"

"That's precisely where *my* modest genius has surreptitiously entered into the complicated mystery equation," Inspector Joe Giralo unabashedly boasted. "And I owe the entire, non-sophisticated, simple answer to *me* thinking about my wife's second cousin!"

"What!" Agent Velardi vehemently balked. "You gotta' be kidding me! Say what, Boss?"

"Yes Sal, my wife's bad-luck second cousin Mark Martino and two other Hammonton losers in 1977 opened a risky boardwalk amusement arcade at Missouri Avenue and the Atlantic City Boardwalk called Wheel and Deal. Summer arcade addicts would stroll-in and play electronic poker machines and boardwalk wheel games to accumulate coupons and win displayed prizes."

"So, what does this lackluster Wheel and Deal amusement center have to do with all of these inexplicable human disappearances on a plethora of boardwalks along the East Coast?" bewildered Sal Velardi intrepidly protested. "Art's right-on-target with his patented cynicism, Boss! You do treat *us* like we're baby cave mushrooms."

"But Salvatore, this rather annoying missing persons' dilemma has truly *mushroomed* into a fantastically colossal kidnapping and murder mystery!" the very venerable Inspector casually insisted. "Think strategically about the general given circumstances. It's all quite elementary, you see. We have an unusual mathematical equation here; a rather peculiar arithmetical formula having *two* lowest common denominators!"

"So far, Chief, *your* completely weird explanation is as clear as Egyptian hieroglyphics, and your obtuse interpretations are about as lucid as Babylonian cuneiform scribbling," distressed Art Orsi strenuously attested. "And for good measure, Boss, throw-in an abundant measure of indecipherable Indian Sanskrit, too!"

Unfazed Inspector Joe Giralo ignored Agent Arthur Orsi's verbal vernacular and then haughtily resumed his insightful dissertation. "First of all, Men, the missing-in-action boardwalk merchants from Coney Island down to Myrtle Beach have all disappeared after 1978, the indisputable year that Atlantic City casino gambling went into effect. Secondly, and more importantly, I was on the right track when I thought about my wife's second cousin and his two naïve partners losing their business lease when their shrewd profit-oriented landlord sold the entire Missouri Avenue block to Caesar's World! And that's exactly what seriously compelled me to make my extremely astute scientific method theory!"

"Which is?" an irritated florid-faced Dan Blachford angrily asked. "Quite frankly Boss, you've been about as clear as muddy Louisiana bayou swamp water so far this morning!"

Inspector Joe Giralo nonchalantly explained to his impetuous crew that after casino gambling had been officially and legally approved in 1976, entire blocks on the Atlantic City Boardwalk were quickly purchased and effectively gobbled-up by large corporations. And naturally, while in pursuit of once-in-a-lifetime windfall profits, avaricious boardwalk landlords were quickly motivated to terminate leases with former small business owners, who suddenly felt alienated and abandoned, ostensibly needing new places to earn a living. "For instance," Chief Giralo finished, "the 2012 Revel opening caused at least a dozen displaced merchants to actively seek new boardwalk opportunities elsewhere!"

"I now see the merit of your impeccable reasoning," Sal Velardi perceptively acknowledged. "So, as a result, the distraught, displaced merchants from Atlantic City needed new frontiers to conduct their various business specialties; new alluring destinations like Seaside Heights and Rehoboth Beach were aggressively pursued. These were new beaches where the evicted boardwalk entrepreneurs from Atlantic City might already have had hard-working family and friends running various amusement arcades, food joints, gift shops, candy emporiums, and beach tee shirt stores!"

"Exactly Fellas', but here's the most salient part *I've* forgotten to present!" a now adamant Joe Giralo deliberately emphasized. "These aggravated, displaced merchants always ran cash businesses where they could skim twenty-five thousand dollars or more each summer from the IRS's scrutiny. Hence, they could approach greedy landlords at other beach resorts, offer them, let's say, a handsome sum of one hundred thousand bucks under the table to successfully evict former tenants, and then as a proposed rental bonus, promise to provide the delighted, compliant landlords an additional twenty-five-thousand-dollar summer surplus payment, which would be over-and-above the past amount that the former merchant/tenant had been paying. That method of extortion utilized by evicted store owners would be very enticing to influence individual boardwalk landlords owning city blocks at beach resorts other than Atlantic City!"

"How could these itinerant, former Atlantic City boardwalk businessmen afford to do this?" Arthur Orsi marveled and inquired. "It doesn't seem economically feasible for them to work for practically nothing! I'm no rocket scientist, and I know that!"

"Very profoundly true, Arty!" Inspector Giralo readily concurred. "Boardwalk store summer rentals have traditionally been exceptionally exorbitant, virtually out of sight! Back in 1977, the going rate on major boardwalks was a thousand dollars a front foot. A meager twenty-five-foot frontage meant a hefty twenty-five thousand rental fee. Today, it's on the average of two-to-three thousand bucks a front foot. Now if a greedy landlord gets an unexpected offer from a displaced Atlantic City boardwalk merchant for three thousand bucks a foot, the in-jeopardy of losing his store merchant might hire a Mafia hit squad to rub-out the eager newcomer for let's say, a handsome hundred grand for a permanent personal elimination expense! And the whole payoff system could easily work in reverse, too."

"Wow!" expressed a very impressed Dan Blachford. "These poor people that own boardwalk businesses probably have to work from Memorial Day to Labor Day just to cover their enormous rental leases, their escalating merchandise expenditures, along with their various employees' salaries, not to mention all of the pressure-related taxes and license fees. So Boss, that's why these affected East Coast beach resorts are attempting to extend their seasons from April to November with enticing promotions and attractive spring and autumn festival tourist packages!"

Then Chief Inspector Joe Giralo shocked his already-astounded agents by revealing that just that same early August 1st morning, he and relentless Matt Riley down in DC had brilliantly figured-out the entire "boardwalk killing and murder spree debacle".

"Just two days ago, a former IRS agent came clean," Joe Giralo informed his still-astonished detective trio. "It seems that the IRS revenue guy had a guilty conscience after he had egregiously violated his federal duty in addition to his solemn government oath. It appears that this rogue IRS agent had accepted a large bribe from notorious Mafia affiliate Carmine Campanella, who as you probably know, owns a slew of boardwalk businesses ranging from Seaside Heights down to Ocean City, Maryland. This disreputable punk Campanella had paid the corrupt IRS fellow a hundred-thousand-dollar bribe to go into the amusement arcades of three competitors and harass them with a federal *gaming tax* attached onto their former games of skill, claiming that the electronic poker machines were now games of chance subject to federal gaming laws, that when applied retroactively for a dozen or more years, upon let's say thirty individual machines," Chief Giralo expounded and then resumed, "would amount to a substantial fine of over a hundred thousand bucks plus accumulated back interest and associated penalties; all owed to *our* most excellent benefactor, good old Uncle Sam!"

"And please allow me to guess the rest," Sal Velardi euphorically interrupted his immediate superior. "One of the arcade guys knew about this demonic thug Carmine Campanella doing the dirty behind-the-scene bribe because Campanella's similar boardwalk arcades in other beach towns were not assessed and taxed by the corrupt IRS guy. But what about the killing of Manny Hammerstein off the Ocean City, Maryland shore, along with the attendant disappearances of the other legitimate shore merchants up and down the whole East Coast?"

"Well Salvatore," Chief Giralo answered with a stern expression upon his stoic-looking visage. "One of the overtaxed arcade owners turned State's Evidence and has voluntarily entered into the Witness Protection Program. This brave amusement games' operator knew all about Carmine Campanella being instrumental in rubbing-out Manny Hammerstein and then stupidly leaving the victim's fishing boat adrift in the *Atlantic*. The arcade gentleman's documented testimony indicates on this official transcript I've just received from DC headquarters that Campanella would have his two bodyguard hit men 'rub-out' a predetermined victim for the nominal sum of $150,000.00 per professional hit."

"Holy Hades!" Art Orsi's voice emotionally boomed. "Has this dangerous Mafia-connected boardwalk crook you've identified as Carmine Campanella been arrested?"

"Ha, ha, ha!" indulgently laughed Inspector Giralo. "Yes indeed. Campanella has been taken into custody. The slippery culprit was captured earlier this morning over in Barcelona, Spain trying to reboard the Royal Caribbean Cruise Lines *Voyager of the Sea,* which had been docked in the city's deep harbor. Campanella and his two diabolical henchmen were heading for scheduled vacation tours in Tuscany, in Rome and on the Anakfi Coast.

Agents Velardi, Orsi, and Blachford stared at each other incredulously in total astonishment. Finally, the FBI Inspector's main agent gathered the wherewithal to utter a summary comment.

"Boss, your keen ability to solve intricate, complex, federal crimes is absolutely phenomenal!" Agent Velardi earnestly announced his well-intended kudos. "And just to randomly think, you did it all without ever soliciting the services of your very close Delta Force friend, Colonel Bob Bauers!"

"Not exactly!" Inspector Giralo facetiously answered and then hardily chuckled. "Sorry to terribly disappoint you, my dear Salvatore; for you see, quite coincidentally, Colonel Bob Bauers had been attending a rather boring NATO conference over in Barcelona. But then, my loyal friend's unrivaled military expertise had been enlisted and soon swiftly utilized by Interpol, and so Colonel Bauers both coordinated and later assisted in the well-executed arrest of this lunatic: narcissistic, ingrate Carmine Campanella along with the vile scoundrel's two despicable Mafia hit men, Louie "the Lance" Lanciano and Denny "the Decapitator" DeLareto. And for all of *our* exemplary scientific method expertise Men," the FBI Chief admirably concluded, "I wholeheartedly say, 'Long live the memory of Edgar Allan Poe, along with my favorite fictional hero, the magnificent French Inspector, Auguste Dupin'!"

"Irrigation Irritation"

Robert and Rita Randazzo had experienced a pleasant week-long Pocono Mountains vacation at Fernwood Resort in Bushkill. In addition to playing golf and swimming, the couple also relished visiting the picturesque Delaware Water Gap situated just below East Stroudsburg; rented and paddled a canoe on the tranquil *Delaware* up near Milford; felt adventurous and tried white water rafting on a mountain river, and also attended various popular entertainment venues at other area resorts at Mt. Pocono, Analomink, and at nearby Swiftwater. For the vacationing couple, the three-hour ride from Fernwood back to Hammonton, New Jersey was especially carefree and enjoyable. Everything including the normally abominable traffic congestion on Route 206 was (in Bob's judgment) "copacetic".

"That was a great escape from reality," the husband commented to his wife from behind the wheel of his Mercury Mountaineer, as the tan SUV sped south by Atsion Lake at noon on Friday, August 5, 2005. "No flat tires, no major complications, and thanks to your sister staying at her high-rise condo' at the Jersey Shore," the Ford/Lincoln/Mercury new car salesman evaluated, "our two teenagers were being expertly supervised while hittin' the surf and walkin' the Wildwood Boardwalk."

"Don't jinx us before we get safely home," Rita Randazzo cynically answered while reflecting her typical Sicilian superstitious demeanor. "I'm a little nervous about certain things, and I don't want you recklessly causin' a reverse black cat situation. When events are goin' smoothly and seem too good to be true," the leery wife related, "just pretend letting matters just be as they are, and start thinking about something else more positive. But Bob, the Poconos and Fernwood were pretty terrific and exciting; but frankly, it's great being back on flat South Jersey land again."

Upon reaching the familiar horseshoe-shaped driveway of 569 North White Horse Pike, Robert stopped and removed the past week's mail from his highway box. The now-relaxed husband then re-entered the SUV, parked in front of his well-kept, gray, two-story colonial house, and next carried the travelers' four pieces of luggage inside. After depositing two bags of dirty clothes in the spacious laundry room, Randazzo lugged the other two suitcases upstairs to the master bedroom. Returning downstairs to the kitchen table, the rejuvenated man-of-the-house casually sifted through the pile of accumulated mail, casually sorting junk solicitations from the more relevant monthly bills and the recent personal correspondence from relatives and friends. Soon, something seemingly important grabbed the husband's attention, and Robert Randazzo anxiously opened the unexpected missive.

"Honey, here's a letter from your old high school boyfriend Brian Raso, Esquire," Bob yelled from the kitchen in the direction of the close-by laundry room. "I haven't seen that guy since your last class reunion, five years ago. Just think. I always beat the wimp up my junior year, and now he's a prominent lawyer and judge over in Mays Landing; and also, Raso's practicing law right here in Hammonton and teaching several night courses over at Atlantic Community College!"

"What does Brian want?" Rita hollered back from two rooms away. "Is he tryin' to sell us a hundred-dollar ticket to the Lions Club Gold Raffle? If so, let's just buy the ticket for a hundred bucks and write it off on our annual income tax statement. If we go to the dinner and drawing, it'll cost us a hundred and seventy smackeroos!"

"Holy mackerel!" Bob exclaimed in a shocked and astonished tone of voice. "We're bein' sued, and your old beau is representin' the plaintiffs. At least that's what's described in the first paragraph of this legal-lookin' document!"

"What's this crazy nonsense all about?" a puzzled-looking Rita Randazzo answered as the alarmed woman of the house quickly exited the laundry room and approached the kitchen in a strident gait. "This rude postal interruption sounds absolutely absurd! Who would possibly be suin' us, and for what reason?"

The husband checked the calendar hanging on the kitchen door leading to the cellar. "Today is Friday, August 5th," the now-aggravated spouse confirmed to his equally upset marital partner. "It states in this lousy letter that at six p.m. on Wednesday, July 28th a certain couple named Philip and Elsie Mangano from Berlin were drivin' by our place when the irrigation sprinklers were runnin'. Some water from one of the three front-line sprinkler heads splashed onto the windshield of their car; frightened the driver, who incidentally was Elsie Mangano, and then their auto' swerved off the highway and abruptly hit a tree. The Manganos' sustained lacerations, bruises, and other injuries in the mishap, and were taken by the Hammonton Rescue Squad to Kessler Memorial Hospital."

The husband further explained from his reading that Mrs. Mangano had sustained several deep cuts on her face that might require plastic surgery, and that her husband had suffered a broken wrist. "The 2001 Ford Focus, which by the way I did not sell to them," the husband emphatically clarified, "requires two thousand dollars to repair, and the attorney's letter also states that we're both completely liable for *that* compensation, also."

The newly arrived vacationers were not-too-thrilled with the disappointing new-found information received in the highway mailbox. Rita Randazzo soon felt nauseous in her stomach. "How long has it been since those sprinklers had been installed?" the still-in-surprise wife angrily asked. "I can't seem to remember."

"If you recall, your cousin Nino had acquired a trench diggin' machine and next, your helpful relative assisted me putting-in the plastic pipes, the risers, and the sprinkler heads before I finally got around to seeding the lawn," Bob Randazzo recollected and reluctantly reported. "That was two years after we also had moved into this home, which was brand new in 1970, so it had to have been in the summer of '72 when the sprinklers were installed. Yes, it was a year before my cousin Steve was born."

"That front line has always been a problem," the peeved wife admitted, "and sometimes the water does squirt-out onto the highway when the wind is blowing from the north. I've warned you to get the nuisance fixed at least a dozen times!"

"Yes Hon," Bob guiltily acknowledged in a disgusted tone of voice. "When the wind's blowin' north to south the water carries about ten feet farther than usual, and some water does land splashing in the right-hand-lane goin' west towards Philadelphia. But that only happens occasionally, maybe three times a summer. If I'm home, I don't run the front line on a windy day. But since I had the irrigation system set on 'Automatic' during our nine-day Poconos hiatus," the male resident of the house mentioned with an element of regret, "then it could be true that we're responsible for causin' the accident and the injuries."

"Our society is becomin' so damned litigious!" Rita instinctively complained. "Exactly how much are these money-hungry people, the Manganos, suing us for?"

"For $250,000.00 if your old beau Brian Raso can prove negligence on our part," Robert Francis Randazzo revealed while again examining the legal language in the lawyer's dispatch. "But the hospital expenses and the damage to the 2001 Ford Focus come to a mere three thousand bucks, which I think we'll certainly be obligated to pay. And that's not counting court expenses too, if we lose the case."

"Will our homeowner's insurance policy cover the unbelievable $250,000.00 negligence claim if the presiding judge is crazy enough to award that exorbitant amount?" the disbelieving wife inquired. "Is there no more sanity in this chaotic world? I hope that Brian doesn't carry a grudge against you and your sophomoric antics when you were a high school senior, nearly forty years ago!"

"I don't know that technical answer!" Bob replied and then hesitated. "Maybe I'll have to get on the horn with our insurance agent and ask him that very same question. And then after I speak with Mike Garrison about the matter," the very concerned husband continued describing his next strategic move, "I'll give my old high school buddy Nelson Donio a call. He's reputed to be the best defense lawyer in town. This ugly lawn sprinkler misadventure looks as if it's goin' to cost us more than a pretty penny!"

"Why couldn't you have gotten a professional sprinkler installer to put in our system?" the wife criticized and indicted as was her bad habit when under emotional duress. "You're always trying to save by cutting corners, and that lousy frugality makes you penny wise and dollar foolish. It always pays to have things done right by professionals in the first place, ya' know."

"Honey, at the time we were strugglin' makin' ends meet right after we first got hitched," Robert snapped back in a defensive baritone. "You were talkin' to Nino at a family get-together, and your good cousin volunteered to help us out. And now all these years later, we're gonna' pay the piper big time! I hope we don't have to declare bankruptcy after the dense smoke clears! This sudden legal challenge might just mean financial ruin for us!"

"You'd better get on the phone and set-up an appointment with Nelson Donio right away," Rita emotionally commanded like a female political dictator. "I hope our defense lawyer doesn't still hold any old high school grudges against you like your old nemesis Brian Raso does! Bob, I think your inglorious past is actually coming back to haunt us."

"Not a chance!" the former high school quarterback replied in an exaggerated attempt to put a positive spin on the bad-topic-conversation. "You just gotta' hope that if Nelson can't perform a minor miracle in this extraordinary case, then at least he could partially rescue us by pullin' a legal rabbit out of his hat; perhaps on the basis of some procedural technicality, or something imaginative like *that* Rita," the ex-star Hammonton High School athlete expressed in a more civil tone of voice. "And maybe there is such a thing as creative justice in the courtroom! Please hand me the yellow phone book in the top drawer. This unexpected dilemma that's all-too-quickly surfaced from nowhere requires instant attention."

Nelson Donio, Esquire was quite sage in regard to breaking-down bizarre cases, especially ones similar to the present perplexing in-progress litigation that was thoroughly vexing Bob and Rita Randazzo. At the first legal consultation, the veteran attorney had convinced the harried couple that the best tact would be to delay the trial for six months in order to frustrate the greedy plaintiffs, and also in order to perform comprehensive background checks on the weird lawsuit's propagators. The very frustrated Randazzos wholeheartedly endorsed the reputable barrister's advice, and as a result, agreed to award Mr. Donio a retainer of one thousand dollars.

Three weeks elapsed, and finally, the Randazzos received a registered letter from their attorney, Nelson Donio. "I'll need some additional money allowance for research and background help I must employ in your rather stranger-than-fiction legal case! I'll have to hire a private investigator to dig-up some pertinent information on the prosecuting Manganos. This proven method of intensive information gathering is common practice in the legal profession. This plaintiff-defendant infighting can get a little dirty and messy at times, and if I need to use past questionable practices that the plaintiffs may have committed, I want to be on solid ground while exploring those particular avenues. So, Bob and Rita," the lawyer's missive specifically conveyed to his new clients, "I'll soon need another fifteen-hundred-dollars to hire two investigative gumshoes I've had satisfactory past associations with. My very competent friend and his new partner are very skilled at their line of work, and I have a hunch that this very necessary P.I. intervention will ultimately yield positive results. Sometimes a client and his or her lawyer have to go the extra mile to outwit and defeat their determined opponents in very difficult Legal War battles; particularly *this* rather fascinating one that you've been inadvertently thrust into."

The autumn months passed by very slowly for Robert and Rita Randazzo, as the worried couple thought about the potential liability outcome of their "unfortunate lawn sprinkler predicament". Soon, Thanksgiving and the Christmas holidays had passed, and on Friday, December 26th the husband received a follow-up call from Attorney Nelson Donio.

"Bob, the case has been scheduled for Thursday, January 6 at 10 a.m. in the court chambers inside the Hammonton Municipal City Hall. I know that this phone call doesn't quite sound like a 'Happy New Year' statement, but that's when the judge is available, and he's tired of me postponing the trial for us. But Bob, there's one good aspect to this court date announcement. The case will be held in private session without any local reporters around to pepper us with annoying questions about the trial. The press just loves 'man bites canine stories', you know, and I think we have one of those in our midst!"

"Can you tell me anything in detail about what your private investigator friend has discovered?" the over-anxious defendant curiously inquired. "After all, Nelson; I am your client, and I am paying the full freight here."

"Believe me Bob, I take my profession seriously, and also the revelation of *that* kind of sensitive information, at least in my mind, constitutes a gross violation of professional ethics established between the on the prowl private investigator and me. His research is still ongoing. But I can tell you this little tidbit. You'll learn what particular facts have been excavated over the past several weeks, either during or after the formal court proceedings," the all-too-honest barrister pledged. "And in addition, Bob. I'll try to see to it that you won't have to testify under oath because you weren't at home during the time of the accident and allegedly, also absent when the automatic sprinklers had been activated."

"Thanks a lot Nelson! Rita and I will see you at Town Hall on the morning of January 6th," the somewhat-relieved Hammonton citizen indicated. "I'll jot *that* important date down on the cellar door calendar, and also in my personal memo' book. If Rita and I have to cough-up a quarter of a million dollars that we don't have, then we'll have to secretly leave town in the middle of the night and move to Afghanistan, or some other remote country like that and start our miserable lives all over again! Nelson, we just can't afford paying any excessive settlement!" Click.

At precisely 10 a.m. on the morning of January 6, 2006, Bob and Rita Randazzo (represented by Attorney Nelson Donio) appeared in Town Hall Municipal Court before the Honorable Judge Vincent C. Curcio in the predominantly Italian community of Hammonton, N.J. The Randazzos waived their right to testify, and then Nelson Donio stood and read an opening statement which maintained that his clients had accepted full responsibility for the "front irrigation sprinkler line shooting water out onto Route 30, the White Horse Pike". The Manganos sat behind a long, rectangular, wooden table on the opposite side of the courtroom, and the self-confident plaintiffs had smug-but-happy expressions on their faces.

356

Judge Curcio then heard testimony from Philip and Elsie Mangano, whose rehearsed glib statements and answers supported each other's account of what had transpired at 6 p.m. on Wednesday July 28th, 2005. The shocked Randazzos were quite dismayed about the flow of events, feeling that Attorney Donio had veritably conceded the case and that they (the defendants) should break with courtroom protocol and speak-up; defiantly, vocally challenging their lack of an organized professional defense.

After the Judge patiently listened to the plaintiffs' common version of what had occurred, Nelson Donio courteously asked the Solon seated at the bench if he and lawyer Brian Raso could temporarily adjourn from the formal proceedings and have a "necessary "sidebar conference" in the honorable Judge's chambers.

A full hour elapsed with only the Manganos, the Randazzos, the court stenographer, and a conscientious bailiff occupying the silent courtroom while the private conference (that the all-too-shrewd Attorney Nelson Donio had requested) was still in progress. Then, the three legal experts all re-entered the courtroom and the dignified proceeding continued with presiding Judge Curcio surprisingly rendering his conclusive verdict from his black leather. swivel chair. All eye scrutiny originating from the four principals involved in the "lawn sprinkler dispute" seriously focused their attention on the judicious man wearing the long black robe.

"Mr. Robert Randazzo, this court warrants that you get your sprinkler system adjusted and immediately move your front line back ten feet so that your irrigation water does not drift-out onto Route 30 on certain windy days," Judge Curcio austerely mandated. "I don't want to see any recurrence of the unfortunate events of July 28, or else the consequences levied upon you will be quite severe next time."

Philip and Elsie Mangano momentarily stared at each other with very evident smirks upon their disdainful countenances. The plaintiffs both believed that their "negligence case" had been bolstered by the Judge's attitude toward Robert Randazzo, and by *his* preliminary negative comments directed towards the nervous defendants. The plaintiffs' scheming minds contemplated that handsome civil damages would definitely be awarded, after initial fault had been legally established. Then Judge Vincent C. Curcio continued disclosing the essence of his decision.

"And now Mr. and Mrs. Robert Randazzo," the prudent enforcer of Hammonton justice addressed the very apprehensive defendants from his elevated courtroom position. "I hereby rule that it is *not* necessary for you to compensate the plaintiffs, otherwise known as Mr. and Mrs. Philip Mangano of Berlin, New Jersey, for either accumulative hospital debts. or for damage done to their automobile. Furthermore, Mr. And Mrs. Mangano," Judge Curcio sternly and forcefully declared, "by virtue of additional evidence presented by the defendants' attorney, I am hereby ordering the two of you to appear in this court four Thursdays from now to answer to certain charges that your reputable lawyer Mr. Brian Raso shall later discuss with you. Secondary facts have entered into this unusual case that clearly demonstrate that malicious fraud might be involved," the notable Judge divulged to the suddenly-stunned plaintiffs. "My clerk will be sending you a letter via certified mail outlining the specific violations to which you will have to answer. This court now stands adjourned!" Judge Curcio determined as he smacked his gavel down upon his elevated mahogany desk's flat wooden panel.

Mr. And Mrs. Philip Mangano appeared quite perturbed and distraught at the case's unexpected disposition, and the disappointed couple vehemently protested the judge's verdict to no avail. Seemingly embarrassed Attorney Brian Raso appeared wanting no part of his belligerent clients' random, acrimonious insinuations.

* * * * * * * * * * * *

An hour and a half later, Bob and Rita Randazzo met with Nelson Donio in the lawyer's plush downtown Bellevue Avenue office. The attorney thoroughly disclosed what pertinent information had been reviewed and analyzed in Judge Curcio's chambers, and then explained in layman's terms why Brian Raso, Esquire had acceded to the final verdict without providing aggressive legal arguments (or challenges) for his vitriolic Berlin, New Jersey clients.

"Bob and Rita," Nelson Donio prefaced his analysis with a broad smile. "Much to my satisfaction, the investment in my private investigator friends indeed paid off quality dividends in your favor. First of all, we caught the Manganos in the middle of a blatant lie."

"This is all rather confusing, so could you please go back to square one?" a rather confused Robert Randazzo insisted. "We had no inkling that the Manganos were lying about the accident! I mean to say, Nelson, they did sustain physical injuries, didn't they?"

"Well Bob, in the beginning neither did I question or challenge their integrity!" the very efficient local attorney admitted. "You see folks, the Manganos had passed your place a first time going west toward Philadelphia, and the couple perceptively observed that the irrigation water was squirting out onto the Pike. The sue-happy pair drove a quarter mile past your home and turned around at the Silver Fox Tavern, thus entering back onto your busy Route 30; and then their vehicle headed back east going toward downtown Hammonton. Next, the wily Manganos turned around at Ideal Clothes Manufacturing Company, and by that time, the vile troublemakers had coyly fabricated a story that each agreed corroborating to the Hammonton police. It always pays to actually have observant honest citizens in your neighborhood."

"But how do those particular occurrences prove that a legally defined lie in court ever existed?" Rita Randazzo piped-in. "I simply don't understand how these separate things involving *them* and *us* are even vaguely connected. There's a missing link here somewhere about the dual turnarounds the Manganos had made on Route 30. And what do you mean by us having honest citizens in our neighborhood? I just don't get it Mr. Donio!"

"You'll see in a minute," Nelson Donio assured his grateful-but-confused clients. "The owner of the Silver Fox Tavern was just finishing-up mowing his lawn when Mr. Mike Paretti noticed the Manganos' red Ford Focus turning around rather wildly in the establishment's driveway. Then, the observant restaurant owner stepped inside his place of business, and five minutes later, heard on his police radio scanner that a car had hit a tree near your residence. The tavern proprietor rushed to the accident scene, and noticed that the dented vehicle was the same one that had recklessly turned around in his restaurant's driveway. Since nobody had been seriously maimed or killed in the accident," Attorney Donio uttered and then paused, "the Silver Fox owner did not issue a statement to the Hammonton Police, because he didn't desire getting immersed in having to make an inconvenient court appearance simply to testify in regard to what Mr. Mike Paretti considered to be a minor observation on his part."

"I see!" Robert Randazzo interrupted. "The Silver Fox owner's statement as told to you, and to your private investigators, proved that the Manganos had turned around in the restaurant's driveway several minutes prior to hitting the tree, so that the connivers could again pass by our property a second time and then deliberately collide into the sturdy oak, blaming the whole incident on *my* errant front sprinklers."

"Now you're cooking with gas!" the very competent attorney enthusiastically praised his astute client. "And when the sneaky Manganos had turned around at Ideal Manufacturing, their all-too-rapid U-Turn had been spotted by the caretaker of Oak Grove

Cemetery, situated just across the highway. The caretaker four minutes later also heard the ambulance call over his police monitor, which Mr. Lou Rizzotte keeps inside his storage garage. And next, my private investigator team obtained the Hammonton police dispatcher's transcript records to enable them to identify the exact time of the rescue squad emergency call, precisely 6:03 p.m. It's a good thing that the people in and around Hammonton are both nosy and concerned, and the residents keep their police monitors active most all of the time."

"Naturally, Nelson, your private investigators had interviewed both the alert tavern owner and the watchful cemetery caretaker," Rita Randazzo concluded and stated. "In fact, my husband and I know both Mr. Paretti and Mr. Rizzotte on a first name basis."

The attorney hardily laughed, and then communicated other interesting facts that had eventually persuaded Judge Curcio to dismiss the Manganos' negligence claim, and that ultimately dissuaded Brian Raso from actively representing his disenchanted, reprehensible clients. Evidence presented in the judge's conference chambers exposed that Philip and Elsie Mangano had previously demonstrated a long history of filing frivolous lawsuits. Mrs. Mangano had once fallen-down outside the Berlin ShopRite Supermarket, and later collected ten thousand dollars for her premeditated tumble that incidentally, happened with only her prevaricating husband as a witness. Then, on two separate occasions, the devious Manganos had become involved in "similar suspicious-in-nature" Berlin, New Jersey area auto accidents.

"The crafty couple would look in the rear-view mirror for a fast traveling car in the passing lane, while both vehicles were approaching a traffic light that was turning yellow," Attorney Donio eloquently divulged. "At the last minute, the Manganos would switch lanes and then be rear-ended when the speeding vehicle in the passing lane jammed on its brakes too late to avoid a violent impact. Berlin Police records describe in detail this insane, dangerous scam happening twice with the Manganos collecting medical expenses, car repairs, and then aggressively suing the other perfectly innocent driver for carelessly operating a motor vehicle. The auto' insurance companies suspected fraud, and alertly filed counter-claims that are still in litigation."

"I had no idea that we were being sued by such deceitful, nefarious people!" Rita Randazzo gasped while shaking her head in total disgust. "Who would ever think that any mature adult could be so furtively greedy, and so harmfully untrustworthy?"

"Anyway Folks, the Manganos have already been convicted for claiming to have their previous car stolen in April of 2000," Nelson Donio informed his now thoroughly delighted, attentive clients. "And Pennsylvania court records indicate that *your* legal adversaries had sold *that* particular vehicle to a notorious chop-shop in Philadelphia, and then collected windfall insurance checks on it, too. That incident was another prime example of the devious pair conspiring to cheat an insurance company out of money while also getting paid by the chop-shop dealer, who incidentally claimed under deposition testimony to be operating a legitimate auto' repair business. And thank goodness the South Philly' chop-shop was recently raided, and the Manganos' records were luckily found, with the convicting data being kept in computer files that the Quaker City police had confiscated. And finally, according to Camden County police records," Attorney Nelson Donio declared and related., "Philip Mangano had broken his right wrist in a Berlin barroom fight on Monday evening, July 26th. His wrist was *not* fractured in the car hitting the oak tree near your home on the White Horse Pike."

"We're sure glad we hired you, Nelson, to take our case," Bob Randazzo praised the eminent attorney. "Ironically, it only goes to prove the maxim 'Honesty is really the best policy'."

"Maybe yes, and maybe no!" Nelson Donio cryptically answered, quite tongue-in-cheek. "It also pays to have the Honorable Judge as my loyal third cousin. Nepotism is quite common in small towns like Hammonton, you know! That's not to definitely say that bein' a blood relative of the Judge had affected the disposition of your unusual case. And besides, *that* distinct blood relationship, Bob," Nelson Donio resumed his extraordinary exposition. "You stand to directly profit from this 'deal', or should I say 'ordeal'. And then Sir, you'll have enough cash left over to fully subsidize your new irrigation system, and to travel first class to faraway Hawaii, too!"

"It sounds like you're talkin' in riddles again!" Robert Randazzo exclaimed. "What on Earth are you referrin' to?" the now-cheerful husband asked the stellar defense attorney. "I must admit, Nelson. Hawaii certainly beats the Poconos any day of the week. But please tell me. Where's all of this new family revenue coming from?"

"Well, Bob; you're a new car salesman over at the Route 30 Ford/Lincoln/Mercury distributorship, aren't you?"

"Why yes, Nelson!" the rather bewildered new car salesman responded. "Yes, I am!"

"Now Bob, I was talkin' to cousin Vince Curcio over the telephone just before you two Hammontonians arrived at my office for your slated briefing conference. And it coincidentally appears that the Judge and I, along with two other town lawyers, are in the market for brand new Lincolns. Congratulations Bob!" Nelson Donio commended. "You've just merited handsome commissions that'll more than pay for your irrigation alterations, for your grand Hawaiian vacation, and for your wise hiring of me and my sagacious Berlin private investigator friends."

"July 4th, 2076"

Colonel Madison strode briskly across a wet pavement inside the vast military quadrangle. His polished knee-high boots made a distinct cadence upon concrete as the very important Army commander swiftly paced past colorful rosebushes and well-trimmed yews. The proud officer's impeccable uniform had neither a wrinkle nor a lint particle. Madison had chosen a military career because he liked order and discipline. The strict-minded disciplinarian fully comprehended that personal appearance meant proper image; that precision meant responsibility; and that punctuality meant loyalty to superior officers.

Madison's destination was the suburban Denver military base's prestigious Officers Club. The colonel desired to arrive early and enjoy a well-deserved drink before the United States Director General delivered his special July 4th, 2076 television address to the American citizens. The country was celebrating its Tricentennial, and the nation's leader's speech would commemorate three centuries of national courage, cultural evolution, and enviable vigilance.

'The epic events of this nation's past struggles must be linked to the glory of the present,' Madison thought as the Colonel approached the Officers' Club. 'All true neo-patriots are anxious to learn of the Director General's State of the Culture speech,' his concerned mind observed and considered.

The Officers' Club was situated on the western fringe of the Denver Military Strategic Institute. Madison had spent the last month at the center, taking courses to strategically prepare for his very challenging G-1 oral and written examinations. The ambitious colonel lived every second of his life in quest of promotion to the highly coveted One-Star General rank. The officer's brain was weary from twelve hours of intensive cramming and studying.

'Competition is extremely keen at the apex of the military pyramid,' Madison quickly determined. 'Only the best minds, best records, and best recommendations will ultimately prevail. Mental discipline is the key to my success,' the prospective One Star General concluded during that warm, drizzling, early July evening.

The officer entered the electronic-controlled glass doors, stepped to the mahogany-facade bar, and was fortunate to find an empty stool. The regular patron showed his impressive-looking military credentials to the bartender, quickly ordered a scotch and soda, and then leisurely perused the room.

On the wall to Madison's right hung the majestic American flag with its thirteen red and white stripes, and its fifty-eight stars.

On the wall to the colonel's right was an enlarged duplicate of the sacred *Ten Amended Amendments* to the *United States Constitution*. Federal Law provided that each person in the land had the right to memorize the ten declarations in order to pass the written and oral tests at age twenty-one, also done in order to qualify for the distinguished high honor of individual citizenship.

"The Director General believes that such regimentation forces each person to be more knowledgeable about the nation's laws, customs, tradition and history," the corporal bartender noted as the meek enlisted soldier alertly observed Madison staring admiringly at the enlarged document hanging upon the wall.

"Yes indeed," Madison agreed as the colonel surveyed the simulated, scrolled script framed on the wood-paneled partition. "Such indoctrination compels the public to have more respect for those in authority. The aspiring masses need leadership to follow; just like sheep need competent shepherds and church congregations need quality pastors."

Madison's alert mind carefully reviewed the *Ten Amended Amendments*. His rote memory had not failed him. Each citizen was required by law to know those magnificent same statements by heart. If challenged by a policeman, a military officer, a superior at work, or a courtroom judge, any voter-eligible man or woman in the country was obligated to state the words verbatim. "Recite Article I," Madison demanded of the corporal bartender.

"Freedom of Judeo-Christian religions shall be granted to all citizens," the bartender answered. "There will be no exceptions."

"Can there be freedom of speech?" Madison imperatively demanded. "Exactly what constitutes the loose expression freedom of speech?"

"Freedom of speech shall exist as long as it does not involve treason, sedition, libel, pornography, or obscene language," the bartender replied under duress.

"And what about the third section on freedom of the press?" the colonel insisted on hearing. "What is the exact function of the Fourth Estate?"

"Freedom of the press shall exist as long as journalism is not negative, and as long as journalism does not undermine important government functions," the man behind the bar seriously emphasized.

"Do citizens have the right to assemble and express their various opinions?" the officer asked.

"Section Four, of Article I explicitly states that citizens have the right to peaceably assemble only to express support for government programs, projects, or edicts," the obedient corporal recited from rote memory. "Negative behavior in the form of protests and violent demonstrations will not be condoned or tolerated."

"You've passed your abbreviated oral examination and retain your citizenship," Madison commended. "I only hope and trust you satisfactorily know the other nine *Amended Amendments* equally as well as you do the first."

Madison was proud of his uniform, of his Army, and of his great nation. The military superior thought it right that only police and army personnel were allowed to carry handguns, and that only *privileged citizens* were permitted to own shotguns and rifles if they officially belonged to a government adjunct State Militia, or to a branch of the Federal Military. 'Order and organization must be the watchwords of our great American civilization,' the dedicated officer mentally generalized.

Captain Jefferson entered the lounge and sat-down on the stool to Colonel James Madison's left. C-1 Thomas Jefferson was preparing for his important CC-1 review to attain the lofty rank that Madison already enjoyed.

"Hello there Colonel Madison," Jefferson courteously and respectfully greeted. "You aren't going to ask me about the significance of Article IX today, are you?"

"I know you're aware that the government could seize a person's property if the federal bureaucracy could determine *just cause;* also, so ordinary citizens have no stipulated assumed rights outside those comprehensively listed in the *Ten Amended Amendments,*" Madison congenially replied. "Even a complete dolt has memorized *that* imperative, and could easily recite any of the items on demand."

"Thank God that English is the only legitimate language allowed to be spoken across the land," the captain commented. "At least we can all understand one another without a lot of foreign gibberish contaminating our culturally preserved communication. Thank God for William Shakespeare's stellar contributions to the English language. Let's not forget Chaucer, either!"

"Yes Jefferson, in plain, pure, uncorrupted English," the colonel agreed. "And the great Director General has eliminated juvenile delinquency because anyone under twenty-one is not a citizen until the candidate passes the standard oral and written tests administered right after their twenty-first birthday. That really eliminated an excess of stupid court cases involving the matter of *juvenile incompetency.* I have to laugh when I consider that illegal, insubordinate behavior used to be called juvenile delinquency. Thank God for the demise of psychology in relation to law, education, and the society in general."

A large portrait of the revered Director General had been conspicuously hung over the officers' lounge cash register. Everyone in the country recognized that *he* was the Supreme Military Commander, and also the Chief-Executive-Citizen in all the land.

"The Director General made a smart move by making it necessary for all citizens to represent themselves in court," Jefferson observed and contributed to the formal discussion. "Lawyers and their sophist-type polemics no longer control the damned country."

"That's absolutely correct," Madison concurred, nodding his head. "Now that private attorneys have been officially outlawed, the court system functions much more efficiently with plaintiffs and defendants appearing alone before military judges. And since non-citizens have no rights at all, the courts aren't constantly tied-up with frivolous civil and criminal cases. And if I may add," the colonel elaborated, "there are no more defiant *juvenile delinquents* maturing into felonious convicts. The new, very efficient system is also considerably less expensive for taxpayers to pay for."

Jefferson inquired why Madison wasn't out jubilantly celebrating the *Fourth of July* and actively enjoying the myriad parades, fireworks, barbecues, and family reunions.

"My family lives on the East Coast," the colonel informed his inquisitive bar companion, "and I wouldn't have time to fly back and forth and then be refreshed enough to take my upcoming G-1 on Wednesday. That formidable examination, as we both well know, represents a wicked challenge to anyone's intellect."

Another colonel from the West Coast entered the Denver Base Officers Club, and promptly occupied the stool to Madison's right. Madison was curious to learn the name of his newly arrived rival for the coveted G-1 rank. He had seen the man talking on several occasions to General Hancock, the Chief Administrator of the Denver Military Strategic Institute. Madison decided to initiate a casual conversation with the newly-arrived military man and gain some personal information.

"I believe you're a friend of General Hancock's," the colonel cautiously began his inquiry. "My name is Madison."

The nation's military officers always assumed the names of American *Revolutionary War* patriots, so the other gentleman knew that Madison's first name automatically had to be James.

"Glad to make your acquaintance, Madison," the aspiring competitor remarked as the officer formally shook his rival's hand. "My name is Monroe. I'm here in Denver for an important briefing. You taking the G-1 too on Wednesday?"

"Yes," the intrigued colonel tersely answered. "And Monroe, if I may say, you look a bit fatigued to be taking the difficult G-1. Have you been traveling?"

"I've just completed a stint up in North Dakota, and I'm now slated to be transferred to Montana next week," Monroe mildly complained. "And I couldn't catch an early plane to Dallas and be back in time for the crucial G-1 tomorrow. My wife's very disappointed I couldn't make it back to Texas for the big holiday festivities, but she fully understands the gravity of the situation."

One of Monroe's statements instantly stimulated Madison's curiosity. He had to delve a little deeper to obtain more pertinent details. "Where were you stationed in North Dakota?" James inquisitively asked. "That's such a harsh territory in winter."

"I had been commander of the Bismarck operations," Monroe revealed. "We processed two thousand miserable cases a day there. They're coming in what seems an endless procession, but I don't mind all of the bureaucratic paper shuffling. In the final analysis, I can see that our society has become safer, much safer with each passing day," Monroe seriously maintained. "That comforting fact makes my daily efforts all the more worthwhile; and so, Madison, I've learned to sacrifice my individual ambitions and subordinate them for the good of the order."

"Bartender," Madison said, "when you have time, get Colonel Monroe a...."

"A screwdriver will be just fine," the very tired officer ordered. "With a double of vodka if you don't mind."

"Is the North Dakota Reservation making significant progress towards the country's much-needed social reform?" Madison wanted to know. "I understand that it's a key part of the Director General's national strategy."

"Yes," Monroe asserted. "And I'm happy to report that we're rapidly eliminating social diseases, and eradicating an abundance of serious mental health problems, too. Our American civilization will prosper as never before once those non-essential *Federal Programs* have their fatty budgets trimmed. Madison, how about you?" Colonel James Monroe deliberately asked. "Where have you been stationed throughout your honorable career?"

"I was superintendent of the Wyoming Rehabilitation Center at Cheyenne," Colonel James Madison proudly articulated, "and I enjoyed the difficult assignment, because quite frankly, I never approved of sexual deviates, gays, prostitutes, pornography, transvestites, or child molesters roaming around freely without supervision. We implemented very effective therapy programs at Cheyenne. Now I'm informed that if I pass the G-1, I'll be relocated right here in eastern Colorado," Madison informed his rival G-1 competitor. "I'll wholeheartedly welcome the change in scenery. I always preferred safe metropolitan areas to rural environments."

Jefferson was eavesdropping on the men's generic discussion. "The Director General's reform methods are really working," Captain Thomas Jefferson confirmed. "I understand that all seven rehabilitation zones are functioning optimally and are nearly filled to capacity. Crime rates are already virtually non-existent on the East and West Coasts," Jefferson authoritatively added. "Our next central focus is going to be cleaning-up the socially contaminated, toxic mid-west cities; especially Chicago, Cleveland, and Detroit."

"It's great to be an American," Madison stated as he held his glass high indicating justification for a toast. "To the greatest civilization in the history of the world. Let's drink to and salute the preservation and stability of the United States. May America live long and prosper well into the future!"

The three officers clicked their glasses. Each *contemplated his* role in implementing the essential sweeping reforms that the sagacious Director General had initiated in the past decade. The all-too-solemn men discussed how brilliant government leadership had devised a national plan specifically designed to obliterate the scourge of immorality. Seven western states had been converted into "much-needed Rehabilitation Reservations" to alleviate the internal "social difficulties" that especially existed in the country's abundant "diseased urban areas".

The three military officers discussed how Alaska had become a detention center for hard-core criminals. The public staunchly supported the very necessary government enterprise because all costly state prisons, jails, and penitentiaries were immediately shut-down. Citizens now felt safe from the epidemic of dangerous felons, murderers, rapists, muggers and robbers that had previously terrorized the general law-abiding population. The chronic repeat offenders were now quickly apprehended and spontaneously transported to barren Alaska in "comfortable passenger trains" for "government counseling" that had been especially developed to accommodate federally mandated "emotional reconstruction".

"And North Dakota has been converted into a 'centrally funded government reservation' to handle mentally retarded, emotionally disturbed, criminal-minded, and physically handicapped people," Monroe authoritatively stated. "The public enthusiastically endorsed the necessary program because it meant the elimination of expensive mental health institutions squandering taxpayers' money all across the country. The Director General has courageously addressed these undesirable, societal dregs that had detrimentally and egregiously been draining the nation's resources and wealth in the past."

"That's right on the money," Jefferson chimed-in. "And the former specialized hospital buildings are now being re-deployed as academic schools and government administration buildings, just like the former prisons are being efficaciously utilized for federally approved rehabilitation training exercises. Everything is running much more efficiently now."

The three officers next discussed how Montana had become the central base for "disadvantaged minorities", and how all unemployed blacks and Hispanics were now automatically transferred to Montana to learn "vital job skills" which would enable them to be more easily absorbed and then socially modified in order to participate in "the great American economic mainstream". "Montana has also become a Mecca for former welfare recipients of all races, besides being a haven for deprived minorities," Colonel James Monroe aptly concluded and related. "It's like the country's new safety net for those deprived and depraved individuals that always seem to fall between the cracks."

Captain Thomas Jefferson noted that New Mexico quickly became one enormous "Indian Reservation" where all tribes were unilaterally forced to emigrate under penalty of arrest for violating new federal laws. The government offered generous economic incentives to all those downtrodden tribes-men descendants that found it expedient to relocate in the "new Red Paradise".

Then Madison told Jefferson and Monroe about the recently constructed "government-effective control installations" currently flourishing in Wyoming. "Millions *of* concerned Americans have responded to the government's legitimate request to have all sexual deviates and perverts therapeutically 'reconditioned'," the austere-minded G-1 candidate disclosed. "The promise of a new beginning has enticed hordes of sex offenders, lesbians, pedophiles and pornography-smut traffickers to the *now*-crowded state. The

Wyoming perverts are exposed to government remedial therapy under the benign protection of strong martial law jurisdiction."

"How do they get there?" Monroe asked. "Wyoming is so far away from western and eastern coastal cities for the millions of immoral deviates in need of the territory's special services."

"Local cooperating police departments now escort identified sex offenders to regional holding centers," Madison explained. "And then the stubborn perverts are transferred to the custody of the military establishment, who soon place the intolerable patients onto comfortable trains, and transport the disgusting vermin safely to Wyoming. It's all a very simple money-saving process, once the basic mechanics of frugality are placed in operation."

Thomas Jefferson had spent three unforgettable years stationed in Nevada, and the young officer next related how the state had been imaginatively modified into an immense senior citizen complex. "Elders over the age of seventy who are not self-sufficient, or who have inadequate savings to independently sustain themselves, are sent there to be provided for by our noble humanitarian government," the informative captain communicated. "And once a month they're even allowed to visit Las Vegas."

"You mean to say that all of the old people that are burdens to their families and to society are now being conveniently sent there," Colonel Madison clarified. "I'm quite familiar with a similar program in Colorado where drug addicts and alcoholics are sent for rehabilitation," James Madison continued his parallel. "Again, local police departments cooperate by rounding-up the worthless, indigent scum, who are then immediately assigned to defend themselves in various low-level 'kennel courts'; and in short time, the degenerate riffraff are routinely and quickly sentenced by local judges, who effectively expedite the bureaucratic legal process; and finally, my dear colleagues," Madison lucidly emphasized, "the pathetic dregs are conveyed by chartered buses to government detention centers, and then magically *railroaded* here to Colorado."

"Madison, I don't know if *railroaded* is the best choice of words to describe the government's urgent system of operation," James Monroe cautioned. "The Director General would prefer that you use the more appropriate term *congregated*."

"Monroe, how many years had you been assigned and stationed in North Dakota?" Madison inquired.

"Four," the upwardly mobile G-1 candidate replied. "The best psychiatrists and psychologists in the entire country have been relocated there. I had the cream of the mental health profession working under my singular command," Monroe bragged. "Despite *their* valiant efforts, only five percent of the mentally ill ever manage to return to society as normal functioning adults. The entire experimental enterprise was an absolute grandiose exercise in futility, and the grossly wasteful project could only be accurately labeled as an extremely extravagant, futile boondoggle."

Monroe took another gulp from his vodka and orange juice and then rambled-on about his "fruitless prairie lands' tenure". His receptive audience gave him their keen attention.

"Most of the insane and emotionally disturbed dregs couldn't show any degree of satisfactory progress," Monroe glibly contributed and substantiated. "It all was extremely frustrating for everyone associated with the colossal project to endure and evaluate. And the physically handicapped were overtly incompetent to begin with, possessing terribly defective motor skills. It was a very sad situation indeed. How were things over in Wyoming?"

"Slow, very slow," Madison carefully admitted. "To begin with, sex perverts have corrupted value systems with weak consciences. Many of the sinful, evil deviates are deranged psychopaths. But we did our best and tried to persevere against the staggering odds," the colonel declared as the speaker stirred the remainder of his second scotch and soda around with his index finger. "Insufferable sociopaths and psychopathic perverts are extremely difficult to rehabilitate into productive citizens. It's more than a Promethean task we were futilely attempting, you know."

"I'm probably getting out of the military in two years," Jefferson intimated. "Now that Canada has officially been incorporated into the United States, I see lots of opportunity for my settling there as a 'new generation pioneer'. Until I hit it big somewhere in Manitoba, I'll be able to live off my modest military pension."

"Good for you Thomas," James Madison commended. "And if I recall, ever since the American West and Alaska had been declared 'Rehabilitation Reservations' back in 2068, the former residents of those associated states were given generous government incentives to move to Canada."

"You can't blame them for preferring Alberta or Saskatchewan to living in Wyoming. And with fanatical sexual deviates residing in North Dakota," crazies and misfits abound throughout the entire West," Colonel James Monroe added with a highly uncharacteristic laugh. "It's a good thing the federal government already owned much of the Rockies, so that the State could efficiently accommodate all of these newly constructed, very essential facilities!"

"Or move to Nevada with its abundance of overcrowded geriatric wards, hospital beds, wheelchairs, oxygen tanks, canes, false teeth, and bedpans," Jefferson relevantly declared from his own personal experience. "Or be unexpectedly transferred to Idaho with all of its terminally-ill patients."

At that precise moment, a large eagle emblem flashed upon the overhead television screen, signaling that the Director General was about to deliver his July 4th, 2076 oration. Whenever the country's leader's image appeared on television screens, all U.S. TV stations were required to broadcast the Chief Executive's significant address live, and no one was permitted to speak in public places in absolute deference to the nation's top citizen.

Army General John Adams, Admiral George Washington, Marine Corps General Nathan Hale, and Air Force General Patrick Henry initiated the ceremony by leading the nation in the recitation of the *Pledge of Allegiance* and in the singing of the *National Anthem*.

Four-hundred-and-twenty-two million devout citizens on the North American Continent and Hawaii joined in the patriotic chorus. Director General Benjamin Franklin then raised his right hand, and solemnly saluted his millions of continental admirers.

The great Chief-Executive-Citizen approached the microphone dressed in *his* handsome military attire. His spotless gray uniform was accentuated by a dark-blue beret emblazoned with fifty-eight stars, and also, a dark blue band around his left arm with a light-blue eagle embroidered onto a background of thirteen red and white stripes complemented the leader's apparel.

"My fellow Americans. It is with great satisfaction that I speak to you tonight on the three hundredth anniversary of the signing of the *Declaration of Independence*," General Director Benjamin Franklin began. "We all should feel both proud and honored, living in the closest functional model of a Utopian society ever devised by man in the history of the world. Our magnificent Republic is our sacred legacy we are creatively molding, and it will be enjoyed and fully appreciated by future generations of law-abiding, moral, ethical, and God-fearing American citizens for many centuries to come."

Everyone listening dared not blink an eye or move a finger or limb. Four hundred and twenty-two million patriotic Americans stood respectfully at attention and listened intently.

"Our glorious Founding Fathers established a noble tradition truly worthy of their descendants' blood, sweat, and tears," Director General Franklin continued his national address. "Our forefathers were very moral and courageous men. The Founders shared a dream of political independence and a hope of abundant Judeo-Christian religious freedom. The Great Men demonstrated enviable conviction and dedication to their inspired *Revolutionary War* liberty cause. Our Founders organized their heartfelt beliefs into the *Constitution of the United States,* a document which, out of necessity, has been recently updated and revised to ensure that the dreams of our Founding Fathers would remain sustainable, viable and living realities."

The camera operator panned the Senate Chamber that was filled with amenable politicians and military brass, all in attendance being loyal to *"the party',* the partisans enthusiastically applauding and appreciating the Chief-Executive-Citizen's wonderful, nationalistic words. The TV camera's lens then again zoomed-in on the charismatic demagogue, whose lips were smiling and waiting for the thunderous applause to diminish inside the historic, filled-to-capacity Senate chamber.

"Our great nation has endured a *Civil War*, two horrible *World Wars*, two major *Depressions,* and widespread internal strife," Director General Franklin reminded everyone. "The *Second Greater Depression* in 2049 was thrice as severe as the famous one that had originated in 1929. The 2049 debacle completely devastated *our* American standard of living. When I first assumed my high office sixteen years ago," Director Franklin expounded, "my principal objective was to create a marriage between government and industry. As history has accurately recorded, the unemployment carryover from the *Second Greater Depression* was virtually eliminated when I, with your honorable trust and support, forced the private sector to assume full responsibility for national job training and for local job placement. Under my no-nonsense leadership, and with your wonderful endorsement, we had established that everyone in the country between the ages of seventeen and seventy *must work* to earn and retain their citizenship status. And in the difficult process, we eliminated the expense of funding half of our high schools and all of our community colleges."

Four hundred twenty-two million patriotic citizens from Maine to Hawaii demonstrated their tremendous affection and appreciation by enthusiastically-but-politely clapping their hands.

"After *my* Neo-American National Party had finally achieved financial stability in the country," the Director General editorialized, *"my* next goal was to reduce the influence of the ever-corrupt legal establishment. I was granted the mandate by Congress to decree that formerly parasitic lawyers and attorneys could only work for government agencies that assisted our citizens; and also, I mandated that those same lawyers and attorneys should be paid no more than public school teachers earn. I'm extremely happy to report that few people sue others in the year 2076, and when a government approved lawsuit does occur, the loser, either plaintiff or defendant, must pay the total cost of the settlement, and the losing lawyer does not get paid anything," the great public orator reviewed. "One fourth of a weekly salary is deducted from the legal loser's earnings statement, and the money is donated to the Neo-American National Party. I believe that I have decisively shackled a great menace that formerly had egregiously promoted frivolous and expensive litigation, a decadent menace that formerly had flourished under wasteful Republican and Democrat rule. I'm quite happy to report that lawyers no longer serve their own special interests. The former greedy crooks are now dedicated professionals serving the best interests of our American citizens. I have effectively converted attorneys from harmful exploiters into national benefactors."

The Director General's poignant remarks had been received with great admiration and gratefulness by his extremely loyal national constituency. The public showed its staunch approval by engaging in even more heightened applause.

"By establishing our seven wonderful 'National Rehabilitation Reservations,' our good God-loving citizens now enjoy wonderful freedom from violence; freedom from drugs; freedom from fear; freedom from sexual deviates; freedom from sin; and freedom from high taxes," Director General Benjamin Franklin indicated. "We no longer have ugly and unproductive prisons, costly mental institutions, expensive old age homes, millions of lazy welfare recipients, juvenile delinquents, costly high schools and unproductive community colleges, and countless wanton criminals terrorizing and preying off of our God-fearing citizens. I have brought essential law, order, justice, efficiency, and stern discipline to this greatest of great nations."

An even louder applause escalated throughout every public place and private home in the fifty-seven contiguous states and Hawaii.

"The chaotic period between 1960 and 2015 had constituted a grotesque time of moral and ethical decay," Director Franklin stated. "Excessive freedom granted by the courts, along with the cowardly judicial system's misguided misinterpretation of the *Constitution*, promoted the diabolical advance of drug trafficking, immoral sexual activity, homosexuality, and general social disorganization. Legality was undermining morality. Lawyers acting as Congressmen passed ultra-liberal legislation which, over that corrupt fifty-year span,

374

weakened the pillars of our noble Republic," Director Franklin emphasized. "Excessive *democracy* was undermining *the Republic's* moral foundation. In 2010, San Francisco alone was over sixty percent homosexual. Under the pretense of democracy, the devil's sinister work was rapidly eroding the very fabric of the highly moral Protestant work ethic; yes, the very engine of American *capitalistic civilization.* With your committed assistance and unwavering support, *we* have courageously put an abrupt stop to all of the vulgar socialistic decadence."

Every attendee in the Senate chamber instantly stood and applauded louder than before, again showing his or her loyal commitment to the Director General's much-needed national improvement mandates.

"If you recall, my fellow Americans, less than twenty years ago the United States was on the threshold of being conquered by a coalition of Arab states, China and Russia," the Director General reminded his captive audience. "But for once, our country was saved by its own corruption when Western ideas caused devastating revolutions inside Russia and China in 2063. Now, my fellow Americans, I am engineering a vital crusade to rid the United States of America of the Western evils and corruption that had led to the Western-influenced downfall of the despicable Bear, Dragon, and Crescent menaces."

Citizens in all fifty-eight states showed their unanimity by again standing and loudly applauding and cheering *their* combined benign leader and political savior.

"From the ashes of the *Second Greater Depression,* our great Neo-American National Party was born. *My Party* was determined to champion the sacred moral cause of our Founding Fathers. *We* are destined to purify America from the cancerous social perils that had previously threatened our God-blessed existence. Together with our loyal political friends," Director General Franklin emphasized, "the Neo-Puritan WASP Party and the Neo-Republic Federalists, along with *your* Neo-American Nationalists, have rebuilt an America than supersedes anything the criminal Republicans and Democrats had ever dreamed possible. I have helped *you* rescue law and order from the jaws of anarchy. Remember always *our* Party's motto and credo, 'The ends justify the means.' May I take this auspicious opportunity to wish all of you a happy and blessed *Fourth of July* holiday. May God bless and favor the United States of America and its leaders."

* * * * * * * * * * * *

When the Director General finished his emotionally stirring presentation, jubilation reigned supreme throughout the land. Cannons boomed, fireworks burst, and merrymakers fired arsenals of firecrackers into the air. American *citizens* in all fifty-eight states unanimously agreed that Chief General-Citizen Benjamin Franklin had indeed meritoriously salvaged the nation's population from the clutches of lawlessness, and from the evils of immorality. It was the Chief Citizen's firm, decisive actions that gained the necessary grass roots' support of *his* appreciative people. The Director General had admirably restructured the federal bureaucracy, and had resuscitated the American free enterprise system from the fierce mandibles of beastly, detrimental socialism.

The citizens were now delighted that only "good news" could appear in newspapers, in magazines, and on television. Killings, suicides, automobile accidents, income tax evasions, robberies, and drug addicts had been forbidden on TV newscasts, and in public print. "Our citizens should only be exposed to positive, moral example," the Director General had insisted in his inspiring inaugural address. "Tabloid journalism shall be forbidden throughout the land," Director Franklin had vigorously promised during his well-received inaugural address.

Madison, Monroe and Jefferson, along with the other hundred or so officers inside the club, habitually stood and applauded their benevolent leader's July 4th, 2076 speech. The well-designed propaganda had appealed to the nation's nationalism and to the citizens' patriotism, the two main components that allowed Chief-Executive-Citizen Franklin's leadership to convincingly resurrect America from the infamous "age of useless struggle and turmoil".

"Bartender, give Colonel Monroe another vodka and orange juice, and I'll have another scotch and soda," Madison ordered. "How about you Jefferson? What's your drinking pleasure?"

"Sorry Gentlemen, but I have to hit the books and cram for my CC-1 exam," the determined captain answered. "Next week this time, I should be able to speak to you two gentlemen on equal terms. If I can't distinguish myself and advance up the ranks to colonel, then I'm definitely headed for the peace and quiet of Manitoba when I retire from the service in two years."

Captain Thomas Jefferson dismissed himself from the company of his eminent new acquaintances. "What did you think of the Director General's speech?" Madison asked Monroe.

"Splendid, simply on target," James Monroe remarked. "Our country desperately needed the regimentation and the regulation our leader provided in order to bring *us* out of the troublesome era of civil unrest," Colonel Monroe pontificated. "Social chaos would have destroyed and plundered this great land. Thirty short years ago, *we* were about to join the ranks of the Roman Republic and czarist Russia. Thanks to Director General Franklin and his Neo-American National Party, we've survived as a fortunate civilization that has risen above crisis, and our citizens have not fallen victim to anarchy. Patriotic Benjamin Franklin is perfectly correct when he asks us all to believe in the triumph of the American Phoenix!"

"True, my friend Monroe," Madison promptly acknowledged. "The Neo-American National Party gave the nation efficiency, and it trimmed waste everywhere. When Director General Franklin abolished the burgeoning Social Security System along with the burdensome welfare system, his weak-hearted critics were quite vehement in expressing their opposition. And of course, you know who prevailed in the end."

"Yes," agreed Madison. "And when our great leader made the *Bank and Mutual Fund Pension Individual Retirement Account* mandatory as a substitute for the inadequate Social Security System, each working citizen has been guaranteed a self-sufficient future free of government control. No more federal tentacles strangling the self-reliant taxpayers' throats."

"And the productive citizens are no longer accountable to those that don't work, don't pay taxes, and don't contribute," Monroe added. "Now that welfare has been eliminated and social problems have been controlled, everything runs like a well-oiled machine. Smooth and mechanical."

Madison proposed another toast. He and Monroe raised their glasses and Madison suggested, "Hail to the independent producers and workers of the United States!" The two new friends drank lustily, and it was obvious that the men were enjoying their new-found camaraderie. Even though the pair would soon compete for the coveted G-I ranking, their thoughts and beliefs were congruent on virtually every major domestic issue.

"That's what I really admire about Director General Franklin," Madison insisted. "The President's pragmatic, and not afraid to implement change. He despises bureaucracy and red tape. Our leader did not hesitate to attack old, flaccid institutions, and was not afraid to do battle against the corrupt legal establishment. Director General Franklin recognized that those malicious forces were detrimentally counterproductive to good government, and the reigning

Commander-in-Chief intrepidly exposed the corrupt lawyer establishment as being detrimental to the national interest."

"You're right again in your assessment," Monroe concurred, "and General Director Franklin had the wherewithal to discredit past Presidents and Congressmen who had pandered to special interest lobbies and to crybaby minorities. Now *that* type of courage required nerves of steel."

"And Monroe," his colleague interrupted, "the Neo-American Nationalists, the Neo-Puritans, and the Neo-Federalists all share the same basic vision for America, but the illusion of three separate political ideologies is still projected to the gullible citizens even though it's just one basic philosophy now. There is no definite choice afforded the people. The three parties are mirror images of one another. That way *the Party* made sure that ordinary citizens could never make mistakes in judgment at the voting booths. It was the original principal reasoning for the existence of the *Electoral College* back in the early days of our Republic. Don't you agree?"

"It sure beats the old Republicans and Democrats," Monroe asserted. "The current system sort of took the politics out of politics, if ya' follow my drift."

"Are ya' doin' anything important tonight?" Madison informally asked his new acquaintance. "I'd like to continue this fascinating conversation and get to know you better."

"No, not really," the other colonel politely answered. "I've gotten the inside dope direct from General Hancock's lips. The G-1 has been postponed because of the extended holiday. Matter of fact, we're not scheduled for the G-1 exam' until July 7th. What did ya' have in mind?"

"That's really terrific news! Let's go out and celebrate the Tricentennial," Madison enthusiastically suggested. "We'll drink-up a storm in honor of the *Fourth,* and then we'll reminisce about our noteworthy military experiences. You can spend the night at my apartment in Boulder."

"Sounds like a decent proposal to me," Monroe assented. "I need to loosen-up a bit after all my grueling G-1 preparation. My mind is wound tighter than a mainspring. We'll slake-down a *fifth* apiece to celebrate the *Fourth*! Pardon the preposterous pun. Ha, ha, ha!"

The men quaffed-down the remainder of their drinks, bid adieu to the amiable corporal bartender, and cheerfully left hefty tips in appreciation of his reliable service.

Madison led his companion into the "Package Goods" section of the Officers' Club, purchased quarts of scotch and vodka, and then escorted Colonel James Monroe to *his* jeep. Colonel Madison hopped into the driver side, started the engine, and headed northwest toward Boulder, a half-hour excursion from the prestigious Denver Military Strategy Institute.

The pair talked about the improved economy, and about the advent of the greatest national prosperity ever. Madison drank from his bottle of scotch, and Monroe imbibed his potent vodka as the men exchanged various childhood recollections and high school exploits. The two military colleagues were feeling no pain when the conversation finally shifted to the rigors and sacrifices associated with austere army life.

"Did you know either General Revere or Colonel Hamilton when you were assigned to duty up in North Dakota?" Madison inquired as his trusty vehicle dangerously veered and wove in and out of dense, oncoming traffic.

"Paul Revere and I were pretty good chums up in Bismarck," Monroe communicated, "but Alexander Hamilton was definitely a loner. He didn't drink or smoke, or share his thoughts. He never hung around the club and mingled with the other officers," Monroe revealed. The passenger paused for a second to gather his scattered wits. "Hey Madison; I'll bet you didn't know that Director General Franklin and Paul Revere grew-up together in Tennessee. Few people know of Franklin's early life. I got the inside scoop right from Revere's mouth."

Noticing that Monroe's quart of vodka was already a third empty, Madison decided to take the longer scenic route to Boulder. The man's questions became less deliberate and less self-censored. His demeanor became more aggressive, more audacious. "You can trust me Monroe, I assure you," Colonel James Madison pledged. "The Director General's early biography and secret records are hidden deep in a National Archives' vault close to the fake *Declaration of Independence* and the *Constitution.* Tell me all about our great fearless leader's illustrious past."

Monroe gulped-down another mouthful of vodka. James began slurring his words as his basic reflexes diminished. The passenger felt he had to share his "exclusive secrets" with his new-found colleague. The half-inebriated, belching officer stated that "Benjamin Franklin" had been a mediocre student in high school, did not excel at any sport, and had dropped out of college his sophomore year. "Good old Ben was an outspoken rebel in the Nashville Tennessee Militia," Monroe divulged. "His great-grandfather was very active in the Ku-

Klux-Klan, and his rebellious father had been an avowed Neo-Nazi. That scenario was Franklin's checkered background."

Monroe further explained that the Klan and Neo-Nazi movements had a profound influence on Benjamin Franklin's rigid attitudes toward society. Franklin had been shrewd enough to realize that the old Klan and Nazi symbols conjured-up negative public images of racial prejudice and of the *WW II* holocaust. Franklin cleverly kept the old right-wing discrimination attitudes, and cunningly attached the old biases to new patriotic symbols. The swastika had been transformed and soon became the blue eagle on the red and white striped background, and the blue berets with the fifty-eight white stars quickly and creatively became the Klan's white hoods and burning crosses in disguise.

Madison's eyes widened. "Franklin had lived a lackluster past, but later in his life, he demanded excellence from everyone else, speaking as the most powerful citizen in the world's most powerful nation," the driver opined and concluded. "Franklin was an opportunist who had acquired power during a great vacuum in American history, the *Second Greater Depression*," Madison continued his critical exposition as the military jeep recklessly entered and exited the yellow center-lines of the rural two-lane highway, the vehicle swerving back and forth. "Old Ben selected loyal advisers whose social blueprints were carbon copies of his own inflexible beliefs. The lawyers, the press, the schools, the Congress and the more aggressive military generals were all deftly hammered into submission. Benjamin Franklin's 'secret police squads' did the real dirty work for his expanding regime."

The men discussed that when Benjamin Franklin finally solved the nearly three-decade-long *Second Greater Depression* by halting *Social Security* payments and by suspending the benefits of all welfare recipients, *he* had adequately plugged the drain (in the weaknesses of applied *democratic socialism*) that had been emptying the basin of the 'free enterprise sink'. The Director General's initial successes, according to Colonel Madison, accelerated his meteoric ascent to supreme power. "The public willingly placed its faith in a maniac who had a distorted 'non-mongrel' vision of what characteristics comprised the 'ideal society'," the erratic driver boldly advanced the party's central political methodology to his fellow officer.

"The New Caesar had his 'hit squads' practice barbarism in the name of 'purification' in order to adequately accomplish his long-range objectives," Monroe drunkenly proclaimed. "Yes, Benjamin

Franklin soon crushed all opposition to his imperial ethnic cleansing doctrines. The complete support of the country's 'citizens' frustrated all those that dared to speak-out against his tyrannical dictatorship," James Monroe declared and slurred.

"Look Colonel Monroe, crime, drugs and social deviation have declined to almost nil," Madison observed and attested as the careless navigator just avoided a head-on collision with an oncoming automobile. "Hospital bills and doctor and dental expenses were drastically reduced after our awesome leader proclaimed that no doctor or dentist could earn more than an average Detroit autoworker. And insurance costs were held-down by the now-famous 'boomerang law'."

"That's a definite veracity if I ever heard one, and I truly remember the implementation of *that* particular innovation," Monroe recollected and reminded his host. "If a 'citizen' sues someone and loses, the plaintiff has to pay the defendant the sum that he had sued for, and all court expenses, too. And the system works because there are no parasitic lawyers around to feather their own nests and exploit other people's problems. It's now just the plaintiff, the defendant, the judge and the excellent boomerang law. What a proficient, streamlined legal model!"

"Yes, most certainly," the jeep driver confirmed, "and with government-appointed conservative judges hearing all the court cases, plaintiffs won only about five percent of the time. Lawyers were quickly unemployed and were no longer instrumental in the legal process, or in the outcome of cases. Citizens saved money by paying less on their insurance payments, and on federal and state income taxes, property taxes and sales taxes," Madison orally concluded. "By shrewd economizing, the precarious condition of the country's economic health had been alleviated."

"Everyone who is productive has more money in their pockets to purchase the more expensive things that were formerly regarded as luxuries," Monroe laughed. "It's no wonder that the Director General is so popular!"

"Yes," Madison concurred as the driver swallowed-down another mouthful of scotch with his right hand; his left hand still gripped on the jeep's steering wheel. "The citizens revere the way Ben Franklin has dismantled the medical, legal. and insurance industries. He's even abolished the *IRS* for its role in the 'lawyer's and accountant's great conspiracy' that was waged against the vulnerable citizens. And don't forget the mass exportation of dependent illegal aliens back to their native countries!"

Colonel Madison entered the passing lane as his jeep-gone-amok climbed a steep grade and skirted around a slow-moving tractor-trailer. His unperturbed, unfazed colleague resumed the pseudo-intellectual conversation.

"Madison, to your credit, what you've just said has much merit," the giddy passenger agreed. "The legal establishment was corrupt and unethical all along," Colonel Monroe slurred and then burped. "Lawyers along with doctors, accountants, insurance companies, and the *IRS* were milking, or should I say *bilking* the citizens of most of their hard-earned dollars," Monroe stammered; "and the Director General hit the nail squarely on the head tonight when he stated that 'the ends justify the means'," Monroe finished. "That's it in a crazy-but-simple nutshell, Madison; the ends justify the means."

"True, my friend. It is much better to live in a strong, safe Republic than in a weak, perilous democracy," Madison professed to his comrade. "There is more respect for law, for order, and for tradition in a Republic. Rome was a Republic that lasted almost a millennium. Democracies are doomed to short life spans because the flawed judicial court systems prevalent throughout a democratic nation's lifespan inevitably breeds anarchy, corruption, and constant change. History is my witness."

Colonel James Madison cautiously studied Monroe's pallid face as the driver's eyes alternated from the ever-curving two-lane mountain highway to his passenger's weary-looking pale features. The coy man behind the wheel was waiting for the appropriate time to widen the base of their dialogue. Each knew an abundance of secrets that the government had been concealing from its uninformed "citizens". America in 2076 was a land of peace, prosperity and justice for "God-fearing, obedient, productive 'citizens', but the New Republic was a demented, totalitarian, hellish nightmare for everyone else.

"Truthfully Monroe," the jeep driver evaluated, "justice is lacking for many in America. I say these comments off the record, of course, but the military is decisively used as a tool to swiftly punish those who violate our *Ten Amended Amendments* to the *Constitution*," Madison determined and genuinely expressed. "We use fascist methods far more brutal than Hitler had ever employed in Germany, over a century ago. There is harsh censorship of newspapers. The government controls the propaganda programming on all television stations, just to begin the many examples."

Monroe hiccupped several times, and then the now-dizzy Army Officer rendered *his* biased opinion about the present state of domestic affairs. "Thank God that rock and roll music and rap have been banned, and everyone can now appreciate Beethoven, Wagner and Mozart's genius," Monroe stuttered and vociferated. "Our young people are now more cultured, sophisticated, and civilized, Madison; and I heard from *your* own lips that in Wyoming, your old bailiwick, only five percent of sex deviates could be 'rehabilitated'. The other ninety-five percent have been executed, and their abominable corpses have been instantaneously decomposed in secret government laser cell chambers!"

Madison sipped some more scotch, and voluntarily confirmed Monroe's speculation about the government's cruel Wyoming genocide operations. The half-inebriated driver admitted to his fully inebriated passenger that leftover human body remains from the "ongoing laser experiments" had been stealthily incinerated in crematoria, and that the human ashes were used as an ingredient in fertilizer production. "A silent, multi-faceted holocaust, Monroe, that's what the clandestine government activity amounts to," Madison confessed. "It's a damned diabolical death campaign. Even though the country and the world out there are obviously better-off and safer, I still feel guilty about my past and present role in all the insanity that's been goin' on throughout old Uncle Sam's America. I still have a conscience, Monroe. Yes, I still have a conscience."

Colonel James Monroe had a similar tale of government savagery to reveal, the misdeeds involving his administrative duties in North Dakota. The drunken passenger communicated that mentally ill, emotionally disturbed, and physically handicapped people, and "former citizens" had been destroyed en mass in Bismarck just like the millions of sex deviates had been exterminated in Cheyenne, Wyoming. The same kind of mass annihilation had been occurring with criminals in Alaska, with Indians in New Mexico, with burdensome, penniless senior citizens in Nevada, and with drug addicts in Colorado. "Whether we approve of the mass extermination or not, we're both unwilling accomplices in this demented, evil treachery," Monroe told Madison before loudly belching three times.

There was a minute's pause in the conversation as each man ruminated about the reprehensible evil known as genocide. The Army men both knew of the numerous government-concealed disgraces, but the jeep's occupants were ordinarily afraid to publicly speak-out against the heinous carnage out of fear of devastating reprisal. Then Colonel Monroe elaborated on the gruesome subject.

"I try to justify my complicity in the totally hellish scheme," Monroe continued, "by rationalizing how civilized, and how cultured the outside society has become. No doubt there is great prosperity, and my wife and children are safe and secure from sickos and from psychopaths disrupting their 'sacred' lives," Monroe stated before imbibing another mouthful of vodka. "My wife and kids are ignorant of the real reasons why they are happy, wealthy, and not threatened by scurrilous criminals and lowlife deviates. Those insidious faulty elements are being systematically eradicated from mainstream American society. I don't know if *that* methodology is good; that is, Madison; good in a moral sense."

"My only consolation," Madison interrupted and then reflexively burped, "lies in the hope that the Director General has created a utopia for productive and ambitious 'citizens' like us to enjoy. Our families' futures, Monroe, will be blessed with the daily celebration of the American dream. For our own families' sake, Monroe, I also advocate that 'the ends do justify the means'."

Colonels Madison and Monroe resumed slurring most of their heart-felt words. More gory, true stories described brutal details of additional government "mass atrocities". Madison's mind and Monroe's conscience were swimming in a wild frenzy of guilt, denial, and blatant drunkenness. "Ten years ago, I was assigned to command one of Franklin's clandestine 'death squads'," Monroe confidentially related. "We assassinated labor union leaders, Congressmen, ministers, social workers, and anyone else that disagreed with the Director General's inflexible social and political agendas. I was a hit-man for the tyrannical government; nothing more, nothing less. Madison, what about you?"

"In the fall of 2070, I along with my Secret Police Unit personally had murdered eight prominent Senators that opposed the Central Executive Department's long-range plans," Madison remembered and articulated. "Forgive me, if I accidentally stammer or stutter," the driver apologized with tears forming in his eyes, "but keeping these things inside my psyche has brought me to the brink of lunacy. I should've seen evil approaching when Franklin began condemning the urban areas and their equally immoral suburbs as being too 'mongrel' and too 'cosmopolitan'."

"I believe you're totally vindicated in feeling that way," Monroe responded. "When power-hungry Benjamin Franklin began discrediting Lincoln for freeing the slaves, and mocking J.F.K. for his civil rights policies, and then vilifying F.D.R. for the creation of the *Social Security Administration*, I should've recognized those criticisms as *sobering* signs of future foul things to come," the drunken rider confessed.

Several moments of somber silence passed. Monroe was in a semi-conscious stupor. Madison could barely keep his eyes focused on the highway. The passenger was mumbling indecipherable jargon as large tears cascaded down his cheeks. The driver steered his military jeep down a crowded Boulder boulevard that was teeming with thousands of *Fourth of July* celebrants boisterously reveling.

Madison's jeep made a hard right hand turn onto a less active thoroughfare. Then, the dangerous vehicle skidded and sped in and out of traffic lanes, weaving down a series of less populated residential streets, the last of which led to a newly constructed Boulder military compound.

The jeep halted at the main gate of the Boulder Drug and Rehabilitation Center. The security *MP* on duty immediately recognized the driver as the Regional Military Commandante, and instinctively gave Colonel Madison a formal salute and motioned for *his* much-feared superior officer to proceed into the compound.

The colonel drove past four recently constructed barracks, and then past the all-too-familiar Central Base Administration Building. The erratic men together hiccupped, and the two colonels found amusement in the other's advanced state of intoxication. Then, five minutes later, the driver stopped at a mammoth, renovated structure situated on the base's northern perimeter.

Madison glimpsed over at Monroe. The other G-1 candidate was now snoring loudly with his empty vodka bottle loosely gripped in the palm of his right hand.

The self-appointed chauffeur gingerly parked his military vehicle next to a side entrance of the enormous "Laboratory Research Building". Colonel James Madison got out and briskly stepped to the vehicle's passenger side, removed the empty vodka bottle from Monroe's weak grasp, and tugged the drowsy, incoherent officer from the front seat.

Colonel James Madison lifted the man's arm around his shoulder, and awkwardly dragged his fellow officer to the Research Laboratory Building's side gray, steel door. The high-ranking madman searched his left pocket with his free hand for his master key, inserted the object into the keyhole, and from rote memory, skillfully turned the lock. Colonel Madison then clumsily dragged and escorted Colonel Monroe down a long, spotless, brown-speckled, terrazzo-tiled corridor.

"What's goin' on Madison?" Monroe muttered in his stupor. "Where ya' takin' me? Ya' sure live in a funny-lookin' apartment building. Hope there's a bathroom with a toilet at the end of this weird hallway!"

Madison did not answer his intoxicated companion's delusional prattle. The obsessed control freak methodically opened a red steel door, and showing little hospitality for his mentally-disheveled guest, rudely deposited Monroe onto the hard, dark-green, tiled floor of the dimly lit room. The large chamber had light-green tiled walls, and a dark-green ceiling to match the Spartan-type floor pattern. "Hey, ya' don't even have windows in your place!" Monroe yelled-out like a dizzy, drunken derelict. "Your damned home looks like an asylum without any damned windows!"

A line of overhead shower-heads made the room seem vaguely familiar to Colonel Monroe's hazy recollection. Madison exited the depository chamber, and then wildly slammed the heavy red steel door shut, successfully locking it behind him. The obsessed maniac then opened a corridor side green door, exposing a narrow passageway that led-up a narrow flight of steps. The scheming perpetrator then slowly ascended the twelve steep planks.

Twenty-five feet down the aisle was a master control panel. Looking through a bulletproof window, Madison peered-down at the disoriented occupant of the chamber below. Monroe staggered to his feet, and wobbled his way to the wall directly beneath a speaker. The shrewd observer inside the elevated booth flipped-up three switches, which activated a microphone inside the control room, and also turned-on loudspeakers inside the chamber below.

"What on earth are ya' doin'?" Monroe shouted-up to his crazed antagonist. The trapped drunken officer stumbled, hitting his head against the green tile wall like a wounded knight weighted-down with heavy armor. "Madison, is this some sort of sick joke? I detest jokes. They're so juvenile! So damned infantile! I demand that you release me immediately, or else this episode will go into your personal file for immediate court martial review!"

"Demand all you want," Colonel Madison calmly responded. "But now you know how *your* poor victims feel right before *you* execute them. Before tonight, killing was so impersonal," Colonel Madison hollered-down to his extremely confused enemy. "All I did was command an order, and *it* was done by obedient soldiers enacting my instruction. Monroe, I want you to know that I hate you more than I hate anybody alive, including the perverted Director General."

"You're jealous of me! That's what this is all about!" Monroe's voice bellowed up to the enclosed control booth. "You know I'm goin' to get the G-1 appointment, and you aren't!" the drunken officer screamed as he pointed a shaking index finger up at Madison.

"The G-1 has nothing to do with it," Madison's firm voice blustered over the loud speakers. "I have my ulterior motives, but it's definitely not the G-1."

Monroe finally became sober enough to realize that his fellow officer was just as deranged as the Director General's evil justice system was. "But why this, Madison?" Monroe asked in the form of a challenge. "You've committed the same atrocities as I have. You were an active participant in the annihilations. You're just as guilty of genocide as I am! If you hate me, you must also hate yourself," Monroe nervously stuttered and trembled. "Why not kill yourself and let me enjoy the honor of the G-1 ranking all by myself."

"Your convoluted logic is the same as the ugly propaganda of the Neo-American Nationalist Party," Madison answered as the incensed psycho stared-down with vindictive eyes at his squirming hostage. "Our eminent Director General has cleverly disabled your God-given knowledge of right from wrong."

"What in the world are you double talkin' about?" the captive in the green tiled room screamed-up. "Stop bein' so damned cryptic and give me a logical explanation! Cease performing this preposterous abomination right now!"

"My poor younger sister was mentally retarded," Madison said into the microphone in a cold methodical voice. "She was sent to Bismarck, North Dakota four years ago. No one has heard from her since that tragic day. Monroe, I really loved my sister in spite of her severe handicap. Do you read me Monroe? I *loved* her!"

The imprisoned colonel was suddenly overwhelmed with terror. He realized the gravity of his dilemma and begged his grief-stricken captor for mercy. Colonel James Monroe sensed, and then felt his fated doom approaching.

"And my step-father was Congressman William Burns, who had obstinately opposed the 'Rehab' Reservations' edict of the Director General. My uncle, Attorney General Jerry Gares, and my cousin, Admiral Gabe Donio had both been murdered in cold blood by death squads Monroe; slimy, repugnant death squads, all of them vilely commanded by you, you repugnant worm!" Madison's voice bellowed-down from the elevated control booth.

Monroe wanted to divorce himself from his past, hideous, covert operations, but it was too late to be remorseful. History could not be changed or altered. "Madison, I was only following orders, just like you had been doing in Wyoming. You would've done the same things had you been me. You *have* done the same things in different settings. I beg your sense of decency; please don't kill me!"

The calm-and-collected colonel standing in the overhead booth still held the absolutely frightened colonel in the green-tiled room below in deep contempt. "Your lame excuses can't save you from my stubborn wrath," Madison declared without hardly any trace of emotion evident in his monotone voice. "My orders are coming from *my* soul, not from *your* Director General, whom incidentally, I no longer consider *my* Director General. But much to your dismay Monroe, I still possess a kernel of dignity in my heart, despite all of the government's grotesque brainwashing. Monroe, I still have a heart, a soul, and a mind. I am no longer a vile killing machine of the state like *you* still are."

"Madison, I beg you, please don't *kill* me!" Monroe screamed. "Pity me and have mercy! I want to live!"

"I can't show you any clemency, Monroe," Madison replied in a trance-like voice. "Because *you* have *murdered* several dear members of my family. I loved each of them dearly. There is still enough humanity in my heart to seek revenge. I lust for revenge. Do you hear me, Monroe? I lust for revenge!"

Monroe openly wept, pleading for his captor to show "Christian forgiveness". But the incarcerated prisoner's begging for compassion fell upon deaf ears.

Madison proceeded with his powerful prosecution. "Monroe, you will die a slow horrible death," the jaded colonel predicted. "I promise that your miserable mind will die before your pathetic body does," the demented madman in the control room slowly and deliberately prattled into the microphone. "I shall cut-off your oxygen supply at just the right moment. Monroe, you'll be reduced from a proud Army Colonel to a babbling vegetable in a matter of five terrible minutes. Do you hear my prophetic words? I hope *that* five minutes will feel like an absolute eternity to you; you heinous, despicable vermin."

Madison pressed a red button that opened overhead gas jets, while doomed Monroe got to his knees, futilely begging for salvation.

"Don't beg *me*, you pathetic, gutless coward," Madison demanded in an almost hypnotic tone. "Beg your Creator for forgiveness; not me. After you've been rendered severely retarded, I'll provide you with fake identity documents," Madison disclosed. "No one in the military will even know or care about you. No one will ever believe that *you* are Colonel James Monroe, craven candidate for a G-1 Star," Madison laughed like a delirious mental patient. "The corporals and the sergeants in North Dakota will only want to see *your* identification credentials. And here they are," Madison declared as the deranged sadist demonstrably held the fabricated, official military documents over his head. "All I have to do is type in the name Howard Esposito on the first line, and sign the three necessary documents myself. Our Director General and his detestable government will then direct its obedient officers to do the rest."

"No, please, No!" Monroe cried and ranted. "Don't have me executed," the captive whimpered, but the prospective victim's earnest pleas were totally ignored.

"You'll be transported tomorrow by a 'comfortable train' to your old base back in Bismarck, where *you* will be exterminated after the psychiatrists find it will be impossible to rehabilitate you," Madison informed his soon-to-be victim. "No one will recognize *you*, Howard Esposito, alias James Monroe, among the thousands of lackluster souls scheduled for massacre by our omnipotent Fascist Republic. If I may humbly quote *you* Monroe, life is often cruel and brutal," Madison nonchalantly uttered in a steady determined voice. "Soon you will enter your vegetable state, maybe a carrot or a cucumber's intelligence perhaps, and if I may humbly quote *our* warped-minded supreme Director General Franklin, 'the ends justify the means'."

"Death and Taxes"

The Delmarva Peninsula is famous for its poultry and chicken cooperatives, its fruit and vegetable farms, its seashore resorts having pristine sandy beaches, its marinas, and its splendid fishing paradises. Delaware, Maryland and Virginia share geographic jurisdictions along the narrow one-hundred-fifty-mile ribbon of fertile sandy soil known as the Delmarva Peninsula. The landmass's unique acronym had been formed from the beginning letters and sounds of the three states that occupy its particular length: Delaware, Maryland, and Virginia.

Delmarva is bordered on the east by the *Atlantic Ocean,* and is flanked on the west by the *Chesapeake Bay.* The scenic seventeen-mile *Chesapeake Bay Bridge Tunnel* connects the peninsula with Norfolk, Virginia to the south. And *that* engineering marvel should not be confused with the lengthy *Chesapeake Bay Bridge* at Annapolis. Geographic places such as Dover, Delaware, Salisbury, Maryland, Assateague Island, Maryland and Chincoteague, Virginia are some prominent landmarks situated on *that* renowned extension of the *Atlantic Coastal Plain.*

Natives of Delmarva often use the pseudonym *Eastern Shore* to describe the popular tourist area east of the *Chesapeake Bay Bridge.* Ocean City, Maryland, a famous beach and amusement resort, occupies the peninsula's eastern fringe and was once connected to Assateague Barrier Island until a fierce storm formed an inlet. The popular seashore resort boasts the claim "White Marlin Capital of the World". Delmarva's bays are reputed to produce the most delicious crab meat east of the *Mississippi.*

The long, narrow strip of sandy soil is home to a special breed of crop and chicken farmers. Most of these hardy Delmarva men are avid bird and duck hunters in the fall, and their special dialect is evident when used in the context of "em our dux" for "them are ducks". The proud fourth generation men value their tendency to be fiercely independent. The down-to-earth, practical farmers feel a wonderful attachment to "Mother Earth's" benign fertility. Peaches, apples, soybeans, corn, and tomatoes grow in abundance along the rich-in-tradition peninsula each summer.

Evidence of intensive farming becomes more widespread as the traveler drives towards Delmarva's interior. A multitude of "truck farms" ship their seasonal harvests to bustling food distribution markets in Washington DC, Baltimore, Philadelphia, Boston, and

New York. The growers are staunch disciples of the traditional Protestant Work Ethic. The proud "self-made men" labor from sunrise-to-sunset, and they are known to voluntarily help each other during times of emergency or dire need.

Clint Abrams operates a thousand-acre fruit and vegetable farm midway between Salisbury and Ocean City, just off highly traveled *Route 50*. Zeke and Hugh, Clint's two stout sons, assist their father in managing the huge estate.

Clint Abrams is one of the most successful produce merchants on Delmarva. He owns a fleet of twelve tractors, four tractor-trailers, six pickup trucks, five water winches, four chemical sprayers, nine forklifts, three durable front-end loaders (with accompanying back hoes), and one enormous packing house featuring a gigantic cold storage facility attached.

Farmers of the Berlin, Maryland vicinity both admire and envy Clint Abrams. The local gentry view the industrious grower as a prosperous model of American free enterprise; indeed, worthy of imitation. Abrams quietly enjoys basking in the radiance of his local legendary prestige. Most of the area's equipment merchants, produce brokers and regular citizens revere Clint's prestigious name. The very successful farmer-baron also has several envious enemies.

One Monday morning in early June of 1999, *IRS* Agent Mark Turner from the Salisbury office drove into the driveway of Clint Abrams sprawling manor. The estate's "new homestead" was accessed from the main highway by a little traveled stone road that originated half a mile off of the busy *Route 50* thoroughfare. The solitude afforded the wealthy grower privacy from the noisy highway, which was used by thousands of tourists and condominium owners (especially during the summer months) on their way to and from the Ocean City, Maryland boardwalk, and the thriving resort's myriad residences, commercial motels, restaurants, and boat marinas also caused the heavy eastbound traffic to occur.

The young federal *IRS* investigator stopped his shiny black government car at the manor house where Clint's cooperative wife Faye gave Agent Turner directions to the farm's greenhouse compound. Clint Abrams was busy watering his three hundred thousand tomato sprouts being nursed for spring planting the following week.

The clean-shaven, on-a-mission federal man, dressed in an impeccable three-piece pinstripe suit, confidently approached the wily old farmer. Agent Mark Turner appeared out of place with his present environment, being entirely too well-dressed as the young, handsome bureaucrat casually walked across the dusty strip of ground between his black government car and the farm's main greenhouse compound. The *IRS* official was heading directly toward Clint Abrams, who according to wife Faye, would be found "tinkering" and "fixing tractors" near one of the ten colossal plastic-covered, steel-framed enclosures.

"Good morning, Sir," the benign revenue collector cheerfully greeted the notoriously cantankerous Abrams. "I'm Agent Turner with the *Internal Revenue Service* Salisbury Office Division," the visitor announced as the young man instinctively flashed his shiny government badge. "You seem to have built quite an impressive operation here," the IRS representative complimented. "Your success is terrific evidence that our free enterprise system is smoothly working."

The sixty-five-year-old veteran farmer surveyed his visitor with suspicious eyes. "I'm workin', but I don't know about the rest of the free enterprise system. Let me tell ya' somethin' son," Abrams ranted. "It all didn't happen by sheer accident. I worked real hard puttin' it all together, and I'm workin' even harder tryin' to maintain and keep what I got from hungry government vultures like you."

"Well Sir, it certainly is a nice place you have here, anyway," the uninvited guest remarked while holding his official black government attache case firmly in his right hand. "It looks like you've done pretty well for yourself over the years."

"Ain't no secret about my farm here," Clint insisted. "Hard work from the mornin' rooster's crow to the old owl's night-hoot. Ya' nine to five business suit fellas' can't understand that kind of dedication, now can ya'? When the noisy five o'clock whistle blows, *you* do too!"

"Now Mr. Abrams, I didn't come here to debate philosophy or wrangle with you," young Agent Turner diplomatically replied. "I just need your cooperation and some information from you, and then I promise, I'll honor your privacy and be on my way."

"Well, you'd better get on with it, young fella'. I'm a very busy varmint with plantin' and field prep' goin' on this time of the year," the grumpy grower bluntly answered. "Every second counts in the spring when you're a farmer gamblin' with moody Mother Nature."

"You planting tomatoes soon?" the inquisitive young fellow asked. "My wife loves to can tomatoes. That practice is becoming a lost art, yes it has!"

"We're way behind on plantin' because of the late spring, and also those bad March storms we had," Clint sneered. "If ya' don't get down to brass tacks soon and tell me your business bein' here, ya' can help me shovel some good-smellin' horse manure next to that barn over there."

Before Agent Mark Turner could communicate the real reason for his visit, the testy, old vehement farmer preempted him. "Remember one important thing, son," Clint Abrams imperatively said. *You* want somethin' from me. That's why you're here. I ain't wantin' nothin' from you. Before I give ya' what ya' want, ya' gotta' pay the piper, and I'm holdin' the cotton-pickin' musical instrument."

The determined *IRS* Agent was not distracted by the rich landowner's typically tough rhetoric. "Mr. Abrams, I'm looking for Agent John Powell who's also out of our Salisbury office," Mark Turner indicated. "Our records show that Agent Powell was right here on your farm examining your tax records three months ago. He's mysteriously disappeared, and hasn't been seen or heard from since that day you had spoken with him. Now please tell me; when's the last time Agent Powell's been here?"

Clint Abrams removed his straw hat and scratched his balding head. "See here, Mr. Turner," Clint defensively prefaced. "I'm not runnin' a missin' persons' service here. I'm tryin' my best to get some early crops planted. Why ya' askin' me all these dumb questions? Go talk to the police!"

"Do you know anything about Agent Powell?" Turner insisted on learning. "I've been temporarily assigned to your case, but if Agent Powell suddenly shows up, he's the one who will conduct your comprehensive tax audit."

"Ya' know Mr. Turner," the old farmer complained. "I don't got no polished fingernails like you city slickers do. And I don't got no hemorrhoids from sittin' on soft leather chairs behind fancy desks all day long. Why come to me? Call the state police! Contact the local sheriff's office! That's who ya' gotta' see about a missin' person!"

Clint Abrams paused to measure the young man's reaction to *his* blistering admonishment. "The local sheriff and his men will set-up roadblocks, and search junkyards for the agent's car," the old farmer continued on his sidebar filibuster. "Son, I think you're lookin' for an orange growin' on an apple tree by comin' here and wastin' my valuable time. You'd be better off goin' on a wild goose chase out in Nevada or New Mexico."

"Mr. Abrams, I didn't come here to antagonize you. There's no need to argue," the undaunted *IRS* man retorted. "All I desire from you is a straight answer. My question has nothing to do with your current tax liability with the government. Now again, when is the last time Agent John Powell had stopped in to see you?"

The embittered fruit and vegetable grower exhibited a fierce uncooperative stubbornness, analogous to that of an ill-tempered mule. "Mr. Turner, maybe this Powell fella' got sick and tired of workin' for Uncle Sam, and maybe the unhappy guy eloped with his pretty secretary to Elkton to get married," the elderly codger prevaricated. "Or maybe the lazy fella' got lucky and hit the big lottery, and then retired without officially resignin' from the government. Maybe your Mr. Powell just flew the coup!"

"Mr. Abrams, you aren't being very cooperative," the now-frustrated tax agent criticized. "Most people realize that the *IRS* is only doing its official business."

Clint Abrams continued his sarcasm without any regard to Agent Mark Turner's objection to *him* being evasive *outside* of mandated tax reporting. "Or maybe your Mr. Powell turned psycho and jumped off the amusement pier over there in Ocean City; or maybe the freakin' fella' had one of 'em sex gender changes ya' read about in the papers, and is now singin' soprano somewhere in an all-girls' choir," Clint facetiously theorized and stated. "Or maybe some rich high society dame took him in as her private gigolo; or maybe Mr. Powell's turned into one of 'em evil pimps ya' also read about in the disgusting newspaper tabloids; or maybe he....."

"Mr. Abrams," the red-faced Agent Turner objected. "You're testing both my fortitude and my patience. I insist you answer my simple question! There's no need to feel threatened or abused by my presence on your farm!"

"No sir, I haven't seen hide nor hair of the fella'," Clint Abrams declared. "Now if ya' please would excuse me, I got some important things to attend to. Life on a fruit and vegetable farm is full of duties and responsibilities; yes; it is!"

Clint Abrams then hobbled his way to the adjacent red barn without the courtesy of saying "Goodbye". Mark Turner realized that a disgruntled, obstinate, vociferous old taxpayer that hated the tentacles of modern bureaucratic government had mercilessly belittled him. 'Seldom do *IRS* agents receive such disrespectful treatment,' the idealistic-but-thwarted novice agent thought. The young man ambled dejectedly to his black government automobile, almost mechanically shaking his head in total frustration.

The insulted *IRS* official climbed inside his black car, started the ignition, turned around in front of the main greenhouse, and angrily sped out of the gray-stone driveway onto a dirt section of the road. A long dust trail followed the black sedan's speeding back wheels.

Clint Abrams turned around and smirked at the visible indication of the departing young man's aggravation. The proud, aging farmer ambled back to his main greenhouse, favoring his bad right leg. More tomato sprouts had to be sufficiently watered, or else they soon would begin wilting.

* * * * * * * * * * * *

Agent John Powell had paid a visit to Clint Abrams "new homestead" thirty-three days prior to Mark Turner's appearance on the sprawling plantation. Powell wanted to interrogate the rich farmer about a previous tax return. The about-to-retire revenue agent casually stepped from his black "government pool" Ford Taurus and casually sauntered-over to the farm's main maintenance garage.

The very resourceful country estate owner was preoccupied repairing the hydraulic system on one of his nine forklifts. Powell attempted introducing himself inside the cluttered farm shop. The agent's salutation was completely ignored by the preoccupied farmer, and no eye contact was made. The self-made millionaire was too engrossed in his enterprise to have his valuable time being bothered with a meddlesome government bureaucrat.

"Excuse me, Mr. Abrams," Agent Powell began his inquiry. "I see you're very busy, but this matter will only take a minute of your time. I do a lot of business with farmers here on Delmarva, and I know that you have plenty to get done."

"Look Mr., if you're sellin' somethin', I'm not interested in buyin' it," the old curmudgeon volleyed back. "Ya' see, I got all I want or need, and then some."

"I'm Agent John Powell from the Salisbury Office of the *Internal Revenue Service*," the distinguished-looking, gray-haired records' inspector declared. "And I want to ask you a few questions about your latest income tax filing. You see Sir, I've been specially assigned to audit your account."

"Lookee here, Mr. *Howell*," Clint Abrams deliberately distorted and returned. "Can't ya' see my arms are elbow-deep in messy grease here? Go talk to my accountant. That's why I hired him, and that's exactly why I pay the numbers guru big bucks to deal with government rats like you!"

"Now Mr. Abrams, let's be reasonable," Case Investigator John Powell politely suggested. "First of all, my name is Powell and not

Howell. Second of all, I honestly believe you're intentionally overreacting a little here."

"Reasonable, ya' say? I hired my *CPA* to deal with monkeys, snakes, rats, and other pesterin' animals of your ilk," Abrams adamantly protested. "Ya' know anything about fixin' hydraulics, Mr. Howell? If ya' do, you're welcome to stay and help me work on this frustratin' dirty repair job."

Agent Powell was shocked at Clint Abrams' arrogant, brusque attitude directed toward federal authority. Ordinarily, taxpayers quivered in their shoes when the *IRS* agent officially announced his presence. The thirty-four-year tax veteran found the landowner's belligerent remarks, along with the obstinate farmer's fearless, hostile reception, a new distasteful experience.

"Mr. Abrams, I can be just as blunt and just as nasty as the behavior you're exhibitin' right now," John Powell indicated. "It's not really my style to get into petty personality disputes with unhappy taxpayers. And honestly, I didn't come here to quibble with you, so please stop being so sarcastic. I can be just as bullheaded and confrontational as you are."

Clint Abrams' normally pale face turned florid. The stubborn farmer became downright argumentative with his uninvited guest, whom the grower regarded as an undesirable trespasser.

"Look Mr. Powell, first of all, I only quarrel with men that make over five hundred thousand dollars a year. That way, I figure I might learn some good ideas from more intelligent men than me," Abrams petulantly yelled at his farm trespasser. "Guys of your low character ain't worth the trouble."

Then, the irate farmer told Powell that the agent actually was *his* employee, and that the rich farmer's taxes helped pay the government employee's salary. and that the prosperous grower didn't trust anyone without any dirt embedded under *their* fingernails because that kind of person had never done a decent day's work in his life.

Much to Agent John Powell's surprise, Clint Abrams spit a large tobacco chaw onto the concrete floor, and the wet clump barely missed the federal man's polished black loafers. "If ya' wanta' talk, come back here at nine tonight when I'm finally caught-up on all my chores. Then, we can have a real nice chat, *Mr. Howell*."

Agent Powell felt quite alienated by the farmer's haughty disposition, and also by his 'Who cares?' attitude. Never before had an irate taxpayer ever addressed him in such an audacious, caustic, condescending manner. The *IRS* man despised the taxpayer's

intentional rancor with a passion. Agent Powell assessed Abrams'
insolence as being both 'reprehensible and inexcusable'.

"See here Mr. Abrams; if your main objective is to humiliate me,
I want you to know that you've failed big time!" the incensed tax
revenue agent exclaimed and persisted. "You know as well as I do
that I can't come and see you nine o'clock at night. My daily business
ends at five."

"Who really cares about your silly nonsense?" Abrams
vociferously bellowed. "I'm still workin' at nine tonight. That's why
I got all that I have. I go the distance and government scum like you
don't wanta' extend yourselves more than ya' have to. Government
workers like you think there's only fifty yards on a football field, or
to put it in baseball terms, it's only thirty-feet to first base."

"Our computer records have determined Mr. Abrams," the
persistent official declared, "that you presently owe the government
two-hundred-ten-thousand dollars in back taxes for last year alone.
And we haven't done retroactive research yet for the previous five
years. That vital fact ought to get your keen attention, if I can't."

The wily Clint Abrams always loved a good debate. The flippant
farmer was more than adequately prepared to do verbal battle with his
now-livid visitor. "You know as well as I do Mr. *Howell* that every
year I reinvest my profits back into equipment on the farm," Clint
staunchly argued. "Just look at all the expensive machines I got sittin'
all around here. That heavy-duty *John Deere* tractor over yonder cost
me over a hundred and fifty thousand, and it's not new, but used.
That's probably more than *you* make in two years," Abrams angrily
berated.

The farmer also then mentioned his ninety-five-thousand-dollar
used bulldozer, and his thirty-thousand-dollar second-hand forklifts.
"And that's without all the fancy gadgets and extras," the proud
grower vehemently embellished his escalating antagonism for his
unwanted visitor.

Agent Powell crossed his arms and grit his teeth to symbolize his
obvious displeasure with Clint Abrams' obnoxious disregard of
federal government power.

"Mr. Abrams, if you'll just allow me to review the paperwork and
the basis for the *IRS's* claim against you, you'll understand exactly
where I'm coming from," the unwelcome, chagrined visitor insisted.
"I'm actually here to expedite matters so that then you can just go
about your regular business as you normally do."

"I ain't got no two hundred thousand cash stashed away to
recklessly throw out the window, now or never," Clint almost

dramatically protested. "And I don't give a pig's squeal about what you're sayin' or accusin'," the rich farmer declared. "And to top it off, ya' all come here and act like it's twenty cents and not two hundred thousand dollars ya' want from me. All because some dumb computer spits-out some wrong information, and tells ya' so, and then it spits out some false numbers to back-up your false claim. Why *Mr. Howell*, that's one large crock of cow manure for me to believe in two human lifetimes!"

Agent John Powell thought he had detected an element of weakness in Abrams' voice, and that the shrewd farmer's hard-shelled constitution was beginning to slightly crack. From years of mentally grappling with infuriated taxpayers, the veteran agent knew that the time was ripe to change his tempo and express sympathy for the unfortunate recipient of bad *IRS* tidings. Sugar often yielded better results than vinegar, once a taxpayer had been softened-up. "Remember Mr. Abrams, I'm only doing my duty," Powell shrewdly attested. "We know for a fact that your prosperous farm grossed over three million dollars last year. Your total operating expenses, including the tractor, the bulldozer, and the forklift, came to a little over a million and a half."

Powell then produced from his Salisbury office portfolio *Xeroxed* copies of canceled checks supplied by Abrams' *CPA,* and the documentation originating from various East Coast produce brokers and commission houses. "Mr. Abrams, if you don't cooperate right now, my investigation might spill-over into *their* financial affairs, and *they'll* blame it all on you. One time, such a case as yours took me eight years and eighty-seven supplementary accounting sessions to finally complete. You don't want to make bitter enemies with *your* many business partners distributing your produce up and down the East Coast, now do you?"

Clint Abrams took umbrage with Agent Powell's more-than-subtle verbal threat. "Just a cotton-pickin' minute!" the old codger hollered. "Both you and *your* government stand for waste. Only carefree Uncle Sam will pay a worthless flunky like you big bucks to go around and pick on honest, innocent people like me. Stop hassling me! You're no better than one of Hitler's Gestapo!"

"I resent *that* insinuating remark!" Powell loudly objected. "I work for the finest and most compassionate government the world has ever seen, and I want you to know that millions of Americans are very proud of their *government*."

Abrams then gave Powell a lecture about how "the *regime*" in Washington could never make a "profit" like hard-working business people do because all the government does is "play Robin Hood" and redistribute money from the productive "haves" to the unproductive "have-nots," who then greedily squander the labor and production of the "haves".

"As long as the money is in *my* hands, it's good money," Clint Abrams opined. "As soon as it goes to incompetent Uncle Sam, it instantly becomes bad money, squandered on stupid government programs and projects, and wasted on lazy people that just refuse to work. Do ya' hear me *Mr. Howell*? I said wasted! Unproductive! No good! That's exactly what *you* pushy *IRS* jerks really represent from coast-to-coast!"

Agent Powell was not accustomed to being maligned in such a vicious manner by such an insolent, cunning, mean-spirited man. The abused and insulted bureaucrat had to bite his tongue to avoid becoming radically unprofessional.

Clint Abrams took a deep breath, and then got back on his soapbox. He told Powell that billions of hard-earned dollars go to "rinky-dink foreign countries" that turn around and then hate Americans for *their* benign generosity. "I read in the papers where Uncle Sam is trillions of dollars in debt," Abrams continued his defiant diatribe. "That plainly means that people's savings in the bank ain't worth a plug nickel if there's a serious depression like the one that happened in 1929. Do ya' think I was born in a sow's eye? Who's gonna' pay for the massive debt that's been accumulatin'? Are you *Mr. Howell?* No siree; it'll be honest, hard-workin' citizens like me that will have to pay-off that very huge debt and get the government off the hook through *my* hard labor and sacrifice."

Agent John Powell was reaching his maximum tolerance limit. Abrams' brash contempt was making the tax collector's heart palpitate. Clint had to be the most despicable, ferocious taxpayer the revenue agent had ever encountered or confronted. Still, Case Investigator Powell had an official duty to perform, and *that* function was his special mission to now reveal to the already livid grower additional aggravating news.

"There's a distinct possibility that the *IRS* might have to make a jeopardy seizure on some of your property should *you* fail to cooperate with my audit," the peeved Agent informed the aggrieved farmer. "I'll organize a team of agents together and supervise the confiscation if I have to. The local sheriff will be contacted, and we'll come onto your property and repossess two hundred thousand in equipment in order to satisfy your massive debt before you could blink your eyes. I'll show you who is the boss, and who holds the dominant trump cards in this frivolous and idiotic power game *you're* recklessly playing."

Clint Abrams gave the tenacious *IRS* collector an ultimatum. "Honestly now Mr. Powell, I ain't got time to chew the fat with you," the irritated grower gruffly prefaced. "I got some necessary tree trimmin' to do, a peach hydro-cooler to overhaul, crops to plant, and not to mention two hundred tons of fertilizer and lime to lay down before sunset."

The very distressed farmer also informed the diminished agent that spray material was to be delivered soon, and that Abrams had a crew of eight Mexicans working on the farm's outer perimeter that needed proper supervision right that moment. "If ya' wanta' discuss this matter further with me, *Mr. Howell*, ya' gotta' come along in my pickup. Ya' demandin' fellas' in fancy suits and shiny patent-leather shoes can't cut the mustard if ya' ever had to make it on your own like I have ta' produce and succeed year in, and year out!"

John Powell reluctantly acceded to Clint Abrams' demand to accompany the mercurial old geezer on some urgent farm business that needed to be conducted immediately. The cantankerous farmer was certainly a hard nut for the very experienced public servant to crack. The elderly, wily grower exhibited no fear of the federal government's mammoth muscles that John Powell had vainly attempted to flex.

Conversely, the old coy Delmarva grower was a strong, rugged individualist who both practiced and worshiped free enterprise self-sufficiency. Clint Abrams wholeheartedly resented those "weak crybaby dependents" that needed Washington or Annapolis's assistance to make a living, or to subsist on the dole, parasitically benefiting from the accumulative labors of others. But Abrams was always abusive to anyone or everyone, (government official (or otherwise) whom the old gent thought violated *his* unalienable right to absolute privacy, and *his* privileged right to privately amass unlimited wealth.

The landowner tossed a small chain-saw into the rear of his late-model red Ford pickup. The power tool landed next to a roll of transparent plastic, which had been used by the farmer to mend greenhouse holes and gaping rips caused by early spring high winds.

The odd pair climbed into opposite sides of the red truck's cab. Suddenly, Clint Abrams was much more rational and much less argumentative than he had been to Agent John Powell back at his farm's coveted repair shop. Seeing a favorable opportunity, the

Internal Revenue official attempted to assess and capitalize on Clint Abrams sudden change in temperament.

The red pickup rambled-down a bumpy dirt road as the occupants conversed. "Ya' know Mr. Powell, the only difference between *you* and a criminal is that you want to steal from me without using a gun," Abrams claimed with a mild chuckle. "That makes you just one level above being a common thief!"

"I'm just defending and enforcing the national tax code," Powell civilly maintained. "It's my sworn duty that I have to contribute every single workday to keep this great country goin'."

"There's only so much taxes a man can pay before he gets fed-up with the feds!" Clint humorously replied as the all-too-volatile driver kept his keen eyes on the meandering dirt road. "I know my history pretty well, Mr. Powell. Yes indeed, I do know my history. George Washington fought the *Revolution* against England because of a small stamp tax, a silly molasses tax, and a tiny tea tax," Abrams lectured his passenger. "The whole *Revolutionary War* was fought to oppose a lot of *tiny* British taxes. Now the bloated United States government over the centuries has become the enemy of the people. Uncle Sam's not satisfied simply stealin' fifty percent of *my* hard-earned money. The Feds' now want to rob me, and put me out of business, and send me into the poorhouse so that I'll need government assistance just like those lazy welfare people in all the big cities do," Clint argued with a mild attempt at persuasion.

"If you'd let me explain," Powell blandly suggested, "I'll be able to tell you exactly where that figure of two-hundred and ten thousand dollars I had mentioned earlier came from. Actually, Mr. Abrams, it might be a lot more when you consider adding-in mounting back interest and penalties, which I haven't exactly fully calculated as of yet. That two hundred and ten thousand might indeed be a low-ball figure."

"Mr. Powell, you're doin' this country more harm than mighty King George of England ever did," Clint Abrams obstinately asserted. "But tell me, where did ya' get that crazy out-of-the-ballpark, exaggeratin' figure ya' say I owe?"

Powell had trouble figuring-out the obscure motivations of his petulant "client". First, Clint Abrams was randomly philosophizing about excessive government waste. Then the "insolent" grower looks at himself as a contemporary John Hancock or Samuel Adams vehemently opposing avaricious taxation. Now, Abrams was inquiring about the exact mathematical basis for his current tax liability. The farmer's oscillating personality seemed much more complex, and much more surreptitious than Agent John Powell had originally imagined it could ever be. The evasive, obdurate, old farmer kept vacillating from one subject to another without much consistent rhyme or reason being evident in his angry logic.

"Mr. Abrams, the *IRS* can't reveal its anonymous sources," the red truck's passenger stated. "You must understand that the service must protect the identity of anyone that confides in us with absolute professionalism and secrecy."

"You really mean to say you protect anybody that rats or squeals on somebody else, and then receives a kickback bonus reward for being deceitful!" the incensed driver clarified. "That makes you a disgustin' filthy rat too, Mr. *Howell!* The tricky Russians, along with the corrupt Chinese Communists, well now; they show me more basic decency than you lousy *IRS* boys have."

"Mr. Abrams, we've discovered that *you* have a lucrative cash flow business where you annually fail to report all of its income," Powell explained. The agent then garrulously disclosed that Abrams' wife Faye ran a wholesale/retail farm market that grossed over two hundred thousand dollars each summer, and that Abrams had only reported a small net income of only twenty thousand dollars. "Sir, we have the goods on you on *that* particular count, too," Powell proudly proclaimed. "You use the farm market to unload all your 'second quality' produce, what you call 'rejects,' fruit and vegetables that you can't send to the wholesale fresh markets in New York, Philly', DC, Boston and Baltimore. You only claim full measure on the *number one* quality produce *you* ship *wholesale* and report annually on your tax returns. You're skimming a lot of money from your cash retail farm market business Mr. Abrams, mucho cash if I might add; and then you're greedily funneling the hidden profits directly into your burgeoning stock market account!"

Clint Abrams had trouble keeping his new red pickup on the curving bumpy dirt road. Agent Powell's comments had really had an unnerving effect upon the driver's general composure. The seasoned farmer exhibited his abundant discontent by ranting about expensive military missiles, and about wasteful welfare programs, and about disintegrating and unproductive urban housing projects. "I'm a WASP Mr. Powell, a White Anglo-Saxon Protestant. But now you lousy, conniving government employees have made me madder than a hornet!"

"You've mentioned hornets and wasps in one breath. Are you some kind of entomologist?" Powell deliberately joked to further irk Clint.

"Speak plain, uncorrupted English," Abrams nastily reprimanded. "I only speak words I know how to spell."

"An entomologist is a scientist who studies insects," Powell academically clarified. "You should know *that* specific term, being the very successful farmer that you are."

A broad smile beamed from Abrams wrinkled face as his thin body bounced up and down inside the truck's cab. Wearing a broad grin, Clint told the *IRS* man that insects were a farmer's best friends. "Bees pollinate my peach, nectarine, and apple orchards," the grower explained. "And I need 'em to help my vegetable crops, too. Ya' don't have to graduate from *Yale* or the *Naval Academy* over in Annapolis to know that basic knowledge!"

A mile further down the dusty trail Clint Abrams' Ford truck entered a side dirt road that soon cut through a patch of woods', and the new trail led to the southern edge of the man's expansive thousand-acre estate. The red vehicle stopped next to a huge apple tree situated all by its lonesome. The driver had a rather germane question for his passenger to answer.

"Before we get out, tell me something Mr. Powell. Who ratted on me? I know how these things work. An informant squeals to the *IRS*," Abrams maintained. "The government then protects the tattler from any retaliation by keeping the weasel's identity confidential. When the *IRS* eventually collects its new-found money, your agency kicks back a commission to the undeserving squealer. You must really like doin' business with liars and cowards."

"I'm not at liberty to divulge that particular operational information," Powell replied before gulping twice to make his raspy voice come-out clearer. "Our sources are strictly classified, and therefore, confidential."

"You're protectin' a yellow-bellied snake," Clint nastily alleged. "There's only one person on Delmarva that would do this wicked thing to me. It's Jason Purnell, isn't it! He's the lousy snitcher! The creep's always been jealous and envious of my success; that no good envious piece of pond scum!"

"I cannot reveal the source," Powell repeated. "The informer has taken the government into his confidence."

"I thought I smelled a stinkin' rat in the woodpile!" Clint indignantly challenged. "What's his commission outa' this caper? What kind of deal did ya' cut with that filthy skunk! Show me some guts Powell! Tell me, or else I'm hereby accusin' ya' of havin' no honor whatsoever!"

"I told you earlier, Mr. Abrams," Powell insisted and emphasized, "that I'm not at liberty to disclose the identity of my sources."

The sly grower informed the federal tax investigator that he and Jason Purnell had been on unfriendly terms for over thirty years. During *WW II,* the Purnell family farm had been the most profitable agricultural business on the peninsula. Over the last five decades, Clint's estate had multiplied in size, becoming almost twice as large as Jason Purnell's total inheritance, and over double his present wealth. "Jason would stoop to a weed's height to blemish my good name," Abrams claimed. "He's got no decent character!"

Before Clint exited the red cab, the farmer picked-up his portable radio and reported, "Unit 1 to Units 2 and 3. I'm out at daddy's old place on a 521. In case ya' boys need me, I repeat, I'm out at daddy's old place on a 521."

"Roger, ten-four," Zeke answered over his radio.

"I hear ya' loud and clear pappy," Hugh soon replied.

"I just called my two sons to let 'em know where my 'twenty' is in case one of 'em needs me for something," Clint elusively explained to Agent Powell. "A 521 is our code for prunin' fruit trees."

The farmer and his unlikely passenger climbed-down from opposite sides of the red pickup's cab. Clint then pointed to the nearby old, venerable, giant apple tree. "My granddaddy planted this here monstrosity back in 1921, right here at the old homestead. The *Depression* times around these parts sure were rough. If ya' wanna' stick around and talk Mr. Powell, I'm gonna' put ya' to work," Clint continued speaking with a forced smile. "We're gonna' prune this here ancient apple tree. It's more of a symbol of the farm's history than anything else."

John Powell slowly ambled over with Clint Abrams to inspect the enormous, gnarled fruit tree. The thing was still in sturdy condition for its age, but its many unkempt limbs obviously required intensive pruning. Abrams then explained to his fascinated visitor that he possessed great reverence for the overgrown apple tree because it was the modern farm's only real link with the huge plantation's humble "founding". The apple tree was Clint's cherished "treasure" that he hoped to pass on to future Abrams' generations.

"Does it still produce quality apples?" John Powell inquired as he marveled at the immense tree's size. "It's the oldest and largest apple tree I believe I've ever seen."

Agent John Powell suddenly felt a hard shove from behind. The surprised farm visitor then awkwardly plunged into a twelve-foot-deep pit that had been skillfully camouflaged by a dense cover of twigs, branches, grass, weeds, and brown leaves. Clint Abrams had deliberately and maliciously shoved the government tax collector directly into the center of the well-concealed trap.

"Mr. Powell, can ya' hear me down there?" Clint shouted as his cupped hands formed a makeshift megaphone around his mouth. "If you'll look on either side of you, Mr. Powell, you'll be able to see the skull and bones from two different skeletons. Do ya' see your new buddies eternally resting down there?"

Powell sat-up in the dark, drab pit and fearfully surveyed the skeletal bones evident on either side of his rude landing place. Fear immediately invaded the man's heart.

"The skinny guy on your right Mr. *Howell* was a certain *FBI* feller' who tried stoppin' my granddaddy from making illegal moonshine during the *Prohibition Era,*" Clint yelled-down to his more-than-apprehensive captive. Abrams verbally rambled on that money was scarce back then, and that the family couldn't even afford beds. "My granddaddy had to sleep on straw, and my pappy didn't have no crib either. Pappy had to sleep in an old wooden orange crate. My granddaddy was so poor he had to put cardboard over some of the window panes to keep the cold winter air out; that's how damned poor he was. No Sir Mr. *Howell.* No damned government welfare programs or food stamps back then!"

Clint Abrams peered-down at his still-stunned, whimpering hostage. The old farmer was very resolute and shrewdly calculating in his purpose. The determined man expressed to his *captive* listener how the family couldn't afford electricity, then a luxury back in "the '20s", and how his daddy had to wear his grandma's shoes to school because the Abrams ancestors were too destitute to afford decent foot gear. "Do ya' get what I'm drivin' at, Mr. Powell?" Clint ridiculed and shouted down into the shadowy pit. "You and Uncle Sam ain't gonna' steal what I had to work hard to get!"

Agent Powell's life, his wife, his three children, along with the distinct prospect of imminent retirement all flashed across *his* very disturbed mind. "Please Mr. Abrams, weigh what you're doin'," the *IRS* official pleaded. "I promise you; I'll never bother you again about taxes. You have my word of honor. Please, get me out of this diabolical hellhole!"

The cunning-but-resolute farmer was not-too-moved by Agent Powell's emotional entreaty. "I seriously doubt whether you have any honor at all," Abrams sarcastically and loudly remarked. "You never thought of how ya' hurt people since ya' started collectin' their hard-earned money for the whore of a government you're working for. It's too late for mercy, Mr. Powell. You had your chance to go away peacefully. But you refused to leave me alone to my own business."

IRS Agent Powell was now on his knees, seemingly like a devout churchgoer praying for salvation. The remorseless antagonist was not-at-all impressed with his hostage's exaggerated supplication. "I've no choice but to kill you," Abrams very mechanically declared. "Notice Mr. Powell, I didn't say the word 'murder'. I said the word 'kill'. Murder is what ya' do to another human being. Kill is what ya' do to an animal. Now then; I got to get rid of ya' once and for all Mr. Powell, right when I was beginnin' to like ya', too! I gotta' kill ya' because I hate my government, but I want ya' to know before you die that I still love my country."

"But my wife, my children. Who will take care of them?" Powell implored and sobbed. "Show me some Christian mercy, please!"

Clint Abrams felt highly motivated to achieve *his* end. The bones of two other government "snoopers" that had preceded *IRS* Agent Powell's intrusion flanked the prospective third victim on either side. Powell was totally petrified at seeing the hideous bones of the eerie-looking dual horrors, and the sentenced tax collector was wondering exactly what circumstances had led to the unidentified individual on his left being killed.

"All those fancy words and your elite college education ain't no use to ya' now," Abrams affirmed and laughed. "If ya' treated your wife and kids anything like ya' treat your victimized taxpayers, Mr. Powell, then in truth, they ain't gonna' miss ya' at all either. No siree, not one bit Mr. Powell!"

The man trapped in the dank, dusky pit was now totally horrified. Powell knew that Clint Abrams was positively serious about engineering *his* death. Despair dominated the captured man's soul. Powell now knew that he should have left the unscrupulous farmer alone. The IRS representative had failed to let the proverbial sleeping dog lie.

"Mr. Powell," Clint Abrams hollered-down to his completely terrified "guest". "That skinny feller' over to your left was a county sheriff who came here to arrest my daddy for runnin' an illegal gamblin' house here on the farm. As you can see, you're in real good company. Now it's my turn to carry on the family tradition of getting rid of trespassin' troublemakers with shiny badges tryin' to throw their government weight around where they ain't wanted!"

Investigator Powell was then absolutely, totally petrified. The prisoner screamed and loudly cried for clemency. His hysterics were exercised to no avail. The government agent cupped his hands over his eyes and wildly wept like an infant. The *IRS* man finally realized that his mortal existence was doomed. Powell had finally comprehended that he had been sentenced to death by Clint Abrams' unique brand of inflexible, unyielding, vigilante country justice.

Clint then limped to his truck, removed his trusty shotgun from behind the seat, loaded it, and pointed the barrel at the intimidated "loser" still weeping in the "elimination pit". Abrams' taunting actions and speech were akin to a cat toying with a mouse before deciding to seal its prey's fate.

"This is gonna' be the end for you, Mr. Powell. You came here actin' like a hungry bulldog, but look at ya' now. You're a scared, pitiful little puppy dog with your tail hangin' between your useless legs," Clint Abrams cackled. "What's it like to feel humiliated and terrified at the same time?"

"Don't shoot! Please don't shoot!" Powell begged and reiterated. "I'll do anything you wish if you'll just spare my life."

"I ain't gonna' let ya' die so easily by just bein' shot execution style," Abrams said with a snicker. "Wait 'til ya' see what I got in store for ya'!"

A distant cloud of dust could be detected heading in the direction of the old revered "homestead apple tree". Zeke and Hugh were coming in response to the recent 521 emergency call dispatch, which was really Clint's secret farm code for "unwanted intruder" prowling around on the premises. Two minutes later, Zeke and Hugh simultaneously leaped-out of a new blue Chevy pickup to survey the present source of alarm.

"Welcome boys," the elder Abrams warmly greeted his loyal sons. "We got *IRS* Agent Powell hunkered-down there in the old burial pit. He's been buggin' me about payin' more taxes to that greedy Uncle Sam fella'. Get that plastic greenhouse wrap and chain saw outa' my truck's flatbed. I'm gonna' clamber-up the old apple tree with my trusty, rusty chain saw."

Zeke and Hugh did exactly as their adamant father had instructed. Powell was praying on his knees in his now-grimy dark-blue business suit. The distraught man looked-up from his bleak hollow, his dirty face showing a pathetic expression of fear that seemed welded upon his waxen-pallid visage. The petrified *IRS* official soon was instructed to direct his attention to an overhead limb of the gigantic, ancient apple tree.

Agent Powell observed a very immense beehive suspended from a high branch directly overhead. Clint carefully climbed-up the revered apple tree while awkwardly toting his small chain saw. As Zeke and Hugh obediently unraveled and cut enough plastic to cover the exposed hole, old Abrams adroitly straddled the sturdy limb that was conveniently positioned directly overhead of Mr. Powell's secluded death hollow.

"Please, spare me!" John Powell futilely cried. "I'm going to retire next year, and I'll see to it that no one from my office ever bothers you again! Please show me mercy!"

"And if they do come around here," Abrams yelled-down, "your ugly bones are gonna' then have some new company down there, too!" Clint paused for a minute to enjoy the sound of Agent Powell sobbing and weeping at the bottom of the hideous hole.

"I feel no guilt or shame about this," Clint shouted-down at the tearful man, now-standing in the pitiful pit. "Mr. Powell, ya' told me during your last visit that there were only two certain things in life, 'Death and taxes'. But now you slithering government skunk, you're gonna' find-out that *your* death is a little more certain than *my* stinkin' taxes are!"

Clint firmly wrapped his legs around several strong apple tree limbs. The incensed maniac then pulled the rope, starting-up the rusty chainsaw's small gasoline engine.

Agent Powell's tongue and mouth were so parched that the frightened man couldn't even utter an indiscernible syllable. The whining chain-saw's rotating teeth easily chewed through the thick apple tree limb (that was suspended above the pit) like a sharp scissors sheering through thin paper. The huge beehive hanging from the apple tree limb suddenly plunged down into the hole.

Zeke and Hugh quickly covered the improvised grave with the transparent plastic, and the sons held the material against the ground so that no angry swarming, imported African killer bees could escape their new confinement. Shrill cries echoed from the execution hollow. Thousands of agitated killer bees buzzed in a wild frenzy around the panic-stricken federal bureaucrat's total anatomy.

The elder Abrams casually shut-off his favorite chain-saw, and then carefully clambered-down from his apple tree perch that had been situated directly above the now plastic-covered pit. Zeke, Hugh and Clint continued to anchor-down the plastic cover with large stones and heavy fallen apple tree limbs.

Ten minutes later, the three conspirators furtively concealed the small crater with twigs, branches, grass, weeds and brown leaves so that the area looked exactly as it had before Agent Powell had swiftly plummeted through its prior concealment. The three family men felt no regret for Agent Powell's unfortunate painful demise.

"Well Pop," Zeke announced with a chuckle. "It looks like we gotta' somehow figure-out how to grow another active beehive on this here old apple tree."

"The guy tried buggin' Daddy," Hugh added with a broad grin, "but we sure fooled him. Daddy *bugged* the life outa' poor, deceased Mr. Powell!"

"That was Agent Powell's last sting operation!" Zeke amusingly noted as the zany older son and Hugh buckled-over, holding their stomachs to contain their wild hysterics.

"Sons, Mr. Powell is no longer employed by the *IRS*. He's now in the *F Bee I*, Ha, ha, ha!" Clint Abrams incessantly laughed. "Most families keep their skeletons in the closet," Abrams declared to his two wildly giggling progeny. "But we Abrams' clansmen keep all our skeletons right in this here pit!"

Amusement was just a temporary distraction to Clint Abrams' austere Protestant Work Ethic. "Enough foolin' around and that's enough frivolity too, boys," the family patriarch commanded. "We got some serious work to do. You two comedians head over to the packinghouse. The old hydro-cooler needs a new sprocket installed."

Zeke and Hugh hopped back into the brand-new blue Chevy pickup as if nothing of importance or consequence had ever happened. Zeke drove the farm vehicle in the same direction from which the brothers had arrived. The obedient sons immediately headed "in-a-beeline" for the farm's packinghouse to begin their assigned major repair job to the peach hydro-cooler project.

Clint Abrams carefully returned his utilitarian roll of plastic and his other property and tools to his flatbed Ford truck. The independent felon next placed his cherished, favorite shotgun behind the driver's seat, and two minutes later, the family patriarch headed back to his estate's spacious manor house.

That afternoon, old Abrams drove John Powell's shiny black "government pool" Ford Taurus to cousin Newt Trimper's junkyard, where the expendable automobile was quickly crushed into a neat metallic cube.

"We fellas' here on Delmarva gotta' stick together," Clint said to cousin Newt. "We's all family here!"

"Clint, thanks plenty for the free piece of decent scrap metal," the amiable blood relative appreciatively replied. "I know you'd do the same for me anytime, if I ever needed some help in an emergency."

"Can ya' give me a ride home Newt?" Clint humorously asked. 'I'm without a means of transportation for obvious reasons."

"I sure can Cousin," Newt Trimper jovially replied. "Just hop into my old reliable tow truck and I'll drive ya' over to your palace!"

Two weeks later, Clint Abrams reached-up on a shelf in his den and pulled-down the *E* volume of his leather-bound encyclopedia set. The curious researcher looked-up the subject "Entomology", and then diligently read the scholarly article. His plain, homely-looking wife entered the den and inquired about her husband's sudden interest in reference book literature.

"Faye, tomorrow I'm gonna' make a special attempt to impress Jason Purnell with my exclusive knowledge of indigenous insects," Clint surprisingly announced to his obedient spouse. "And I want Jason to meet a new young fella' in the area named Mark Turner."

"I do declare," Mrs. Abrams said. "You turnin' into a bookworm after all these years hatin' colleges and school teachers. And I thought you and Jason weren't on the best of terms? Seems very strange, indeed. Things are really changin' fast here on Delmarva, I must say!"

"Faye, we got beehives all over this here farm, and I've located two new ones just this past week," Clint casually disclosed. "And I'm gonna' courteously invite my old nemesis Jason Purnell over and show the fool just how important bees are in runnin' a big agricultural operation."

"I'm glad to hear that both you and Jason are now on favorable speakin' terms," peace-loving Faye Abrams happily replied. "It ain't good havin' enemies!"

"And Faye, Mr. Mark Turner already knows about my big bee problem as well as another fella', *his* good pal Mr. John Powell," Clint revealed.

"Mr. Mark Turner, that name sounds awfully familiar," Mrs. Abrams answered, her fuzzy mind trying to focus and concentrate. "But I just can't seem to place him anywhere, though."

"And Faye," Clint Abrams typically stated in his characteristic Eastern Shore drawl. "I've now decided I owe Jason a real big favor. We farmers out here on Delmarva gotta' cooperate and share ideas in order to survive. It's about time old Jason Purnell and me became good friends. The subject of bees, beehives. and apple trees is actually a good place to start *our* new friendship!"

"Time Vigilantes"

Michael Daniels stood erect before the austere-looking judge and next to his state appointed defense attorney inside the crowded *Camden County Courthouse*. A solemn-but-confused expression ornamented Daniels' rather small facial features. The bailiff stood at attention upon the raised platform, just left of the judge's elevated bench. The black-robed New Jersey public official austerely stared-down at the accused through thick bifocals, loosely resting on the bridge of his nose.

"Michael Daniels; raise your right hand and place your left palm over the *Holy Bible!*" instructed the bailiff. "Now, do you swear to tell the truth, the whole truth, and nothing but the absolute truth, so help you God!"

"Yes sir," came the almost inaudible reply.

"Michael Daniels, how do you plead?" Judge Matthew Dixon asked the nervous defendant.

"I think not guilty," the shy young man answered in a low hoarse voice. "Yes; I believe I should plead not guilty."

"Are you certain?" the seemingly inflexible courtroom judge adamantly asked. "Could you speak a little louder and repeat your plea for everyone present to distinctly hear. And please don't say the word *think*. It's a subjective word that suggests uncertainty. Let's try it all over again. Now Mr. Daniels, you should either tersely plead guilty or not guilty!"

"I plead not guilty!" the defendant accused of first-degree murder firmly stated.

"Counselor, have you adequately advised the defendant of his *Constitutional Rights* and of the possibility of a lesser voluntary manslaughter plea bargain should he have instead pleaded 'guilty'?" the by the book judicial authority asked the tall, lean defense attorney. "If found guilty, the defendant could receive a greater sentence than if he had pleaded guilty."

"Yes, Your Honor," Attorney Mark Brookes respectfully replied. "The defendant is very obstinate in that particular matter, insisting that he had been unaware of any malicious intent on *his* part upon committing the alleged act."

"But Counselor, must I remind you that twenty-one other highly suspicious deaths had occurred at the *Echelon Mall* on the evening of May 20, 2002! Twenty-two people, many of them children, teenagers, and perfectly healthy adults suddenly collapsed and died for no apparent reason. If convicted," Judge Dixon continued, "Michael Daniels might also be implicated in the other twenty-one bizarre, mysterious deaths."

"In all due respect, Your Honor," Attorney Mark Brookes slowly indicated, "my client claims to know nothing about the other twenty-one inexplicable deaths that had transpired at the *Echelon Mall* on the night of Monday, May 20, 2002. The county's *Medical Examiner* and the best forensics' professionals in New Jersey haven't a clue as to a satisfactory, logical explanation for the exact cause of the other twenty-one deaths, other than simultaneous cessation of vital signs," the gaunt-looking defense lawyer nobly stated. "The exact cause is a baffling enigma, even to the state's most talented expert investigators. The cause is too difficult to discern for even the most sophisticated and knowledgeable medical specialists to identify."

"Very well then, Counselor," the dignified judge sanctimoniously replied as the legal authority now sat still as a statue in his elevated black leather chair. "Do you have anything else to disclose before I direct the witness to take the stand and ask the prosecutor to proceed with his opening statement?"

"Yes, Your Honor, and for the record," Attorney Mark Brookes further elaborated, "I would like to have it entered that the identity of the victim remains unknown. The deceased had no wallet, no credentials, no *Social Security* card, no driver's license, and no credit cards in his possession. The only things *he* had in his pocket were ten and twenty-dollar-bills, four-hundred-and-seventy dollars total cash. The fingerprints on the bills matched none on record anywhere. The anonymous victim was shopping alone at the time of his demise, and no one in the mall knew his name. And," the State Appointed Counsel proceeded with his introductory remarks, "my young client believes that the murder victim had possibly been involved in the killing of the twenty-one other victims at the *Echelon Mall,* and that the nameless murder victim possibly had an accomplice in performing those nefarious criminal acts."

"Is *Exhibit A* the device believed to be the murder weapon?" the judge prudently asked the well-prepared county prosecutor. "I'd like to examine it when the questioning commences."

"Yes, Your Honor," the chief Camden County District Attorney responded. "If you'll notice," District Attorney Jeffrey Jensen suggested, holding the unique object up to the judge while wearing sheer plastic surgical gloves, "our chief investigators believe that this instrument is some ingenious, multi-functional weapon, some sort of organic tissue disintegrator," the county prosecutor expounded.

"When pointed at a person, we believe the device activates a distinct invisible death ray that instantly makes heart, liver, and kidneys stop functioning. Our forensics' experts have experimented with this instrument at the *SPCA,* and satisfactorily demonstrated its properties by effectively killing three rabid dogs and two diseased cats that were about to be put to sleep."

A roar of laughter broke-out from the huge audience seated in the crammed courthouse. Judge Matthew Dixon pounded his gavel on his elevated desk-podium yelling, "Order in this court! Order in this court! Any further spontaneous gallery outbursts will result in immediate removal, and I hereby instruct the bailiff and the other court security officers on duty of my serious intent!"

After absolute silence had been re-established, Judge Dixon again addressed the accused. "Michael Daniels, before I accept your earnest plea, clarify one thing for me. Did *you* know that the object in the prosecutor's hands was a murder weapon at the time of the alleged murder incident?"

"No, Your Honor, I didn't!" the defendant emphatically answered. "It looks rather peculiar, doesn't it; sort of like a microphone with a flashlight head at one end, with three strange switches in the middle. That's really all I know about the thing, other than it was only in my hands for about ten seconds. It looks like something science fiction that you would see on Star Trek."

"Very well then, Mr. Daniels," Judge Matthew Dixon assented. "The court accepts your plea of *Not Guilty*. We shall now hear opening statements and relevant arguments for Case Number 2943, State of New Jersey, County of Camden versus the defendant, Michael Anthony Daniels."

* * * * * * * * * * * *

In the year 2370, the *Democratic* and *Republican* parties had become extinct because their political persuasions no longer met the changing socio-economic needs of American society. The fledgling *Neo-Puritan Party* came into power in the United States in 2376, following a bloody and devastating thirteen-year civil war between the radical left-wing *Libertarians* and the conservative right-wing *New Age Moralists*. Within a year, stringent elements were set into motion to prevent a repeat of, or a continuation of, the horrible national catastrophe that had been courageously fought between cities *(Libertarians)* and rural towns *(New Age Moralists)* all over the entire nation.

In 2377, *District Military SWAT* squads were authorized to dispatch "moral vigilantes" to patrol city streets, slums, ghettos, and drug-infested middle-class urban neighborhoods. Those crusading "behavioral reformers" were not only assigned to enforce the nation's new laws, but also dispatched to monitor the accepted practice of America's customs, traditions and favorable social habits. When law and "social order" had been forcibly re-established throughout the land, "moral vigilantes" were then delegated in teams of two to time-travel to the past. Their assigned objective was to punish "ancestral violators" that did not conform to the "high moral standards" based on "common sense" that constituted the rigid principles of the newly implemented *Neo-Puritan* philosophy.

Zentar and Grel were veteran "moral vigilantes" who had been working together for seven years, ever since the quelling of the last significant *Libertarian* upheaval. The two highly-decorated time-warriors ambled to the designated "Year 2002 Locker Room" to change into light-dyed blue denim jeans, black tee-shirts, and spring denim jackets to simulate the clothing worn by males of the era that the militant time travelers would soon be visiting.

"What's your assignment?" Zentar asked Grel. "Or is it the usual search and destroy mission? I'm glad we both have only ten more years until retirement."

Grel opened a sealed envelope that contained and described his "Vital Instructions." "It says," the Time Vigilante read aloud, "proceed to *Echelon Mall,* Voorhees, New Jersey, May 20, 2002 from seven to eight p.m. Grel, you are hereby delegated and elevated to the important and distinguished *Non-Smoking in Public Places Patrol.* Efficiently eliminate anyone you find smoking in public. Feel free, Officer Grel, to exercise your judgment when it comes down to life-or-death situations."

"That's only right," Zentar agreed with the new edict formulated by the area *District Moral Code Commander.* "People should be more considerate of those that don't smoke. I mean," Zentar momentarily paused to further organize his justification, "I mean Grel, it's bad enough that people are so stupid destroying their own lungs and bodies with hungry cancer cells caused by tar and nicotine. But if the lunatics are so addicted to tar and nicotine chemicals, then they should be smart enough to only smoke cigars and cigarettes in the privacy of their own homes. People should have the decency to not inhale and exhale contaminated toxic fumes in public places and jeopardize the health of innocent human beings."

416

"You're right on the money," Grel concurred with his loyal partner in moral law and social values' enforcement. "If people are ignorant enough to abuse the health of others by expelling quantities of smoke into the air," the time vigilante haughtily hypothesized and opined, "then Zentar, those same stupid people must face the severe consequences without the expense of court appearances, police reports, and jail incarceration. We just zap them with our *Internal Organ Destabilizers*," Grel stated as the time policeman examined his splendid weapon, which looked somewhat like a black microphone with a flashlight head attached on the front end.

"Aren't you going to ask me what *my* special assignment is?" Zentar coaxed, as the experienced assassin ripped open *his* "Confidential Orders" instructional envelope. "You know Grel, we both spent an entire week studying the speech patterns and mannerisms of these year 2002 male freaks, and I feel no compunction about killing the defective units right there in their antiquated shopping mall environment."

"Okay, you're my reliable partner," Grel admitted to Zentar. "So naturally, you're heading to a place called the *Echelon Mall* with me. But what specific detail must *you* home-in on? Are you going to kill the passive smokers inhaling the nicotine and tar from the active puffers? What about the repugnant public spitters?"

"Ha, ha, ha," Zentar bellowed in a rare display of emotion. "I've been assigned to the *Elite No Kissing in Public Patrol*. Anyone caught showing affection in public is to be executed on the spot. Grel; everyone knows that showing affection in public breeds self-centered spoiled, bratty children, and makes infatuated adults such repulsive ingrates that they're then instinctively governed by hormones and not by logical reason. Hey Grel," Zentar expounded. "Tell me; how many people you've killed this year while on *Vigilante Patrol?* Have you kept a record?"

"Why yes," Grel acknowledged and confirmed. "I've killed three hundred and fifty-six in the past twelve months, mostly while on 'Affection Stakeout' patrol, and a thousand seven hundred and fifty-three total for all of my various *Vigilante Patrol* assignments."

"Wow! You're several hundred executions ahead of me!" Zentar exclaimed with sincere admiration. "I'll have to accelerate my eradicator button on this particular expedition," the moral crusader candidly declared as the futuristic hit-man made a last minute adjustment to a side dial on his very lethal laser weapon. "I have some accelerated catching-up to do. Ya' know Grel," Zentar concluded and disclosed. "I like these blue denim jeans I have on a lot better than our soft-plastic uniforms we have to wear daily. Maybe I'll stay a while, retire, and live-out my life as a freelance assassin in the year 2002!"

"Don't become too corrupted by the crime and moral decay of the year 2002," Grel earnestly warned, "or I might soon be assigned by the *District Commander* to stalk and exterminate you! Now make sure you have the five-hundred dollars in 2002 cash in your possession in order to buy food and merchandise at this Echelon Mall place!"

Zentar and Grel believed in the importance and the necessity of their assigned "morality enforcement patrols". In their briefing from Captain Dorn, they had learned that Year 2002 Americans were reprehensibly egotistical, so despicable, so unappreciative, and also so completely and intolerably aberrant of the prime fundamentals of peaceful social organization.

Moral Patrols were often officially commissioned to journey to the past and assassinate inconsiderate individuals caught smoking, kissing, loitering in public places, cursing, or spitting on public sidewalks, or acting uncouth, boisterous, and obnoxious inside public areas and squares. The Time Vigilantes' actions were justified from their point of view because both men had been wholly indoctrinated into a strict moral discipline code that made each hunter think unilaterally in identical idea-interpretation-reaction patterns. Both Grel and Zentar behaved and obeyed the edicts rendered by the all-powerful military authorities as if the two "Time Vigilantes" were similar, well-synchronized murder machines.

"I particularly enjoy exterminating fat people," Grel proudly boasted. "There's no satisfactory reason or explanation for anyone weighing three hundred pounds and walking around a commercial shopping mall eating a triple-scooped chocolate ice cream sugar-cone. When I see a person like that, I instinctively deviate from my prescribed orders and zap that lousy violator dead right on the spot."

"Now you're talking my language," Zentar related and agreed. "*Neo-Puritans* have the right idea, and I'm glad the party emerged victorious from the civil war, and totally vanquished the major opposition parties. Fat people, invalids, ugly people, and lame cripples all carry bad genes," the cyberpoliceman confidently maintained and shared. "Eliminate the ingrates as the *Internal Security Council* has intelligently mandated, and then big expensive *future* drains on our fine government's treasury, and on our now strong economy, have been swiftly excised out. Cancel-out problems in the past to ensure a moral and prosperous future; well Grel, that's

418

my philosophy, along with the *Internal Security Council's* omniscient positive thinking, too."

"Just remember," Grel reminded his cold-hearted, hell-bent-for-leather comrade, "you've been delegated by the government to kill violators kissing in public. Zentar, as a general rule, you're not allowed to terminate corpulent, lame, ugly, or feeble wheel-chaired senior citizens at random on this specific scouting foray deep into enemy territory. You're to only kill *those* kinds of idiots if you don't come across a lot of inconsiderate public kissers. And above all else," Grel joked while showing little conscience or morality, "don't kill any smokers. That violation is *my* personal responsibility on this mediocre mission."

America in the year 2380 AD happened to be a tranquil civilization devoid of the ravages of "frustrating social diseases". The ultra-right-wing *Neo-Puritans* had transformed men, women, and children into "Reverse Transcendentalists", or a society that valued thinking over feeling. The edicts and mandates coming out of Washington had maintained: "Man is a rational, intellectual creature capable of learning, discovering, analyzing, studying, and inventing." Expression of feelings or emotions while in public areas was regarded by the *Neo-Puritan* government as an extension of "overt animal monkey behavior".

Expressions of feelings and emotions were not only at first discouraged, but after the brutal "moral revolution", were later heavily suppressed. *Neo-Puritan* government officials both despised and deplored demonstrations of affection in public. And when violators were caught on tape by spy cameras located at every city intersection and at every town traffic light across the continental United States, then the self-centered "criminals" were promptly apprehended by "Storm Police", and then put into stocks and placed on public display in the center of town, or in a city square to be publicly scorned and ridiculed by law-abiding citizens. The "immoral criminals" were then mocked, spit upon, slapped and humiliated by amused bystanders and by righteous passing citizens.

Zentar and Grel were both aware that all aspects of life had to be logical and rational, including law, morality, behavior, and even death. Everything had a scientific explanation and had been transmitted as "basic educational truth" to the public via schools, and also via the government-controlled mass media. The entire society was functioning in a precise manner like a well-oiled machine.

According to the *Neo-Puritan Party* leadership, the elimination of "animalistic emotional behavior" would make the achievement of "rational reality" more readily attainable. Scientific principles such as "cause and effect" were taught as factors that govern human behavior, as well as being prevalent elements in technology also; so if a "criminal" committed a public fault, then his or her action was pragmatically judged to be the "cause" of a predictable "effect" (punishment and public ridicule). The inflexible codes of the *new* social sciences had been shrewdly molded and elevated to be *exact sciences,* similar to chemistry and physics, and psychology. Religion and sociology were banned subjects in all of the nation's colleges and universities. Such practices were narrow-minded "New England Retro-History", but nevertheless, the ethical codes were extremely effective conditioning methods of the *Neo-Puritans.*

"Are you ready to enforce social justice upon idiotic fools and insane hypocrites in the year 2002?" Grel asked his highly motivated companion.

"Our beam transmitters are pre-programmed to the Men's Room just outside the Food Court at the *Echelon Mall,* Voorhees, New Jersey. Check your gauge coordinates for accuracy," Zentar advised his vigilante colleague. "It's almost the designated time to initiate our essential 2002 mission that's specifically designed to eradicate future evolving decadence!"

"Everything is showing desirable in our preliminary gauge readings!" Grel alerted. "Let's synchronize our time-space alteration beams and do some time traveling."

"All right, contact, and away we go!" Zentar directed. "Let's have a fruitful blast into the past!"

* * * * * * * * * * * *

Three men were washing their hands in sinks, and a teenage boy was combing his hair as Zentar and Grel suddenly crystallized behind the four 2002 occupants in the men's lavatory mirror's reflection. The pair of futuristic space-time visitors immediately turned right and stepped out of the *Echelon Mall's* tidy Men's Room in a well-disciplined military cadence, as if nothing extraordinary had ever happened in the mall bathroom.

The four rather bewildered individuals looked at one another with astonished expressions upon their faces, all sharing the same "mass hallucination" and "group illusion". The inadvertent spectators were all shrugging their shoulders in disbelief at what their eyes had just perceived, but what their bedazzled minds could be comprehend..

420

Inside the crowded "Food Court Pavilion", Zentar and Grel decided it was time to split-up, promising to rendezvous again at 8:30 p.m. in the same tidy Men's Room for the return passage to Precinct Headquarters, 837 Arch Street, Philadelphia, Pennsylvania, calendar year 2380.

"See you in an hour," Zentar predicted to his very efficient killing comrade. "Don't get lost in any lingerie departments!" the very capable Time Vigilante facetiously added.

"Make sure you don't expire any smokers," Grel reminded his determined. patriotic colleague. "And don't be a maverick. Only focus on zapping kissers with your *Internal Organ Destabilizer,* and leave the nasty despicable smokers to me."

"You do have a propensity for manufacturing your own brand of ludicrous propaganda," Zentar volleyed back. "You'd make a damned good politician in this age we're visiting, now that lawyers in the future have been made illegal!"

Grel meandered to his left at the *Echelon Mall* Food Court's congested custard and ice cream concession, and Zentar remained stationary inside the colorful "Food Court Pavilion", searching for potential recipients of his formidable death ray. 'This isn't exactly a random killing spree,' the well-trained assassin evaluated. 'Random means to kill anybody violating the country's future moral codes, but I'm especially in quest of people showing excessive affection in public at the wrong time, and at the wrong place,' Zentar rationalized and considered. 'I'm not governed by any narrow time schedule or by any specified itinerary to perform my vital service. I only have a valid agenda that will make future generations more cerebral, and less animalistic and emotional. Raw emotions are merely extensions of the basic animal state of existence.'

Zentar alertly observed a young couple embracing in a long customer line in front of the *Food Court's* pizza concession. 'The imbeciles must be low-mentality teenagers. infatuated with one another's *animal magnetism,*' Zentar speculated and concluded. 'Married couples usually are tired of each other after a month of sex and don't care to show public affection like these unfortunate adolescent morons are about to demonstrate.'

Predictably, the acne-faced high school students' mouths came close together, and in another three seconds, their lips met. Soon, the young lovers were engaged in an extended kiss. The futuristic commando was very adroit at his chosen trade, and without even raising his deadly weapon to his eyes, Zentar easily extinguished the two young "Cupid lovebirds" with two instantaneous waist-high invisible laser jets speedily pulsating from his remarkable weapon.

No one milling around the *Food Court Pavilion* ever noticed Zentar's efficient evil executions, which had indeed been performed very stealthily and quite deftly. Two youthful bodies collapsed to the tan-tiled mall floor, and then a chorus of hysterical screams permeated throughout that corner sector of *the Food Court Pavilion.*

The successful time traveler assassin casually sauntered in the direction of the custard and ice cream station situated in the middle of the *Echelon Mall* Food Court, just adjacent to the colossal double-decked indoor shopping center's main traffic corridor. 'Grel and I will be out of here is less than an hour once we meet our separate quotas,' the confident killer reckoned. 'And the incompetent 2002 police won't be able to coordinate mall camera pictures from all of the selective assassinations for at least two hours. Even if the moronic cops foolishly cordon-off all entrances and exits to the mall,' Zentar slyly speculated, 'we'll both easily escape *their* wimpy dragnet by simply disappearing into *time* while shrewdly eluding being trapped in *space.*'

In front of the *Pretzel and Donut Factory* concession, Zentar spotted a male and a female passionately kissing. It didn't matter if they were husband and wife, or simply an engaged couple about to be married. Public affection was a definite taboo that had to be purged from the Year 2002 in order to guarantee society's future "mental health" in the Year 2380. Zentar wasted little time reacting to the capricious public display, exterminating the "self-centered cretins" rather promptly and effectively.

'Silly frivolous fools!' Zentar evaluated. 'The dolts ought to know better and have more consideration for the public that has to be unnecessarily exposed to *their* juvenile antics. *They* should know that in the future, television shows, movies and soap operas aren't allowed to have kissing scenes in them. Dumb sub-human numbskulls!' Zentar imagined. 'In the future, people simply *like* each other, and are compelled by law to *like* everyone in their society. *Love* is too strong of a word to use in 2380 AD. *Love* is just an ideal, a distant longing for a girl, or for a woman, like *Don Quixote* had felt in literature for *Dulcinea,*' chauvinist Zentar mentally assessed. 'That's what *love* should really be in the Year 2002, but the word *like* is exactly how the abstraction *love* is described in 2380, and in *my* society, *like* never involves affection!'

As Zentar reached into his jacket to again wrap his right hand's fingers around his trusty "violators' zapper", the futuristic visitor wondered what it would be like to actually kiss a woman. Realizing the folly of his rampant, curious imagination, the dedicated space-time patrolman squeezed the side of his awesome weapon, and in five brief seconds, a pair of invisible death rays had "destroyed" the "two human examples", soon lying motionless on the tile floor.

The very dangerous time commando scanned the area above the store facades for mall surveillance cameras. After completing *his* cursory camera inspection from a location twenty feet above the fallen affection victims, Zentar wandered-off and strolled to another section of the mall, pretending to be one of many apathetic eyewitnesses that wanted nothing to do with the travails and fates of the already dead mall patrons. Shouts and gasps were heard as alarmed and appalled merchandise shoppers rushed to the scene to view the macabre, charred spectacles lying on the elaborate brown-tiled floor designs.

Three hundred feet down the busy mall corridor, Zentar encountered two gay women holding hands. Lesbian behavior was regarded as "an abomination" by the rigid-morals' *Neo-Puritan Party,* which staunchly condemned all forms of homosexual activity. 'The lesbians don't even have to kiss each other for me to be motivated to kill them,' the time visitor wickedly thought. 'This human vermin disgusts me, and turns my stomach sour. I can even taste the foul, putrid, digestive juice pumping its way up to my parched mouth! I hate scummy queers even more than I despise public affection!' the futuristic soldier's twisted mind diabolically imagined and decided. 'I can't wait to zap these scurrilous, licentious female violators!'

In another ten seconds, two additional corpses lay prone on the brown-tile floor amidst yells, hollers, and shouts from exasperated mall shoppers that happened to be ambling about in the vicinity. Zentar chuckled to himself' as the matchless impostor slyly feigned looking inside a glass partition of an exclusive men's store, coyly studying several pair of fancy-dress shoes in a display window. 'Don't need those suckers!' the assassin thought with a wide smirk appearing on his face. 'I'll take combat boots any day,' the Time Vigilante grinned as his eyes glanced-down at the "silly" brown penny loafers on *his* feet.

Two very distraught security guards followed by three anxious Voorhees Township policemen sprinted by the shoe display in the opposite direction, all racing toward the most recent crime scene. Zentar nonchalantly shuffled his way toward the expansive entrance to a prominent department store. 'Those ugly female faggots got exactly what the lowlife deserved,' the specialist killer mentally reviewed with great satisfaction. 'If they want to be lesbians, then the damned perverts should be lesbians outside of public scrutiny in the privacy of their own homes. In the year 2380,' Zentar mused, 'even popular songs don't mention the words' kiss, affection, or love, and I'm exclusively thinking about heterosexual relationships. But those female freaks who just expired are on their way to *Hell* right now, and that's precisely where the lecherous sinners belong! The *Devil* already owned their souls before I punctually eliminated them from this Earth!'

Zentar then stepped inside the enormous, well-stocked department store and advanced through the perfume, jewelry, and panty hose departments. In front of the dual ascending and descending escalators, the callous, human automaton's eyes witnessed a young kindergarten age girl dashing-up to an elderly woman yelling "Grandma', Grandma!" The affectionate young girl gave her grandmother a massive kiss on her lips, and the elderly woman wholeheartedly reciprocated.

'There's no depth to *their* simple, childish minds; even as elderly adults', the enraged observer concluded. 'All the two dunces know how to do is express shallow ideas of a need for security to each other!' Zentar angrily conjectured with his eyes blazing red. 'They'll now be instantly executed on the basis of lacking mental depth and of showing a lack of regard for others in this insane public mall environment.'

The unbridled exhibition of genuine, natural affection had caused animosity to well-up inside Zentar's consciousness, and ten seconds later, two still bodies lay dead on the department store floor amidst resounding screams from horrified mall customers, and completely stunned sales personnel.

Zentar next entered and then took the elevator up to the second floor and exited into the gigantic department store's sporting goods section. Immediately, the Time Vigilante's perceptive eyes detected and focused on a mother loudly smooching her baby's face, and the overt sound of exaggerated affection and loud cooing only intensified the time assassin's rage. 'Stupid, immature, frivolous, asinine, behavior!' the commando's hateful mind criticized. 'That foolish woman doesn't realize that true happiness comes from achieving, from producing, from inventing, from thinking, and from exploring the limits of *rational* human intelligence. That kid will never be able to have the patience and the discipline to ever sit-down and write a book, or to accomplish anything great in life that requires plenty of thought and preparation,' Zentar mentally concluded and analyzed. 'And that simpleton mother doesn't realize that true happiness results from satisfaction being derived from success. A kid who is too secure is afraid to fail, and failure is necessary to build character and integrity over time,' Zentar convinced himself as his mind reiterated certain moral axioms that military instructors had incessantly inculcated into *his* very complex thought patterns. 'What ever happened to parent-centered families? Child-centered families breed demanding, doltish offspring that are lazy, contented, egocentric, and that are falsely praised for just existing. The little morons are undeservedly doted-on for not achieving anything special in life or for that matter, ever achieving anything mediocre!'

Before the highly trained Time Vigilante again administered his fatal death ray, some other negative thoughts swam through his very upset mind. 'Lazy spoiled brats are the result of this silly and ridiculous affectionate behavior, this repulsive mental sickness! Instead of children imitating mature parents, parents in this derelict. socially chaotic age of 2002 are absurdly imitating immature children. and the adults are acting like undeveloped two-year-olds themselves! Whatever happened to the all-too-truthful notion that children should be seen and not heard, or touched?'

A minute later, the fawning mother and her affectionate infant lay dead in front of the sporting goods department's pyramid baseball bat display. After a sales clerk screamed and desperately yelled for assistance, a crowd of delirious and hysterical curiosity seekers gathered around the helpless victims, who both soon would be riding in the local coroner's hearses rather than in hospital ambulances.

The extremely proficient time murderer nonchalantly paced to the front of the department store where seven beleaguered police officers frantically rushed by *his* slow, methodical gait. 'Life in my future time might be cold, calculating, and analytical,' Zentar reckoned, 'but it's certainly more objective and rational than a human existence in 2002. Little is subjective and emotional in 2380, and I especially *like* it that way. Everything makes perfect sense in *my* world. It bothers me when adults act like children; that is, when parents and grandparents should be setting models of mature behavior for youngsters to imitate,' Zentar reasoned and justified. 'The people of this peculiar age are so primitive and so un-evolved. The parents slobber all over and delight in licking their babies' faces much the same way as primitive apes do with their young. It looks so sloppy, and it sounds so awful when they suck on each other, as if the ignoramus mother and the clueless kid were mutual sweet candy lollipops. And it sounds and looks like a mother monkey licking and sucking her helpless and hapless chimpanzee offspring. That's exactly what this inferior kissing business looks like and what it sounds like,' the Time Vigilante determined as mass turmoil and confusion abounded all around him. 'These damned mentally underdeveloped humans of 2002 haven't yet evolved beyond the gorilla level of jungle existence! Human intelligence must ultimately triumph over animalistic feelings!'

Zentar's cruel heart lusted for more sensational homicides, so the human killing machine ventured into the mall's *McDonald's* and unobtrusively sat-down at a booth without ordering anything. According to schedule, in fifteen minutes he would be meeting Grel, who had been creating *his* own premeditated havoc with unwary smokers all over the panic-stricken mall.

Glancing to his right, the conscience-less time slayer observed two small children across the aisle. The moral vigilante surreptitiously suspected that the two were perverted brother and sister siblings as they were innocently and voluntarily kissing one another. As usual, the toddlers' parents were preoccupied chatting, and the pair of apathetic adults and their pristine children were totally oblivious to the killing machine's cunning scrutiny.

'What's wrong with the people of this wretched era?' Zentar contemptuously wondered. 'They all seem to want to be targets of my wrath, and the inane dolts all appear to have definite death wishes. Don't they know that they're exchanging millions and millions of germs and spreading infection with their slimy tongues and wet mouths constantly licking each other like retarded human ice cream cones?' the crazed highly-disciplined homicide enforcer remembered from one of his introductory military indoctrination lectures. "It's now time for my intervention!"

Then, the moral vigilante's temper escalated to an even higher level. 'Affection merely breeds complacency and a false sense of security,' Zentar thought and truly believed. 'It never leads to suspicion and the enactment of intelligent survival behavior. That's why lions rule the grasslands, and antelopes don't. The carnivorous lion is more intelligent than the weaker herbivorous antelope. The lion is the hunter, and the antelope the targeted prey. Don't these stupid people understand that only intelligent and wary creatures survive in a world fraught with competition, danger, struggle, and survival of the fittest! Darwin had it right. Too much security will lead to societal decay and to cultural decline!' Zentar vengefully considered. 'These disturbing, entitlement-oriented 2002 kids will never enjoy the much more meaningful abstractions in life such as honor, happiness from achievement, justice, courage, courtesy, beauty, creativity, and truth. All these spoiled conditioned brats know is security resulting from affection in a dependent welfare state, and too much security is evil, and will eventually lead to *Western Civilization's* decline and collapse!' concluded the brainwashed moral vigilante to his very receptive will and *Neo-Puritan* value system. 'I know the human history that will follow *this* disturbing age, and these motley dullheads do not!'

Zentar instinctively reached into his denim jacket's pocket and removed the power source for his deadly death ray *Internal Organ and Tissue Disintegrator* in order to swiftly enact his sworn moral responsibility. The killer's first impulse was to warily gaze to his left to ascertain that his villainous act would not be observable to any normally inattentive *McDonald's* diners.

Much to *his* utter astonishment, Zentar's eyes recognized Darf, a member of the *Libertarian Party's* Stealth Secret Police, aiming *his* lethal death ray gun directly at the enemy that the Time Vigilante had readily identified, and had been astutely stalking inside the *Echelon Mall* promenade.

The Darwinian concept of 'Survival of the fittest' dominated Zentar's machine-like, precision mind, and as the heartless assassin quickly ducked-down under the booth's table, Darf's ray blast flashed across the *McDonald's* seating area, beaming just above the intended victim's lowered head. Ironically, Darf had performed Zentar's duty by inadvertently and unintentionally killing the little boy and his assumed sister affectionately kissing one another in the adjacent *McDonald's* booth.

Seeing an opportunity for a quick escape, Zentar slid-out of his smooth, green, leather booth, crawled a distance of ten feet on the floor, rose to his knees, and then hustled as fast as his legs could carry him out of the fast-food establishment. In his haste to safety, the distressed Time Vigilante had accidentally left his extraordinary zap disintegrator gun behind during all of the tremendous, chaotic mass confusion.

Michael Stephen Daniels, a mentally challenged-but-dependable *McDonald's Restaurant* employee, recognized that Zentar had left his personal property lying upon the light green leather seat. Daniels ceased wiping-down the top of a neighboring table, ignored the delirious exclamations of shock and fright emanating all around him, picked-up the strange, black, alien weapon, and instinctively pursued its owner into the main mall shopping area.

"Sir, Sir, you left this inside the store!" Michael Daniels shouted at the top of his lungs. "Please stop and let me give it to you!"

A young child broke-away from his mother's grasp and wobbled directly into Michael Daniel's path. The mentally challenged high school special needs student leaped into the air to hurtle over the wandering toddler, and when the teenager's right wrist made contact with the brown rectangular tiled floor, the deadly weapon was activated and accidentally discharged. An invisible ray was emitted, and the laser beam instantaneously paralyzed the fleeing Zentar, who immediately dropped to the cold tile floor and was dead as a stone within ten seconds.

* * * * * * * * * * * *

Judge Matthew Dixon carefully studied Michael Stephen Daniel's pallid face and asked Camden County Prosecutor Jeffrey Jensen to remove *his* surgical gloves and then hand them to him, so that the court official could closely examine the "alleged murder weapon".

"May I remind the judge that the defendant Michael Stephen Daniels is a mentally challenged high school student working part time at *McDonald's* on a special state-sponsored school work program," Defense Attorney Mark Brookes glibly objected and interrupted. "There is nothing documented in Mr. Daniels' school records that suggests that the youth has shown a violent disposition!"

Judge Matthew Dixon next carefully inspected the alien lethal ray expeller, but the curious Solon's right thumb slid against an inconspicuous side-control, and coincidentally, the "flashlight head" had been pointing straight into the unsuspecting judge's face. A secondary invisible ray-beam was instantaneously ejected, and the Honorable Judge Matthew Dixon mysteriously vanished from sight.

The flabbergasted bailiff and the amazed police guards on courtroom duty rushed forward with drawn revolvers. The shocked courtroom audience was unaware that Judge Matthew Dixon had accidentally teleported himself' to the year 2380 where his "good workable mind" would be thoroughly infiltrated, indoctrinated and retrained to become a member-in-progress of the "Honorable Neo-Puritan Moral Vigilante Police Patrol".

"Salientia"

Artemas Walsh enjoyed a carefree existence, but the lazy, greedy man was never fully satisfied with his life's mediocre status. Walsh always wanted more: more property, more wealth, more material comforts, and more power. The quixotic dreamer drove a black *Mercedes* sedan, but desired a red *Ferrari*. Instead of being content with a more-than-adequate two hundred fifty-thousand-dollar annual living allowance, Artemas often complained to his rich wife that he needed "at least a half-million cash flow to merely make ends meet."

Artemas Walsh was a former pharmacist that had sold his profitable business on Bellevue Avenue in downtown Hammonton, New Jersey after marrying the former Vanessa Harper, who had obtained a colossal fortune from her former husband Girard "Jerry" Jamieson, the wealthiest investment banker in southern New Jersey. As part of the complicated divorce settlement, Vanessa had acquired Jamieson's massive home situated on the southern bank of the tranquil *Mullica River* in Sweetwater.

"Artemas; I don't know what's wrong with you besides you possessing all your egocentric propensities," Vanessa criticized one late August morning at the breakfast table overlooking the very scenic, cedar-colored *Mullica*. "Most working men can support an entire family on fifty thousand dollars a year, but you keep lobbying me for a preposterous half-million. Everybody of any repute in these parts calls you exactly what you are; 'a lazy married gigolo'. Did you know that?"

"Now Vanessa," Artemas diplomatically began his suave rebuttal, "I've always been faithful to you, and the half-million is less than three months interest on your fabulous annual investment income. Even in a recession year, you still make over three million on your most enviable and lucrative Merrill Lynch stocks, bonds, mutual funds, and money market portfolio."

"Vanessa, I think you're being entirely too unreasonable!" Artemas squawked. "I only have around twenty more years to live, and I want to live those remaining two decades with a degree of style and elegance!"

"I'd like more coffee, Paul," Vanessa indicated to the household butler who had just entered the room. "Now Artemas, I married you for love; something I never got from my nasty ex-husband. I was hoping that our marriage would produce at least one child, but regrettably it hasn't. Do you realize how unfulfilled my life has been being a woman without producing any children?" the wife sniffed in frustration, seeking a modicum of sympathy. "Why thank you Paul!" the woman commented after her second cup of coffee had been poured. "Paul, you can go and get the boat ready to cruise down the river. Get Giles to help you," Vanessa politely commanded. "Then, when you're finished, remember to clean-up the kitchen area. I want to see it spotless."

"Yes Madam'," the amiable butler answered with a forced smile. "The yacht will be ready to cruise in less than fifteen minutes. I'll notify Giles immediately."

"Vanessa, you know that I still love you dearly," Artemas rather melodramatically declared, "and I regret that our relationship has not provided you with the son or daughter you so rightly deserve. You're still a very beautiful woman in my eyes, and I want you to kow that you'll always be my beauty queen!"

"Save your false flattery!" the fickle wife indignantly chastised. "You're beginning to sound like one of those tawdry dime-a-dozen soap opera actors that thrive on noontime television. Arty," the pampered woman continued her monologue. "I happen to be much more sophisticated than you give me credit for. And if you persist in making your unwarranted demand for more money, then I'll diminish your allowance down to a hundred-fifty thousand. Do I make myself absolutely clear?" the haughty woman firmly stated.

"A hundred and fifty thousand!" Artemas protested. "I'd be a pauper! I'll have to go on welfare!"

"That was the pre-nuptial agreement we had signed, and if we should divorce, you'll only get two hundred thousand as a permanent severance. So, it's in your best interest to simply love me, keep your annual stipend, and be quiet about our arrangement. Otherwise," the curt woman insisted with a determined menacing expression on her face, "you'll have just enough money after our separation to purchase a second-hand pharmacy, and then have to diligently labor the rest of your life like a common citizen."

"I wasn't really complaining *that* bitterly," Artemas returned in a more apologetic tone of voice. "But you're acting and sounding like a spoiled diva! Vanessa; I thought that maybe a minor cost of living adjustment over the next ten years would be something picayune for you to consider; that's all!"

"Look and listen, Arty," the alert-and-defensive wife maintained. "Unfortunately, most women cannot have love and money both at the same time. It's usually either one or the other, so you extend to me the love part, and I'll show my appreciation by giving you fifty more grand than the negotiated two hundred and fifty thousand a year," Vanessa bluntly negotiated. "That figure, incidentally, if you recall, was our initial oral agreement five years ago, and the new modest fifty grand adjustment will not be changed or modified. Do you understand?"

"Perfectly," the subordinate husband reluctantly agreed. "I was only hoping you'd be a little more receptive to my very reasonable half-million-dollar request!" Then, the freeloading man of the mansion had a random secret thought pop into his head. 'I'm glad I had that vasectomy performed right before our marriage and right after Vanessa put me through a sperm-count test. She'll never have a principal heir to her colossal fortune besides me.'

"Well, Arty, maybe if you accompany me on *my* yacht down the river to *Harrah's Casino* this afternoon," Vanessa proposed, "then I'll be generous enough to give you ten thousand free dollars to predictably lose at the gambling tables. Or you can save the little stipend toward your fantasy red *Ferrari* if you desire that small option. Is it a deal?"

"You drive a hard bargain," the all-too-clever woman's second husband admitted. "But I have no viable choice here other than to allow you to be parsimonious. It's a fairly decent deal. Ten thousand gambling cash is okay with me."

After breakfast had been completed and partially digested, the argumentative couple prepared for their twenty-five-mile eastern river excursion down the *Mullica* and across the wide bay to the much-heralded Atlantic City Marina District.

"Is Paul or is Giles going to pilot us down the river?" Artemas asked his attractive wife as the always-dueling pair later that morning descended the spiral staircase from their master bedroom overlooking the placid *Mullica*. "Sometimes, I enjoy being the captain. I'm quite capable of performing that duty, you know!"

"Paul will be at the helm," Vanessa curtly replied. "Giles has some serious assigned tasks to perform around the house. He and Glenda must get the dining room table set for us to entertain the Smiths tonight," the wife sternly reminded her spouse. "We should be back from the casino by five this afternoon, and then still have ample time to get ready to greet our important guests at eight."

"I was hoping Giles would be our captain," Artemas commented and expressed. "He's a much better navigator than Paul is and knows the river rather well. Why can't just the two of us go? I can steer the boat as well as either Paul or Giles can?"

"Because your principal job is to cater to me and my preferences and keep me amused for several hours," Vanessa directly answered. "I need you to gossip with me, to order our mixed drinks, and to attend to my psychological and emotional needs. If I wanted Giles to do those things, I would have married him instead of you!" the egotistical woman rebuked her *first mate* quite thoroughly. "And besides, Arty, I think that Paul is a better, more skilled river navigator than either Giles or you!"

"Sorry I asked!" Artemas exclaimed and protested. "I often feel like I'm not your devoted husband at all! I'm treated more like another one of your nondescript kiss-up pompous servants!"

"My three employees only make thirty-five thousand a year each, plus free room and board in the servants' cottages. Why couldn't *you* be like Paul?" Vanessa rankled as the combative couple finally reached the base of the winding steps leading to the resident's huge foyer. "Paul's been happily married to Glenda for fifteen years now, and never has a bad word to say about anyone or anything. His temperament is divine, while yours is borderline abominable!"

"I guess you're right, as usual, Doll," Artemas hesitated and then artificially concurred. "I suppose I don't know how lucky I actually have it. I need you to constantly remind me of how privileged I really am," the husband insincerely flattered. "Maybe in the final analysis, I should be a lowly chauffeur like Giles, or an ordinary butler like Paul?"

"Next time Artemas, don't sound so sarcastic when you pretentiously reply to one of my pertinent, true observations!" the domineering wife warned. "I might make you ride around in a two-year-old *Jaguar* instead of in that brand-new black S-Class *Mercedes* I bought for you last month."

"Dave Smith has the top-of-the-line *Porsche!*" Artemas enviously insisted. "Why can't I have a *Ferrari?*"

"Because Dave Smith has a very profitable construction company business and you only have wild, worthless, ambitious fantasies, that's why," Vanessa emphatically snapped back. "And most Americans have trouble trying to keep-up with the Jones, but apparently *you*, my miserable, covetous louse of a spouse, you have fanciful ambitions of keeping up with the Smiths!"

The irritated woman had then reached the back door facing the picturesque river, and Paul dutifully and obediently held it open. As soon as Vanessa set foot outside the mansion onto the top deck step, she let out a very boisterous shriek.

"What's wrong?" Artemas instinctively shouted. "You've scared Paul and me half-to-death!"

"It's an ugly, filthy, slimy frog!" Vanessa deliriously screamed. "It's absolutely horrible! How hideous! Get that grotesque-looking pest away from me right this instant!"

Artemas and Paul stared at the turf and inspected the small harmless creature that had frightened the wits out of the still-hysterical woman of the house. Then her husband broke out into a mild laugh. "Vanessa, this poor innocent animal isn't even a frog. It's only a harmless lost horned toad."

"What's the difference!" the woman angrily countered. "It's still hideous-looking and disgusting! I told you to get that atrocious thing out of my sight, and I meant it! You're making me rapidly lose both my temper and my patience! I insist that you kill it!"

"Vanessa; frogs have longer back legs than toads do," the husband academically disclosed, "and a toad's skin is usually darker, drier and rougher than a frog's. A toad's skin is usually more scaley and more-warty than a frog's skin is, wouldn't you agree Paul?"

"Er, no comment or opinion on the matter, Sir," the family butler wisely and judiciously responded. "All I know is that frogs and toads eat a variety of insects. In a strange way, they do sort of serve a constructive purpose."

"That's exactly right, Paul," Artemas agreed. "And the creatures use their long sticky tongues to snare their unwary prey. Most frogs and toads have skin that gives-off a poison that could make an aggressive cat or dog go unconscious. I think I once read *that* salient fact in *Readers Digest*. Or was it *National Geographic?*"

"That's enough silly conversation on this rather sick subject!" Vanessa strenuously objected. "I refuse to go to any restaurant that has frog-legs on the menu. I hate the vulgar, slimy animals with a passion," the 'river diva' vehemently attested. "And their bulging eyes are most despicable when they eerily glare at you; I must say that the word 'horrific' is actually the best word to describe their ghastly appearance."

"Is that why you never like to dine at *Frog Rock Inn* over in Hammonton?" her husband realized and asked. "Because of the establishment's trade name?"

"Precisely," Vanessa readily confirmed as the frightened toad hopped into some nearby exotic shrubbery. "Frogs are a nuisance, regardless of whether you call them toads or frogs! It's that plain and simple. Now Artemas," the pampered wife commanded in a nastier tone of voice. "Escort me to the boat while Paul gets the engines warmed-up. I believe I need a couple of martinis after that very horrendous experience!"

"Vanessa, you gotta' expect seeing a frog or two around here since we live right on the riverbank," Artemas logically concluded and maintained. "They come with the territory! They're part of the natural environment, and I believe that the critters are adequately protected by state conservation laws."

"Arty, I married you strictly for romantic reasons, and all of this garrulous nonsensical talk about frogs is quite distinctly remote from sharing romance, wouldn't you agree?" the distraught wife replied with rancor evident in her voice. "Try being a little more discreet and sentimental! Start showing me more basic respect!"

"I promise to avoid the annoying topic for the remainder of the day," Artemis volleyed-back with a short wink directed at Paul, who was pretending to ignore the entire feuding exchange. "Frogs and toads will be taboo topics in today's conversations!"

The river trip from Sweetwater to *Harrah's Casino* was quite pleasurable, despite the former arguing and bickering. The banks on both sides of the *Mullica* were scenic, exhibiting beautiful homes, extensive pristine pine-barrens, tall reeds, and an occasional small business catering exclusively to river traffic. First, the yacht cruised under the Lower Bank Bridge, and several miles further east, glided underneath the newly-reconstructed Green Bank Bridge. After slowly passing by several "No Wake" zones, the ocean-worthy yacht picked-up speed where the channel widened, as the craft approached the *Garden State Parkway Bridge;* and soon the sleek boat was zipping past Chestnut Neck Marina on the right and, then pounding against small waves while moving across the familiar wide bay en route to *Harrah's Casino*.

"Arty, rub my tender shoulders," Vanessa asked while holding her third martini. "That terrible experience with that sordid toad has made my neck muscles tense, and has given me a mild headache. I require some gentle TLC!"

"All right Sweetie," the compliant husband responded, thinking about his upcoming ten thousand dollar gambling fun fest. "I'm glad it's a calm Monday morning; and I'm thrilled that we virtually have the entire river and bay all to ourselves."

"Yes," Vanessa promptly acknowledged, "because obviously Arty, on weekends every riffraff that has a rowboat or a canoe ruins it for the good people that live on the *Mullica*. Saturdays and Sundays are veritable nightmares to all of us that love this very special area," Vanessa aptly noted. "A little gentler with the fingers, please, Arty.

434

Oh, that feels so much better. I do believe that this little down river excursion is going to be a four-martini-trip."

Paul then deftly moored the forty-foot-long, dual inboard, luxury cruiser at a *Harrah's Marina* slip. Vanessa gave Artemas a check for his ten-thousand-dollar gambling allowance, which the husband foolishly elected to lose at the craps and roulette tables rather than save for a hefty down-payment on an expensive, red *Ferrari.*

After dining on an array of seafood and luscious desserts in the casino's exquisite Fanta-Sea Reef Restaurant, Vanessa returned to the casino floor, and much to her broke husband's chagrin, the demanding wife won thirty-thousand-dollars at the roulette and craps tables, while Artemas had to swallow his pride watching his 'arrogant spouse' demonstrate fantastic good fortune. At three in the afternoon, the aristocratic couple boarded their comfortable, well-appointed yacht for the hour and a half upriver Mullica cruise back to rustic Sweetwater.

"Since your total winnings came out forty thousand ahead today," Artemas began after concocting two dry martinis inside the boat's immaculate walnut-paneled cabin, "can't you give me half of today's earnings?"

"My dear extravagant loser of a husband," Vanessa scornfully sneered, "Stop acting like a silly prince about to turn back into a, pardon the expression, back into a reprehensible frog. I'd prefer your company much better. Arty. if you acted like a royal prince making me feel like a regal queen! Right now, you remind me of a repulsive horned toad! That's why I'm afraid to kiss you Arty! You might turn into a disgusting, damned human-sized frog!"

'Jennifer Smith is looking better and better every time I see her,' Artemas secretly thought. 'Maybe I can make a little time with her tonight after dinner, and get something going on the side. Vanessa is becoming an absolute witch, and she's really beginning to irritate and peeve me.'

Glenda had carefully prepared a delicious meal of prime ribs, crab-meat sauteed in butter, and mixed stir-fried vegetables. Giles and Paul poured the diners imported French champagne, and the conscientious servants then brought-out the entrees to Vanessa and Artemas, and to David and Jennifer Smith; the servants' efforts exquisitely culminating the splendid four-course dining event. The table conversation soon switched from current business contracts and proposed corporate partnerships to Vanessa's great dread of frogs.

"You know David," the haughty, rich woman cautiously began. "I'm very much afraid of frogs and toads. Ever since I was a little girl, I still remember a school field trip to the Philadelphia Zoo, and there was a repulsive snake and frog exhibit there," Vanessa recollected and shared. "I simply abhor slimy creatures like lizards, snakes, frogs and alligators. They instantly turn my stomach sour!"

"Well, I have to admit that reptiles and amphibians aren't the most glamorous-looking animals, that's for sure," David Smith added as the successful businessman sipped his third glass of delicious, sparkling champagne. "Generally speaking, those useful bug-eaters are quite innocent and will never bother you, Vanessa; that is, unless you first disturb them. Respect nature, and nature will respect you; so to speak."

"I wholeheartedly agree with David's rather perceptive remarks," Artemas contributed to the dialogue. "Frogs and snakes are really a benefit when you consider that they help keep the insect population in check." Then the self-appointed Casanova stared across the table at attractive, blonde-haired Jennifer Smith, and her radiant blue eyes seemed to verify in *his* mind that 'the doll' had been completely enamored with Artemas's overwhelming charm, and also with the suave gentleman's extremely captivating personality. Jennifer toyed with her long blonde tresses draping over her shoulders in response to her new admirer's casual eye flirting.

"I don't care what either of you men profess on the repugnant topic," Vanessa steadfastly maintained. "Frogs and snakes, and other slithery vermin, aren't worthy of our attention, or our conversation. I think we should now retire to the recreation room and listen to some soft classical music while I tell you both about my exceptional good luck at *Harrah's Casino* this afternoon. Come along Artemas. You can act as our official bartender!"

After the combination dinner and business session had ended, the Smiths finally departed the luxurious, opulent mansion on the *Mullica* just before midnight, and soon their silver *Porsche* exited the U-shaped driveway and headed southwest in the direction of Pleasant Mills Road and Hammonton.

Vanessa inspected the spacious, custom-designed kitchen and made sure that the servants had put all of the expensive china and silverware away into their appropriate cabinets and compartments. Then the wealthy dame retired to her personal, pink-decorated spa where she intended to enjoy an hour-long bubble-bath and ponder David Smith's tempting investment proposal involving the construction of forty-eight condominium units on the *Atlantic* at the southern end of Brigantine.

While Vanessa was preoccupied with pursuing her personal pleasure, Artemas strolled to the estate's walnut-paneled library, poured himself a glass of blackberry brandy, reached-up, and then out of sheer curiosity, grabbed *Encyclopedia F*. The intrigued researcher thumbed through the five hundred and sixty pages of academic articles until the playboy eventually located the heading designation "Frogs".

'I want to learn all I can about the fascinating topic,' the sensitive-but-frustrated husband thought. 'Let's see; it says here that frogs belong to the class Amphibia, and together with toads, constitute the order Salientia. Some frogs like the bullfrog can live for fifteen years. Since frogs are cold-blooded animals,' the engrossed reader evaluated, 'they often hibernate in the wintertime.'

Artemas eagerly read much more information about the nature, behavior and habits of Salientia for a full forty minutes, absorbing every minute detail that had then been exposed to his hungry mind. 'Perhaps I can use frogs to upset Vanessa for making me feel inferior to her selfish whims all the time,' the conniver secretly speculated and pondered. 'My delicate ego feels stunted, and it demands more success, and definitely more gratification than I'm currently receiving from Vanessa. The shrew doesn't realize that my hungry spirit needs continual satisfaction, too, just like hers does. I'm sick and tired of daily being crushed like a ripe grape. I think I know exactly how to achieve those beneficial things I'm seeking!'

The following morning at eleven, Vanessa had scheduled Giles to drive her to the *Hamilton Mall* over in Mays Landing so that she could peruse the more-ritzy stores to purchase jewelry and a wardrobe of formal dresses to complement the sixty ensembles she already owned. Giles had already backed the black *Lincoln* sedan into the U-shaped driveway, and as was her superstitious custom and habit, Vanessa exited the mansion via the three-car garage.

"Ahhhhh!" the wealthy woman boisterously and deliriously screamed her healthy lungs out. "Get those damned disgusting monsters out of the garage immediately!"

Artemas heard his wife's shrieking and swiftly dashed into the large garage to investigate her particular cause for alarm. A long black snake was in the process of consuming a puffed-up bullfrog head first, and only the slimy creature's legs were visible gyrating around outside the hungry reptile's chomping jaws.

Artemas quickly grabbed a nearby shovel, and then the attacker firmly held the flat-blade down against the wriggling snake's ugly neck. The master of the house firmly pressed down, quickly lifted the shovel and then repeatedly thrusted and pounded the metal garden tool against the reptile's neck and throat as hard as the attacker could, until the serpent's head was completely severed from its still-writhing body. The disoriented-but-lucky bullfrog had inadvertently been rescued. The dazed creature managed to squirm out of the dead snake's jaws, regained its senses, and then abruptly hopped out of the open garage door and into some nearby bushes.

"How horrible! How absolutely nauseous!" Vanessa hysterically ranted. "I'm so upset that I'll spend at least fifty thousand on jewelry and dresses at the mall; just to pacify my great anxiety!"

The black snake's body was still flopping about in a corner of the garage. Much to Vanessa's aggravation, Artemas once more thrust the flat-ended shovel against the wiggling form, and again wildly severed the black reptile's back. Next, the motivated spouse carefully scraped-up the dismembered head and the other bloody viper remains onto the shovel's flat surface, rushed out of the garage, paced quickly to the mooring dock, and then flung the creature's three disconnected sections into the *Mullica*.

"Here's an unexpected snack!" Artemas yelled to imaginary carnivores living in the river's depths. "Feast your eyes and then your hungry stomachs!"

"Oh Artemas!" Vanessa yelled upon her husband's return to the garage. "You're so brave! Now I know you'll always be there to protect me from encroaching danger! You're my knight in shining armor! My champion! My Sir Galahad!"

"Just remember Vanessa; that's just a fringe benefit that comes along with the total package," her money-hungry husband bragged. "I must say darling; I rather enjoyed that particular enterprise. I never imagined that killing a dangerous animal could be so thrilling! I must confess, Vanessa, that I had been overwhelmed by my sense of survival and by my need for self-preservation! The encounter actually brought out my primitive instincts! I think I now want to take you on an African safari and go after some big game animals!"

"Oh Arty, that terrible snake incident was the most dreadful graphic, raw thing I've ever witnessed in my entire life," Vanessa dramatically gasped, "and I expect *you* to do something about this sudden frog and snake invasion, right now! Call an exterminator about the epidemic infestation! Call a whole fleet of them if you have to! I need the disgusting things eliminated, immediately!"

"Vanessa, I must assure you, it was just a bizarre coincidence," Artemas calmly and deliberately answered. "And I trust that all of our remarkable confrontations with toads and amphibians, and reptiles

438

and the like have already occurred today." Then the valiant husband interrogated the chauffeur.

"Giles, Artemas said, "didn't you see the snake and the frog when you had entered the garage to get the *Lincoln.*"

"No Sir; the slimy animals were in the corner opposite the passenger side and outside of my viewing range. Then I was preoccupied raising the garage door with the remote control while backing-out, and I never again looked forward," the somewhat flustered chauffeur defensively explained.

Six hours later, Vanessa Harper had completed her intense shopping spree at the *Hamilton Mall,* and the rejuvenated woman returned to Sweetwater with a stunning diamond necklace and a half dozen designer evening gowns. The arrogant woman's obedient husband greeted her with a polite kiss on the cheek.

"Well now, Vanessa. Have you gotten over this morning's extraordinary amphibian and reptile encounter?" Artemas frivolously joked. "Actually, it even has made me a little jittery."

"You would have the audacity to remind me of that sickly, horrid ordeal!" Vanessa automatically chastised. "You ought to show a bit more compassion for the terrified woman who incidentally adds a bright luster to your rather boring, mundane existence."

Giles carefully carried the six new designer evening gowns up to the master bedroom, and gently placed the boxes on the automatic electric king-size bed just as Vanessa had instructed. Five minutes later, the wealthy woman strode inside her spacious walk-in closet and let-out a nerve-piercing yell that would have frightened King Arthur's Sir Galahad. Her husband, the chauffeur, the butler, and the maid all immediately responded to the startling summons.

"Look Artemas! There are two hideous frogs defiantly sitting in my closet! Do something about this horrendous situation right this minute!" the highly distressed wife ordered.

"Well. I'll be damned!" her unsympathetic husband exclaimed in sheer astonishment. "The frogs are either looking for a place to hibernate for the winter, or they're getting ready to croak, no pun intended. I'll take care of your little dilemma right away!"

Vanessa insisted that her spouse contact an exterminator at once to rid the premises of the newly-developed pestilence, but the former pharmacist was hesitant to honor her verbal mandate.

"Honey, exterminators only concentrate their specialized efforts eliminating certain annoying insects like nasty termites, roaches, and ants," Artemas stated as if he were a renowned authority on the subject. "And quite frankly, Dear; frogs and snakes are protected by strict environmental laws. If we kill off any frog or snake families, every conservationist in South Jersey will smear *your* good name in every imaginable newspaper and tabloid. You don't desire to be interviewed by prying *Action News'* reporters on the dumb subject of frogs, now do you?"

"There must be something we can do instead of being constant victims to this rash of horrendous, unwanted animal intrusions!" Vanessa stubbornly insisted. "I hereby demand that something tangible be done right away to alleviate the aggravating menace, environmentalists or no damned lousy environmentalists!"

While Giles and Paul trapped the new-found amphibian trespassers in small cardboard boxes, and then dropped the frogs into a lidded trash barrel, Artemas related to his spouse a story an acquaintance had once shared with him at a local diner.

The friend happened to be a driving school instructor and was stopped in front of the Hammonton Post Office while teaching a woman from India how to park alongside the curb. The female driving student detected a black cat crossing the street and spontaneously informed the instructor that the animal was about to viciously attack the car. A minute later, the aforementioned feline leaped onto the automobile's hood and began hissing, screeching, and clawing-away at the terrified Indian lady sitting petrified on the opposite side of the windshield.

"What does *that* crazy tale have to do with me?" Vanessa challenged as Giles and Paul silently left the master bedroom with a waste container holding captured frogs' that were destined to be deposited in lidded containers in the trash bin placed outside the river mansion.

"Well, I have an interesting theory about certain animal behavior," Artemas offered. "Animals, no matter whether they're cats, dogs or frogs, can instinctively sense when a human is afraid of them. They exploit that negative emotion by going into an attack mode as the cat had done with the frightened Indian lady, and as the frogs are presently doing with you," Artemas surmised and non-persuasively lectured. "There really isn't anything complex or elaborate about it," the husband matter-of-factly continued his commentary. "Vanessa; if you would just discipline yourself to not be intimidated by common frogs and toads, then *they* will sense your indifference and finally the creatures will decide to leave you alone. I really suspect that your anxiety is part of the central problem!"

"Well, for the record, I place little credence in your shallow pin-headed frog theory," Vanessa candidly admonished her husband-tormentor, "and furthermore, poor-advice Artemas; I'm hereby personally appointing *you* to somehow solve this very disturbing frog phenomenon."

"Will there be anything else you might need, Madam?" the loyal maid inquired as she entered the bedroom.

"No Glenda, you may leave now," Vanessa stated in bland tone of voice. "I believe that we've seen a sufficient number of frogs these last several days to last an entire decade. That will be all Glenda."

After the maidservant had left the spacious bedroom, Vanessa seriously addressed her happy-go-lucky, frivolous, totally annoying husband. "Artemas, why can't we have a good marriage like Paul and Glenda do? They seem so happy and pleased with their mediocre and lackluster existence. And although *we* have so many luxuries and financial assets to enjoy," the addled wife observed and declared while showing melancholy hazy eyes, "it all goes to prove that money by itself cannot guarantee genuine happiness!"

"The servants just pretend to be compatible when in our presence," Artemas cynically replied, "but I've heard an occasional dispute erupting from the first servant's cottage. Yes Vanessa; Giles has told me in confidence that he has listened to more than a few arguments emanating from inside the adjacent, *mosquito*-infested cottage down near the river. That's why we need frogs around, Dear; to defend this lovely setting from destructive river bugs and bothersome gnats," the prevaricating husband emphasized. "They're very useful in keeping the insect population at a minimum."

"I suppose you're finally right about something," Vanessa commended in a rare utterance of marital praise. "Perhaps I'm overreacting a bit about the overall dilemma, and should show more tolerance for nature's lower-level creatures. Every time I'm prompted to scream from encountering a cruel frog sighting," the wife acceded and compromised, "I'll simply remember the moral of *that* interesting story about the unfortunate lady from India and the overly-aggressive black cat."

Two days passed without any significant Salientia incidents, and life on the *Mullica* returned to routine, aristocratic doldrums for the former Vanessa Harper. The area socialite did an exclusive interview with an *Atlantic City Press* reporter on her renowned philanthropic activities, and the former debutante attended a humanitarian-oriented conference in Cape May on the need for the mentoring of orphans by economically successful adults, with Vanessa receiving a plaque award for providing handsome donations to alleviate terrible family living conditions that often existed in area foster homes. Although the themes were contrary to Vanessa's contempt for the lower classes futilely trapped in the highly competitive socio-economic-debt maze, the Sweetwater woman actively participated in the widely publicized venue to project her public image as being a concerned, generous, responsible, patriotic American citizen.

Returning from Cape May, Giles steered the black *Lincoln* sedan into the U-shaped asphalt driveway. Vanessa triumphantly entered the house's huge laundry room via the three-car garage. But then four lazy, stationary frogs sitting on the brown tile floor adjacent to the washing machine greeted *her* arrival with several loud croaks. The petrified woman let out a wild scream that almost burst her lungs, and the sudden shriek virtually ruptured Artemas and Gile's delicate eardrums.

"Get those scummy, filthy creatures out of my house right this instant!" Vanessa imperatively bawled. "We've never had this type of lousy amphibian problem before just recently. It's an epidemic; an evil deplorable, despicable epidemic, I say!" Remove the pests immediately!" the local socialite bellowed.

"Vanessa, I do believe you have a distinct phobia about helpless toads and frogs," Artemas theorized and professed. "Now try not to get too out-of-control and bent out of shape about a very ordinary insignificant bugaboo!"

"Phobia? Bugaboo?" Artemas's perturbed wife loudly replied in amazement and bewilderment. "You have the unmitigated audacity to casually label this vile epidemic, this cruel plague we're suffering through, 'a phobia' and a mere 'bugaboo'!"

"Yes Doll; an irrational fear, that's precisely what you're feeling and exhibiting an unnecessary reaction toward," her unsympathetic husband calmly declared. "There's nothing at all to be afraid of. Quite frankly, I think you should seek professional assistance. Perhaps a highly skilled psychiatrist or relaxologist?"

"I refuse to honor your ridiculous suggestion under any and all circumstances!" Vanessa retorted with a trace of belligerence evident in her quavering voice. "This inexplicable outbreak of frog sightings is quite inordinate to say the least Artemas; and you're now advising *me* that there's nothing peculiar about this weird series of events! I'm beginning to question your credibility, and also my own perception of reality," the rattled wife stammered with trembling lips and shaking hands. "I'll agree to see a competent medical doctor, but certainly not any quacky shrink or sociologist!"

"Giles and I will take care of these innocent croakers," Artemas, the domestic problem solver softly indicated. "Your harrowing shouting was so loud that you probably scared the living daylights out of our nearest neighbors on the other side of the river."

The next two days only intensified Vanessa's distraught mental condition. The spoiled lady had ventured-down to the basement to place an old dress into the last of three trunks of "disposable junk clothes" she had intended to donate to the *Salvation Army,* when the rich dame accidentally interrupted the presence of eight frolicking frogs apparently having a noisy family conclave. And then, when the nervous woman entered the pink marble-walled spa-room to take her nightly bubble bath, much to her dismay, Vanessa discovered sixteen frogs merrily hopping around inside the usually immaculate deep pink tub. The rich dame emitted another ear-piercing shriek upon making her most recent disturbing find.

"Artemas, I think I'm going stark-raving mad!" the distressed female boomed. "My heart's pounding so rapidly I think it's going to rupture its aorta. Please take me to Aruba or Hawaii, or Bermuda to escape this terrible perpetual nightmare!"

"Honey, I hate to mention it, but there're probably scads of frogs in Aruba, in Hawaii, and in Bermuda, too! I'm certainly no authority on the habitats of animals," Artemas pessimistically qualified, "but I'm willing to wager that both frogs and toads very capably adapt and live just about anywhere, except probably in the Arctic and Antarctic regions of the world."

"Paul, please set-up an appointment to see Dr. Carver's office over in Egg Harbor," Vanessa instructed her normally-reticent butler. "He's got an excellent reputation. and can prescribe some effective medication to soothe my jangled nerves. so that I don't go into cardiac arrest the next time I see an errant toad or frog. Dr. Carver will be able to allay my anxiety, or remediate my depression; or whatever it is that I'm experiencing and fearing!"

"Madam, would you like me to sterilize the tub and then run your hot water?" Glenda asked. "You need to unwind."

"Just wash and clean the tub good with disinfectant," the wealthy woman in the pink velvet robe directed. "I think I'll skip my regular bubble-bath tonight. And also, Giles," the still-disturbed woman imperatively continued her instructions, "I want *you* to collect and remove these sixteen hateful specimens, drive down the river to Port Republic, and toss the vile demons in the water. Hopefully, the salt water downstream will kill them instantly."

"Yes, Madam," the family chauffeur politely answered. "Consider your request finished and done!"

Paul had arranged an appointment for Vanessa Harper to visit Dr. Jonah Carver, who then prescribed a strong medication and a vial of sleeping pills to enhance the woman's frayed coping mechanisms. When the unsettled mistress finally returned to the twenty-four-room Sweetwater mansion accompanied by Giles, the now-apprehensive Vanessa Walsh thought that she had heard a low, dismal sound originating from within the living room's stone fireplace.

"Giles, please open the hearth doors," the prominent socialite requested. "A wayward bird must've fallen down the chimney and might be trapped and fluttering its wings inside. That happened once before, I believe, about three years ago."

The accommodating chauffeur gently opened the tempered glass doors, and the servant immediately detected thirty-two stationary frogs listlessly sitting inside. Giles frantically slammed the dark-tinted-glass doors shut. Vanessa let-out a fierce, ear-piercing scream in spite of the strong medication she had swallowed and nursed-down with a bottle of cold mountain spring water on the ten-mile drive back from an Egg Harbor City pharmacy.

Artemas hastily zipped into the expansive living room to aid and comfort his extremely emotionally, disheveled wife. "Don't you see Vanessa," the husband declared as he held his distressed spouse tightly in his arms. "There's some sort of weird mathematical progression going on here. First, there was one frog in the garage with the black snake. Then there were two more in the closet, four in the laundry room, and eight…"

"In the cellar," Giles chimed-in. "Sixteen interrupted your bubble-bath Madam, and thirty-two are presently located in the fireplace. That means that…"

"Sixty-four will haunt us somewhere in this house the next time!" Artemas predicted. "But where?"

"Oh Artemas; take me away from all of this wicked mental cruelty!" Vanessa insisted. "I desperately need to salvage my waning sanity! Maybe a change of environment will accomplish that end!"

"Giles and Paul, get an old laundry bag, open the fireplace doors, and collect all thirty-two nuisances," Artemas ordered like a Parris Island marine drill instructor. "Then, take the bothersome pests to Chestnut Neck Marina near the Parkway Bridge on the bay. Throw the frogs into the saltwater twelve miles far away from Sweetwater," the man-of-the-house stepped-up to the plate and austerely assigned.

"Oh Artemas; please hold me tight again!" Vanessa worriedly requested. "How could those creepy, obnoxious amphibians have gotten into the fireplace?"

"I believe that there must be a hole or crack in the masonry, or perhaps a brick might've come loose somewhere at ground level," her husband hypothesized and suggested. "It's late Friday. and quite hard to get a qualified builder over to evaluate anything. I'll call Jim Bishop early Monday morning to come over and give the entire chimney a thorough inspection. He's without a doubt the best brick and masonry contractor in the area," Artemas concluded and recommended. "I'm sure he'll have a valid explanation for this crazy frog-infestation anomaly. If the chimney requires repair, he's the best around to do it."

"I'll not be able to rest until this horrifying, grotesque riddle is completely solved!" the affected wife whimpered as her egocentric nature temporarily melted-away, and her suppressed sincerity finally surfaced from her subconscious. "It's more than a riddle, Arty; it's an absolute diabolical mystery!" his worried spouse intensely sobbed between long deep breaths.

On Saturday morning, Artemas and Giles piloted the fabulous yacht downriver to Port Republic to buy fresh fish, crabs, clams, and oysters from local fishermen and trappers. The carefree pair returned from their combined boating and seafood expedition at five p.m. Vanessa had been distracted from her frog misadventures and had spent the entire afternoon entertaining three distinguished members of her socially prominent weekly "Bridge Club", and for some inexplicable reason, the popular socialite had used the appropriate occasion to vent her mounting fear of, and her hostility for, Salientia, to her captive audience.

Later that afternoon, Artemas and Giles entered the mansion from the property's river dock. "How was your cruise downriver, Arty?" Vanessa inquired. "You were gone the whole day. I really missed your valued company."

"Terrific!" Artemas related, stretching his arms above his head to crack several vertebrae near his neck. "I piloted the boat on the way down, and Giles handled the chore on the way back. We finally landed at Chestnut Neck Marina, and then bought six beautiful sea bass from several ocean anglers," the itinerant husband announced. "And the oysters, clams, and crabs we were able to buy came from licensed bay and river trappers, guys that have legal floating claims' markers for their registered river cages over beyond Port Republic."

That night, the sometimes-incompatible couple enjoyed a regal candlelight dinner featuring freshly broiled sea bass, crab-meat sauteed in butter, and delectable river oysters and bay clams.

Vanessa's table articulations seemed quite poised and confident to Artemas, who was also feeling quite relaxed.

"Here's a special toast to recognize Glenda and Paul!" Vanessa proposed loud enough for the loyal servants to hear in the mansion's kitchen. "Without a doubt, they're definitely the two finest cooks on the entire river!"

"And let's not leave venerable Giles out of being officially recognized and saluted!" her talkative husband added while raising the sparkling champagne contained inside his tall stemmed glass. "He's without a rival, and indeed, the finest and most reliable chauffeur and yacht river pilot in all of South Jersey!"

That evening Vanessa enjoyed her standard one-hour bubble bath and appeared unruffled from the nightmarish frog duress the afflicted woman had been enduring the entire week. Artemas constantly reminded his neurotic spouse that she should faithfully take the strong medication that Dr. Carver had prescribed, along with the two powerful sleeping pills.

"Where are the medicine and the sleeping pills?" the now-sedate wife asked. "Are you sure I need the medicine? Honestly, I feel doped-up and giddy already."

"You most certainly do!" Artemas curtly encouraged. "There're too many fears lurking in your subconscious mind, and only a good night's sleep will enable you to avert having a terrible nightmare."

"Tell me, when did you obtain your psychiatry diploma?" the wife sarcastically asked. "And where are my damned pills?" Vanessa wanted to know. "I just checked, and they aren't in the medicine chest above my vanity!" she clamored.

"I think that we had put them inside the kitchen cabinet that's next to the refrigerator," Artemas recollected and mentioned. "We placed them there because *you* always swallow-down your tablets with a large cold glass of water. There's a plastic container of fresh cold water inside the 'fridge. Do you want me to pour it for you?"

"No thanks, Arty," Vanessa defiantly replied, not wishing to be dependent on her husband in any way. "Haven't you noticed? I'm a big girl and perfectly capable of performing that perfunctory pill-taking task all by myself!" the very proud woman orally responded.

Several minutes later, the fastidious wife exited the master bedroom, glanced-up, solemnly admired the majestic crystal chandelier in the hallway, and then descended the magnificent spiral staircase to the mansion's ground floor. Vanessa confidently walked across the multi-colored Italian tile slates that graced the kitchen

446

floor, her pink slippers rhythmically flopping against the hard surface. The woman of the mansion was both calm and collected.

Upon reaching the wooden-facade refrigerator, the river aristocrat paused for a second, garnering sufficient courage to overcome her latent frog phobia. 'First, I'll swallow the two nerve pills, and next the two sleeping pills. Then, I'll get a glass from the cabinet and open the refrigerator door to grab the plastic pitcher of cold water.'

The paranoid woman was able to conquer her initial fear, gulped-down the four aforementioned, prescribed medicine tablets, and then deliberately reached for the refrigerator's metal handle. The thirsty female thought she had heard a muffled thump that ten seconds later was followed by a discernible dull thud. The anxious resident hesitated, took a very deep breath, assessed her curiosity, and upon opening the door, let-out a savage scream in reaction to what her shocked eyes suddenly beheld.

Vanessa quickly slammed the wood-paneled door shut, felt very faint, and then her knees buckled. The wife slumped to the floor, panic-stricken, and soon became unconscious.

"Wake-up Honey, snap out of it!" Artemas implored as the rescuer rapidly splashed cold water onto Vanessa's face.

"Ahhh!" the wife ranted and shouted. "Those heinous despicable frogs! How did they ever get into the refrigerator?"

"I don't know! I just don't know!" her husband answered in reiteration. "Giles and Paul; gather-up the frogs in an old burlap potato sack and have them removed from this haunted house this very second. You're going to be okay, Vanessa," Artemas reassured his almost-psychotic wife. "Everything's going to be all right!" the husband promised as he knelt-down and held and caressed his female critic in his strong arms.

"Help me to my feet!" Vanessa commanded. "And get me a glass of fresh cold water from the faucet to wash-down those four pills I had just taken."

Glenda poured a tall glass of cold water, plopped five ice-cubes inside, and then gently handed it to her exasperated employer. Vanessa ravenously drank half the liquid down. Soon, Giles and Paul returned from their comprehensive frog ejection assignment. After a few minutes of somber conversation, the three servants departed to their respective river cottages, and Artemas then gingerly escorted Vanessa up to the master bedroom.

"Here Vanessa," the husband recommended, "please take another sleeping pill. I guarantee you'll be out like a light bulb in five minutes. You've been through a lot of suffering tonight, Vanessa,"

Artemas courteously added, "and the only satisfactory remedy that I can think of is a good sound sleep."

"I've been thinking. Perhaps you *are* worthy of that new red *Ferrari* after all!" Vanessa decided and remarked. "Maybe by next summer, Arty, I'll be inclined to buy *us* one! A new adult toy, that's what that dream machine of yours will be!"

"Anything you say, my dear," the receptive husband readily agreed. "Now here's the rest of that glass of water you had neglected to finish downstairs. You'll definitely feel much better in the morning. Just take this one additional sleeping pill, and your vexing hardships will evaporate into thin air!"

The stressed-out wife removed her pink velvet robe, placed the additional sleeping pill into her moist mouth, and quickly chugged-down the remainder of the glass of cold water. In ten minutes, the eccentric woman's eyelids were shut with her troubled mind drifting-off into placid Dreamville. Midnight soon passed, and during the early hours, Vanessa heard an owl hooting, and soon reluctantly opened her eyes. Mrs. Walsh slowly glanced at the red digital read-out on her alarm clock. 'Four a.m.,' she drowsily thought. "It's too early to rise and drink some coffee."

Suddenly, the all-too-wary lady felt uncomfortable, because her husband's left arm was now heavily weighing around her waist. She reached down to touch Artemas's hand, but was literally shocked to feel a dank, slimy appendage. Vanessa reached over to the bedside lamp table, turned on the light, flipped her body over, and then let-out an ear-shattering shriek. The unsettled woman immediately comprehended that she had been sleeping in *her* bed with a terribly loathsome human-size frog.

Almost traumatized, Vanessa quickly leaped-out of the bed and fled into the wide hallway to swiftly descend the spiral staircase steps. The afflicted woman flicked-on the crystal chandelier lights, and then her throat and larynx emitted another delirious spine-shivering scream. A second human-size frog was standing stationary at the foot of the stairs with its arms symbolically open and extended, beckoning the disoriented lady to descend the steps to engage in a disgusting embrace.

A gunshot was heard, and before Vanessa's senses could interpret exactly what was transpiring, the giant frog at the base of the spiral staircase fell upon the black marble floor. Paul suddenly appeared at the foot of the stairs and he yelled, "Get down!"

A second shot from the butler's revolver whizzed by the stooping woman and entered the chest of the first human-size frog, which instantly lost its balance and tumbled-down the steep steps, roughly colliding into Vanessa near the bottom. The jolting impact made the two forms roll down the additional seven steps, until three hapless bodies were lying prone in the massive mansion's foyer.

* * * * * * * * * * * *

Vanessa Harper finally awoke from her deep coma two days later inside an *Atlantic City Medical Center* private room. Paul was sitting in a blue leather chair beside the totally confused woman. The faithful butler gathered his wits, and very meticulously divulged to his ordinarily demanding employer the incredible explanation for the most peculiar chain of events that had hospitalized Artemas Walsh's worldly and vociferous wife.

"What happened Paul?" Vanessa asked in a weak and almost submissive voice. "I trust you to tell me. Where am I?"

"You're resting in the A-Wing Ward of the *Atlantic City Medical Center*, Pomona Division," Paul replied in a stilted-but-subdued, benign voice. "You had fallen down the steps after I had shot your husband in the chest!" the butler candidly informed.

"What!" Vanessa exclaimed in a loud disbelieving tone of voice that got the nurses' attention sitting at the main work desk down the corridor. "You'd better tell me the whole story right now! And it better be believable! Are you a murderer? Is my husband dead?"

"No, only wounded!" the grim-faced manservant answered.

"Well then Mr. Paul; you'd better start this strange story at the very beginning!" the shocked woman patient impatiently insisted.

Paul explained that *he* had become very jealous because his wife Glenda was having an affair with Giles. The amorous chauffeur and greedy Artemas had been conspiring against Vanessa to eventually drive her insane, and then have her institutionalized at nearby Ancora State Hospital. The unscrupulous pair had been cruelly and deliberately exploiting Artemas's wife's fear of frogs in a concerted effort to transform her obvious paranoia into an abnormal state of emotional instability. The two plotting men wearing frog costumes had schemed-up a dastardly plan designed to shock Vanessa into an undeniably psychotic state of mind.

Upon learning about the sinister plot that had been deviously planned and organized against her, lying quite still in her hospital bed, Vanessa gathered-up sufficient strength to ask her favorite servant to provide additional details to the complex, perplexing puzzle that her now-feeble mind envisioned. "Paul, I solemnly pledge that you'll be rightfully rewarded for your allegiance to your most grateful employer!" the emotionally disturbed lady disclosed.

"Thank you, Madam," Paul graciously replied with a broad smile. "You've always been good to me."

"I had never suspected Paul that your wife Glenda and Giles were having an affair," Vanessa related and then negatively shook her head in disapproval. "Perhaps in the future, I ought to be more observant of my servants!" she weakly jested. "Now, I can fully understand your motive for shooting Giles. But why did you also shoot Artemas?"

Paul lowered his eyes, inhaled a deep breath, and then said, "Because Madam; *he* was also having an affair with my promiscuous wife, the sex-crazed whore! I felt intense animosity toward both Artemas and Giles these past six months. But now, I must confess Mrs. Walsh, that I'm completely overwhelmed with guilt."

"Paul, I had suspected that Artemas was having an illicit affair with Jennifer Smith, but I had never zeroed-in on with whom else he might have been with," Vanessa grieved and disclosed. "That no good two-faced philanderer. Yes Paul, I had thought of Jennifer Smith, but then she had called me at home the other day. She asked me to take her into my confidence," Vanessa explained to Paul. "Then Jen described how she resented Artemas attempting to flirt with her, and that the amorous cad had made improper advances and promises to my friend over the phone when David Smith was coincidentally out in Los Angeles on business. That's when I became suspicious of the frog scenario and of my husband's possible role as a heartless accomplice in it. Because I couldn't trust Artemis, I publicly used the name Vanessa Harper, and not Vanessa Walsh."

"Then you weren't fooled by the imaginative frog conspiracy?" the butler incredulously asked. "I must confess Madam, I had been a part of the conspiracy until I realized that I couldn't betray you, or indeed, until I couldn't withhold my anger about the sinful, lustful love triangle between Glenda, your husband and Giles any longer."

"I see it all clearly now," Vanessa replied and understood in a more docile tone of voice. "Giles was the second frog at the base of the stairs. All along, I tried being logical about the odd frog invasion. I knew quite well that it was impossible for frogs to suddenly appear in some queer mathematical order from one to two; from two to four; from four to eight; from eight to sixteen in the bathtub, and then doubling to thirty-two in the fireplace, not to mention possibly sixty-four of the unsightly creatures inside the refrigerator. Paul; how many grotesque frogs were actually inhabiting my wood-paneled refrigerator when I had opened it?"

"Er Madam, your estimation is on-the-money and quite accurate! I believe there were sixty-four of the elusive amphibians stuffed inside. At least, that was the original plan!" Paul guiltily elaborated. "Artemas evilly schemed-up the creative frog scare-tactic after *you* had been fazed and unnerved by that first small *toad* you had initially confronted."

Vanessa then explained to Paul that she had become additionally wary from the unbelievable skein of frog misadventures, and consequently, the suspicious wife was put on defense when a gossipy woman from Port Republic had called her on the phone and personally thanked Mrs. Walsh for Artemas generously buying her son's living frog collection for a hundred dollars. "Were the same frogs being used over and over again during the bizarre hoax?" Vanessa curiously asked her loyal butler.

"Yes Madam!" Paul shyly verified and then cleared his throat. "If you, Madam had to stay in a mental hospital from all of your ungodly duress, the plan was for Artemas to seize control of your finances after you would be declared mentally incompetent by psychiatrist friends of your husband. But on the other hand, if you were to die from extreme fright," the humble butler proceeded with his incredible explanation, "the game plan was then to cash-in on the one-million-dollar insurance policy Artemas had quite secretly taken-out on you!"

"Only a mere one million! That's an absolute disgrace!" Vanessa balked from her hospital bed. "Why that conniving scoundrel of a husband! Why that's peanuts out there in the real world!"

"It might be chickenfeed to you, Madam, but at the time, to the three of *us,* it seemed like a real bonanza!" Paul clarified his answer.

"What have the township police said about the shooting incidents?" the concerned socialite inquired. "The newspapers will have a picnic with this totally bizarre story! My good reputation will be ruined!"

"Well, they're releasing as little information as possible to the press to avoid a juicy gossip scandal," the all-too-honest butler reported and confided. "The authorities are chomping at the bit to interview you to obtain the rest of the vital facts, which of course, I had conveniently pretended to be unable to supply. They've documented my partial story that I had told them, pending *your* testimony in court. I simply related to the Mullica Township investigators that I had committed both shootings," Paul disclosed to his bedridden employee. "I trust Madam that you'll support my version. There are two detectives standing in the hallway making sure that I don't escape from this room. You should know I still have a guilty conscience about severely wounding Mr. Walsh and Giles."

"Would you want me to fire Glenda?" Vanessa asked.

"Yes Madam. I cannot live with or trust a wife that's addicted to promiscuity and that habitually practices wanton infidelity," Paul sadly explained. "Love is not sex, and that's the long and short of the matter. I still have my scruples about *that* distinction!"

"Very well then, consider Glenda no longer in my employ," the hospital patient supportively declared. "And furthermore, Paul; how would you like to own a nice red *Ferrari* as *my* heartfelt reward for saving my life and also for salvaging my mind?"

"That sounds marvelous Madam; quite marvelous!" the butler amply agreed. "I promise to put the sporty vehicle to good use!"

"Well, that's quite wonderful!" the semi-reclined hospital patient acknowledged and smiled. "I'll arrange its purchase as soon as I'm released from this cheap, tawdry hospital bed! How pedestrian this uncomfortable bed is! It doesn't even have a massage or a heat button; let alone silk sheets and satin pillowcases!"

The local township police accepted Vanessa's affidavit, and later, also her deposition as being truthful documentations, and two months thereafter, Paul was free to drive his spanking-new red *Ferrari* all over the East Coast on his weekly day off. Glenda and Giles were both abruptly and simultaneously fired, and Vanessa Walsh, disgusted with her surname, immediately filed for divorce from Artemas. Everything was copacetic in the *Mullica River* mansion until a Monday in early October. Paul was rudely awakened by an intense shout coming from Vanessa's master bedroom.

The servant speedily left his small riverbank cottage and swiftly rushed into the brick mansion accompanied by Jacques, the new butler, and *his* wife Hilda, the new maid. The three employees promptly dashed-up the spiral staircase, flicked on the light that illuminated the overhead crystal chandelier, opened the master bedroom door, and were appalled at what their doubting eyes perceived. A hundred and twenty-eight ugly, slimy, sickening frogs were sitting stationary on Vanessa's magnificent bed, croaking and creepily staring at the horrified mistress, who apparently was too terrified to move even a muscle while sitting-up as still as a statue, and violently quivering with her eyes bulging-out of their sockets.

"Texas High Noon"

The three and a half-hour Continental Airlines flight from Philadelphia, Pennsylvania to Houston, Texas was quite smooth and comfortable, and then the secondary briefer air excursion via the same airlines from Houston down to Brownsville was quite pleasurable, despite the general fatigue experienced by the four traveling FBI companions. The entourage was en route to an October week-long federal crime prevention conference to occur at the South Padre Island Convention Centre Hall.

After renting a white *Ford Expedition* at the diminutive Brownsville Texas Airport, the four government agents were soon motoring the twenty-five miles north along the Gulf Coast from Brownsville up to semitropical South Padre Island. Non-business "shop conversation" merrily ensued and abundantly flourished between the combination driver/team captain, Inspector Joe Giralo and his trio of very capable law enforcement subordinates, FBI Agents Salvatore Velardi, Arthur Orsi, and Dan Blachford. The latter pair had been occupying the deluxe SUV's spacious back seat.

"It's a good thing I had the foresight to reserve this large *Ford Expedition* from AVIS a week ago," Inspector Giralo loudly opined. "It was the only SUV available from the AVIS lot back at the tiny Brownsville Airport."

"Check-out all of the oil refineries and oil rig repair facilities along this Texas coastal highway," Agent Sal Velardi commented. "I never imagined that those ocean-worthy oil rigs were so gigantic up close. I suppose that everything requires some maintenance and repair; even these huge, monstrous oil drilling platforms."

"This highway is low-lying and must flood-out occasionally," Agent Art Orsi observed and stated from the rear. "Say, Guys; just listen to the names of some of these parallel streets in South Padre: Retama, Mesquite, Acapulco, Campeche, and Esperanza. Sounds like a definite Mexican influence to me. And according to this map I'm holding," Agent Orsi expounded, "the island has three major north south highways: Laguna Boulevard on the bay side; Padre Boulevard up the island center, and then Gulf Boulevard situated closest to the alluring Gulf of Mexico."

"I'm more interested in good restaurants serving delectable food dishes than in commonplace street names," Agent Dan Blachford contributed to the casual, ongoing, four-way dialogue. "According to this informative local cuisine guide, Ted's Restaurant at 5717 Padre

Boulevard has tremendous breakfast meals. And then there's other unique eateries such as Louie's Backyard located on the bay, the Sea Ranch Restaurant to be found at the southern tip of the island, Scampi's, Amberjacks, and Blackbeards towards the middle of the island, and if we really want some simply scrumptious Italian food," Blachford characteristically embellished, "we can always cross over the causeway to Port Isabel and gobble-down some tasty pasta at either Gabriella's or Marcello's! I gotta' also add that this terrific eatery selection must also include the attractive restaurants inside the Pearl, the accommodating hotel where we'll be staying when not attending the various Convention Hall conference sessions."

"And if we want to go casual or do supper less expensive," Sal Velardi chimed-in while recollecting his beforehand studying of various local dining establishments, "there's always the infamous Dirty Al's Marina next to the Sea Ranch, and if we really get desperate, there're several area Whataburgers, Texas's big answer to Burger King and McDonald's."

"We're lucky it's October, and not March or April down here in South Padre," Inspector Joe Giralo nonchalantly related after his right front tire made hard contact with a massive highway pothole. "Those hormone-driven college kids invade the island from all over the country. South Padre is sort of the new Fort Lauderdale during the annual rites of spring 'Animal House' celebrations."

For the next several miles, the three weary passengers politely listened to the driver's reminiscences of what circumstances were like when the Inspector had first joined the FBI ranks back in 1974. "In the beginning, computer data bases were few and far in between," venerable Inspector Joe Giralo vaguely recalled. "And hand-held communication devices and cell phones were mere science fiction stuff that appeared in fantasy magazines, and also on the original episodes of *Star Trek*. The first computers were a form of calculators, designed for computing or determining sums in addition, products in multiplication, and quotients in arithmetical division. And because of certain space-age fantastic advances in computer software technology, and in Internet communications, criminals are much easier to track-down nowadays, especially with most of the cowardly fools stupidly bragging about and inadvertently confessing their gross felonies on Internet social media. Google, Yahoo, Facebook and Twitter have made it much easier to find and arrest dangerous criminals."

"I really think it's now siesta time!" Agent Velardi complained.

"I know I'm boring you fellas', so I'll intentionally bore you three amateur sleuths even more by speaking briefly about my wife, who incidentally this morning accidentally backed into several pylons in the town chain store's parking lot. A thousand-dollar expense, and that's a very mild, conservative estimate. Thank goodness I have a low three-hundred-dollar insurance deductible applicable on the two-family vehicles."

"Women; you can't live with them and you can't live without them!" Agent Art Orsi philosophized and blandly articulated. "I had spoken with my wife via cell phone when we were waiting in a lounge area for our connection flight from Houston down here to Brownsville. Well anyway," Orsi gladly pontificated, "Carol was out walking our white miniature poodle Murray down at Hammonton Lake Park when seven or eight angry Canadian geese suddenly popped out of a fern growth clump, and the large creatures began wildly squawking, thrashing, and quarreling incessantly."

"Maybe there was a snapper turtle trying to attack one of them," Inspector Giralo conjectured and commented as the garrulous driver unsuccessfully swerved and rumbled over another huge, obscured pothole. "Everything's immense down here in Texas, including the oil rig platforms, the hamburgers, and the potholes!" the man behind the steering wheel jested in defense of his suspect driving skills.

"Well anyway," Art Orsi continued with his fairly intriguing narrative. "Carol picked-up Murray and high-tailed it to her car. It's bad enough when you're assaulted by muggers and thugs, but apparently now, my wife has to worry about squads of belligerent Canadian geese and invisible antagonistic snapper turtles that might wildly vex her daily routines!"

"Well, yesterday my wife received an e-mail from a cousin who lives in Baltimore," Dan Blachford declared, thinking that he also had a decent spouse story to disclose. "The e-mail stated that her cousin, along with her cousin's family, were vacationing in London when they were maliciously robbed, mugged, and stranded without any I.D.s, or important passport credentials, which were also heisted. My better half was about to wire the cousin two thousand dollars to cover air transportation for five back to the States. It's a good thing she had called and told me about the strange situation, which I immediately recognized as a vile Internet e-mail scam. Boss," Agent Dan Blachford specifically addressed impatient Inspector Giralo, "This felonious international wiring of money has generated an intolerable number of crafty cons and hoaxes upon the unassuming public, and many honest, trustworthy, and unwary victims are being harmfully swindled out of millions of greenbacks daily!"

"That was quite some story involving your good-hearted wife almost being taken advantage of!" Agent Sal Velardi indicated to Blachford from the front passenger-side bucket seat. "But believe me. I have a pretty exceptional recent wife story that totally reeks with government bureaucracy!"

"Don't keep us in suspense!" Art Orsi implored, fighting-off the onslaught of drowsiness. "Tell us an even more spectacular wife tale before we violently rumble over another gargantuan pothole!"

"Yesterday my beloved spouse had to go for jury duty in Atlantic City," Agent Velardi prefaced his spectacular tale. "As you know, in Atlantic County criminal cases are held in tranquil Mays Landing, and civil cases are tried at the Atlantic City Courthouse, which unfortunately borders rather dangerous, high-crime neighborhoods."

"That's precisely right!" Agent Orsi quickly interrupted and acknowledged. "A juror could easily get mugged walking the five perilous blocks from the assigned high-rise parking lot on New York Avenue to the courthouse on North Carolina Avenue. And the human environment is definitely not the best! I've done *that* precarious trek on two occasions myself!"

"Regardless of the obvious, Art!" a somewhat perturbed Agent Velardi forcefully short-circuited his impetuous colleague. "My wife is sitting there in the crowded Atlantic City Courthouse jury selection room among a group of one hundred and twenty prospective jurors. Thirty names are called, and twenty-three candidates are eventually rejected for various reasons after they had been generally interviewed by the assigned judge. Finally, after the next twelve random lottery names had been completed, the eighth jurist was finally accepted, much to the relief of my wife and the remaining prospective citizens that were sitting obediently inside the congested courtroom!"

"So, tell me Sal, what's so extraordinary about *that* basic situation!" Dan Blachford challenged Velardi. "Your beautiful wife was an exemplary, courageous, typical citizen for braving a hazardous five-block trek through an unsavory neighborhood only to be inconvenienced for around four hours of bureaucracy to then learn that she won't again be called for jury duty for the next three years! What's so dramatically unusual about that?"

"You're absolutely right about the bureaucracy aspect of the judicial process!" Agent Sal Velardi promptly agreed. "We do indeed live in a litigious-oriented culture! But then my faithful wife had to silently sit there with full knowledge that she would be rejected for jury duty because of various real conflict factors. First of all, the lawsuit involved an auto' accident at the intersection of the White Horse Pike and Pleasant Mills Road at the all-too-familiar Hammonton Lake highway bend. My wife's older brother had been involved in a similar auto' collision at that exact same place several years ago. That related fact would automatically disqualify her!"

"Okay, is that all?" Inspector Joe Giralo gruffly replied, showing only mild empathy for his agent's rather mediocre revelation. "If the accident being reviewed happened in the town of Hammonton, the courthouse clerk should've realized that no one from Hammonton, including your wife, should ever be eligible for placement on the jury and then inconveniently called to Atlantic City in the first place; only to eventually be dismissed by the judge!"

"Well, no Boss! I mean, there is plenty more to this weird scenario," Velardi proceeded with narrating his graphic description. "The aggressive plaintiff doing the suing was once a lackluster student of *our* daughter, who as you know, teaches fifth grade at the Hammonton Elementary School, so obviously, *that* additional element represents a new conflict of interest right there. And also," Agent Velardi enthusiastically elaborated, "the father of the attorney representing the plaintiff had once been a lawyer on my wife's father's behalf. Is that new development a totally bizarre coincidence or what? Kathy would've been disqualified for *that* conflicting relationship, too!"

"Is there anything else of relevance to report?" a somewhat irritated Joe Giralo requested fathoming, solely out of general courtesy. "Remember Gentlemen, to genuinely clarify and balance matters, we're all indispensable parts of the widespread town, county, state, and ever-burgeoning federal bureaucracies. Quite confidentially, Men. I find being a meager minuscule cog inside the enormous government wheel rather repugnant and personally insulting! That's how I interpret my IRS reality!"

"Listen Chief," Agent Sal Velardi intoned, much to the chagrin and dismay of his three fully exhausted traveling companions, "Yes Sir; there is another salient dynamic to be introduced here. The defendant accused of slamming her vehicle into the rear of the plaintiff's automobile happened to be a party-animal distant cousin of my wife, so *that* very relevant familial connection certainly would've also disqualified *her* from participating on the jury panel. And to top it all off," Velardi firmly finished, "the defendant's lawyer had been attending several graduate night classes with my wife at Rowan University, over in Glassboro!"

"Thanks for keeping me slightly awake for the past five minutes!" Dan Blachford grumpily expressed to Sal Velardi. "Say, that must have been Port Isabel we just motored through. And that steep elevation in the road ahead must be the Queen Isabella Causeway! Holy cow! According to the map on my handheld computer, we're going to cruise a mile and a half over the Laguna Madre directly into the heart of South Padre Island. With the bright lamp lights on this bridge, just look at how gorgeous the placid blue-green bay water appears down there!"

"And did you catch the docked shrimp fishing fleet on the right, and the Pirate Cove Fishing Pier on the left; not to mention the impressive Port Isabel lighthouse," the suddenly energized driver orally conveyed to his rejuvenated audience. "This small port, along with nearby South Padre Island, is often referred to as the Shrimp Capital of the United States."

"I can't wait to sink my teeth into a juicy well-done steak, let's say at Blackbeard's Restaurant, or at Louie's Backyard Buffet!" Agent Art Orsi directly suggested.

"I'll even settle for a giant two-handed meal at the nearest Whataburger!" Agent Sal Velardi concluded and shared. "I think it takes two hands to handle a Whopper, but it must require four appendages to lift a colossal-sized Whataburger from one of the joint's tables up to your mouth!"

* * * * * * * * * * * *

The FBI agents' two fifth floor rooms at the Pearl Hotel were quite cheerful in appearance. and were more than adequate to accommodate their basic needs. The initial three days were rather humdrum and nondescript in nature. with all four convention participants attending various educational seminars and associated conferences on such difficult topics as Border Security, Internet Pornography Interstate Illegal Trafficking, Internet Illicit Gambling and Vice, and finally, A Comprehensive Analysis of Across State Lines' Drugs, along with discussions of Kidnapping and Prostitution Violations. Early on Thursday morning, the four-member team was enjoying a peaceful, eclectic breakfast at Ted's Restaurant on north Padre Island Boulevard.

"I hope we have some free time to visit the Sea Turtle Rescue Aquarium tanks sometime later this week," Agent Dan Blachford proposed. "At the site, they have giant sea turtles being expertly rehabilitated after losing an essential appendage to hungry sea

458

predators, along with a variety of other injured turtles from other species that are also being salvaged from the Gulf."

"And I have a strong desire to spend a half-day at the famous Schlitterbahn Beach Waterpark, that's really not too far from the Pearl," Agent Salvatore Velardi chipped-in and vociferated. "It's widely promoted as one of the major water-slide parks in the whole United States. I know from watching a deluge of local TV advertisements that the venue's a tremendous hit with the Spring Break college crowd!"

"We do have all Sunday to ourselves after the federal convention closes," Inspector Giralo answered. "And since it's our special free time allotted all to ourselves, I won't even have to be granted permission from Chief Riley's office back in DC. So, allow me to allay your innermost fears, Sal. I won't prevent you from exploring your addictive need for juvenile splish-splash entertainment! But while you're frantically cavorting-around at the waterpark and hanging-out with twelve and fourteen-year-old acne-faced kids, I'll either be snoozing in my hotel room or exploring the Turtle Rescue Clinic with Dan and Arty."

After paying their group bill and giving the gorgeous Mexican waitress a well-deserved ten-dollar tip, the four G-men, now possessing satisfied appetites, re-entered the white *Expedition* SUV and immediately headed south in the direction of the modern-architecture designed Convention Hall Centre. A rare moment of silence was swiftly interrupted by Agent Arthur Orsi, who was presently acquiring some significant New Jersey information from the classified FBI closed-circuit data base.

"Boss, here's some extremely disturbing news from the Garden State," astonished Agent Orsi began verbally sharing his recently obtained knowledge. "An adult female was casually out jogging in Somerville up in North Jersey when both her and her car mysteriously disappeared. There's been no trace of Mrs. Carolyn Simmons since Tuesday afternoon. And in a second peculiar incident, Ms. Martha Zimmerman and her SUV are missing from the Harrah's Parking garage in Atlantic City."

"These women are very vulnerable to being attacked, especially when walking or exercising alone while on some sort of daily or weekly schedule cycle," Inspector Giralo evaluated and emphasized from his standard stationary position behind the steering wheel. "Most women can easily be overpowered by a weapon-toting male villain out there, the nefarious weasel taking his bitter enmity toward the world out on an unsuspecting female target!"

"And Boss, there's much more to this ugly developing trend," Agent Orsi excitedly replied. "Up in the Middletown, New Jersey Shopping Center, a woman by the name of Jennifer Carlson was apparently kidnapped, and she's disappeared along with her late model black Mercedes. And also, up in the Mt. Calvary Cemetery in Asbury Park, a victim named Denise Jenkins is missing-in-action since Wednesday, along with her 2010 Ford Thunderbird. There's a definite heinous pattern being demonstrated here!"

"Perhaps Riley will send us back early to the Garden State to help solve this recent sinister crime wave," Inspector Giralo speculated and related. "As I've mentioned, these women don't realize it, but they're vulnerable, especially with the economy being depressed like it is, and with a lack of prosperity existing virtually everywhere. And I gotta' admit," the Inspector generalized. "Women jogging or speed-walking alone in cemeteries are really susceptible to being mugged, raped, robbed, or kidnapped. The lurking culprits know that the ladies are usually wearing earphones while doing their daily graveyard strolls, and that they're also carrying their keys to their locked cars with them. When the woman approaches her parked vehicle, then...."

"Then the dastardly criminal comes-out from behind a huge stone mausoleum and viciously attacks the gullible female before she even knows what's been occurring. She's knocked-out, probably with a blackjack or wooden pistol handle, and then mercilessly dragged inside her compromised vehicle. Of course, the barbaric robber has already gotten her easily accessible car keys. He can now pilfer the vehicle, unload it for cash at a Mafia chop-shop, sell the woman into sex slavery, and then quite obviously, easily steal all of her pocketbook money," Agent Blachford stated.

"Oh no Inspector! Here's the latest in this terrible skein of devastating events!" Art Orsi exclaimed as the astute agent closely examined new FBI news flashing onto his laptop computer screen. "An unwary Waterford woman named Marilyn Passarella has disappeared from inside the Hammonton Oak Grove Cemetery at 7 a.m. Eastern Time, just last Friday morning. Again, there's no sign of her anywhere. It's as if alien space invaders have cruelly abducted the middle-aged lady, and unscrupulously purloined her red 2012 Cadillac sedan in the process."

"Great bunions!" Inspector Joe Giralo instinctively yelled. "I just bought eight burial plots in Oak Grove Cemetery last month as an investment. "And women should be extremely careful when either entering or exiting their vehicles in cemeteries; in high rise-parking garages; in shopping center and mall parking lots, and also in innocent-looking city and town scenic parks. I strongly recommend Guys that we all soon call our endangered wives and advise them to not walk, jog, or shop alone until these pernicious fiends committing the despicable atrocities have been apprehended, interrogated, and incarcerated by the appropriate authorities.”

* * * * * * * * * * * *

After enjoying solid nutritious breakfasts of bacon, eggs, and toast and coffee on that early October 2013, Saturday morning, the four visiting FBI agents sat outside on comfortable chairs on the Pearl’s balmy patio deck and predictably engaged in typical, general tourist conversation. Agent Salvatore Velardi, the possessor of a huge culinary appetite, commented on one of the hotel’s most outstanding features.

“Just look at that Palpapa Bar and Grill sitting there in the middle of that enticing outdoor swimming pool,” Velardi pointed-out. “Hotel guests simply swim over to a circular, raised, concrete seat and sit in waist-deep water around the bar. They then eat delicious grilled hamburgers and drink a variety of savory tropical cocktails, including my favorite, chilled pina coladas. It’s sort of like a nifty aquatic Whataburger, especially designed for aristocratic guests.”

“Sal, I know you’re my only man who brought along a bathing suit on this particular business/education excursion,” Inspector Giralo reminded his underling disciple. “But this evening, we’re going to feast at the hotel’s Beachside Bar and Grill, and partake of terrific stunning views of the Gulf of Mexico from inside! Expensive appetizers and desserts will be included as my treat!”

After returning to their fifth-floor rooms to prepare for the slated Saturday morning seminars, with the impending Power Point discussions concentrating on Mexican Gun Smuggling and on Modern Day Money Counterfeiting, ten minutes later, agents Blachford and Orsi knocked loudly on Inspector Giralo and Agent Velardi’s hotel room door.

“Boss, there’s been a flagrant rash of female abduction incidents over in Florida,” Art Orsi anxiously revealed. “I’ve jotted-down the pertinent details the old-fashion way; right here on my trusty notepad. Five ladies have disappeared while performing similar daily routines just like the victimized females up in Jersey. One wife vanished while in Indian Harbour’s principal shopping center; that is, according to the husband who had planned to meet her there and was in cell phone contact with his spouse just three minutes earlier. Another inexplicable disappearance was in Arcadia's Morgan Park; the third suspected kidnapping was in the Ocean Center Parking Garage in Daytona Beach; the fourth apparent felony was outside Jupiter's Driftwood Plaza Mall; and finally," exhaled an exasperated out-of-breath Agent Arthur Orsi, "the fifth comparable crime occurred in Hollywood at the tranquil Queen of Heaven Cemetery!"

"That's right, Arty!" Inspector Giralo instantly verified. "There's a Hollywood, Florida in addition to the more famous Hollywood, California. And again Fellas', these major, brazen muggings and thefts have been systematically executed in designated cemeteries, in diverse parking garages, in quiet parks, and in various crowded shopping center mall parking zones."

"And Boss," an equally charged-up Dan Blachford spoke. "I've just thought of something that might be uniquely relevant to this weird riddle. The five horrendous events in New Jersey happened in five separate communities, and the five violations in Florida also occurred in five distinct municipalities. This *number five* abduction factor might be more than just an interesting coincidence!"

"Dan might've discovered some material evidence that links these diabolical illicit acts, that are oddly transpiring in different states!" Sal Velardi hypothesized and remarked. "Here's some new information currently coming into FBI Headquarters from five affected towns and cities in sunny California."

"This whole scenario is becoming more fascinating and confounding by the second!" Joe Giralo assessed and concluded. "Hurry-up Guys with the new pertinent data being received!"

"Again, just like in the bewildering New Jersey and Florida examples, five communities have been affected in different sections of the Golden State," Velardi announced as the reader intensely studied the new-found language appearing upon his special government-issue laptop. "One targeted woman regrettably vanished while supposedly power-walking in the Davis Central Park. A second selected female vanished into thin air in Modesto's Vintage Faire Mall. And another unlucky young woman met her unexpected fate at Inglewood Park Cemetery. The fourth bull's eye victim had just exited her *Nissan Maxima* at the Garden Walk Parking Garage in Anaheim; and finally, the fifth felony misdeed can be traced to the San Francisco Bay area, Alameda County; the hostile abduction happening inside the Mt. Eden Cemetery in the formerly tranquil community of Haywood."

"Again, five towns geographically remote from each other, but all located in a separate state," Art Orsi confirmed and gasped. "This whole grotesque pattern involving the number five is developing into quite a difficult, perplexing dilemma!"

"Men, I still want the three of you to attend those monotonous seminars being conducted over at the Convention Centre," Joe Giralo imperatively instructed his loyal subordinates. "But in the meantime, I have two essential things I plan to do up here in this isolated room. First, I want to get in touch with Riley up in Washington concerning this intricate, national crime wave. Secondly, I desire doing some preliminary work on deciphering Art's new 'conundrum', which if I remember accurately, the curious term 'conundrum' being a sophisticated word frequently used by Sherlock Holmes when speaking to his rather clumsy associate in serious crime fighting, Dr. Watson!"

"Okay Chief!" Sal Velardi automatically concurred. "My brain is in a total shambles' state, trying to figure-out this enormous enigma. I'll be thinking about all of the relevant facts while pretending to be listening to a battery of bureaucratic, lackluster presentations over at the Convention Hall Centre."

"Sal, please try using your cerebrum and not your cerebellum!" humorously advised the sometimes-haughty Inspector Giralo. "We fragile humans can never achieve becoming too sagacious when being both influenced and auto-controlled by an overactive medulla oblongata!"

* * * * * * * * * * * *

Later that momentous Saturday afternoon, Agents Velardi, Orsi and Blachford arrived back from the academic FBI conferences and landed back at the aforementioned Pearl Hotel. The ambitious-but-fatigued threesome immediately proceeded directly to Inspector Giralo and Velardi's assigned room.

"Have you been communicating with Chief Riley?" Dan Blachford spontaneously wanted to ascertain.

"Yes, but first," insisted Giralo while exhibiting a prodigious, stern expression on his stellar Italian countenance, "I believe that I now have this entire female abduction crime spree somewhat figured-out. Now Men, here's the dramatic evidence along with the accompanying underlying theory I'll soon endeavor explaining to you. Here are the five first letters of the New Jersey cities and towns I've scribbled onto this sheet of paper during my initial perfunctory observations," the esteemed Inspector commenced his extraordinary verbal exposition. "Now then, you three accomplished Gumshoes. I occasionally spend some much-valued leisure time working-out certain scrambled words that appear in the *Atlantic City Press* and *The Philadelphia Inquirer* morning newspapers. I want you three detective geniuses to focus your eyes on the first letters of 'M' for Middletown, 'S' for Somerville, 'A' for Atlantic City, 'H' for Hammonton, and 'A' for Asbury Park. Let's see exactly how brilliant you three fellas' are at practicing fundamental, elementary problem solving!"

"Holy mackerel, Chief!" Sal Velardi impulsively shouted in sheer amazement. "The five letters you've just provided can be used to form the word 'Hamas'."

"Now let's cautiously scrutinize the five first letters taken from the five Florida towns and cities," Giralo directed his apostles like a veteran classroom teacher cleverly guiding his or her students. "We have the given appellations Indian Harbour, Arcadia, Daytona Beach, Jupiter, and finally Hollywood!"

"This is absolutely mind-boggling!" Art Orsi impulsively yelled. "The five letters could be easily rearranged to amazingly spell-out the word 'Jihad'!"

"Now let's carefully analyze the five California towns and cities," calmly directed the head FBI investigator. "Together, we have Davis, Inglewood, Modesto, Anaheim, and Hayward. What related word can be unscrambled from the five disarrayed nouns?"

A full thirty seconds had elapsed before Agent Dan Blachford mentally recognized and then exuberantly revealed, "Mahdi!"

"What's a Mahdi?" Sal Velardi wondered and asked.

"Well Men, an hour ago I did some comprehensive research on the esoteric subject, and I've gleaned the following applicable facts," Inspector Giralo pragmatically divulged to his now-captivated audience. "Mahdi refers to a Muslim warrior/prophet, formally named Muhammad al Mahdi. The Muslims as you might be aware," Joe Giralo confidently elucidated, "are divided into two sects that often disagree with each other: namely, the Sunni and the Shi'ites. The Shi'ites believe that the Mahdi, commonly also known as the Twelfth Imam, will exit from a sacred well that he has been staying down inside for the past seven hundred or so years, ever since the Great Crusades that had been warred between Christianity and the Muslim faith. The conflict between the Christians and the Muslims, of course, was over which religion would have dominance over Jerusalem and the Holy Lands!"

"Hey, I've heard of the Mahdi," Art Orsi equivocated. "He's a kind of Apocalyptic religious figure who is believed will successfully lead the Muslims against the West at the end of the world! His presumed ultimate supernatural power is worshiped by the Shi'ites, but the Madhi's assumed authority isn't fully accepted by the minority Sunni Muslim element!"

"Exactly true, Arty!" an impressed Inspector Giralo indulgently commended. "According to my' recent research, the Shi'ites believe that the Mahdi is being protected by Allah, while being preserved for centuries down inside that sacred well, which the crusading prophet had entered after being inspired by Heaven to do so. Now, the Iranians are Shi'ites, just like most of the Iraqis are, but their culture and their history are somewhat dissimilar from the Iraqis. The Iranians speak Farsi, and the Iraqis and the Sunni tribes speak Arabic! But unlike the Saudi Arabians, most of the Shi'ite Iranians adamantly believe that the Mahdi will lead them to victory over the Western infidels at the start of Armageddon; that decisive battle signaling the prophesied end of the world!"

Then suddenly, Sal Velardi hollered, "Wait a minute, Guys!" as new information was being transmitted into his laptop from the FBI's Washington Headquarters. Everyone stood motionless inside the illuminated room, the three G-men having their mouths agape as Inspector Giralo furiously wrote-down the newly-obtained data exclusively pertaining to the Lone Star State of Texas.

"Lubbock; South Plains Mall, Odessa; Sunset Memorial Gardens, Amarillo; Parking Garage at Rick Husband Airport, Laredo; Lake Casa Blanca International State Park, Houston; the Galleria Shopping Mall, Brownsville; Riverside Park, Harlingen; Ashland Memorial Park, and finally, Sunland Park Shopping Mall, El Paso!" reported Agent Velardi.

"Okay Men, at least we can now discard the all-too-simplified five letter words' theory!" Inspector Giralo quickly determined and communicated. "Let's look at the assorted letters and see if a plausible word can be derived and constructed. We have an 'L' for Lubbock; an 'O' for Odessa; an 'A' for Amarillo; an 'L' for Laredo; an 'H' for Houston; a 'B' for Brownsville; another 'H' for Harlingen; and an 'E' for El Paso! Now, what esoteric knowledge could you three erudite individuals extrapolate from this simplistic puzzle? The present elusive word evidently has two Ls along with two H letters!"

After a full minute's pause, Agent Orsi bellowed-out "Eureka!" in a similar manner that the Greek scientific sage Archimedes must have exclaimed the same word in Syracuse (Sicily) many years back in ancient BC history.

"Boss," Orsi ecstatically prefaced. "If you simply add a letter 'Z' to the cryptic formula, then the word 'Hezbollah' can be readily formed and identified! The scrambled word is *Hezbollah,* but with the 'Z' missing!"

"Quick Dan; research on Google how many towns in Texas have names that begin with the letter Z!" Giralo urgently commanded. "I think we've meticulously found the Rosetta Stone that'll crack open this formerly, most confounding affair!"

"Inspector, there are only two very small Texas towns that begin with the letter Z!" Dan Blachford reported. "The tinier one is Zephyr with a diminutive population of around two hundred residents; and the other remote village is Zavalla, having around a thousand or so country native inhabitants."

"Okay Men, we have little time to squander!" Joe Giralo related. "Dan, you and Art will be dispatched directly to Zephyr, while Sal and I will head a quick expedition over to Zavalla! I've already been in touch with our miraculous savant Matt Riley, and he's given his advanced okay for us to leave South Padre immediately should new essential facts surface. And Guys, they certainly have!"

"I guess this means that I won't be partaking of the tremendous water-slide park and viewing the injured Sea Turtle Clinic?" Agent Velardi pretentiously complained.

"Sal, you can wear your zany-looking three-tone bathing suit in Zavalla if you'd like!" Inspector Giralo hardily laughed. "And I'm glad you didn't embarrass us by cannonballing into the hotel pool with that hideous-looking, poorly designed swimsuit on!"

* * * * * * * * * * * *

Inspector Joseph Giralo and Agent Salvatore Velardi hitched a free ride with the Texas Ranger Highway Patrol. A fast cruiser transported them at speeds reaching 100 mph from South Padre Island down to the Brownsville Airport, their excursion leaving Agents Blachford and Orsi fully liable for returning the rented white *Ford Expedition* SUV.

Two civilian passengers had been bumped from the scheduled flight at the Brownsville Airport, and the irate, displaced couple vehemently protested to airline employees, with their vociferous, cackling objections delivered completely in vain. The non-turbulent one hour and fifteen-minute Continental flight from Brownsville to Houston went without any further turmoil for Giralo and Velardi, with *that* city having the nearest major metropolitan airport to

Zavalla, which is located approximately twenty-five miles southeast of Lufkin, population 35,000. At the ever-bustling Houston International Airport, the relentless-in-pursuit FBI men impatiently retrieved their baggage from a rotating luggage carousel, and then earnestly rented a *Ford Taurus* from AVIS.

On the several-hour high-speed ride to Zavalla, Inspector Giralo reviewed a few salient points with his conscientious understudy, whose eager mind was busy absorbing in sponge-like fashion virtually everything the FBI Chief had to say.

"Sal, according to all reliable available records," Giralo amiably introducing his standard dissertation style, "I've neglected to mention to you one essential-but-consistent fact. In each separate abduction incident, the time that the crime had been committed was exactly at *high noon* on a Friday! However, some of the information was not efficiently corroborated, and not quickly entered into our thoroughly independent computer data base; and that's why there appeared to be certain time discrepancies as to the exact days of the week the sensational kidnappings had been occurring. And Salvatore, since this last Texas 'Z' felony had a lot of letters to spell-out the clue word 'Hezbollah', I conjecture that there must be at least eight Arab or Iranian hit teams maneuvering around the Lone Star State in full operation. That's why the 'Z' ninth Texas kidnapping is probably in progress right now!"

"Why do you conclude that this ongoing craziness all is so?" Velardi asked, his mind temporarily swimming in a veritable quandary. "Wait a minute Chief! Your contention means that a number of hit-teams have been accountable for enacting the individual atrocities! I now see and fathom your logic! There must be a total of nine hit squads!"

"Precisely Sal! After studying necessary background knowledge about the Muslim religion," the speeding Inspector orated and then hesitated as he wildly rounded a highway bend, "Friday noon prayers are without a doubt the most sacred in the Islam religion. The Muslim faithful are summoned to prayer by an announcer sporting the title 'muezzin', who proudly stands high in a mosque minaret while chanting and reminding the faithful to pray to Allah from the tower!"

"I see, now," Agent Velardi understood, nodding his head. "And if no mosque minaret is in the vicinity, then the insular Muslim will turn in the direction of Mecca or Medina; both religious cities situated in Saudi-Arabia!"

"I have an imaginative assumption about exactly what's going on here," the FBI Chief intimated. "But I'll reserve my right to relay my thesis to you until after the abominable perpetrators have been arrested and summarily sent to prison. I hereby predict Sal that the next attempted kidnapping will happen at noon today at the Hanks Creek Recreational Park in somnolent Zavalla, Texas. Since we'll be arriving there after noontime, Matt Riley has intelligently alerted the Army, and they've cooperated by dispatching a very competent Delta Force Unit led by the legendary commander, my old college friend, Colonel Bob Bauers! But just in case of a judgment error," wily Inspector Joe Giralo qualified, "another Delta Force Team led by Colonel Joe DiFilippo will handle the second military assignment and coordinate efforts with Blachford and Orsi over in Zephyr, which I think is in No Man's Land somewhere in the center of this mammoth state."

Upon reaching their "Z" destination, Hanks Creek Recreational Park in Zavalla, Texas, the determined Inspector abruptly stopped his black *Ford Taurus* in a cloud of dust; his vehicle halting next to an Army jeep. The new arrivals to Zavalla were cordially greeted by gregarious Colonel Bauers.

"It was a common saying in the Old West when riding up-front in a pursuing posse going after the bad guys; you either make dust or you eat dust!" Joe Giralo jested. "It seems, Bob, that my rental car just made dust!"

"It took you guys longer-than-expected to get here," Colonel Bauers mildly reprimanded. "Anyway Joe, my men along with four Texas Rangers have, with minimal resistance, already apprehended the two suspects, a Middle East fella' with the monicker Muhammed Aarif, and *his* extremely dangerous accomplice, an imported illegal alien terrorist with the name Jamal Abdul Samad. I looked their oddball names up on the Internet, and the first guy's name means 'Praised Knowledgeable', and the second guy's appellation means 'Servant of the Eternal'. The pair of really weird name descriptions apply to two formidable vermin that have mutually declared jihad on the United States of America!"

"Just as I had shrewdly surmised!" Inspector Giralo stated in an exhilarated manner as the FBI investigator turned his sweating head, now facing an astonished and beleaguered Agent Salvatore Velardi.

"So Boss, kindly tell me more significant details. What was your secret theory to which you had confidentially alluded to me about an hour ago?" Agent Velardi both questioned and requested learning. I just gotta' know!"

"The whole enchilada all makes very rational sense now!" Joe Giralo maintained, speaking specifically very loud for both Colonel

Bauers and *his* subordinate to hear. "The two apprehended evil, pathetic Arabs certainly have Sunni names. This vital fact means that by using the terminology 'Hamas', 'Jihad' and 'Madhi', those totally deplorable, desperate *Sunni* idiots have futilely tried to cover their tracks, making it furtively look like bellicose *Shi'ite* Muslims had been responsible for the plethora of terrible crime abductions that have been brutally terrorizing innocent and unassuming American women! What diabolical scoundrels!"

"The Love Tree"

Walter Steward had been an academically-oriented student at Edgewood Regional High School, Tansboro, New Jersey. Walter never was insolent or rebellious to adult authority, and his teachers praised the young man's very evident dedication to his studies. Steward made the "all A's" Honor Roll every semester since the start of his sophomore year, was elected president of the *National Honor Society* at Edgewood High, and graduated from that South Jersey educational institution in 1999.

After receiving his Edgewood diploma, the industrious scholar attended the *College of New Jersey* in Trenton, and the young scholar had one more year of preparation to successfully attain a Bachelor of Arts degree in communications. Everyone that ever knew Walter believed he had the potential to become an acclaimed journalist, but young Steward's true aspiration was to take the art of "mundane journalism" a plateau higher and author creative novellas, novelettes, and novels. 'First, I must find my writing voice and writing style so that I can distinguish myself from the rest of the competition, and then I'll ambitiously pursue a rewarding literary career,' the dreamer with a passion for writing secretly thought.

All through three years of college at the prestigious Trenton, New Jersey campus, the shy South Jersey young man dated Cindy Tyler, an attractive high school acquaintance that had also attended Edgewood Regional. The two lovebirds saw plenty of each other during the summer months, where each labored at menial jobs to help their struggling parents pay for expensive "college extras". Cindy worked the cash register at a popular local *WaWa* convenience store, and Walter was promoted to assistant manager at a downtown Hammonton hardware store that had not yet been eliminated from doing business by the town's *Wal-Mart*.

"One more year of demanding college courses, and we'll finally be thrust into the adult world," Walter told Cindy as 'the avid dreamer' drove his favorite female on a late evening June date seven miles west to Atco to view a popular feature film at the area's most frequented multiplex cinema. "One more year and we can escape the curse of middle-class mediocrity and monotonous employment drudgery. I can't wait to earn my college sheepskin and get a high-paying job in the real world."

"Yes Walt. Then we can have real professional careers that pay decent *real* salaries," Cindy predicted in her typical optimistic, upbeat mood. "I mean, I just make two dollars an hour more than minimum wage," the pretty brunette complained to her beau. "$9.15 an hour. And *you* only make a dollar an hour more than I earn, and you're supposed to be the assistant manager of a thriving hardware business. And you'd make about the same at *Wal-Mart,* at *McDonald's,* or at *Burger King.* What a lousy bummer!"

"I honestly believe the future will be much better and brighter for both of us," Walter hopefully expressed. "I meant to say, Cindy, that *our* future together will be better and brighter with lots of opportunities as soon as we obtain our diplomas and show the world what we can do. There's a lot more I can achieve in journalism, or in the literary world, than what I'm accomplishing now selling paint, hammers, screwdrivers, brooms, rakes, wrenches, and shovels at Charlie's Hardware on Bellevue Avenue in very ordinary, metropolitan downtown Hammonton, that's for sure."

"Walter, there's something I feel I have to tell you," Cindy communicated in a more serious tone of voice, speaking just as her steady date was pulling his drab gray '92 *Mazda Protégé* into the Atco Fourteen Multiplex Theater's enormous asphalt parking lot at the congested junction of Route 30 and Route 73.

"No Cindy, we've discussed the matter at least a hundred times. We can't get married until we both graduate and accumulate a little nest egg," Walter spontaneously joked, shrugging his shoulders to further emphasize his main point. "Is that the plan which you wanted me to do? Propose to you tonight?" the aspiring writer facetiously asked. "Quite frankly, Cindy. I'd like to do just that right this minute, but honestly now; we're simply not ready yet for matrimony; that is, of course; I'm speaking from strictly a financial point of view."

"No, silly; just drive safely to a parking space and keep both hands on the wheel," the girlfriend suggested and mildly admonished. "I realize that patience is a virtue. Soon, you'll be able to junk this gray '92 *Mazda* for a brand-new *Acura, Lexus,* or *Infiniti.* I'll even settle for a *Nissan Altima.* But Walt, I want you to know that I have great faith and confidence in your potential! "

"What did you really want to tell me besides the fact that you value certain automobile status symbols?" Walter Steward curiously asked his very special girl. "That it's wrong for us being too impetuous about starting a family, and also that 'haste makes waste'? I suspect that you must be a devout disciple of Poor Richard and Ben Franklin!"

"Oh, nothing especially urgent right now," Cindy reluctantly answered. "We'll talk about it when the time is right. I don't want to spoil tonight's double feature fun."

Walter found a suitable parking space, and then glanced at *his* cherished girl loyally sitting next to him, suddenly noticing a large red mark on Cindy's left arm. "Where did you get that nasty bruise?"

"Oh, I accidentally banged my arm yesterday when I was rushing around the deli's meat display case to quickly get to the cash register counter," Cindy nervously explained. "And I guess the collision was more damaging than I had originally thought. I almost broke my arm, just so a regular *WaWa* customer could get cancer after buying a carton of cigarettes and five losing lottery tickets."

"All the more reason to escape out of our nowhere jobs and get our college diplomas, our wonderful tickets out of mass society drudgery," Walter logically concluded and stated as the positive-thinking boyfriend shut-off the gray automobile's engine. "Then the sky's the limit for us, Cindy. You can work with your mind and not have to worry about getting banged-up flitting around a stupid convenience store serving caffeine and nicotine addicts, and sugar-rush junkies price-inflated products that maliciously clog-up their cardio-vascular systems. In fact, Doll, with a little luck, you might someday wind-up owning a whole chain of *WaWa* franchises!"

Cindy Tyler rendered a brief smile that superficially camouflaged the deep emotional distress that had been troubling her mind and spirit. The attractive girl's cinema escort sensed that something was definitely wrong, but for the sake of harmony, Walter decided not to belabor the unknown specific topic of discussion if Cindy was not ready to share her soul about it that evening, and honestly divulge to young Mr. Steward exactly what was destabilizing her emotions. The temporarily reticent pair exited the ancient gray *Mazda Protege* and ambled through the huge parking lot to get in line and purchase their movie tickets.

After work the following day, Walter called his favorite female on the phone. Cindy sounded very jittery, and her concerned boyfriend detected an element of despondency in her vague and evasive replies. The young man's cognizance of his girlfriend's present uncharacteristic mental condition soon changed from general concern to basic worry.

"Are you sure everything's all right?" the intelligent soon-to-be college senior asked from his bedroom telephone. "I sense that something major is really aggravating you. We've always been truthful with one another! That's what a good relationship is all about, and it's called *trust,* Cindy. Would you like to talk about it?"

"Walt, I feel that we should stop seeing each other and possibly begin dating other people for a while," Cindy Tyler surprisingly proposed. "That's what I've been considering lately, especially the other night over at the Atco movies."

"Cindy, your idea is so absurd! So crazy!" Walter shockingly answered. "You've been my only love since we were acne-faced Edgewood students. I absolutely adore you! I don't want to go out with anyone else! And it's my gut reaction that you don't actually mean what you're saying. Please stop being so anxious and state directly what's bugging you," Walter loudly insisted. "After all, we're both honors communications' majors and ought to know how to understand one another."

"That's exactly what I mean," the sobbing blonde-haired girl sadly replied. "You've never dated any other girls besides me, so how do you know I'm the one you wish to spend the rest of your life with? As they say in novels and in the movies, variety is the spice of life."

"Don't be ridiculous!" Walter protested and mildly reprimanded. "Why are you saying these weird things to me now? What's really annoying you? Cindy, this is not-at-all like you! Your logic is, how should I say, well, it's very obtuse. I guess that the nomenclature *nebulous* would be the best word to describe the odd gibberish you're telling me."

"Walt, I don't want to see you until we're back in Trenton, strolling together on the old familiar college campus," Cindy Tyler very emphatically stated. "We're becoming much too serious about getting engaged, and the whole thing is making me extremely nervous. Even my parents are worried! Perhaps we aren't ready to make *that* big move, yet."

"I just can't believe that what you're saying you sincerely feel and believe in your heart," the former prom queen's faithful and studious four-year companion challenged. "Has another guy I don't know about recently entered the picture? Level with me and please stop being so evasive and skittish! I can handle truth Cindy, once I comprehend what it is!"

"Let's consider this blunt phone conversation a minor lovers' quarrel," the extremely upset girl insisted. "More of a lovers' disagreement than a lovers' spat! Please don't call me again until after we get back to the college campus," the soon-to-be senior sorority girl insisted. "Walter; right now I need to clear some thick, dense cobwebs from my mind so that I can think more clearly."

Then after making the rather strange statement, the desk phone in the young woman's bedroom was very deliberately and forcefully placed into its cradle. "Cindy! Cindy! Is there some secret fraternity guy you've met on campus! Is it some handsome Casanova that magically stepped into the convenience store and swept you away? Cindy! Cindy! What's going on here?" Click.

On Tuesday, July 2, 2002, the perplexed, jilted lover drove his faded gray 1992 *Mazda Protégé* to Charlie's Hardware on Bellevue Avenue and parked his weather-worn vehicle in the employees' sector of the back lot, conveniently situated directly behind the all-too-familiar store. While at work, the assistant manager could not smoothly concentrate on performing even his most routine daily duties. The normally dependable summer employee made several clerical mistakes tabulating sales on the cash register tape, prepared three separate customers the wrong shades of house paint, and then in the back-room coffee lounge, usually "calm-and-collected" Walter Strward very erratically communicated with fellow employees, his strange language patterns showing a distant mind that was preoccupied with distractive matters other than the commonplace hardware store shop talk.

Seeking some semblance of emotional security, and also reacting to a need to connect with his inner self, that afternoon the disturbed young man visited his favorite place of asylum, a special requiem from the hectic and confusing crazy South Jersey world. Walter drove his gray 92 *Mazda Protégé* off of *Route 561* down Hall Street through the village of Winslow, entered a dirt road that paralleled the busy *Atlantic City Expressway,* halted his shabby vehicle behind a hedgerow, and then after exiting his old reliable automobile, the befuddled young man entered a familiar wooded area of the New Jersey Pine Barrens.

'At last; sanctuary from boisterous demanding retail customers, from belligerent bosses, and from the general chaotic American society,' Walter contemplated. 'Now my mind can clearly focus on my relationship with Cindy and attempt to figure-out what weird mystery is gnawing away at her soul. She and I would always come here to picnic and neck, and this remote place has special meaning to me,' the sentimental-but-jealous lover thought, and then meditated. 'Now I finally have time to ponder the course of recent events.'

Walter paced further into the woods and followed a narrow sandy trail deep into the interior, his deliberate footsteps entering a pristine, natural environment which consisted mostly of tall pine and deciduous trees, along with an occasional clump of dense briar bushes. A hundred feet inside the dense woods was a clearing, and situated in its center was a massive, majestic oak tree having a gargantuan, gnarled trunk. The fascinating object was what Cindy and her beau had affectionately nicknamed "The Love Tree," and whenever Walter felt he needed to escape the rigors and pressures of human civilization, the young man visited the very special spot to regain peace of mind. The magnificent oak was by far the largest tree Walter had ever seen, and its stately height, its thick bark, and its incredibly dense girth suggested that it was indeed one of the oldest trees to be found anywhere in New Jersey.

'I wonder what's really wrong with Cindy?' Walt sighed as the melancholy college student tried dealing with his troubling, disconsolate mood. 'Is there another guy in her life? Does she really believe we're getting too serious? Does she really want to date other college guys as she's said? Is she afraid of marriage and adult responsibility? Has she contracted an incurable disease? Is she really speaking from her heart?' The highly upset young man considered all of those possibilities as he respectfully touched "The Love Tree", and slowly felt its irregular coarse bark.

The saddened lover glanced to his left and his sad eyes perceived the initials W.S. + C.T. The four letters had been carved inside a heart, and *that* particular nostalgic sight brought a brief smile to the young man's lips. 'It took me half a day to etch those eye-high letters and form the surrounding heart with a sharp penknife blade,' Walter fondly recollected. 'Cindy adores this marvelous tree just like I adore her; and she also treasures this rather juvenile artistic heart as much as I do. What could be behind this strange shift in her attitude toward me? It goes a lot deeper than a simple change in mood,' Walter reflected and assessed. 'It's definitely an ugly shift in her usually predictable behavior! And *that's* precisely what's bothering me! I can't comprehend why I've been temporarily exiled from Cindy's life until we go back to college in September. Do I have leprosy, or what? There must be some feasible explanation to account for my girl's erratic conduct, but what the heck is it? It's all so damned inexplicable!'

After staring at the lovers' initials engraved into the huge tree's bark, Walter had a sudden impulse to climb the mammoth oak. His immediate desire was to sit on a high sturdy limb and curiously watch the heavy *4th of July* traffic heading-down to the Jersey shore on the bustling *Atlantic City Expressway,* which was only three-hundred-feet away from the mighty Love Tree. 'I have to think this entire scenario out,' a confused Walter Steward considered as the local Winslow resident carefully ascended the twisted, knotty base of the ancient-but-stately deciduous. 'Right now, I don't have a clue as to why Cindy is acting the way she has been. Oh well; I suppose I'll soon be able to engage in a little mental reverie.'

After clambering a dozen-feet up the right side of the immense oak tree, the climber's left foot made contact with a dry decayed limb that was about to snap; and instantly, the young adventurer realized that he had to rotate his ascension to the opposite side of the Love Tree in order to avoid a swift plummet caused by his body weight. 'Only two limbs higher on this side and I'll be able to perch my hindquarters on that strong-looking branch up there,' Walter keenly imagined. 'I would've had to eventually maneuver around to this side anyway, since I'll now be facing the eastbound shore traffic heading to Atlantic City, Ocean City, Avalon, Stone Harbor, Wildwood and Cape May,' the sentimental forest visitor determined.

When the panting, sweating climber finally reached the desired limb, Walter swung his tired body around, and gently plopped his buttocks upon the designated 'thick limb'. Steward now had an excellent, clear view of the congested eastbound *Expressway* lanes, which brought a certain sorrow to his spirit, making the young fellow recall riding the highway with his cute sweetheart down to beaches, bars, casinos and boardwalks, all located at the ever-popular Jersey shore. But unfortunately, the distraught young man's present woeful, emotional condition offered disconsolate Walter Steward very little mental consolation or satisfaction.

Looking up above and marveling at the tree's unique bark pattern, Walter soon made a startling discovery. A second more ancient set of initials had been carved into the giant oak tree, and when the observer stood erect to engage in further examination, amazingly, the newly discovered set of initials happened to incredibly be W.S. + C.T., which ironically were also situated inside a carved heart.

'This whole oak tree experience is really a tremendously peculiar coincidence,' Steward thought and evaluated. 'The same initials inside a heart about twenty feet higher than the ones I had carved. I never saw *these letters* before, because I had never attempted climbing this tree, of course, since Cindy and I always laid our blanket in the sand and sat and picnicked on the giant oak's other side. This whole love scenario is all getting quite bizarre and mysterious,' the accomplished tree explorer decided. 'The date below the initials reads July 4, 02. Now I remember that I had inscribed *our* initials on July 4, 00. This entire queer coincidence is totally bizarre. and logically impossible!'

Out of mounting curiosity, Walter Steward had an inspiration to clamber up to an even higher elevation upon the extraordinary and impressive "Love Tree". 'It's a good thing tomorrow is Wednesday, my day off!' Walter reckoned, acknowledging his general fatigue. 'And Thursday's a national holiday, but I'm in no mood to be patriotic this July 4th. At least I'll have two full days off from monotonous work tedium, so I should be able to again get my mind and my act together. I gotta' watch-out though; some of these higher limbs are rather treacherous. A fall from this treacherous height could be fatal!'

Now very exhausted, the stubborn on-a-mission climber finally managed to ascend another twenty feet up into the colossal oak. Walter turned his body and gracefully parked his rear end on a seemingly sturdy, rigid limb. Because of less foliage, Steward could now easily observe the heavy shore-bound 'bumper-to-bumper' traffic whizzing by on the *Expressway.*

As Walter's eyes casually searched the branches above, his alert pupils noticed a most stunning and phenomenal sight. Three feet above the young fellow's head were the all-too-familiar initials W.S. + C.T. again carved inside a heart.

The astounded trespasser felt dizzy, as a fresh supply of blood intensely rushed-up from his heart to his neck and brain. Steward precariously stood on the thick limb and held on tightly to another solid oak tree appendage in order to achieve a better scrutiny of the third set of initials, which had been coincidentally carved inside Cupid's famous symbol. Steward then anxiously scraped-away some accumulated algae discoloration from the bark, and in amazement, his eyes examined the astonishing similar date that had been inscribed: 'July 4, 1802.'

"Oh my God!" Walter panted as his lungs suddenly gasped for more oxygen. 'Could the second set of initials have been *July 4, 1902*? I gotta' examine some old public records and do some vital research on this totally perplexing riddle. I won't rest until I find-out the identities of the other two W.S.'s and C.T.'s that were carved into the giant oak in consecutive centuries!' Steward thought, with his rejuvenated heart rapidly thumping inside his chest.

As Walter sweated profusely and breathed heavily atop the rigid limb, Cindy Tyler's rejected boyfriend suddenly became frightened, and Steward's body movements instantly froze. A red-tailed hawk swooped by the branch on which the depressed lover was standing, flew across the clearing, and then skillfully landed inside another tall oak tree. Squealing along with frantic animal crying was heard, and

478

finally, the petrified observer standing erect upon the tall "Love Tree" limb fully comprehended what was graphically occurring. A targeted squirrel had been swiftly and viciously attacked and killed by the voracious red-tailed predator that happened to be hungry and flying in pursuit of a delicious forest meal.

'I'd better get-down from this high perch as soon as I can!' Steward neurotically realized. 'That ferocious hawk could've taken my eyes out, and could've punctured my temples with its sharp talons. That dangerous bird could've easily killed me standing at this height. I'm definitely out of my familiar environment and am rather vulnerable invading *his* territorial domain.'

The alarmed young man took another wary glance at the preoccupied hawk pecking-away into the soft abdomen of the unfortunate forest squirrel, inhaled five deep breaths, and next slowly and methodically descended the awesome "Love Tree".

After finally reaching good sound terra firma, the jilted lover cautiously ambled in the direction of his gray vehicle, which had been parked next to the summer-green hedgerow that incidentally separated the forest from the *Expressway*. The still-petrified young fellow eventually gathered-up sufficient courage, and then eagerly sprinted the last hundred feet to the safety of his archaic automobile, frantically opened the driver's side door, roughly hopped inside the vehicle, violently slammed the door shut, and then sincerely prayed and thanked heaven that he had escaped imminent hawk danger, and was grateful that he was truly still alive.

On Wednesday, July 3rd Walter Steward woke-up early, and instead of waiting to eat a breakfast prepared by his devoted mother, the hardware assistant manager drove his gray *Mazda* over to the rustic Red Barn Restaurant on *Route 206* to indulge in a private meal of pancakes, sausage and eggs, and while there, to further meditate about his failing love life.

"Hi Walter," Evelyn (the Red Barn proprietor) greeted her occasional patron. "Where's Cindy? She's always with you," the owner innocently inquired." Is your girlfriend sick?"

"Oh, my significant other has gotta' work today over at the *Route 30* WaWa convenience store," Walter all-too-truthfully answered. "Today's Wednesday, and lucky for me, I have the day off from working at Charlie's."

"How come you're up and around so early on a day that ya' don't have to work?" the inquisitive lady asked. "Ya' got a two-day vacation from retail misery, don't ya'?"

"I'm goin' into town to do some research for a term paper I want to write next semester," Walter creatively fibbed. "The county library is open today, and since tomorrow's the *Fourth of July,*" the breakfast customer imagined and creatively stated, "I'll have to get all the information I need today. I'm doin' a required paper for next semester's sociology course on people that lived a hundred and two hundred years ago in this pinelands area, and in the challenging assignment, I'll have to compare occupations and lifestyles of South Jersey residents through the course of the last two centuries; that is, right up until the present."

"Oh, I see," Evelyn said, sounding quite impressed. "You know Walter, when Margaret Mead was a young woman, she had lived in Hammonton over on Fairview Avenue, and the world-famous anthropologist had done ground-breaking research on early Italian immigrants that worked on local farms, mostly owned by British settlers coming-down to South Jersey from New England. But I gotta' admit, your assigned study does sound pretty interesting, too. The Hammonton Historical Society Museum is closed today, and also tomorrow, because of the big Independence Day holiday. Maybe you'll have better luck goin' to the *Hammonton Gazette,* or to the *Hammonton News* rather than to the county library to acquire the historical data that you need!"

"Hey Mrs. Hamilton; that's a really terrific idea!" Walter exclaimed. "I'm glad I came here for breakfast. I do know the editor of the *Gazette.* He's a friend of my dad's. And while you have your pad out, I'll have bacon, two eggs over light, coffee, orange juice and toast. Excuse my apparent gluttony, but I'm pretty hungry this morning!"

* * * * * * * * * * * *

At nine-thirty, Walter thanked Evelyn Hamilton for her constructive suggestion to retrieve the information Steward was in quest of at the *Hammonton Gazette* offices, so after paying his breakfast bill and leaving a rather generous tip for a starving college student, the very thankful patron departed the landmark Red Barn Restaurant, re-entered his gray *Mazda Protége,* and drove south on State Highway 206 directly toward "metropolitan downtown Hammonton". The motivated college student parked his car on Horton Street, quickly exited the lackluster sedan, and then rapidly sauntered to the Bellevue Avenue entrance to one of the small town's two competing newspapers. Walter Steward rang the doorbell, and

480

the *Gazette's* Editor-in-Chief descended the twenty steep steps to answer the visitor's inquiry.

"Hi; is Gabe Donio the publisher in?" Steward asked Gina Rullo, the newspaper's Editor-in-Chief. "I'd like to speak with him. Mr. Donio knows my dad pretty well, if that carries any weight. They're in the local Lions Club together."

"No; Gabe's out of town, down the shore at the Atlantic City Press Club speaking to area reporters about the rewards and travails of newspaper journalism, and he won't be back in town until after four," the courteous editor informed. "May I help you?"

"Why yes," the nervous Winslow Village resident replied. "My name's Walter Steward, and I'm a senior at the *College of New Jersey up in Trenton.* I'd like to gather some background information about people that lived in this area from 1800 to around 1910. I'm doing some preliminary research for a prospective term paper I might write next semester."

"Gabe has often mentioned your father to me," Gina Rullo recalled and orally conveyed. "I've seen you around town. Don't you work in the hardware store down the street?"

"Yes; I'm the assistant manager at Charlie's Hardware," Walter proudly responded and verified. "So far, that's my biggest accomplishment in life, but I hope to achieve greater ones in my future career."

"Yes, Walter. I've seen you many times working in the store," the Editor-in-Chief recalled and declared. "I believe on a Saturday back in early May you sold me two gallons of mint-colored paint for my new apartment above Varga's Pharmacy."

After Walter verified Gina Rullo's accurate sighting recollection, the genial journalist invited Steward upstairs to the *Gazette* offices, and related where and how the newspaper's unexpected guest could obtain the biographical information he had claimed he sought. "You'll find old copies of the *Hammonton News* on microfiche listed in chronological order in *that* file cabinet drawer," the Editor-in-Chief politely indicated. "The issues date back to the late 1880s. Do you know how to use the reading machine for the microfiche?"

"Yes, I had learned that in high school, and I've often used this type of machine for my college research papers," the vernal visitor confidrd and related. "I'm thinking about pursuing a career in journalism. I think it's nice that the town's other newspaper has shared these old files with the *Gazette.*"

"That's great! You say that you have aspirations of becoming a reporter, Walter!" Gina Rullo praised with a broad smile. "And yes, the town's newspapers do cooperate with one another, even though we're competing for subscriptions and advertisements. Jim Calder, our cub reporter, is in the room right next door, so if you need anything, just give him a hoot," the Editor-in-Chief advised. "I'll tell him you're here. Is there anything else you'll need to know?"

"Where can I find data on area people that lived before 1880?" the ambitious future journalist asked.

"In the bottom drawer to your right you'll find old newspaper articles from the *Philadelphia Inquirer* and from its older parent newspaper; both sources list obituaries and also important news articles of bygone days, presented in an organized, chronological time sequence," cooperative Gina Rullo voluntarily shared with the newspaper's inquisitive visitor.

"Thanks, plenty," the college student said. "And if I require any more help, I'll ask Jim over in the next room."

The young man began his intensive search immediately after the very helpful Editor-in-Chief excused herself to answer a phone call about an automobile accident that had just occurred at the intersection of Central Avenue and Third Street, in front of the local police department.

Steward ignored the newspaper data for the years 1910-2002, and with a bit of luck, managed to locate the *Hammonton News'* July of 1902 headlines. And soon, Walter's intensive delving found the newspaper's "Obituaries" and front-page articles. The researcher's sweaty hands trembled and blood surged to his head as Steward gleaned certain pertinent facts from two principal articles. On July 4, 1902, a lumberyard employee named Warren Sawyer had murdered his fiancee Charlotte Tennyson in a Winslow Village woods; and then at nighttime, the killer dismembered her arms and legs at the country sawmill that had been employing him.

Walter could again feel blood pulsating in the veins and arteries networked around his neck, and the area history reader was aware of an intense throbbing and pounding behind his all-too-sensitive ears. 'My God! W.S. had possibly murdered C.T. below the Love Tree!' Walter speculated and rationally understood. Warren Sawyer had killed Charlotte Tennyson!'

The investigator's quivering hands then closed the top drawer and opened the one directly below to his right. Inside the compartment, the news explorer found an obituary from a mid-July *Pennsylvania Evening Post* edition. "On July 4th, 1802, a trapper and fur trader named Wesley Skinner had murdered *his* longtime lover Catherine Townsend in a forest clearing just south of the village of Winslow,

New Jersey. The motive for the horrible crime," the article further stated and described, "was believed by authorities conducting the investigation to be jealousy."

'My God! I would never harm Cindy in any way; let alone murder her!' Walter thought to himself in a trance-like stupor. 'I wonder if she knows about either Charlotte Tennyson or Catherine Townsend? I gotta' meet-up with my old girlfriend and learn why she's acting so peculiarly. But Cindy's strange behavior sounds more like a simple female hormone problem that she must be suffering from. Women's feelings are fragile, and certainly, people's emotions are not logical all the time,' Walter intelligently concluded. 'I'll now return all *Gazette* materials I've just examined; and all the equipment to their proper places. Then I'll go home to Winslow and arrange to meet Cindy after she finishes work at the convenience store. I just have to learn the true reason for her drastic change in temperament toward me! I can't stand living with all of this upsetting new-found uncertainty! And the news about the Love Tree is very disturbing!'

Since Jim Calder (the cub reporter) had been dispatched with a camera and a notepad to the Central Avenue and Third Street motor vehicle accident scene, Walter announced his departure to the multi-tasking Editor-in-Chief, who had been seated in her small office behind her cluttered desk, assiduously reading the morning mail.

"Did you find what you were looking for?" Gina Rullo congenially asked the all-too-introspective visitor.

"Yes, and the information I obtained will be most beneficial in the development of my upcoming sociology class thesis," Walter fibbed with a now-pallid face. "I put everything back exactly where I had found it. Tell Mr. Donio I said *hi* and *thanks*."

"Okay, Walter. It's been a real pleasure meeting you," Gina Rullo cordially answered. "And be sure to sign your name in and out as a visitor on the ledger that's on Jim's desk. We like to keep track of public relations matters such as your visit today."

"Okay, I'll do that!" the still-unsettled young man agreed. "It's been nice meeting you."

"And Walter, if you have to do a journalism internship, stop by for an interview!" the newspaper woman cordially invited. "Our paper does have an active intern program, you know!"

"Thank you! I'll remember that!" Steward politely acknowledged. "Hope to see you shopping again in the hardware store. Be sure to ask for me the next time to stop in. Good bye now."

When Walter returned to his Winslow Village home, the under-duress young man stepped out of his gray *Protége,* walked to the road mailbox, and obtained the morning mail. Since his parents were both working that Wednesday, the returnee had the house all to himself. Walter Steward entered the kitchen, leafed through the pile of junk solicitations and utility bills, and then his nervous fingers held a letter addressed to *him* from his erratic-minded heartthrob, Cindy Tyler. The recipient frantically opened the envelope and read:

My Dearest Walter,

I have not been myself these last few days, and I want to tell you why. I would never do anything to hurt you, but something very disturbing is tearing my soul apart. Please meet me tomorrow morning, July 4th 10 a.m. at the old Love Tree. Then I'll tell you everything you need to know and why I can't see you until we return to college in Trenton.

My love always,

Cindy

That evening at supper, Walter was taciturn when the younger Steward impatiently listened to his normally laconic father complain about *his* abusive boss at the local glass factory. Then, the depressed son tolerated his chatterbox mother reviewing the litany of domestic chores she felt obligated to perform from cooking the meal, to washing the dishes, to ironing Mr. Steward's white shirt for a formal presentation he had to make on Friday morning to important company executives. "All of this added responsibility after having to be a lowly receptionist slaving my life away inside a hectic doctor's office," Mrs. Angela Steward complained to male deaf ears. "Thank goodness tomorrow's a national holiday!"

That night Walter tossed and turned in bed, thinking about what missing puzzle piece had been plaguing Cindy's mind, and why she adamantly refused discussing the sensitive matter over the telephone. 'Tomorrow will be the moment of truth!' the *jilted lover* concluded as the emotionally tortured sufferer grabbed his pillow tightly and then closed his eyes.

On Thursday morning, July 4th, 2002, Walter Steward hopped out of bed early, shaved, combed his hair, and stepped downstairs to prepare himself a bowl of cereal and milk. After gulping-down his quickly assembled breakfast, the apprehensive fellow sulked, feeling that he was now a jealous 'jaded lover' being shunned and neglected by his former faithful sweetheart. While cleaning-up the table and then washing the ceramic cereal bowl, Walter was careful not to make any noises that might disturb his parents, for the two adults were sleeping late that *Independence Day* holiday, resting from the general fatigues of their menial jobs, and from performing their myriad household responsibilities.

The still-anguishing college senior checked his watch. '9 a.m.,' Walter nervously thought. 'Just enough time to brush my teeth, get out of this bathrobe and into a tee-shirt and jeans, take a ride around Winslow and vicinity to clear my fuzzy brain, and then finally drive out to the forest fringe and meet Cindy at the Love Tree.'

Walter left a note for his parents' perusal, which stated that their son would be home for supper. The 'rendezvous man' exited the side kitchen door, entered his dull gray *Mazda Protégé*, fired-up the sick-sounding engine, and then slowly backed-out of the resident's asphalt driveway as carefully and as noiselessly as possible. The befuddled young motorist departed the somnolent village of Winslow, and took Hall Street in the direction of Winslow Junction, an abandoned railroad station that had experienced its glorious heyday in the 1930s Great Depression era.

'Cindy and I used to come to the Junction, sit in the car, and openly share our personal hopes and our dreams,' Walter fondly recollected. 'Of course, that was before we ever started frequenting the Love Tree.'

After a half hour of nostalgically studying the hulking freight cars, locomotives, and boxcars that were decades removed from their New York to Atlantic City triumphant zenith days (while now resting on rusty metal switching tracks), the modern-day dreamer snapped-out of his mental trance and mentally determined that it was time to reconnect with Cindy Tyler (and with fickle destiny) at the incomparable "Love Tree".

The young man's heart had mixed feelings of joy, apprehension, and rejection, and his emotions alternately vacillated from frustration to despondency as the confused driver left obsolete and archaic Winslow Junction behind in his rear-view mirror. Walter was now somewhat-elated with the prospect of reuniting with Cindy Tyler, but conversely, his mind was paranoid about the pattern of horrible murders recorded on the oak tree, both occurring on the two past *4th of Julys,* and the driver's heart was still feeling inconsolable from being repelled over the telephone by his longtime steady girlfriend.

The gray 92 *Protégé* pulled-off of Hall Street and onto the winding dirt road (with the tall hedgerow) that paralleled the *Atlantic City Expressway.* Cindy's '90 white *Chevy Cavalier* had not yet arrived at the secluded site, so Walter instinctively trekked into the familiar woods to once again view the resplendent "Love Tree", having the three sets of identical lovers' initials strangely etched into its bark. 'This is more than a remarkable arcane coincidence! The three cupid hearts had been drawn a full century apart from one another.'' Walter apprehensively analyzed and concluded. 'It's something mysterious; something like reincarnation, or something eerie and uncanny like out of the *Twilight Zone* movie. And I've never been superstitious my entire life, but I am right now!''

As Walter fondly touched his and Cindy's carved initials and the two-dimensional heart that surrounded the four letters, the interloper heard the muffled sound of an automobile engine rumbling in the distance. A door slammed and then thirty seconds later, Cindy Tyler came dashing up the sandy path, sprinting like a female Olympian through the dense pine-barrens' woods. The frantic girl's face was exceedingly pale as if she had just encountered a conflict with a very hostile, pursuing ghost.

"Oh Walter, Walter!" the young woman screamed as she darted towards his open arms. "Hold me! Please hold me!" the hysterical frightened female wildly cried.

"Cindy, what on Earth is wrong? Yes, I think I know," the perceptive young man uttered as Walter impetuously comforted the delirious sorority girl by stroking her long blonde tresses with his left palm, while hugging his former 'significant other' with his other hand. "I'm not going to harm you; even though we have the accursed initials W.S. and C.T.; I promise, I'll never hurt you in any way."

"Oh Walter, just hold me! Please hold me!" Cindy repeated as the young woman persistently whimpered and sobbed. "I'm so terrified for your sake, for my sake, and for our sake!"

"What happened Cindy at this tree in the past will never happen to us," the boyfriend solemnly pledged. "I vow that I'll never abuse you in any way!"

"Walter, somehow I feel we just aren't understanding each other! It's not *you* I fear!" the girlfriend cried as she failed to fathom exactly what Walter was all-too-vaguely prefacing and ranting. Tears flowed from Cindy's bloodshot blue eyes and slowly rolled-down her cheerless cheeks. "I love you Walter with all my heart and with all my soul, and I'll always want to be by your side through thick or thin!"

"Then what in the world is bothering you?" the very confounded Love Tree worshiper desired to know, as the very perplexed Love Tree advocate continued stroking Cindy Tyler's long blonde hair.

"Why won't you speak to me on the telephone? Why have you asked me to wait until we get back to Trenton to resume our former romantic relationship? Please communicate a rational answer!"

The thoroughly delirious girlfriend finally calmed-down enough to divulge what had recently transpired at the *WaWa* convenience store. The regular manager had gone on summer vacation, and his replacement was mean and nasty to all the store's employees. The ill-tempered, temporary boss had asked Cindy to go out on a date, and when she refused and related that she already had a steady boyfriend, the rejected new manager went ballistic. The belligerent beast had threatened to find-out where Walter lived, and then threatened to send the hardware store assistant manager to either the hospital, or to the local morgue.

"Why couldn't you have told me this pretty vital information on the telephone?" Walter asked and insisted. "I can defend myself if I have to from that distasteful WaWa bully!"

"Because my parents knew that I had been upset about something," Cindy sobbed and explained. "They suspected that *we* were having a lovers' quarrel. I didn't want Mom and Dad to know that this crazy monster wanted to injure or kill you, wanted to beat me up, and that the repulsive ogre threatened to burn my family's house down, just like he had predicted he would do if I didn't go out with him. And I want you to know, Walter, that I didn't! Oh Walter, I'm so upset by all of this worry! What can *we* do?"

"Why didn't you just call the police? Tell me straight-up Cindy. Is the WaWa idiot the same arrogant jerk who had bruised-up your arm right before we had gone to the Atco movies?"

"Yes; and I was too afraid to tell you about *his* nasty temper. He's a mentally-disturbed lunatic; a real absolute demented maniac!" Cindy ranted in a still-distressed manner. "I didn't notify the police because then it would be only my word against *his*. The cops can't protect you against someone that has vowed to hurt both *you* and *me*, unless the police can catch the bully in the act. *He* would've claimed that I was just a disgruntled employee trying to get her benevolent boss in trouble by fabricating a wild, fictitious, phony story. Walter, I didn't know what I should do while dealing with this totally freaky, out-of-control psycho!"

"Who is this brash creep?" Walter asked. "What's his name? Is he from out of town?"

"His name's Bill Slaughter," Cindy revealed and wept. "He's from Cherry Hill. I assure you Walter; this nutcase maniac is much more dangerous than the obnoxious brash bully you think he is. Bill's ruthless, and has evil eyes that strike terror in my heart whenever he doesn't get his stubborn way. Now, what did you mean about the other sets of initials carved on the Love Tree?"

"Bill Slaughter," Walter wondered and repeated while failing to grasp or fathom his girlfriend's question about similar initials' combinations being carved into the giant tree's bark at three different heights. "At least his initials aren't *W.S.* Hey; wait a minute, Cindy! Bill Slaughter; the two names together sounds like a lot of nonsensical B.S. to me! Hey now, what's this, Cindy?"

Without any warning, fifty feet away from the Love Tree, a portly male stepped-out from behind a clump of tall pines. The sinister-looking antagonist was short, stocky, fat, and muscular. The hostile villain quickly approached the petrified college students, and the depraved instigator was wearing sheer plastic surgical gloves and was brandishing a shiny revolver in his right hand.

"Yeah; you're somewhat right, *creep*; my initials *are* W.S., and that's no *B.S.* either!" William "Bill" Slaughter verified while gruffly addressing Walter in a loud, brash bass voice. "Fancy meeting you here, Cindy! Ha, ha, ha!" the heartless, callous stalker exclaimed and then cackled.

"Now just please wait a minute; can't we be reasonable!" Walter implored the madman. "Shouldn't Cindy have something to say in this matter? Why don't *you* just ask her what *she* wants and thinks, and then learn to live with it?"

"Okay Cindy," the obsessive, rejected stalker replied with a snicker. "I followed your cheap white *Chevy* all the way out here in the sticks, and now I've suddenly found myself a bonus. I can kill your boyfriend right in front of your eyes, and if you don't become *my* woman, then I'll have to kill you, too! The ultimate choice is all yours, sweetheart!" the insane lunatic shouted with bulging eyes sticking-out from his hard thick skull.

"In that case, I'd rather die and be with Walter in Heaven than have to have anything at all to do with *you* down here on Earth; you contemptible brute; you vulturous monster!" the beleaguered girlfriend impulsively screamed in an extremely desperate and passionate state of mind.

"Are ya' sure that's the way it's gotta' be!" mendacious William Slaughter bellowed in a disappointed tone of voice. "Look and listen, Hon. When I can't get what I want, I flip-out and either hurt or kill people! I've always gotten what I desired, and if I can't *possess* you, then I'll just have to destroy the both of you, and that's all there is to it! Plain and easy; simple and practical; the long and the short of it!

As you two punk college kids would say, 'the alpha and the omega'! Ya' both gotta' be eliminated!"

"Love is mutual commitment!" Walter vainly insisted and futilely philosophically argued. "Love is not being someone's personal property, or it's not having a partner who's an obedient slave! True Love means to give more than to receive!"

William Slaughter menacingly waved his handgun and ordered Walter and Cindy to separate from their embrace, to stand fifty feet apart, and then to "get down on your knees". The convenience store substitute manager then gave his dream girl one final chance to live and breathe. "Cindy, are you sure you won't go out with me?" Slaughter begged his WaWa dream girl. "This is your last chance to live to see tomorrow!"

"You can't make her do anything against her God-given free will!" Walter bravely-but-foolishly objected. "Cindy has a beautiful mind, and she knows how to use it!"

"That's what the hell *you* think, Punk! You can't tell me what and what not to do! Nobody tells me that! Not even the Pope in Rome!" the totally fanatical, obsessive/compulsive mental case bellowed.

The about-to-be-felon stepped over to where Walter was kneeling in the white, sandy, pine-barrens soil. The potential murderer diabolically pointed the revolver to the terrified lover's right temple, and then maliciously pulled the trigger. Blood and brain tissue exploded out of the young man's forehead as Walter Steward's limp body toppled-over onto the forest's hard ground.

Cindy rose to her feet and quickly ran five steps in the direction of her fatally wounded boyfriend. Feeling betrayed, William Slaughter heinously discharged another lethal bullet from the .38 caliber revolver that instantly penetrated the young woman's heart. Cindy clutched her chest, and then also slowly collapsed upon the white sandy ground.

The guiltless, cold-blooded killer then wickedly placed the pistol into the dead male's right hand and squeezed tightly until the psychopath was certain that the young man's fingers had made a detectable fingerprint impression on the murder weapon. In the killer's warped mind, the savage dual executions then appeared being a case of a brutal murder-suicide committed by a jaded, jealous lover. The remorseless assassin next removed his sheer plastic gloves, contemplated his totally reprehensible crime, stared-up at the stately "Love Tree", and lastly, maniacally smiled while assessing the magnitude of his most evil deed.

On October 4, 2002, the mendacious murderer returned without conscience to the aforementioned crime scene, which the area newspapers had erroneously reported as the setting for an "apparent murder-suicide". At the bottom of the desolate Love Tree, amidst ankle-deep fallen leaves, pernicious William "Bill" Slaughter carefully studied the initials W.S. and C.T. that Walter Steward had carved into the bark inside the heart perimeter.

The possessive psychopath then quickly removed a penknife from his brown leather jacket, and showing uncharacteristic patience, the cold-blooded killer etched-out the date July 4 '02, just below the etched heart. To complete his evil enterprise, the cunning murderer next traced and carved a neat isosceles triangle around the eternal symbol of love. His wooden-hearted evil deeds completed, William Slaughter, like a remote-controlled robot, trudged back to his black automobile and sped-away from the remote pine-barrens Village of Winslow, New Jersey, the newly-promoted convenience store manager motoring twenty miles northwest to the glitter and sophistication of suburban Cherry Hill.

"The Price of Bigotry"

The popular South Jersey tavern had two dozen workmans' pickup trucks in its parking lot, and each one had a green and white rear bumper sticker reading: "I Love Deer Huntin' in the New Jersey Pinelands." At five-fifteen on an April 2002, Friday afternoon, Tom Morris sauntered into the *Pine Barons Bar* on *Route 322,* the Black Horse Pike in Folsom, New Jersey. The hard-working tradesman meandered his way through the slew of patrons (mostly plumbers, electricians, carpenters and masons) enjoying cold mugs of beer before returning home to their bossy wives and spoiled, bratty kids. Tom spotted a recently vacated bar stool next to an old Hammonton High School football teammate, Harry Watkins, an air-conditioning and heating contractor.

"Hi Harry; mind if I sit down next to you," Tom Morris politely asked Watkins. "It's been a real hectic day, and I could use a few cold brews to refresh my energy supply. I'm exhausted from just completing a really big commercial installation job over in Vineland that I've been working on for two whole weeks."

"Not at all Tom," Harry Watkins receptively answered. "Have a seat and spill your heavy heart out, Jim," Harry then said to the alert bartender, "Jim, kindly give me a refill and give my old buddy Tom Morris here a…"

"A bottle of *Coor's Light*," the newcomer appreciatively replied. "Ya' know Harry, the funniest thing happened to me today, and I wasn't on my way to the Roman Forum," the highly proficient electrician offered to relate with an exaggerated laugh. "It's a real tale off the beaten track."

"Tell me about it, Tom," Harry Watkins implored. "I need a good chuckle to balance-out all the abundant turmoil and strife in my accursed life. Why couldn't I have been born a Rockefeller or a Carnegie? Being Bill Gates' twin-brother wouldn't be such a bad idea either!"

After Jim the bartender laid down two bottles of *Coor's Light* in front of Tom Morris and thirsty Harry Watkins, the garrulous electrician narrated his humorous anecdote to the also fatigued heating and air-conditioning contractor.

"Harry, I was diligently workin' on the gig I was tellin' ya' about over in Vineland this afternoon, when nature suddenly called," Tom Morris prefaced his amusing anecdote. "I rushed to the Port-a-John in an all-too-sudden total downpour; laid my radio communicator next to the hopper; pulled my dungarees down, and when I turned my butt around to finally sit, I accidentally knocked my radio right into the toilet hole. Isn't that pretty hilarious?" Tom Morris rhetorically asked Harry Watkins. "My portable radio had plopped smack-dab into the center of the portable latrine's crapola!"

"That *is* pretty damned funny," Harry Watkins admitted and laughed. "Did you proceed to bombard your portable radio with fecal waste matter?"

"Well, my construction boss on the project decided to call me at that exact moment, right in the midst of this afternoon's torrential April shower," Tom commented and hardily laughed, "and *his* booming voice was coming directly from the radio's speaker in the hopper hole. I had to listen to *his* crap coming right from the crap hole during a major South Jersey thunderstorm."

"Did you ever manage to retrieve your coveted radio?" Harry giddily giggled. "Ya' know Tom, this crazy story could definitely make the humor page of *Readers Digest.*"

"Well, yes. I did manage to retrieve my communications' device," Tom conceded with a broad smirk exhibited upon his tanned face. "I very intelligently wrapped my right hand in a lot of toilet paper, reached-down into the smelly hole, grabbed my still-squawking radio, and just had enough time to turn my butt around and plop-down on the toilet seat and successfully do my business. What a bizarre adventure *that* experience was when a bolt of lightning simultaneously hit a nearby tree, and the blast scared the livin' crap out of me even more!"

"That was pretty smart to be able to act that quickly under extreme duress," Harry Watkins complimented and chuckled. "You already had the toilet paper in your hand to wipe yourself after you had so ingeniously salvaged your cherished radio. Jim," Watkins hollered to the busy bartender, "better bring us two more chilled *Coor's Lights* before our overactive mouths become parched from doin' too much talkin' and laughin'," the jovial, independent heating and air-conditioning contractor ordered.

Harry Watkins glanced-up at the bar's overhead television set, and his mood quickly shifted from general cheerfulness to deep disgust. "Just look at that ugly scene, Tom," the contractor requested. "In almost every damned commercial, a white guy has to have a black jerk for his best friend, whether they're riding in a car, partying at the bowling alley, or simply sittin' in a bar like us right now. That sort of contrived nonsense really turns my stomach sour. It's a form of government regulated social modeling. It's all designed to make the average, hard-working white American like you or me believe that that's the ideal thing to do. The white guy has to always have a black guy as his best buddy. It's deliberate social engineering, I say! And it doesn't reflect the true reality of American society."

"I see it on TV all the time, but I don't actually think or worry about it that much," Tom Morris acknowledged as he imbibed another mouthful of delicious brew from his cold brown bottle. "It doesn't upset me any more, Harry, because I'm used to seein' it on nearly every damned commercial and sitcom. I've sort of become acclimated to it!"

"Well, it still annoys the hell out of me," Harry indignantly persisted. "I ain't got any close black friends, and really don't ever want to have any close black friends, either. Just look around this bar, Tom. Ya' see about seventy guys in here, all hard-working white fellas'. That's the way I like it and understand it," Watkins pontificated. "Those damned commercials we see on TV don't show true America. At least, they don't reflect the reality I live in and want to live in. It's all the networks' conformity to government politically correct propaganda, that's what the heck it is!"

Tom tried to sidetrack discussing the core of the controversial issue, stating that the government, civil rights leaders, Hollywood, the main street media, and *MTV* were attempting to bring about social change to promote better harmony between the country's races. Harry Watkins was not quite as amenable to accepting the revolutionary cultural transformation as was his more adaptable electrician friend Tom Morris was.

"I mean Tom," Harry persisted in his prejudice, "every TV football panel has to have three black guys and one white gay analyzing the game, and every newscast has to have a black weatherman and sports commentator. Ya' know," Watkins continued his very critical evaluation, "you'd think that when watching local and national network TV that blacks were the majority and that whites were the minority in America; when actually, the country's population is only 17% Afro-American! Ya' know Tom," the all-too-biased heating and air-conditioning guru continued his negative diatribe, "this crazy nonsense is all being done just to placate the damned blacks. We bust our tails every day to pay half our incomes to the federal government so that *Uncle Sam* can wastefully redistribute our hard-earned money to lazy mookers living high on the hog; many on welfare, and food stamps. It's all a damned shame."

"Isn't *that* last comment of yours a little over the top?" Tom Morris weakly challenged. "Now Harry, I didn't hear stuff like this coming out of your mouth when we were playing football for Hammonton High!"

"Look Tom; if constantly complaining squawky blacks don't get their way," Harry Watkins theorized and insisted, "the potential anarchists threaten to riot and burn-down the cities like they did in the '60s. As I just mentioned, every damned TV news program has to have at least one black anchor-person or weatherman on it simply to give the program being broadcast into *our* homes the appearance of racial balance. The stinkin' government is trying to model an artificial ideal that they're selling, but I'm not buying! Nobody in the year 2002 should ever be disadvantaged, because everyone has *equal* opportunity to be educated in the public schools! But I'm tellin' you Tom, the word equality is solely a political idea. When the idiots in Washington try applying *it* to economic, to wealth, and to education, equality then becomes socialism!"

"Unfortunately, that's the way the country's been heading, and there's little that either you or I could do about it," Tom Morris diplomatically generalized and shared. "I mean Harry; everybody's so concerned about being politically correct that they no longer challenge racial and cultural integration as long as it doesn't seem to interfere with their own personal lives and happiness," Tom Morris somewhat-sympathetically summarized. "Live and let live seems to be the new *white* philosophy that's out there. The blacks are somewhat organized, and if the whites do the same, then naturally, they'll be instantly accused of racism!"

"But *it* does interfere," Harry Watkins adamantly maintained and persisted. "The uplifting of the black race takes away half your happiness in the form of excessive taxes. And it's not only blacks. It's lousy Hispanics, too. Take your warm states down south and out west. In another thirty years, Hispanics and blacks will be the majority in California, Texas, Florida, New Mexico, and Arizona," Watkins slowly orated as if Morris was taking accurate dictation. "Who do ya' think the panderin' politicians in those states are gonna' cater to? And please tell me Tom, who's goin' to have to pay the freight bill for all the social programs needed to house and educate the minorities, and to absorb the Hispanics and illegal aliens into American mainstream civilization? If *we* obediently go along with it," Harry vociferously emphasized, "we're throwing in the proverbial towel; conceding defeat and signing our own death certificates. The way it is now *Uncle Tom*, we might never see a Republican president again unless the GOP candidate has the mirror-image same platform of the Democrat that the RINO nominee is running against."

"I agree we're heading there somewhere down the line in the future," Tom reluctantly concurred before imbibing another delicious mouthful of cold beer. "But what really can be done about it, Harry? It's all quite futile as I see it! If you openly object, resist, or oppose the social change that's evolving out of Washington and Hollywood, you're automatically labeled a racist. No one wants to be accused of practicin' discrimination, now do they?"

Harry Watkins stood-up from his soft bar stool, got on his imaginary soapbox, and began lecturing to the now-embarrassed Tom Morris how blacks were both an economic and a cultural drag on American civilization, and also on free enterprise capitalism. His inflexible long-winded dialectic encompassed American education, the entertainment and music worlds, sports, economics and American politics. Harry's single listener was becoming uncomfortable being exposed to *his* friend's inexhaustible bigotry.

"Tom, do you watch the Philly' news channels at night?" Harry finished-up and inquired.

"Why yes," Morris admitted. "I also watch the New York news on cable, along with the movie channels."

"Well, Tom bo. I call what we see at 11 o'clock nightly the *N News*," Harry declared with a forced smile. "All ya' see is ugly niggers lookin' like apes and gorillas killin' and robbin', and kidnappin', and shoplifting, and drug trafficking. It's a total disgrace to Western Civilization and to American Christian tradition," Watkins criticized and argued, now getting the attention of other tradesmen seated around the bar. "The crimes are the same each night, and the only thing that changes is the names of the dumb uneducated mookers that are committing them," the angry speaker insisted. "That's precisely why we gotta' keep the belligerent, ignorant mookers in the city and out of the pristine New Jersey pine-barrens. We gotta' prevent the pinelands from being niggerized."

"You're sounding like an absolute racist now," Morris protested. "White people commit crimes, too. Just look at those thugs that run our largest corporations, and how they cheat and bilk their stockholders while making millions by selling stock option bonuses that they never paid for in the first damned place."

"That's very true," Harry acceded before swallowing-down another tasty mouthful of beer. "But white-collar crime isn't violent crime that kills and destroys innocent people. City blacks have the monopoly on shootin' and murderin'," Watkins bellowed inside the still-noisy country tavern. "Thank goodness it's mostly always done to other mooker victims. But the jive city punks are now movin' into the suburbs, and we'll soon be deluged with them operatin' in our tranquil rural neighborhoods; thanks to the generosity of good old Uncle Sam over in Washington DC. That's what the government is tryin' to accomplish, Tom. The feds call it racial integration. I call it reverse slavery."

"Did you say reverse slavery?" Tom Morris exclaimed in mild astonishment. "How so?"

Harry Watkins ordered two more *Coor's Lights,* and continued his critique of blacks and minorities "infesting and infecting America". First, the cultural maverick said that blacks were showing-up on television with white Irish surnames like Sullivan, O'Leary, McGee, Kelly and Kennedy. Next, Watkins strenuously objected to his kids having to study black history in school and black and Hispanic literature written by obscure minority authors in their English classes. Tom Morris (and now several other tradesmen) patiently-but-uneasily listened to Harry Watkins' very biased litany.

"Kids don't read quality stories by guys like Jack London, Edgar Allan Poe and Charles Dickens anymore," Harry loudly editorialized to his now slightly-upset bar companion. "White literary masters are taboo in the politically correct school curriculums. My eighth-grade daughter had to read a story in her literature book last night with a shallow plot written by a Hispanic author that had a vocabulary of only about a thousand English words," Harry bitterly rankled. "Even Mark Twain's great work is coming under criticism by politically correct pundits that claim *Huckleberry Finn* is basically racist. What an absolute farce! It's a total travesty that's affectin' the whole school curriculum all over our damned country!" Watkins lectured to Morris. "The mooker lovers and the power-hungry politicians that cower to the black crybabies are becomin' too influential and goin' entirely too far with their holier-than-thou propaganda, and their excessive taxation on us."

"But how is it that you're callin' this new type of democracy we're livin' in 'reverse slavery'?" Tom Morris insisted on knowing. "I don't see the relevant connection."

Harry digressed from his main theme and expounded on the fact that a channel existed on cable television titled *BET (Black Entertainment Television)* and that if someone were to feature a network called *White Entertainment Television,* it would automatically be labeled "divisive and racist".

"You have a choice whether or not to watch *BET,* don't you?" Tom Morris rationally challenged. "Harry, you and I aren't forced to watch it, are we?"

496

"You're right on that small point, Tom, and that's why I watch a lot of *AMC, American Movie Classics,* and *Turner Movie Classics* also," the all-too-biased air conditioning contractor disclosed. "Old films from the '40s and '50s have mostly white people in them, and if there's an occasional black or two, they're usually presented in a subordinate role like a butler, a chauffeur, a cook, or a maid."

"I'm surprised that the *NAACP* hasn't tried to eliminate *AMC* and *TMC* from the airwaves because their movies show mostly '30s, '40s and '50s' whites," Tom Morris alertly opined to his highly perturbed and opinionated acquaintance. "I'm afraid, Harry, that you and your values are living back in the 1950s!"

Then Harry Watkins went on a propaganda sermon (rampage) explaining how virtually every white kid on television in need of help had to have a black coach, a black guidance counselor, or a black teacher to assist him or her back onto the righteous path of life. "The all-wise black authority figure is the only one in the whole town that has the capacity or the wherewithal to straighten-out the troubled Caucasian kid's emotional problem, caused by *his* insensitive, incompetent, and totally prejudiced white parents," Harry Watkins boisterously emphasized to Tom Morris. "And the white kid's overwhelming psychological problems had to usually be caused by his or her biased white parents, or by his or her narrow-minded white friends!"

"But how does this all tie in with your theme of reverse slavery?" Tom again challenged his former high school football squad pal. "Harry, please be a little more specific and less divergent. I mean, you're jumping all over the damned place making rash comments and generalizations without providing specific examples."

The temporarily thwarted racist then delved into the subject of reparations being advocated and endorsed by white college professors, by "treasonous" white lawyers, and by traditionally white *Ivy League* academic universities like *Harvard* and *Yale.* According to Harry Watkins, the primary purpose for those most recent gross reparations proposals was to engineer social "politically correct change", and to send the dynamic white race on an unwarranted "guilt trip" where Caucasians have to defray more and more outlandish, exorbitant expenses to pacify militant blacks, and to subsidize *their* indigent existence. The new "outrageous racial scenario" would allow opportunistic white lawyers to handsomely profit from the intended, excessive reparations' settlements generously conferred upon undeserving blacks; many of the current flimsy legal claims dating back to the antebellum period prior to the historic *Civil War*.

"Okay Harry, I admit you have a somewhat valid general point," Morris recognized and compromised. "But again, exactly how does this reparations' compensation thing amount to reverse slavery?"

"Tom, it's not only reverse slavery! It's also reverse discrimination," the half-inebriated heating and air-conditioning contractor rambled on and elaborated. "The lousy *Harvard* and *Yale* lawyers are sayin' that black slavery was condoned in the American South before the *Civil War,* and that it was a crime against humanity. And now fifteen generations later, you and I are expected to pay for something that happened over a century and a half ago!"

"What's wrong with that?" Tom Morris spoke-up in defense of modern, twenty-first century, government morality. "Wasn't the practice of black slavery a *crime* against humanity? Man's inhumanity to man, so to speak?"

"Tom," Harry Watkins symbolically admonished while shaking his head in disappointment, "don't you get it? Individuals commit crimes upon other individuals. A government can't commit a crime like these fancy lawyers are insistin'. Just like on television, when a mooker shoots another mooker in a drug deal gone sour," Harry argued. "Now Tom, *that's a crime!* And besides *that* rather obvious fact, the Confederate government had been dissolved over a hundred and fifty years ago. They're the ones the lawyers should be suing for reparations for blacks for the *crime* of slavery. The *Union* was the parent of the present *USA*, and it was the Union that freed the damned slaves *after* the Confederate states had seceded from the damned Union!"

"I think I now see your point much better," Tom Morris benignly and politely stated. "But aren't we just talkin' semantics here? I mean Harry, it's only a definition of terms and words, and stuff like that's being disputed. The bottom line is that slavery was a grave injustice and compensation might actually be required and justified."

"An alleged *injustice* that happened over a century and a half ago!" Harry Watkins vociferously balked. "Since being liberated, the blacks have had over twelve generations to get their act together, and they've dismally failed. My ancestors came into Ellis Island in the 1890s, over forty years *after* the damned *Civil War*. Why should I have to pay for *alleged injustices* that my great-grandparents had never been here to commit? It's absolutely insane!" Watkins adamantly maintained. "The only *injustice* about this reparations' issue is that you and I might have to pay niggers for social crimes our benevolent family-oriented ancestors never performed."

"But everyone sort of agrees that slavery had been a gross abomination," Tom Morris answered while deftly playing the role of Devil's Advocate. "Why are *you* so concerned about something that might not ever materialize?"

Harry protested that if whites didn't organize and resist the reparations' claims, and if Congress caves into pressure from lawyers and "squeaky wheel 'give me more grease' minorities" because of "general white apathy and disorganization", then the results would be economically catastrophic for the white working man.

"Those little semantics you've alluded to like *crimes of government* and *social injustice* are gonna' cost *us* plenty if someone doesn't have the guts to stand-up for the working white man's rights," Watkins coarsely debated. "We're talkin' about billions and billions, possibly trillions of dollars, if this ridiculous slavery reparations bill ever passes through Congress. The do-gooders pushin' this absurd criminal social justice movement are mostly white lawyers and politicians out to line their own pockets with fees they'll eagerly charge for their totally undesirable services. Remember Tom," Harry Morris gravely stressed and pontificated, "most of *your* politicians and lawmakers are damned crooked greedy white lawyers to begin with. They're definitely more evil crooks than your worst corporate executives are!"

"Well Harry, wasn't slavery an injustice to begin with?" Tom returned. "An atrocity of the worst magnitude, if my memory of history still is workin' correctly?"

"Those slaves lived better on the southern plantations than they ever would have as primitive spear-chuckers terrorizing the African jungles," Harry unconvincingly exhaled. "They had roofs over their heads and adequate food in their bellies on the plantations. Come to think of it, Tom. Southern slavery was actually a form of social welfare givin' blacks free room and board," Watkins haughtily related and believed. "This reparations' issue is nothin' to trifle with. The lawyers are promisin' the blacks something for nothin' without ever workin' for it, and you and me gotta' build more houses and work more hours just to help pay for all the damned craziness!"

"I've heard enough of your bitter white propaganda for now," the electrician replied to his obviously prejudiced bar colleague. "I gotta' run and take the wife food shoppin'. Talk to someone else Harry about this terrible black extortion conspiracy you're so damned paranoid and worried about. As long as it doesn't interfere personally with my life, I don't really care too much about it."

"Okay Tom, nice talkin' and sharin' a few brews with ya'," Harry Watkins answered in a relatively hostile tone of voice. "If ya' ever have a change of heart on this issue, just give me a call."

After Tom Morris staggered and almost stumbled out of the popular drinking hole establishment, Harry Watkins began giving the carpenter to his left a tin ear about how black urban culture exhibited on *MTV* was thoroughly corrupting the norms of American suburban society by infecting and "niggerizing" the minds of gullible suburban white kids. "I believe in separate-but-equal for the races, the policy that existed back in the '50s," Harry uttered in a half-drunk baritone. "And many black people out there don't like mixed marriages or datin' members of other races either. I have a teenage daughter, and I told her that if she ever dated a black mooker, I'd disown her."

"Here Harry; have another beer," the new-found listener offered. "Bartender? Give this guy dying of thirst and holdin' court over here another *Coor's Light.*"

"As I was sayin', I was watchin' a recent play production of *Hamlet* on public television," Harry remarked to local carpenter Jack Simpson. "And when the camera panned the audience, there wasn't one black person in the whole damned amphitheater. Spuds don't give a crap about Shakespeare, or about proper English, or about white culture. The light bulb, the automobile, the computer, the radio, television, good literature, you name it Jack. They were all invented or created by ambitious white people," the intoxicated racist blustered.

"So, what's your point?" the instigating carpenter asked. "I don't get the object of your flamboyant rhetoric!"

"The point Jack is that my kids and your kids have to study all day long in school about some black guy named George Washington Carver, who found a hundred impractical uses for the peanut. The kids in her class also spend valuable class time reading about Harriet Tubman and other slaves that were rescued by whites in something called the Underground Railroad," Harry Watkins wildly and insistently vociferated. "Einstein, Lincoln, Newton, Edison, George Washington, Henry Ford, and O. Henry are reduced in importance in schools because they happened to have been white men. I tell ya' Jack, this nation's goin' to the dogs if we don't do somethin' quick to stop it. And another thing," Harry Watkins opined to his thoroughly puzzled and captive listener, "I was at a *Broadway* stage show that had twenty dancers, and there *has* to be one black guy dancin' with a

500

gorgeous white doll. Well Jack, my wife and I got out of our seats and walked out of the theater in protest. Why couldn't the black idiot have a black girl to dance with? I know five hundred people sittin' in that same damned audience wished they had the courage to do the exact same thing as my wife and I had done, and step the hell out of there. But they've been indoctrinated by television to accept what they personally dislike! Whites have been conditioned into cultural submission by the mass media and by ruthless influential politicians!"

"Is that why the others didn't leave the auditorium?" Jack Simpson asked. "What say you, Harry?"

"Because the white fools all have to be politically correct," Harry declared. "And they've sold their souls to the government in exchange for the right to pay higher taxes to fund black advancement, both now and in the future! They've all been totally brainwashed, conditioned and made into dunce-like Washington brainless clones!"

* * * * * * * * * * * *

On the night of April 24th Harry Watkins' telephone rang. and the answerer was surprised to hear Tom Morris's distraught voice on the other end calling from the emergency ward of Hammonton's Kessler Memorial Hospital. The caller was virtually hysterical, ranting and raging his larynx and lungs out.

"Tom, you sound awfully stressed-out! Calm down and tell me what's wrong?" Harry demanded in a fairly sober voice. "What's troublin' you?"

"This afternoon, my wife Barbara was driving my son to *Little League* practice when a drunken black imbecile in a 1975 van ran a red light and smashed into her car," Morris panted over the phone. "Barbara's in serious condition with a broken arm, and the doctors think her spleen has to be taken out. Her immune system is gonna' be affected for the rest of her life if that happens! And my son Steve's got three broken ribs and a sprained ankle, and is gonna' miss the entire summer baseball season. If *they* weren't wearin' their seat-belts, the cop conducting the *accident* investigation says that both my wife and my kid would've been killed. Accident my foot!" Tom Morris vehemently yelled over the phone. "Harry; this freakin' accident was caused by a drunk mook driver; a friggin' black derelict on wheels without two cents to rub together to his name. The intoxicated drunken 'cloud' had no damned car insurance, no valid registration; but he did have an expired driver's license."

"You sound like you need a sedative," Harry sympathetically suggested. "You can always sue the state for allowing the drunk nigger to terrorize the highways. You sound like you're frazzled! But, then again, you and I will have to pay for any successful settlement in the form of higher state taxes! Is there anything else that's botherin' ya' that ya' need to get off your chest?"

"I gotta' admit that you were probably right in what you had said at the piney bar," Tom reluctantly conceded. "If I sue the state, I wind-up suing myself and you, because who is the state anyway? It's the honest law-abiding taxpayers that have to foot the bill for a ton of illegal and immoral nonsense like this unnecessary traffic accident. Harry, why does white responsibility have to carry the weight of continuous black negligence?"

Tom Morris's poignant words resonated well with Harry Watkins receptive all-too-discriminating ears. "How can I help you, Tom?" the notoriously prejudiced tradesman asked his now-confused and distressed caller.

"Harry, do you remember the theme of that conversation we had at the *Pine Barons Bar* on the *Black Horse Pike* a couple of Fridays ago?" Morris uttered with evident animosity dwelling in his heart. "Do ya' recall what we discussed?"

"I Sure do Tom," Watkins recollected and verified. "I really did some redundant sounding-off that afternoon. I guess I was bent out of shape over my wife's use of her credit cards after I had just paid the high annual federal income tax bill that was due April 15th. I can't deduct credit card interest on my *IRS* tax return anymore! I'm sick and tired of *our* government always trying to punish *us* and constantly taking away *our* rights and privileges!"

The perturbed caller explained that Harry Watkins had told him to keep in touch should Tom's attitude towards certain parasitic elements of American society change. "Well Harry," Tom Morris declared, "I'm so damned angry and fit-to-be-tied right now, and I need to talk to someone like you that empathizes with me," the revenge-oriented electrician intimated to his new-found pal. "Where can we meet?"

"My wife is goin' to the *Hamilton Mall* tonight to do some spring shopping with one of her friends, and she's takin' our daughter Lisa with her," Harry remembered and conveyed over his business cell phone. "Tom, you can come over to my place between seven and ten this evening to discuss things in detail. We'll have the house all to ourselves. Can ya' make' it?"

"Sure, you still live in Pennypot at the end of Folsom Road?" the still-irate caller asked the wrathful bigot listening on the other end.

"Yeah; right behind the Pine Crest Restaurant and Motel," Harry confirmed. "You've been to a couple of parties and backyard lawn picnics at my place if I recall."

"See ya' after seven," Tom Morris promised. "I need to channel this rage I'm feelin' into avenging my wife and son's unnecessary injuries. This regrettable tragedy has hit home, and all the things *you* were preaching about at the *Pine Barons* now make good logical sense. Now it's become a very personal crusade, if ya' know what the hell I mean. See ya' after seven Harry." Click.

At a quarter after seven, Tom Morris's white-paneled van with its green and white pinelands' bumper sticker pulled into Harry Watkins' driveway in the Pennypot section of Folsom, a Hammonton, New Jersey satellite borough. The man of the house invited the still-incensed visitor inside the middle-class dwelling. Harry Watkins stepped to the refrigerator, obtained two twelve-ounce bottles of *Coor's Light,* and handed one to the extremely jittery visiting electrician.

"This morning, I got into a little argument with my son Steve over him wearing a football jersey with a black guy's name on it," the irritated tradesman began his narrative. "I hope my kid *now* sees the merits from where I'm coming from after his close brush with death that had been caused by that worthless irresponsible drunken shine."

"It peeves the heck out of me, too," Harry contributed to the already-slanted discussion. "We gotta' keep the spuds out of the pine-barrens; that's my friggin' opinion. It's all quite that simple Tom. Keep the damned black city scum in the damned cities so that we can safely sit home on our sofas and watch the jungle scumbags conduct their insane, tribal, city warfare every night on *Action News.* Scum killin' scum ain't no big deal, as long as it stays in Philly' and in other foul places like the damned Bronx and Chicago! "

Tom inquired whether all blacks should be targeted by *their* joint racism, or should the two conspirators just ferret-out lower classed "mookers" that were on drugs or alcohol, and that committed crimes to support their immoral, detrimental habits. "Harry, I now believe you when you say they're a direct danger to law and order. A direct threat to civilization itself," victimized Tom Morris maintained.

"Tom, we're both New Jersey Pineys at heart," Harry observed and articulated while further identifying with his out-of-kilter friend's apparent excessive angst. "Some liberal critics might call us country hicks, or even local rednecks, but we got strong values and convictions that so-called college educated, politically correct Americans lack. We're the new underground patriots of this country, ready to sabotage government tyranny once we're commanded by law to finance all of the loafers on welfare, and all of the decadent drug users that have to be rehabilitated!" Harry Watkins ranted. "Do ya' follow me now with all this outrageous reparations' crap, too?"

Tom raised and lowered his head in almost a trance-like state to tacitly show that he agreed with his new colleague's contemporary, and almost seditious statement.

"Are ya' ready to talk some turkey?" Harry Watkins asked his perplexed visitor. "I got some hot stuff to tell ya'."

Tom Morris then came out of his momentary stupor and disclosed that he basically supported Harry's general contentions, but *he* had certain doubts about bringing harm to suburban black professionals in the legal, business and medical fields. "I mean Harry," Tom objectively remarked, "professional blacks have bought into the free-enterprise system and can afford payin' small fortunes for expensive homes that you and I help build. The upper-class blacks do contribute to *our welfare!*"

"Don't kid yourself Tom," Harry bluntly answered. "They're still black. They aren't pathetic mookers, rug heads, and jive rappin, niggers like ya' see causin' havoc on *Eyewitness News,* but they're more like contemporary pioneers coming into our pinelands' area to stake claim to new territory, which is to you and me, *our* territory. The spud-headed niggers and mookers of the scum black lower class will follow the black professionals into the suburbs, and eventually into the Jersey pinelands to settle and to cause social chaos," Watkins pragmatically predicted. "The *N News* will gradually make its way right into *our* sacred backyards, and consequently, corrupt our kids' Amerucan morals. It already has affected your family with your son and wife's misfortunes, not to mention the negative effects of rap music all over the damned country. In fact, Tom. I just saw your wife's accident on the Atlantic City cable channel. Your family is already victimized by the nasty *N* problem that's now invadin' *our* cherished deer-huntin' turf! It's basically up to guys like me and you to stop the upcoming epidemic black invasion of our beloved pinelands bailiwicks."

Tom next asked Harry exactly what type of offensive and defensive action *he* had in mind, and if any "white trash" were to be also designated and targeted for Piney retribution. Morris then listened attentively to Harry Watkins' egregious grand scheme. The cohorts strolled to the kitchen refrigerator where Harry removed two more bottles of *Coor's Light*, handed one to Tom, and then the pair resumed their impromptu two-man conference.

"Out west and also in the southeast, there're many white militia cells that are involved in scarin' out blacks from enterin' *their* neighborhoods," Harry confidentially related. "Now Tom, it's not done blatantly with white hoods and crosses like with the old *KKK* in the old South. It's done more subtle now, and each white militia cell coordinates its own activities and acts independently of all other cells," Watkins carefully explained. "But when *they* strike, the rest of us automatically know why and how it was done when we read about the attack incident in the newspapers, or see the results of *their* clandestine activities on national network news."

"Sort of like the radical Arab al Qaeda cells causing havoc all over the world," Tom realized and mentioned. "You're suggesting that *we* act like terrorists?"

"If it's a choice of *you* or them being the victims, which will you choose?" Watkins shrewdly indicated and advanced. "And Tom, you've already been horribly victimized once by nigger scum this afternoon! What more proof or evidence do ya' actually need? Do ya' need to re-mortgage your house to pay for black parasites' expensive need for social welfare and economic justice in order to convince you of the urgent need to act now?"

Thomas Anthony Morris took a deep gulp from his cold brown beer bottle and asked his determined confederate what the name of the newly founded organization was going to be. The visiting electrician listened attentively to his friend's standard. Inflammatory, prejudiced comments.

"I propose that our little club should be referred to as *DEN*. That stands for *D*rugos,' which obviously includes drug distributors; *E*nvironmentalists, and *N*iggers. They're gonna' be our targeted enemies, and we're gonna' destroy their houses, and make it look like it was an accident, just like the patriotic white militia groups are now surreptitiously doin' out West and in the South."

"Why declare war on environmentalists?" Tom questioned his paranoid and partially-insane companion. "Greenies want to conserve the New Jersey pinelands and restrict the land use. Conservationists want to protect the environment."

"Because Tom, these lousy environmentalists want to limit *our* freedom, that's why," the obsessed contractor explained. "Our property values will always be low because no one can build near us unless they build on ten acres of ground like some rich black football players and wealthy black professionals and rappers can easily afford to do," Harry crudely maintained.

The guest then reminded his host that the ten-acre pinelands' ordinance pertained to the need to conserve the precious water under the pine-barrens, and Harry Watkins immediately took umbrage with Tom Morris's direct contention.

"Tom, the last three years we've had a drought restriction and could not water our lawns because of lack of rainfall," Harry rambled and blustered. "Did you know. Tom. that there're over seven trillion gallons of fresh pristine water lying under these precious Jersey pinelands? I said 'over seven trillion gallons of pristine water'. We live above what is known as the Cohansey Aquifer," Watkins informed his avid, almost-mesmerized listener. "You and I own our worthless land, but not the valuable water deposits underneath it. You and I have wells, but the New Jersey governor says we're not allowed to water our lawns from the seven-trillion-gallon water reserve, because of crazy state and local drought restrictions. Isn't that absolutely ridiculous?"

"Why is that?" Tom Morris inquired before finishing-off his second brown bottle of brew. "You got my ears listenin'!"

"Because the seven trillion gallons of fresh water is bein' saved for Philly' and New York' niggers, that's why!" Harry Watkins yelled in an exasperated voice, accompanied by an exaggerated madman expression upon his grim face. "If the reservoirs outside those cities run dry, our seven trillion gallons of water will be available to keep all of the spud-heads in New York and Philly' happy, so that they don't riot and wreck-up the downtown business and historic areas, and then destabilize the whole damned country. City blacks are quite connected with all of this environmental bull that's bein' crammed down our lily-white throats!"

"So there really doesn't have to be any drought restrictions in the pinelands after all?" Tom concluded and asked. "It's all like a gigantic canard; a tremendous lie being perpetrated on us!"

"Exactly; it's all a big preposterous government scam!" Harry Watkins attested while generously handing Tom Morris his third cold beer. "That's why after we scare off the leeching mookers, the drugos, and the conservationists, our next enemies are gonna' have to be social deviates like gays, the state and federal governments, and the greedy, avaricious lawyers that run the state and national politics."

"This is dangerous business that you're askin' me to collaborate with you on," Tom seriously and defensively commented. "Are the drugos and drug distributors we target goin' to be white or black?"

"I haven't decided on that particular minute detail yet," Harry related, showing some rare indecisiveness. "But our first targets are gonna' be the rich dude, fat cat blacks movin' into the various ritzy South Jersey developments we're presently workin' in. Then Tom," Harry Watkins continued describing his bizarre lunacy, "after we become established and secretly sponsor some subordinate-but-independent militia cells, we'll then go after the detrimental conservationists and the ruthless drug distributors that are makin' millions in the subterranean economy that's presently causin' us to spend half our incomes on wasteful government programs. All of this unethical crap is happening because the burgeoning subterranean economy contributes no taxes to the IRS!"

"Didn't you once say that blacks should be separate-but-equal?" Tom Morris meekly challenged his new anarchistic partner. "These rich blacks can live wherever they want if they have the damned money. Can't they?"

"Tom, remember your wife and kid being in the hospital and why they're both suffering in there," Harry reminded his emotionally disheveled guest. "And by 'separate-but-equal', I mean that blacks could live in fancy houses if they can afford them, but they should all live in the same development and not become rabid Afro' pioneers seeking new frontiers; that is, *our* sacred pinelands. The professional blacks are gonna' be the vanguard that's gonna' niggerize and integrate *our turf;* city black scum will soon follow the initial *N pioneers* directly into the pinelands! Do I make myself perfectly clear?"

"When do we get started on implementing the secret project?" the anxious and emotionally-disoriented visitor asked. "I need to get even as soon as possible."

Harry Watkins remarked that the electrician and the heating and air-conditioning specialist would work together to clandestinely rig certain heaters and electrical circuits to short-out, to wildly spark, and then to ignite major house fires. Watkins also recommended that *they* break into the empty houses where black contractors have been working to avoid *FBI* suspicion and scrutiny. "Here's a list of prominent black contractors who recently have constructed homes for black professionals. Tom," Harry continued, "we're goin' to burn those fancy new black-owned homes to the ground, one by one. Are ya' ready to start our own secret militia cell Tom?"

"After what had happened this afternoon to my wife and kid, I'm more than ready," Tom Morris firmly agreed as the now-vindictive electrician firmly shook Harry Watkins' right hand. "I can't wait to read the daily papers to see how other white militia cells throughout the country are stealthily getting their important jobs done. I'm glad we had this confidential talk, Harry. It's time to stop talkin' and to start actin'!"

* * * * * * * * * * * *

The area newspapers and *Action* and *Eyewitness News* incidentally reported a rash of sundry house fires mixed-in with the regular blend of murders, thefts, kidnappings, drug arrests, and urban suicides. The *Atlantic City Press* covered the story of a home going up in flames in late April and the *Camden Courier-Post* had a front-page article describing an electrical fire to a wealthy black family's new residence in Glassboro. And then the *Hammonton News* and the *Hammonton Gazette* had feature headlines depicting a furnace exploding in Waterford Township, and each town paper reported that fortunately, no one was at home during the "mechanical and electrical malfunction".

"That will discourage these spooks, shines, and mookers from infiltratin' into our pinelands' paradise," Harry said to Tom on the way to their next subversive "housewarming". "This special job we're executin' tonight is goin' to require a huge demolition crew on the scene tomorrow mornin'."

"Are ya' sure no one's at home?" Tom Morris nervously asked his demented mentor. "I don't mind scarin' the crap out of our victims, as long as nobody's killed or seriously injured."

"The black family is out of town visitin' relatives," Watkins divulged to his partner-in-destruction. "I guarantee that they won't be home until tomorrow mornin'."

"You said black family and not niggers," Tom questioned. "Is there a difference?"

"Sure is," the driver of the white commercial pickup truck confided. "Niggers are what ya' see and hear on *MTV,* and what ya' see and hear interviewed on *Action News.* Niggers are the urban scum ya' see white suburban kids imitatin' with the gaudy earrings, the baggy pants, and the jungle body piercing, and the outlandish tattoos, along with *their* despicable rap lyrics," Harry elaborated. "Black Americans have evolved above the nigger state; got good educations, and drive around in expensive *Acuras* and *Mercedes*. Tom, we gotta' stop the upscale blacks from infestin' the suburbs, because they're just the first wave of Afro-Americans soon to be followed by the scumbag city niggers; that is, right after you and me start payin' the unfair reparations to finance their radical move into the sparse Jersey pinelands."

The white truck pulled-up into a prestigious, mostly Caucasian housing development, featuring a variety of homes listed at four hundred thousand dollars and up. One black family had recently moved into the upscale "yuppie" Pitman, New Jersey neighborhood, and that singular gossip had reached Harry Watkins by virtue of the white tradesmen' contracting network. "There it is across the street," the heating and air-conditioning technician pointed-out to his expert electrician colleague. "Let's make this trip short and sweet. Tom, ya' got the skeleton key to get in the back door?"

"Right here in my left front pocket," the extremely bigoted man's partner-in-hate-crime nervously answered.

Only three other handsome houses were occupied on that newly asphalted street in the just-being-built development, and the two devious men made their furtive entrance into the targeted premises without any apparent detection. The stealthy arsonists quickly descended the basement steps, and using flashlights, the two dedicated saboteurs got busy rearranging the wiring in the master switch-box and in the heating-air conditioning unit to eventually cause a continuous flurry of sparks to be emitted from each. If the defects were not discovered within an hour, the house would then go up in a huge blaze.

"Okay, Harry. I think we've done the necessary damage," Tom neurotically determined and shared. "Let's fly the coop!"

"Another sensational accident for the dumb teleprompter-reading commentators on *Eyewitness News* to report," Harry snidely laughed. "But the best part, Tom, is that there won't be any eyewitnesses squealing on *our* secret white clandestine activity on *Eyewitness News*."

The men stealthily scurried out the elaborate home's sturdy back door, and quickly hustled to Harry's white commercial pickup truck, innocently parked across the dark street. Both men jumped inside the vehicle's cab, still wearing their tool belts and their white plastic surgical gloves. Watkins speedily turned-on the ignition, and then a fantastic explosion blasted-out from the truck's engine, sending the white hood, motor, debris, human body parts, and fire and smoke bursting into the chilly night air. Both saboteurs had been instantly killed by the violent detonation.

* * * * * * * * * * * *

The following day, *Action* and *Eyewitness News'* reporters converged on the scene of devastation to cover the strange deaths and the damages done by the booming explosion. Pitman Police had already arrested two Afro-American suspects. The alleged bomb riggers were members of the radical black hate group *REP,* which specifically targets *R*ednecks, *E*uropeans and *P*ineys. According to the *Philadelphia Inquirer* Metro Page, South Jersey News article, "Apparently the black supremacist group had randomly isolated and then followed the white men's truck to the plush suburban housing development. While the workmen had inexplicably been parked outside a particular house, their truck engine then violently exploded. Evidently, heated debris from the blast shot across the street and ignited the plush house, which quickly burned to the ground before the Pitman Fire Company and the Pitman Rescue Squad personnel could respond to the extraordinary dual emergencies. An intensive police investigation is presently being conducted into the extraordinary incident."

Harry Watkins and Tom Morris had both learned all-too-late that excessive racial discrimination has its own definite high price. Hate begets hate, and bigotry begets bigotry. Those that live by prejudice often attract enemies that endorse the same type of antagonism toward them. Haters of other races often die by the prejudices of their avowed radical enemies, either performed by intention or performed by coincidence. And finally, everyone including New Jersey Pineys should be careful of what endorsement (by association) their telltale bumper stickers might suggest to criminal elements flourishing and prospering in American society.

"The Rings of Saturn"

At 11:30 a.m. on September 4th, 2002. a dark brown *UPS* truck rumbled into Michelle Celia's driveway to deliver a heavy package to 230 Marlyn Avenue, Hammonton, NJ. The attractive brunette was just drying herself off with a bath towel after exiting the shower, and was ready to don her newly-ironed police uniform. Michelle did not hear the series of knocks on her back kitchen door, so the *UPS* driver left the wrapped carton on the red-tiled floor inside the porch's screen door. Michelle's thirteen-year-old son Todd had been attending his first day of fall semester classes as a seventh-grader at the Hammonton Middle School, so the lad wasn't home to answer the door bell ring. The single-parent patrolwoman was mildly surprised to discover the 'box item' that had been delivered and placed on her back porch.

'What's this?' the surprised lady officer wondered as Michelle examined the package. 'It's from California. I don't have time to open it now because I'm almost late for my work shift. Chief Leadley will rip into me pretty good if I'm tardy. I'll stop home and check-out the carton on my four-o-clock break. But whatever is inside certainly weighs a heck of a lot!'

Then Patrolwoman Michelle Celia connected two distinct ideas. 'September 6th is my birthday, and this is probably a present from Aunt Marie out in San Diego,' the female crime-fighter presumed as she again hastily glanced at the California marking on the shipping label. The lady cop then lifted-up the bulky package and carried it into her kitchen, placing it in the center of the recently-wiped breakfast/lunch/supper table. 'Good old Aunt Marie never forgets my birthday!' Michelle very affectionately thought. Then the conscientious patrolwoman finished tidying-up her work uniform, locked the back kitchen door, exited the screen porch, and ambled over to her seven-year-old *SUV*.

Michelle Celia was the town's only female patrolwoman, and through perseverance and dedication, she had eventually won the confidence and the respect of her fellow male officers, who all politely treated her as an accepted peer. Michelle had retained her maiden name after undergoing a difficult emotionally-charged divorce proceeding with Dante Pagano, who turned-out to be a deadbeat dad, neglecting to honor his court promise to pay seven hundred dollars a month child support. Todd's mother had been awarded custody of the boy because the judge had noted Dante's pathetic history of accumulating chronic gambling debts, and *his* extensive bad reputation for womanizing outside the sacred vows of *Holy Matrimony*.

It was tough for Michelle to make ends meet on just a single-mother's salary. The town required that police personnel had to reside in the community where they served, so the female officer struggled to maintain her neat Marlyn Avenue brick home, and was considering the idea of another marriage as much out of economic necessity as out of a need to be loved, honored, and obeyed.

The gorgeous brunette patrolwoman backed her white *Jeep Grand Cherokee* out of her driveway, took Marlyn west to Bellevue Avenue, turned left, and then drove seven blocks to the Third Street traffic signal where the officer made another left turn. Five minutes later, the woman had already parked her *SUV* behind the Central Avenue police department, which was located below the Hammonton Town Hall. Michelle hastily scampered down the steps to avoid being tardy for duty.

"Sorry Michelle," Chief Leadley bluntly articulated, "but your patrol car is being serviced over at Crescent Tire. It needs new brakes and a new muffler. You'll have to partner with Officer Santoro until we get your cruising wheels back later this afternoon. Our back-up car is also in the shop being overhauled."

"That's all right, Chief!" Michelle amiably acknowledged. "Mark and I get along pretty well, and he's a proven true-blue professional. We've investigated many *Route-30* car accidents together, and also participated in at least seven complicated drug busts in the more unsavory sections of town. Mark and I never quarrel. And he'll be good company until I get my patrol car back!"

"Good. I expect to see you both out on your cruiser beat in five minutes," the Chief curtly replied. "As you know, I'm more into law enforcement than I am into my staff's social chemistry, if ya' know what I mean! I just can't help it. *You can call me old-fashioned, Michelle,* but that's just the way I am, and probably always will be!"

"Why should I call you 'old fashioned Michelle' when I know your name is Chief Donald Leadley?" the lady patrolman joked and giggled at her weak attempt at stand-up comedy.

Michelle Celia had had her eyes on Mark Santoro for quite some time, a tall, dark, handsome Italian, and the only eligible bachelor her age on the force. Michelle had known Mark when he was a Hammonton High School senior and she a junior, but his ultra-shy and mild-mannered personality was one that was a hundred percent committed to "loyalty to duty". The female officer dreamed of Mark some day proposing marriage, but the bashful patrolman would have difficulty asking the beautiful doll for a single date; let alone a trip down the church aisle straight-up to the altar.

"Hi Michelle," Officer Mark Santoro genially greeted his female colleague and partner for the day. "The Chief wants us to patrol the area between Central and the White Horse Pike this morning."

"Accident alley," Michelle immediately noted. "We're averaging three-a-day now on the busy *Route 30* strip. I'm getting arthritis in my right hand from writing so many thorough collision reports and comprehensive traffic violations."

"I guess you can call that arth-*write*-us!" her partner-for-the-day drolly jested, while awkwardly formulating an inane play-on-words.

The two defenders of justice entered the three-year-old patrol car, and then the male officer fired-up the loud engine. "There must be an easier way of making a living," the consummate policeman complained as Santoro steered his daily cruiser onto congested Central Avenue. "I mean, I really enjoy my job and really like the challenges connected with police work. But you're absolutely right Michelle," the driver qualified. "There's entirely too much bureaucracy and paperwork involved with each passing day. Everything has to be justified in detail, or else Chief Leadley puts us on the proverbial carpet."

"And all documentation and traffic citations have to be prepared in triplicate!" Mark's female partner-for-the-day smartly responded and added. "I need my own personal, professional copier and reams of paper just for completing all the reports! Maybe I'll try requisitioning a Xerox machine next year on my annual budget sheet, and watch the Chief's toupee skyrocket off his bald head and blast right through the ceiling."

The patrol car was rounding the corner of Third Street and Fairview Avenue when a rare moment of silence existed between the pair of ten-year veterans. Michelle was about to mention what a peaceful trouble-free morning it had been when the dispatcher's baritone voice came over the police car radio.

"An alert neighbor reports an attempted breaking and entering at 230 Marlyn Avenue. Mark and Michelle, you're to proceed immediately to the scene and apprehend the suspects. Initial information is that the trespassers are a male and female in their forties, quite possibly of Hispanic descent."

"Roger, Sam!" Mark acknowledged and confirmed. "10-4! Over and out!"

"Michelle, that's *your* place that Sam just described!" Officer Santoro exclaimed as the driver simultaneously put on the patrol car's red flashers, and aggressively pressed the pedal to the metal. "How could anybody be so stupid trying to burglarize a cop's home! I swear that most criminals' IQs are progressively getting lower all the time. Einsteins they are not!"

"They might be Mexican or Puerto Rican farm workers looking for some easy drug money," Michelle theorized and expressed, "but we won't know for sure unless we can catch them red-handed in the act and interrogate them. I hope the culprits speak some English!"

"Do you know any Spanish?" the anxious cop behind the wheel asked. "I can't speak a word of it. I had taken French as a second language way back in high school. Mr. DeFiccio liked me, and luckily gave me a D for simply showing-up and smiling at him every school day."

"Only a few phrases to get by on introduction," the driver's all-too-honest colleague/passenger revealed. "I was lucky to get a C in my Spanish I class from Mr. Taylor, and a B my sophomore year from all-too-generous Mr. DeFiccio."

The speeding patrol car swung a right onto Linda Avenue, which led to Elvins. Mark next turned right onto Bellevue, the town's main avenue. A quick left was negotiated just past the Colonial Court Apartments complex, and then the roaring patrol car was soon zipping along heading east on Marlyn. The cruiser zoomed-down the ordinarily somnolent residential street, buzzing past modest ranch and two-story colonial houses. In twenty seconds, Mark's vehicle veered into Michelle's asphalt driveway at the designated 230 Maryln Avenue address.

The officers hastily leaped out of the patrol car, and swiftly raced to the back porch door. The two investigators discovered that the kitchen door had been jimmied-open, and so the patrolmen aggressively entered the premises, instantly surprising the two interlopers caught red-handed committing their felonious act. A well-dressed man (in a gray pinstriped business suit) was collared holding the heavy brown *UPS* package, and both *the culprit* and his female companion (wearing a black dress) were shocked to realize that *they* had been so easily detected and apprehended. Michelle and Mark steadily held their revolvers, pointing their weapons directly at the unsuccessful and thoroughly guilty thieves.

"Caja en mesa y manos arriba!" Michelle loudly commanded in stilted Spanish.

The Hispanic man immediately placed the heavy package on the kitchen table, and then raised his hands above his head. The suspect's female accomplice quickly mimicked *his* example. Mark proceeded to first handcuff the trespassing gentleman, and then do likewise to *his* lady associate.

"Como se llama?" the intense female cop asked the very embarrassed man in English accented Spanish.

"Alfredo Torres," the suspect reluctantly admitted.

"Y sus nombre, Senora por Senorita," Michelle questioned.

"Yolanda Flores," Alfredo again replied in a seemingly disgusted tone of voice.

"Ustedes es esposo y esposa?" the lady patrolmen sternly fired back.

"Si," Alfredo volunteered. "Para viente y cinco annos!"

"Mr. and Mrs. Alfredo Torres have been married for twenty-five years," Officer Celia informed Patrolman Santoro. "Donde viva, ustedes?"

"El Cajon, El Cajon!" Alfredo answered. "En California!"

"Tu tiene identificacion?" Michelle firmly interrogated.

"No tiene. Yo tengo nada! Lo es en mis coche," Alfredo Torres responded in a defiant manner.

"Que es ustedes en esa casa?" Michelle demanded to know in the best Spanish she could muster.

"Porque lo es aqui. El Cajon! El Cajon! Lo es aqui! Los anillos de Saturno! Los anillos de Saturno! Lo es aqui!" Alfredo repeatedly confessed.

"Why does he want to give *Lois a key*?" Mark Santoro honestly asked his fellow on-the-spot investigator. "Is his wife's name Lois? I thought it was Yolanda?"

"No Mark," the officer's partner laughed and corrected. "Lo es aqui means 'it is here'. El Cajon! The box!"

"Do you mean to say that these two trespassers live in a box and they broke into *your* house looking for the box's key?" Patrolman Santoro marveled and chuckled as the capable cop expertly stuck his reliable revolver back into his waist holster.

"No silly," Michelle said and chided with a smirk that held back a hardy laugh. "According to my knowledge of geography, El Cajon is a small city outside San Diego. I know *that* because my Aunt Marie lives not far away from there in Mission Hills. And there must be a box in this *UPS* package I received this morning via UPS. It's probably a gift from my Aunt Marie. The second reference to 'el cajon' you had heard probably refers to *the box*."

"I see, so there're actually two El Cajons," Mark stated and understood with a contrived smile. "The town where these two persons of interest live, and the name of the box in the package on the kitchen table. Maybe these two villains know your Aunt Marie?"

"Let's take them down to the station and book them for further questioning," Michelle intelligently suggested. "Unfortunately, I've just about exhausted my entire Spanish vocabulary. We'll need an interpreter to get additional information out of them. Maybe Detective Martinez can interrogate these two suspects, and get some more pertinent details. Jerry's family was from Puerto Rico, but I think he can communicate with Mexicans much better than I can."

"Okay; let's escort them out to the patrol car," Patrolman Santoro recommended. "They're both under arrest for breaking and entering and for suspicion of intent to commit robbery."

Officer Santoro reached inside of Alfredo's custom-tailored suit jacket pocket and pulled-out an envelope. Inside was a neatly drawn map with detailed Spanish directions to "230 Marlyn Avenue, Hammonton, New Jersey".

"The suspects even have a neat little treasure map leading right to your home," Mark indicated to Michelle. "These foreign banditos are getting more and more sophisticated every passing day. But by their dress and general appearance, I doubt very much if *these two* are migrant farm laborers coming here to pick peaches, tomatoes, peppers, and blueberries. These two folks look like *seasoned* criminals and not *seasonal* crop pickers."

"Remind me to call a locksmith and have the latch on my door changed," Michelle politely requested of her uniformed companion. "They must've used that screwdriver laying on the kitchen counter to pry the door open. It's not one of mine!"

"Roger Wilko!" Mark amiably replied while giving his fellow officer an impromptu mock salute. "We'll take along the screwdriver as evidence. And please specify you want a deadbolt lock installed on your back door. Say Michelle, where did you learn that *manos arriba* stuff? I gotta' admit; that particular vocabulary phrase seemed pretty impressive!"

"I remembered it from the classic movie *Butch Cassidy and the Sundance Kid*," Santoros' fellow officer laughed. "Paul Newman tried saying it when he and Robert Redford were attempting to rob a Bolivian bank. That was really a hilarious scene!"

Alfredo and Yolanda Torres were taken into custody and detained inside two Hammonton Police Department jail cells; both situated beneath the outdated Town Hall. The couple finally confessed through an interpreter that they had parked their 2001 black *Lincoln Continental* in the *McDonald's* parking lot on Woodlawn Avenue and *Route 30,* and had trekked the three blocks to 230 Marlyn Avenue to then rob the female cop's house.

"Not your typical Mexican migrant workers following the crops up the east coast from June to October, that's for darned sure," Mark Santoro declared to his partner-for-the-day later that afternoon at police headquarters. "According to authorities in El Cajon, the unscrupulous intruders own a pawnshop in that city and actually live in a small palace," Mark related to Michelle, who was also sipping coffee during their afternoon break. "What motivated them to trespass onto your humble property and contemplate committing robbery? We'll discuss that scenario some more in the privacy of the patrol car."

"Good idea!" Michelle concurred before imbibing another mouthful of Folgers Instant. "It all does seem to be quite a weird riddle! Perhaps a vital clue can be found inside the mysterious package I had received."

Mark drove *'Car Seven'* out of the police station's entrance en route to the local doughnut haven where the two hungry anti-crime warriors purchased some high-calorie snacks from the employee manning the Dunkin' Donuts drive-through window.

"Have our amigos Alfredo and Yolanda been tested for drugs?" Michelle inquired as her partner again pulled into her driveway after acquiring two lidded cups of coffee along with four mouth-watering chocolate-covered doughnuts for quick consumption during their next slated fifteen-minute break.

"No, I don't think this particular break-in crime is drug-related," Mark speculated and stated. "These people specifically broke into your house for a purpose other than drug money or searching for items to steal to fence for drugs. I'm almost certain of that! They both appear to be too sophisticated, and too educated, to commit an amateur break-in!"

"The trespassers had the map to my place with the Spanish directions," the female cop recollected and mentioned, "and they're probably on a rampant crime spree stretching from coast to coast. I'm sure Alfredo and Yolanda just didn't cross the continent simply to target my rinky-dink residence for a commonplace *UPS* package hit. Let's be logical for a minute. There're hundreds of mansions in this affluent town worth robbing compared to my tiny dump. Let's have the snacks and java Mark, and then I'll curiously open the package and see what's contained inside."

"Good idea. Could I use your desktop computer for a few minutes?" Mark Santoro requested. "I want to see what that 'antillos *day sad turn no*' means in English. Sounds like a tropical resort somewhere near Aruba or Cancun!"

"Try spelling the phrase this way: a-n-i-l-l-o-s d-e S-a-t-u-r-n-o," Michelle constructively advised. "I think I know how it's spelled, but in all honesty Mark, it's definitely way out of my very limited Spanish vocabulary and grammar range."

The two compatible cops voraciously ate most of their doughnuts inside Michelle's modest kitchen, and then each officer gulped-down the remainder of his and her twelve-ounce-coffees. After the keepers-of-the-peace were delightfully finished swallowing-down their delectable pastry snacks, Mark casually stepped to the desktop computer in the den, while Michelle rapidly began opening the recently arrived mystery package. A moment later the patrolwoman was absolutely fascinated by what her eyes perceived. A splendid jewelry chest having three tiers of velvet-covered trays had been discovered inside the brown cardboard box.

The first compartment contained thirteen gold-banded rings. Twelve were labeled with designated zodiac signs. The second thin sliding shelf contained twelve corresponding gemstones with no given identifications, and the third moveable drawer had a dozen arcane zodiac constellation symbols. The all-too-curious female cop instinctively shut the three drawers when she heard Mark turn-off the computer in the adjacent room.

"Well, what was in the box that was so valuable and important to Alfredo and Yolanda?" Officer Santoro uncharacteristically asked. "Was it loaded with tacos, enchiladas and burritos?"

"It's just a chest of rather cheap costume jewelry of some sort," Michelle imaginatively fibbed. "It must have some special cultural significance to them to want to steal it. The items in the ordinary-looking jewelry box don't look like stuff you'd buy on Fifth Avenue in Manhattan; that's for sure!" Michelle creatively commented. "What did *you* discover on the computer?"

"Antillos de Saturno means 'Rings of Saturn'," Mark disclosed with a puzzled expression featured on his face. "I researched it on a Spanish-to-English online dictionary. Are these itinerant people into astronomy or what? I'm very disappointed Michelle. I thought that *that* package you had opened would have a small telescope *you* had to assemble," Patrolman Santoro smiled and jested while shrugging his shoulders upwards to the level of his chin, showing feigned regret.

"Well, I'm going to keep the odd gift anyway since it had been addressed and delivered to me," Mark's temporary partner disclosed. "I'm certain it's a present from my Aunt Marie out in San Diego. It's just a rather bizarre coincidence that the felons are also from the same area of California."

"Is your aunt's return address on the package's shipping label?" Mark perceptively asked. "I would logically think that tiny piece of information could easily solve your little source riddle."

"No; the address on the carton is 370 Zodiac Boulevard, probably the store that had sold the costume jewelry gift to Aunt Marie. You aren't trying to implicate my seventy-two-year-old-aunt in this small town breaking and entering case, are you?" Michelle facetiously accused with a prodigious smile upon her countenance. "Mark, I think you have better things to think and worry about."

"Okay, I do admit; no harm no foul!" Officer Santoro plausibly answered. "I never graduated from prosecutor's school, nor do I ever want to!" the handsome Italian keeper-of-the-peace amiably replied. "Now let's get back on the beat and find some more crime before crime manages to find us again!"

* * * * * * * * * * * *

At 8:15 that night, Michelle drove her white '95 *Jeep Grand Cherokee* into her driveway, removed her keys, locked the doors, and then entered her modest brick home that she was struggling to maintain on a single parent's public servant mediocre income. The young lady bent-down and picked-up a second *UPS* parcel that had been left on her back porch, and then carefully entered her home. A plain red sweater sent from San Diego by Aunt Marie had been contained inside the second delivery.

Michelle's next impulse was to closely examine the unique ebony jewelry box's particular jewelry contents. The homeowner quickly scrutinized the thirteen sparkling gold rings; then Officer Celia admired the dozen dazzling precious gemstones in the second-tier drawer, and finally closely admired the twelve silver horoscope symbols stored inside the third velvet-lined tray, all of which highly intrigued her.

'I'll use the encyclopedias and then also the computer to research some pertinent things about these beautiful items,' the fascinated woman thought. 'This is some sort of peculiar riddle that must be deciphered. I won't be able to sleep until I match-up all the missing pieces and develop some meaningful, plausible rhyme or reason.

Todd ate an early supper over at Jimmy Sandler's place, and now he's at Hammonton Hawks' football practice at the lake,' Michelle remembered. 'This gives me a precise time window to academically do some initial research and then fully investigate this very strange gemstone enigma!'

Michelle had the next day off from work because Chief Donald P. Leadley had penciled her in to be on patrol the following Sunday. The Chief had traded assignment days, so Officer Celia would be substituting on Sunday for a patrolman that would be away on vacation. The exchange of days now seemed to be a blessing in disguise, and the very anxious policewoman couldn't wait to open her encyclopedias and learn more about zodiac signs, and to perform some preliminary research on the subjects of gems and astrology. The single-mother was scheduled to pick-up son Todd at Hammonton Lake Park on Egg Harbor Road after Hammonton Hawks' football practice, but in the meantime, Michelle had to also prepare a supper of mashed potatoes and pork chops.

"Mom, why are you so pleasant and peppy tonight?" Todd asked as he hopped into the white *SUV* just after football practice. "Has Dad sent some child support money in the mail?"

"No Todd; I had a very relaxing day at work, and have more energy than usual," the mother cunningly replied. "Tomorrow I should be back to being my same old miserable, demanding self. In fact, I guarantee it."

"Well Mom, I have some good news for you," Todd excitedly mentioned. "I'm now a starting offensive guard on the football team. Coach Attanasi and Coach DiDomenico just broke the terrific news. Isn't that cool?"

The following morning before school, Todd had a pertinent question to ask his mother. "Mom, what's in the weird-looking box in your bedroom?" the boy innocently asked.

"Oh, just a birthday present from Aunt Marie," the working mom deceivingly responded. "Did you remember to buy your mother a birthday gift?" the parent challenged, cleverly reversing the tables on her suddenly alarmed son.

"No Mom; I promise to buy you somethin' nice at *Wal-Mart* this weekend after our first game," Todd replied with a trace of guilt apparent in his high-pitched voice. "I've been savin' my allowance money since Christmas, though."

"*Wal-Mart?*" the boy's mother indulgently laughed. "Well, it's not exactly *Sak's Fifth Avenue or Tiffany's,* but I guess it's better than nothing. A new pair of bedroom slippers would be just fine. Any other questions before school?”

“Yes; why is that man changing the lock on the back porch door?” the alert and inquisitive son asked. “Is our house on lock-down like the middle school often is?”

“Oh,” the mother hurriedly answered while her astute mind was formulating a feasible explanation. “I accidentally bent the key while entering the back porch door yesterday on my afternoon break and decided it was time to get a new lock put on. I promise to provide you with a duplicate key as soon as the new lock’s installed.”

That day, while Todd was at school, and that night, while Todd was practicing as starting right offensive guard on the Hammonton Hawks football squad, Michelle Celia was assiduously engaged in her intensive computer and encyclopedia research. Her first task was to coordinate the twelve labeled golden zodiac rings with their corresponding dozen silver constellation symbols, and then also with the glittering birthstones relating to the twelve months of the calendar year. The anxious investigator soon learned that the jewelry chest was actually a kind of kit, and the three distinct sets of information that she had meticulously gleaned from the three-tiered trays had to be correlated into a dozen separate zodiac files.

At seven p.m., the locksmith returned to 230 Marilyn Avenue, rapped on the back door, and a half hour later, announced that he had finally completed his routine deadbolt lock installation. “Thanks for your prompt service call,” Michelle readily acknowledged. “How much will that be, Frank?”

“Don’t worry,” Frank Fucetola, the town’s reliable locksmith cheerfully answered. “I had to go and pick-up some special materials to finish the job. I’ll send you a bill in the mail once I get everything itemized. How dumb those two characters must’ve been, breaking into a policewoman’s house!” the handyman heavily laughed. “And the home of a very crackerjack, top-notch policewoman too, if I might add.”

“Thanks again, Frank,” Michelle said and smiled. “I always respond favorably to compliments, especially when they’re stated with sincerity.” The resident then accepted three keys to the new deadbolt lock, closed the back porch door, and then rapidly paced to the den to resume her zodiac knowledge exploration, using the *Internet* and her trusty set of 1960 era encyclopedias.

‘Let’s see now,’ Michelle thought while studying the twelve gemstones and comparing them with a color-page of pictures in her *World Book Encyclopedia G.* ‘The twelve gemstones in the second tray all match-up with the twelve birthstones listed in the book. But the zodiac signs are not exactly identified according to months. For example,' she considered, 'I'm a Virgo because my birthday is today, September 6th, but Virgo goes from August 24th to September 23rd in the newspaper horoscopes. Since more days in the sign Virgo are in September than in August, I assume that the ring for September should be constructed of the plain golden band for Virgo in the first tray. Then, that should be joined with the sapphire gemstone for the month of September from the second tier, and with the silver virgin symbol for Virgo from the chest's bottom third drawer. This whole puzzle is becoming mighty interesting!'

Michelle carefully removed the three particular items from the three-tiered drawers, and amazingly, the dark blue sapphire stone fit perfectly into a grooved-out slot on top of the golden band. And then similarly, the two-dimensional silver 'Virgin Image' snapped perfectly on top of the sapphire gemstone into four tiny slits in the topside of the band. 'Since it's September, I made myself a beautiful Virgo ring. I hope it brings me good luck,' the now-enamored gem researcher wished.

The woman's diligent research was instantly interrupted by her sudden realization that it was already eight p.m. 'Oh no! It's almost time to pick-up Todd at Hawks' practice. I gotta' hustle over to Hammonton Lake Park.'

Michelle Celia slid the newly assembled ring onto the fourth finger of her ring hand, pretending it was a wedding band presented by Mark Santoro. After admiring her recently assembled creation, the dedicated policewoman readily exited her neatly-maintained brick home, latched the new dead-bolted back kitchen door, and then gathering her scattered wits, drove a monotonous mile to the town's principal park to retrieve starting right guard Todd Celia.

"Oh Michelle," Jimmy Sandler's chatty mother hollered and hand- signaled her friend at the park's football bleachers. "The girls missed talking with you up in the stands tonight."

"Oh, hi Madge," the *SUV* operator answered from the driver's seat. "I had to stay at home while a locksmith finished changing my back door's bolt. In this day and age, you're never safe enough from prowlers and burglars. Even savvy police officers need added protection from scheming, nefarious crooks!"

"They'd be both stupid and crazy to try anything at your place," Madge indulgently laughed. "You would practice some advanced self-defense karate maneuvers on them, and then savagely body-slam the violators just like the versatile athletes do on television professional wrestling.”

The following Saturday afternoon was the *Hammonton Hawks* first scheduled football game against *Egg Harbor Township*. It was late in the fourth quarter, and the score was tied 14-14, but the *Hawks* had the ball with only thirty seconds remaining on the game clock. “I *wish* the *Hawks* could score a touchdown and claim an early season victory,” Michelle innocently commented to Madge. “*Egg Harbor’s* the toughest opponent we’re goin’ to face all year.”

“If only I had a magic wand,” Madge said with a smile. “I’d surely use it right now!”

‘I *wish* Todd could score a touchdown, but he’s an offensive lineman and not the team quarterback; an end, or a halfback,’ Michelle imagined.

The next play was third down. The Hammonton quarterback had called a “fake reverse *Statue of Liberty* pass to the tight end” in the offensive huddle. The team leader retreated back pretending to pass, and as the slot-receiver came around to fake grabbing the ball from the quarterback’s right hand, the player accidentally knocked the football out of *his* grasp. The pigskin bounced and rolled around on the turf, and then the bouncing pigskin popped-up into the hands of a very surprised Todd Celia, who then zigzagged, rambled and hustled totally unimpeded through heavy opponent traffic sixty yards directly into the *Egg Harbor Township* end zone, just as the umpire’s game watch expired.

The Hammonton crowd enthusiastically screamed and cheered encouragement during and after the sensational twenty-second exhaustive accomplishment. Madge Sandler and Michelle Celia threw their arms around each other and jubilantly jumped up and down in recognition of Todd’s unexpected, wonderful contribution to the *Hawks’* dramatic victory.

“Michelle, that’s a beautiful ring you’re wearin’!” Madge noticed and praised. “Where did you get it?”

“It came from California *UPS*,” her completely thrilled, very proud friend explained. “My dear Aunt Marie sent it as a birthday gift. It’s got my sapphire birthstone in it, and a unique Virgo zodiac figure attached also. I just love it!”

“Well then, happy birthday!” Madge genuinely congratulated. “And tell your fine son he couldn’t have given you a better present than that incredible touchdown he just scored!”

The possessor of the spectacular zodiac chest decided that the ring of the month should only be worn at home when ‘off police duty and off parent duty.' 'I don't like when people become too curious and ask too many questions,' Michelle determined. 'I'll just keep and cherish the rings all to myself in my bedroom.'

Soon, it was October, and being a little tired of the August 24-September 23rd Virgo ring, on October 1st Michelle disassembled the Virgo image and the dark blue sapphire stone, and carefully placed the items in the appropriate drawers of the ebony jewelry chest. Then, she meticulously constructed the regal-looking Libra ring, which consisted of a light blue and earth toned opal gemstone and a silver set of scales to snap on top of the precious mineral. To supplement her knowledge and appreciation of astrology, the off-duty policewoman feverishly read various texts and articles on zodiac signs on the *Internet*.

'It states that astrology is based on the four primary elements of ancient and medieval philosophy,' Michelle ambitiously read. 'People that are of the air element are least emotional and value mental activity and thinking over passion. There're three distinct air signs: Aquarius, Gemini and Libra. I'll wager that Mark is an air sign, because the handsome guy is much more rational and aloof than he is openly affectionate.'

Then, the suddenly avid reader explored the topic Virgo and discovered that it was an earth sign along with Taurus and Capricorn. 'Earth sign people tend to be practical and believe in permanent relationships. That's me, but unfortunately, my deadbeat ex-husband never valued that sort of commitment. Dante must be a water sign, a Pisces, a Scorpio or a Cancer. It states on the computer screen that water sign individuals are moody, emotional, sensitive of criticism, and very intense when aggravated,' Michelle assessed and considered. 'Let's see now. I know that Dante's birthday was on July 15th. That makes him a Cancer, and his peeved personality fits the water sign description perfectly.'

Quite contented with her academic findings and with her subsequent hypotheses, Michelle continued her delving into the very interesting 'arcane' subject matter. 'Todd's birthday is April 10th. That makes him an Aries, which is a fire sign along with Leo and Sagittarius. Fire sign people tend to be warm, motivated, assertive, and energetic. That matches Todd's characteristics to the exact detail,' Michelle deducted. 'I'm glad I'm becoming more interested in something besides tedious police work. At this incredible rate, I'll be an authority on astrology within a week.'

The next day, at the town police station, Michelle confronted Officer Santoro before the two entered their separate parking lot patrol cars. "Say, Mark; would your birthday happen to be in October? I'll bet you're a Libra! If not, then I'd wager you're probably a February Aquarius or a June Gemini!"

"Are you into crystal balls or are you now hanging out with crackpot fortunetellers?" Mark marveled and chuckled. "I'm really quite impressed, I must say! You're right on the money with your first guess. My birthday's October the 6th. I'm a Libra according to the morning horoscope page in the Atlantic City Press. How did ya' know *that* esoteric detail about my life, Michelle?"

"Oh, just a woman's intuition I suppose," the lady officer coyly answered with a forced wry smile. "I'm becoming an avid student of astrology, and it's all pretty interesting once you master the fairly odd terminology. Of course, I'm just looking into it for amusement purposes only, but contrary to popular opinion, there seems to be more science to it than art, I must say."

"Just don't turn into a mean old witch before Halloween," Officer Santoro joked. "Broomsticks are becomin' more and more expensive all the time, and quite frankly, they're now out of vogue."

On October the 8th Michelle was looking out from her kitchen window at her neighbor's ugly, dilapidated house. The Marlyn Avenue resident inadvertently glanced-down at her earth-toned opal Libra ring and uttered, "I *wish* Mr. Jacobs would spend some cash and fix up his house. My property value would probably go up twenty thousand dollars if *he* decided to make the necessary investment and improvement."

Two days later, a team of skilled carpenters, plumbers, electricians, roofers, and siding-installers showed-up on the Jacobs' property. After three days of intensive labor, the reclusive neighbor's former decrepit-looking residence looked like one that belonged in a fancy home renovation magazine. "Gee Todd, just look at our neighbor's new black roof, green vinyl siding, and the addition of a spacious recreation room. My prayers have been answered, and if I ever sell my place, I'm guaranteed to make a handsome profit because of Mr. Jacobs' new mini-palace," Michelle articulated to her somewhat disinterested son, who was busy reading and analyzing the contents of a *Batman* comic book.

November soon rolled around, and Todd was worried that he wasn't going to make the school honor roll because of a C he expected to earn in science class. Michelle casually glanced at her new topaz ring with a scorpion attached to the gemstone and *wished* that Todd would get an A on his last science test of the semester to qualify making the honor roll. A week later, Todd came home in an exceptionally ecstatic mood, and the excited lad enthusiastically presented his stellar first marking period report card to his mother.

"Look Mom; I got a B in science and made the honor roll! This is almost as thrilling as scoring that lucky touchdown against *Egg Harbor Township*!" the energized boy blithely related.

"I knew you could do it if you just applied yourself!" the mother exclaimed, while forgetting all about her whimsical November wish a week before. "Here's a ten-dollar bill as a bonus-reward, and it looks like we're goin' over to Bruni's Pizza to officially celebrate your amazing academic achievement. Call Jimmy Sandler on the phone and tell him I'm willing to treat the two of you honor roll geniuses to anything on the menu."

In early December, Michelle had trouble making ends meet. First, she had to pay her hefty November property tax bill, then her water pump went haywire, and had to be replaced, and next, she needed a new heater because the old one had a crack in its furnace wall and was emitting a small trace of carbon monoxide. The no-nonsense gas company inspector instantly condemned the furnace until a new one would be installed.

As the very depressed woman stared at her December Sagittarius turquoise ring (having a kneeling silver archer mounted on its golden crest), the tearful patrolwoman *wished* that Chief Leadley would promote her to corporal, so that she could receive a two-thousand dollar raise in addition to her standard yearly salary increment. 'He's always criticizing and finding fault with my reports,' Michelle lamented. 'He's such a fussy nitpicker when it comes to personnel qualifications. I wish *he* would commend my job performance once in a while. I hate to admit it, but I'm rapidly developing a self-destructive inferiority complex!'

On the second Friday in December, Chief Donald P. Leadley summoned Patrolwoman Michelle A. Celia into his office so that the head cop could deliver some very favorable news. "Michelle, you're the only woman on the force, and I want you to know you do one heck of a job. Without a doubt, the men all hold your loyalty to the department in high regard."

"Thank you, Chief," the somewhat-stunned and flattered lady officer verbally acknowledged. "I always try to be fair with the public, and perform my duties to the best of my ability."

"It gives me great satisfaction to hereby announce that you've been promoted to the rank of Sergeant," The Chief happily declared. "I'm recommending your good name to the town council at the next scheduled meeting. Michelle, you'll probably have your stripes no later than the first week of January. And it's not because you're a woman," the chief insisted and emphasized. "Gender had nothing to do with it. It's simply because you're a really effective and outstanding police officer!"

"How much will my salary increase be?" the highly elated lady officer requested knowing. "I can't believe that I've passed right by the rank of Corporal and have swiftly ascended the pay scale from Patrolman to Sergeant!"

"Well, you've definitely jumped Corporal rank and will indeed become a Sergeant," the Chief stated as the head honcho closely examined the pay-scale chart. "So, that means you'll get five thousand dollars more a year plus your standard increment. Figure on a nice seven thousand dollar pay raise!"

"Thank you so much for the wonderful recommendation," Michelle appreciatively replied to the normally stoic Chief-of-Police. "I'll try my best to confirm your confidence in me!"

'I wonder if my Sagittarius ring had anything to do with my most recent success,' Michelle speculated. 'There seems to be a strange connection with *wishes* I've secretly made that had eventually come true. I'll try a little experiment when I go home.'

The totally lighthearted policewoman arrived at her modest residence, placed the aforementioned Sagittarius ring (with the turquoise gemstone and accompanying archer) on her finger, and wished that a million dollars would instantly appear on her bed. When Michelle Celia glanced around her bedroom, no stacks of bills were piled on her plain, white, cotton bedspread. 'It was only *wishful* thinking,' the disappointed woman sullenly concluded. 'It all must've been a series of strange, ironic coincidences. Astrology doesn't control the universe, or the galaxy, or even the more diminutive solar system I live in, for that matter. It is I who controls my own destiny, and not some silly zodiac ring! How foolish of me to give these rings any special credence at all!'

In early-January, eight inches of snow had fallen on the ground after a fierce mini-blizzard had hit the Mid-Atlantic States. Michelle carefully placed the three principal elements of her Sagittarius ring back into their respective trays. Next, the Police Sergeant skillfully assembled her Capricorn finger-ornament, consisting of the standard gold band from the first tray; the reddish garnet stone insert from the second; and finally, the silver goat zodiac snap-on accessory from the jewelry box's bottom third tier. 'I must wear this good luck charm only when at home,' the woman possessively thought. 'I much prefer asking questions rather than answering them. I *wish* that Mark would become motivated to get a romance going and ask me out on a date. I believe he really wants to do so, but can't get up the gumption to call and suggest it. Perhaps I should reverse the tables and call him.'

Ten minutes later, the kitchen wall phone rang. "Hello Michelle; it's me, Mark," the caller pleasantly identified himself. "I figured I'd give your phone a ring and learn what's happening in your secluded life. How are things going?"

"Gee, hi Mark!" the call's recipient surprisingly exclaimed. "What's up? Arrested any celebrities or Congressmen today?"

"I've been meaning to ask you out for the longest time," Mark prefaced, "but I haven't been able to muster the courage. Would you be interested in dinner and a show at *Harrah's Casino*? I know a person in the ticket sales' department who owes me a big personal favor, who can get us good seats."

"That sounds tremendous, Mark!" the suddenly euphoric lonely woman responded. "When can we make the Atlantic City scene? I need a change in venue badly!"

"What about, let's say, two Fridays from now?" Mark persuasively suggested. "I can make the arrangements tomorrow."

"Really terrific!" Michelle mildly shouted into the receiver as the New Age Astrologer stared in admiration at her fabulous, new Capricorn zodiac ring. "I'll get my sister to have Todd stay at her house over on Tilton. Consider it a date."

"Thanks," the spirited caller declared. "You don't know how relieved I am getting this matter over and done with. I've always had this great formidable fear of being rejected."

"You're definitely number one in my book," the still-happy policewoman exclaimed. "And I'm very glad you called and made the totally romantic offer," the enraptured woman aptly encouraged.

After putting the bedroom phone down onto its cradle, Michelle came-up with an interesting explanation for the latest remarkable coincidence. 'Maybe each ring has the power to grant one wish a month; the first wish I accidentally or deliberately make on *that* associated month. In February, I'm going to test my new theory and determine its accuracy,' the newly appointed Sergeant imagined and decided. 'I'll intentionally make a wild, ridiculous *wish,* and then wait and see if the unexpected event actually materializes.'

February arrived with Mother Nature featuring another cruel, blustery winter snowstorm. The possessor of the very extraordinary jewelry case systematically dismantled her Capricorn ring with the accompanying garnet gemstone, checked the encyclopedia to verify amethyst as the official Aquarius mineral; very methodically inserted the new stone into its appropriate slot, and then snapped the silver water-carrier zodiac symbol over it. Looking at the sparkling ring, Michelle very seriously and maliciously thought, 'I *wish* Dante were dead. He's never paid any child support, has constantly abused me verbally, and is an absolute discredit to the whole human race.'

Thirty minutes later, the telephone rang. "Hello," the woman of the house said as she inspected and continued admiring the newly assembled, magnificent Aquarius ring glittering on her finger.

"Michelle, this is Mary Pagano, your former mother-in-law," the voice on the other end of the line sobbed. "I have some disturbing news. Dante died from a massive stroke around a half-hour ago," the very upset woman grieved. "I know you and my son didn't hit it off too good from the start, but I thought I would give you the courtesy of a call to inform you of the bad news."

"Oh my God!" the former daughter-in-law gasped, attempting to disguise the verification of her immoral vindictiveness. "I just can't believe this has happened!" Michelle exclaimed, as she intently gaped at the magical ring. "He's so young!"

"Check the *Atlantic City Press*," Mary Pagano whimpered in a faltering voice. "The obituary and church service should appear in Wednesday's paper, once I make the funeral arrangements."

"Sorry again to hear the terribly bad news," somewhat-distraught Michelle Celia replied in a monotone voice, feigning genuine sympathy. "I'll put in for a personal day and definitely attend the funeral," she promised.

After terminating the conversation with her former mother-in-law, Michelle poured herself a *Southern Comfort* double on the rocks', plopped-down in her living room's soft, black, leather chair, and then studied the fantastic ring on her right hand's fourth finger. 'I'll bet each ring allows me one wish per month,' the lady of the house conjectured in a very melancholy frame of mind. 'Of course, that's precisely what happened without me ever realizing the exact connection. The Virgo ring compelled Todd to score the touchdown; the Libra ring influenced Mr. Jacobs to repair and renovate his house, and the Scorpio ring caused Todd to pass his science test and make the honor roll,' the lady cop objectively reviewed and summarized. 'And then, the Sagittarius ring made my wish for a promotion and a substantial salary raise come true; the Capricorn ring had the power to persuade Mark to ask me out to Harrah's Casino, and the Aquarius ring amazingly brought about Dante's unexpected death. I'm going to personally capitalize on my magic rings starting in March. Now, I know why Alfredo and Yolanda Torres so badly wanted to pilfer the contents of this unbelievable and indispensable, unknown sorcerer's jewelry chest.'

In early March, Michelle Celia eagerly disassembled the Aquarius ring with the amethyst gemstone, and then very adroitly pieced together the three parts to her new Pisces ring. 'Chalcedony is another name for bloodstone,' her keen mind excitedly thought after deriving the appropriate terminology under "Birthstone" from *Book B* of her archaic-but-trusty *World Book Encyclopedia.* 'This nifty fish decoration is especially charming,' the policewoman imagined while delighting in adoring her newest jeweled creation on her ring finger. 'I'll methodically test my theory on a small scale,' she thought. 'I still have six wishes left, so I have plenty of time to be selfish and become a multimillionaire,' the female dreamer mused. 'I wish I hit a jackpot the next time Mark and I go out on a date to an Atlantic City casino.'

On March 16th Mark Santoro and Michelle Celia had just enjoyed a sumptuous dinner in *Harrah's* Fanta-Sea Reef buffet restaurant. "That shrimp, crab-meat, and lobster combination dinner was out of this world," Michelle's escort indicated as the couple left the swanky buffet restaurant and stepped out onto the very busy and noisy casino floor. "Now it's time to have a little adult fun."

"Let's do some serious gambling," Michelle slyly suggested. "I feel a little lucky tonight."

"Okay, but remember; we're only salaried public servants," Mark reminded his voluptuous date. "And we don't have excess cash to fool around with. Let's just play twenty dollars each in the slots. That's my limit."

"All right," his gorgeous date replied. "I read that if you don't hit on the first five attempts, then you should change slot machines. If you don't hit in the next five tries, then you ought to leave the casino before you go broke."

"Sounds like an extremely good system to me," low-level gambler Santoro readily agreed. "Let's try our luck! Nothing ventured, nothing gained!"

Mark lost his twenty dollars on three separate quarter slot machines, while his amused date watched his frustration mount. Then Michelle stated that she would play the dollar slots where the payoffs were much higher, as well as the higher odds against her. The casino visitor frivolously dropped three-dollar tokens into the slot and pulled the handle. The wheels rotated, and much to her date's astonishment, three large red sevens appeared in the machine's window. A series of bells, whistles, and buzzers went-off. A slot machine attendant dutifully arrived on the scene and notified a floor manager, who then proudly announced that Michelle had just won a huge twenty-thousand-dollar jackpot.

"That's absolutely wonderful and rather phenomenal, too!" Mark raved as the Hammonton patrolman amorously hugged his new-found love partner, with his whispered words paying tribute to her fabulous, instant luck. "It's almost as if you knew you were goin' to win big, and that you knew exactly what machine to play, and when to play it!"

"I just had a silly hunch," Michelle skillfully lied. "I always trust my instincts. I guess I'm a trifle superstitious in that respect. Sometimes, I think I'm a witch, so you might've been partially right about that oddball Halloween joke of yours. I know that Todd thinks I *am* a witch at times," the elated winner lustily laughed. "Now Mark, you can have your personal suspicions, too!"

The diligent casino cashier very professionally handed the extremely grateful slot winner a fifteen-thousand-dollar check after the federal and state income taxes had been withheld, and after the winner had signed bona fide legal documents attesting to *that* specific fact. Michelle anxiously rummaged through her handbag and then handed the casino floor supervisor a hundred-dollar tip for graciously assisting her in obtaining her fortuitous windfall.

"What are you going to do with the money?" Mark asked. "That was quite a bonanza you just won!"

"Prudently put it in the bank towards Todd's college education," Michelle informed. "He wants to go to *Rutgers,* and that should cover most of his first year's tuition in case he doesn't earn that football scholarship his mind is set on."

Right up to March 20th, certain disturbing thoughts persistently haunted Michelle Celia's delicate psyche. 'Will the rings continue to be effective if I persist in using them for personal gain? When I get to the thirteenth ring, should I wear it? Will the thirteenth ring restart the good-luck cycle, or will the unlucky number stop my monthly wish-come-true rotation? Oh well; I have five more months to make my deepest dreams become reality,' the policewoman-turned-astrologer pensively considered.

On April 2nd, the jewelry chest's possessor resolved that it was time to dispense with the bloodstone Pisces ring, and begin integrating the three components that would constitute the diamond Aries zodiac ring. 'I didn't want to do anything foolish on April 1ˢᵗ,' the superstitious woman reviewed in her mind. 'The 2ⁿᵈ of April seems to be a more opportune time to take aggressive action than to attempt any experiment on *April Fools Day.*'

Without exhibiting any hesitation, Michelle Celia confidently ventured to Tapper's Stationery Store on the corner of Bellevue Avenue and Second Street to purchase a New Jersey Pick 6 Lottery ticket. An affable clerk behind the counter greeted her. "May I help you?" the young woman asked.

"Yes; I feel a bit lucky today. I'd like to buy a lottery ticket," Michelle presumptuously indicated.

"Are you sure you want only one?" the courteous-but-busy red-haired young lady questioned.

"Yes," Michelle casually replied, fully knowing the outcome was certainly in her favor. "It only takes one ticket to win, doesn't it? And I'm hereby betting that the next ticket you sell is going to be *my* special winner."

"Do you want a *Pick 6* ticket or an *Instant Winner* card?" the girl asked. 'You have a choice to make."

"Give me an *Instant Winner* rub-off," Michelle replied with certitude while honoring an inkling she suddenly experienced. "I don't want to seem too greedy winning five million dollars. Fifty-thousand will be perfectly all right with me."

The fairly amused cashier instinctively smiled, ripped-off an *Instant Winner* rub-off from a roll kept behind the cash register, and traded the ticket for three dollars. The purchaser then removed a dime from her dungaree pocket and scratched-off the surface to confirm what she had already known. "Here's a fifty-thousand-dollar winner," off-duty Sergeant Celia matter-of-factly reported to the suddenly astounded store clerk. "Just explain to me how I can get my little payoff," the winner nonchalantly requested to the more-than-mildly stunned salesgirl.

Mark Santoro soon heard about Michelle's exceptional good fortune while "shooting the bull" at a local coffee shop, and soon called his favorite girl on the phone to congratulate her propitious timing; first demonstrated at *Harrah's Casino,* and now at Tapper's Stationery Store.

"It's just totally bizarre and pretty uncanny!" the lady sergeant cackled and prevaricated to her admiring boyfriend. "And I just saw in the *Philadelphia Inquirer* that a drawing for a new *Hummer* is to be held May 15th. I'm goin' to enter the contest by ordering a newspaper subscription, and then possibly win the chief sweepstakes' prize. When you're on a roll, Mark, ya' gotta' keep tossin' the dice! I'll just wait and see what happens next in the good luck category!"

"What are ya' goin' to do with your fantastic lottery payday?" her fellow officer and now steady-companion asked. "Now you not only outrank me in position on the force and command a higher salary, you've also surpassed me in the good luck department, too!"

"I intend to deposit the entire sum in the bank and earmark it for Todd's college education," the exhilarated law-enforcement officer haughtily replied. "Now, all I have to do is focus on winning that mean-lookin' *Hummer!*"

* * * * * * * * * * * *

May 1st couldn't have arrived sooner on the kitchen wall calendar for Michelle Celia. The lady cop systematically took apart the beautiful diamond Aries ring, and then expertly coordinated the three new parts, and organized them into the exquisite emerald-stoned Taurus zodiac ring. 'I *wish* to win the newspaper subscription contest's grand prize, the colorful yellow *Hummer,'* the ring possessor mentally commanded to the inanimate object. 'More specifically, I wish to win the *Philadelphia Inquirer* sweepstakes' grand prize yellow *Hummer.'*

When the telephone rang on May 15th at seven p.m., Michelle had just finished washing the supper dishes and cleaning-off the formerly cluttered kitchen table.

"Mom, it's for you!" Todd informed.

"Is it Mark on the phone?" his harried parent asked.

"No; it's a lady from the *Philadelphia Inquirer!*"

"Ms. Celia, this is Karen Watson speaking from the *Philadelphia Inquirer* subscription department. I'm calling because I want to confirm your subscription to our fine newspaper. All of your documentation has been properly filled-out. Delivery will commence next week once everything is activated."

"Great!" Michelle replied with pretentious emotion. "I'm looking forward to all of the nifty features your newspaper has to offer. Thank you so much. Good bye."

A day later, the telephone again rang. "Mom, it's the *Philadelphia Inquirer* again. Should I just hang-up on them?"

"No Todd," the mother impatiently reacted. "Just hand me the phone! And I want to check your science homework when you're finished doing it!"

The mustard-yellow *Hummer* was delivered to 230 Marilyn Avenue the following spring day, and the vehicle was the talk of the very active gossip mill in every Hammonton beauty parlor, gas station, and barbershop. People chattered and chatted all over town about the casino jackpot, about the lucky scratch-off lottery ticket, and now about the policewoman's winning of the much-coveted *Hummer* all-terrain vehicle.

On June 3rd, Michelle casually placed the three parts to the Taurus emerald zodiac ring in the required tiers of the ebony jewelry chest, and next deftly put the ring, the alexandrite light green stone, and the silver image of twins together to build the extraordinary collection's intricate-looking Gemini ring. The assembler then impetuously *wished* for a hundred thousand dollars worth of splendid jewelry, diamond-studded earrings, watches, necklaces, mink coats, designer cocktail dresses and evening gowns, and those elegant luxurious items instantly appeared on her bedroom dresser and in her already cluttered closet rack.

'All these items are tax free!' Michelle merrily thought while feeling the 'magical gifts' and thoroughly appreciating her great euphoria. 'But I can't share my wonderful secret with Mark or Todd. Oh, how I'd love to tell both of them, but I fear that it might reverse my good fortune and possibly have disastrous adverse effects!'

To celebrate the *4th of July* in a non-patriotic manner, Michelle Celia disconnected the segments to the now powerless Gemini ring. Then, she skillfully pieced-together the much-anticipated Cancer zodiac ring comprised of a brilliant ruby and a four-pronged silver crab attachment to snap into place onto the zodiac chest's next plain golden band. 'Only one more month,' Michelle regretted. 'And then I'll reach the dreaded thirteenth ring. Thirteen has always been an unlucky number.' But then her conniving mind objectively rationalized the total situation. 'It's the *4th of July* holiday, and the country was founded on thirteen colonies, so *thirteen* might not be such a sinister, evil number after all!'

Michelle peered at the majestic red-stoned ring on her finger, stared into her bureau mirror, and solemnly wished in an almost hypnotic mind-state that a million dollars in cold cash would suddenly appear neatly stacked in "an obelisk shape" on her plain white cotton bedspread. The wisher turned around and immediately observed a wonderfully high three-dimensional pyramid formed from twenty-dollar bills at the base, and fifty and hundred dollar bills respectively comprising the center and the apex of the marvelous cash matrix. 'I can now retire from the police force if I want to,' Michelle merrily mused. 'I'll hide most of the money in the attic, and store the rest in the suitcases I've stashed in the cellar before Todd rides his bike home from baseball practice. After my son graduates from *Rutgers,* Mark and I will be able to live like royalty anywhere in Mexico!'

The lazy, hot "dog days of August" couldn't have arrived quicker for the apprehensive and now-obsessed woman police sergeant. Michelle was becoming increasingly bored with the monotony and tedium of her humdrum behind-the-desk office duties at the police station, and fantasized 'early retirement' after completing the minimum twenty years of service. Then, she and Mark could enjoy in Mexico the enormous wealth created by her most omnipotent and benevolent zodiac ring collection.

'I *wish* I could have anything I want whenever I want for the remainder of my life,' Michelle secretly and covetously desired. 'I can't endure the mounting suspense. That's my final wish before I get to wear the mysterious thirteenth ring.'

Michelle Celia was reading the latest weekly edition of the *Hammonton Gazette,* and in the *Lost and Found* section a brief classified ad stated: "Magician's magic ring chest has been lost. Substantial reward will be given for its safe return, including the thirteenth ring. Please respond by writing to A. and Y. Torres, 370 Zodiac Blvd., El Cajon, CA 92021. Please return items immediately to rightful owners, or face possible negative supernatural consequences." An identical ad also appeared in the *Hammonton News'* classified section.

'I refuse to return the ring under any and all circumstances,' Michelle stubbornly thought. 'Yolanda and Alfredo want that invaluable thirteenth ring for some greedy, ulterior reason. I'll bet it extends the powers of the twelve zodiac rings, and quite possibly re-initiates their monthly generosity for another full year's cycle,' Michelle contemplated and surmised. 'I'm not going to surrender those almighty privileges to anyone; handsome reward or no handsome reward. Those two doltish amateur crooks could go to the nearest California beach and start pounding sand all day and all night long as far as I'm concerned!'

The almost-possessed female could not resist the strong temptation that soon had overwhelmed her better judgment. Filled with audacity and bitter defiance, Michelle compulsively removed the Leo yellowish-green peridot ring from her finger, avariciously grabbed the enigmatic thirteenth golden band from the first velvet-lined tray, and very deliberately placed it on her finger. She closed her eyes and wished that the rotation of the remarkable 'zodiac 'baker's dozen' rings' would regenerate their already demonstrated powers, to be effectively employed by her for a lucky second-year-cycle. 'These sensational rings are safer in my possession than in the hands of those two clumsy, incompetent quacks that tried heisting them from my house,' Michelle reckoned in defense of her sensitive ego. 'And I have the superior imagination to put the Rings of Saturn to good use right here in good old Hammonton.'

When the fanciful dreamer opened her eyes, the woman was absolutely horrified and deeply angered. Her opulent jewelry was no longer on the dresser beneath its mirror, and the splendid three-tiered jewelry chest had completely disappeared. Upon further inspection of the bedroom environment, Michelle's expensive clothes' wardrobe along with her luxurious mink coat collection had incomprehensibly vanished from the walk-in closet. Looking at her now-naked finger, the jinxed thirteenth ring was no longer there.

Additional frantic searches around the house soon revealed that the suitcases in the cellar, and the cardboard boxes in the attic were now devoid of large denomination bills. The only remaining evidence of Michelle's past good fortune were her mustard-yellow *Hummer* still parked in the driveway, and the money that had been set aside for Todd's college tuition that still was safely deposited in the local bank.

The following afternoon, at her four p.m. break-time, a very disenchanted and emotionally disturbed Michelle Celia drove her police cruiser into the driveway at 230 Marlyn Avenue. The pallid-faced, depressed sergeant collected her mail from inside the front porch postbox prior to entering her home via the back kitchen door. Two letters immediately caught the despondent woman's attention.

Michelle opened the first missive with great anxiety. "Your first supplemental payment is now due on your new *Hummer*. As you know, the *Philadelphia Inquirer* ran a sweepstakes that you had entered, and the paper paid half of the vehicle's total cost. Everything had been explained in the small print that appears at the bottom of your entrance coupon. Your first moderate monthly payment is to the amount of $700.00."

The now totally-outraged, seething woman then violently ripped open the second envelope. Inside was a small map with English directions to the new location of the illustrious Rings of Saturn; presently in the custody of Alfredo and Yolanda Torres, 370 Zodiac Blvd., El Cajon, CA 92021.

The following morning, Michelle Celia physically confronted Mark Santoro in the asphalt parking lot behind the Hammonton Police Department. "Mark; I desperately need your help," the ranking officer began while deftly camouflaging her current livid disposition. "I want you to go on a wonderful vacation with me to San Diego during our October breaks. And don't worry. I'll pay for the total expenses."

"I just can't believe it," Mark quite spontaneously sighed and then replied. "I was thinking of asking you to accompany me down to Jamaica for a little recreational romance, but I suppose a San Diego hiatus is just as good if not better than the Caribbean. I've always wanted to visit the Hotel Del Coronado, and also tour La Jolla. As you probably know, that's Spanish lingo for 'The Jewel'. I've taken-up your excellent lead Michelle, and have been brushing-up on expanding my Latin American vocabulary!"

"That's really great news, my good amigo!" the impressed and rejuvenated female officer answered with a rather weak smile that covered-up the intense hurting her heart felt deep inside. "I'll call my travel agent early next week and make jet and hotel reservations. Mark; I'll fully explain why we're going to San Diego on the plane flight out to California!" Michelle genuinely promised. "But please get ready for the adventure of your life!"

"The Christian Republican Left"

Powerful members of the Fraternal Order of Constructionists had in 2040 AD founded the exclusive "Society of the Christian Republican Left". The newly-established secret brotherhood believed that the United States of America had sinfully drifted away from its original "divinely inspired purpose and direction". The new-found movement started in Delaware, the nation's "First State," and its three most influential members were Samuel Wilkes, a prominent Dover and Wilmington banker; William Rogers, a devout right wing conservative Anglican minister; and Richard Adams, a very wealthy "old money" importer/exporter.

The "CRL" had its historical roots in certain fundamentalist chapters in Rehoboth Beach, Lewes, and Bethany Beach, all Atlantic seashore resort communities having religious origins; and then "the growing movement" spread-out from those respective Delaware communities, gradually establishing clandestine chapters (exclusively chartered among White Anglo-Saxon European stock Americans) in Dewey Beach, in Fenwick Island, in Milford, and in Smyrna. From those humble origins, the fledgling organization gradually matured to having a membership of over one million serious advocates and adherents in all fifty states. The CRL had little to do with liberal "left wing politics.," which its ultra-conservative membership virtually unanimously abhorred. The unique oxymoron title "Christian Republican Left" received its appellation from the cartel's founders' secret salutation of deliberately greeting one another by shaking their left hands.

Samuel Wilkes, the renowned Delaware financier, William Rogers, the fire-and-brimstone Episcopalian televangelist, and Richard Adams, the affluent and dynamic international products and commodities dealer met on July 4th, 2155 in Wilkes' luxurious penthouse atop the Star of the Sea Condominiums, overlooking the Rehoboth Beach boardwalk and beach, with the tranquil Atlantic Ocean gleaming in the background. The trio of determined men shared parallel philosophical opinions in regard to what they considered the "corrupt denigration of American democracy by immoral socialist left-wing Democrats".

"In five short years, it'll be 2160, the 540th anniversary of the noble Pilgrims' landing in Massachusetts at Plymouth," Minister William Rogers reminded his all-too-adamant colleagues. "This nation was gloriously founded on the idea of religious freedom; yes

Gentlemen, on the premise of *Christian* religious freedom long before the Constitution was savagely perverted to allow Arab radicals and terrorists to roam about freely from mosque to mosque with designs of undermining our national security. Yes, my esteemed Colleagues; in the beginning," William Rogers lectured and emphasized, "Massachusetts and Rhode Island belonged to the Pilgrims and the Puritans; Pennsylvania to the Quakers and other devout Protestant denominations; and the Maryland Colony to the Catholics. Just look at what Godless deviations have occurred in the United States of America since our mostly Mason founding fathers had authored and endorsed the Declaration of Independence and had later conducted themselves admirably in the Revolutionary War! The last hundred years have been a dangerous, immoral, precipitous slide down an extremely slippery slope!"

"Your God-inspired comments, William, have hit the bull's-eye right in the center of the target area," Samuel Wilkes commended the fiery Reverend Rogers. "Hopefully, in the new national era, *we*, the rightful leaders of our *ordained* organization, will ensure that Thanksgiving Day will be the new 4th of July. Our country will experience a political and spiritual Renaissance, just like Italy and Europe had a magnificent cultural Renaissance in the 1400s," the banker enthusiastically prognosticated. "We must engineer and initiate our plan so that we can use our political and financial clout to have a rebirth of Christian values in America. We must take back our country from the atheists, the gays, the blacks, the woman's rights advocates, and the anti-war dissidents," Samuel Wilkes implored his co-conspirators. "Our nation must have a much-needed rebirth, and then quickly revert back to its original purpose for existence. America must return to possessing a moral compass firmly based on the Ten Commandments, and our country's philosophy should *not* be predicated on exploiting dangerous liberal interpretations of the First Ten Amendments. Our numerous enemies," Wilkes reminded his associates, "both our internal and international adversaries," the wealthy financier qualified, "have, with the collaboration of soulless, amoral and greedy lawyers, advanced *their* sinful causes and agendas. The abusers are using the Bill of Rights along with the rest of the sacred Constitution to pervert and traduce our fundamental national values. Indeed Gentlemen, our heritage is in serious jeopardy! Wouldn't you agree with my assertions, Richard?"

"Yes; without a doubt," the very rich and on-a-mission Richard Adams concurred with the very prestigious Samuel Wilkes. "The Pilgrims had inadvertently landed on the Cape Cod peninsula at

Provincetown before heading onward to the Massachusetts mainland, and ironically, today, Provincetown along with *our own* Rehoboth Beach are havens for gays and lesbians, avowed practitioners of debauchery who believe that they're free to openly practice their vile Sodom and Gomorrah licentious lewdness in public. These arrogant in-your-face sinners are both unabashed and unashamed of their baneful, disgusting, reprehensible behavior. Now Gentlemen," the prominent banker continued his narrative, "it's up to us as dedicated directors of the CRL to put a stop to this disgraceful demonstration of evil before the wicked travesty ravenously consumes America from sea to shining sea."

"And getting back to history, then the thirteen eastern colonies became the thirteen original states with our Delaware being one of them," Minister William Rogers reviewed and stated. "I say in all good conscience that America is doomed to the fires of Hell unless this blessed land returns back to its Puritan roots and its Christian family values. It's no longer sufficient simply being the minority Right Wing Neocons, Gentlemen. Our Christian Republican Left must gain control of the United States, and return our blessed land to the same sober, ethical state of mind that existed back in Philadelphia in 1776. Now Gentlemen," the rhetorical manipulator of words continued his didactic narrative as if *he* were occupying a church pulpit, "I firmly believe that 13 is a lucky Heavenly-favored number. We should start our Bible-inspired campaign by first purging sin out of Delaware, and then systematically cleansing the remaining twelve original colonies of Satan's evil practices. Yes, I insist that 'ethic cleaning' shall begin with 'ethnic cleansing!' Are our honorable militias in the northeast ready to conduct their separate crusades against God's avowed enemies? Are they ready up in New England?"

"Yes Sir!" the dedicated-to-the-cause Samuel Wilkes confirmed to William Rogers. "All of our eager-for-action commando units are prepared to assassinate the thirteen targeted governors; the twenty-six Senators, and the other listed dangerous Congressmen, diplomats, lawyers and judges. The CRL will soon have control of the entire eastern seaboard, in a year flat, I predict," Samuel Wilkes flagrantly boasted to his impressed comrades. "Especially with the support of our most elite members being in charge of all thirteen National Guards from Georgia right up to New Hampshire and Maine. And my capitalistic Wall Street associates are chomping at the bit to lead and finance the inevitable insurrection, just like patriotic Stephen Girard had used his personal fortune to help the Patriots' defeat the British during the War of 1812."

The three CRL leaders then discussed the methodology that would accomplish their immediate, sinister objective; that is, to gain dominion of the original thirteen eastern seaboard states. First of all, "incentive loans" would be offered to inner city blacks to get the "riffraff" out of urban areas from Boston down to Atlanta, and to strategically relocate "the ghetto masses" in warm states like Florida, Texas, Arizona, New Mexico, and California. As Samuel Wilkes aptly described it to his CRL comrades, "This much-needed purging of the thirteen Atlantic Coast states will be similar to the old nineteenth century adage of 'forty acres and a mule'. I'm certain that our monetary fifty-thousand-dollar bribes will easily accomplish *our* purpose. Once our military allies take over the East Coast, soon the state militias will become stronger than the regular Army, Navy, Air Force and Marines. Thank you, 'Article 2' of the U.S. Constitution for your benign assistance, ha, ha, ha!"

Then Richard Adams added to Samuel Wilkes' observations and predictions. "Yes, Sam; and then the Harlem Project will be initiated where those urban blacks that didn't cooperate with our sugar-coated money compensation incentive offers will be biologically and chemically 'exterminated' by General Townsend's very competent New York Militia, or to use more benign nomenclature, the obstacle known as 'the ghetto dwellers' will be effectively and permanently 'eliminated'. And then the Newark, Jersey City, Philadelphia, Washington DC, Baltimore and Boston 'Sister Projects' will be swiftly implemented. In many respects, my fine Gentlemen," the wealthy importer/exporter gloated, "Hitler had the right idea attempting to make Germany exclusively Nordic Aryan. But in our case here in America, the burden-to-society blacks, gays, atheists, Mexicans, drug addicts, and chronic alcoholics will be systematically dispensed with. Our vigilant State Militias will handle *that* essential responsibility. Just think Gentlemen," Adams proceeded with his profound propaganda. "All of the ugly sinfulness that the present United States indifferently tolerates will be effectively eradicated so that our 'New National Order' can rise to power and begin flourishing. All of the corrupt symbols of our parasitic, wasteful, politically correct government must be quickly erased," the famous importer/exporter maintained as if Richard Adams was Patrick Henry reincarnated. "And when the Capitol Building, the Supreme Court Building, and the White House are proudly burned just like the German Reichstag had been set ablaze in 1933, then..."

"Then, true measured freedom, responsible liberty, and a new rigid, inflexible justice system will become reality once more; and

America will again be able to lead the world in triumphing over evil by becoming a worthy model for every sinful European country to imitate," Minister Roger Williams pontificated. "America will once again be the true leader of the Free World."

"Excellent point! Great speech!" Richard Adams exclaimed and praised the venerable man of the cloth. "Just look at Japan and China, for instance! Those Oriental countries have no so-called sanctuary cities to accommodate illegal immigrants! They're all basically exclusionary; thus, allowing their own gene pools to prosper. Those self-protecting countries are not interested in mongrelizing *their* cultures and *their* civilizations by allowing too many outsiders to contaminate their populations' gene pools by *liberally* allowing natives of their lands to intermarry with foreigners," Richard Adams persuasively elucidated. "Tokyo and Beijing have been achieving right along what Adolph Hitler had failed to accomplish in Nazi Germany. In order to compete with the proliferating Chinese and the ambitious Japanese on a worldwide scale, *we* must first..."

"Cleanse our fifty states of all harmful non-Christian, unproductive and evil elements so that WASP America can be both revived and rejuvenated; therefore, giving *us* an even playing field on which to compete with our Japanese and Chinese economic and military rivals," Samuel Wilkes firmly indicated to his political soul-mates. "We'll scrupulously transport the Mexican and other dark-skinned Hispanic infections to the warm states to join the blacks, gays, drug addicts, atheists, criminals and other malignant sub-cultures. As much as I hate to admit it, the Nazis had the right idea! We must purify America by first purifying our mongrel gene pool. We've reached a stage in *our* historical evolution where our country's laws are contaminating our basic moral principles. Laws should be absolute, and not arbitrary. God's laws should always prevail over man's defilement of it!"

"Agreed! Bravo! Bravo!" Richard Adams praised his banker colleague's rambling, extemporaneous oration. "Within a year our marvelous plan will go into effect. We'll save America from itself if it's the last thing we'll ever do! And if our critics vociferously balk and claim that *our* adopted methods are 'discrimination', let it be said and known that throughout history good has always discriminated against evil. When things are black and white with little gray area in between," Adams pompously resumed his garrulous discourse, "then nothing is subject to interpretation, and everything is completely understood by the general populace. But please remember, Gentlemen; all black officers are to be excised from the State Militias within the next year, and when the thirteen separate rebellions occur all at the same time, the whites in the regular Armed Services will also rebel and chase-out blacks and Hispanics, and gays from *their* infected ranks. If all goes according to the prescribed script," Adams hypothesized and concluded, "then Friends, I predict that the much-warranted takeover of the United States of America should occur in less than two months of ongoing internal strife and intense conflict."

"Plato was absolutely right in what he had so eloquently expressed in his *Republic!*" William Rogers sagely concluded and shared. "Only honorable and moral people should be eligible for citizenship, which should, in the final analysis, be an earned *privilege* based on individual performance and good reputation, and not be predicated on an automatic *right* conferred upon a person at birth. And the major difference between a republic and a democracy is that in a republic there is respect for law, organization and tradition," the renowned televangelist communicated. "That's exactly the kind of patriotism that conservatives do best, Gentlemen! We patriotically *conserve* our revered American way of life! Too much democracy will ultimately only lead to open anarchy! American Democracy has really become wicked socialism in disguise!"

* * * * * * * * * * * *

In mid-September, Samuel Wilkes and Richard Adams delegated the talented William Rogers to author the "New American Manifesto" that would represent the official blueprint outlining the future direction and function of the United States of America. "You'll be like *our* own Thomas Jefferson; wonderfully organizing the requisite ideas we've been diligently discussing over the past five years," Wilkes congratulated the thoroughly elated Episcopalian preacher. "You'll give much-needed definition and meaning to our presently fragmented CRL *revolutionary* ideas. You're a born wordsmith; Bill!"

"We'll meet again a week from today at eight p.m. sharp for dinner and a detailed progress report at the Embers Restaurant on 24th Street and Philadelphia Avenue down in Ocean City, Maryland!" Richard Adams suggested to William Rogers and Samuel Wilkes. "The resort city will be virtually devoid of the annoying tourist crowd, and we'll have the entire place to ourselves to review last minute details to the essential document that *you,* dear William, will be assiduously drafting. What do you think Reverend Bill?"

"I do believe that the thoroughfare Philadelphia Avenue in Ocean City, Maryland above 17th Street is called Coastal Highway," the always precise William Rogers respectfully corrected his less meticulous CRL ally. "17th Street marks the boundary between old Ocean City and New Ocean City, which as *you* know, had been annexed into the ten-mile-long stretch of beach way back in the 1960s, if my nebulous memory still accurately serves me. And conversely," the acclaimed minister proceeded, "the New American Manifesto will clearly mark the boundary between the old dysfunctional America, and the new necessary and vibrant Christian Republican Left America, that's impatiently waiting on the horizon to happen."

"Yes, Reverend Rogers," Samuel Wilkes readily conceded to the minister while simultaneously endorsing Richard Adams' proposal about the next scheduled meeting of the CRL intelligence committee. "I'll get a room at the newly renovated Holiday Inn up near the 62nd Street Bridge; you know, the *Route 90 Expressway* into north Ocean City. Reverend Bill; you're welcomed to join me and stay in my suite," the pompous banker invited the appointed wordsmith. "The food in the Reflections Restaurant at the Holiday is gourmet to say the least, and I promise that the treat will be on me. Or Bill; we could dine at Phillips Seafood Restaurant instead if that's what you'd prefer."

"No thanks!" the highly focused church minister William Rogers politely declined. "When visiting Ocean City, my wife and I usually stay at the old Atlantic Hotel; four blocks up from the inlet on the boardwalk between Wicomico and Somerset Streets. It's a quaint, old-fashioned, casual hotel featuring Tiffany lamps in the lobby, and it's located just north of the town's only amusement pier," the preacher further elaborated. "The Atlantic's reduced fall room rates are much more reasonable than the ones at the much more exorbitant Holiday Inn!" the frugal and thrifty minister added. "My dear wife's wild spending habits, and her frequent mall excursions keep me operating on a rather strict budget. My spendthrift spouse is far from being parsimonious!"

"After you finish writing the New American Manifesto," Samuel Wilkes remarked to Puritanical William Rogers, "then you could put together the Second Constitution of the United States! You certainly have the fine language and grammatical acumen to do precisely that, you know!"

* * * * * * * * * * * *

In mid-September, the Reverend William Rogers occupied the desk inside his modest third-floor room at the landmark Atlantic Hotel, while his extravagant wife Esther was out shopping looking for season closeout bargains in souvenir and casual apparel shops situated along the popular Ocean City, Maryland boardwalk. The televangelist meticulously organized his random ideas, and then laboriously commenced incorporating them into his 'highly focused principles' that would constitute the first draft of "The New American Manifesto".

'Let's see now,' Rogers imagined while looking out the window overlooking Somerset Street. 'Freedom of speech; freedom of press, and freedom of religion will be limited only to white European ancestry Christian Republican Lefts. As an exception, Italians (and Sicilians) are to be accepted as part of the standard 'Occidental Christian heritage'. And *those* specially described and listed *privileges* must be earned and maintained, all according to one's accomplishments and one's contributions to the general society. They are not *unalienable rights* as is currently believed and practiced. Citizenship will not be automatically conferred at birth! And I must remember to include the statement that two felony convictions will result in the immediate loss of citizenship and prestige. Yes, *that* specific condition must be a veritable reality not subject to either debate or change!'

According to the particulars of the "breakthrough document" being developed by William Rogers, certain *revolutionary* elements were essentially introduced into and defined in the New American Manifesto. 'Radicals and anti-government Arabs, along with Hindus and Buddhists, will either be deported from the country or be conveniently transported to Florida, Texas, New Mexico, Arizona and California,' William conscientiously contemplated. 'After the apathetic urban dwellers from the original thirteen states have been removed from their all-too-comfortable slums, and sent to the warm climate states, then the 'Red States' family-oriented areas in the former 'Bible Belt' are to be rid of welfare recipients, atheists, gays and lesbians, felons, blacks, drug addicts, dope distributors, Hispanics, and also of indolent Indians parasitically living on reservations. Those disposable, welfare-dependent individuals will then be immediately transported to New Texas, which would ultimately become the new 'American Reservation' reserved for all of the formerly undesirable elements of society. I must make certain that in the New America, law and order, and family values, must take precedence and prevail over all else.'

William Rogers next concentrated his cerebral activity on other articles to be neatly synthesized into the New American Manifesto. 'The 'undesirable elements' living in Florida, New Mexico, Arizona and California will be conveyed under military and police supervision to myriad security barracks in New Texas. When all of the 'non-productive individuals' living off the welfare of the productive white citizens of America have been herded and corralled into New Texas, then the central 'Red States', and also Florida, New Mexico, Arizona, and California could then smoothly join the thirteen original states, and be efficiently absorbed into the new United States of America, which would ultimately consist of fifty prosperous and indigenous Christian Republican Left districts. The country will finally be ethnically and ethically cleansed, and we'll let the exiled lawyers down in New Texas figure-out how *that* deliberately isolated mass of wasteland will be able to survive on its own productivity with its millions of new imported, worthless residents no longer being a perpetual burden and drain on the incomes and lives of productive and conservative, God-fearing white Christian Republican citizens.'

On September 23rd at precisely 8 p.m., the three Christian right-wing confederates met at the aforementioned Embers Restaurant to orally review the articles that were to be included in William Rogers' initial draft of the "New American Manifesto".

"The spirit of the Louisiana Purchase and the pursuit of our enterprising pioneers' most august Western Movement, Manifest Destiny, must be re-captured, identified, and expressed in the 'New American Manifesto," Samuel Wilkes firmly instructed the greatly inspired and highly motivated William Rogers and Richard Adams. "Two years from now, our great New America will be born! It'll rise like the proverbial Phoenix from the ashes of despair! Yes, sir, Gentlemen, Darwin was positively right in making his extraordinary assumption! Everything must have renewal in order to adapt, endure, and survive. But first," Samuel Wilkes prefaced while switching to a more sociable subject of conversation. "Let's enjoy our succulent surf and turf dinners before our New World patriot seated next to me returns to the Atlantic Hotel and continues authoring his immortal document. I predict that someday, the old wood-framed Atlantic Hotel will be revered in public school classroom textbooks throughout America as being the new Independence Hall!"

"I'll drink to that!" importer/exporter Richard Adams echoed his political sentiments and religious convictions as the investor slowly raised his stemmed glass of Merlot wine. "Here's a toast to the ascension of the CRL to political and military prominence," the adamant co-founder proposed inside the nearly empty Embers main dining room. Then Adams addressed Samuel Wilkes in a low soft voice. "And I trust that you, Mr. Wilkes, have orchestrated the Second Great Depression stock market crash while secretly collaborating with your trustworthy Wall Street cohorts."

"Yes Richard, that'll be the first operational phase of our nice grandiose scheme," the influential banking tycoon smiled and lowly answered before sipping down a mouthful of red wine. "Once the stock market fails, everyone will be out of work; cash flows will cease; bills won't be paid; people will lose their mortgages, abandon their houses and their properties; and poverty will become rampant and on such a widespread scale that anarchy throughout the land will prevail. Consequently," Samuel Wilkes uttered and paused to gauge the impact of his words on his perceptive audience of two; "yes consequently, Gentlemen; the average starving American will gladly be willing to be transported at *our* expense under military and police supervision to warm climates states in the south and southwest. Then our little Christian coup can be satisfactorily put into motion with little political opposition.

"How could you be so sure?" asked wealthy importer Richard Adams. "You make it all sound too easy."

"Since the designated scum won't have any money to live, and since we'll promise them food, shelter, and welfare in the warmer states," Samuel Wilkes chuckled, "they'll wholeheartedly cooperate with our foolproof plan. And then, several months after the other states are cleansed of their heavy scum burdens, namely sin, crime and government waste, and after all of the social deviates have finally been transferred from Florida, New Mexico, Arizona and California to New Texas," the banker specified, "*we'll* promptly and gladly shut-off the welfare and funding valves. And soon, the disgusting vermin and their exploitative lawyers will start killing one another in New Texas, once the old economic system is no longer working in *their* favor. What poetic irony! Parasites will be killing parasites! Ha, ha, ha!"

"I have to get back to the Atlantic Hotel and finish-up my all-important first draft," William Rogers ambitiously disclosed, just as the Embers' waiter brought the three extra-large cherries' jubilee desserts to the table. "The sacred words 'In God We Trust' will have a much more tangible meaning, once I get through with modifying and refining the Manifesto's exact language. I just can't wait to finish-up the masterpiece!"

548

                    * * * * * * * * * * *

Reverend William Rogers had driven across Delmarva from
Ocean City, Maryland to Baltimore to conduct some personal
business. Before departing from the "Eastern Shore" beach town, the
televangelist had promised his wife Esther that he would be returning
to the resort early the following morning. But the famous minister's
meeting with an Episcopal Church Council wound-up ending early,
so the TV preacher decided to return to the Atlantic Hotel and finish-
up his New American Manifesto in order to show copies of the
completed manuscript to Samuel Wilkes and to Richard Adams the
following afternoon.

'I'll coordinate the last seven paragraphs, and have the language
typed-up on my laptop computer by noon tomorrow morning!' the
anxious minister thought. 'I'm slated to meet again with Sam and
with Rich at Phillip's Seafood Restaurant tomorrow evening at 8 p.m.
to give them copies of the final draft. I hope that Esther hasn't spent a
small fortune gallivanting around the myriad Ocean City malls and
various shopping emporiums.'

Upon entering his third-floor Atlantic Hotel room, the nationally
acclaimed televangelist was speechless when his arrival had barged-
in on discovering his unfaithful wife in bed with the notorious
importer/exporter tycoon, rich importer Richard Adams. Immediately,
the dumbfounded intruder interrupting the romantic interlude,
garnered his courage, and had the wherewithal to demand an
immediate explanation from his cheating wife.

"Esther! How could you do this vile wicked betrayal to me!
You're a Jezebel! A sinful Delilah! What has happened to your sacred
wedding vows?" the jilted preacher vehemently accused and ranted.
"Where is your loyalty to our marital relationship?"

"Never mind the meaningless small-talk!" Richard Adams
answered as the discovered paramour slowly climbed out of the
ancient bed in his boxer shorts, and next pointed and waved a
handgun at his new protesting enemy. "You bungling Idiot! You
would have to come back to your room early and spoil everything
you had going for yourself!"

"What do you mean Richard?" the still-shocked Reverend
William Rogers nervously asked as his emotions-in-turmoil did a
complete vacillation from anger to fear. "Now don't do anything
drastic or rash that you might regret! Please put the gun down!"

"Well now, my dear Reverend William, or should I call you
Father Billy Boy," Adams condescendingly proceeded with his

derision. "For your information, I've already shot and killed Sam Wilkes this morning when I accidentally discovered him lying in the sack with my wife in my condo' up in Bethany Beach. His body's already been disposed of, dropped off twenty miles at sea into the deep Baltimore Canyon between Rehoboth Beach and Cape May; his corpse was chained to a heavy slab of utilitarian concrete. The ocean predators will have a nice little surprise feast, that's for damned sure! Now unfortunately, for your ignorant, naïve sake, sanctimonious Reverend Bill, it looks like you're gonna' have to be my second shooting victim of the day!"

"Now Richard, please control your fierce temper and calm-down a bit! Don't get yourself into a dangerous rage and throw a tantrum!" Reverend William Rogers futilely pleaded. "Things can be worked out. An amicable solution can be arranged! Isn't that right, Esther? You don't even have to apologize to me!"

"That's what the hell you think!" an incensed, livid Richard Adams snidely returned. "Why do you suppose your adorable wife always wanted to go out shopping? Certainly not to spend *your* petty cash all over the Delmarva Peninsula! Wake up Billy Boy!" the man holding the revolver chided and admonished. "Esther desired to escape your lunatic, sanctimonious sermons and your irrelevant gospel ranting because your charming wife preferred being in bed with me!" Adams vehemently remarked and then snickered.

"I can't believe all of this is happening!" appalled and confused Reverend Rogers cried.

"It's *my* damned money Esther has been spending at the area malls all these years. And when I caught Sharon in bed with that nefarious skunk Sam Wilkes," Adams angrily confessed to Rogers, "I felt that I had to instantly eliminate the amorous impostor out of sheer jealousy and spite. It was without a doubt a strange double love triangle going on, with Wilkes hitting on Sharon; and with me hitting on Esther; and with *you* not suspecting *my* secret activity one second, simply because you were too foolishly trusting and unassuming about human nature, and you were too involved in your televangelism. and too engrossed in *your* propagation of the Christian Republican Left campaign to ever notice that your wife absolutely hates you!"

"Spare my life, and I'll forget that this regretful incident ever happened!" the TV preacher begged on his knees like as ancient Greek suppliant. "Have clemency! Please show me some generous Christian mercy!"

"You gullible, idealistic, quixotic Ignoramus!" Adams hollered across the hotel room. "You're just a dogmatic, religious Zealot; a clueless, moralistic, self-righteous Ideologue! True; the melting pot concept has been a two-century-old American façade; a national canard; a lousy ongoing myth!" Adams bellowed to Rogers. "And you're quite right in thinking that republics last over centuries but democracies flare-up, but then predictably soon die out. Republics breed cultural unity and democracies die because of cultural *diversity,* which is obviously the complete opposite of *unity!"* the irate madman rambled through several standard CRL talking points. "Plato be damned, along with all his confounded academic, Greek philosophical rhetoric!"

"What are you trying to say?" William Rogers jealously stammered. "You're speaking wild gibberish! Your jargon is too vague, too nebulous for me to comprehend! Now Richard, at least I have a clear conscience and am not a contemptible hypocrite like someone I know. Don't I always speak the truth?"

"You petty, inconsequential demagogue! Soon you'll be joining our old pal Samuel Wilkes in Davy Jones' very wet nautical locker. You'll also be fish chum at the bottom of the Baltimore Canyon," Adams augured. "Don't you get it Billy Boy? You're now the second disposable man being routed-out of *our* convoluted triumvirate! I'll soon have full control of the entire CRL! You're to me Billy Boy, exactly what Leon Trotsky had been to Vladimir Lenin and to Joseph Stalin! You're the jackass author of the movement, who incidentally is now considered expendable! You contemptible Dupe! Ha, ha, ha! And Esther here loves and honors me, and your fun-loving wife totally despises you! And all the while, you were too blinded by your impractical dreams and aspirations to ever fathom *that* salient truth!"

"I'll do anything that's feasible to appease you, but please don't pull the trigger!" the now paranoid minister implored the wanton murderer. Have mercy; please Richard, have mercy!"

"Your desperate cowardly pleas are all cried in vain, you repulsive craven Puritan; you deplorable, straightlaced, idiotic Prude! But face reality and experience your impending fate, Billy Boy!" Richard Adams imperatively dictated to his next murder victim. "I'm going to first tie you to that wooden chair, and next I'll shove a gag down your throat, and then you're gonna' emotionally suffer watching me making mad passionate love to your attractive wife!"

"No, Richard! Stop it! Stop it!"

"And then my fine-feathered, holier-than-thou Mr. Preacher Man; after you've agonized through witnessing *that* very special debauchery," the power-hungry tormentor arrogantly bragged, "you'll finally realize the vast discrepancy existing between academic/political/religious philosophy and real-life biological gratification!" Richard Adams loudly articulated.

"What are you saying Richard? I don't fathom the meaning of your nebulous words?"

"It's your final chance to get real before you die, Reverend Billy Boy! But your great agony and anguish will all be done in vain! Yes, Reverend Bill!" the power-hungry narcissist indulgently laughed. "What a marvelous reversal! The shrimp and the lobsters will be having *you* for supper! Say your final prayers Father Bill! Soon your soul will be fully prepared to meet your Maker! Get ready for your Last Supper, but *you* are going to be the food!"

"Global Warming Thwarted"

What real mental abnormalities constitute a madman's mind? Paranoid? Neurotic? Chronic Angst? Psychotic? Delusional? Schizophrenic? Insanity? Fanaticism? How about a combination of any of the aforementioned conditions? One thing is for certain; a poor person is labeled "crazy" when exhibiting any of the states of mind already indicated, but a wealthy person having the same identical emotional dysfunction (as a pauper demonstrates) is automatically identified as an "eccentric" and not as a "lunatic".

An obsessive/compulsive, multi-billionaire, crazed human being named Jefferson Mason existed. The eccentric tycoon had become one of the wealthiest men in the world, hitting it big in computers and office networking equipment. Mason had later intelligently parlayed his vast amassed fortune into lucrative real estate investments in America, Europe and Australia.

Jefferson Mason had been a shy young man back at Glassboro State Teachers College in the mid-'50s. The bashful, aspiring history teacher seldom dated co-eds at the mostly female-attended institution, and rarely socialized with the more masculine male classmates, staying isolated in his dorm' room with his eyes focused in textbooks the full four years of his career preparation. Upon graduating with stellar honors, self-conscious Jefferson decided that American education (along with tolerating its brazen, defiant, insolent *students)* was not his forte, so the shy dreamer boldly risked failure and opened a retail electronics store in a Vineland, New Jersey strip mall.

The frugal fellow saved every penny Jefferson could accumulate. Mason invested his money wisely, and soon thereafter, had a chain of profitable stores in seven South Jersey towns. Never marrying or showing any interest in female companionship, in the early 1970s, Jefferson Mason sold his thriving retail operations, and the ambitious entrepreneur immediately became active in the computer software distribution business, his efforts eventually branching-out into computer networking. By 1980, success upon success had the enterprising risk-taker listed by *Forbes Magazine* as one of the ten wealthiest capitalists in the entire United States.

While in his sixties, Jefferson Mason had been quite actively altruistic, and often engaged in donating to myriad charity and philanthropic causes around the globe. But as the introverted, balding, gaunt-faced recluse turned seventy-five, Mason avariciously hoarded money like a fanatical miser, and abruptly ceased making his generous contributions in assisting his fellow needy human beings. But the laconic Mr. Jefferson Mason had no heirs to leave his immense fortune to, and the self-pitying hermit often contemplated *his* particular station in life, while perpetually brooding about the advent of his death. Jefferson remained a virtual recluse, residing in his deep subterranean compound, which was situated a thousand feet below his walled-in Princeton, New Jersey mansion.

'All of my blood relatives are dead, and I have no children, grandchildren, nieces, or nephews to be beneficiaries in my will,' the lonely, distraught American aristocrat pondered and lamented. 'But the press doesn't know it, but I have contracted incurable cancer, and the malignancy's already spread to my lymph nodes. According to the medical experts, I only have around six months to live, and I absolutely refuse to have detrimental chemotherapy or radiation done. I've now dismissed my butler, my chauffeur, my maid, and my gardener, all for one obvious reason. None of them will be able to discover my marvelous stealthy plan that I've surreptitiously and ingeniously arranged. It's time to make another stealthy entry into my personal diary.'

Dear Diary,

Allow me to describe Phase I of my foolproof, perfect, secret plan. My physical double (whom I've promised to pay the sum of five million dollars) has arrived at Cape Canaveral to be launched with a crew of international astronauts into orbit around the Earth. My look-alike facsimile has passed all of the physical tests, and even has my blood type of O Positive. NASA wants to see how a specimen my advanced age can endure the rigors associated with living in outer space.

On the crew's third day circling the Earth, I'll have my Russian military contacts stationed outside Moscow launch a guided missile (I say missile because a GPS missile is much more accurate than an ordinary rocket), and the projectile will obliterate the orbiting space laboratory (with my victimized double inside) right out of the outer atmosphere. The press and the TV media will erroneously report that I've been killed in outer space.

I predict that the U.S. government will accuse Russia of committing the diabolical act, which incidentally, Dear Diary, only cost me an additional ten-million-dollar bargain bribe to complete. General Zinkoff will soon go incognito, and escape to a remote unknown destination; have plastic surgery performed, and then my old, loyal Cossack acquaintance will settle-down comfortably in either Mexico or in Canada with his small fortune, which of course I'll have deposited in that secret Swiss bank account that I've coyly established in my Russian friend's name. But World War III will be temporarily averted, mostly because the Russians will argue that one of their own astronauts had been killed in the spectacular space laboratory explosion.

Jefferson Mason smiled and then sipped some blackberry brandy from an ice-cube filled glass, while mentally rehashing "Phase II" of his dangerous, unscrupulous strategy. 'I'm seventy-five years old, yet I still strongly desire to live. I find the idea of imminent death quite repulsive! The finest medical attention available can't extend my life beyond what my widespread cancer is currently dictating.'

Then, the scheming, doomed man seriously thought about his futile health predicament some more. 'My liver and lungs have already been invaded by cancer, and will soon start showing symptoms of the dreaded disease. And here I am with seventy-five years under my belt, a mere grain of sand in the Universe's infinite hourglass; its incredible age spanning thirteen billion-years; not to ignore the Earth's very impressive four-five-billion year-existence! I could very well be the richest man on Earth, yet who really cares way out there beyond the solar system in the far extremities of the Milky Way, or anywhere else in any other distant galaxies?

Sighing about his imminent demise, the hermit multi-billionaire resumed his sulking rumination. 'Indeed,' saddened Jefferson Mason imagined, 'my death only really matters if Earth is the only damned planet in the galaxy, or in the Universe, that has developed intelligent life! Then, me being the wealthiest human on Earth would have some relevance and significance, after all! But that's why Phase II of my brilliant plan must be carefully implemented. I refuse to have the world, and all its inferior minions, continue on living, while I'm assuredly going to perish within the next several months!'

Jefferson Mason consumed another mouthful of delicious brandy and then meditated some more. 'Yes; Phase II will be a fabulous prelude to the end of the world according to Jefferson Mason. Why should others with less ability, less motivation, and less savvy outlive me? I'll be safe and secure down here in my underground bunker, much safer than Adolph Hitler ever was in his! Yes;' the emotionally-warped maniac considered and then grinned. 'General Zinkoff has arranged by virtue of another meager five-million-dollar bribe to have his close comrades at several Russian military bases fire-off six ICBMs with nuclear warheads pointed directly at New York City, Washington DC, Chicago, Los Angeles, San Francisco and Philadelphia. And then certainly, the vigilant U.S. military will retaliate with overwhelming vengeance, and soon, the debacle known as World War III will be initiated, thanks to my brilliant cunning. I'll survive the global devastation down here in my air-conditioned, generator-operated compound, while all sorts of havoc, catastrophe and destruction will be occurring up on the surface.

Then, the wealthy, sick, madman continued his bizarre meditation. 'No more Princeton University; or Dartmouth; or Cornell; or Harvard; or Yale, for that matter, ha, ha, ha! Completely annihilated! Ha, ha, ha!' the crazed psycho snickered. 'All of that ongoing colossal calamity occurring on all continents, magnificently initiated and orchestrated by me, the most powerful, indispensable man in the whole wide world; who, by virtue of my clever acumen, will stubbornly endure the terrible global holocaust; and then, I'll live six months or so longer than any other human being on the planet, including the President of the United States, and his soon-to-be asphyxiated secret service storm-troopers! Ha, ha, ha! I'll outlive everyone, even though I have only a hundred and eighty or so precious days remaining.'

The following morning, after partaking of a cereal, toast and orange juice breakfast, Jefferson Mason again took pen-in-hand and opened his personal autobiographical black leather diary that might never be read by another human being. 'I don't know why I'm keeping detailed records for posterity, when quite probably, there'll be no damned posterity,' the elderly, maniacal, disease-infected fiend thought and chuckled. 'Oh well, I'm writing these splendid words for my own personal satisfaction, and not for anyone else's individual reading pleasure. I remember when I was a kid, my parents had an atom bomb shelter built in the basement of their home with adequate food and provisions to last a full month. But I have to admit that my sturdy, well-constructed, self-sufficient subterranean compound, along with its adequate food, liquor, and water supply, will last as long as I will, basically, six-to-ten lonesome months! Ha, ha, ha!' Of course, while the rest of humanity will be dead!"

Oh, My Dear Diary,

Only two more anxious days before my sagacious scheme will be launched into most-wonderful action. Much to my meticulous organizational skills, the unwary world's apathetic population has no knowledge or suspicion of their prospective extermination. After my duplicate likeness is blown out of the atmosphere from inside the orbiting International Space Laboratory tomorrow morning, like clockwork, Phase II will go into operation with World War III rapidly ramping-up to warp speed. And while the Americans and the Russians are having their savage Armageddon with their awesome ICBM exchanges and bombardments, I'll then systematically commence with Phase III of my in-genius machination.

Yes indeed, in the past year, I've also satisfactorily bribed criminal and espionage elements along with certain Muslim terrorists all over the globe, who out-of-spite, have great animosity for Americans, and for American freedoms. The result of my well-planned methods will cause a gigantic dust veil to envelope the entire Earth; a tremendous cloud so incredible in size that it'll make the meteor concussion that had eliminated the dinosaurs seventy-to-ninety million years ago seem like mere child's play. Yes, Dear Diary; a sequence of hydrogen bombs will crash into various targeted volcanoes around the planet with such fantastic ferocity that Global Warming will become much more than a contemporary buzzword, or popular catch phrase.

Phase III will mean that tremendous nuclear explosions will occur to Mt. Etna in Sicily; to Mt. Vesuvius outside Naples; to Stromboli, also in Italy; to Krakatoa in Indonesia; to Mauna Loa in Hawaii; to Mount Fuji in Japan; to Popocatepetl in Mexico; to Mont Pelee in Martinique; and finally, to U.S. Mt. St. Helens, Mt. Shasta, Mt. Hood, and to Mt. Rainier, all situated in America's northwestern region. Such a gargantuan dust cloud shrouding the sun's rays would immediately envelop the whole globe. Soon, the polar regions and their massive glaciers will melt, but hopefully, that occurrence with happen well-after the human population will have been totally exterminated, or should I say 'eradicated,' to politely use a much more benign term. Only I, Jefferson Mason, shall miraculously escape the total horrific devastation and cleverly

outlive the remainder of the human race! This I promise, my
dear diary.'

'Yes, thanks to my need to survive, an incredible 'greenhouse
effect' of such enormous and monumental proportions will make the
disappearance of the prehistoric dinosaurs seem like a trivial,
geological event,' the psycho-minded egomaniac concluded. 'And a
secret is only a secret if it is kept by only one person, and not
ridiculously shared. That's precisely why I prefer to act as a lone
wolf! Of course,' Jefferson Mason greedily reasoned, 'my
knowledgeable and wholly competent Arab and Russian co-
conspirators are in on separate parts of the clever ruse, but they hate
Americans with a passion, and will gladly participate in my grand
design, just to slaughter as many millions as they can by firing-off the
already acquired projectiles at selected volcanoes. I had illicitly
obtained the missiles on the black market from Pakistan, from Iran
and from North Korea, and soon thereafter, my well-connected
contacts clandestinely smuggled the lethal devices into my state-of-
the-art launching facilities, conveniently hidden in strategic places all
over the world. Those selfsame, formidable weapons of mass
destruction that I've furtively obtained had been originally purchased
by my former agents and international employees,' the mentally ill
psychopath recalled with a smile.

The lunatic billionaire took a deep breath, and then analyzed his
particular physical, sick plight some more. 'Yes; only the self-
centered doctors over at the University of Pennsylvania Hospital
know of my grave medical problem, but they're bound by the
physician/patient privilege to not reveal any pertinent information
about my deteriorating physical health to anyone. Even though my
thoughts are sometimes erratic and disconnected,' the deranged
fanatic speculated and rationalized, 'I'm still a veritable genius, and
therefore, rightfully deserve to outlive the more inferior members of
my mostly mediocre species.'

And then Jefferson Mason thought about the lack of love and
romance in his life, and justified his fabulous prosperity and his
current aversion towards his fellow man by wickedly reckoning, 'I
had to stay focused on my great dream of ascending above the
competition and totally winning in the end,' the delusional,
egocentric, rogue-scoundrel assessed. 'A nagging wife and bratty
children would've taxed my creativity, and would have put a strain on
my financial resources. If I had to be dedicated to *them*, I could've
never accomplished what I had done. I had very intelligently devoted

my entire existence and energy to pursuing the Queen of Diamonds, and I obstinately refused to be subordinate to, or be henpecked by the very demanding Queen of Hearts.'

And indeed, for a fleeting minute (during a rare moment of sentimentality), Jefferson Mason recalled his Oakcrest High School heartthrob Charlene Wilson, and his Glassboro State College dream girl Gina Thomas; each of whom later had led lackluster lives, had married, and divorced rather ordinary husbands; and both females soon became typical mothers trapped in totally mundane, miserable, middle-class existences; the women living and drowning within a Darwinian world teeming with boundless opportunity and abounding in intense individual and corporate competition.

'But ten years ago, I did send Charlene and Gina checks for a million dollars each, but then I deliberately ignored both their efforts to contact and personally thank me for my fine generosity. I deliberately shunned having close associations with others, especially women; *that* very necessary practice being employed so that I could concentrate my enviable talents on achievement and on being exclusively objective in my proclivities; and consequently, my sacrifices and endeavors were blessed by me not having bothersome emotions influencing the outcomes of my keen decision-making. And just look what I've attained and what Charlene and Gina have done with their very lackluster pathetic lives!' Jefferson Mason concluded. 'They've both been content being minor cogs inside of small wheels, not ever realizing that they could be big wheels themselves! I'm glad I didn't waste my life endeavoring to be just like everyone else in this dull and drab convoluted world! On the contrary, I've always derived satisfaction from being productive, self-reliant, resourceful, and successful!'

The progressively disconsolate man then thought about Princeton, New Jersey, and about the excellent university, and how he had often declined giving guest lectures at the institution out of his fear of public speaking, and also, out of disdain for close human contact. And then attempting to switch his ever-deteriorating mindset from the negative to the positive, Jefferson Mason recollected living in San Diego, of visiting the outstanding Balboa Park Zoo there; of appreciating the architectural splendor of the Hotel del Coronado, and of viewing the beautiful rugged cliffs and placid coves along the La Jolla coastline without anyone (close to him) to share those most pleasurable sites. 'Yes, I do miss Southern California after living there for twenty-two marvelous years,' the melancholy maniac sobbed. 'The trips and vacations to Palm Springs and Palm Desert, the great restaurants on Palm Canyon Drive and on El Paseo, all fond recollections, but definitely, irrelevant and minuscule to the enormous task at hand. Why should other less deserving people enjoy the amenities of those terrific places when I must die a mere half-year from now! If there's a God in heaven, I must curse Him for my rapidly spreading cancer!'

* * * * * * * * * * * *

The emotionally unstable, mercurial-tempered, multi-billionaire suddenly became temporarily elated, sitting inside his isolated deep bunker compound, a full thousand feet underground. The crazed spectator curiously viewed on his giant flat-screen television evolving news reports of the mammoth International Space Laboratory's recent explosion. Mason poured a glass of blackberry brandy and contemplated the successful implementation of Phase I of his twisted plot to survive the remainder of his doomed species.

'Yes; my unwary physical double has just been erased from existence!' the obsessed villain summarized. 'Everyone will think that I've been blown to smithereens with all my atoms, cells and molecules instantaneously scattered into outer space in a unique sort of contemporary, astronomical cremation, ha, ha, ha! But obviously, I've not been blown into oblivion as everyone now believes! To the mini-minded populations of the world, my passing will be just a momentary bit of gossip and tabloid dissemination, and nothing more. But I intend to have the last laugh on so-called 'civilization'; yes, I most certainly will! Ha, ha, ha! The pea-brained inhabitants of Planet Earth will soon become hysterical rats desperately scampering all over creation, desperately seeking shelter from inevitable extermination! Much to their frustration, the pathetic masses will soon be learning histrionics instead of history inside my experimental well-contrived Earth laboratory! Ha, ha, ha!'

The mentally superior yet emotionally underdeveloped iconoclast had very methodically taken the time to deactivate the elevator leading-down from his palatial mansion to the well-equipped and handsomely furnished subterranean "survival compound". That strategic precaution would ensure that Jefferson Mason would indeed out-live his fellow man. 'Yes, tomorrow morning, World War III will commence, and it'll soon be followed with missiles impacting into Mt. Vesuvius, Krakatoa, Mt. St. Helens, Mt. Rainier, Mt. Etna and the rest of geography's most important and destructive volcanoes. I'll mastermind the end of humanity and not leave it up to definite incompetents like Satan or Jesus Christ!'

And then Jefferson Mason's defective mind reflected on the present state of mortal affairs some more. 'Perhaps I'm Vulcan reincarnated, the defunct and obsolete Roman god of fire and metallurgy; yes, the Roman resurrection of the Greek god Hephaestus,' the mentally sick fiend hypothesized. 'Yes, now I distinctly remember learning in my college Greco-Roman Mythology class that the word 'volcano' had originated from the god Vulcan's name, ha, ha, ha! Yes indeed; I am the very capable author, producer and director of this morbid, tragic play now spawned into progress! Let Mt. Stromboli and Mt. Hood violently erupt and completely pollute the atmosphere, all occurring at my omnipotent command! My supreme powers are limitless! My invincible will is final! I shall ultimately prevail! Ha, ha, ha!'

* * * * * * * * * * * *

A series of extremely loud explosions suddenly rocked the underground bunker, and soon tons of debris descended into its well-fortified interior. A team of thirteen Delta Force commandos stormed into the compound with weapons and searchlights, just after the emergency generator had failed, and the overhead and wall lights had gone out. Soon, the lifeless body of Jefferson Mason was discovered beneath a fallen beam and underneath large fragments of crumbled concrete. The evil architect of the world's end had swallowed a cyanide capsule just before the elite squad of soldiers had forcefully entered the area, so the wily multi-billionaire had died of his own volition and not from the series of powerful military blasts that had been detonated.

"The nutcase fanatic's dead!" Major James Nelson determined upon feeling Jefferson Mason's neck. "No pulse evident on his frail wrists, either! Forensic tests will determine exactly how this perverted humanitarian had died, but the important fact is that he's dead, and that the world's no longer in jeopardy from his demented insanity! What a diabolical plan his vile mind had hatched! Better him being dead and not us, Captain!"

"Yes, indeed Major," Captain Gene Donohue agreed and verified. "It's a good thing we managed to bypass the deactivated elevator and climb-down that elevator shaft with our high-powered stun grenades intact! And it's also a good thing that the Russian authorities and our Arab intelligence agents found-out about this nefarious monster and his devious blueprint for international calamity," Captain Donohue knowledgeably added. "This demonic predator absolutely loathed his fellow man, and fortunately, the vindictive knave wound-up destroying himself in the process! And Mr. Mason had everything going for himself too, but then the fiend became too selfish, too excessively covetous, and...."

"And despicably wanted to start World War III and next eradicate his fellow man as if we all were disgusting insects and fleas," Major Nelson confirmed with a serious-looking frown showing on his grim, gritty face. "And there're hundreds of other crazy loons with all kinds of grievances out there, having similar weird notions and delusions of grandeur; but luckily, those random culprits have less money and less resources than this psycho Mr. Jefferson Mason possessed. Most of the country's most bitter enemies are without a doubt anarchistic socio-paths having demented concepts of what's right and what's wrong, finding fault with everything *outside* of themselves! If this loon's nightmare had reached fruition, and had not been expertly foiled by our superb intelligence network," Major Nelson emphasized to Captain Donohue, "then *we* would've been sent back to Neanderthal times, with us and our accursed descendants again living in caves and going back to being slaves to a primitive, subsistence existence. Culture and civilization would've had to begin all over again!"

The well-trained Delta Force commando soldiers all stood there, totally amazed at what had just happened, and contemplated what had almost transpired had *they* not so decisively acted and violently intervened. Then, the attack squad's fearless second-in-command had something salient to say.

"Major Nelson; you're assuming that some people would've survived the unparalleled worldwide destruction!" Army Captain Donohue conjectured and then stated to his immediate superior. "And Major, everyone out there in the media all along had been deceived and felt that this twisted-minded maniac had been a benign benefactor to humanity, and also a kind contributor to society's greater good! Philanthropist my eye! Now we fully understand this loose cannon Jefferson Mason for what he actually was, and for what he really represented. Needless to say, a harmless benefactor and philanthropist he was not!"

"This delusional old codger's malicious strategy wasn't just a fascinating whim or an idle idiosyncrasy," Major Nelson evaluated and verbally communicated. Thank God that this mentally ill crackpot never got the chance to employ Phase II and Phase III of his perverted, heinous plot, or else, Captain Donohue," the commanding officer of the undercover mission maintained, "we wouldn't be standing here having this casual conversation right this minute!" Major Nelson convincingly and solemnly replied. "We'd both hopefully be in Heaven and asking St. Peter at the fabled Pearly Gates exactly how the *hell* we ever got there!"

"Triple Jeopardy"

Ever vigilant FBI Inspector Joseph Giralo was quite fatigued from his grueling daily work schedule that involved apprehending major East Coast felony criminals, and now the veteran federal law enforcement official and his wife Gina were anxiously looking forward to a weeklong bus excursion originating from the Senior Tours Bus Terminal on Route 9 in Cape May Court House, New Jersey. Upstate Michigan was the land tour's principal destination, and also its culminating tourist experience: the site of the famous and historic Grand Michigan Hotel, which majestically occupies a picturesque ridge on tranquil Mackinac Island. The world-renowned vacation resort is ideally located midway between the mid-western state's Lower and Upper Peninsulas.

After boarding the huge white bus along with the other dozen bleary-eyed, early rising passengers, Joe and Gina were ready to commence their great adventure at precisely 5 a.m. on a mild September Saturday morning. The husband and wife sat impatiently in their soft blue seats and watched out the window as Mike the bus driver dutifully loaded the group's luggage into the modern, deluxe vehicle's right-side storage compartment. The FBI Inspector seemed rather content coping with his "rooster time existence".

"It's great being a regular, non-government civilian for the next seven days. And Hon, you just can't get any bus better than this one anywhere in Jersey," the somewhat-relaxed man commented to his devoted spouse. "This is one of those new 'kneeling buses' that has an impressive spiral boarding entrance. I don't know if you had noticed it or not, Gina, but the front steps had actually lowered several inches to allow us to conveniently step inside, and then move up the aisle more easily. How long until our first rest stop? I could use some hot coffee to wake me up?"

"Well Hubby, according to the itinerary I'm holding in my hand," Gina Giralo alertly answered, "we'll be stopping at the King-of-Prussia rest stop on the Pennsylvania Turnpike in about three hours. The local bus tour company had to team-up with a couple of other regional operators to fill-up this bus. Other passengers will be picked-up at the Shore Mall just outside Atlantic City, and later at the Wyndham Hotel on Route 73 in Cherry Hill," Mrs. Giralo prattled and informed. "Then it'll be across the Delaware River via the Betsy Ross Bridge to the Neshaminy Mall, where the remainder of the group will be picked-up along with our special tour guide."

"This trip looks like a real bargain, costing only eleven hundred dollars a person," Joe Giralo reminded his very upbeat traveling mate. "Where are we staying the first night?"

"At a La Quinta Inn in an Ohio town called Macedonia."

"I hope we don't run into King Philip, or his conquest-minded son, Alexander-the-Great," Joe jested as the FBI Inspector curiously stared through the passenger window and noticed Mike slamming shut the side luggage door. "This might sound stupid, but I've done more than my share of up-front combat with enough local *barbarians* during my thirty-year career working for Uncle Sam. I hope that folks traveling the busy Interstates in Ohio and Michigan don't think we're a part of a traveling high-jacked sequestered jury," the husband facetiously quipped.

"Why do you say that?" Gina asked, anticipating one of her spouse's incessant, ridiculous jokes.

"Because on the side of the bus is painted the words Senior Tours, Cape May Court House," Giralo replied before giggling. "You know me Hon. Always thinking about some aspect of the law and some oddball facet of the American justice system."

At eight a.m. (and on schedule), the bus rumbled into the King-of-Prussia rest area on the Pennsylvania Turnpike, and Joe and Gina stepped-out to enjoy some hot coffee and fresh doughnuts during their half hour stop. In the midst of their light conversation, the wife gave her loyal companion some background on what Senior Tours had planned for the week besides a "glorious three-night stay" at the splendid Grand Michigan Hotel.

"After the first night in Ohio at the La Quinta Inn, we'll be occupied Sunday afternoon viewing the many exhibits at the Ford Museum in Dearborn, just outside Detroit," the excited woman reviewed. "Then, right next to the museum is Greenfield Village, a wonderful re-creation of the place where Henry Ford had lived his childhood. I won't go into all the details of what's in the museum, or inside the village, because I want to see how surprised you'll be when we view them. Our tour guide Julie told me five minutes ago that we'll be on our own for the entire museum and village explorations. Next, we'll be staying the night at an area Ramada Inn before heading out to Frankenmuth in the center of Michigan."

"What's Frankenmuth?" the puzzled husband wondered and asked. "It sounds like a gift the Three Wise Men brought to Bethlehem, or it might just be a distant relative of Victor Frankenstein. Or perhaps it's a gross mispronunciation of the dangerous monster's *mouth?*"

"No Silly!" Gina corrected, revealing a cute grin upon her lips. "I read in the informative trip brochure that 'Franken' refers to the German people that eventually settled in central Michigan, and that 'Muth' is a German word meaning courage; so together, Frankenmuth means the bravery of the original German settlers. The place is a really neat Bavarian-style town in appearance, and I think you'll actually feel like you're in a Black Forest village rather than meandering around in the middle of a Midwestern State."

"That all sounds pretty terrific, and exactly what I need; a nice change of pace from our hectic New Jersey environment," Joe opined. "Now tell me Dear; did you bring along that new deck of cards of yours? I'm even willing to play a game of 'Phase Ten' to pass the night in Macedonia; that is, if there aren't any major baseball or football games on the TV."

Julie promptly sauntered over to the Giralos' rest stop table and announced, "Our bus leaves in five minutes! Mike's already had his standard two cigarettes and an extra-large cup of coffee, so the nicotine and the caffeine will keep him wide-eyed for the next two and a half hours until we reach western Pennsylvania and have a chance to view the beautiful Allegheny Mountains. After another casual rest stop," Julie continued her narrative, "it's then into Ohio, and finally off to rural Macedonia and supper at a Cracker Barrel Restaurant; followed by a restful night at the very comfortable La Quinta Inn. And after a decent continental breakfast to be eaten just off the lodge's lobby," Julie concisely expressed, "Sunday morning it's off to Dearborn. Don't forget Folks. Except for the nights at the Grand Michigan Hotel, you can only take your two carry-on bags into the several motels where we'll be staying."

"Thanks Julie," Joe replied with a smile. "What does La Quinta mean in English? Is it a number?"

"No; but just like we have different words for 'house' like 'home', 'abode', 'dwelling' and 'residence' in English," the knowledgeable tour guide stated and then paused to further emphasize her point; "La Quinta means 'country house' in Spanish, and it's a synonym for regular words like 'casa' and 'hacienda'."

"Pardon my ignorance when it comes to foreign languages," Joe indulgently laughed as the vacationing FBI Inspector rose from his red, plastic, snack area seat. "But even a broken clock is right twice a day! Ha, ha, ha!"

* * * * * * * * * * * *

Late Sunday morning, Mike used his reliable GPS device to leave a very congested Interstate having plenty of new infrastructure construction, and then the man behind the wheel skillfully navigated his ultramodern bus through downtown Detroit, heading west in the direction of Dearborn and the aforementioned Ford Museum and adjacent Greenfield Village. Since the outside temperature was approaching an unseasonably high eighty-degrees, most of the bus entourage, including the smart-thinking Giralos, decided to amble through the village first, and then later, enjoy the air-conditioning that would be provided inside the immense museum.

Train tickets were purchased at the village's main station, and the New Jersey duo stepped aboard the third carriage car of the *Edison*, which was a small refurbished steam locomotive that had been manufactured during the past century. Gina explained to her somewhat-interested husband that one of Henry Ford's closest friends was inventor Thomas Alva Edison, so naturally it made perfectly good sense that the train engine appropriately bore *that* particular famous last name.

Most everyone riding the colorfully painted train cars decided to exit at the second depot stop, which amazingly was a full-scale recreation of Michigan's legendary Port Huron Railway Station where incidentally, a young Thomas Edison had become a twelve-year-old "news butcher" on a train owned by the then prominent Grand Trunk Railway. Young Edison was quite ambitious, and the industrious lad sold newspapers, candy, peanuts, and various sandwiches on a popular rail route that ran from Port Huron all the way down to Detroit.

According to a brochure Gina had been reading, one day young mischievous Tom tried conducting a difficult chemical experiment in the baggage car, when a stick of phosphorus accidentally caught on fire. The appalled and angry conductor entered and roughly grabbed the boy, vigorously boxed Edison's tender ears, and then mercilessly kicked the non-penitent youth off the train at the next station. That particular ear abuse led to Edison being nearly deaf, but later in a separate railroad incident, another conductor on a slow-moving train helped Tom clamber aboard by lifting the adolescent up by the ears, thus additionally contributing to Edison's virtual deafness that regrettably accompanied the very famous inventor throughout the remainder of his curiosity-oriented life.

"Last year my class read a short story about the amazing Thomas Edison," elementary school teacher Gina Giralo recalled and related to her somewhat-apathetic spouse. "The theme was that Thomas

Edison had often said that he didn't mind being almost totally deaf because the lack of sound afforded him the luxury of thinking and concentrating better. Edison really was quite a remarkable man."

"And I remember from a high school science class lecture that Edison had kept plenty of clocks on the walls and tables of his New Jersey laboratory, but none of them ever had the right time," the husband shared. "Everyone on his staff working on their various projects forgot all about time, and quickly focused their undistracted attention upon individual tasks at hand. Perhaps I'll remember to do a similar thing in my FBI office when I get back home."

Greenfield Village was indeed rather spectacular for the first-time visitors to experience. After stepping away from the realistic-looking Port Huron Railway Station, the New Jersey couple stopped their trekking for several minutes, and enjoyed listening to the calliope music emanating from an enormous children's amusement carousel house, that was strategically situated towards the center of the spotless, clean-street village.

Other delightful surprises were seen and soon entered. One brick building was a facsimile of the original H.J. Heinz office and processing plant; another attractive edifice was a rendition of the Wright Brothers Store in Dayton, Ohio, and also several foundries had been meticulously erected inside Greenfield Village to show the public the tremendous economic "factory progress" that had been made during the great American Industrial Revolution.

And next, the two enamored visitors strolled around the grounds of Henry Ford's birthplace, a handsome white country house with a fine rotating windmill occupying the back yard; the eye-appealing property being quaintly situated next to a replica of Thomas Edison's gray laboratory building in Menlo Park, New Jersey, where marvelous inventions such as the phonograph, the light bulb, and the motion picture film projector had been conceived during the extraordinarily dynamic early stages of the twentieth century.

But the most truly wonderful aspect of anachronistic-looking Greenfield Village was yet to come. At a booth, the Giralos purchased tickets to climb into an authentic, well-maintained Model-T Ford that was still functioning as if it was a brand-new transportation machine. A fleet of fifteen Model-Ts of different designs (ranging through the years 1915-1927) was available to the visiting public. Every Model-T had a chauffeur, and the knowledgeable drivers took captivated tourists on refreshing fifteen-minute rides all throughout the immaculate, cement-paved, wide streets of absolutely incomparable Greenfield Village.

"Nothing at all like this unique attraction exists back in Jersey," Giralo noted to his wife. "I'm not exaggerating when I say that *this* inspirational ride is borderline sensational."

"Yes, Sir. The Model-Ts became obsolete in the late 1920s, and the design was then followed by the upgraded, more-sophisticated Model-A Ford," eavesdropped and commented Ben, the Model-T operator. "Don't ask me why the early Fords are in reverse alphabetical order, because I can't academically answer that question. But it's a known fact that the Model-A definitely came into production right after the Model-T became extinct."

"Regardless of the chronological order," Joe Giralo declared with an air of certainty evident in his tone of voice. "Tell me now, Ben. Are the buildings here in Greenfield Village all miniature models of the original structures?"

"Actually, many of the main structures are the same size as the originals, and have been carefully dismantled; and after being specially transported here, they've been gingerly reassembled stone by stone, brick by brick," Ben conveyed to his fascinated audience of two. "It was quite a colossal undertaking to say the least, but just like good old Henry Ford had achieved during his remarkable life-time, the almost-impossible engineering feats represented here in Greenfield Village could only be accomplished with extra diligence and perseverance. When you have a chance, be sure to walk through the several large machinery buildings where the theme 'machines making machines' is the key message."

"Positively incredible!" Joe Giralo evaluated and exclaimed, contrary to his normally placid demeanor. "*Special* is the only word I can think of to describe this pretty unbelievable place! Positively incredible!" The visiting Inspector repeated.

After passing through the Main Pavilion's exit turnstiles, Joe and Gina strolled hand-in-hand like two newlyweds over to the nearby Ford Museum, which also offered its appreciative guests many outstanding attractions. And after taking photos of each other standing in front of the sentimental-in-appearance Oscar Mayer Weinermobile, the rejuvenated pair swallowed-down delicious hot dogs at the adjacent Oscar Mayer food concession.

Other exquisite exhibits were visually enjoyed including a reproduction of a '50s Texaco gas station; an original Golden Arches McDonald's walk-up Restaurant advertising 15cent hamburgers; the actual Rosa Parks bus that was still in mint condition; a walk-in '50s diner, and the historic Presidential limousines of Franklin D. Roosevelt, John F. Kennedy, and Ronald Reagan. But besides the giant generators, turbines, tractors, airplanes and powerful steam locomotives occupying strategic spaces, the main highlight of the Ford Museum (for the Giralos) happened to be the nearly two hundred classic American automobiles on display; the array including a vintage white Dusenberg; a terrific-looking Rolls Royce Phantom; a sporty red Jaguar Roadster; a fantastic Bugatti; several memorable Cadillacs and Packards, along with a contingent of nostalgic-looking, shiny '50s Chevy Corvettes and sporty classic Ford Thunderbirds.

"Did you see the rear seat of F.D.R.'s limo'?" Gina asked. "It had three buttons positioned on a back seat console; one each for NBC, ABC and CBS, the three dominant radio networks of the awesome 1940s' decade!"

"Wow!" Joe Giralo merrily exclaimed, showing his new-found exuberance. "President Roosevelt had a form of push button radio remote control several years before television had ever been invented. I suppose that those three useful network buttons were really high tech' state-of-the-art back in the Big Band, art deco days of the 1940s. Glenn Miller really had it right all along. This fabulous out-of-this-world Ford Museum has really gotten me out of my tedious work doldrums and 'In the Mood'."

* * * * * * * * * * * * *

Midway into the third day of scenic early fall traveling, Mike steered his mammoth bus into the town of Frankenmuth, and the weary passengers all checked into their various rooms at the Drury Inn at 260 South Main Street. That evening, a tasty chicken and beer supper was enjoyed at the extra-large-sized Bavarian Inn, owned by the same family as the landmark Zehnder's Restaurant situated across the street, which proudly promotes itself as the largest family restaurant in the entire United States. The waiters at the Bavarian Inn wore green feathered hats and knee socks with short pants, traditional German festival apparel known in and around 'Old World' Munich as 'lederhosen', while the pretty waitresses were garbed in attractive cotton dresses that were being referred to as being called 'dirndl.'

But much to everyone's appreciation, after a delectable pastry/ice cream dessert had been served and consumed, the Jersey tourists re-boarded the dependable bus, and Mike drove the now-spirited delegation to the magnificent Bronners Christmas Land on the east end of Frankenmuth. Upon its nighttime arrival, the bus passed up and down a series of parallel lanes that featured a brilliant spectacle of flickering and blinking lit Christmas decorations: angels, elves,

Magi, a North Pole setting, Bethlehem manger scenes, Santa Clauses, glistening snowmen, colorful giant boxed gifts, impressive toy soldier guards, and the like. The bus's radio was instantly tuned to a certain lively FM frequency, and everyone aboard cheered when the thrilled passengers heard the loud refrains to "We Need a Little Christmas", "Here Comes Santa Claus" and "Frosty the Snowman", with the entire fantastic circuitous lane route requiring three full songs to finally complete.

After a quick breakfast the following morning, the energized group spent several hours walking around downtown Frankenmuth, viewing and taking pictures of the elaborate Glockenspiel Clock situated on the side of the alpine-in-appearance Bavarian Inn, the very splendid time apparatus chiming twelve bongs at noon. And simultaneously, the Giralos and their traveling party were treated to seeing character figures mechanically moving-out one by one from the high-elevated clock, and then methodically reenacting a rendition of medieval history's legendary perfect pest exterminator, the classic "Pied Piper of Hamelin". Later that afternoon, Mike again conducted the forty-eight bus travelers to Bronners, the colossal-sized Christmas store that advertised itself as being open for business three hundred and sixty-one days of the calendar year.

"This building is incredibly gigantic; at least ten times as big as anything like it I've seen back in Jersey," Gina observed and stated. "Joe, this place Bronners claims to be the most prodigious Christmas paradise in the whole-wide world, and now I believe that their assertion is, without a doubt, a hundred percent true."

"Yes, and the only thing saving us from getting lost inside this phenomenal building are the huge overhead red and white ceiling signs that tell us what section of the store we're shopping in; ranging from area #1 to area #12. And Gina," Joe Giralo added. "I just got an idea. I think I'll get my office's two secretaries these matching Michigan State and University of Michigan stockings to hang from their fireplace mantels. The two schools are bitter rivals ya' know; especially during football season."

"And about a half an hour ago, I had seen some cute Christmas tree ornaments that I'd like to purchase. They're located over in Section 7," the wife indicated. "I had always thought that the Yankee Candle Christmas Shop we had visited in Connecticut on our last fall bus trip up to the Beacon Resort in New Hampshire was massive, but this whopping place is at least three times as big."

The Giralos lazily spent the remainder of the afternoon sampling various red and white wines (offered in plastic jiggers) at the town's

St. Julian's Winery, and that evening, the couple played two games of 'Phase Ten' in the Drury Inn's 'Card and Recreation Lounge' with another husband/wife twosome they had met on the trip, Jim and Janice Heisler from Buena, a rustic South Jersey borough just south of Hammonton.

And finally, after indulging in a good night's sleep and partaking of the usual continental breakfast, the rested Jerseyites toting their various carry-on bags, climbed aboard the long white bus and then settled into their respective seats. Loquacious tour guide Julie Setzer provided her attentive audience with essential background about the Grand Michigan Hotel, along with picturesque Mackinac Island.

"The name Mackinac has a French pronunciation, and it's really sounded-out as the word *Mackinaw* would be enunciated in English," Julie educated her listeners over the bus's microphone. "Ironically, Mackinaw City is the town from which you'll take your ferry ride three miles across the channel to Mackinac Island, having the exact same pronunciation; but obviously, spelled differently. There're three ferry services shuttling people and goods back and forth from Mackinaw City to Mackinac Island: Arnold, Starr Lines and Shepherd's Ferry."

"How far is the island from the famous Mackinac Bridge?" an elderly male senior citizen seated in the back of the bus hollered his question. "My uncle worked on that super five and a half-mile long span way back in the mid-1950s."

"Actually, you'll be able to see the Mackinac Bridge from certain parts of the Grand Michigan Hotel property," Julie communicated over the bus's intercom. "The span is quite an engineering marvel. Now here's something fairly interesting I just thought of. The Michigan people that live on the state's Northern Peninsula are called 'Oopers', a name given by the residents living on the Lower Peninsula. And the folks living on the Lower Peninsula intentionally gave *them'* that designation 'Oopers', the local term being a deliberate misspeak of the word 'Uppers'. Conversely," Julie lectured on, "the Upper Peninsula residents refer to their Lower Peninsula Michigan neighbors as 'trolls'; probably referring to the fairy tale The Three Billy Goats Gruff, the very popular children's story having a mean-spirited troll threatening the three crossing goats from below a bridge."

"I think the Mackinac Bridge goes over one of the Great Lakes," a gentleman sitting in the fourth row (right hand side) blurted-out. "Would you know which one?"

"Well, let me see now," Julie politely thought and answered. "The Mackinac Bridge separates Lake Superior on the left and Lake Huron on the right; that is, presuming we're facing the Upper Peninsula. Yes, that's correct," the knowledgeable tour-guide clarified. "Facing north, Lake Superior would be on the left and Lake Huron would be on the right."

"Do the locals call *us* tourists anything weird?" an inquisitive-but-vociferous woman in the central bus section asked Julie. "I mean, *we* at the Jersey Shore call summer tourists 'shoebies' because during the Great Depression, the day-tourists would come into Atlantic City on a train, carrying their modest already-prepared lunches on their laps in shoe boxes."

"Why yes!" Julie quickly understood and laughed. "Tourists are referred to up here as 'fudgies' because there's a variety of at least thirty fudge shops selling their delicious sweet confections to visitors, both in the shops in Mackinaw City and also in the many fudge stores on Main Street on Mackinac Island."

"How will our luggage get from the bus to the Grand Michigan Hotel?" the curious woman's apparently worried husband wanted to know. "I understand that there aren't any cars, trucks, or buses allowed on the island."

"You're right!" Julie concurred with a smile. "When the famous Grand Michigan Hotel was built back in the late 1880s, the island's town council passed an ordinance stating that no new-fangled, noisy, horseless carriages would be allowed. So, from that day forward," Ms. Julie Setzer courteously explained, "the only way around Mackinac Island is by foot, by bicycle, or by horse and wagon, with many of the transportation carts looking like colonial-era stage coaches. During the peak summer months, around six hundred horses take people around Main and Market Streets, the island's two chief thoroughfares. The horses are usually arranged in sets of two, but if you want to take a ride to the higher parts of the island, the horses will be in a team of three."

"But you didn't answer my question! How will our luggage get from the bus to the hotel?" the stubborn, impetuous elderly fellow persisted as his perturbed wife gave him a dig into his ribcage with her bony left elbow.

"Dock workers will take the luggage from the bus's storage compartment, put the pieces onto carts, and then carefully wheel the carts onto an awaiting Shepherd's Ferry. When the boat makes the three-mile trip across the bay to the island," Julie suavely conveyed to her traveling flock, "several horse-drawn wagons will be loaded with your suitcases; and I assure you, then your items will be safely delivered to the hotel, where you'll find your luggage in the hallway just outside your assigned rooms."

"I saw some postcards of a few wonderful houses on Mackinac Island and the homes look like the bread and breakfast places in Cape May," Gina told Julie. "Many of the houses show a lot of external gingerbread designs."

"Yes; even the incomparable Grand Michigan Hotel flaunts a Victorian appearance," Julie Setzer articulated through the bus's overhead speakers. "And the hotel's magnificent front porch overlooks a flower-laden terrace facing-down towards the water. The famous porch is over six-hundred-and-fifty feet long, the largest hotel porch in the world. And the Grand Michigan's spacious dining room easily seats seven-hundred-and-fifty guests for supper and breakfast. And Gentlemen," Julie purposely reminded her male passengers, "this next announcement is very important. You *must* wear a suit or formal jacket with a tie if you wish to be seated and eat supper in the resort's extraordinarily elegant main dining room."

"It sure beats enjoying informal dining at Burger King!" vacationing FBI Inspector Joe Giralo whispered into Gina's ear and then characteristically chuckled.

"And now, Folks," the charming tour guide proudly announced. "You'll be seeing the widely acclaimed 1980 movie *Somewhere in Time*, starring Christopher Reeve and Jane Seymour. The film's a classic time-traveling adventure where a young playwright goes back in time to the early 1900s, and has a dramatic love affair with an actress of that era who had done stage performances at Mackinac Island's Grand Michigan Hotel. And a lot of the movie's scenes had been filmed on location at the Grand Michigan!"

* * * * * * * * * * * *

The scenic three-mile Shepherd's Ferry ride across the placid channel from Mackinaw City to Mackinac Island was both swift and invigorating for the picture-taking passengers recently departed from their bus. A trio of two horse-pulled, open-air carriages (capable of seating eighteen passengers each) met the eager tourists at the central Mackinac Island docking terminal. Another three wagons that had been differently designed to specifically convey cargo had six strong workmen diligently loading-up the group's bulky luggage pieces, and after everyone was accounted for by Julie, the Giralos and their highly motivated traveling colleagues were soon riding down Main

Street, enthusiastically viewing its many souvenir shops and casual eating establishments.

"Looks a little like a typical Jersey Shore boardwalk without any evidence of any boardwalk!" Joe instinctively quipped. "Julie was right! There're fudge shops galore here! And there were plenty more too operating over in those tourist-trap shopping centers back in Mackinaw City. If we were to stay on this island paradise for a full month, I'd probably easily weigh seventy-five more pounds than I do right now!"

"Stop being so cynical!" Gina coyly chided her all-too-garrulous husband. "Learn to relax and forget your eminent FBI identity for a few days! Look Joe! The driver's turning the corner at the end of Main Street, and we're now going onto Market! And you just have to admire those stately Victorian mansions up on the high ridge overlooking the water! And just look at the architecture of that beautiful church steeple!"

Upon arriving at the regal-looking Grand Michigan Hotel, the New Jersey guests were warmly greeted by an employee/guide, who then led the awed group through the well-decorated and extra-large main lobby; through a beautiful green-draped, oval-shaped sitting lounge, and next directly into the venue's sophisticated entertainment room where orchestra music was played nightly after supper.

Various hotel speakers and guides then addressed the assembled visitors, describing and discussing in detail the myriad amenities available to guests, explaining the "no-tipping policy"; then lecturing about the exotic botanical gardens surrounding the majestic edifice, and finally, a woman greeter enthusiastically elucidated about the hotel's inimitable Paul Bunyan outdoor swimming pool.

When the Giralos' finally reached Room 132, their three pieces of luggage had already been delivered outside their door. Each of the hotel's three hundred and seventy guest rooms had its own sophisticated décor, and no two sleeping chambers were identical. And the window view of the property's flowers, shrubs, well-manicured lawns, stately coniferous trees and gardens, along with an abundance of astonishing deciduous tree varieties was indubitably stupendous, and none-the-less, extremely breathtaking.

"Joe, just look at the gorgeous dark green drapes, matching mint-colored wallpaper, and accompanying light green, silk-cushioned background above the bed's headboard," Gina marveled and gasped. "And the contrasting green and white table lamps, and the thick, rich rug match perfectly. I'll bet this place had a separate interior decorator for each room!"

"And besides, the bed's soft, and the mattress seems more-than-adequate. When do we eat supper?" the lesser-intrigued spouse desired receiving some feminine response about a matter the FBI Inspector considered to be very important. "My stomach's actively growling for some fine cuisine."

"Joe; did you see the framed caricatures of all the U.S. Presidents hanging along the wall down the first-floor corridor," the wife asked as she zipped open *her* Totes carry-on bag. "And just a couple of doors to our left is the Presidential Suite. I wonder if anyone famous is staying in it?"

"Maybe it's the President of Somalia, or perhaps the Yemen Ambassador to Cuba!" Joe pessimistically replied and then characteristically laughed. "I'm famished Honey! Perhaps I won't be so sarcastic after I have the highly publicized five-course dinner!"

The patient wife totally ignored her mate's brazen attempt at demonstrating typical male negativity, so she shrewdly decided to change the subject. "Well Honey, what did you think of the movie we had seen on the bus, *Somewhere in Time*?"

"I'd have liked the film a whole lot more if Christopher Reeve had fallen in love with a female in his own 1980s past and not be smitten by Cupid's arrow with an attractive lady in the year 1912," Joe Giralo aptly criticized. "I mean, I think that Jane Seymour is an excellent actress, but quite frankly, I prefer TV reality shows to science fiction fantasy, time-travel love stories. I liked Christopher Reeve better when he played Superman."

"Have it your own way without the culinary magic of Burger King!" Gina Giralo wittily retorted. "You probably think that Oscar Mayer hot dogs are the greatest thing going since ancient man invented the fork and knife!"

"Now you're talking!" the FBI official officially on vacation bellowed. "Let's unpack our stuff and then get ready for supper in the main dining room. I can't remember the last time I wore a jacket and tie at a restaurant. Maybe it was a tuxedo at a wedding, but definitely, not a suit and tie for dinner!"

"You'll have to start some intensive dieting when we return to Jersey," Gina diplomatically mentioned and predicted. "I don't want you getting diabetes!"

"But really and truly, I have to apologize to you, Honey! The filet mignon on tonight's menu is several levels above either a frankfurter or a charcoal-broiled slab of meat. And honestly Gina. I don't know why they call the round things hamburgers," Joe Giralo awkwardly introduced his next comical remark. "Ham comes from a pig, and steak happens to come from a cow. The round food in a bun should rightfully be called 'steak-burgers' and not hamburgers!"

* * * * * * * * * * * *

The first full serene day on Mackinac Island (for the Giralos) was a rather nondescript pleasant one. After the couple consumed a sumptuous breakfast in the hotel's nearly eight-hundred-seat main dining room, Joe and Gina ventured outside to partake of the early brisk Northern Michigan autumn air. The pair slowly descended wooden steps, leading them through the eye-appealing terrace area, and then ambled-down to the massive Paul Bunyan Swimming Pool to inspect the many other recreational facilities that were conveniently provided to satisfactorily accommodate the Grand Michigan's thousand or so catered-to, pampered guests.

Julie Setzer was standing outside the hotel's main entrance with her names' checklist clipboard, and at precisely ten a.m., three red and yellow painted horse-drawn carriages were ready to take the forty-eight New Jersey tourists on a "horizontal cross island journey" to the "Carriage House", where fifteen minutes thereafter, a fleet of three horse' carriages was available to transport the delegation to the island's higher elevations. There, the tourists could observe marvelous panoramic views of Lake Huron, along with them snapping impromptu pictures of the natural rock "Arch Formation" located towards the island's summit.

Next on the itinerary was a tour of historic Fort Mackinac, and nearby were the dull, white ramparts that were emblematic of the Governor's Summer Mansion, where James Heisler remarked to the Giralos, "Mitt Romney probably spent many of his youthful years there since his father George was once the Michigan Governor."

The afternoon hours sped-by rather rapidly, as the Giralos and the Heislers casually meandered around parallel Main and Market Streets; doing light shopping at the sundry souvenir stores, and occasionally munching the irresistible fudge "free samples" randomly being offered on employee-held trays to targeted pedestrians. Pizza and Coca-Colas were purchased at a snack bar, but Gina warned Joe that he was limited to two slices, so that the weight-conscious food connoisseur would not spoil his upcoming five-course lobster tail feast back at the hotel.

That evening, after the sumptuous seafood-style dinners were consumed, the remainder of Tuesday night had the formally dressed Giralos and Heislers sitting on sofas in the expansive color-coordinated lobby and drinking cocktails, while listening to an accomplished pianist playing a selection of popular 1940s and '50s melodies. And then after playing three fun-packed games of Phase Ten in the hotel's recreation area, the card playing couples retired to their respective first-floor rooms for the night. Everything was copacetic with the world, and FBI Inspector Joseph Giralo's mind was finally devoid of solving the plethora of illicit criminal activity habitually plaguing American society.

On Thursday morning, Joe was suffering from a mild case of acid reflux, so the ailing epicure thought he would rest-up and recover from his brief malady inside Room 132, while his energized wife accompanied the Heislers on a walking tour of the hotel's majestic gardens, their prime objective being viewing the property's many deciduous trees exhibiting their wondrous red, brown and yellow autumnal hues.

The husband promised Gina that he would be feeling better after a few cups of "Room Service Coffee", and the traveling Inspector also mentioned that his spouse should not worry about his general health during her three-hour absence. Giralo picked-up a copy of the *New York Times* main stories that had been left under the suite's door, and feeling his newly-acquired lackadaisical disposition, the calm and collected vacationer waited for his pot of coffee to be routinely delivered by room service.

* * * * * * * * * * * *

At nine-thirty, a loud, frantic rapping upon Room 132's door interrupted Joe Giralo's peaceful coffee consumption. The FBI man opened the portal, and the occupant was somewhat-astonished to perceive the normally debonair, suit-and-tie head hotel manager impatiently standing in the hallway.

"Mr. Giralo," the exasperated hotel executive said all out of breath. "I'm Giles Martin, the Grand Michigan's chief operating officer. May I come in?"

"Why of course!" the surprised Inspector replied, closing the door behind the unexpected visitor's entrance. "Is everything okay? You do appear to be more than a trifle alarmed!"

"I understand that you're an experienced inspector with the FBI. Our desk records indicate *that* much Inspector Giralo, and I've already verified *that* formerly confidential information through our local police department, which incidentally also drastically needs your immediate assistance."

"Mr. Martin, exactly what is wrong?" the now thoroughly interested hotel guest asked. "What matter is of so much paramount importance and concern?"

"A most serious epidemic of colossal proportion has broken-out among the horse population here on Mackinac Island," panic-stricken Giles Martin boisterously disclosed. "Just about all of our six hundred horses are terribly sick with colic, and with influenza symptoms, and our town veterinarians are going crazy attending to all of the afflicted animals. And besides that," the agitated hotel manager impulsively expounded, "the entire transportation system on the island has been shut-down. This is a colossal nightmare dilemma in progress, Inspector Giralo; an unimaginable, worst-case scenario, and its basic origin, or should I say 'its real cause', *we* certainly find exceptionally baffling. That's why, Inspector Giralo, I'm here in your room to both urgently request and solicit your reputable expertise."

"But Mr. Martin, by your vivid description, I'm not so sure that a genuine FBI crime has actually been committed here on this island," Giralo politely answered. "To be perfectly candid, I'm usually involved with kidnappings, ruthless murders, interstate prostitution and drug smuggling, money counterfeiting, along with major assassinations and multiple homicides performed in adjacent neighboring states. Horse epidemics might just be out of my law enforcement background realm; and the infections that you've depicted might just be a result of a rather bizarre-but-rare, widespread contagion that's going on."

"The horses are biting their stomachs in response to the colic, and others inside their stables are nauseous and lethargic; apparently suffering from their own flu symptoms," the virtually delirious and animated hotel executive reported. "If you can't help us, truthfully Sir, I don't know who else can!"

"Well, Mr. Martin, what about the hotel's CEO? Is he around for me to interview?"

"He's away attending a national conference at the Greenbrier Resort out in White Sulfur Springs, West Virginia, and quite confidentially," Giles Martin pontificated, "I'm afraid to divulge the exact magnitude of the current horse catastrophe to him!" the desperate and now-neurotic man-in-charge of daily operations nervously ranted.

"Well then, what about your Board of Directors? Can I consult with and interview them about this urgent horse matter?"

"Unfortunately, Sir, the Board is spending a week at the Hotel Del Coronado near San Diego where off-the-record, they're doing a little espionage work checking-out *that* facility's various amenities, including the food menu," the now-neurotic and distraught hotel administrator reluctantly shared. "They won't be back until next Monday, and I'm afraid to contact them about the bad news; but I'm sure they'll soon learn about the calamity from another source!"

"Now, Mr. Martin. How about your Corporate President? Is he to be found anywhere in Michigan?"

"This is all indeed very embarrassing for me to endure," the fit-to-be-tied, emotionally encumbered hotel executive apprehensively complained. "Our illustrious President is over in Dixville Notch, New Hampshire, and he's anonymously staying at the famous Balsams Resort while sizing-up the competition. Is there no compassion, or rhyme or reason in this heartless world?"

Just then, Giles Martin's cell phone rang three times, and the man's anxiety level instantly heightened to its crescendo level. The hotel manager's facial expressions, along with his florid complexion, suggested to Inspector Joseph Giralo that the executive's secretary on the other end of the line was communicating additional negative news to the completely harried fellow.

"Mr. Giralo, I think I need to swallow-down at least a dozen aspirins. My secretary Ms. Gibson just informed me that the famous small photograph/portrait of Jane Seymour has been stolen from the downstairs Hall of History. And in addition," miserable Giles Martin continued his ongoing tale of woe, "I've recently learned that three priceless paintings from the mezzanine level art gallery have also been pilfered and have been nefariously replaced with authentic-looking counterfeits."

"I usually get involved with counterfeit money distribution, but if there's evidence or suspicion that these valuable heisted paintings have crossed state lines," Inspector Giralo qualified his complicated explanation, "then I'll be obligated to cut my vacation short and get immersed into cracking-open these new-found riddles of yours."

The usually composed and normally unfazed hotel manager's cell phone again rang, and the already besieged and flustered Giles Martin hesitated before finally responding to the three rings. Obviously, more horrible information was being transmitted to *his* ear, because the perplexed man's facial skin was gradually turning from red to purple. After ending the disturbing telephone call, the beleaguered, perspiring, frantic executive had more catastrophic developments to sadly convey to his now-fascinated listener.

"Oh my God, Inspector Giralo!" the chagrined about-to-go-insane manager screamed while dramatically holding the sides of his head.

"Duchess Priscilla from Denmark is staying with her cousin Princess Natasha two doors down from you in the newly renovated Presidential Suite. I feel like fainting and collapsing on the rug, Mr. Giralo. Their cache of diamonds, of sapphire necklaces, and of jeweled pendants, along with their emerald and ruby gemstone rings, have suddenly been mysteriously purloined from their exclusive room's safe. What an unprecedented career shattering nightmare I'm experiencing!" the extremely delirious gentleman related to his objective-minded Grand Michigan guest. "This entire sequence of events is absolutely scandalous; not only for me, but also for the respectable reputation of this distinguished hotel! It's unprecedented and horrendously devastating upon the long-honored history of *this* truly noble and esteemed establishment!"

"Okay, Mr. Martin; you've now overwhelmingly convinced me to personally and professionally intercede in your terrible crisis!" Inspector Giralo declared. "I'll immediately notify my superiors in Washington of the problems here on the island. I strongly suspect that definite criminal activity is going on here; bizarre occurrences that are evidently on the cusp of being suspiciously pernicious! The events you've just described have to be more than a series of unorthodox coincidences! This complex puzzle now is much greater than a simple case of grand larceny!" Inspector Giralo firmly maintained. "The present circumstances absolutely warrant and justify my pledged Justice Department services! The Duchess and the Princess are both foreign dignitaries that have inadvertently become felony victims. The fact that royal foreign aristocrats have been robbed now makes *your* very unenviable hotel plight into an important federal investigation matter!"

* * * * * * * * * * * *

Much to Giles Martin's utter astonishment, FBI Inspector Joseph Giralo showed-up without an appointment at the hotel director's office early on Friday afternoon, and the man-on-a-mission was bearing some wonderfully propitious news. After being greeted by the somewhat relieved upper echelon executive, the highly skilled federal investigator orally delivered a most stunning exposition.

"Well, Mr. Martin, I've cracked your seemingly strange and inexplicable conundrum wide open, and I'm quite happy to tell you that the overall case has been solved."

"Please divulge what you know, and how you've managed to achieve your amazing results so quickly," Giles Martin reflexively insisted. "For example, what was the horse sickness hysteria all about? What culprit, or should I say *culprits,* were responsible for such a despicably cruel deed?"

"When you had first told me about the unusual colic and influenza epidemic affecting your Mackinac Island work horses, I immediately suspected that some sort of ruse, or should I say, some sort of deliberate diversion had been set into motion," the experienced FBI sleuth remarked. "And when you later found-out about the missing Jane Seymour portrait stolen from the Hall of History, and about the Duchess and the Princess's cherished jewels being burglarized, then those two separate revelations fully confirmed my theory about a clever cover-up horse malady canard being slyly enacted."

"Before you proceed with revealing your discoveries, did you work alone on this case?" Giles inquired. "That prospect would seem to me to be a relevant part of the mystery riddle."

"Yes, Giles. I must confess that I did have competent assistance," Joe Giralo curtly answered. "FBI command in Washington assigned and dispatched a trio of fine men operating up here in Michigan to help me, Agent Arthur Orsi out of Flint, and Salvatore Velardi and Dan Blachford out of Saginaw. The three ambitious agents immediately drove-up here to Mackinaw City, and the investigators conducted comprehensive interviews with the local merchants; most of whom were proprietors and employees of shops on Central Avenue, on Huron Street, and in the Mackinaw Crossings shopping mall. Several conversations from trustworthy people at the Sweet Tooth Confectionery Store, at Joann's Fudge Shop, at the Michigan Peddler, and at the Mackinac Bay Trading Company provided *us* with key information that then led to the acquisition of essential clues and additional vital evidence. Once that specific knowledge had been gleaned and fed into our sophisticated national police data base computer system," Inspector Joe Giralo attested, "the remainder of the well-conceived plot was quite fairly easy to decipher."

Mr. Giles Martin demanded that Inspector Giralo slow-down his general recollection, and precisely state the pertinent facts in their exact chronological order. The cooperative investigator promised to comply with the still-mentally disheveled manager's entreaty.

"Well, as I had already stated Giles," Joe Giralo proceeded with his sage analysis on a more personal basis. "Just as I had suspected, the abnormal horse epidemic was basically a creative canard to divert *your* attention from high level felonies that were in the making. Now Giles, I've noticed that most of your summer employees here at the hotel are from Jamaica and from the Dominican Republic, and a few more from Haiti."

"That is quite true," Giles Martin readily verified. "The hotel annually closes for business in mid-October. Most of the imported summertime help then all return to their native lands, while the Island's working horses are carefully transported to various farms in the Upper Peninsula for the winter. Only about five hundred brave, hardy souls stay around on Mackinac for the extremely frigid, snow-laden months."

"Anyway Giles, after I learned about the art collection counterfeit replacements, and about the replica phony Jane Seymour portrait being exchanged for the original one, along with the snatched jewelry from your royal guests staying in the luxurious Presidential Suite," Inspector Giralo keenly elucidated, "I immediately thought about your employees and about their countries of origin. A background check on various merchants across the bay over in Mackinaw City established that a certain art gallery dealer there by the name of Mortimer Benton had once owned a pawnshop in Montego Bay, Jamaica, and that Mortimer's eldest son Clyde..."

"Once was a lower management clerk here at the hotel who had been dismissed two years ago because Clyde Benton had gotten into a heated dispute with my younger brother, Ted, who was *his* immediate boss at the time! We don't tolerate or allow insubordination to occur here! That's our strict company policy!"

"So, Giles; now we have two distinct motives: Aggrieved Clyde Benton wanted his revenge on the hotel management team, and diabolical Mortimer Benton loved the hotel's art collection, and ultimately, schemed to steal its three most valued canvas treasures," the Inspector plausibly explained. "But don't you see, Giles? It was the missing and substituted for Jane Seymour Portrait that got me hot on Mortimer Benton's trail."

"How did that narrowed-down pursuit come to be?" the still bewildered hotel administrator asked. "There are still several missing components to this rather confusing jigsaw puzzle!"

"Agents Orsi, Velardi and Blachford had discovered over in Mackinaw City that Mortimer Benton was infatuated with *that* very desirable Jane Seymour portrait, ever since the clever *con-artist* had first cinematically viewed in 1982 what later became his passionate obsession, his favorite movie, *Somewhere in Time*. In Mortimer's conniving mind," Inspector Giralo revealed and then paused, "my hypothesis upon initial instinct was that nothing was going to prevent this scheming thug Mortimer Benton from confiscating and possessing *that* coveted Hall of History object. But then, I logically reasoned that the other art masterpieces along with the opulent jewelry would eventually be fenced, with the obtained money being used for desperate Mortimer Benton to pay-off his huge gambling and loan-sharking debts before the ruthless Detroit Mafia closed-in on their pathetic 'mark'."

"And I guess that since Mortimer Benton once owned a pawnshop in Montego Bay, Jamaica," Giles Martin surmised and expressed, "the slippery conniver, just like his volatile son Clyde, the devious rogue also was able to speak Patois, the language often used by the island's natives that had been handed-down from their colonial-era Jamaican slave ancestors; who didn't want *their* vindictive masters to understand what they were plotting or communicating. To the British colonists of Jamaica, the words spoken in Patois all sounded like stupid, garbled gibberish."

"And since Clyde and Mortimer Benton both spoke this contrived language Patois pretty fluently," Inspector Giralo eloquently concurred, "the reprehensible Benton thieves were able to bribe and persuade some of your hotel's less loyal employees to temporarily poison the island's horses; to snatch and replace the three expensive art works; to steal the precious jewels from the Duchess's Presidential Suite; and finally, to stealthily swipe and switch the authentic Jane Seymour Portrait inside the Hall of History."

"And naturally, a former pawnbroker would have direct access to unscrupulous trading fences, and also access to illicit underworld dealers, along with fraudulent contact with numerous nefarious-minded business connections that would be able to easily dispose of the artwork trove at a handsome profit, and to also...."

"To also chop the brilliant diamonds, rubies, emeralds and sapphires down to be dispensed with on the thriving global black market," Joe Giralo clarified. "Now, also Giles. I've learned that Mortimer's brother, Nigel Benton, owns and operates an import/export business over in Alpena; thanks to the dedicated research of FBI Agents Orsi, Velardi and Blachford. But I still need to dig deeper into Mortimer's strategy in order to excavate more salient facts that will enable me to fully implicate Nigel Benton directly to Mortimer and Clyde's felonious Michigan activities."

"And I must say, *that* imaginative horse epidemic diversionary ploy really had us officials here on the island going on a frustrating wild goose chase, just as it had originally been designed by the unscrupulous perpetrators," Mr. Giles Martin concluded and orally conveyed. "For several days, pandemonium had been rampant all over Mackinac. And oh yes, Inspector Giralo; the Chief-of-Police just notified me a half hour ago that a Jamaican room-cleaning maid he's described as a definite 'person of interest' is now under interrogation for her possible participation in the incredible grand larceny, royal jewelry theft caper."

"Yes, and I must admit, even the crafty crooks were surprised when the flu and colic epidemic proved to be more widespread than the culprits had ever anticipated or imagined," the very skilled Inspector nonchalantly verbalized to his most recent admirer. "And to add a new dimension to the confounding ugly mess, another disgruntled former hotel employee named Milo Ransom has already confessed to being a secondary co-conspirator in the elaborate crime scenario. Up to yesterday," Giralo informed Martin, "Milo had been employed as a maintenance crewman on Arnold Ferry Services boats. But after devious Mr. Ransom admitted to smuggling and transporting the jewelry, the original canvas paintings, and also the singular Jane Seymour portrait from Mackinac Island back to Mortimer Benton's art gallery in Mackinaw City, I'm obligated to report to you that *our* subordinate villain Mr. Milo Ransom is currently out of a criminal job, and the adventurous lowlife is now on the local judge's docket, and scheduled to be sentenced to a minimum of six months jail time."

"Most remarkable and extraordinary detective work!" Giles Martin sincerely commended his veteran crime-fighting guest. "If it weren't for you coincidentally vacationing here at the Grand Michigan, *we'd* still be struggling with a mammoth mystery on square one!"

Just then, the elated manager's land-line phone rang, and Ms. Gibson stated over the desk speaker that Inspector Joseph Giralo's boss wished to converse with the new Mackinac Island hero.

"Hello, Joe! And may I add congratulations, too!" Chief D.C. Inspector Matthew Riley praised and complimented over the desk speakerphone for everyone present inside the hotel manager's office to hear. "My reliable sources have informed me that you've become a veritable champion of justice up there in Northern Michigan!"

"All in the line of duty, Sir, but quite frankly, I didn't expect all of the wild excitement to transpire in the middle of my late summer vacation! It's all been a little surreal to tell you the candid truth, Matt! But the Duchess and Princess's gemstones have been recovered intact, and also the stolen paintings from the hotel's art gallery, along with the original Jane Seymour portrait, are all now safely back in the possession of their rightful owners," Joe Giralo respectfully replied.

"Honestly Boss, we have to commend Agents Orsi, Velardi and Blachford, who truthfully did most of the difficult gumshoe groundwork investigation. Everything appears to be back to normal on the Island. But what's up Chief? Anything new developed that I should know about?"

"Well now, Joe," Giralo's no-nonsense, straightlaced superior driveled on. "Since your well-earned Michigan hiatus has been abruptly interrupted with the outlandish Mackinac Island crime spree adventure, I want you to know that I've received special permission to have your vacation at the Grand Michigan Hotel extended for an additional week; expenses all paid for by good old Uncle Sam. Such fine compensation couldn't have happened to a more deserving guy. Nice going Inspector! You have my sincere congratulations! I now only wish that I could be so lucky! I should change my last name from my Irish nationality to Italian!"

"Why that's positively wonderful news, Chief!" the very satisfied Sicilian Inspector boomed into the telephone speaker. "My wife Gina is positively enamored with this place, and she'll be absolutely thrilled to be relaxing here for another seven days. In fact, my better half and I are seriously thinking about moving up here to Northern Michigan after I retire from government service!"

"And that's not all!" Chief Inspector Matthew Riley expeditiously vociferated. "As an added bonus reward, at noon a week from tomorrow, we've arranged for a limo' to pick-up you and Gina at the Mackinaw City central loading pier, and then a hired chauffeur will drive the two of you down to a cute German town in central Michigan called Frankenmuth, where you'll both be treated to another free and fully paid week at a certain lodge; here it is on a sheet of paper sitting on my cluttered desk," Chief Riley said as the FBI administrator fumbled through some irrelevant letters and associated memos. "It's called the Drury Inn. What do you think about those apples, Joe? Talk about living the 'Life of Riley!' Ha, ha, ha! Pretty neat stuff, huh?"

"Why, er yes; it most certainly is, Chief!" the totally shocked and astounded FBI Inspector uttered. "I'm almost flabbergasted! My Uncle Manfred is from Bavaria, and I can't wait to tell him all about my good fortune, being able to hang-out in a German town right here in idyllic Michigan! Thanks a million, Chief! I can't wait to relay the good news to my wife! Another week up here in this green paradise is like a full month relaxing at a desert health spa! Thanks again for the good news Matt!" Click.

The following morning, Inspector Giralo was feeling a bit sluggish, suffering from mild indigestion. The Investigator was all alone, peacefully sipping his morning coffee inside Room 132, when a loud knocking on his first-floor hotel room door interrupted the gentleman's intense reverie. Deja Vu! Standing in the hallway was the very distressed hotel manager.

"Mr. Giralo; a very terrible horse epidemic has just broken-out on the island!" a perspiring Giles Martin announced. "I've learned through our confidential records kept here at the Grand Michigan that you work for the FBI. It's a very urgent matter I have to tell you about! A serious emergency situation has emerged involving the island's six hundred horses suffering from colic and influenza, and the dire matter must be immediately addressed! May I come in?"

About the Author's Books

Jay Dubya is author John Wiessner's pen name and also his initials (J.W.) John is a retired New Jersey public school English teacher and he had taught the subject for thirty-four years. John lives in southern New Jersey with wife Joanne and the couple has three grown sons. John is the creator of fifty-five books.

Jay Dubya has written adult satires *Fractured Frazzled Folk Fables and Fairy Farces* and *FFFF and FF, Part II*. *Black Leather and Blue Denim, A '50s Novel* and its sequel, *The Great Teen Fruit War, A 1960' Novel* and *Frat' Brats, A '60s Novel* are adult-oriented literary endeavors constituting a trilogy.

Pieces of Eight, Pieces of Eight, Part II, Pieces of Eight Part III and *Pieces of Eight, Part IV* are' short story/novella collections featuring science fiction, paranormal and humorous plots and themes. *Nine New Novellas* is the companion book to *Nine New Novellas, Part II, Nine New Novellas, Part III* and *Nine New Novellas, Part IV*. And *So Ya' Wanna' Be A Teacher* is a satirical autobiography describing the author's thirty-four-year educational career in American public schools.

Ron Coyote, Man of La Mangia is adult humor and the work is an imaginative satire/parody on Miguel Cervantes' Don Quixote, published in 1605. *Mauled Maimed Mangled Mutilated Mythology* is a work that satires twenty-one famous ancient tales. *The Wholly Book of Genesis* and *The Wholly Book of Exodus* are also adult satirical humor. *Thirteen Sick Tasteless Classics, Thirteen Sick Tasteless Classics, Part II, Thirteen Sick Tasteless Classics, Part III* and *Thirteen Sick Tasteless Classics, Part IV* are adult satirical rewrites of famous short fiction.

John has also authored a trilogy of young adult fantasy novels, *Enchanta, Pot of Gold* and *Space Bugs, Earth Invasion*. *The Eighteen' Story Gingerbread House* is a new collection of eighteen diverse and creative children's stories.

Jay Dubya likes '50s rock and roll music and he also enjoys pop' songs by the Beach Boys', Fleetwood Mac, the Eagles, the Rolling Stones, ELO, John Mellencamp and by John Fogerty.

Author Biography

Born in Hammonton, NJ in 1942, John Wiessner had attended St. Joseph School up to and including Grade 5. After his family moved from Hammonton to Levittown, Pa in 1954, John attended St. Mark School in Bristol, Pa. for Grade 6, St. Michael the Archangel School in Levittown for Grades 7 and 8 and then Immaculate Conception School, Levittown, Pa. for Grade 9. Bishop Egan High School, Levittown Pa was John's educational base for Grades 10 and 11, and later in 1960, the aspiring author graduated from Edgewood Regional High, Tansboro, NJ. John then next attended Glassboro State College, where he was an announcer for the school's baseball games and also read the nightly news and sports over WGLS, GSC's radio station.

John Wiessner had been primarily an English teacher in the Hammonton Public School System for 34 years, specializing in the instruction of middle school language arts. Mr. Wiessner was quite active in the Hammonton Education Association, serving in the capacities of Vice-President, building representative and finally, teachers' head negotiator for 7 years. During his lengthy teaching career, John had been nominated into "Who's Who Among American Teachers" three times. He also was quite active giving professional workshops at schools around South Jersey on the subjects of creative writing and the use of movie videos to motivate students to organize their classroom theme compositions.

John Wiessner was very active in community service, being a past President of the Hammonton Lions Club, where he also functioned for many years as the club's Tail-Twister, Vice-President and Liontamer. John had been named Hammonton Lion of the Year in 1979 and in 2009 received the prestigious Melvin Jones Fellow Award, the highest honor a Lion can receive from Lions International.

John also was a successful businessman, starting with being a Philadelphia Bulletin newspaper delivery boy for two years in the late 1950s in Levittown, Pennsylvania. After his family moved back to New Jersey in 1959, John worked at his grandparents and his parents' farm markets, Square Deal Farm (now Ron's Gardens in Hammonton) and Pete's Farm Market in Elm, respectively. He later managed his wife's parents' farm market, White Horse Farms in Elm for three summers.

Also in a business capacity, for 16 summers starting in 1967 John Wiessner had co-owned Dealers Choice Amusement Arcade on the

Ocean City, Maryland boardwalk and also co-owned the New Horizon Tee-Shirt Store for eight summers (1973-'81) on the Rehoboth Beach, Delaware boardwalk. In addition, "Jay Dubya" was a co-owner of Wheel and Deal Amusement Arcade, Missouri Avenue and Boardwalk, Atlantic City. And then, for 18 summers beginning in 1986, John had been the Field Manager in charge of crew-leaders for Atlantic Blueberry Company (the world's largest cultivated blueberry farm), working both the Weymouth and Mays Landing Divisions.

After retiring from teaching in 1999, writing under the pen name Jay Dubya (his initials), John Wiessner became the author of 55 books in the genre Action/Adventure Novels, Sci-Fi/Paranormal Story Collections, Adult Satire, Young Adult Fantasy Novels and Non-Fiction Books. His books exist in hardcover, in paperback and in popular Kindle and Nook e-book formats.

In January of 2022, John Wiessner (Jay Dubya) was nominated into Marquis Who's Who in America, and in April of that same year, was one of nine distinguished Who's Who in America members honored with receiving Lifetime Achievement Awards, all nine sharing a news article of recognition appearing in the Wall Street Journal.

Google: Jay Dubya, books
Google: Walmart, Jay Dubya

www.ingramcontent.com/pod-product-compliance
Lightning Source LLC
Chambersburg PA
CBHW070728120726

47910CB00001B/24